STONEWIELDER

A NOVEL OF THE MALAZAN EMPIRE

Ian C. Esslemont

A TOM DOHERTY ASSOCIATES BOOK
NEW YORK

This is a work of fiction. All of the characters, organizations, and events portrayed in this novel are either products of the author's imagination or are used fictitiously.

STONEWIELDER

First published in Great Britain in a limited edition by PS Publishing LLP and by Bantam Press, a division of Transworld Publishers

A Tor Book
Published by Tom Doherty Associates, LLC
175 Fifth Avenue
New York, NY 10010

www.tor-forge.com

Library of Congress Cataloging-in-Publication Data

Esslemont, Ian C. (Ian Cameron)
Stonewielder : a novel of the Malazan empire / Ian C. Esslemont. — 1st Tor ed.
p. cm.
"A Tom Doherty Associates book."
ISBN 978-0-7653-2984-4 (hardcover)
ISBN 978-0-7653-2985-1 (trade paperback)
I. Title.
PS3605.S684S76 2011
813'.6—dc22

2011007400

First Tor Edition: May 2011

Printed in the United States of America

10 9 8 7 6 5 4 3 2 1

To Gerri
with love

ACKNOWLEDGMENTS

Greatest gratitude to Gerri for her unswerving support. Thanks to Derick Burleson for graciously allowing me to adapt one of his pieces to this setting. I would also like to acknowledge the fans of the World of Malaz, its readers, and those active on its online forums. Your energy and enthusiasm keep Steve and me inspired.

CONTENTS

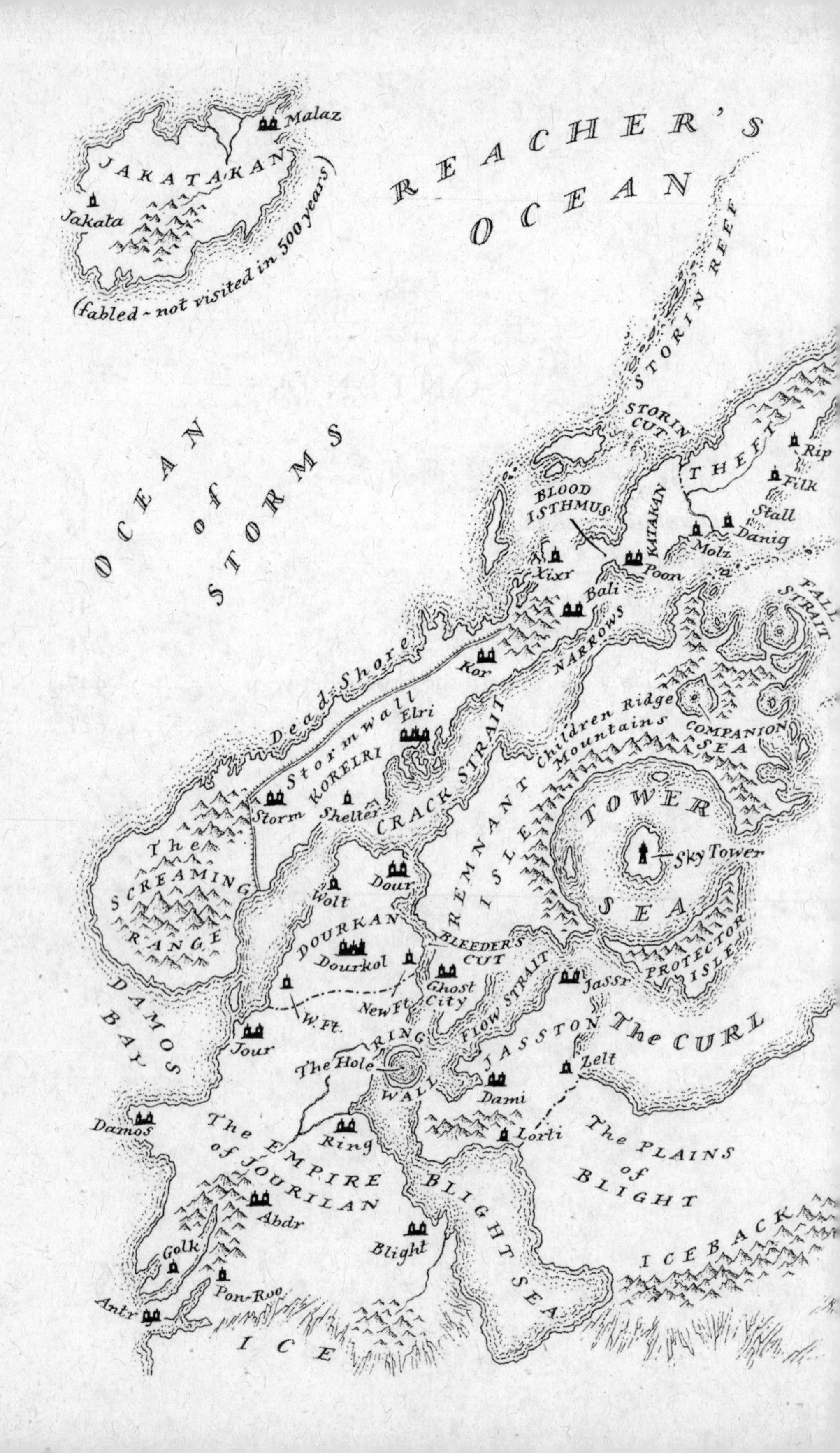

Malaz
JAKATAKAN
Jakata
(fabled - not visited in 500 years)
REACHER'S OCEAN
STORIN REEF
STORIN CUT
THEFT
Rip
Filk
Stall
Danig
Molz
KATAKAN
Poon
BLOOD ISTHMUS
Xixr
Bali
OCEAN of STORMS
NARROWS
FALL STRAIT
Kor
Dead Shore
Stormwall
Elri
KORELRI
Storm
Shelter
CRACK STRAIT
Children Ridge
Mountains
COMPANION SEA
REMNANT ISLE
TOWER'S SEA
Sky Tower
PROTECTOR ISLE
The SCREAMING RANGE
Wolt
Dour
DOURKAN
Dourkol
BLEEDER'S CUT
Ghost City
Jassr
FLOW STRAIT
New Ft.
W. Ft.
DAMOS BAY
Jour
RING WALL
The Hole
JASSTON
The CURL
Zelt
Dami
Lorti
Damos
Ring
The EMPIRE of JOURILAN
The PLAINS of BLIGHT
BLIGHT SEA
Abdr
Blight
ICEBACK
Golk
Pon-Roo
Antr
ICE

The LANDS of FIST
SKOLATI
WILDERNESS
FIST SEA
PIRATE'S SEA
Grest
Steel
Dorik
Lorest
Falt
Fort Drii
Aamil
Homdo
Thol
ROOL
Lallit
Paliss
Haft
Gost
FIST
Three Sisters
Banith
Aliss
Zestr
BLACK WATER STRAIT
Mald
Kren
Ebon
Black City
Dorl
MARE
Rivdo
SENDER'S SEA
Cast
Dim
Drak
Shade
Shroud
STYGG
Sty
Kevil
Shale
EBON MTNS
BLOOD MARE OCEAN
N
East Watch
The DEEP WILDERNESS
The ELDER CONTINENT
RANGE
ICE
ICE ISLAND SEA
TUNDRA
ICE

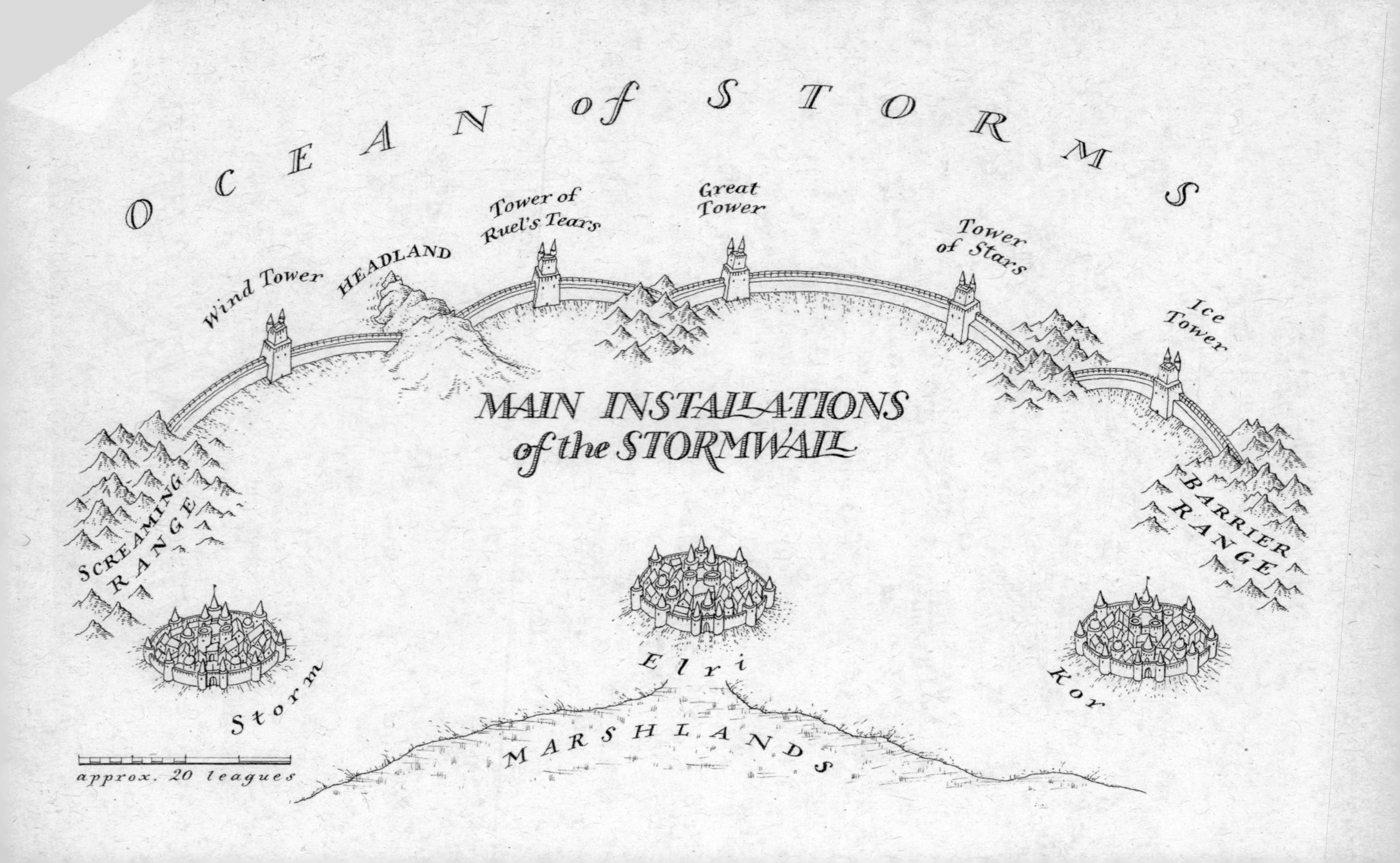

OCEAN of STORMS
Wind Tower
HEADLAND
Tower of Ruel's Tears
Great Tower
Tower of Stars
Ice Tower
MAIN INSTALLATIONS of the STORMWALL
SCREAMING RANGE
BARRIER RANGE
Storm
Elri
Kor
MARSHLANDS
approx. 20 leagues

DRAMATIS PERSONAE

Of the Malazan Expeditionary Force

Greymane / Orjin Samarr	High Fist, Commander of Expeditionary Force
Kyle	Adjunct to the High Fist
Nok	Admiral, Commander of Naval forces
Swirl	Admiral of Moranth Blue forces
Rillish Jal Keth	Divisional Fist of the Fourth Army
Khemet Shul	Divisional Fist of the Eighth Army
Devaleth	Cadre mage

Malazan 17th Squad, 4th Company, 2nd Division, Fourth Army

Betteries	Company Captain
Goss	Sergeant
Pyke	Heavy infantry
Yana	Heavy infantry
Suth	Heavy infantry
Lard	Heavy infantry
Dim	Heavy infantry
Wess	Heavy infantry
Len	Saboteur
Keri	Saboteur
Faro	Scout

Others

Urfa	Lieutenant of 4th Company saboteurs
Twofoot	Sergeant of the 6th
Coral	Sergeant of the 20th
Tolat	A Barghast scout of 4th Company

Of the Malazan Sixth Army

Yeull 'ul Taith	Overlord
Ussü	High Mage and Adviser
Borun	Commander of Black Moranth
Enesh-jer	Envoy of the Overlord

On the Stormwall

Hiam	Lord Protector of the Stormwall, Commander of all Korelri
Quint	Senior officer (Wall Marshal) of the Stormwall
Shool	Aide to Hiam
Toral Stimins	Master Engineer
Iron Bars	Champion of the Stormwall, and Crimson Guard Avowed
Corlo	A prisoner and Crimson Guardsman
Jemain	A prisoner and member of Bars' crew
Hagen	Ex-Champion of the Stormwall
Tollen	A Malazan prisoner

In the Kingdom of Rool

Bakune	Chief Assessor of Banith
Karien'el	Lieutenant, later Captain, of the City Watch
Hyuke	A city watchman
Puller	A city watchman
Starvann Arl	Abbot of Our Lady the Saviour Cloister and Hospice
Ipshank	An ex-priest of Fener
Manask	A thief

Of the Jourilan Army of Reform

Beneth	Spiritual leader
Hegil Lesour 'an 'al	Commander of the cavalry
Martal	Commander of the army, the 'Black Queen'
Ivanr	Ex-Grand Champion of the Jourilan Imperial Games
Carr	A lieutenant of the army

STONEWIELDER

PROLOGUE

The Elder Age
Height of the Jacaruku Crusades
The Many Isles

ULI KNEW IT FOR A BAD OMEN THE MOMENT HE SAW IT. HE'D been readying his nets for the pre-dawn fishing when the unnatural green and blue aura bruised the sky. It appeared out of the lightening east and swelled, becoming more bloated with every passing moment. The bay was choppy as if as agitated as he, and he'd been reluctant to push his shallow boat out into the waves. But his family had to eat, and cramped stomachs belch no end of complaints.

Through the first of the morning's casts he kept his face averted from the thing where it hung in the discoloured sky, blazing like the baleful eye of some god. The catch that morning was poor: either his distraction, or the fish fleeing the apparition. In either case he decided to abandon the effort as cursed, threw his net to the bottom of the craft, and began paddling for shore. The blue-green eye now dazzled brighter than the sun; he shaded his gaze from the points of alien light glimmering on the waves. He paddled faster.

A strange noise brought his frantic, gasping efforts to a halt. A great roaring it was, like a landslide. He glared about, searching for its source. The alien eye now seemed to fill half the sky. No remnant of the sun's warm yellow glow touched the waters, the treed shore, or the dark humps of the distant islands. Then, with unnatural speed, the surface of the bay stilled as if cowed. Uli held his breath and ducked side to side in his tiny craft.

The eye broke apart. Shards calved trailing blue flames, arcing. A roaring such as he had never before endured drove him to clap his hands to his head and scream his pain. A great massive descending piece like an ember thrown from a god's fire drove smashing down far to the east. A white incandescent blaze blinded Uli's vision. It seemed as if something had struck the big island.

Just as his vision returned, another glow flashed from behind. It threw his shadow ahead like a black streamer across the bay. Turning, he gaped to see a great scattering of shards descending to the west while others cascaded on far above. He rubbed his pained eyes – could it be the end of the world? Perhaps it was another of the moons falling, as he'd heard told of in legends. He remembered his paddle; Helta and the little 'uns would be terrified. He returned to churning water with a desperate fury, almost weeping his dread.

The hide boat ground on to mudflats far sooner than usual. Mystified, he eased a foot over the side. Shallows where none had ever stretched before. And the shore still a good long hike away. It was as if the water were disappearing. He peered up and winced; in the east a massive dark cloud of billowing grey and black was clawing its way up into the sky. It had already swallowed the sun. Untold bounty lay about him: boatloads of fish gasping and mouthing the air, flapping their death-throes.

Yet not one bird. The birds – where had they gone?

The light took on an eerie, darkly greenish cast. Uli slowly edged round, turning his head out to sea, and all hope fell from him. Something was swelling on the waters: a wall of dirty green. Floods such as the old stories tell of. Mountains of water come to inundate the land as all the tales foretell. It seemed to rear directly overhead, so lofty was it. Foam webbed its curved leading face, dirty white capped its peak. He could only gape upwards at its remorseless, fatal advance.

Run, little 'uns, run! The water comes to reclaim the land!

* * *

Approx. 400 years BW *(Before the Wall)*
The Empty Isles

Temal pushed himself upright from the chilling surf and crouched, sword ready. He gazed uncomprehendingly around the surface of the darkening waters, wiping the cold spray from his face. *Where have they gone? One moment he's fighting for his life and the next the sea-demons disappear like the mist that preceded them.* Weak coughing sounded from his flank. He slogged among the rocks to lift a soaked comrade: Arel, a distant cousin. Though almost faint with exhaustion, Temal dragged the man to shore. Survivors of his war band ran down to the surf to pull both to the reviving warmth of a great bonfire of driftwood.

'What happened?' he stammered through chattering teeth.

'They withdrew,' answered Temal's older sword-brother, Jhenhelf. His tone conveyed his bewildered disbelief. 'Yet why? They had us.'

Temal did not dispute the evaluation; he was too tired, and he knew it to be true. He had less than twenty hale men in his band and too many of those inexperienced youths.

'They will return with the dawn to finish us,' Jhenhelf continued from across the fire. Temal held his old comrade's gaze through the leaping flames and again said nothing. At their feet Arel coughed, then vomited up the seawater he'd swallowed.

'What of Redden?' one of the new recruits asked. 'We could send for aid.'

Faces lifted all round the fire, pale with chill and fear.

'They could be with us by dawn . . .'

'Redden is just as hard-pressed as us,' Temal cut in strongly. 'He must defend his own shore.' He glanced from one strained face to another. 'Redden cannot spare the men.'

'Then—' began one of the youths.

'Then we wait and rest!' Jhenhelf barked. 'Arel, Will, Otten – keep watch. The rest of you, get some sleep.'

Grateful for the support of his old friend, Temal eased himself to the ground. He thrust his sandalled feet out to the fire and tried to ignore the agonizing sting of salt licking his many cuts and gashes. He felt the heat work upon him and hunched forward, hand across his lap at the grip of his sheathed sword, and through slit eyes he watched the mist climb from his drying leathers.

He had no idea why the damned sea-demon Riders attacked. Despite them, it was an attractive land. The peninsulas and islands were rich and cultivable. It was ready to be wholly settled but for a few ignorant native tribals. His father and his grandfather before him had fought to keep their tenuous foothold. As leader of his extended clan he had to think of the future: enough futile wandering! They would hang on to these islands and all the lands beyond. Dark Avallithal with its haunted woods had not suited, nor the savage coast of Dhal-Horn, nor the brooding Isles of Malassa. Here flew their standard. Here his forebears burned their boats. He would not allow these Riders to force them out; they had nowhere to go.

Temal jerked awake, knocking aside Jhenhelf's touch. It was almost dawn. 'An attack?' He struggled up on legs numb and stiff.

His lieutenant's face held an unfamiliar expression. 'No.' He lifted his chin to their rear, to where the grass-topped cliffs of the shore rose; to the meadows and forests and farmland beyond, all of which would soon be dead and withered should the sea-demons be allowed to work their witchery unmolested.

Everyone, Temal noted, stared inland, not out to sea where they should be keeping watch for the first pearl-like gleams of the Riders' approach. 'What is it?'

Jhenhelf did not answer, and it occurred to Temal that the strange expression on his friend's coarse, battle-hardened face might be awed wonder. He squinted up to the top of the cliffs' ragged silhouette. A figure stood there, tall beneath dark clouds in the red-gold of the coming dawn's light. The proportions of what he was seeing struck Temal as strange: whoever that was, he or she must be a giant to rear so high from so far away . . .

'I'll go,' he said, his gaze fixed. 'You keep guard.'

'Take Will and Otten.'

'If I must.'

Dawn was in full flush when they reached the crest, and when they did Will and Otten fell silent, staring. Though the shore breeze was strong, a repulsive stench as of rotting flesh struck Temal. He clenched his lips and stomach against the reek and forced himself onward alone.

The figure was gigantic, out of all proportion, twice the height of the Jaghut or other Elders he'd heard talk of, such as the Toblakai or Tarthinoe, and vaguely female with its long greasy tresses hanging down to its waist, its thrusting bosom, and the dark tangle of hair at its crotch. Yet its flesh was repulsive: a pale dead fish, mottled, pocked by rotting open sores. The fetor almost made Temal faint. At the thing's side rested a large block of black stone resembling a chest or an altar.

Temal glanced out to sea, to the clear unmarred surface gleaming in the morning light, where no hint of wave-borne sea-demons remained. He glanced back to the figure. *Dark Taker!* Could this be *she*? The local goddess some settlements invoked to protect them? That many claimed offered sanctuary from the Riders?

The broad bloodless lips stretched in a knowing smile, as if the being had read his thoughts. Yet the eyes remained empty of all expression, lifeless, dull, like the staring milky orbs of the dead. Temal felt transformed. *She has come! She has delivered them from certain annihilation at the lances of the sea-demons!* Not knowing what to say he knelt on one knee, offering wordless obeisance. Behind him Will and Otten knelt as well.

The figure took a great sucking breath. 'Outlander,' it boomed, 'you have come to settle the land. I welcome you and offer my protection.' The Goddess gestured with a gnarled and twisted hand to the block at her feet. 'Take this most precious sarcophagus. Within rests flesh of my flesh. Carry it along the coast. Trace a path. Mark it and build there a great wall. A barrier. Defend it that behind it you may rest protected from those enemies from the sea who seek to ravage this land. Do you accept this my gift to you and all your people?'

Distantly, Temal felt cold tears trace lines down his face. Hardly trusting himself to speak, he gasped: 'We accept.'

The Goddess spread her ponderous arms wide. 'So be it. What is done is done. This is our covenant. Let none undo it. I leave you to your great labour.'

Temal bowed again. The Goddess lumbered south in prodigious strides that shook the ground beneath Temal's knees. She was gone in moments. He did not know how long he remained bowed but in time Will and Otten came to stand with him. The sun bore down hot on his back. Sighing, he straightened, dizzy.

What had he done? What could *he have done?* No choice. They were losing. Each year they were fewer while the enemy seemed just as strong, if not stronger. But her mere approach had driven them back.

Will found his voice first. 'Was it a Jaghut? Or *her*? The Goddess?'

'It was her. She has offered her protection.'

'Well, she's gone now – they'll be back,' Otten said, ever sceptical.

Temal gestured to the basalt coffin. 'No. She's still here.'

'What is it?' Otten asked, reaching for it.

'*No!*' Temal pushed them back. 'Get Jhenhelf. And Redden.'

'But you said they were to keep guard.'

'Never mind what I said. Listen to me now. Get them both. Tell them to bring wood and rope.'

'But what of the demons?'

'They won't be back. At least, not near us.' He extended a palm to the black glittering block. Heat radiated from it as from a stone pulled from a fire. *Flesh of her flesh. Good Goddess! Gracious Lady! May we never fail you or your trust.*

* * *

Korelri year 4156 sw (Since the Wall)
Year 11 of the Malazan Occupation
Kingdom of Rool
Island of Fist

Karien'el, a lieutenant of the City Watch, led Bakune under the wharf to where the young woman's body lay tangled in seaweed at the base of the jumbled rocks of the breakwater. The lieutenant, ever conscious of rank, reached up to aid the man across the slippery rocks though he himself carried more years than Bakune, newly installed Assessor of Banith.

With Bakune's arrival at the chilly wave-pounded shore the men of the Watch straightened. A number quickly cinched tight helmets, adjusted leather jerkins and the hang of their truncheons and their badge of honour: swords – albeit shortswords – which they alone among the subject peoples of Fist were allowed to carry by the Malazan overlords. Also conscious of rank, in his own way, Bakune answered the salutes informally, hoping to set them all at ease. It still did not feel right to him that these men, many veterans of the wars of invasion, should salute him. Uncomfortable, and hugging his robes to himself for warmth, he raised a brow to the Watch lieutenant. 'The body?'

'Here, Assessor.' The lieutenant led him down to the very edge of lazy swells and blackened, seaweed-skirted boulders large as wine tubs. An old man waited there, sun and wind-darkened, kneeling on scrawny haunches, tattered sandals on filthy feet, in a ragged tunic with a ragged beard to match.

'And this one?' Bakune asked Karien'el.

'Brought us to the body.'

The old man knelt motionless, his face flat, carefully watchful. The body lay at his feet. Bakune crouched. Newly cast up; the smell did not yet overpower the surrounding shore stink. Naked. Crabs had gnawed extremities of hands and feet; had also taken away most of the face (or deliberate disfigurement?). Very young, slim, no doubt once attractive. A prostitute? Odd marks at the neck – strangulation. Faded henna tattoos – a common vanity.

Without looking up Bakune asked: 'Who was she to you?'

'No one,' the old man croaked in thickly accented Roolian.

'Then why the Watch?'

'Is one anonymous dead girl not worth your attention?'

Bakune slowly raised his head to the fellow: dark features, kinky greying hair. The black eyes in return studied him with open, what others might term impertinent, intent. He lowered his head, picked up a stick to shift the girl's arm. 'You are a tribesman. Of the Drenn?'

'You know your tribes. That is unusual for you invaders.'

Bakune peered up once again, his eyes narrowed. 'Invaders? The Malazans are the invaders.'

A smile empty of any humour pulled at the edge of the old man's lips. 'There are invaders and then there are invaders.'

Straightening, Bakune dropped the stick and regarded the old man directly. As a trained Assessor he knew when he himself was being . . . *examined.* He crossed his arms. 'What is your name?'

Again the patient smile. 'In your language? Gheven.'

'Very well, Gheven. What is your – assessment – here?'

'I'm just an itinerant tribal, vaunted sir. What should my opinion matter?'

'It matters to me.'

The lips hardened into a straight tight line; the eyes almost disappeared into their nests of wrinkles. 'Does it? Really?'

For some odd reason Bakune felt himself almost faltering. 'Well, yes. Of course. I am the Assessor. It is my duty.'

A shrug and the hardened lines eased back into the distant, flat watchfulness. 'It's more and more common now,' he began, 'but it goes far back. You all blame the Malazan troops, of course. These Malazans, they've been here for what, ten years now? They walk your streets, billet themselves in your houses and inns. Visit your taverns. Hire your prostitutes. Your women take up with them. Often these girls are killed for such mixing. Usually by their own fathers or brothers for smearing what they call their "honour"—'

'That's a damned lie, tribal scum! It's the Malazans!'

Bakune almost jumped – he'd forgotten the Watch lieutenant. He raised a placating hand to the man who stood seething, knuckles white on the grip of his shortsword. 'You said *usually* . . . ?'

The man's lined face had knotted in uncompromising distaste; his gnarled hands remained loose at his sides. He seemed unaware of, or indifferent to, how close he was to being struck down. Luckily for him Bakune shared his disgust, and, generally, his assessment as well. Gheven nodded his craggy head up and down, and the tightened lips unscrewed. 'Yes. *Usually.* But not this time. Much of the flesh is gone but note the design high on the right shoulder.'

Bakune knelt, and, dispensing with the niceties of any stick, used his own hands to shift the body. The henna swirls were old and further faded by the bleaching of the seawater, but among the unremarkable geometric abstracts one particular symbol caught his eye . . . a broken circle. A sign of one of the new foreign cults outlawed by their native Korel and Fistian church of their Saviour, their Lady of Deliverance. He tried to recall which one among the bewildering numbers of all those foreign faiths, then he remembered: a minor one, the cult of the 'Fallen God'.

'What of it? You are not suggesting that just because of one such tattoo the Guardians of Our Lady—'

'I am suggesting worse. Note the bruises at the throat. The cuts at the wrists. It has been a long time, has it not, Assessor, since the one who you claim protects you from the sea-demons, the Riders, has demanded her payment, yes?'

'Drenn filth!' Karien'el grasped the man by the neck. Iron scraped wood as his sword swung free of its scabbard.

'*Lieutenant!*' The man froze, panting his fury. 'You forget yourself. Release him. I am assessing here.'

Slowly, reluctantly, the officer peeled his fingers free and slammed home the blade, pushing the man backwards. 'Same old lies. Always defaming Our Lady despite her protection. She protects even you, you know. You tribals. From the sea-demons. You should stay in your mountains and woods and consider yourselves blessed.'

Gheven said nothing, but in the old man's taut, almost rigid, mien Bakune saw a fierce unbowed pride. The dark eyes shifted their challenge to him. 'And what is your judgement here . . . *Assessor*?'

Bakune retreated from the shoreline where stronger waves now cast up cold spray that chilled his face. He pulled a handkerchief from a sleeve to dab away the briny water. 'Your, ah, suspicions are noted, Gheven. But I am sorry. Strong accusations require equally strong evidence and that I do not see here. Barring any further material facts the murder remains as you originally suggested – a murder or a distasteful honour killing. That is my assessment.'

'We are finished here?' Karien'el asked. His slitted eyes remained unwavering on the old tribesman.

'Yes. And Lieutenant, no harm is to come to this man. He did his duty in calling our attention to an ugly crime. I will hold you personally responsible.'

The officer's sour scowl twisted even tighter but he bowed his accord. 'Yes, Assessor.'

Climbing back up on to the breakwater walk Bakune adjusted his robes and clenched his chilled fingers to bring life back to them. Of course he'd seen the marks encircling the neck, but some things one must not admit aloud – at least not so early in one's career. He regarded the lieutenant who had followed, one boot on the stone ledge, ever dutiful. 'Report to me directly the discovery of any more such bodies. Or rumoured disappearances of youths, male or female. There may be a monster among us, Karien.'

A salute of fingertips to the knurled brow of his iron helmet. 'Aye, Assessor.'

The officer descended the slope, his boots scraping over the boulders, cloak snapping in the wind. Bakune hugged himself for warmth. The coast, Lady, how he hated it: the chill wind that smelled of the Riders, the clawing waters, the cold damp that mildewed all it touched. Yet a positive review here could lead to promotion and that posting in Paliss he hoped for . . . yet another good reason for discretion.

He looked for the tribesman down among the wet boulders but the man was gone. Good. He didn't want a beating on his conscience. What an accusation! Why jump to such an assessment? True, long ago the ancient ways sanctioned such acts in the name of the greater good – but all that had been swept aside by the ascendancy of Our Saviour, the Blessed Lady. *And in their histories it is plain that that man's ancestors practised it, not ours! Thus the long antipathy between us and these swamp- and wasteland-skulking tribals with their bastardized blood.*

Perhaps in truth a killing by an enraged father or brother, but without sufficient evidence who can assess? In lieu of evidence the locals will decide that this one, like all those prior, was plainly the work of their bloody-handed murderous occupiers, the Malazans.

From between tall boulders Gheven watched the two walk away. The Watch officer, Karien'el, lingered, searching for him. That did not trouble him; he intended to be moving on in any case. In the eyes of the Roolian occupiers of this land they called Fist he was officially itinerant, after all. And why not, since he was on pilgrimage – an itinerary of sacred paths to walk and sites to visit, and in walking and visiting thus reinscribing and reaffirming? A remarkable confluence of diametric attitudes aligning.

He turned to go. With each step the dreamscape of his ancient ancestral land unfolded itself around him. For the land was their Warren and they its practitioners. Something all these foreign invaders, mortal and immortal, seemed incapable of apprehending. And he too was finished here. The seeds had been sown; time would tell how strong or deep the roots may take.

If this new Assessor was true to his calling then Gheven pitied him. Truth tellers were never welcome; most especially one's own. Better to be a storyteller – they at least have grasped the essential truth that everyone prefers lies.

* * *

Korelri year 4176 sw
Year 31 of the Malazan Occupation
Kingdom of Rool
Island of Fist

The occupant of the small lateen-rigged launch manoeuvred it through the crowded Banith harbour to tie up between an oared merchant galley out of Theft, and a rotting Jourilan cargo scow. He threw his only baggage, a cloth roll cinched tight by rope, on to the dock, then climbed up on to the mildewed blackwood slats. He straightened his squat broad form, hands at the small of his back, and stretched, grimacing.

An excise officer taking inventory on the galley pointed his baton of office. 'You there! You can't tie up here! This is a commercial dock. Take that toy to the public wharf.'

'Take what?' the man asked blandly.

The dock master opened his mouth to respond, then shut it. He'd thought the fellow old by his darkly tanned shaven head, but power clearly remained in the meaty thick neck, rounded shoulders, and gnarled, big-knuckled hands. More alarmingly, faded remnants of blue tattoos swirled across his brow, cheeks, and chin, demarking a fiercely snarling boar's head. 'The boat – move the boat.'

''Tain't mine.'

'Yes it is! I saw you tie it up just now!'

'You there,' the fellow called to an old man in rags on his hands and knees scouring the dock with a pumice stone. 'How about a small launch? Battered but seaworthy.'

The elder stared then laughed a wet cackle, shaking his head. 'Haven't the coin.'

The newcomer threw a copper coin to the dock. 'Now you do.'

The excise officer's gaze flicked suspiciously between the two. 'Wait a moment . . .'

The old man took up the coin, cocked an amused eye at the excise officer and tossed it back. The newcomer snatched it from the air. 'Talk to this man,' he told the officer, turning his back.

'Hey! You can't just—'

'I'll be moving my boat right away, sir!' the old man cackled, revealing a dark pit empty of teeth. 'Wouldn't *think* of tying up here, sir!'

Walking away, the newcomer allowed his mouth to widen in a broad frog-like grin beneath his splayed, squashed nose.

He passed Banith's harbour guardhouse, where his gaze lingered on the Malazan soldiers lounging in the shade of the porch. He took in the opened leather jerkin of one, loosened to accommodate a bulging stomach; the other dozing, chair tipped back, helmet forward over his eyes.

The newcomer's smile faded. Ahead, the front street of Banith ran roughly east–west. The town climbed shallow coastal hills, its roofs dominated by the tall jutting spires of the Holy Cloister and the many gables of the Hospice nearby. Beyond these, rich cultivated rolling plains, land once forested, stretched into the mist-shrouded distance. The man turned right. Walking slowly, he studied the shop fronts and stalls. He passed a knot of street toughs and noted the much darker or fairer hues of mixed Malazan blood among them, so different from the uniformly swart Fistian heritage.

'Cast us a coin, beggar priest,' one bold youth called, the eldest.

'All I own is yours,' the fellow answered in his gravelly voice.

That brought many up short. Glances shot between the puzzled youths until the older tough snorted his disbelief. 'Then hand it all over.'

The squat fellow was examining an empty shop front. 'Easily done – since I own nothing. This building occupied?'

'Debtors' prison,' answered a girl, barefoot, in tattered canvas pants and dirty tunic, boasting the frizzy hair of mixed Korel and foreign parentage. 'Withholding taxes from the Malazan overlords.'

The man raised his thick arms to it. 'Then I consecrate it to my God.'

'Which of all your damned foreign gods is that?'

The man turned. A smile pulled up his uneven lips and distorted the faded boar's head tattoo. His voice strengthened. 'Why, since you ask . . . Let me tell you about my God. His domain is the downtrodden and dispossessed. The poor and the sick. To him social standing, riches and prestige are meaningless empty veils. His first message is that we are all weak. We all are flawed. We all are mortal. And that we must learn to accept this.'

'Accept? Accept what?'

'Our failings. For we are all of us imperfect.'

'What is the name of this sick and perverted god?'

The priest held out his hands open and empty. 'It is that which resides within us – each god is but one face of it.'

'Each god? All? Even Our Lady who shields us from evil?'

'Yes. Even she.'

Many of the gang flinched then, wincing, and they moved off as they sensed a more profound and disquieting sacrilege flowing beneath the usual irreverence of foreigners.

'And his second message?' a girl asked. She had stepped closer, but her eyes remained watchful on the street, and a sneer seemed fixed at her bloodless lips.

'Anyone may achieve deliverance and grace. It is open to all. It cannot be kept from anyone like common coin.'

She pointed to her thin chest. 'Even us? The divines of the Sainted Lady turn us away from their thresholds – even the Hospice. They spit at us as half-bloods. And the old Dark Collector demands payment for all souls regardless.'

The man's dark eyes glittered his amusement. 'What I speak of cannot be bought by any earthly coin. Or compelled by any earthly power.'

Perplexed, the girl allowed her friends to pull her on. But she glanced back, thoughtful, her sharp brows crimped.

Smiling to himself again, the newcomer took hold of the door's latch and pushed with a firm steady force until wood cracked, snapping, and the door opened. He slept that night on the threshold under his thin quilted blanket.

He spent the next morning sitting in the open doorway, nodding to all who passed. Those who did not spurn his greeting skittered from him like wary colts. Shortly after dawn a Malazan patrol of six soldiers made its slow deliberate round. He watched while coins passed from shopkeepers into the hands of the patrol sergeant; how the soldiers, male and female, helped themselves to whatever they wanted from the stalls, eating bread, fruit, and skewered meat cooked over coals as they swaggered along.

Eventually they came to him and he sighed, lowering his gaze. He'd heard it was bad here in Fist – which was why he'd come – but he'd no idea it was this bad.

The patrol sergeant stopped short, his thick, dark brows knitting. 'What in the name of Togg's tits is a Theftian priest of Fener doing here?'

The newcomer stood. 'Priest, yes. But no longer of Fener.'

'Kicked out? Buggery maybe?'

'No – you get promoted for that.'

The men and women of the patrol laughed. The sergeant scowled, his unshaven jowls folding in fat. He tucked his hands into his belt; his gaze edged slyly to his patrol. 'Looks like we got an itinerant. You have any coin, old beggar?'

'I do.' The priest reached into a fold of his tattered shirt and tossed a copper sliver to the cobbled road.

'A worthless Stygg half-penny?' The sergeant's fleshy mouth curled.

'You're right that it's worthless. All coins are worthless. It's just that some are worth less than others.'

The sergeant snorted. 'A Hood-damned mystic too.' He pulled a wooden truncheon from his belt. 'We don't tolerate layabouts in this town. Get a move on or I'll give you payment of another kind.'

The priest's wide hands twitched loosely at his sides; his frog-like mouth stretched in a straight smile. 'Lucky for you I no longer have any use for that coin either.'

The sergeant swung. The truncheon slapped into the priest's

raised open hand. The sergeant grunted, straining. His tanned face darkened with effort. Yanking, the priest came away with the truncheon, which he then cracked across his knee, snapping it. He threw the shards to the road. The men and women of the patrol eased back a step, hands going to swords.

The sergeant raised a hand: *Hold*. He gave the priest a nod in acknowledgement of the demonstration. 'You're new, so I'll give you this one. But from now on this is how it's gonna work – you want to stay, you pay. Simple as that. Otherwise, it's the gaol for you. And here's a tip . . . stay in *there* long enough and we sell your arse to the Korelri. They're always lookin' for warm bodies for the wall and they don't much care where they come from.' He eased his head from side to side, cracking vertebrae, and offered a savage smile. 'So, you're a priest. We got priests too. Guess I'll send them around. You can talk philosophy. Till then – sleep tight.'

The sergeant signalled for the patrol to move on. They left, grinning. One of the female soldiers blew a kiss.

The priest sat back down to watch them as they went, collecting yet more extortion money. The street youths, he noted, were nowhere in evidence. *Damn bad. Worse than he'd imagined. It's a good thing the old commander isn't here to see this. Otherwise it would be the garrison itself in the gaol.*

He picked up the two shards of the truncheon, hefted them. *Still, mustn't be too harsh. Occupation and subjugation of a population – intended or not – is an ugly thing. Brutalizing. Brings out the worst in both actors. Look at what he'd heard of Seven Cities. And this is looking no better.*

Well, he has his God. The priest's wide mouth split side to side. *Ah yes, his God. And a browbeaten and oppressed population from which to recruit. Fertile ground.* He edged his head sideways, calculating. *Yes . . . it just might work . . .*

* * *

First year of the rule of Emperor Mallick Rel 'The Merciful'
(Year 1167 Burn's Sleep)
City of Delanss, Falar Subcontinent

Sitting across from his hulking grey-haired friend, Kyle squeezed his tumbler of wine and tried to keep his worry from his face. The long, stone-hued hair that had given his friend his old nickname, Greymane, now hung more silver than pewter. And though he attacked his rice and Falaran hot peppered fish sauce with his usual gusto and appetite, Kyle could see that his strained finances must be taking their toll: new lines furrowed his mouth, dark circles shaded his eyes, and Kyle swore the man was losing weight.

They sat on a terrace overlooking an enclosed courtyard of raked sand where racks of weapons boasted swords of all makes plus daggers, pole-weapons and staves, as well as padded hauberks, helmets and shields. Everything, Kyle reflected, one might need for a fighting academy.

Except pupils.

So far, Kyle didn't think Greymane, who now insisted on his original given name, Orjin, had attracted more than thirty paying bodies to his new school. Kyle didn't count himself; he'd tried paying for all the lessons and sparring he'd been privileged to have from the man, but Orjin wouldn't accept a penny. The three cousins who'd come along with him and Greymane had also tried to help, but after their version of 'training' broke bones and bloodied noses Orjin asked them to quit. Bored with hanging around, Stalker, Coots and Badlands had said their goodbyes and shipped out on a vessel heading west. Kyle's guardian spirit, or haunt, seemed to have also drifted off: Stoop, the ghost of a dead Crimson Guardsman, one of the Avowed, those who swore a binding vow to oppose the Malazan Empire so long as it should endure. And that vow, which granted them so much, extended life and strength, also bound them in death, chaining them to the world. But over the months he too had faded away, returning, perhaps, to his dead brethren. Kyle had thought he saw a kind of disappointment in the haunt's eyes when it appeared that last time to say farewell.

So over the months he'd spent his time talking up Orjin's school at every chance. He suspected, though, that his friend wasn't interested in what the regular burghers and farmers of the markets, inns and taverns thought of his new academy – he had his eyes on a far more elevated, and moneyed, tier of the local Delanss society.

Small chance there. Delanss, capital city of the second most populous island of the Falaran subcontinent and archipelago, boasted prestigious long-established schools: Grieg's Academy, the School of the Curved Blade, the Black Falcon School. Academies that rivalled the famous officers' school of Strike Island. And privately, Kyle did not believe his friend would ever manage to push his way into such a closed, tightly knit market in what seemed such a closed, tightly knit society. As far as he could see, this region's capitulation to its Malazan invaders seemed to have amounted to no more than changing the colour of the flags atop the harbour fortress.

Greymane – Orjin – tore a piece of greasy flatbread and used it to sop up the last of his sauce; he looked as though he was about to speak, but chewed moodily instead. Kyle sipped his white rice wine, thought about asking whether any classes were scheduled for the day, decided he'd better not.

It seemed to him that all this must be especially galling since his friend had to hide his past. A past that would have officer hopefuls battering down his doors should they know of it. Unfortunately, word of his past career as an Imperial Malazan military general, a Fist, and subsequent outlaw from that same Empire, would have him a hunted man on this subcontinent as well.

A sound from below turned Kyle's attention to the practice floor. A man had entered. He was dressed in the rounded cloth hat, thick robes and bright jewellery of just that social stratum Orjin was so keen to attract; the fellow gazed bemusedly about the empty school. Following Kyle's gaze, Orjin peered down, then shot upright from his chair, sending it crashing backwards. 'Yes, sir!' he boomed. 'May I be of service?'

The man jumped at the bellow trained to penetrate the crash of battle, squinted up, uncertain. 'You are the master of this establishment?' he asked in Talian, the unofficial second tongue of the archipelago.

'Yes, sir! A moment, sir!' Orjin wiped his mouth, disentangled himself from his fallen chair and headed for the stairs. Crossing the practice floor, he bowed. 'How may I help you, sir?'

Kyle finished his wine and followed. He stopped at the base of the stairs, leaned against the banister of unfinished wood. The fellow wore the full fashion of the local aristocracy: multiple rings at his fingers, thick silver chains round his neck over fur-trimmed robes with fur cuffs. His hat consisted of wrapped dark burgundy cloth set with semi-precious stones. His goatee was finely trimmed, and while looking Orjin up and down he stroked it, showing off the large gems in his rings. 'What are your credentials?'

Orjin bowed again. He looked what Kyle hoped was properly severe and professional in his tanned leathers. 'I served in the Malazan Fourth Army, sir, and attained the rank of captain before injury at the Battle of the Plains.'

The man's brows rose. 'Truly? Then you were there when the Empress fell?'
'Yes, sir. Though I did not witness it.'
'Few did, I understand. What, then, is your impression of this new Emperor, Mallick Rel?'
Orjin glanced back to Kyle, cleared his throat. 'Well, sir, I'm not a politician. But I was glad that he did not prosecute the officers who had rebelled against the Empress.'
The man's calculating gaze seemed to say, *Because you were among them?* 'He's Falari, you know.'
'No, sir. I did not know that.'
'Yes. And I will tell you this – there were many of us here who were not in the least bit surprised at the news of his, ah, advancement.'
'Is that so, sir.'
The man shrugged uneasily beneath his layered furred robes. 'Anyway . . . Your rates?'
'A half-silver per hour for individual instruction.'
The man's mouth drew down. 'That is much more than I was expecting.'
'Ah, but . . .' The big man motioned to Kyle. 'I can also offer instruction from my compatriot here, who was of the famed mercenary company, the Crimson Guard.'
The nobleman eyed Kyle thinly. 'And now employs those skills breaking arms.'
Orjin actually winced. 'Yes, well. You can always withdraw should you not judge the instruction beneficial.'
'It is not for myself. It is for my son.'
'I see. His age?'
'Still a boy, really . . . but rowdy. Undisciplined.' He tilted his head as he stroked his goatee. 'But you look as if you might be able to handle him.' He nodded thoughtfully. 'Yes. Thank you. Until then.' He bowed.
Orjin answered the bow. 'I look forward to it.'
The man left. Kyle ambled across the floor to Orjin's side. 'Think we'll see him again?'
'Could be.'
'He didn't even ask to see your papers.'
'Perhaps he knows how easily all that bullshit can be forged.'
'Maybe.' Kyle eyed his friend sidelong. 'A half-silver per hour? Pretty steep. I couldn't afford you.'
The man smiled wolfishly and his glacial blue eyes glittered with

humour. For a moment he had the appearance of his old self. 'He looked as if he could spare it.'

Kyle laughed. 'Aye. Tomorrow, then.'

'Yes – sword and shield work.'

Backing away, Kyle waved the suggestion aside. 'Gods, no. There's no skill in that.'

'No skill! There's ignorance speaking. Do you in, that ignorance might one day.'

'Not before I knife it.'

'*Knife?* Useless against anyone in a shred of armour.'

Kyle paused. 'I'll—' A knock sounded just as he was reaching for the doors. Frowning, he opened one of the wide leaves. Three men, plainly dressed, bearing expensive Falaran-style longswords and daggers, the blades straight and slim. Three more! Must be Greymane's – Orjin's – banner day. He nodded to one. 'Morning.'

This one, a young swell in a broad-brimmed green felt hat, looked him up and down and made no effort to disguise his lack of approval. 'You are this new weapon-master?'

'No.' Kyle motioned up the tunnel. 'He's it.' He stood aside. The three men entered, leaving the door ajar. The indifferent condescension of that act – as if the three were used to others opening and shutting doors for them – moved Kyle to stroll along behind them, curious.

He stopped in the mouth of the tunnel that led to the court. The three had met Orjin at a weapon rack. 'You are this new weapon-master, Orjin Samarr?' their spokesman asked in a tone that was almost accusatory.

Orjin turned, blinking mildly. His eyes glinted bright like sapphires in the shade. 'Aye? May I help you? You would like a lesson, perhaps?'

The three exchanged glances, their mouths twisting up, amused. 'Yes,' the fellow in the green hat began, backing off and setting a gloved hand on his sword. 'You can help us settle a wager my friends and I have made . . .' The other two stepped aside to Orjin's right and left. Kyle pushed himself from the wall, edged closer to a weapon rack. '. . . as to whether any foreigner could possibly provide fighting instruction in any way approximating that quality with which Delanss has been so blessed.'

Orjin nodded his understanding. He drew a bound stave from the weapon rack, sighted down its length. 'I see. Well, normally I charge a half-silver for lessons. But perhaps the three of you would like to go in together on a group rate—'

They drew, snarling. Orjin sprang upon the one on his right, the stave smacking the man's right hand, and he yelped, tucking it under an arm. Orjin spun to face the other two. Kyle drew a wooden baton from the weapon rack, tossed it end over end while he watched.

Using a two-handed grip, Orjin parried, the stave blurring, knocking the slim double-edged blades aside. The fellow in the felt hat furiously threw it aside and drew his parrying dagger. The clack of the stave against the blades echoed in the court. Kyle listened for the telltale catch of iron biting wood, but so far Orjin had managed to avoid that particular danger. The man's face was reddening and Kyle stopped tossing the baton.

Too early; far too early for any exertion to be showing. '*They're* using knives,' he observed conversationally.

Orjin shot him a glare, his cheeks puffing. The three danced around him while he shifted slowly, knees bent, stave cocked. 'Now, normally,' he began, 'none of you would have occasion to meet an opponent using a two-handed weapon . . .' One lunged in, and Orjin's stave smacked his face, sending him tottering aside. Orjin returned his guard on the remaining two. 'Normally, it is too slow and awkward to move from side to side across the body. A nimble opponent should—' The same one charged, slashing. Orjin's stave parried, dipped, and came up into the fellow's groin. The man fell like a string-cut puppet. Kyle winced in empathetic pain.

Sweat now sheathing his face, Orjin faced their spokesman, who smiled, acknowledging the lesson, and immediately attacked. Parrying, Orjin dipped his head, shouting his encouragement. 'Yes, yes! That's right – draw the point aside, prepare the gauche for the hidden thrust!'

A warning shout from Kyle died in his throat as the hand-slapped fellow re-entered the fray to grip Orjin from behind. Kyle was amazed by the foolhardiness of the move; the bhederin-like Orjin was half again as broad as any man he'd ever met.

Shrugging, Orjin wrenched an arm around to get the man in a headlock and threw him over his shoulder stomach up like a sack of grain. Stave in one hand, he faced the spokesman. 'Now you have the advantage – a one-handed opponent!'

The spokesman did not hesitate. His booted feet shushed and thumped the sand as he dodged, feinting, circling the ponderously shifting Orjin. Kyle kicked himself from the wall. *Shit! He's really gonna try it!* The longsword scraped up the shaft of the stave, holding it aside, and he stepped in the gauche, thrusting, but Orjin spun, the blade sawing shallowly across his side as the legs and boots of the man across his shoulder smashed into his assistant, sending him flying aside. Orjin tossed the man on to his sprawled fellow and stood panting. He touched his side gingerly and flinched. 'The lesson is . . .' he drew a heavy breath, 'that you all should've attacked at once, regardless.'

Kyle watched the big man's chest rising and falling. Out of breath already? Not good. No, not good at all. He replaced the baton.

As the spokesman struggled to rise Orjin put a booted foot to his backside and sent him tumbling to the tunnel. 'I'd charge you. But I suspect you're all incapable of learning anything.'

Gathering up their fallen weapons, they backed off to the exit. Kyle bowed as they passed. 'Honoured sirs!' They merely glared and mouthed curses. Kyle ambled out to Orjin, who was cleaning up. 'Winded already . . .'

The man shot him a glare. 'Been a while.' He found a rag, wiped his jowls.

'A little dust-up like that shouldn't—'

'Drop it.'

Kyle's brows rose. *Short-tempered too.* 'So I'll be by tomorrow afternoon then for that sword and shield work. What do you say? Full armour too?'

Orjin made a face. 'Very funny. Now get out of here. I have to get cleaned up.'

Kyle saluted and backed away.

But he'd been serious.

*

In a shaded narrow alleyway a few streets down, the young tough, his green felt hat in one hand, dabbed a silk handkerchief to his bleeding nose and mouth and faced the richly dressed Delanss noble in his furred robes and thick silver chains. With a ringed hand the noble edged the young man's head aside to examine one cheek, tsked beneath his breath. 'So he did manage to handle you . . .'

'Father!'

'So, what do you think? Is he the one?'

'He must be. He lifted Donas like a child.'

'Very well. I'll send word. Until then, hire men to keep an eye on the school.'

The young man bowed.

'And no retribution! No crossbows in the night, or knives in the market. They want him alive.'

The young man rolled his eyes. 'Yes, father.'

The noble stroked his grey-shot goatee, studied the young man. 'I must say I am impressed by the man's control. He put you down without breaking any bones at all. He showed great restraint in the face of almost intolerable insult.'

'*Father!*'

* * *

First year of the rule of Emperor Mallick Rel 'The Merciful'
(Year 1167 Burn's Sleep)
Stratem Subcontinent

At dawn, Kuhn Eshen, called Kuhn 'The Nose', master of *Rich Tidings*, a Katakan freetrader, dropped anchor offshore from the town of Thickton and spent an anxious morning waiting to see whether the stories of the lands of Stratem being open once more to the outside world were true.

As the hours passed the usual small boats made their way out, offering fresh fruit, bread, fish and pigs. Boys and girls swam the cold waters, offering to lead the crew to boarding houses or brothels, or to act as general guides about town. All good signs of a growing openness to trade. By noon the larger open launches were oaring out, bearing merchant agents. These men and women Kuhn greeted. He offered a taste of the Styggian liqueur he'd brought, and showed bolts of Jass broadcloth. They listened with barely concealed eagerness to his talk of Korel; news only a few weeks old rather than the two or three months it usually took for any word to reach this stretch of the isolated Sea of Chimes.

One woman among them, however, mystified Kuhn and he kept a wary eye on her. She stood leaning self-contained against the side. Dressed in dark leathers, with a sword belted at her side, her long auburn hair pulled back and fixed with a bright green tortoiseshell clip, she almost looked to be a military officer of some sort. She took no interest in his wares; instead she watched his crew as they in turn eyed the thickly treed shore. Some few garbled stories had reached Korel lands concerning events on their southern neighbour. Word of a band of hireswords carving out a private kingdom. But all that had been long ago. Still, he wondered: could she be one of *them*?

After expressing an interest in board feet of the local hardwoods, in tanned hides, and furs, Kuhn spent a time doling out news of Korel lands. The crowded circle of locals hung on every scrap – true or not. He was talking of the Stormwall when his audience went silent and all eyes edged aside, glancing past him. He turned.

The woman in dark leathers had come up behind him. She was watching him expectantly, her sharp chin raised. 'I'm sorry . . . ?' he stammered.

'I said what was that . . . what you were just talking of.'

'Just the latest news from the Stormwall, honoured lady. And you are . . . ?'

'I represent the governor of this province – Haven Province, of Stratem.'

'Truly? A governor?' Kuhn looked to a nearby agent who was nodding seriously, his thick neck bulging. *Intriguing. This news could be worth much in certain ports of Korel.* 'And this governor – does he have a name?' Closer now, he saw that she wore a single piece of jewellery high on the left of her chest – what looked like a dragon or snake wrought in silver.

The woman's thin lips edged sideways in an almost cruel knowing smile. 'You first.'

Ah. Going to be that way, is it? Kuhn shrugged, and rested his forearms on the ship's gunwale. 'Certainly, m'lady. My news is always free. It's half the reason we traders are welcome wherever we go. I was just speaking of the Stormwall. The ranks of the Chosen have thinned, you know. But this last season a new champion has arisen on the wall. The Korelri are full of his exploits. They call him Bars – odd name, that.'

The woman's reaction made Kuhn flinch. She fairly paled; a hand rose as if to shake him by the throat but to his relief merely clutched air. '*Bars*,' she hissed aloud in an almost awed whisper. She threw herself over the side, slipping down the rope ladder by her hands alone. Landing jarringly in a launch, she immediately ordered it away. She even lent a hand at an oar herself and it was all the rest of the burly crew could do to keep up. All this Kuhn watched bemusedly, scratching his scalp. 'Who in the name of the Blessed Lady was that?'

'That was Janeth, warder of the town.'

'Warder? What does that mean? Is she your ruler?'

A shake of the head. 'No, gentle sir. We have a council. She enforces the laws. Her men guard the coast. Arrest thieves and killers – not that we've had a killin' here in some time.' The agent warmed to his subject, crossed his arms on the gunwale. 'Last season raiders from your neighbour Mare came through. They show up from time to time. She and her men drove them off.'

Kuhn eyed the retreating launch. Drove off Mare raiders? Her and how many men? So, law enforcement and protection. Agent of this self-styled governor. A king by any other name? News indeed for the Korelan Council of the Chosen concerning their once sleepy southern neighbour. 'And this provincial governor. He has a name?'

An easy shrug beneath bunched hides. 'I heard him called "Blues" once. We just call him the Lord Governor. He's living in an old fort called Haven. Hasn't been around lately. Not that I'd know him to see him.'

Enough for now. Smiling easily, Kuhn slapped the agent on the arm. 'Well, thank you. See you this evening?'

'Oh, yes. Esta's house. She runs a clean place. Best ever. You'll see.'

Best ever? My friend, I very much doubt that this muddy backwater could offer any attractions rivalling those of infamous Danig of Theft, or legendary Ebon of Stygg.

BOOK I

The Sea

The so-called Malazan 'empire' began as a thalassocracy. That is, rule by sea power. In the undignified scholarly scramble to identify and distil the empire's early stages this truly defining characteristic is usually overlooked. Yet the Malazan expansion was undeniably one of sea power and this was the key to its early successes. It was also the key to one of its early failures: the ill-conceived incursion into the archipelago and subcontinent known variously as Fist, Korel, or the Storm-cursed. For this archipelago was itself a supreme sea power, if non-expansionist. And in the end of course it was the sea that so definitively, and with such finality, put an end to all hostilities.

Imperial Campaigns (The Korel Occupations)
Volume II, *Fist*
Imrygyn Tallobant

CHAPTER I

What is an old man but a pile of fading leaves?

Wisdom of the Ancients
Kreshen Reel, compiler

Year 33 of the Malazan Occupation
Korelri year 4178 sw
North of Elri, Korel Isle

THE DESK OF THE LORD PROTECTOR OF THE STORMWALL IS CONstructed of planks taken from the wreck of a Mare war galley that the Stormriders, the enemy, had captured and used in an attempt to ram the wall. It had been one of their most successful stratagems of the recent century. Over thirty of the Chosen gave up their lives in holy martyrdom to stem that breach. The Lord Protector of the time, one of the few non-Korelri ever to have attained that august office, ordered the desk built to serve as a reminder to all his successors that while the Stormriders had for centuries thrown themselves against the wall in so far predictable, even repetitive tactics, one must never become complacent regarding them.

Lord Protector Hiam, the current holder of the highest office of the subcontinent of Korel, latest in an unbroken line reaching back to the first holder of the title, the legendary Founder, Temal-Esh, ran a hand over the smooth warm surface of this desk, thinking about its all too salient message from the past. During the height of the Riders' assaults frost limned its corners as if it carried still within it the memory of its subverted purpose. That had been one of the most perilous moments for the Stormwall, yet at least it was a threat from without. And that was a peril Hiam would gladly exchange for the one facing them now.

Glancing up, he saw his aide, Staff Marshal Shool, patiently waiting through his woolgathering. He cleared his throat. 'So, Shool, more falling recruitment estimates.'

Helm in the crook of one arm, dark azure cloak folded up over the other, Shool bowed and sat. He set his plain helm down. 'Yes, Lord Protector.'

'With retirements, casualties, and the usual attrition – where does that put us for the coming fall?'

'Even shorter than last year.'

And that year shorter than the one before. An undeniable trend that spoke of ultimate unavoidable disaster to anyone inclined to trace that particular trajectory into the future – but Hiam was not one so inclined. The Lady, their Preserver, would save them as she always had. He knew that common opinion blamed the thinning numbers on these invaders, the Malazans. A belief he did nothing to discourage precisely because he knew the trend reached back far before their arrival.

He crossed to the slit window overlooking the central and strongest sweeping curtain length of the leagues-long Stormwall. The glittering surface of the Ocean of Storm lay iron-grey and summer-calm. How many times had he stood here and wondered what that surface disguised? Were the enemy now likewise regarding them? Or did they withdraw between raids to some unimaginable depth or cavern to sleep away the intervening months? None knew, though poets and jongleurs speculated in endless romantic ballads and epics.

With the Lady's aid may he yet wipe these Riders from the face of the earth.

He turned from the narrow slit in the arm-thick stone wall. 'More provincial levies, Shool. Press them hard. Remind Jasston and Stygg of their obligations.'

Shool picked up his helmet and turned it in his hands. He seemed to study the blue-dyed leather wrapping and the silver chasing of the Chosen Stormguard. 'You are expecting an offensive from the Malazans with this new Emperor?'

'I am expecting an offensive, Shool,' Hiam said levelly, 'but not from the Malazans.'

The helmet froze. Shool dropped his head in acquiescence. 'My apologies, Lord Protector.'

From a hook next to the window Hiam lifted the heavy layered wool cloak he wore year round, both in the dire biting wind of winter and in the simmering heat of summer. 'Shall we?'

Shool stood hastily, bowing. 'Yes, Lord Protector.'

They exited the main donjon to step out on to the wide, windswept main marshalling surface of the wall, fifty paces wide. Seaward rose a thinner wall, lined by staircases of stone and topped by a walkway and parapets – the outer machicolations. The grey granite blocks of the wall's construction glittered dark from a recent rain and pools reflected the overcast sky.

Distraction, Hiam told himself. These Malazans. Nothing more than a distraction from their true calling – their God-given purpose. Never mind that too many seemed unduly impressed by that Empire's accomplishments elsewhere. But they were no fleabitten barbarians gawping at the mysteries of ordered infantry, nor decadent city-dwellers to be intimidated or bought; they were the Stormguard, the Chosen, defenders of all the lands from its greatest enemy.

They would not be overborne. They could not.

A Chosen met them just outside the doorway. He stood wrapped in the thick dark-blue cloak that was their unofficial uniform, crested helmet on his head and wide leaf-bladed spear held tall. Wall Marshal and Quartermaster, Quint of Theft. He bowed to Hiam and his dark, scarred features twisted in what the Lord Protector knew passed as the man's smile; he inclined his head in acknowledgement.

As they made their inspection tour, Hiam could not help noting troubling details even as he passed them over without comment: cracked steps in ill-repair; torn baskets that ought to be replaced; thin frayed rope past its best years; the tattered edges of Quint's cloak and his cracked sandals. Lack of maintenance, lack of equipment. All problems adequate funds could solve. But what monies the Stormguard did pull in through tribute, taxation and levies it poured entirely into acquiring warm bodies to man the wall – in any manner it could.

And that flow of tribute and taxation was diminishing. Particularly now with the presence of the invaders, the Malazans, emboldening resentful neighbours such as Stygg and Jasston to neglect their ages-old treaties and agreements.

'How go repairs, Marshal?' Hiam asked.

Quint's scarred face – the gift of a Rider's jagged blade – twisted down even further. Beneath his cloak he shifted his arms, cradling the spear haft. 'Slow as fastidious whores in a brothel, these labourers.'

Hiam could not keep an answering wry smile from his lips. The man had the reputation of being most ferocious Stormguard on the wall. Together they went all the way back to induction, though Quint preceded him. 'They aren't volunteers, like the old days.' *Unlike us.*

An answering grunt was all the marshal would allow – an informality none other would dare before the Lord Protector. 'If they worked a fraction as hard as they complained we'd have every job done by now. You should hear them, Hiam. How they give enough in the winter without having to provide work gangs in the summer. Yet not one man of them has ever stood the wall. We rely more on foreign levies now than on true Korelri. It's a damned disgrace is what it is. It wouldn't surprise me . . .' His voice trailed away, then he gave a harsh laugh. 'Well, their song always changes when the snow flies, hey, Hiam?'

Hiam had glanced up to see Quint's gaze on Shool's shocked face. Yes, old friend, we aren't alone. Going to say you wouldn't be surprised if Our Lady turned her face from us for our sins, hey? We're now the old dogs grumbling about how standards have fallen, just as did our instructors and superiors before us.

Stopping, Hiam nodded to Shool. 'That's all. I'll look at the inventories later.'

Shool bowed. 'My lord.'

Quint watched him go. 'Too soon from the tit, that one,' he growled.

'He did his season.' Quint grunted, unimpressed. 'So, give it to me straight, Quartermaster. Not your usual sweet-talk.'

''Sa bloody cock-up, is what it is. We're behind schedule everywhere. There's a crack in the facing east of Vor you could shove a man through. But,' and he bared yellowed uneven teeth, 'I could say the same thing about a woman I knew from Jourilan.'

'Master Stimins?'

Quint let go a snort of exasperation. 'Let me tell you about Master Engineer Stimins. Last week he drags me down the wall behind the fifth tower north of Storm, and he points to a little course of sand in the rocks. The man's pulling his hair out over some tiny dried-up rivulet while I'm trying to find enough masons to fill gaps!'

'He's worried about the foundations.'

'Foundation my arse. The wall's as heavy as a mountain. It can't fall down. Anyway, it's just a place to stand – it's the men and women defending it who count. And we need more of them.'

'Lady bless that, Quint. So, what about the latest crop? How are they shaping up?'

'As useful as eunuchs and seamstresses. But we'll knock them into line. The usual prison scrapings from Katakan and Theft aren't worth the food we buy to feed them. The Dourkan and Jourilan contingents are pretty solid, as ever. Mare has sent a shipload of Malazan prisoners. We even have some debtors from Rool – the Malazans continue to allow it, apparently.'

'They get their cut, I'm sure. Speaking of them, how's the current champion?'

The quartermaster shook a sour negative. 'We can't count on another season out of him. He has the death wish. I've seen it before.'

'Too bad. He accomplished some amazing feats.'

'True. 'Cept he laughs like a lunatic every time we call him Malazan.'

Nodding to himself, Hiam listened to the wind carrying the distant metallic clinks of mallets on stone, the calls of foremen, and the low heartbeat of the quickening autumn surf. His arms were sweaty beneath the sweltering cloak. 'Very good, Quartermaster. I won't keep you from your duties any longer.'

Quint tilted his head suspiciously. 'Where're you off to?'

'To find our good Master Engineer.'

'Ha! You'll likely find him on his hands and knees, sniffing around our foundations like a dog, no doubt.'

'Carry on, Wall Marshal – and stay out of Stimins' way.'

'With pleasure.'

It was not until late that afternoon that the Lord Protector finally tracked down Master Engineer Stimins. And – true to Quint's prediction – the man was sniffing around the base of the wall. By that time Hiam had picked up an escort: two veterans, Stall of Korel and solid Evessa out of Jourilan, whom many suspected of carrying more than a drop of the old blood. They'd arrived care of Quint, whose message was that it was unseemly for the Lord Protector to be wandering about without guards. Hiam did not bother pointing out that it was just as unseemly for Quint to allow the Master Engineer to do so.

He heard Stimins long before he found him, among the huge tumbled boulders of the slope that graded back from the wall's rear. 'You're a pretty one,' he heard the old fellow coo, and he didn't have to wonder what the man was addressing. 'Very nice, very nice.' Stumbling along with him, their spears clattering, Stall and Evessa shared a glance and rolled their eyes.

Hiam wondered if he was stalking a parrot.

Eventually, circling round a tall boulder, he found the man hunched down on all fours like a pale spider investigating a crevice for food.

'Master Engineer . . .' Hiam began.

The man jumped, and glared about myopically beneath bushy white brows. 'Who's that? Who?'

'It's Hiam, Stimins.'

'Oh, young Hiam. What in the Lady's name are you doing down here?'

'Looking for you,' Hiam observed tartly.

'Ah! Well, whatever for?'

Hiam crooked his head to motion away his escort. Bowing, they moved off to lean back amongst the tumbled boulders, arms crossed over the hafts of their spears. 'Your report.'

The engineer was fiddling with small rocks in the palm of one hand, turning them round and round. 'Report? What report?'

The Lord Protector slapped a hand to the hot gritty side of a boulder. Dried bird guano streaked the stone white and patches of lichen grew green and orange. 'Your report on the state of the wall!'

'Ah. That report. Well, it's not conclusive yet. I need to study things further.'

'That's what you said last year, and the year before that.'

The snowy brows rose over pale, watery blue eyes. 'I did? Well, there you go.'

'With all due respect, Master Engineer. We no longer have the time for the luxury of conclusiveness . . . Your current assessment will have to do.'

Stimins sniffed his disapproval. 'That's the trouble with you younger generations – no patience to do the job right. Things are off to the Abyss in a broken wagon, they are.'

Hiam crossed his arms, and his cloak fell open to reveal the broad scarred forearms, the dire gouges and deep scrapes in the bronze and leather vambraces. The Master Engineer extended his bony hand, clenched, knuckles knotted in joint-ache. Hiam held his own out, open. Two small stones fell into his palm.

'My report,' Stimins said.

Mystified, Hiam studied the two stones. Taking one in each hand he found that they fitted together exactly: two halves of the same piece. 'What's this? A broken rock?'

'Shattered cleanly in half, Lord Protector. By the corroding cold itself.'

Now Hiam regarded his Master Engineer. 'The cold? How could it do such a thing?'

Stimins raised his hands for patience. 'Let me correct myself. By frost. By moisture, freezing suddenly. Explosively.'

Hiam thought of casks of water left out during the worst of the assaults, how some exploded at the touch of the Riders' sorceries. 'I see . . . I think.'

'All up and down the wall,' Stimins continued, his voice becoming dreamy, 'freezing, thawing, year after year. But not the mild slow advance of nature, mind you. The forced unnatural fist of the Riders slamming winter after winter. Pounding the wall to slivers.'

'How—' Hiam coughed to clear his throat. 'How long do we have?'

The old man, his face still unfocused, shrugged his maddening disregard. 'Who is to say? Another one hundred years – or one.'

Struggling to contain himself, Hiam threw the stones to clatter among the boulders. 'Thank you for your report, Master Engineer.' *Though it be utterly useless to our current crisis*. 'And I remind you that such information is to be shared only between you and me.'

The old man blinked his confusion, his brows crimping. 'But of course, Lord Protector.'

'Very good. Carry on.' The Lord Protector left his Master Engineer scratching his thin hair and frowning among the rocks.

His escort, Stall and Evessa, straightened from where they leaned among the menhir-sized boulders. Stall tossed away a handful of pebbles. 'Odd noises among these stones, hey, Evessa?'

'The strangest echoes, Stall.'

* * *

Ivanr hacked his farm out of the unsettled far south of Jourilan, hard up against the foothills of the immense mountain chain some named the Iceback range. Wanderers and religious refugees fleeing south from the cities often passed his field. Many claimed that the Priestess was nearby but still Ivanr was surprised when she appeared one day.

Her voice startled him as he was bent over weeding his garden and he straightened, blinked the sweat from his eyes.

'Ivanr,' she said, 'what is it you fear about me?'

He studied the slip of a girl-woman in her dirty rags before him. A foreigner come to convert an entire land. He saw a face lined and drawn by a suffering no youth should be asked to endure; limbs emaciated, almost warped by the tasks that had been exacted from them. And yet the undeniable aura of power hovered about her, warning off any who would consider a challenge. Shrugging, he returned to his weeding.

'Priestess, I do not fear you.'

'Yet you resolutely avoid me.'

He gestured broadly to his field. 'I have work to do.'

Dry leaves shushed as she closed. Her bare feet were dirty, her robes no more than mud-smeared tatters. 'As do I. Could it be, Ivanr, that you fear I may have other work for you?'

'You have plenty of others to choose from.'

'Yet here I am speaking to you.'

He straightened, towering over her, and she raised her chin to meet his gaze. Her tangled black hair blew about her face like a cowl. He had to flinch from the depths of those compelling eyes. 'Well, you're wasting your time.'

'You presume to know what I am doing? They mock you, you know. Call you farmer. Dirt-grubber. Coward.'

'And I grow things called tomatoes, beans, marrow.' That raised a brief haunted smile. 'You do not need me. I'm told you have many of the aristocrats. The pure-blooded ruling families.'

'True. Sons and daughters of the highest Jourilan names have marched up to my modest fig tree. "Teach me," they demand. "Instruct me in this new way we hear of." Already perhaps they are too far down the wrong path. But I cannot show them that – only you can.'

He studied his dirt-smeared hands; cut and bloodied, calloused, nails broken. *Just as during all those years of training and duelling.* 'They won't listen to me. I'm . . . of the wrong background.'

'Ah yes. That taint so shameful to the Jourilan. Mixed blood. Do you know the name of your ancestors, Ivanr?'

He shrugged, his gaze hooded. 'My mother said her people were of the Red-Rock tribe of the Thoul-Alai. That is all I know.'

The Priestess's voice hardened in sudden outrage. 'Your people were of the Toblakai, Ivanr! Blessed of the children of the Great

Mother! Some of you survive, isolated, in pockets here and there, despite the best efforts of all those who have stolen your lands.'

'Stolen? Strong language for an outlander.'

Now the Priestess hugged her angular frame, the lines at her mouth deepened in shadow. 'It is a story not unfamiliar to me.'

Ivanr stared wonderingly. *So, a vulnerable side. An opening up. Careful. Seduction bears many faces.* 'Immaterial. What's done is done. Nothing can bring back the past.'

'I would never seek that.' Her words were softer now, her tone closer to that of her true tender age. He felt the wounds that she carried and something within him ached to hold her, to soothe that pain.

Dangerous indeed.

'The question is how to proceed into the future. You, Ivanr, the warrior champion who defied the call to the Stormwall. I have heard many rumours as to why. But I have my own theory . . .'

His gaze found a flight of crows crossing over the face of the distant Jourilan central plateau. Smoke obscured the north horizon; he shielded his eyes, squinting. *Burning already – damned early.* 'It was cowardice – leave it at that.'

'No. It would be cowardice to leave it at that.'

He let his hand fall. She eyed him levelly, almost coolly, and he felt himself shrinking under that steady gaze. *Such suffering scoured into that lined hatchet face that should be unmarred! And a haunting glow as well – the lingering hint of the revelation everyone whispers of? Who is he to dare dispute this one's choices? But surely he must be unworthy! How could he, who once gloried in conflict, possibly serve Dessembrae, the Lord of Tragedy, or any of these foreign gods?*

'I couldn't. I'm not—'

'Not worthy? Not pure enough? Not dedicated enough? Not . . . certain? None of us is. And none who is certain interests the Lord of Tragedy. *Those* minds are closed. He requires the mind be open.' She now seemed to eye him sidelong, almost mockingly. 'It was your open mind that led you to your conclusion, to that intuitive flash that so changed you, yes?'

'I don't know what you're talking about.'

'You saw instinctively, on your own, the uselessness of it all.'

Gods, this woman was dangerous! How could she know? And yet – wasn't this the essence of her sermonizing, her own message? He ran a hand across his slick forehead and said, his voice hoarse,

'Dangerous talk, Priestess. Talk that can get a man, or a woman, put to death.'

'So you *are* afraid . . .'

He offered a half-smile. 'Of the Jourilan Emperor's torture pits, yes.'

'*They* aren't the enemy. The enemy is ignorance and hate. Aren't these worth opposing?'

Pure idealism. Ye gods, where does one begin with such a one? His gaze found the peppers ripening at his feet. 'Priestess,' he began, slowly, 'you don't really think you're the first, do you?' He waved to encompass the fields. 'The Lady Our Saviour has kept a tight watch on her garden all these generations. She weeds thoroughly. And ruthlessly. No unwelcome invader has been allowed to take hold. I've seen it before.'

The Priestess raised her gaze, and perhaps it was day's late argent light, or a reflection of some kind, but the eyes flared as if molten.

'Have you not wondered,' she asked in a low voice, 'why you must constantly weed in the first place?'

He cocked his head, uncertain of her tack.

'It is because the weeds are far hardier than the crop you're trying to raise.'

Ivanr found that he'd flinched away. He paced the field, stepping between the plants. *Damn you, woman! How dare you plague me with such outrageous demands! Haven't I done enough? But perhaps walking away wasn't enough. Perhaps walking away was never enough.* He stopped his pacing. Turning to her, he could only offer his mute denial.

She approached gently, as if afraid he would flee, and proffered a hand. 'Take this. And come to my fig tree. Sit at my side. Listen to the message that has come to me. I believe you are already far down the path.'

When he would not raise his own hand she took it and pressed an object into it. Her hand was a fraction the size of his, yet far harder. As sharp and unyielding as stone slivers. She walked away, the long tatters of her robes dragged behind through the stalks. Ivanr opened his hand. A square-cut iron nail like a sword in miniature, with a lace of leather drawn through the small loop that was the grip and pommel. The symbol of the cult of Dessembrae.

Word of the heresy of polytheism had come north down the mountain foothills only a few years ago. It had been twice that time since

Ivanr had refused the Call and thrown down his swords in the dust of the training grounds at Abor. They'd imprisoned him, beaten him almost to his death, cursed him as half-breed Thel scum – not that his background had mattered while his sword served. But they would not kill him; not great Ivanr whom they had lauded as the greatest Jourilan champion in living memory.

And so it was that he had found himself blinking in the unfamiliar bright sunlight with only the rags about his loins to his name. The guards who had prodded him from the wagon threw a skin of water at his feet and told him that if he returned to the city he'd be killed out of hand. The wounds on his lashed back split open as he knelt to pick up the water.

He had walked south. At first he thought he'd simply keep walking until his feet brought him to the vast glacier wilderness held in abeyance by the Iceback range. Where he would no doubt have perished. But when he reached the foothills he came across many more of his kind, clustered in small family camps around smoking firepits, digging the earth beside the road. Some purebred, some mixed – remnants, those bearing the mark of the prior inhabitants of the land. Some markedly tall, like himself, others broad and low to the ground. The Thoul-Alai, or variously 'Thel' or 'Thoul', as the invaders had parsed. And so he decided that here was perhaps where he belonged. He selected a section of a hardscrabble unfavourable hillside, and planted.

The local ranchers who raised a breed of cattle called Baranal thought him mad and regularly ran their beasts through his field. His fellow Thel also thought him touched; none of them farmed. But it seemed to him that a society reliant on a way of life no longer viable, namely hunting and gathering, really ought to adapt. He judged farming a reasonable substitution.

Then word came of this new cult. Blasphemous! They deny the Goddess! They speak against the Stormwall! This priestess who led them was a witch who enslaved men with sex. They held orgies at which babies were murdered and eaten.

It seemed strange to him that everyone should be so ready to believe that a cult that preached nonviolence should also be murdering babies. But from what he'd seen in life there was much insanity surrounding religion.

Then the first of the prisoner gangs came shuffling along the road that ran through the valley beneath his hillside. A corpse suspended from a gibbet swung at the head of the column. After working the day with his back pointedly turned to the valley, Ivanr finally threw aside his digging tools and walked down to where the Jourilan captors had staked the chain gang. An officer of the detachment came out to meet him, flanked by troopers.

'These are the heretics?' he asked.

'Yes.' The officer watched him narrowly; Ivanr saw many of his brother and sister Thel among the shackled prisoners. None raised their heads.

'They are for Abor?'

'Yes.'

'Execution?'

'Yes.'

'The usual? Stoning? Crushing? Public garrotting and impalement? Or just plain crucifixion? Violent ends for people who swear to nonviolence.'

The Jourilan officer's gaze hardened even further. 'Is that an objection?'

'Just an observation.'

The officer motioned him off. 'Then observe from far away.'

A month later Ivanr was sitting in front of his sod-roofed hut sharpening his tools when a file of dusty beggars approached. An old man led them, of pure Jourilan invader stock, haggard and unwashed, but holding his head high and walking with a firm stride, planting a walking staff strongly before him. He stopped his band of followers a discreet distance off then stepped up and leaned on the staff.

'Spare a drink of water for those who thirst, stranger?'

Ivanr set down his sharpening stone. He scanned the horizon for any Jourilan patrol. Saw none. 'Aye.' He carried out a small keg of captured rainwater and a tarred leather cup. The old man bowed, took a small sip, then handed on the keg to his band. The entire time, the dark eyes slitted in his sun-burned, lined face did not leave Ivanr's.

'You are from the south?' Ivanr asked.

'Aye.'

'You carry word of this new faith?'

The cracked and bloodied lips climbed with faint humour. 'We follow the Priestess and bring the word of her teachings. Word of the new faith revealed to her. A faith that embraces life. Rejects death.'

'You reject death?'

'We accept it. And thereby deny it any power over us.'

'And you are headed north?'

'Yes. To Pon-Ruo.'

'I think you'll find what you deny waiting for you there.'

Again, the half-smile. 'Death awaits us all. The question, then, really should be how to live.'

'You mean survive?'

'No – how to live one's life. Harming others is no way to honour life.'

Ivanr, who up until then had merely been amusing himself, shivered at those words. The old pilgrim did not seem to notice; he gestured to Ivanr's fields. 'Farming honours life.'

Ivanr waved the man off. 'Take the water and go.' He walked away.

'You cannot hide from life,' the old man called after him. 'You harm yourself and give power to that from which you turn.'

'Go!'

The old man bowed. 'We honour you for your gift.'

Just go, damn you!

* * *

Of all the places to die in Banith, Bakune believed that this was very probably the ugliest. He could almost smell the madness that must have driven the old woman to her death here in this dead-end alley. What he could not avoid smelling was the stale sweat, the animal fear, and the dried piss.

She'd been a nun in attendance at Our Lady the Saviour Cloister and Hospice. That much the Watch had ascertained. A woman gone mad to end her life in a frothing twisted heap at the back of a garbage-strewn alley, fingers bloody and torn where she'd clawed at the stone walls.

And he'd almost missed this one.

The Watch hardly bothered to call him in any more. Just another corpse. The Assessor came, poked about, asked his obtuse questions, then went back to frown and potter over his reports. What was the use? For his part, Bakune saw that while the Watch respected his judgements from the bench, all the same they wished he'd just stay in his chambers. After all these years it was becoming, well, an embarrassment.

But there was something different about this one. What was a nun of the temple doing outside in the middle of the night? How had she gotten out without anyone noticing? And why? Why lose herself in this warren of alleys? Lunacy, he supposed, was the easy answer.

But too glib for his liking. The temple revealed little of the finer points of its faith, let alone its inner workings. How could this embarrassment have escaped its self-policing? No doubt the madwoman had been under virtual house arrest for some time now, perhaps locked in an ascetic's cell. A visit to the cloisters might just be in order.

He straightened from the stiffened corpse to find that his escort, two soldiers of the Watch, had retreated to the mouth of this ratrun of an alley, where it met a slightly larger and less choked back way. Sighing, Bakune stepped over the rotting garbage and dumped nightsoil to join them.

'A right reek,' the moustached one offered – as close to an apology as any of the street-level patrolmen might offer him.

'I want to talk to the Abbot.'

The two shared a flicked glance, and in that quick exchange Bakune was chagrined to read the true bankruptcy of his influence and reputation: babysitting the Assessor while he pottered among alleyways was one thing, allowing him to pester the Abbot of the Cloister of Our Lady was another altogether.

He was chagrined, yes, but not surprised. The City Watch valued action and quick results. To him, the blunt brutal truncheons at their sides were fitting weapons for the blunt and brutal instruments of state that carried them. 'You need not accompany me.'

Again the flicked glance. 'No, Assessor,' the less dull-looking of the two drawled. 'It's our job.'

'Very good. Let's hope the Abbot is available on such short notice.'

The Cloister of the Blessed Lady was the third most revered holy site on the island of Fist, after the caves of the Ascetics near Thol, and the Tabernacle of Our Lady at Paliss. Neither Mare nor Skolati possessed any such sites worthy of pilgrimage. The Cloister was raised around the very bare rock where it was said the Lady herself shed blood on her holy mission to forestall the sea-borne enemy.

Bakune headed to the pilgrim route that twisted its way from the waterfront docks to the Cloister's double copper doors. The cacophony reached him first. Touts and hawkers bawled to catch the attention of the penitents as they tramped the ancient path that climbed the hillside to those beaten-panelled doors. Bakune, followed by his guards, joined the file. Shop fronts, stalls, and modest laid carpets lined the narrow Way of Obtestation. Each displayed a seemingly infinite array of charms, blessed bracelets, healing stones, bones of this or that monk or nun or saint, swatches of cloth taken from the backs of noted devouts who passed away in frenzied rapture – anything and everything, in short, that might tempt pilgrims come to enhance their spiritual purification.

He brushed aside sticks thrust at him laced with charms like small forests of beading. 'Cure the ague, rot, and the clouding blindness!' a tout yelled. A flask hanging from a tall stave was swung at him. 'Blessed waters from the Cloister's fount! All-healing!' He knew that to be truly efficacious such waters must be taken from their source, but first-time pilgrims knew no better.

A grimed street urchin yanked at his robes. 'Inspect the holy virgins?' The leer was startling on a face so young. One of the guards sent the boy on with a kick.

Bakune could only shake his head; it had been a long time since he'd made his own obligatory visitations, but he did not remember the whole thing being so, well, seamy. He paused to turn, and, brushed by the shoulders of those who passed, heads lowered in contemplation, looked back the length of this arc of the Way, taking in not only the hawkers and purveyors of religious goods, legitimate or not, but the food sellers, the inns, the stablers, all the many services the enterprising citizens of Banith provided the steady year-round stream of visitors. In this unimportant seaside town it was frankly the one and only going business. To threaten the flow would be to threaten the city's very lifeblood, and Bakune felt a cold chill creep upon him in the face of so visceral a reaffirmation of what he'd always appreciated intellectually.

His escort drew up short, eyed him quizzically then exchanged bored glances. Turning back without comment, he waved them on.

Near the Cloister the press thinned. Here high-priced shops behind narrow doorways catered to the wealthier pilgrims – merchants themselves, perhaps, or the wives of highly ranked civil servants from Dourkan or Jourilan. Here also patrolled Guardians of the Faith in their dark severe robes, armed with iron-heeled staves. The order had begun as a militant cadre of the faith in response to the Malazan invasions. It was charged with the duty to protect the pilgrims, and the faith itself, from backsliding and corruption. In Bakune's eyes it was the worst of the innovations brought about by the pressure of foreign occupation – perhaps because the order was a sort of rival religious police adjudicating what was permitted behaviour and what was not, and perhaps because it saw itself as above the earthly laws represented locally by none other than himself.

As he came to the tall double doors of the Cloister grounds, the sight of so many of the Guardians loitering about brought to Bakune's mind that during his entire approach he had not seen one trooper of their erstwhile occupiers, the Malazans. Politic, that: keeping away from the pilgrimage route where tempers might flare.

Two Guardians stepped forward to bar the open doorway. 'What business in the Cloister?' one demanded.

He cocked a brow; since when had they begun interrogating visitors? 'My business is my own. By what right do you ask?'

The man bristled, clenching his stave tight. 'By right of faith.' He eyed Bakune up and down, taking in his dark cloak, cloth trousers, brocaded satin vest, and clean linen shirt. 'You are no pilgrim. What is your business?'

'I'm dying of the bloody-lung.'

The Guardian flinched, but recovered, raising his chin. 'That is not a matter for jest. Men and women are dying of that very affliction in the Hospice, praying for Our Lady's blessing and her healing waters even as you make light of it.'

Bakune was impressed by the speed with which the man had charged the high moral summit, though the move was by far too naked and bold. Bludgeons. Like his own guards, even now dragging themselves up the cobbled way, these too were yet mere blunt instruments.

Sighing his irritation, he pulled off one moleskin glove and extended his hand. 'Assessor Bakune. I am come to see the Abbot.'

The Guardian frowned over the ring of office. Belatedly, Bakune realized that he might as well have thrust a live polecat at the man for all he understood of the significance of the seal of a magistrate of the state. Yet a survivor's instinct told the man that perhaps there may be something to all this and he nodded, grudgingly, and stepped aside. That, or the overdue arrival of Bakune's two guards of the Watch, both licking grease from their fingers.

Bakune entered beneath the wooden vaulted ceiling of the tunnel that led to the grounds. The other Guardian, perhaps the brighter of the two, had run ahead to bring word of his arrival. Past the tunnel, shaded colonnaded walks beckoned to the right and left, while ahead lay the gravel paths of the manicured gardens and walks of Blessed

Contemplation. Beyond, to the right, rose the three storeys of the wooden Hospice of Our Lady, largest of such installations in all Fist, eclipsed only by that servicing the veteran Chosen of Korel. To the left, over the tops of the hedges and ornamental trees, reared the tall spires of the rambling Cloister itself. A city within a city, complete with its own schools, administration, kitchens and bakery, nunnery, library, orphanage, even the Hospice to shelter its aged and dying brothers and sisters.

Bakune chose to wait outside. He drew off his other glove to better appreciate the blossoms of the late-blooming winter-lace, whose tiny white flowers were considered melancholy as their appearance signalled the coming of winter. He appreciated their delicate scent. His guards sprawled on a bench and eyed the more hale inmates of the Hospice shuffling back and forth on their constitutional walks. Eventually, as Bakune knew he must, if only for the sake of form, came Abbot Starvann Arl, trailed by a gaggle of his higher functionaries and staff.

They embraced as the equals they were – at least in principle. Starvann, head of the Cloister, with authority over all matters of faith locally, answerable only to the Prioress herself at the capital, Paliss. And Bakune, Assessor and magistrate, the highest local legal authority, answerable only to the High Assessor at the same city. Yet what a difference; Bakune was rendered a bare grudging sort of assistance from the City Watch while Starvann commanded all the staff of the Cloister, numbering perhaps more than a thousand – plus the authority of the order of the Guardians of the Faith themselves. Yes, Bakune reflected tartly, equal in principle only.

'Bakune! Good to see you. We meet too rarely. How gracious of you to visit us.' The Abbot captured Bakune's hands in a surprisingly bone-hard grip. Then the smile behind his thick beard faded and his startling pale eyes clouded over. 'I know why you have come,' he said sadly.

Bakune raised a quizzical brow. 'You do?'

Starvann gave the Assessor's hands one last painful squeeze before releasing them. 'Sister Prudence. Word came to me only this morning.' He pressed a hand to Bakune's back and gently but firmly urged him on. 'Come, let us walk the grounds . . . forgive me, but I find it refreshing.'

'Certainly.' Bakune allowed himself to be steered on to a path between low evergreen shrubs. The Abbot clasped his hands behind his back. His plain dark robes brushed the gravel as he walked. His dress was appropriately severe and august, his only ornament a diadem suspended from his neck in the starburst sigil of the faith of the Blessed Lady.

'She is dead, then?' he asked, head lowered.

'Yes.'

'Then she has at last found peace with Our Lady.'

'Yes. Did you say Sister . . . Prudence?'

The head rose, and the long grey hair blew in the mild breeze. 'The name she chose when she joined the order as a child.'

'Ah, I see. May I ask—'

'How I knew she had passed on?'

Bakune cleared his throat, had to narrow his gaze in the light of the man's unearthly pale eyes. 'Well . . . yes.'

The gentle smile returned and the Abbot squeezed his shoulder. Bakune knew he should be reassured by the smile and flattered by the personal attention, but somehow he was not. The suspicious adjudicator's voice that spoke to him when in the magistrate's chair murmured now: *Why should he bother?*

We've met before. It is merely professional courtesy.

And you feel gratitude for this condescension, do you not?

And he wondered in his most ruthless self-analysis: was this jealousy?

Bakune glanced behind and had to strangle an urge to laugh. The Abbot's entire entourage was now bunched up behind his two ambling guards, one of whom was exploring the cavity of a nostril.

The Abbot continued his slow pacing. Gravel crackled beneath his sandals. 'She has been with us all her life. We have had to – how shall I put it? – *restrain* Sister Prudence for some time now. When she escaped from the Hospice we all knew how it would end. A terrible act. Terrible. But,' and he took a slow deep breath, 'no doubt the Lady has taken in her troubled spirit and now protects and soothes her.'

'Yes. Of course. May I ask – what were her duties?'

Starvann paused and turned. His tangled brows rose. 'Her duties? Why, no different from those of all her sisters. Devotional, of course. Praying for and easing the suffering of those within the Hospice. She rotated through the kitchens and cleaning duties as do all the sisters. And she served within the orphanage as well. I remember she was particularly fond of working with our young charges.'

'I see. Thank you, Abbot, for your time.'

Starvann bowed. 'Of course. Thank you for coming personally. Your attention is noted.' He gave a small bow.

Bakune bowed in answer; his audience was over. *The man actually thinks I came seeking to impress him with my diligence!* And something moved him to press his case – perhaps that very condescension. 'Had she a particular friend, Abbot? Within the order, I mean?'

Caught in the act of turning away, the Abbot frowned. He made a vague gesture. 'There might have been a friend – Sister Charity, I believe.'

Though the Abbot was now walking away, Bakune again raised his voice: 'And where might I find this Sister Charity?'

The Abbot's lips thinned. His entourage had pushed past Bakune's guards and were now ushering him off. 'She left the order years ago,' he said slowly. 'Good day.'

Bakune bowed, murmuring, 'Good day,' but no one remained but his guards – who had their hands tucked into their belts while they watched the crowd shuffle away. 'Looks like we're finished here,' he told them.

'Looks like,' one drawled.

'I want to see your captain now.'

Sharing a glance, the two rolled their eyes.

* * *

A year ago Kyle quit the mercenary company he'd fought with since he was taken from the tall grass steppes he'd known all his youth. Now, trying to get by in Delanss, the capital city of the island of the same name, he suddenly discovered the pressing need for something he'd never known before: cash for room and board. He met this problem by agreeing to serve as a hiresword for a fellow named Best. The job consisted of little more than warming a bench, drinking the man's ale and sleeping at his tavern while occasionally intimidating people stupid enough to have borrowed money from him.

This night as usual he was drinking in the common room when his immediate boss, Tar Kargin, stomped downstairs and waved together all the regular muscle. 'Got a job. Straight from Best.' He led the way out on to the darkening, rain-slick cobblestone street.

Tar, broad as a boat, lumbered down the middle of the way flanked by his chosen enforcers and followed by Kyle, who marvelled at the way the fellow, perhaps by dint of plain dull-witted obstinacy and towering self-absorption, could bully everyone and everything from his path. Not only all late night pedestrians of the capital city melted aside, but also men drawing carts, stevedores grunting under heaped bags and bales, even horse-drawn carriages which were diverted at the last instant lest they flatten, or be flattened by, him. Astonishingly, he even forced aside an ass leading a blind man on a rope.

'Got your trophies?' he demanded of Kyle without turning his bull neck.

Kyle gritted his teeth and reluctantly drew the grisly, stinking belt from a pouch and hung it round his neck. Tanned, wrinkled-up *things* hung from it – ears perhaps, or noses. He wasn't sure and frankly didn't want to know. Best had dug it up from somewhere and made him wear it when on the job. Said it frightened everyone good. What frightened Kyle was the smell.

They stopped close to the waterfront in front of a row of darkened two-storey shop houses and Kargin banged on a door. 'Bor 'eth! Open up! I know you're in there! Open up!'

The three thugs grinned at Kyle and thumbed the truncheons they carried pushed down their shirt-fronts. Kyle crossed his arms and for the hundredth time cursed this civilized innovation called work. He didn't think much of it so far.

A vision-slit opened and an old man peered out. 'Oh! It's you, Kargin. You know, it's funny, but I was just—'

'Stow it and open up.'

'But tomorrow I'll—'

'Today's too late.'

'I swear, tomorrow—'

'If you don't let me in now, next time I won't ask so nice.'

'Oh . . . well . . . if you must . . .' Locks rattled and jangled. The thick door slowly swung until Kargin thrust it wide and stepped in. The thugs followed and Kyle brought up the rear.

They jammed into the foyer of a shop that in the dim light of the old man's lantern looked stocked with fine imported goods. A shelf next to Kyle held goblets of various sizes and shapes. Kargin gently reached out to take the lantern from the old man, Bor 'eth, and set it high on a nearby shelf. He motioned for one of his boys to shut the door. The old man's smile slipped as the thug shot the bolts.

'I'll pay, Kargin – you know that. I will.' He tried to smile again but only looked frozen and terrified. 'It's just that business is slow right now . . .'

'Slow . . .' Kargin raised and lowered his great bulk in a sigh heavy with weary patience. He waved Kyle forward. Kyle remembered to set his face in his best sullen glower. 'See this lad here?' Bor 'eth nodded uncertainly. 'He comes from a savage distant land where they don't think twice about killin' one another. Don't value human life. Not like us civilized people here. See that belt?' Again an unsure nod. 'Those are the ears and noses and . . . other things he's cut from the men he's killed.' Peering up, the old man flinched back, pulled the quilt he'd thrown about his shoulders tighter. 'I'd just have to snap my fingers like *that*, and he'd have your ears . . . What do you think about that?'

The old man clutched his neck and glanced from face to face as if wondering whether this were a joke or not. 'Really?' he gasped, his voice high and quavering. 'Amazing . . .'

'*Take his ears!*'

Kyle launched himself forward and grasped a handful of the old man's thin orange-grey hair, pressing the edge of his knife just under one ear. The fellow screeched like a hoarse bird, flailed uselessly at Kyle's arms. Kyle turned a glance on Kargin.

The big man let out a great belly-laugh and took Bor 'eth from Kyle's hands. He held him in a tight hug. 'But I won't let him do that this time, Bor 'eth! Why would I do such a thing to a paying customer, right?' The old fellow was fairly sobbing and clung to Kargin as if he'd just saved his life. 'No . . . that's what I'll do to you if you don't bring the money to Best tomorrow. *This* is what I do to those who are late.' He nodded to the thugs and, grinning, they pulled Bor 'eth from him.

'What . . . ?' the old man gasped.

'Break his hand.'

Laughing, the lads hefted their truncheons, and while one held the squirming man's hand on a counter the other two raised the weapons.

'No . . . please . . . In the name of Soliel . . .'

'I am being merciful, Bor 'eth.' He gave a curt nod. One truncheon whistled down to smack the counter. The old man shrieked. The second truncheon swung and landed with a wet bang. Bor 'eth went limp in the thug's arms. The lad shook him until he roused. 'Again,' Kargin said. The batons rose.

Kyle examined the goblets while the thugs shattered the merchant's hand. All this pain and trouble over coins; he'd grown up without any on open plains where his people hunted for the food they needed and made the tools they used. They had some coins and other bits and pieces they kept for trade, but other than that he'd grown up without the need. From what he'd seen in his travels since, his people had been better off without this one particular advance of civilization. And if someone pressed such a need upon him, he'd just walk away.

Kargin raised a hand. Kyle glanced over; released, the old man slid down to sit rocking back and forth, cradling the bloody broken thing that was his hand to his chest. Kargin motioned to the door. Kyle set the rose-hued cut-crystal goblet back in place on its shelf.

Out on the street, as they walked back to Best's, the night air cold and crisp after a light rain, one of the young thugs sidled up to Kyle and grinned, exposing his broken uneven teeth. 'Did you see that?' he asked.

'See what?'

'Pissed himself, the old guy. Wet those expensive robes of his,' and he laughed.

'Congratulations. You beat an old guy into pissing himself.'

The grin fell away. The young tough tossed his long hair from his pimply face. 'You ever do any of that stuff Kargin says – cuttin' ears and such?'

Kyle set his mouth in a leer and leaned close. 'All the fucking time.'

Close to the front of Best's inn, Kargin stopped and waved everyone on. 'Too bad about your friend,' he said to Kyle.

Kyle stopped, untied the string of fetid trophies and slowly lowered it into its bag. 'What do you mean?'

'That fellow you used to chum with, the other foreigner. The merchant houses he got to put up the money for his place . . . they foreclosed on him. Closed him up tight.'

Cinching the pouch, Kyle glanced over. 'Really?'

'Uh-huh. When I heard the news, I wondered . . . what would you have done if it was *his* place we went to visit tonight?'

Kyle hefted the feather-light pouch. 'Nothing. I wouldn't have had to do anything because he would have scattered you lot like geese.'

The chief enforcer for Best, the man who controlled most of the blackmailing and extortion in the city, seemed to peer down sleepily at Kyle over the great bulk of his chest. His nostrils flared as he snorted. 'Some kinda hot ex-mercenary you've turned out to be. I ain't seen fuck-all that impresses from you yet.'

'And you won't. Here,' Kyle flicked the pouch at him, 'keep your ears on. See you around.'

'I don't think so,' the man called after him. 'He'd be in prison right now 'cept someone bought his debts – and that someone ain't from around here . . .'

The man's sly rumbling laughter followed Kyle down the darkened street.

Some Falaran legal documents, all ribboned and weighted by wax seals, hung nailed to the door of Orjin's school. Kyle tried the door and found it unlocked. Just inside the tunnel he stopped to study the empty practice floor; the sand shone in the moonlight like glittering quicksilver.

'Orjin?' he hissed. 'Orjin?' Movement from the shadows. A figure staggered into the pale light, sword held slack and low in one hand. *Great Harrier preserve us! What's happened?* He ran to him, grunted as the man's extraordinary weight sagged on him. 'What's happened? Are you wounded?'

Something banged from Kyle's head, sloshing. He snatched an earthenware jug from Orjin's hand. 'What's this?'

'No more of your talk!' the man bellowed hotly in his ear. 'Keep your contracts and writs! Dare to face me like a man, Dead Poliel take you!'

'Oh for Hood's sake!' Kyle pushed him away. He should've smelled it, but the last months spent sitting in a common room had blunted his nose.

Tottering, Orjin swung the slim Darujhistan epée, almost cutting Kyle. 'Come on! Arm yourself! We'll settle this the old-fashioned way!' He crossed to a weapon rack and heaved it over in a ringing clatter of ironmongery. 'Take your pick! As you see – there's plenty!'

'Orjin . . . Greymane . . .'

The man blinked, weaving. 'What's that? Greymane? *Greymane?*' His head sank chin to chest and for a time he seemed to study all the fallen swords glowing silver in the moonlight. 'That man is dead.'

'Orjin . . . I heard someone's coming. Someone from *elsewhere* – that can only mean the Malazans. They've found you.' He stepped closer. 'Now come on. Let's go. There's nothing for us here. I hate this place. These people would bend over for donkeys if they had gold. Let's go.'

Orjin breathed out a noisy wet sigh and eased himself down amid the blades. He hung his head. His long unkempt mane shone just as bright as the tangled iron. 'No. I'm finished. Let them come.' He waved broadly to encompass the surroundings. 'This was always my dream, you know, Kyle. Retire. Open a fighting college. Teach something of what I've learned.' At random, he picked up a longsword, a heavy northern Genabackan weapon; sighted down the blade. 'But no one really wants to know what a bellyful of war teaches.'

Looking down at the man, Kyle considered trying to wrench him up but didn't think he'd be able to budge his bulk. He knelt to his haunches. 'Listen, Orjin. Hood take these merchants and gangsters. They're no different from each other. Let's just go! Hire on to the first ship we come to in the harbour – who cares where it's headed.'

'No, no. That's a young man's game. I'm too old. You go.'

'No one's after me.'

'Then what are you doing here?'

'I'm here because—' A small sound, the scuff of a foot on sand, turned Kyle's head. Four figures emerged from the gloom of the entrance tunnel. All were dressed alike in dark leathers and bore two blades at their sides, one long, one short. Kyle straightened, taking up the nearest weapon as he did so, a sturdy heavy-bladed cutlass. 'Who are you?'

'Whoever *you* are,' one answered, waving him away, 'stand aside.'

The accent was not Malazan. It didn't resemble any accent Kyle had ever heard in all his travels. At the voice, however, Orjin's head snapped up, and he said to Kyle, his words suddenly stone-cold sober, 'Go, now. Leave us.'

'Go? Who are these guys? Hired killers?'

'Killers, yes.' Orjin stood, gathering up a long slim blade in each hand. 'But not for gold or treasure – hey, Cullel?' A gleaming bright hungry grin from the spokesman answered Orjin. 'You kill for something else, don't you? For religious faith alone.'

'We exterminate heretics,' Cullel assented, his voice a low purr. The four slowly spread out, walking the perimeter of the practice floor.

'Where in the Abyss are these lunatics from?' Kyle demanded.

'They are Korelri. Veterans of the Stormwall. They've been given special dispensation to hunt me down. Yes, Cullel?'

'Hunt you down?' Kyle asked.

Orjin shifted to put his back to Kyle's. 'Yes.'

'But I thought the Malazans wanted you.'

'Ah . . . well . . . them too.'

'Wonderful.'

The four now occupied each of the sides of the practice yard. As one they drew their weapons, the long and the short blades.

'Get rid of that and use your fancy blade,' Orjin told Kyle.

'I . . . don't have it.'

'You don't—' Orjin sent an exasperated look over his shoulder. 'Why in the Abyss not?'

'Gentlemen . . .' Cullel called softly.

'It was stolen from my room.'

'*Stolen?*'

'Gentlemen!'

'Well, we're in a right fix now, thanks to you,' Orjin grumbled.

'Thank you,' Cullel said. 'Now, before we execute our duty it is my obligation to inform you, Greymane, that you have been tried in absentia by the High Council of the Chosen, Defenders of the Lands of Korel and All Greater Fist and Beyond, and have been found guilty of making pacts with the enemy. And that you did enter into said pacts and covenants with the daemonic Riders wilfully, and of your own cognizance.'

'*Pacts?*' Kyle whispered to Orjin.

The man gave a beefy shrug of acquiescence. 'I talked to them.'

'Them – the Riders? *You really cut a deal with the Stormriders?*'

'Gentlemen! Decorum, if you please. The discharge of justice is a solemn responsibility.'

'Justice?' Kyle barked, offended by the idea. 'You're damned up yourself, aren't you?'

Distaste twisted the man's blade-narrow face. 'Very well. Judgement has been delivered. And now, the sentence . . .' He nodded to his fellows.

They advanced together, blades raised. So much for justice, Kyle decided – four against two. Entering the moonlight, the four Korelri suddenly blazed as the slanting rays revealed that their armour, fittings and scabbards were all studded and filigreed with thin curving traceries of the finest silver.

It chanced that Kyle faced Cullel. Shifting his sandalled foot, Kyle kicked a scarf of sand for cover and parried the other Korelri. Instantly, he knew he faced the best swordsmen he'd ever met. He could barely deflect their attacks. Light cuts welled blood on his forearms. A thrust tore into his thigh and he almost fell. They even worked as a team: he could only watch while they coordinated their attacks to draw him out and expose his side – *Wind take it! There is nothing I can do!* He sensed Orjin, behind, going down to one knee. *Hit already?*

Then Greymane was up and the two swordsmen facing Kyle flinched, seeing something beyond him. One of the Korelri behind Kyle snarled his pain while the other flew into view, tumbling loosely over the sand as if tossed by a ferocious blow. Then Orjin stepped in front of Kyle, swinging a two-handed dull-grey blade that Kyle had only seen once before. Cullel parried, but his sword blade shattered like brittle bronze and Orjin's swing continued on to smash into his side, crumpling him. The last remaining Defender yelled ferociously and leapt, only to be impaled on the thick blade. Orjin kicked the man from the coarse, gritty-looking weapon, and shook the blood from its length.

Kyle took in the four fallen men, then Orjin's ragged, two-handed sword. 'Where by all the Queen's Mysteries did that come from?'

A wet laugh sounded from where Cullel lay. It raised Kyle's hackles. He squeezed the bloody cut in the leathers over his thigh and limped over.

'What's that? You have even more to say?'

'So it is true . . .' the man gasped. Blood welled up with the word. 'The claims are true. *Stonewielder* . . . He betrayed all humanity for that artefact.'

'Bullshit!'

The man's eyes widened with a fevered light. 'No. His reward. Ask him, though he'll no doubt lie.' He fought to say more but blood now filled his mouth and he gasped in a coughing fit, straining for breath. His body clenched rigid then slowly eased, relaxing, falling limp.

Kyle raised his eyes to Orjin. 'Well?'

The big man simply walked off and knelt to pick up the fallen gourd of wine. When he straightened, the blade was gone. Kyle crossed the floor. 'Where is it?'

'Where's what?'

'The sword.' He scanned the ground but saw no sign of it. 'Where'd it go?'

'Never mind, Kyle. Leave it alone.' Orjin took a deep swig from the gourd.

'But . . . what is it?'

Orjin wiped his sleeve across his mouth, sighed. 'Damned useless is what it is.'

'Useless?'

Waving aside all discussion, Orjin crossed to a bench, sat heavily. As his leg was steadily numbing Kyle decided to join him. He took the gourd and sipped to wet his caked mouth, spat. 'So? Did the Riders give it to you?'

Orjin nodded his slow assent. 'Yeah. They gave it to me. Not for any damned pact or deal or anything. We just talked and they gave it to me.'

'Just like that.'

The man turned his head to glare one-eyed. 'Don't be trite. One night I climbed down the cliffs to the edge of the Ocean of Storm and waited – you try that one night. Eventually, some showed up. They speak Korelri . . . there's irony for you. Anyway, we talked. They claimed they weren't the enemy at all. I pointed out that attacking the Stormwall for generations tended to give the appearance. They said the Korelri were denying them access to their own territory and blocking some kind of ancient obligation, or holy pilgrimage . . . or some such thing.' He cleared his throat, waved a hand. 'Anyway, I couldn't really make it all out.'

Kyle got the impression there was more to it, but apparently this was all the other would say – for now. He took another sip. He rested his eyes on the four still figures gleaming in the moonlight. 'How come they can speak Korelri if they're such sworn enemies? Do they take captives from the wall or something like that? Torture them in their undersea lairs?'

Orjin leaned forward to give him a long hard look.

'What?'

Orjin snatched back the gourd. 'You've listened to too many romances. It's rotted your brain. No, the thought occurred to me too, so I asked. They said they'd always listened to the men on the wall and to sailors on ships.'

'Well then, why don't they just yell from the water then? Talk to them?'

'They said they tried that but the men always ignored them, called them liars and sirens and such. So they stopped.'

'And the sword?'

Again the beefy shrug. 'They were grateful I'd talked to them so they offered it as a gift. I said sure.'

'So what is it? Where's it from?'

Orjin finished the gourd, tossed it aside. 'They didn't know. Said they'd found it deep at the bottom of the Cut far beneath the sea. They did say it was very old, and I agree.'

'But you never use it.'

He edged his head side to side. 'No. It's too powerful. Too dangerous.'

'But you *have* used it – I remember, against that warlock.'

A small thoughtful nod, eyes ahead, perhaps also studying the mute meaning of the four dead Defenders of the Faith.

'So, that name I'd heard for you – Stonewielder.'

'Yeah. A few called me that before I was arrested by Malazan High Command.'

'But . . . I thought you were in command of Malazan forces in Korel.'

'Military, yes. The marines and regulars. But there was a civilian authority. A governor. Hemel. Hemel 'Et Kelal. A Bloorian nobleman. Never did know what happened to the man. Anyway, he and a gang of minor officers denounced me for treating with the Riders . . . and that was that.'

'And then?' Kyle asked, fascinated, almost forgetting the pain clenching his leg.

Orjin waved it all away. 'Never mind. Ancient history.' Groaning and wincing, he stood. 'I'm out of wine and you need that leg looked at.' He held out a hand. 'Let's go.'

Kyle pulled himself upright, held on to the man's shoulder as he limped along. 'So we'll sign on to a ship?'

'Trake no! We're going to get your sword back.'

'But I told you – someone stole it from my room.'

Orjin shook his head. 'Kyle . . . you're too trusting.'

'What do you mean?'

'Best is one of the heads of Delanss' black market. The man's a thief. He stole it.'

'He said he'd get it back for me!'

Orjin stopped short and peered down at him for a time. 'And then he suggested that you might as well do some work for him in the meantime . . .'

Kyle gave a sheepish shrug. 'Something like that.'

'That settles it. Can you walk?'

'Yeah – some.'

'Okay. Head to the waterfront. Wait for me there. I'll be back with your sword and then we'll have to be off right quick.'

'Grey— Orjin, I can't let you do that.'

'Might as well make it Greymane, Kyle. I took a stab at being plain old Orjin Samarr once more, but it didn't take. So it's Greymane again. And it'll be Greymane who'll be visiting Best tonight.'

Kyle peered about at the silent rain-slick street, the moonlit shop fronts. 'Grey, it's not worth it. Let's get out of here while we can.'

'Not worth it? You know that's a lie. Your friends in the Guard, Stalker and his cousins, they told me who gave you that weapon. So we both know it's worth it.' His pale blue eyes, buried deep in their sockets, flashed something that might have been amusement. 'We're both burdened by blades that are more than we would want.' He motioned Kyle on. 'Get us berths on a ship leaving at dawn!'

Kyle watched him go, then limped for the waterfront. So Stalker had told him – or he'd asked. In any case, it was true. Osserc, a being Kyle's people worshipped as a patron god of Wind, Sky and Light, had given him the blade. Since then he'd discovered that Osserc was merely – merely! – a powerful entity, an Ascendant. Such as the Tiste Andii leader Anomander, Son of Darkness, or as some name the Enchantress, the Queen of Dreams.

But now Kyle considered all its power more trouble than it was worth. He couldn't even draw the thing without calling extraordinary attention to himself, just like Greymane. And now the damned fool was off to get himself killed . . . and for what? Maybe, it occurred to Kyle as he hobbled along, the man was doing it to prove a point to himself – that he *could* do it.

It was close after dawn and Kyle was sitting high on the afterdeck of a galley out of Curaca when he spotted the renegade. The ship's bone-mender was wrapping his leg but he sat up, yelling: 'There he is! Let off! Go!'

'Aiya!' the old woman shouted, and gave his leg an agonizing squeeze. 'Sit still!'

From the railing, the mate warned, 'Your man better be worth it.' Then he called, 'Cast off all lines!'

The big man was jogging down the wharf, a long wrapped object in one hand. Behind him, between buildings, erupted a mass of armed men and women, civilians and city guards alike. The bone-mender let go a wild cackle at the sight.

'Wide Ocean below!' the mate swore. 'Your man's stirred up a hornets' nest! What's he done?'

'You know Best, the black marketeer?'
'That cockroach? Yeah.'
'Well, I think my friend has kicked him in the balls.'
The mate grinned and turned to his men. 'Look lively and ready pikes to repel boarders!'
The old crone laughed again. Her riotous cackle unnerved Kyle far more than he thought it should.

*

A Delanss nobleman entered the ransacked and empty practice quarters of Orjin's School of Swordsmanship and tucked his hands into his thick robes behind the heavy silver links of rank. Everything, he noted, had been stripped overnight. 'Hello?' Blood stained the sand but he saw no signs of the bodies. 'Anyone here?'
'Yes.'
The man jumped, and turned to where a woman stepped forward from the shadows. She wore plain dark clothes and soft leather shoes. She was a very deep brown, her hair tightly curled and cut short. Something about her reminded the nobleman of the Korelri he'd just dealt with, though he knew this woman for no Fistian. Perhaps it was the stink of fanaticism that seemed to hang about them both.
'I apologize for this Orjin fellow. I had no idea he was so unstable. I heard that he bulled his way through Best's entire bodyguard and proceeded to hold him by one hand over a privy hole until the man handed over one just one particular item. It's not my fault he went berserk.'
The woman lazily dismissed his concerns with a wave of a long-fingered hand. 'Do not worry yourself. You would have been paid in full even if the Korelri had managed to kill him.'
'Even then?'
'Yes. Because then we would've known he was no longer the man for us.'
The nobleman raised both brows. 'Really? And now – after he has wounded over twenty men, overcome a patrol of the city guard, and thumbed his nose at all civilized authority – what do you know now?'
The woman's deep brown eyes seemed to laugh at him, and more, to do things that only the most recent of his mistresses was able to accomplish with just a look. She said, smiling, 'That he is exactly the one we want.'

*   *   *

The lock to Corlo's cell ratcheted and the door opened. A Korelri officer in their silver-chased, blue-black armour waved him out. He wasn't one of the regulars Corlo knew. Idly, the thought occurred to him that he had yet to meet a female Korelri Chosen – the order must somehow disapprove or work against their promotion. He swung his feet from his pallet. 'What is it?'

'Come with us.'

He pointed to the metal torc at his neck. 'Take this off.'

The officer snorted. 'You think us fools, warlock?'

Not so much fools, Corlo reflected as he followed the man into the hall, *as inexperienced.* These Korelri were so unfamiliar with mages they were willing to sink fortunes into collars alloyed with a touch of the magic-deadening otataral ore for when they might actually come to meet one. Was it irony, the mage wondered, that the source of that ore was the invaders themselves, the Malazans? A squad of Korelri crossbowmen crowded the hall, covering him. *Inexperienced and fearful.* They seemed to actually think the talents of magery must somehow be connected to their traditional enemies, the sea-demons. *Rather ignorant here behind their wall. But then, that's what happens when you raise walls. And the Lady no doubt stands behind their beliefs.*

'Where are we going?'

'Quiet, Malazan. Move.'

By now Corlo had long given up trying to enlighten his captors on politics outside their isolated islands. The subtleties seemed beyond them, or they really just didn't give a damn. Yes, he was a native of the Malazan Empire, from Avore, in fact, before the old Emperor wiped it from the map. But more important, he was also a member of the Crimson Guard. A mercenary company dedicated to the destruction of that very Empire. Or at least he used to be; and the company was once. Now, he didn't know – none of his surviving companions knew.

The officer and his escort led him out of the complex of cells and grottoes that honeycombed the Stormwall here north of Fortress Kor, then up wide twisting sets of stairs to the barracks behind the rock field that tumbled down from the wall's base. It was a sunny day but the shadows were chilly, reminding Corlo that winter was coming and with it another season standing the wall. After a few turns he knew where he was being taken and his chest clenched: *Oh, please Burn. He hasn't tried again, has he?*

Sure enough, the way led to the walled barracks of those favoured prisoners who stood the wall. Here captives from all over the globe, men and women of proven ability and cooperative spirit, lived in relative luxury and ease. Here his commander in the Crimson Guard, Iron Bars, ranked an entire suite of rooms all to himself. *Not that he's all that cooperative.*

At the door to Bars' rooms Corlo's escort thrust an arm across the hall. 'If you value the life of your friend,' he warned, 'you'll remind him of where his best interests lie.'

Corlo edged the man's arm aside. 'He's my friend.'

Behind the narrow slit of his blackened iron helm the man's dark brown eyes remained unconvinced. We can do without you lot, Corlo read in the hard unswerving gaze. The man lifted his chin to the guards. One unlatched the door.

Corlo pushed aside the heavy iron barrier on to a scene of chaos. Shards of pots and smashed wooden chairs and tables littered the polished floor. Drying pools of wine stained the stones and tossed salvers of fruit and bread lay amid the trampled wreckage. Whimpering brought his gaze down to a girl hunched next to the door, arms wrapped around her knees.

He raised her up and she stood shivering, hugging herself. *No, he couldn't have . . .* He lifted her chin. Kohl had run from her eyelids and was smeared across her face. She would not meet his gaze, but he saw only fear and confusion in her demeanour. *Like nothing you've ever run into before, hey, child? Yeah, he's like that.*

He gently handed her out to the guards then crept forward through the mess of shattered furnishings. The remains of glass carafes and fine ceramic jars crackled beneath his sandals. He heard the door pulled shut and secured behind him. Eventually, after searching the main room, he found his commander slumped beneath a barred window, unshaven, hair lank with sweat, a wide-bladed knife held to his neck. The man flashed his teeth like a wild animal upon seeing him.

Corlo pointed to the blade. 'That won't work.'

The fixed smile was ghastly. Bars let the weapon clatter to the floor. 'They don't know that.' His voice was a hoarse croak.

Corlo didn't bother asking what had happened. He simply leaned back against the wall, crossed his arms and studied the man, hoping that beneath his regard Bars would come to feel something. *Please let him still be able to feel – something.*

But the man would not look at him; his gaze roved about the remains of the broken and smashed furniture as if wondering how much it might all cost. 'I can't go on like this, Corlo,' he said, finally, into the long silence. 'I'm dying.' And he laughed, making Corlo wince. 'I'm dying but I cannot die.' Beneath sweat-tangled hair he shot a quick glance at the mage. 'Like the irony of that?'

'Walk away.'

An impatient shrug brought a long silence. Bars reached out to a stoneware jug and took a long pull. 'I won't leave any of you behind.'

'They know that.'

'So. What to do.' He rested the jug on his lap.

Corlo studied his hands clasped at his sash, glanced up. 'They won't kill us. They say they would, but they won't. I've been listening – they need everyone they can get.'

Bars' gaze narrowed; they were edging into old territory. 'To go where . . .'

'Stratem—'

The jug exploding over his head made Corlo duck. 'Fuck Stratem!'

Saying nothing, Corlo straightened, flexed his neck to ease his nervous tension. Bars fell back, frowned after a time at the course of his own thoughts. 'We were so close. I could sense the Guard Brethren at the end there. I sensed them turning away from the mission to that scum Skinner. And he mocked me. He mocked me!' The man pressed his hands to his hanging head. 'The Crimson Guard betrayed its vow and left us to rot. And . . . I . . . still . . . can't . . . die!'

Corlo could only remain silent. *So. The foundation at last. Betrayal. Failure. Helplessness and futility. What could he possibly say?* Feeling ill with self-loathing, he reached for his last remaining tool – the one his captors employed for the very same purpose. He straightened from the wall, pressed his sweaty hands to his sides. 'For the men, Bars. Hang on.'

His commander bit down on a convulsive laugh. He pushed his hands up through his hair so ferociously Corlo thought he meant to tear it out. 'Yes. Well. Back to that.'

'No choice.'

'No. None.'

Corlo allowed himself a shallow nod of assent. 'I'll tell them to clean up.'

Bars said nothing; Corlo thought his eyes looked empty, as if the man had retreated to somewhere far away. He gingerly edged his way to the door, which opened to his knock.

'You can clean the place up, but leave him alone.'

The Korelri Chosen simply motioned him to follow. The curt ingratitude raised no anger in Corlo; it was shame that burned in his chest as he descended the barracks stairs. *I am the same as you*, he told the iron-armoured back of his guide. *No, perhaps I am even worse. I am a collaborator. A traitor who conspires with the enemy in the enslavement of my friend.*

For a hundred years ago the original men and women of the Crimson Guard had sworn a terrible vow: the eternal opposition of the Malazan Empire. And thereby was granted them something approaching immortality – so long as the Empire should endure. But even so Corlo knew they could die. If Bars really want to, he could do it. The wall is high and the waters cold. Nooses throttle. Long thin blades pierce the eye and the brain behind.

That was his fear. That the man would just give up. Most would have by now, probably. But Bars had never given up in the past – that had always been his strength as an Avowed in the Guard. That was what Corlo was counting on.

The man just had to be reminded of it from time to time.

* * *

An inhabitant of Malaz city on the isle of that name, out during a night of its frigid autumn rains – a drunk, or a baker, or a night watchman, should there have ever been a night watch in Malaz – might have seen a slim cloaked figure lingering before the iron gate of an abandoned house of particularly evil reputation. The Deadhouse, the locals called it, when forced to acknowledge its existence at all. A house where none live, where the grounds are humped with the mounds of countless burials, and where those who enter never leave.

Such a wet and chilled witness might have seen the figure place a hand upon the gate, obviously intending to enter where no resident would ever dare, and then might have heard a shout, a woman's voice commanding, '*Hold!*'

No doubt at this point any resident of Malaz, who ought not to have been out in the first place in such fell weather and at such a time, would have had the sense to withdraw, to leave these callers on night-time errands to their dark business, and to speak of such things to no one. And so they would not have seen the taller of the two, revealed as a young woman, take the hand of the speaker, an older woman in a shawl, and kiss it.

Kiska stretched out her legs and peered about at the cramped and cluttered nest of shelves and boxes and stacked burlap sacks that was Agayla's spice shop. To think as a child it had once seemed roomy to her. She rubbed a towel over her damp short hair and gave a gentle snort; that had been a long time ago. Still, each breath – and she sniffed the heady, redolent melange of countless spices – reminded her of that home.

Her aunt Agayla returned carrying soup on a tray. Not a true blood relation, but close enough for those less bureaucratic days when anyone could take in anyone and damn the local authorities who could go jump in the bay anyway. Her long hair was touched by more grey than Kiska remembered. Her arms were even thinner and more wiry than they had been, but for all that she looked remarkably well preserved.

The woman regarded her now over the steaming bowls. Her narrow severe face was set in hard disapproval.

'I wasn't about to kill myself, Agayla.'

A dark brow arched. 'Oh? What *were* you about to do then?'

'It's . . . complicated, auntie.'

Both brows rose. 'Ah. *Complicated*, is it?'

'Auntie! I . . .' She searched for words in the face of the woman's censure, and failed. She waved a hand. 'Never mind.'

'Drink your soup.'

Feeling exactly like the sullen resentful child she must have been more than a decade ago, Kiska scooped up the bowl and spoon. It was delicious, of course. The best meal she'd tasted in years. A twisted bunch of twigs floated on the surface that she nudged aside to sip the broth. Sage? she wondered, inhaling its sharp breath.

'I've heard, of course,' Agayla began, setting down her own bowl. 'And I am deeply sorry.'

Heard? Yes, Kiska imagined the woman had. Who hadn't? The High Mage Tayschrenn, possibly the greatest practitioner of the age, sucked into a void and cast out not even the gods knew where. And she, his bodyguard, left alive to face the truth of her complete, and abject, failure. She must be the most storied failure since Greymane. Yes, there was no doubt Agayla had heard. She herself had yet to bolt awake every morning without seeing it.

'They were Avowed, girl. That you faced them down at all is remarkable.'

'Yet I wasn't good enough.'

'Console yourself with the fact that there are few who would have been.' The woman gathered her long mane of hair over one shoulder and began pulling a shell comb through it. Kiska watched. Despite her resentment, she felt the magic of the familiar ritual stealing over her as her limbs relaxed, and the knot of her shoulders eased. She remembered standing behind the woman on so many nights doing that very brushing, counting every stroke. 'So what did you intend?' Agayla asked, after a time.

'A proposition for whoever opened that door.'

The brushing paused; dark eyes regarded her, glittering. 'A proposition of what?'

'A service for a service. They help me find him and I will serve them.'

The woman set down the comb. 'A very dangerous gamble.'

'What? Entering the grounds?'

'No. Dangerous should they, or it, actually accept your offer.'

To hide her irritation at that familiar high-handedness, Kiska looked away, to where sacks of some sort of dried leaves sat slumped and threadbare. 'It is no longer for you to say, Agayla. I was Tayschrenn's bodyguard for a decade. I travelled with him to negotiate treaties. Met an ambassador sent from Anomander Rake himself. I have visited Darujhistan where we met a delegation of ex-Free City mages. I now know you for a talented practitioner in your own way, Agayla. At least here on this island. But this is a very small island. And these are larger matters.'

The woman's thick dark brows climbed higher than Kiska had ever seen. 'Oho! I see the way the tiles have fallen now. Quite sufficient, am I, for curing the pox? Or helping out the local girls who have gotten themselves into trouble, yes?'

'No offence, auntie – but have you even left the island?'

Agayla knotted her hair into one long braid. 'This island hedge-witch can be of no help to one like yourself who has moved in such high and mighty circles, hmm?'

'Agayla . . .'

'Just call the wind and make my candles, shall I?'

Kiska simply hung her head and waited for the storm to blow itself out. Eventually she said, studying her hands on her lap, 'That's not what I meant.'

'You're young yet, child,' Agayla said, her voice softening. 'Full of yourself. Quite certain you know the way of things now that you've seen the world. When in truth you've hardly even begun your education.'

Kiska's head snapped up. 'Don't treat me like a child. I may still be so in your memories, but I have moved on. I am a grown woman now and I will make my own decisions.' She steeled herself for more argument but it never came. Her aunt merely inclined her head, conceding the point.

'True. To me, you will always be that child whose cries I soothed, whose hands I guided. Nothing can ever change that.' She bound up the thick coil of her hair. 'So enough talk for tonight. Sleep. Your bed remains. Things may look different in the morning.'

And Kiska eased back into her chair, let her hands rest on her lap. She *was* tired. The soup was a warm caress in her stomach. Nodding, she stood and made her way to the rear of the shop where a narrow stairway led up to her old room.

'Sleep,' Agayla murmured to her retreating back, her eyes narrowed once more. And more softly yet, 'And dream.'

When she was alone, Agayla crossed the shop to the latest tapestry stretched upon her loom. She set her feet on the pedals and pushed the shuttle across the weave, then reset the pattern. She worked on towards dawn, the frame rattling as the threads crossed, the wooden shuttle making its countless passes. As she worked she cast her mind far from the task at hand; her fingers moved automatically; her gaze was unfocused, seeking deep into the dazzling pattern emerging from the weft.

'Enchantress,' she entreated. 'This lowly servant would seek counsel. Bless this one with your guidance.'

For every pass of the shuttle was a prayer sent; every shift in the woof a revelation. 'O Queen—'

And came the answer, that cool gentle voice so familiar: *Greetings, Agayla Atheduru Remejhel. Most valued servant. Always I welcome your wisdom.*

'My Queen. I beg an audience. News has come. Though my heart is heavy with the weight of it, I may have an answer to that problem we have spoken of.'

And the answer came, full of understanding and thus sharing in that same heaviness: *Bring her.*

Agayla clamped her hands upon the loom, stilling the mechanism. She blinked to return her vision to the dawn's light. It took many slow breaths to calm the hammering of her heart. *An audience. It has been so many years. Oh, Kiska . . . what have I done? Yet how else could I stop you?* She saw before her how her tears darkened the polished wood.

* * *

At night in an alley in Banith, four men dressed in loose dark clothes crouched, whispering. 'All we have to do is walk in!' said one. 'The door isn't even locked.'

'This foreigner *claims* he keeps it open,' added the second, aside.

'It's open. What are we waiting for?'

After a moment's silence, the third cleared his throat. 'It's consecrated ground. We shouldn't spill blood there.'

'Consecrated to *what*?' said the first. 'Some nameless foreign entity? The man's a charlatan. A fake. He's just pocketing everything. It's a mockery.'

'No one's seen him take any coin from anyone,' pointed out the third.

'He eats, doesn't he?' the first answered. The third nodded, conceding the argument.

'Perhaps he eats what his followers provide,' a new voice rumbled from the deeper gloom within the alley.

The four spun. Eight blades glittered in the starlight.

'Whoever you are, stranger,' said the first, 'turn round now and walk away. Listen to me. I'm giving you this one chance.'

The figure moved closer and the faint silver light revealed a huge shape, unnaturally tall and wide, much of his height coming from a great mane of tangled black hair. 'As you can see,' the newcomer said, 'turning around is out of the question for me. You'll have to back out yourselves.'

'Are you a fool? Can't you see?'

'Yes I can – better than you, I suspect. As to being a fool . . . no, I am a thief.'

‘A thief?’ the second echoed in disbelief. He looked the giant figure up and down. ‘How could you possibly steal anything?’

‘Oh, that’s easy. Like this,’ and the figure leaned forward, lowering his voice. ‘Give me your money.’

The four exchanged confused glances, then all chuckled. ‘You’re trying my patience,’ the first warned, his voice tight.

‘No. I’m trying to take your money.’

The grins fell away. The first and the second, paired side by side, edged forward, blades extended. ‘Go now – or die.’

‘As I said, I cannot back up. And besides, one of my favourite foot-stalls is there across the street.’

‘Die a fool then!’ The two lunged. Blades thudded home, driven with force. The broad figure grunted with the strength of the thrusts. Then the two assailants loosed surprised exclamations as they yanked on the blades. ‘Stuck!’ one snarled. The newcomer swept his arms closed, crashing together the two men who fell, senseless.

‘There. Now, you two?’ the immense figure invited, stepping over the fallen shapes. The remaining pair stared for an instant at this astounding vision, then turned and ran.

‘Damn,’ the huge man said into the emptiness of the alley. He made to turn but his bulging front and back lodged against the walls of the narrow alley and he cursed again in a different language. After grunting and straining to turn round, he abandoned the effort and carefully walked backwards. He felt behind himself with each step until the two fallen attackers lay before him once more. ‘Simplicity itself,’ he said, and brushed his hands together. ‘Now then.’ He bent, grunting, reaching with a hand for one of the unconscious shapes. Sighing, he straightened then tried again with the opposite hand. He reached, cursing and hissing. His fingers clawed the air just above the shoulder of his prey.

Gasping, the man straightened to suck in great breaths. He pulled out a cloth and wiped his glistening flushed face. ‘Ah, of course!’ he murmured, smiling, and patted the loose robes that hung down over his wide armoured chest and stomach. He found a dagger grip standing out from his side and he yanked on it, grunting. After several tries he managed to withdraw the blade. He studied it, impressed. One of the fallen attackers groaned then, stirring, and the fellow reversed the dagger and threw it down to crack pommel-first against the man’s head. Then he found the second blade and began yanking on it, snarling and grumbling beneath his breath again.

'What do you think you're doing here, Manask?'

The giant flinched, jerking the dagger free and dropping it. He blinked mildly at the squat muscular newcomer before him. 'Ipshank. Fancy meeting you here.'

The man scowled, the lines of tattoos on his face twisting. 'I live here, Manask. This is my temple.'

'Ah!' Manask took hold of another lodged dagger. 'Is that what you call it?' He pulled on the weapon, wrenching it from side to side. 'But I recall . . . hearing that . . . Fener is no more!' The blade came free and he studied it, pleased.

'I've found a new god.'

'Oh? A new one?' The tall man held out a hand, thumb and forefinger close together. 'Perhaps a tiny baby one?'

'Spare me your scepticism. I see you still have your, ah, armour.'

Manask clasped his wide sides. 'Why of course. It's like my own flesh and blood.'

'Exactly,' Ipshank answered beneath his breath. He kicked at one fallen man. 'Who's this?'

'Ahhh!' Manask murmured, holding up the dagger. 'A question very pertinent for you.' Bending, he pushed the blade through the clothes of one fellow, then raised the weapon to bring the unconscious man into reach and grasped him with his free hand. All this Ipshank watched expressionless, arms crossed.

'You are making powerful enemies, my friend,' the big man explained as he rifled the attacker's clothes. 'These men work for the City Watch.' A pouch of coins and other weapons were tucked into pockets hidden all about Manask's loose robes. Finished, he dropped the fellow and bent to the next.

'I don't want you interfering. You'll only ruin everything.'

Manask peered up, grinning, 'Oh? Ruin what?'

Ipshank mouthed a silent curse. 'Nothing.'

'Oho! I knew it!' Manask straightened with the second assailant. 'A new scam. I'll have your back again – just like the old days.'

The priest raised his face to the night sky and the boar's face superimposed in faded blue ink stood out in sudden relief. He gave a suffering sigh. 'No, Manask. No more tricks. No more deceits. I'm finished. Retired. Do me a favour now and don't hang around.' Down on the littered cobbles the first attacker groaned, mumbling something and wincing his pain. Ipshank kicked him across the temple.

The big man let the second fellow drop. 'Now don't get greedy.

We've always split the gains. You're not going all priestly on me, are you?'

'How many times do I have to tell you? There'll be no proceeds from this operation, Manask. Not the tangible kind, in any case.'

Manask clasped his fingertips across the top of his great bulging front and peered down at the squat man before him. His tangled brows knitted together. 'Oh dear. You *are* going all religious in your old age, aren't you? Very well. If you must indulge your guilty conscience. Temples do as well as any other racket – better than many.'

Ipshank pressed his fists to his forehead. 'How many times do I have to . . .' The fists fell. 'Never mind. Do as you will. As far as I'm concerned we're no longer associated. Don't expect anything from me.' And he marched away, grumbling under his breath.

Manask stood for a time in the dark alley, fingertips clasped and brows clenched. Then a sly smile blossomed on his long face and he raised a finger, chuckling. 'Ahh! So that's how we're going to play it! I see it now. A falling out! Very good. No one will suspect.' He chuckled more, tried to turn and jammed his stomach on the brick wall. 'Damn! Curse it to the Dark Taker . . .' He clasped his front in an attempt to squeeze himself, hissing and puffing. 'Oh, to the Lady with it!' He began feeling his way backwards. 'Oh yes,' he murmured as he retreated into the gloom. 'We'll fleece these Fistians to the bone, my friend. I can smell it in the air, the turmoil, the tension, and – oh dear – what have I stepped in?'

CHAPTER II

Point to the sky
Point to the ground
Point to the ocean all around

Spin your top
Spin your top
All fall down!

Children's rhyme
Traditional
Korel Isles

HIS NAME WAS NOT SUTH, BUT THE MALAZAN RECRUITING OFFICER at the station kept open year round just north of the Dal Hon lands shortened it into that and so was he entered into official Malazan rolls. He didn't care. Names others chose to call one did not matter. People would use whatever forms of address they wished. These were merely terms imposed from without. For Suthahl 'Ani, the only thing that really mattered was what one named oneself.

And perhaps it was this indifference to names and the petty rivalries and contests for status among the new recruits, male and female, that prevented Suth from attracting yet another name – a nickname to be used within the ranks like so many of the recruits': Dim, Worm, Lard, Roach or Thumbs.

He'd joined because of the stories of great battles up north, but when he got there all the fighting was over. Only the talking remained – too much talking for his liking. Boasting and storytelling. The cheap puffery of those who were cowards on the field, for only those who ran or hid from the fighting could have survived the slaughters they described.

Now he and a handful of recruits had been assigned their squads. After basic training on the march, he, Dim, and Lard ended up in the 17th Squad, 4th Company, 2nd Division, Malazan Fourth Army, encamped in the hills and coastline around the capital city, Unta. He felt privileged; instead of squatting under ponchos or makeshift tents in the rain, the 17th actually inhabited a thatch-roofed fisherman's cottage, either abandoned, or seized. He wondered if perhaps the reason the squad rated such luxury was the man who met them in the night and beating downpour just outside its doorway.

He wore a battered janzerian cuirass with scaled armoured sleeves. A well-worn longsword hung peace-strapped at his belt. The rain ran down the mail coif under his plain iron helmet. Pale, mild eyes looked them up and down from beneath the dark rim of that helmet.

'Welcome to the 17th,' the man said in a surprisingly soft voice. He spoke the common Imperial dialect, Talian, close enough to Suth's own Dal Hon. 'I'm your sergeant, Goss. You three are here because you're classed as heavies, and the 17th has always been a heavy infantry squad.' He pointed to Lard. 'What's your name, soldier?'

'Weveth Lethall,' said Lard.

Their sergeant looked the hulking fellow up and down again. 'You sure? Not Fatty? Or Bhederin? Or Ox?'

'We call him Lard,' said Dim, grinning good-naturedly.

'And you?'

'Dim.'

'Right.' He raised his chin to Suth. 'You?'

'Suth.'

'Suth? What kind of name is that?'

'It's a name.'

'Well, that it is. Okay, you three can sleep inside. I'll see about getting you kitted out.' And he remained, motionless, in front of them. It seemed to Suth that the man was waiting for something. Then he remembered his training and he saluted. Dim and Lard followed suit. Goss answered the salute. 'Right. See you later.'

Their sergeant disappeared into the sheeting rain. Suth, Dim and Lard exchanged glances. Lard shrugged and headed to the open doorway. Suth and Dim followed. Inside, embers glowed in a stone hearth, old straw lay kicked about over a beaten dirt floor. A small, rat-faced fellow sat at a table of adzed planks, smoking a pipe. It was warm and humid and stank of sweat and manure. Lard headed to an inner door.

The little man's eyes followed him. 'Un-uh . . .' he warned, his small pointy teeth clenched tight on the white clay pipe stem.

'The sergeant told us to sleep in here,' Lard said, testy. Suth wiped the rain from his face.

'I know what he said. You three sleep here.' He pointed to the floor.

'What? On the floor? In the dirt?'

'That or outside.' He blew smoke from his pinched nose. 'Your choice.'

'And who're you?'

'Faro's the name.'

'Why in Hood's name should we listen to you?'

''Cause it would be smart to play along till you know the rules.' And he bared his tiny white teeth.

Shrugging, Suth sat next to the hearth and gathered up an armful of straw. Dim sat heavily across from him, grinning. He leaned close: 'Just like home!'

Suth said nothing, but it was in fact just like home, hugging the firepit for warmth after minding the herd in the rain all day.

Lard sat awkwardly, cursing and grumbling. 'Gave up a god-damned warm bed for this! Should've stayed home. Fucking choices I make.'

Suth lay down facing the glowing hearth, ignoring the stink of his soaked leather jerkin, his itching wool trousers, and heavy sodden rag wraps at his legs. He hoped to all the Dal Hon gods that the man would soon shut up.

A kick woke him to light streaming in the open doorway. He'd managed to sleep despite the scratchy clothes these Malazans had issued him, despite his hunger, and despite the massive passing of gas from his two ox-like companions. Someone was leaning over him, offering something – a beast's horn.

'Take it, it's hot.' He was an older fellow, a veteran, not their sergeant, his voice dry-sand hoarse.

'Thanks.' It was hot. A kind of weak tea. 'I'm new.'

A tired indulgent smile drew up the man's lips as if to hint at all the oh-so-smart comments he could make in response to that painfully obvious statement, but that he was far above scoring such easy points. A grey beard, hacked short, surrounded that mouth, and dark eyes peered out of deep wells of hatched lines. 'Len's the name. Sapper.'

'Suth.'

'Good to have you.'

Suth peered down at his snoring companions. 'Let 'em rest,' said Len. 'Have to brew up more tea.'

The sunlight glare from the door was obscured and Suth shaded his gaze and stared at what he saw there. It was singularly the most unfavoured female he had ever set eyes on. She wore a dirty tattered uniform of a grey jupon over old leathers, was skinny to the point of malnourished, and even the bulging eyes that appeared to look in both directions at once couldn't draw all attention away from a mouthful of uneven, yellowed teeth. 'Where's Hunter?' she demanded.

'Out. What's the word, Urfa?'

The bulging eyes swivelled to focus on Suth; she appeared to ignore Len's question. 'More heavies,' she announced, her mouth drawing down, musing. 'Heavies and saboteurs is all we got. Hardly any lights or cav. Looks like it's shaping into an assault on strong fortifications. Maybe south Genabackis.'

'South Genabackis is a pest hole,' Len observed. 'And there ain't nothin' there worth assaulting. Not even their women.'

'There's Elingarth.'

'No one's that stupid.'

'There's that island off the coast. Saw it on a chart once. Somethin' like . . . "the Island of the Seguleh".'

Len choked on his own horn of tea. 'Sure, all fifteen thousand of us might manage to take one fishing village on *that* island.'

She smiled, showing off her ragged teeth. 'Just lookin' on the bright side. Anyways, word is we're shipping out so pack your bag of tricks and have one last screw with whichever sheep it is you found.'

'The one better looking than you, Urfa,' said Len, smiling.

'Must be that old goat smell on you.'

Grinning, Len saluted and she responded. 'Tell Hunter,' she said and left.

Dim grunted then, blinking and smacking his lips.

'Who was that?' Suth asked.

'Lieutenant Urfa. She commands the sappers, the saboteurs, in the company.'

'Lieutenant?'

'Aye.' Len kicked Lard, who grunted. 'There's tea to brew,' he told them. 'Gotta find Hunter – that's Goss – the sergeant.'

Suth saluted. Len waved it aside. 'See you later.'

While Dim and Lard fussed over the pot on the hearth, Suth went out. A heavy low morning mist obscured the hillsides. It mingled with the thick white smoke of the countless fires of an army encamped and burning any wood it could scavenge, all green and unseasoned. In the distance the waters of Unta Bay seemed to lie motionless, dull and grey. A flotilla of ships of all sizes jammed the shallows. Their transport? The damp cold bit at Suth and he rubbed his arms for warmth; it was never this bad on the steppes.

Ox-drawn carts lumbered past, moving materiel down to the shore. Squads of soldiers marched by in that direction as well. One woman approached upslope, against the tide. She was tall – *strapping*, his father might have said – and she carried loose bundles of gear under her arms. She wore a padded leather shirt and trousers such as might be worn under heavy metal armour. She dropped the bundles on the dry porch of the cottage and nodded to Suth. Her olive complexion and hacked-short night-black hair identified her as Kanese, the only nation able to war with any success against his own Dal Hon league of kingdoms. But the women of Itko Kan were supposed to be tiny demure things. This woman was a giant, fully as tall as he, with the breadth across the shoulders of a heavy sword wielder.

'Yana,' she said, introducing herself.

'Suth.'

'Suth? That doesn't sound Dal Honese.'

'It's not.'

A grunt of understanding. Dim and Lard staggered out, blinking. Lard turned to the wall, untied the lacing at the front of his trousers and let loose a great stream of piss that hissed against the mud-chinked planking.

'Next time try the privy out back,' Yana drawled.

Lard turned, tying up the lacing, and winked. 'Gonna hold it for me too?'

'Not even if I could find it.' She motioned to the bundles. 'These are for you, armour and weapons.' Suth knelt at the nearest, began untying the leather strapping. Rolled around the outside was a padded leather and felt undergarment, called an *aketon* by his people, fully sleeved. When he pulled it over his head it hung down to his knees. Inside the bundle he was amazed to see two halves of a cuirass of banded iron, a hauberk with mailed sleeves, and a sheathed longsword. When he forced his arms through the hauberk and pulled it down, it hung just shorter than the aketon. Next he pulled on the cuirass and began lacing up the open side. He was stunned; among his own people only a king could afford such a set. How the Malazans had acquired such bounty, however, was revealed by the black stain of dried blood on one side and the gap between bands where a broad blade had penetrated.

Lard was holding up his own shirt of scaled armour and scowling. 'What is this beat-up old shit?'

That comment offended Yana far more than the earlier jibe. She eyed Lard the way he was examining his armour. 'Goss had to beg and trade all night to pull this gear together so you'd better appreciate it. It's that or nothing.' She turned to Dim. 'What do you say?'

The man actually blushed beneath his tangled dirty-blond hair. 'Good as Burn's own blessing.'

'And you, Suth?'

'Far more than I was expecting.'

Yana grunted. 'Damn right. Well, you're heavies, and of the 17th. So you should at least last the first exchange.' She raised her chin, peering in past them. 'Pyke – you still in there?'

A muffled complaint answered.

'Pack everything up. We're shipping out.'

'What am I? The Hood-damned servant?'

'You're last, is what you are. As usual. Okay, you three,' she motioned to equipment piled at one end of the porch, 'pick that up and come with me.'

Dim saluted but Yana stared, her brown eyes narrowing. 'What was that for?'

'You're not the, ah, corporal?'

'No. Pyke is.'

Dim hiked up his bundled armour and a roll of gear. 'But you're actin' like it, 'n' all.'

'That's because Pyke's a worthless lazy bastard, that's why.'

'I heard that, you sexless bitch!' Pyke yelled from within.

Yana ignored the disembodied voice. 'C'mon, let's go.'

They followed Yana. Suth adjusted his belt and sheath one-handed, a roped bundle under one arm. Around them the press thickened until they could advance no further and they joined one of many ragged lines of men and women squatting and sitting on the trampled muddy grass among rolls and crates of packed equipment.

'Where're we headed?' Dim asked.

'They don't tell us,' Yana answered mildly, scanning the nearby faces. She nodded and greeted many.

'A woman came by earlier to talk to Len,' Suth said. 'A Lieutenant Urfa.'

Yana grunted. 'There's a crazy one. Get us all killed, she will. Sappers an' their cracked schemes.'

Lard was examining his weapon, a heavy cutlass. 'There was a guy in the cottage last night. Said his name was Faro.'

The woman was quiet for a time. 'Faro's a killer. The kind who'd be executed in peacetime, if you know what I mean. Stay out of his way. He answers only to Goss.'

'And Goss – his other name is Hunter?' Suth asked.

She turned to study him. 'Where'd you hear that?'

'Urfa said it.'

Yana grunted her understanding. 'Well, forget it. It's not a name for you.'

The morning warmed, the mist burning off. Clouds of tiny flies tormented everyone. The cacophony of lowing and complaining animals, shouting men and women, and screeching ungreased cart-wheels kept Suth from dozing. He watched all the materiel being carried across long plank walkways laid over the mudflats out to waiting launches. He did not know ships – had only seen the ocean twice – but the vessels anchored in the bay did not seem to have a military cut to them. They looked instead like lumbering, ungainly merchant scows.

'I'm sorry, ma'am, but I am so hungry,' Dim finally announced after sighing and grimacing in vain. 'We haven't eaten since yesterday noon.'

Yana grunted again – it seemed her normal way of communicating. She stood. 'I'll see what I can roust up. You lot stay here.'

Noon passed and Yana did not return. Suth wondered whether they'd met everyone in their squad; he suspected not. A gang of men and women came and sat among the crates and bundles of equipment piled just ahead of them, then collected it all and began moving off. Suth, Dim, and Lard watched until they started gathering up their own squad's gear in the process. Lard jumped to his feet. 'Hey! That's ours.'

The others froze. 'Don't try an' be smart,' said one fellow, offended. 'We left all this here earlier.'

Suth and Dim stood. Lard grabbed one bundle. 'Well, these ones are ours.'

'Piss off, It's all the same, okay?'

'Then leave it,' Suth suggested gently.

The gang – a full squad, Suth assumed – set everything down and straightened. Eight against their three. A challenging fight. He began unbuckling his sword belt.

The eight glanced to one another, smiling slyly. 'Don't be fools,' the spokesman said. 'It ain't worth it.'

'As I see it,' Lard said, 'you can either leave the gear or take a beating.' He smiled as well. 'Your choice.'

The eight began spreading out in a broad circle surrounding them. The spokesman, a scarred squat veteran, remained. He raised his hands, open and empty. 'All right. You got more than talk?'

'I got this,' Lard said, and he swung one great fist.

The spokesman ducked under the wild swing and his fist cracked against Lard's head. Suth winced at the solid smack of the blow. Lard straightened up to his full considerable height and rubbed his jaw. 'Good shot.'

A crowd drawn from the nearby lines gathered around. Suth heard bets shouted, and a name, Keth, repeated. Lard swung broadly again, and again Keth, if that was his name, easily evaded the blow to hammer Lard with solid blows to the stomach and head.

But nothing fazed the big man as he relentlessly stalked the quicker fellow. Eventually, Lard caught Keth by one arm and drew him into a great hug, lifted him over his head, and brought him down crashing on top of a crate that collapsed, shattering. Amid a shower of sawdust and cloth rags a handful of small dark green globes rolled out on to the mud.

Immediately, everyone was silenced. Eyes bulged, staring. Suth glanced about, bemused. As quickly as it had come the crowd vanished. Even the other squad picked up their stunned comrade and melted away. Suth and Dim went to Lard who was puffing, winded, wiping at the blood running generously from his split brow and cheek.

'Dumbass heavies,' a woman grumbled, and they turned.

Two of the crowd had remained, a woman and the saboteur, Len. Ignoring the three of them, they knelt at the broken crate.

'This shouldn't be here,' the woman said, and her gaze snapped up, glancing about.

'Lifted,' Len said, his voice a croak.

The two shared looks that struck Suth as fully the most gleeful and evil he'd seen in a long time. They scrounged blankets and ponchos to quickly cover the wreckage. Suth, Dim and Lard watched, bemused.

Everything covered, Len finally turned to Suth, though his gaze kept darting about the flats. 'Dim and Lard,' Suth introduced his companions. 'Len.'

'Keri,' Len said, indicating the woman. She nodded while one by one gently wrapping the globes in rags and packing them into a shoulder bag.

'I need another bag,' she told Len, who nodded and began searching among the gear.

'What's going on?' Suth asked.

'Munitions,' Len said. He looked up. 'Know what I mean?'

Suth had heard of them; he nodded. Lard grunted his understanding, even conveying a measure of wonder. Dim just looked confused.

Shortly after Keri and Len had finished packing all the munitions Yana came up with a burlap sack in one hand. This she handed to Suth. 'Share it out.' To Len, 'What happened here?'

The two saboteurs looked as if they were not sure which story to try. Suth said, 'Some crates got dropped.' Len shot him a wink.

Yana grunted her disinterest. 'Clean up and we'll go. I found Goss. We got our berth assignment. Pick everything up.' She eyed Lard. 'What in Soliel's mercy happened to you?'

The man wiped blood from his mouth, offered a defiant smile. 'I fell down.'

Their berthing was aboard the converted Cawnese merchant caravel, *Lasana*. Here Suth was introduced to the remaining members of the squad, Wess and Pyke, both heavy infantry. In fact, the *Lasana* was fairly groaning under the weight of heavy infantry. It carried some four hundred men and women of the 4th Company, nearly all heavies, with a sprinkling of saboteurs. It looked to Suth as if Urfa's predictions were correct; wherever they were headed the Malazans must be counting on an ugly fight. Wess was already asleep in one of the rows of hammocks assigned. It was a mystery to Suth how the man could be sleeping given the shattering chaos of loading. Pyke was a tall lanky veteran who ignored the three newcomers. Everyone shoved their gear into hammocks until Yana told them not to because they'd be sharing them with others rotating in eight-hour shifts. Len motioned to pegs where, like bodies impaled in the dark, kit bags of clothing and pieces of armour swung already.

'Where's Goss?' Yana asked Pyke.

'Up top.'

'Okay.' To everyone: 'Stow your gear and head up top to keep this area clear.'

Suth pulled off his armour and hung it but Len took it down and handed it back. 'Clean, repair, and oil it.'

'I have nothing to use.'

'I do.'

'Thank you.'

The old saboteur waved that aside and headed back out to the companionway. Suth followed. He had to hunch almost double to manage the cramped quarters. They found the deck crammed with soldiers. So thick was the press that the sailors found it almost impossible to do their tasks. There was little work for them, however, as departure was delayed and delayed and then delayed some more. It was the night tide before any of the vessels began making their slow, awkward way out of the bay.

Suth and Dim sat with Len, their armour across their laps, as the man educated them in the care of their newfound riches. Half the time, though, Suth listened to the rumours circulating around them. They were headed north to Seven Cities to consolidate its pacification. To north Genabackis to relieve the 5th. East, to central Genabackis to occupy some rich city called Darujhistan. Or on to south Genabackis to initiate a new front.

Finally Suth asked Len, 'Where *are* we headed?'

The veteran just frowned over the leathers he was sewing. 'Doesn't matter. Everywhere's the same for us.'

Suth understood the cold reasoning behind that, yet this was a good deal farther than he'd ever imagined his vow to join the Malazans would take him. 'Where do you *think* we're headed?'

Len looked up, squinted into the clouded eastern night sky. 'Well, it sounds to me like all this speculation on where we *might* be headed is shying scared from one of the possibilities. The one no one wants to consider.'

'Which is what, old timer?' a nearby soldier asked, and he raised a hand to silence his companions.

Len shrugged. 'That we're headed south, to Korel lands.'

'That's just so much horseshit!' the soldier yelled. Everyone began talking at once. Suth watched, amazed, as this version became the new rumour, to spread like ripples over the crowded deck, outward to the rear and to the front, raising shouts of alarm and even horror as it went.

'Go to Hood, old man!' shouted the soldier who'd asked for Len's opinion in the first place.

Len merely offered Suth a knowing grin. 'See how you should always keep your mouth shut? People only want to hear what they want to hear.'

Suth agreed. It had also occurred to him that all the speculation involving Genabackis and some city named Darujhistan seemed to be where the speakers *wanted* to go more than where they thought they *might* be going. Everyone wanted to head to overseas postings in Genabackis, or even Seven Cities.

His own personal philosophy on life told him that, therefore, that was *exactly* where they were not headed. This name, Korel, he'd heard once or twice before. It was always mentioned more as a curse than anything. It was considered the very worst, the ugliest of all the holdings of the far-flung Malazan Empire. Well, he'd joined to be tested, and it looked as though he might be headed into one of the sternest trials of his life. That was good. It would be a waste of his time otherwise.

* * *

The street orphans were out playing on the courtyard across the way from the temple. Ella squatted on the threshold, preparing the midday meal while keeping one affectionate eye on them. She could hardly believe that just a few years ago she ran with her own gang of urchins. She saw hardly any of them any more. The Watch beat Harl to death as a probable thief. Peek disappeared entirely; and the pimps took Tillin. That would have been her fate had she not started listening to the priest.

It was here she had run when the trolling party had come for her: hired thugs on a sweep for young girls and boys to feed the brothels and slave markets all across the archipelago. And it was on this threshold that the priest faced them. One unarmed man against seven armed, and they backed down. She pounded the pestle and shook her head. The priest. She still could not understand him. He was like nothing from her experience as a child, abandoned to fend for herself on the streets of Banith. An extremely narrow education, she could admit. A school of casual violence, constant hunger, exploitation, and rape.

Yet not once had the priest indulged in similar practices – the stronger exacting what they wished from the weaker, including sexual gratification. Not that the man was a eunuch. It seemed that he simply refused to accept all the old, traditional ways of doing things. 'Haven't got us very far, have they?' he once told her.

Giggling brought her attention back to her surroundings. A crowd of dirty grinning faces in a half-circle before her. 'Lunch time, is it?' Obeying the rules of the street, the feral children said nothing lest they misstep and lose their chance for a meal. They grinned instead, as if happy, and 'made cute' as they used to call it in her time. But in their too-bright shining eyes she saw the merciless torment of constant nagging hunger. She reached to the basket at her side, folded back the cloth across it, and distributed the small flatbreads she'd baked earlier that day. Laughing, they snatched their prizes and ran, shoving everything into their mouths before anyone, or anything, could steal it from them.

One young girl remained. Her clothes were finer than the rest, though just as torn and grimed. The bread remained in one hand. She watched Ella with large dark eyes, curiously calm and solemn. Ella returned to preparing the priest's meal. 'What is it, child?' she asked.

'Is this the house of the foreign holy man?'

'Yes.'

'Is it true that he eats babies?'

She stopped her pounding. '*What?*'

'That's what everyone says.'

Ella rocked back on her haunches, eyed the crowded square, the small day-market, the touts and hawkers jostling pilgrims just off the boats as they milled, organizing a procession to the Cloister. 'So that's what they say . . .' she breathed.

'Yes. They say that at night he changes into a beast and steals babies from houses and eats their hearts.'

'What do you think?' Ella asked, strangely unnerved by the child's grisly imagination.

The girl pushed her tangled hair from her pale brow. *Very pale – not of Fist? Fathered by a Malazan occupier perhaps? As she suspected she had been herself?* The girl cocked her head, thinking. 'Oh, I don't think he does any of *those* things. I think he's much more dangerous than that.'

Ella stared anew at this strange child. What an odd thing to say. But the child just smiled, her eyes almost mocking, and twirling a pinch of hair in her fingers, 'making cute', she wandered off. Watching her go, Ella was struck most not by the child's precocious self-possession, her assured manner, or what she'd said. Rather, it was the fact that of the pack of hungry street urchins careering around her, most by far bigger and older, not one attempted to snatch the bread held so casually in one small hand.

Later she was arranging the sauce and boiled fish on a platter for the priest when everything changed out among the crowd in the square. A child of these streets, and sensitive to their moods, she stilled as well. The urchins were gone, as were the older idlers; the shouting of the merchants had quietened, as had the general talk. In the hush Ella heard the approach of a measured tramp of boots. A Malazan patrol.

Even the pilgrims paused in their reverences, hands raised in supplication to the towers of the Cloister. The column entered the square from a side street, marched across the broad open expanse. All eyes followed its progress. A standard preceded them, a black cloth bearing the Imperial sceptre. Their surcoats were a dark grey edged in blood red. As the column tramped past the front of the temple a detachment separated and halted. It was led by a figure familiar to all those of the Banith waterfront, Sergeant Billouth, main extortionist and strong arm of the local commander, Captain Karien'el.

'The priest here?' Billouth demanded in accented Roolian.

She bowed. 'I'll see . . .'

'Yes?' It was the priest in the doorway, a robe open to his waist showing his thick chest and bulging stomach, both covered in a thick pelt of bristle-like hair and the blue curls of tattooing. Ella looked away; she'd glimpsed before that the marks extended well beyond his face, but never guessed they descended quite so far. 'What is it?'

'We're looking for a man,' Billouth said, and he crossed his arms over his studded leather hauberk, a pleased smile growing on his lips. 'A criminal fugitive. A thief. Big fellow. Said to hang out in the neighbourhood.' He leaned forward, lowering his voice. 'Know anything that could help us?'

The priest's expression didn't change. 'No.'

Ella lowered her gaze.

'Really? You wouldn't be withholding information, would you? Because when we catch this fellow and squeeze him . . . Well, that would be bad news for you.'

'I don't know what you're talking about.'

Billouth ran the back of a hand over his unshaven jowls. 'If you say so. But I think we'll be talking again real soon,' and he winked. Straightening, the sergeant raised his voice. 'Thank you very much for all the information, Priest. A lot of locals will end up dancing on the Stormwall thanks to you.'

Ella gaped. *But he'd said nothing!*

Billouth waved the detachment onward, saluted the priest.

Bastard, the priest mouthed.

Ella stood watching the Malazans march away, their wicked grins at the trouble they'd stirred up, hating them. The priest took the tray from her. 'Thank you, Ella.'

'They want you gone.'

'Yes.'

'Why don't they just . . . you know . . .'

'Get rid of me?'

'Yes.'

His wide frog mouth twisted up. 'They've tried. A number of times. Right now it's an uneasy truce.' He shrugged. 'But why should they bother when they can get the locals to do it for them?' He ducked inside.

Ella gasped, seeing it now. She followed him inside. 'Rumours! They're spreading rumours about you!'

'Yes. Them and someone else. The priests at the Cloister, I imagine.' He sat cross-legged on a mat to eat.

'But why should they do that?'

He shrugged again. 'They're on top and I'm an unknown to them. Any possible change is a threat to their position. So their reaction is to suppress.'

Ella rounded on the entrance as if she would march out to confront them all. 'But why? You let the homeless kids sleep here. You give shelter and food to the debtors.'

'And I extort money and sex for the privilege, yes?'

She lowered her gaze, feeling her own face heat. 'I'd heard that one too.'

He nodded thoughtfully, chewing. 'They might even believe it, seeing as in their hearts they know that's what they'd do in my place. But that's not what I'm here for.'

Surprising herself, she asked in a small voice, 'What are you here for?'

Still nodding, he spoke, his gaze lowered to his food. 'I've seen religion from the top and from the bottom, Ella. I've been intimate with faith all my life. And it occurs to me that the transfixion of ecstasy, the transporting feeling of being one with a god, is the same everywhere. It matters not what image or idol is bowed to or hangs on the wall, be it the cowled figure of Hood, or a severed bull's head. It's all the same because the sensation, the feeling, is the same as it comes from within all of us. From inside. Not without.' He looked up, his gaze narrowed. 'That's the important point. It is a natural innate emotion, a human quality, that can be exploited. That's why I'm here.'

At some point Ella had clasped a hand to her throat as if to assure herself that she could still breathe. Taking that deep breath, she bowed to the priest and left the empty room for the cool outside. In the small front court she forced her chest to relax, drawing deep the refreshing air to stop her head from spinning. That eerie child was right. This man was somehow much more dangerous than anyone could possibly suspect.

And the question for her was, dare she follow? She saw how till now her life had been nothing more than a mad scramble to fill her stomach, avoid danger, find shelter. Now something more had been shown her; so much that she'd never even suspected existed in the world. She felt as if she'd been granted a glimpse of something terrifyingly huge, yet also awe-inspiring, impossibly grand. Oddly enough she felt humility in the glimpsing of it rather than the puffed-up self-importance she'd met in those claiming to be filled with the spirit of the gods. Was this sensation what the priest meant? If so, she knew immediately she would follow without hesitation. It felt right. Which, she supposed, was its strength, and its danger.

* * *

Ivanr spotted the mounted column when it entered the north cleft of the valley his fields overlooked. He could run, he supposed, abandon his home and all he'd worked so hard to build these last few years. But something prevented him. A kind of obtuse stubbornness that asserted itself always at the most inconvenient of times. Besides, there was a chance that they weren't after him anyway. So it was that the column of Jourilan cavalry encircled him while he leaned on his hoe amid his field of beans.

Its captain drew off his helmet and the felt cap he wore beneath, then pushed back his matted sweaty hair. He inclined his head in greeting. 'Ivanr of Antr. We arrest you in the name of the Jourilan Emperor. Will you come peaceably, or must we subdue you?'

He peered around at the encircling cavalry. Twelve armed men. Quite the compliment. He shaded his gaze to study the captain. 'And the charge?'

Within his cuirass of banded iron the captain offered a shrug of complete indifference. 'You have been denounced for aiding and abetting the heretic cultists.'

Ivanr nodded, accepting what he knew to have been inevitable. Eventually, he knew, word would have reached the Emperor's secret police, or the Lady's priesthood, that he looked the other way while refugees and travellers drank from his well and slept in the lean-to shelters he'd erected in his fields. They'd probably tortured it out of one they'd caught. 'And should I cooperate? What then?'

'You will be tried.'

So. A show trial. A very public demonstration that no one was above the law, not even disgraced past grand champions. At the moment, though, he faced twelve armed men and the capital was a long way off. Anything could happen in the intervening time. He dropped his hoe. 'I'll make no trouble.'

'A wise decision, Ivanr.' The captain motioned to his men. Two dismounted. One took a rope from his saddle. They approached carefully. Ivanr held out his fists together. They bound him at the wrists.

The leather of his saddle creaking, the captain turned to study the surrounding valley slopes. He replaced his helmet. 'They said you'd lost your fire, Ivanr. That you'd sworn some kind of vow never to take another life. But I couldn't believe it – I'd seen you fight, after all.' The trooper tied the rope to his cantle, remounted. The captain shook his head. 'Hard to believe you're the same man I saw that afternoon out on the sands, taking on all comers. You were untouchable then.' He regarded Ivanr for some time from beneath the lip of his helmet, his heavy gaze almost regretful. 'Better, I think, had you died then.'

He motioned to a nearby tree, bare-limbed, black and grey. 'That one will do.'

The troop kneed their mounts. The rope snaked taut then yanked Ivanr forward. 'Captain! You mentioned something about a trial?'

The captain looked back. He reached a gloved hand into a pannier and pulled out a rolled scroll. 'Didn't I mention it had already occurred? You were found guilty, by the way. We're here to fulfil the sentence.'

This, Ivanr told himself acidly, he should have seen coming as well. As the captain said – he was definitely losing his edge. Well, the captain had had his little surprise. Now it was time for his, and quickly. Jogging, he twisted his wrists, testing the rope, and found they'd bound him no more thoroughly than they would have any other prisoner, which was a mistake. Grunting with the effort, and the accompanying pain, he twisted his arms around the binding at the wrists until the rope snapped. Two long paces brought him level with the trooper leading him. Taking a grip on the saddle he pulled himself up to kick the startled man from his seat. He felt ribs snap beneath his heel.

Shouts of alarm all round. The mounts milled, kicking and nervous. 'Just kill him!' the captain shouted, disgusted.

Ivanr yanked a levelled spear from one trooper, swung it to slap the rump of a mount that reared, startled, dumping its rider. Ducking under another spear, he jabbed with the butt to knock the breath from a fourth rider, and very possibly rupturing internal organs. The captain charged past, swinging his blade. Ivanr blocked with the spear haft, twisting to whip the iron shank beneath the blade across the back of the man's neck, pitching him on to his horse's neck where he hung, seemingly unconscious. Ivanr swung again, knocking aside a number of thrusts, took hold of another spear to yank its wielder backwards off his mount, pulling himself from his feet in the process. That may have saved his life as the blades of two passing troopers hissed over him.

He picked up another fallen spear, kicked a groggy trooper to keep him down. The next two riders he unhorsed with his spear, leaving four to mill about him, swinging. If they'd simply dismounted and surrounded him he knew he'd have faced far worse odds. As it was, they'd given up the main advantage of the mounted troop's charge. Now they merely impeded one another on their horses. They cut down at him while he ducked and thrust. Kicked-up red dust coated everyone. It stuck in Ivanr's throat and stung his eyes. Dodging, keeping them in each other's way, he thrust and jabbed them from their mounts one by one until the dust drifted aside and the last of the riderless horses ran off. Only he was left upright. He kicked two who looked to be rousing then found the captain where he'd fallen from his mount. He pulled the man's helmet off and cuffed a cheek.

'Captain?'

The man's eyelids fluttered. He groaned, wincing. Dirt smeared the side of his face from his fall. The eyes found their focus. 'I thought you'd sworn some kind of vow,' he said, accusing.

'I swore that I'd never kill again – not that I wouldn't fight. I think you'll find that none of your men are dead. Though a few might die if you don't get them attention soon. I suggest back the way you came, to the village of Doun-el. I believe there's a priest there.'

'You mean I should do that rather than track you.'

'It's up to you.' Ivanr yanked off the man's weapon belt. 'Now I'm going to teach you the proper way to tie someone up.'

'We will track you,' the captain swore while Ivanr turned him over and pulled his hands behind his back. 'Others will be sent. Killers, the Emperor's executioners.'

'They are all welcome to try to follow me. Now, must I gag you?'

The captain's sullen silence told Ivanr that the fellow was smarter than his performance to this point had indicated. He bound the rest of the men – they'd get free soon enough by helping one another. After this he gently gathered up the reins of the nearest horse and mounted. Swinging south, he snatched up the reins of a second for a spare mount, and headed off. He knew he ought to prepare more carefully, take the time to rifle all their packs and gear, but they were struggling and he didn't know how much more punishment the poor fellows could take.

He made a show of heading south, keeping himself visible for some time to the lower slopes. After two days he swung east.

In the foothills Ivanr passed barley and millet fields still unharvested despite the waning season. The rutted cart paths he followed proved oddly free of traffic, given this time of trade and readying for the coming winter.

He did meet one riderless horse ambling carefree down to warmer climes. From the state of its matted and burr-laced coat he imagined it had been free for some time and this surprised him; horses were rare, and he with two was already a wealthy man. This runaway he did not bother tethering. Though it was friendly enough, nosing his palm for treats, it looked bloated, ill. It had probably eaten a great number of plants it shouldn't have. Ivanr sent it on its way unmolested. As he crested a hillock his last view of the valley behind was of a vast expanse empty but for the solitary mangy horse walking north.

Past the hillock he came to a farmstead and a hamlet nestled beyond in a forested valley. No smoke rose from the home's cobblestone chimney. The door stood ajar into darkness. A nearby corral was empty. He considered investigating, but with a flick of the reins decided against. His mount was pushing through the tall untended grasses next to the homestead's courtyard when a woman's shrill scream stunned him and shocked his horse into its own panicked rearing shriek. Ivanr ended up on his back, the wind knocked from him, while both mount and spare galloped off.

He straightened to watch the two horses making their way up the track to the hamlet, then turned to search the grasses. 'Hello? Who's there?'

A second sudden shriek and an explosion of pink flesh that made him jump as a brood of piglets and its sow burst from cover. Ivanr exhaled to ease his tensed shoulders. *What an eerie noise those animals make.*

He followed the brood to their old pen, its woven stick walls pushed down. But his grin slowly fell away and his chest clamped even tighter than before; jumbled and trampled bones, hair, and sinew there in the dried mud resolved itself into the remains of several adults and children, all gnawed, consumed by the pigs.

He flinched away, his stomach rising.

All the forgotten gods . . . what has happened here?

The open house beckoned but he turned away. *No, no thank you. Sometimes it is best not to know.* Though the silent and still hamlet did nothing to quell his unease, he followed his mounts into town.

No one walked the streets. Doors were barred, window shutters set. It was peaceful enough but a stink hung over the place, a whiff of charnel rot. They were waiting for him at a central dirt square. The men of the hamlet, armed with an assortment of spears, pikes, staves, wood axes, and a few swords. More of the villagers stepped out to bar his way behind.

A young fellow in the dark robes of a priest of the Lady came forward, bowing slightly. 'Greetings, stranger,' he called.

Ivanr gave his own wary greeting. 'There are bodies in the farmstead beyond.'

The priest appeared genuinely shocked, his hand going to his thin black goatee. 'There are? I am *very* sorry to hear that.' His gaze slid aside to narrow on one old man. '*All* the unfortunates were to have been brought together for cleansing.'

This accused villager paled, his hollow unshaven cheeks turning even more sickly, and he bowed and fled.

The slim priest returned his attention to Ivanr. 'And what of you, stranger? Surely you do not follow any foreign perversions of our one true faith.'

Ivanr gave an easy shrug. 'Of course I have always been faithful to Our Blessed Lady.'

The priest shared Ivanr's easy manner. 'Of course. So, I can assume then that you have no objection to proving your devotion through a trial of fidelity.'

Ivanr eyed the crowd of villagers encircling him; he could easily win through, but where were his mounts? His supplies? 'And this trial involves . . . ?'

'Simplicity itself.' The priest's lips drew back hungrily over yellowed rotting teeth. 'A red-hot iron bar is placed in your hands and you must grip it while reciting the Opening Devotional. Naturally, Our Blessed Lady who protects us all will also preserve you – should your faith be pure.'

'And should it prove . . . insufficient?'

The priest's thin lips drew down in regret. 'There has been a marked lack of purity among the flock of late.' He gestured Ivanr to follow. 'Come, I will show you.'

The crowd parted before the priest, who led him to the well at the centre of the commons. The festering stink that had been sickening Ivanr now rose to a choking reek of rotting flesh that made him gag. He covered his nose and mouth with the sleeve of his forearm. The priest nodded his understanding.

'Offensive, yes, but you get used to it. I know it now as the sweet scent of cleansing.' He gestured for Ivanr to peer into the well. 'Come. Do not be afraid. Welcome deliverance unto Our Lady.'

Though he knew exactly what he would see, Ivanr could not help but look down the stone-lined pit. A strange fascination demanded that he bear full witness to what had occurred. Flies in a churning dark mass choked the opening. He waved them aside one-handed and edged forward. At first he saw nothing. Then, as his eyes adjusted to the gloom, he saw that the well was not nearly so deep as he'd assumed. Something filled it. The dark mass of protruding limbs, heads, and bent torsos of a mass of human bodies stuffed the well to just below its lip. Ivanr flinched away, fighting down the bile clawing at his throat.

'*This is monstrous!*'

‘We are doing the Lady’s work.’ The priest raised his voice, shouting to everyone, ‘The faith must be protected! Heretical doctrine must be cleansed!’

‘*Heresy?* Who says only one god must be worshipped?’

The priest now directed his response to the crowd: ‘And where were these so-called *gods* when our ancestors were being wiped from the land by the predations of the demon Riders? Where was this ancient sea god some go on about now? This god of healing? Or this earth goddess? All the multitude of others? Where were they then?’

Yet the crowd remained silent, more cowed than enthusiastic. It seemed the priest’s fanatical zealotry did not extend to them. Their faces did not shine with the conviction of true believers. Hunger, exhaustion, and days of constant fear had clawed them into a grey pallor. It seemed to Ivanr that they possessed a sullen suspicion directed more at each other than at him. *They are terrified of this man, and their own neighbours. They have woven a bitter existence of constant mutual dread spiked by explosions of bloodletting.* He eyed their drawn faces, sweaty grips on makeshift spears, and fevered gazes. Could they have been browbeaten and dominated into believing anything? Following anyone?

‘What is this?’ Ivanr demanded and snapped out a hand to grasp the priest’s robes at his neck. The man squawked and batted at the grip. Ivanr yanked as if tearing something then raised his hand high, a small object dangling there. ‘Look!’ he bellowed. ‘Look what this man wears secretly beneath his robes!’

The object swung on a leather thong. The token given him from the hand of the Priestess herself: the sword symbol of the cult of Dessembrae.

Ivanr felt all eyes shift to the priest. The young man glared back, scornful. ‘Fools! How stupid can you be?’

Wrong tack, my friend.

Faces twisted into masks of rage as long-suppressed anger and resentment found a path to release. Too late the priest realized his position and raised a hand for pause. It was as if that hand had motioned *Begin* as countless spears and sharpened hafts of broken tools punched into him. Ivanr was shouldered aside, so eager was everyone for a share in the man’s death. With the shafts of their weapons they levered up the still-twitching figure and thrust him over and into the well. Standing back, they raised those wet gleaming tools and looked at one another, amazed by what they had accomplished.

Then all those eyes shifted to him.

Ah . . . the flaw in the plan.

Squeaking of wood on wood announced the return of the old man into the square. He was pushing a wheelbarrow, a shovel resting in it. He set down the barrow to gape at everyone.

'And there's his lackey!' Ivanr shouted.

With a beast-like throaty snarl the crowd went for the man. He ran, showing a good set of heels for a skinny old fellow. Ivanr found himself all alone in the square.

Now where are my blasted horses . . .

He tracked them down easily enough; fed and watered in a corral. As he led them through the hamlet complete murderous chaos raged. Neighbour slew neighbour as all past feuds, grudges, and outright hatreds erupted in an orgy of stalking and stabbing. Soothing his mounts, he passed bloodied corpses splayed across thresholds, trampled on the narrow cobbled ways, and slumped against walls. Men, women, even children.

He reflected that there seemed no stopping once all restraint was gone. And that chute was slicked by blood.

As a stranger, and no part of their feuds, Ivanr was ignored. Only once did he stop, and that was before a child, a young boy, standing in a doorway, blood from a gash in his head wet down his shoulder and shirt-front. The solemn regard of the youth's deep brown eyes shook Ivanr more than all he'd seen. Stooping, he picked up the lad and set him on his spare mount. The boy did not complain; said nothing, in fact. Ivanr's relief was palpable when they reached the cool breeze of the open pastures above the hamlet. Looking back, he saw black smoke pluming from here and there about the town.

Complete and utter collapse. The natural consequences of religious war? Or something more? Who was to say? It was all new to these lands where the Lady had ruled unquestioned for so many generations. Perhaps the eruption was natural, given how hard the Lady and her priests had clamped down, and how long.

He regarded the youth, who sat awkwardly, his thin legs wide, feet bare and dirty. *Probably his first time on a horse.* 'What's your name?' But the boy just stared – not sullen, flat rather – emotionless. *Am I to have no answers from you either? So be it. Spurn me as Thel half-breed, would they? Then to the Abyss with these Jourilan peoples and lands, and all their gods, new and old, with them. I am done with them.*

Ivanr turned his back. The higher slopes of the foothills beckoned, and the snow-sheathed heights of the Iceback range beyond glittered in the slanting amber light of the passing day.

* * *

'It was quick – if that's any consolation.'

Hiam looked to his Wall Marshal, Quint. The man was staring down at the broken equipment and bodies smashed on the rocks below. The indifference on his scared face troubled Lord Protector Hiam. *His callousness again. Was that why the man was passed over for command when the old Lord Protector chose?* Turning away, Hiam waved to the Section Marshal, Felis, the only woman he knew of to have risen so high in the order. 'What happened?'

Felis saluted and drew off her helm, revealing short brown hair that grew low on her forehead, almost to her brows. 'Witnesses say equipment failure. Old rope. I take full responsibility, of course.'

Shameful. What would his predecessors say to see the order so reduced? 'The builders?'

'Theftian labourers. Part of their imbursement.'

Hiam once more peered down the dizzying slope of the curtain wall. A cold wind buffeted him. He examined where the boards and ropes hung tangled, swinging before a long dark rent, a fissure in the face of the set cyclopean blocks of the wall. 'And that break?'

'Largest in these three west sections,' Quint answered.

He saw it in his mind's eye: the specially sized block being lowered to the workers suspended below on their planks, where they would fit and set it. But something went wrong – the block fell, smashed through the workers to crash to the breakwater. And now there was no time to cut a new one. The frost was already upon them.

The fiends could dig their claws into this gap to pull the wall apart.

The answer came reflexively, as it should. He trusted his instincts. 'We'll set the Champion in this section.'

Quint did not disappoint. 'Hiam! That is, Lord Protector! The centre bears the brunt. It's always been the champion's post.'

Hiam offered his deputy, the Wall Marshal, an amused smile. 'You're telling me things I don't know?'

Quint's bright gaze shifted to the Chosen nearby. His look told Hiam: *If we were alone right now . . .* 'They'll read something into the change. You mustn't underestimate them.'

The Lord Protector's smile broadened: that had always been *his* message. The Wall Marshal was obviously not above appropriating arguments. Anything to win the skirmish. 'They might. We'll watch their patterns, just as usual.' The Wall Marshal was not appeased, but he did clamp his lips shut – a temporary withdrawal perhaps. The rain that had been long promised by the day's low-hanging clouds scudding in from the north came spattering down. Hiam pulled his thick cloak higher and tighter. 'Section Marshal Felis . . .' The woman saluted. 'My apologies that we could not provide you with adequate materiel to sufficiently defend your command. I am sorry.'

Felis appeared stricken to the bone. 'Sir! I take full responsibility! The inspection—'

'Was more than thorough, I'm sure. No, do not blame yourself, Marshal. Please convey my regrets to the rest of the Theftian crew and commend them for their efforts.'

The Section Marshal saluted smartly, her eyes fairly shining. 'Yes, Lord Protector.'

Hiam answered the salute. 'Dismissed.' He invited Quint onward. 'Since we're here, let's have a look at the Tower of Ruel's Tears.'

'Yes, Lord Protector.'

Wall Marshal Quint walked quietly at the side of his commander. Once more the man had shaken him by his seeming casual disregard for tradition and the hard-won wisdom of their predecessors. Was he not aware that thousands had died for the priceless knowledge of where best to place their defences and how best to deploy for every situation? Yet of course Hiam knew, perhaps better than he did himself; the man was, after all, a student of history. A reader of scrolls and books, unlike him.

He was a man of the spear. He had but two answers for all that existence could possibly throw his way: either the butt or the blade. Nothing need be more complicated than that.

Yet the protectorship had not come to him. Despite five seasons' seniority. Was he not the Spear of the Wall? Was his service not storied? Now lately he wondered: was there something he lacked? Some quality unfathomable to him? On days such as this Hiam would make him think. That woman, Section Marshal Felis – a woman! Were they in truth that short of men? Yet by his words of support the Lord Protector had won her, helm to sandals. She was his now, would do anything for him. He saw it in her eyes. Hiam could do that with just a word or a glance – what was this the indefinite quality? And most important, was it what was needed by the Chosen at this time?

Or was it the butt or the blade?

They entered the Tower of Ruel's Tears. Guard chambers on the first floor, beds to double as an infirmary. Up the circular stairs they came to dormitories. Chosen jumped to attention. Hiam and Quint answered their salutes.

'All well here?' Hiam asked.

'Yes, sir,' the ranking Chosen present responded, a Wall Provost, or sergeant, by the look of him.

Hiam pointed to a guard across the low-ceilinged room. 'Allan, yes?'

The guard smiled, pleased. 'Yes, sir.'

'Ramparts of the Stars, three seasons ago. That was quite the scuffle, yes?'

'Yes, Lord Protector. A cold one.'

'Good to see you. Carry on.' Hiam brought his fist to his heart in salute.

'Sir!' rang the shouted response.

They continued up the stairway past further levels of dormitories, these empty, awaiting the arrival of the season's contingents from abroad. Beyond these they came to an armoury jammed with racks of spears, swords, and a few sets of spare armour – boiled leather cuirasses mainly. At the walls stood barrels of the weapon of last resort: tar, pitch and rare alchemicals for a barrier of flame. Above this the stairs ended at a trapdoor to the uppermost chamber. Hiam pushed it open and stepped up. Quint followed.

Here broad windows faced all directions, all closed now by sturdy wood shutters bracketed in iron. At the centre of the small open chamber stood a stone pillar topped by an iron sleeve that could be raised and lowered by a lever. Hiam bent down, examining it. 'This was tested this summer?'

'Yes. Tested and inspected.'

'Good. If there is one thing we mustn't stint on, this is it.'

'Yes.' Their communication system. An oil flame within could be made to burn exceedingly bright with the addition of certain mineral powders. Raising and lowering the sleeve allowed them to send coded messages up and down the length of the wall. Simple communiqués: attack, help, all-clear.

Quint examined his tall commander: grey coming into the beard and in the unkempt mane of thick hair. Yet seemingly young in his mannerisms. Not an outstanding spearman, it had to be said. But there was a certain something about his eyes and expression. Quint had always felt comfortable around the man, though he rarely felt comfortable around anyone. He crossed his arms under his cloak. 'You didn't drag me up here to discuss our communication system.'

A wry smile. 'No. And direct as ever. Reassuring, Quint. You've been quiet of late.' He went to the shuttered window facing north, unlatched it and stood peering out. 'No, word has come via my ever-efficient Staff Marshal Shool of the Jourilan and Dourkan contingent.' He turned, leaning back against the window ledge, hands clasping the edges of his thick cloak. 'They have been halved.'

'Halved. *Halved?* Well, what's the point of that? Do they *want* to be overrun? They might as well send no one for all the use!'

Hiam raised a hand in agreement. 'Yes, Quint. Yes. But what's done is done. We cannot conjure up any further men or women. We can expect only some three thousand spears from Jourilan and Dourkan. That puts our strength for the coming season at some twenty thousand spears of active-service men and women. Twenty-five, if we pressed every possible standing body. Including, I suppose, even our Master Engineer Stimins.'

Despite the news, Quint barked a laugh at that vision. 'It may be all worth it just to see that. But,' and he slid a hand up from within his cloak to stroke his gouged chin between thumb and forefinger, 'as you say, there seems nothing to discuss in all this. What's done is done.'

'Yes. There's nothing to discuss,' and the Lord Protector's expression hardened, 'save how we will respond to the fact that we are now below half-strength for the coming season.'

Quint shrugged easily. 'Then there is nothing to discuss. We will defend. We are the Chosen, the Stormguard. Ours is a sacred responsibility to defend all the lands.'

Hiam pushed himself from the wall, nodding. 'Very good, Quint. I knew that would be your answer. I merely wanted to have this out in the open between us. We are in complete agreement. We fight. We defend to the last man and woman. There is no alternative.' He squeezed Quint's shoulder, peered about the chamber. 'You know this tower is named Ruel's Tears because a millennium ago the Lord Protector of the time, Ruel, was said to have thrown himself from this very window after having been overcome by some terrible vision?'

Quint nodded; he'd heard the legend.

'Some say his vision was of the ultimate defeat of the Stormguard. Had you heard that?'

Quint could only pinch his chin savagely; he'd heard that whispered a time or two.

Looking off as if he could see beyond the walls of the small chamber, Hiam said softly, 'I never could understand such a reaction, Quint. All I feel is admiration. I sometimes think that if I were to die of anything, it would be of unbearable pride . . .' He smiled then, looking away. 'Very good, Wall Marshal. We are in accordance.' And he started down the stairs.

Only later, long after he and Hiam had walked in silence completing the day's inspection tour, did it occur to Quint that the discussion of Ruel's Tears in truth had not at all been for Hiam to test his reaction to the news of this season's shorthandedness; rather, it had been to reassure him, Quint, of Hiam's own steadfast resolve in the face of such news.

For it was not in Quint's nature ever to bend or to waver – neither the butt nor the blade allowed for that. However, in the months ahead he may come to wonder on the like determination of his Lord Protector. And Hiam had just neatly anticipated and eliminated any such misgivings on the part of his second in command. As he hung his cloak and sat watching the fire in the common room of the Tower of Kor, it occurred to Quint that perhaps there was more than met the eye to the indefinable quality that made Hiam the Lord Protector.

* * *

Rillish was playing with his toddler, Halgin, in the courtyard of his house just outside the hamlet of Halas when a column of Malazan cavalry came up the dirt road from the village. Straightening, he motioned the nanny to take the lad then walked out to meet them. They took their time. The grey dust of west Cawn coated their travelling cloaks and the sweaty flanks of their mounts. As they drew closer Rillish could see by the torc high on the leader's arm that the commander was a captain, which was unusual for such a small detachment. His wife, Talia, broad with child, appeared at his side. 'You needn't come out,' he told her. 'It's nothing, I'm sure.'

'They wouldn't be here for nothing,' she said grimly.

The captain motioned a halt and nodded a greeting. She pulled off her gloves and batted the dust from her cloak. 'Fist Rillish Jal Keth?'

'That promotion was honorary only. I'm retired.'

The captain pulled off her helmet and the padded leather hood beneath. She was fair, startlingly so, her long white-blonde hair tightly braided. For the life of him Rillish could not place her background. Few on Quon were so pale, and there was something in her voice, the accent unusual.

'That retirement was voluntary. Under terms of service you are still in reserve. The Empire, sir, did not let you go.'

'*That fat toad on the throne . . .*' Talia hissed beneath her breath.

Rillish raised a hand for quiet. 'I'm sorry, Captain, but there must be some misunderstanding. Firm agreements were made in the terms of my service and retirement. I am finished with the Empire.'

The captain gave a judicious nod. 'That may be true, sir. But, as I say, the Empire may not be finished with you.'

Talia's hand found his, hot and sweaty. He squeezed. 'There is nothing, Captain, that could induce me to return.'

'Nothing?' The captain peered about the yard, the modest garden plot, the fields, the paddock of horses, before finally returning to him. 'Perhaps there is somewhere we can talk, sir?'

Rillish shrugged. 'Well, we can go for a walk if you wish.' He released Talia's hand. 'But I believe you've come a long way to no profit. You may water the mounts, of course, and perhaps we can find something for your troop.'

'You are kind, sir.' She turned to the detachment. 'Stand down. See to the horses.'

Dismounted, the woman was as tall as Rillish, and far older than he'd thought, perhaps close to his own fifty. The lines around the eyes and mouth gave her age away. 'And you are?'

She saluted. 'Peleshar is my full name, but I go by Peles. At your service, Fist.'

Rillish let the rank reference pass. 'Peleshar . . . an unusual name . . .'

She nodded. 'I am from south Genabackis.'

Rillish was surprised and impressed. 'You served in One-Arm's host?'

'No, sir. I saw action in the Free City campaigns. Then I served in the liaison contingent to the Moranth.'

Even more impressive. A record of service that should warrant a rank far higher than captain. And the Free City campaigns – those went far back indeed. He managed to stop himself from being so gauche as to ask just how far back, and invited the captain to accompany him.

'I'll see what we can pull together for the troopers,' Talia said, her gaze hard on the captain.

Peles bowed. 'My thanks.'

They stopped at the paddock. Suspicious of the stranger, the horses snorted and edged away. The captain studied them with admiration. 'Fine mounts. They are Wickan?'

Watching the horses as well, Rillish smiled his affection. 'Yes. You are in the cavalry?'

A laugh. 'Fanderay, no. I have had little exposure to horses. My people are not riders. We have other . . . specialties. I am a commander of marines.'

Rillish nodded, brushed drying bark from the still-green wood of the fence. 'So, Captain. Why are you here?'

'I am only the messenger, of course. I was asked to deliver this.' She held out a slim, tightly bound scroll. 'I am told it is from Emperor Mallick's own hand.'

Rillish regarded it without moving. For a moment he feared it was poisoned. Then he mocked himself, thinking, why would the man bother when he could just dispatch his Claw assassins to kill them in their sleep? He took the scroll, broke the seal, and read.

It was a long time before he lowered the short note.

Captain Peles had not moved nor spoken the whole time. She had merely watched the horses, her surprisingly thick forearms resting on the paddock fence. *Patient, this one. We might get along at that.* Rillish returned the scroll. 'Very well, Captain. I accept. As he knew I would, no doubt.'

'Yes, Fist. So I was told.'

Rillish turned to face the yard where his wife and the servants were sharing out bread and cold meats. 'Now the hard part, Captain.'

She nodded, clearing her throat. 'I'll ready my men and women.'

Before he even got close enough to speak, she knew. Her face stiffened and she turned away to enter the house without a word. Rillish followed, but she was gone, fled to some back room. He went to the storeroom where his gear lay rolled in leather. He dug about for his blades, his father's old Untan two-edged longswords. He found them under the shelves, wrapped in oiled rags. When he straightened she was in the doorway. Tears glistened on her cheeks.

'What did he offer?'

'Everything.'

She gestured savagely to the surroundings, the house, the yard. 'You have everything you need here – don't you?'

'Yes.'

She wiped the tears from her face. 'Isn't it enough?'

'Yes.' He closed to hold her but she backed away. 'This is all I need, Talia. But he offered to give it all back – *everything*. How could I refuse?'

Her mouth tightened to a slit and she spat, 'We don't want it.'

He lowered his gaze, pulled one blade a short way from its scabbard, then shoved it home. When he looked up she was gone.

Captain Peles had halted her detachment a short way down the dirt road. With the help of his foreman, Rillish saddled his favourite mount, then led it out into the yard. Here Halgin waited with his nanny. When the toddler saw him he broke free to run. Rillish knelt to hold his shoulders. The lad peered up, his gaze as blue and open as the sky. Rillish kissed his forehead. He could hardly find his voice. 'I'm going away for a time, son. What I'm doing, I'm doing for you, and for little Nil or Nether to come. I want you to know that I love you more than I could ever say. Goodbye for now.'

He straightened but Halgin grabbed his leg and would not let go. In the end the nanny came to pull the howling lad away. Mounting, Rillish searched for Talia but didn't see her anywhere. That hurt, but he teased the reins to start down the road.

When he reached the detachment, Captain Peles raised her chin to motion back behind him and he turned. She stood there. The captain signed for her detachment to move on.

He watched her. For the longest time they remained unmoving, studying one another over the stretch of dusty dirt road between, she motionless beside the unfinished gate to their little yard hemmed in by the house and paddock. Such a small allotment, hardly enough to get by, let alone prosper. He thought of his family's many estates in Unta. The largest, hard by the Gris border, a man could not cross in a full day's riding. All that had been his before the Insurrection, before his choice to side against the Empress's edicts on the Wickan pogrom had stripped him of it. Now the Emperor offered it all back for his return to active duty – and just *where*, he believed he knew. And he'd accepted. Not for himself of course, but for Halgin. It would be his legacy now. He hoped his son would have better luck of it than he or his father before him.

He raised a hand in farewell and she answered, slowly. He lowered his arm and turned away.

* * *

In the end Kiska had no idea why she agreed to Agayla's request that she accompany her up-island for a walk among the windswept hills. Perhaps it was the daytime sight of the Deadhouse: if anything even more foreboding in the full glare of the sun and even more unsettling to her senses now than she remembered from her youth.

Could this tomb-like dilapidated hulk really be of the Azath? A mysterious network of dwellings, caves or houses, call them what you would – *structures*, of some sort – that some claimed pervade creation? All she knew of them was what she had overheard speculated about in Tayschrenn's presence, and that precious little. In fact, she remembered scholars who had approached Tayschrenn for his knowledge of them and their outrage at his opinion that the Azath were not a matter for human investigation. 'They are waning,' she heard him say once. 'We should let them go in peace.'

She rested a hand on the low wall of piled fieldstones surrounding the house's grounds and thought of another night, seemingly so long ago, when she had faced the brooding presence last. That night saw the only known successful assault upon an Azath; and that by the most cunning – and probably most insane – mage of their time. The Emperor himself. All other would-be assailants through the ages, human, daemon, Jaghut, now crowded the many mounds humping the dead grounds, enslaved to the house.

Agayla was probably right. Perhaps but for the older woman's intervention she too would now be rotting within one of those burial mounds. That would have been the most likely outcome. Too perilous a throw by far. She turned away to head to the river road to join Agayla for their walk. She would spend the day with her then say her farewells. Another tack, then, towards finding Tayschrenn. Genabackis, perhaps. The Moranth may be of help.

Leaving, she noticed an old man squatting against a stone wall across the way; his great thick arms hung over his knees, and a white thatching of scars criss-crossed his bald pate. The man's gaze followed her as she left. She thought he looked vaguely familiar: probably from her youth on the island.

She met Agayla just outside the town proper, where allotments and garden plots widened and irrigation channels of set slate bordered the flint road. The fields were dull now with dead stalks. Low bruised clouds pressed overhead, cast up from the south, the Strait of Storm. The chill winds hinted at worse to come.

Her aunt carried a wicker basket on one arm, a shawl over her shoulders. 'Remind you of the old days?' she asked, and brushed wayward strands from her face.

'I suppose so.'

Agayla headed off without comment in her swift energetic walk that Kiska recalled from those old days. Following, she pulled her thick lined cloak tighter and felt about for her gloves. After a time she called, 'Mushrooming, are we?'

'A little late for that. Roots mainly. Some stalks. Like the arrow.'

Kiska wouldn't know an arrow plant if it jabbed her in the eye.

They climbed inland. Agayla struck off the road, following a narrow dirt path that wound between low brush. Looking back, Kiska caught glimpses of the town and the bay beyond before it was cut from view by an intervening hillock. She began to wonder just how far her aunt intended to take them.

At last she pushed through a dense stand of alder, their limbs cast backwards by the constant sea winds, to find Agayla sitting on a lump of rock before a circle of tall standing stones.

'There you are!' her aunt announced, patting the rock next to her. 'Come sit with me.'

Kiska shrugged within her heavy cloak and came to stand next to her aunt. 'Agayla,' she began, awkwardly. 'This has been . . . pleasant. But I really must be getting back to town . . .'

The woman raised a hand for silence. 'Shh. It's almost time. Now sit.' She produced an apple from the basket.

Kiska grudgingly sat. 'Time for what?'

'This circle is sacred to many gods. Did you know that?' Before Kiska could reply, she continued, 'In the old days people were sacrificed here.'

Kiska eyed her aunt, wondering what the old woman was on about. Her mind wasn't starting to meander in her old age, was it? She bit into the apple.

'Ah . . . here we are.'

But Kiska had felt it too. She stood, dropping the apple, and slipped her hands into her cloak to rest where twin long-knives hung sheathed tightly to her sides. A shimmering was climbing between the stones . . . a wavering curtain of opalescent light. It fluttered to life around the circle's full circumference.

'What is this?'

'Mind your manners now,' Agayla said. She was pushing back her hair, adjusting her shawl.

Kiska eyed her, mistrustful. 'What's going on?'

Agayla stood before her, looked her up and down then gently laid a hand on her cheek. The palm was warm, smooth, and dry. It seemed as if the woman was examining her face for something and Kiska had no idea what it was she sought. 'We are about to speak to one of the greatest powers presently at play here in this world,' she began. 'No – hush. Many name her a goddess but to me she is more, and I suppose less, than that. Not like Burn or Fanderay or Togg. Not some ancient entity or force that has come to represent what we choose to cast upon it. She remains a real living person whose influence transcends others' because she is here, now, and can intervene directly as she sees fit.' She gave Kiska's chin a squeeze and gently edged her head side to side. 'So behave yourself. Speak only when you are spoken to. Bow. Show some of those fancy manners you should have learned in Unta.'

The woman released her and Kiska shook her head as if to recover from some spell or blow. Greater influence than the gods'? What could her aunt possibly be on about? She eyed the shimmering barrier. 'Who then? What mage?'

Agayla laughed. 'Oh, Kiska. Not *some* mage or magus. The greatest. The Enchantress. The Mistress of Thyr. The Queen of Dreams.' And she took her niece's hand and led her through the curtain of light.

The brilliant glare momentarily blinded Kiska, and as she blinked to clear her vision she slowly became aware of her surroundings. It was the circle of standing stones she knew, but surrounded by a shimmering reflective silver border. And, standing at its centre waiting to meet them, a woman wrapped in loose pale blue cloth that was draped about her in countless folds. Kiska held back, dazzled by the vision of this diminutive, slim, raven-haired beauty. How could this be real? She'd heard that this woman walked with Anomander generations ago. Yet was she not the greatest enchantress of the age?

She could appear as she wished and this was her choice; it was up to her, Kiska, to take from it what she would.

Agayla shared no such hesitation. She knelt before the woman, murmured something that sounded close to an invocation. But the Enchantress laughed and raised her up with her hands, saying, 'Do not kneel before me, Agayla. Surely you of all people have not fallen to the cult of worship.'

Agayla bowed. 'I give homage where I choose, m'lady.'

The Enchantress turned her glance upon Kiska. 'So this is the one.'

The force of the woman's attention struck her like a blow. Kiska found she could not order her thoughts. It was as if she were standing before a titanic waterfall or a storm front at sea; all she could do was stare, awestruck by the vision.

The woman had advanced and taken her hands, one in each of her own. 'You would follow a perilous trail, Kiska.' She searched her face as Agayla had and nodded as if having satisfied some unspoken question. Motes of gold seemed to float in her eyes. 'It is good you do not pursue this out of some sort of infatuation. For I do not see him capable of such feelings. Still . . .' She regarded Agayla. 'For her to travel alone . . .'

'I can think of one or two I would trust,' Agayla said, frowning. 'But they have taken on other duties.'

'There is someone I can call upon—'

'I can take care of myself,' Kiska blurted out.

Agayla glared her irritation. The Enchantress waved a hand. 'That is not the question. You must sleep sometime. And a lone traveller is too much of a temptation. Fortunately I have someone in mind . . .' and she gestured aside, inviting.

A man stepped through the barrier. He was of middling height but wiry and obviously powerful. Under desert robes he wore armour Kiska recognized as the style of Seven Cities, a mix of boiled leather and mail. His dark flat features and long black moustache sealed his identity as a son of that region. The most ridiculous weapons hung strapped at his belt: two morningstars. 'Who is this?' she demanded.

Again her aunt glared for her silence.

The man appeared similarly unimpressed. He indicated Kiska with a lift of his chin but addressed the Enchantress. 'When we made our deal I told you I was done with protecting.'

'I do not need anyone's *protection*.'

The Enchantress raised a hand. 'This is . . . which name would you prefer?'

'Damn fool comes to mind,' the man ground out. Yet he bowed. 'Jheval.'

'This is Kiska. She is searching for someone. And it is a mission that has my blessing. The man she wishes to locate may be of interest to you, Jheval. He is Tayschrenn, once High Mage of the Malazan Empire.'

The man's eyes widened and he almost stepped backwards. 'You would ask *me* to help find *him*?'

'The gratitude of the Empire would no doubt be extraordinary if he could be found and brought back to them.'

Those dark eyes narrowed then within their many wrinkles and a decidedly wolfish grin climbed his lips in a way that Kiska found hardly reassuring. 'Thank you for your concern . . . m'lady,' she said, 'but I do not need this fellow.'

'You will fail if you go alone.'

The finality of that pronouncement chilled Kiska.

'How are we—' Jheval began, then corrected himself. 'That is, how is the man to be tracked down?'

The Enchantress gestured to a burlap sack atop the broad stone at the centre of the circle. Kiska could not recall seeing it there before.

'The Void that took the High Mage opened on to Chaos and there your trail will take you. When you reach its borders open this. The thing within will then lead you on.'

Kiska wrapped the sack in her cloak. It was dirty, as if it had been buried. From what she could glimpse inside all it seemed to contain were broken twigs and a few scraps of cloth.

'I can send you on your way from here,' the Enchantress said. 'Is that acceptable?'

'Thank you, m'lady,' Kiska said, bowing.

Jheval grunted his agreement.

Agayla, whom Kiska had thought uncharactisterically quiet all this time, now embraced her, kissing her cheeks. 'Be careful,' she whispered. 'I see in the weave that this search will not be the simple task you believe. You may not know what it is you are really after.'

Kiska would have spoken, but she was silenced by the tears that brimmed in her aunt's eyes. A moment ago she would have thought such a thing impossible. *I never thought of her as old before yet now, suddenly, I see her so. Time is cruel.*

The Enchantress motioned aside. 'You will see hills. Keep them to your left.' Kiska bowed again and turned away. Jheval followed, his hands tucked into his leather belt.

After the two had gone, the Enchantress gently brushed a hand across Agayla's face. 'Do not cry, Weaver.'

'I fear I have sent the child to her death.'

'I cannot see into Chaos. But what she has taken as her failure has wounded her to her core. I can only hope she will come to forgive herself.'

'So much is on its way, T'riss. I see it in the weft. The knots ahead come so thick they may choke the shuttle. The cloth may part.'

'It may. We can only do our best to see to it that it only tears in certain places.'

Agayla smiled then, perhaps at her fears. 'Yes. It will be a new order.'

The Queen of Dreams' face hardened as she looked off into the distance. 'Yes,' she said, her voice taut with something almost like distaste. 'Let us hope it will be a better one.'

* * *

It took Bakune two months of questioning, searching archives, and squeezing minor city officials to track down the family name and possible current residence of the family of Sister Charity. Whether the woman yet lived remained to be discovered.

He left his offices at noon on foot, wrapped in a plain wool cloak. He took the west road until it exited the town proper and here he turned off the way, down towards the coast where a ghetto of shacks and huts spilled down the slope. Dogs raged at his heels, knowing full well he did not belong. Dirty half-naked children stared at him, many obviously the half-breed by-blows of Roolian mothers and the Malazan occupiers. Young toughs collected in the muddy narrow paths, staring silently at what he imagined must be quite the apparition of a Roolian citizen wandering lost in the maze of their neighbourhood. At every turn round a staked tent or wattle and daub hut the crowd seemed to grow until he faced a solid wall of young men and women, dressed no better than the urchins, many carrying wasted limbs, milky blinded eyes, ugly swellings, and other disfigurements of illnesses – all from the filth of their poverty, no doubt.

'I'm looking for the Harldeth family,' he called to one of the young men. 'Harldeth. Do you know the name?'

Blocking Bakune's way, the fellow just stared. His mouth was twisted in a harelip and Bakune would have suspected him slow but for the unaccountable hostility simmering in his gaze. 'Stranger,' a weak voice called from a nearby hut. Bakune ducked his head to squint into the darkness.

'Yes?'

'Enter.'

He had to crouch almost double to slip within. He found an old man cross-legged on a woven mat next to a dead blackened hearth. The man was bare-chested despite the gathering cold of autumn. Bakune introduced himself, and was invited to sit. The stink of smoke and old rotten food made him almost gag; he elected to crouch on his haunches. After the old man had sat regarding him for a time, his night-black eyes unreadable, Bakune prompted again, 'Yes? You know the Harldeth?'

'I know the family.'

'Will you take me to them?'

'Why do you seek them?'

'I'm assessing a death. I need to question Lithel Harldeth. She was once a nun in the Cloister. I'm told her family now lives out here.'

The old man cocked his head. 'So, you are assessing a death . . . Where is the Watch? Where are their truncheons? Where is your signed confession?'

Bakune pulled away, offended. 'That's not how we do things. We assess to apportion the balance of innocence and culpability.'

The old man just gave a sad indulgent smile. 'You should spend more time out here, Assessor Bakune.' He struggled to rise, pulling up a tall walking stick, which he held horizontal. 'Come.'

Outside, the old man made some gesture and the crowd backed away. Bakune looked sharply at him; he wore only dirty trousers and jerkin, his grey hair hung stringy and bedraggled, yet his wiry limbs, dark as stained wood, held an obvious strength. A stone on a thong round his neck was the man's only decoration other than the old branch he held as a staff. A thin cold rain had begun to fall that the old man ignored, though it chilled Bakune. 'Do I know you?' he asked, struck by a sudden vague recollection.

'No, Assessor. You most certainly do not know me. This way . . .'

Surprised yells sounded up the mud path the way Bakune had

come and the crowd parted there to reveal his two Watch guards, their cloaks pulled back from the shortswords hung at their sides.

'Who are these?' the old man asked.

Bakune sighed. *Lady-damned fools! They'll ruin everything!* 'Guards that the Watch captain insists follow me around.'

The old man's dark eyes slid to Bakune; the indulgent, almost pitying smile returned. 'Guards, Assessor? Or minders?' He started off before Bakune could respond.

The path the old man followed was bewilderingly twisted, probably deliberately so. His two guards plodded along behind, hands at their belts. Each muddy trail they took between crowded shacks seemed identical to the last. Everyone ignored Bakune now, going about their daily business, carrying bundled firewood, earthenware pots of water. Women cooked over low smoky fires.

Then the old man stopped abruptly at a wattle and daub hut, no different from any other. He gestured within.

'Thank you.'

He did not answer, only motioned inside once again.

Within, a family sat eating. Startled, Bakune nearly backed out until the woman present, mother Bakune assumed of the four wide-eyed children, pointed to a woven reed hanging farther within. Bowing, Bakune edged around the staring family and brushed the hanging aside. A thick cloud of smoke blinded him. He had entered what proved to be no more than a tiny nook, and he pressed a fold of his cloak over his nose and mouth. Eventually he made out a low shape hunched before some sort of altar cluttered with burned-down candle stubs, clay lamps, small rudely shaped statues, and stands of smouldering incense sticks.

'Lithel Harldeth?'

The shape, which had been rocking gently from side to side and crooning to itself, stilled. The head rose, questing. 'Who is there?'

'Assessor Bakune. I am investigating the recent death of Sister Prudence. I'm told you knew her well.'

'So, she is dead. We've been waiting many years.' A gnarled hand went shakily to the altar, pointed to one crude statue. 'Look here. The Great Mother Goddess. She has had countless names, though Lady is not one.' The hand moved to another. 'The Great Sky-Father this one is called, though Light is his aspect. Here, the Great Deceiver would push forward – not realizing that to succeed would spell his dissolution. Here, the Beast of War stirs again – what shall be the final shape of its rising? Here, the Dark Hoarder of Souls. He has my friend now – may both of them come to know peace. And here, the newcomer, the Broken God, watching and scheming from afar.'

Bakune recognized these ancient names and titles from his research into the indigenous peoples of the archipelago – all their old animistic spirits of earth, air, and night. All vaguely similar in character to the foreign Malazan faiths, of which, presumably, they were distant relatives. All the old pagan beliefs that had multiplied indiscriminately before the arrival of the Blessed Lady and the one true faith.

'What would you call evil, Assessor?' the old woman suddenly asked.

Bakune was rather startled by the question. Breathing in the heady, dizzying smoke he eased himself down to his knees. Vaguely, he wondered what drugs might be mixed in with the exotic woods and herbs being burned here. He'd already realized that he would get no straight answers from the crone, and could hardly press her. 'I don't know. The simple-minded would answer whatever is opposed to them. Whatever current enemy or rival they might face at the time. For my part I believe true evil lies in actions. In deliberate harmful acts.'

'Spoken as a magistrate. And it must be said that there is some wisdom in your approach. However, can an act not be harmful in the immediate, yet beneficial in the long term? Could such an act be said to be evil?'

Bakune waved the choking coils of smoke from his face. The last thing he expected was to be challenged to a philosophical debate. 'Again, I do not know. I suppose the harm would have to be weighed against the ultimate benefit accrued.'

The old woman turned her head to regard him directly. Her dirty hair hung like a veil before her face. 'Exactly. It would have to be . . . assessed.'

Bakune suddenly felt stricken. 'What are you getting at, Lithel?'

The woman turned away, rocking. 'I have meditated long and hard on this vexing question, Assessor. There is really only a small set of final responses. My distillation is a refinement of one of them. True pure evil, Assessor, is waste. It is the blunting of potential, the cutting off of a person's or a people's promise, or options, for development. It is, emblematically, the death of a child.' The old woman's head sank. 'Look then, Assessor, to the children.'

'Lithel? Lithel?'

The old woman once more crooned to herself, and now Bakune could hear the ancient burnished pain in her moaning.

Outside, Bakune straightened, coughing. One of his guards offered a water skin and he took it with gratitude and washed out his mouth.

'What did you hear?' the old man asked.

'Exactly what I did not want to hear.'

The old man's smile climbed free of any reserve. 'Good. We are done then. And Assessor . . .'

'Yes?'

'Do not return. Do not try to find this dwelling again. Because you never will.'

Bakune narrowed his gaze on the man. 'You would threaten a magistrate?'

'No threat. A fact.'

The guards snorted their disbelief. Bakune shrugged. His gaze caught the stone at the man's neck. Engraved on it was a circle with a line across its middle like the line of a horizon. The very sigil scratched on the statue Lithel had named the Great Mother Goddess. Bakune motioned to the necklace. 'The symbol of the old pagan Earth Mother.'

The old man's hand went to the stone. 'Yes. The old faith. I am of the Drenn.'

Bakune could not shake a feeling of familiarity. 'I feel that we *have* met before.'

'Perhaps briefly. Now, this way.'

The old man, who once gave his name to the Assessor as Gheven, stopped within the boundary of the shanty town and watched while the magistrate and his minders climbed to the west road. He was surprised, pleased and saddened all at once at having met him again. Surprised by the man's resilience in keeping to his principles in the face of all that had confronted him for the length of his career; pleased to see him cleaving still to the path to justice – as he interpreted it at any rate – and saddened because he knew what all this would cost the man should he continue along the path as he, Gheven, hoped he would.

It was sad but necessary. Pain would be inflicted but was it not all to the greater good? A thorny question, that. One he did not feel qualified to settle.

Back in his office, Bakune settled into his chair and rested his head in his hands. His guards had drifted away once they'd reached the city centre and the blocks holding the mayoral palace and the courts. He didn't know whether to be grateful for their dedication or to curse them for it. The old man's insinuations had slid deep along the paths of his own suspicions. His secretaries appeared at his doorway, thick folders in their hands, but Bakune waved them off.

Rising, he crossed the office and locked the door. He went to a cabinet next to the desk and unlocked it. From the top shelf he pulled out a roll that he laid on his desk. He pulled the ribbon holding the cloth tight and unrolled it. It was a map of Banith that Bakune had ordered drafted years ago. On it, over the years, the Assessor had painstakingly painted in red dots the exact location of every murdered girl and boy he had personally visited, or that he could reliably place. The red dots lay in a thin spread throughout the city; no district was entirely free of their stain. The bright crimson, however, was thickest along the shore, where many bodies were dumped. But not evenly, not randomly. Over the years the marks clumped, observably so, into three main clusters. One to the west, one to the east, and one due south near the centre of the town's waterfront. Leading more or less straight up from each cluster ran a main road into town. And if one traced each road one's finger would end up right at the centre of town where lay the holy Cloister of Our Blessed Lady – near which, revealingly enough, not one bloody dot was to be found.

Bakune sat and stared long and hard at the map, his chin nearly touching his chest. *Damn you for doing this to me. You're killing me. Dot by dot, you are surely killing me. Please, won't you please just stop. Just go away.*

He pressed his fingertips to his throbbing temples and sat motionless, staring. By the Blessed Lady, what could he possibly be expected to do?

* * *

Around noon the ship's captain came to talk to Kyle. He was dozing under the shade of an awning, his leg raised and bandaged, when he became vaguely aware that he wasn't alone any more. Cracking open one eye he saw a wiry fellow gazing down at him, old, grey hair all unkempt, the light dusting of a moustache at the mouth, and a pipe clamped tight between the lips. Multiple gold earrings shone at the lobes and gold bracelets cluttered – *her?* – wrists. 'Yes?' Kyle asked, wary.

'All comfy, are we?'

'Yes, thank you. Your bone-mender knows her business.'

A smile of appreciation stretched the thin lips. 'Speaking of business . . .'

'Ah. You are the captain?'

'Yes. June. Cursed June, they call me.'

'Kyle. Cursed? May I ask why?'

A rise of the bony shoulders. 'Had seven husbands is why.' The woman tilted her head to examine him up and down. 'Can't place you, I have to say. There's something of the Wickan about you with the moustache an' your dark hue an' all. But not quite.'

'Perhaps we're distantly related.'

'P'rhaps.'

Kyle took a pouch from his belt and held it out. 'All I have for transport to your next port of call.'

She hefted it, frowning. 'Not much . . .'

'My companion may have some coin as well.' A noncommittal grunt. 'Where are we headed, may I ask?'

'East to Belid. Five days' sail.'

'We're grateful.'

The woman grunted again, letting loose a stream of smoke. She clearly itched to ask their background and what lay behind their flight, but was also clearly old and canny enough to know she'd get no satisfaction. She nodded instead in a guarded, vaguely welcoming way, and continued on.

The bone-mender, Elia, thumped herself down next to him on the burlap-wrapped cargo tied down on the deck. 'What think you of our captain, then?'

'Rare to see a woman captain.'

'Not at all here in Falar. Curaca ships are all owned and run by the city an' the city demands profits an' tight management. Men captains just get drunk or gamble away the margins. Not like the womenfolk. What say you to that?' The old woman cuffed his shoulder.

'I'd say that anyone who'd voluntarily go to sea must be addled.'

The woman whooped, laughing. 'Spoken like a true son of the plains, Kyle.'

He eyed her, wondering whether that was a probe. 'She said they call her cursed – is that true?'

'Yes, it's true. But here's the kicker . . . is it true because she's had seven husbands, or because she's had seven husbands?'

Kyle could only stare, his brow tight. *What in the name of the Hooded Harrower?* He shook his head. 'How is . . . my companion, Orjin?'

'Oho! Orjin, is it? Sleeping like a whale below. Four of the crew couldn't move him.'

'Any wounds?'

'Nothing serious. And he's seen his share of Denul rituals.'

'What do you mean by that?'

'I mean that the man's far older than he looks, and heals far faster than most.'

'I suppose that's where his money went,' Kyle suggested, looking away.

'I suppose so.'

Three days later, just after dawn, a crewman woke Kyle where he lay in a hammock below. Groggy, rubbing his face, he climbed the short steep stair to the deck. Above, a low cloudbank reflected the gold and pink of sunrise. The waters of the Storm Sea were high, but not choppy. It occurred to him that every region seemed to have its body of rough water or gales, its 'storm sea'. Forward stood Captain June, the mate, Masul, Elia, and Greymane. He joined them; Greymane gave him a tight, concerned glance.

Captain June pointed to the south-east, just off the bow. 'Friends of yours?'

Kyle squinted into the light: three dark shapes emerging from the glare of the sunrise. Large vessels, many sails. 'Who are they?'

'Malazan men-of-war,' said June. 'They seem to be coming on an intercept and we can't outrun them. We're no sleek raider.'

'Wouldn't suggest you try, Captain.'

'No?'

'No,' affirmed Greymane.

June's expressive brows rose. She drew heavily on her pipe. 'Ain't going to be any hostilities, are there? 'Cause my people won't participate in anything like that.'

Greymane pushed a hand through his tangled silvery grey hair. 'No, Captain. No hostilities.'

'Hunh! All right then.' She turned to the stern. 'Steady on!'

'Steady on, aye!'

Kyle moved until he stood next to Greymane. His eyes on the distant ships, he asked, 'What's it going to be?'

The man let go a long growled breath. 'Don't want these fellows to suffer. Can't swim. So, we'll let them come abreast then board the first and take them one by one.'

'Not two at a time?'

He glanced sideways at Kyle. A straight smile pulled at his mouth. 'Let's not get carried away.'

It was a fleet of Malazan men-of-war, tall and moderately broad for greater stability, commissioned for war at sea. From the soldiers lining the high railings, the stern- and forecastles, Kyle estimated that each of the twenty vessels carried some four hundred marines. Much larger troop transports could be seen in the east, convoyed, lumbering south in long straight columns. Even from this distance something struck him as odd about the vessels: they appeared just too damn huge, and of an odd hue, almost that of the waters they rode.

To Kyle it looked like an invasion assembled to take a continent. 'Have you ever seen the like?' he murmured to Greymane, awed.

After a time the man answered, a strange, almost resigned note in his voice. 'Yes, Kyle. I have.'

No fool, Captain June ordered sails furled. A launch appeared, lowered from the nearest warship. Greymane and Kyle watched while it crossed the distance between the vessels, oared by some eighteen marines.

June ordered a rope ladder thrown over the side. Three officers crowded the launch, including one obvious Moranth Blue. The first pulled himself aboard easily to stand comfortably on deck, hands clasped at his back. An obvious veteran, short and stocky with a bald sun-darkened pate, and a high officer by the hatching on the silver torc on his arm. His mouth was thin and tight and had the look of rarely being opened. 'Permission to come aboard,' he asked of no one in particular.

June let out a gust of smoke. 'Could hardly refuse, now, could I?'

The man's mouth did not move.

The second officer was a Dal Honese woman in dark silks, a small silver claw sigil at her breast. The sight chilled Kyle even though the woman's pasty-greyish face and hand clutching the gunwale took somewhat from the power of her presence. The Moranth Blue climbed aboard easily despite the weight of the chitinous plated armour, to stand silent and self-contained. He – or she – nodded a greeting to Captain June.

Greymane broke the protracted silence. 'I gather I am under arrest.'

The Malazan officer's hairless brows rose. 'Under arrest? Not at all, Commander.'

Commander? Kyle wondered.

Greymane shared Kyle's confusion. He gaze flicked from face to face. 'Not under arrest?'

'No.' The man saluted. 'Fist Khemet Shul at your service, sir. Leading the convoy.' He indicated the Claw. 'Reshal. And this is Halat, liaison for the Moranth Blue *Bhuvar* – that is Admiral – Swirl.'

The Moranth Blue bowed to Greymane. 'An honour.'

Greymane's glacial eyes had narrowed to slits. 'Why did you call me Commander?'

In answer, Reshal drew a scroll from her shirt and held it out, her left hand supporting her right, and bowed. 'A missive from Emperor Mallick Rel the Glorious to be delivered personally to your hand.'

Greymane regarded the proffered scroll as one might a bared dagger. Yet, reluctantly, he took it. Kyle waited while the man read. Reshal swallowed hard and straightened, jaws clenched tight and hands pressed to her sides. Kyle thought he'd seen her eyeing him earlier and grinned at her condition. Her answering smile seemed to promise a knife-thrust – later.

Greymane lowered the scroll. He glanced at Kyle, attempting to reassure him with his gaze, which Kyle thought alarmed. 'Insane, Captain. Utterly insane. Twice it's been tried and twice the Riders and the Mare galleys destroyed the fleets. This one will manage no better.'

Shul bowed, accepting the point. 'As you say, Commander. However, this time the Emperor has offered a contract to the Moranth. And they have delivered.' He looked to Halat. 'Liaison?'

The Moranth Blue bowed. Aqua hues churned over the polished plates of his armour as he moved. 'We will break the Mare blockade, Greymane,' he said, his voice hollow within his masking helm. 'That is our promise.'

'You are certain?'

'Or we will die trying. Such is our word.'

'Then – I accept the commission.'

Shul saluted crisply. 'Very good, Fist. Your invasion fleet is assembling off the coast of Kartool.'

'Are *you* the insane one?' Kyle demanded the moment they had time alone in the empty crew quarters. 'How could you accept – after the way they treated you?'

Squeezed on to a bench, the big man raised an accepting hand. 'Yes, Kyle. I understand.' He examined an empty carved wood cup, almost invisible in his wide shovel-like hand. 'Believe me, I used to feel the same way.' He took a great breath, turned the cup in small circles on the table before him. 'But I'm older now. That attack from the Chosen, and the Malazans finding me now . . . I'll never be able to hide. And perhaps I shouldn't have run in the first place. I had people in Korel. People who depended on me. One fellow, Ruthan he was called, he was ready to fight, but I hope he followed my warning. When I was forced to leave . . . well, it's always gnawed at me. Like a betrayal. I've sometimes found myself wondering – are they still alive?'

Kyle filled Greymane's cup and one for himself from a jug of watered wine, and, ducking under hammocks, sat. He studied his friend across the table. The man's long dirty hair, now the hue of iron in this dim light, hung almost to the table. He was unshaven, his wide jowls grey with bristles. Old. The man looks old, and tired. Was this some sort of misguided effort to fix past failures? But from what he understood the failures were not of his making . . . Still, it was obvious he felt responsibility.

Responsibilities. Duties. Why was it that those who took on such burdens did so of their own accord? Kyle supposed that, in the end, those were the only kind that truly mattered. Like his sitting here now across from his friend. No one had asked. He need not accompany the man. His hand slid to the sword at his side. Burdens willingly taken on, he decided, come to define the bearer.

'So you are in charge then?' Kyle finally said into the relative silence of the creaking hull planks and the waves surging past.

'Of all land operations, yes. Once we arrive – Hood! Should we arrive.'

'But not the fleet?'

'No.'

'Who is?'

Greymane offered a half-smile, his pale sapphire eyes holding a tempered humour. 'You will have a chance to meet a living legend, Kyle. The name will mean nothing to you seeing as you're a damned foreigner, but the naval assault will be commanded by Admiral Nok.'

But Greymane was wrong. Kyle had heard of *him*.

CHAPTER III

Master of violence!
And violence mastered.
Companion to darkness.

Hail the Warlord!
Hammer fell
and fist heavy.

What ancient seams
Does he mine when
Night thoughts turn
To fault, fracture,
And that which must be done?

Lament for the Warlord
Fisher Kel Tath

COURTIERS IN BRIGHT FINERY ONCE CROWDED THE RECEPTION hall of Fortress Paliss, capital of the once sovereign Kingdom of Rool. Tapestries lined its stone walls. Long tables offered up delicacies and wines from distant exotic lands in this, the most powerful state on Fist – rival to Korelri.

Once.

Now, the broad hall stood empty, dark and cold. A single occupant – other than his guards – sat at one bare table, his back to a blazing conflagration roaring within a stone fireplace four paces across.

Ussü entered and crossed the wide unlit hall. Shadows danced over him, flickering from the distant fire. His master, Yeull 'ul Taith, commander of what remained of the Malazan Sixth Army,

Overlord of Fist, sat as no more than a silhouette of night, awaiting him.

With Ussü walked Borun, Black Moranth, leader of a contingent of that race shipwrecked on Fist some fifteen years ago and now Yeull's second. Commander of what the locals cursed as Yeull's 'Black Hands'.

Ussü noted how Borun's armoured boots grated on the stone while his footfalls came in comparative silence. He looked down to his leather sandals almost hidden beneath layered robes. *Quiet. Hidden. And so it has always been. Who was to know that he, Ussü, once a mage of little note within the Empire, now pursued power by other, darker, means?*

They halted before their commander. Yes, commander, *now*. Yeull 'ul Taith. Overlord. High Fist, after a fashion. First went Greymane – ousted on account of his outrageous leanings. Then that Imperial-appointed governor – what had his name been? Found dead. Then Fist Udara – but her suicide had appeared genuine. And now Yeull – clinging on like a man gripping a plank in a storm. Terrified of betrayal. Yet hanging on just the same, even more terrified of letting go.

Yeull straightened, a thick bearhide wrap falling from his shoulders. His long black hair hung wet with sweat over a pale scarred face. Dark eyes darted between Ussü and Borun. 'Yes? What is it?'

'News, m'lord. Of a kind.'

Yeull leaned in his tall chair, draped an arm over its back. 'Look at you two.' He gestured to Ussü: 'White,' then to Borun, 'and black.'

Ussü favoured pale hues such as ivory and cream. And his hair was long and thoroughly grey. While Borun was, of course, black.

'Is one to suggest caution, the other haste?'

'M'lord . . .'

'Is one to prove trustworthy, the other . . . well . . . not so trustworthy?'

'M'lord!'

The dark eyes sharpened. 'Overlord.'

Ussü bowed. 'Yes, Overlord.'

'What is it?' He poured himself a glass of wine from an earthenware decanter. 'Is it cold in here? I feel cold.'

As he stood before the roaring bonfire sweat now prickled Ussü's underarms, chest and face. 'No, m— Overlord. I am not cold.'

'No? You're not?' He tossed back the glass in one swallow. 'I am. To the bones.'

'He is calling for you.'

Yeull looked up from studying the empty glass. 'What? Someone calling me? Who?'

'The prisoner,' Borun said, his voice a coarse growl.

Yeull set down the glass carefully, straightened in his seat. 'Ah. *Him*. What does he want?'

'He must have news for us, High Fist. Something to offer, in any case.'

'It is cold – I swear it is cold.' Yeull turned aside. 'More wood for the fire.'

Ussü turned a quick look to Borun but could see nothing within the vision slit of his lowered visor. These Moranth and their armour! The man must be sweltering.

'So?' Yeull demanded. 'Why are you here speaking to me then? Speak to *him*.'

'He will only talk to you.'

'Me?'

'Yes, High Fist.'

'Out of the question.' The High Fist drew the bearhide cloak tighter about his shoulders.

Ussü suppressed his irritation. 'We have been through this before, High Fist. It must be you. None other.'

The man was looking aside, his gaze distant, almost empty. 'It will be cold down there. So far below.'

'We will bring torches.'

'What's that? Torches? Yes. Fire. We must bring fire.'

They walked the dark empty halls of Fortress Paliss. Guards – all Malazan regulars – saluted and unlocked doors to the deeper passageways. Ussü noted the many grey beards among them. They were none of them getting any younger, including himself. Who would carry on? They had trained and recruited thousands of soldiers from among the Rool and Skolati citizens, organized an army of over seventy thousand, but hardly any of the locals held a rank above captain.

Original Malazan officers constituted the ruling body. It was, in effect, the permanent rule of an occupying military elite. Yet their generation was passing away. Who would take up the sceptre – or the mace, in this instance – of rulership? Most had children, grown to men and women now, but these formed the new pampered aristocracy, not the least interested in service, or the world beyond their own sprawling estates. No, it seemed to Ussü more surely with every passing year that the local Fistian and Korelri policy was simply to ignore these invaders until they faded away. As surely they would, soldier by soldier, until nothing was left but for mouldering armour and dusty pennants from forgotten distant lands high on a wall.

The stalemate of initial invasion had ossified into formalized relations. It seemed that as far as the Korelri were concerned the Malazans simply ran the island of Fist now, as had the last Roolian dynasty before them. A mere change in administration. Frustration was not the word. Failure, perhaps, came closer to describing the acid bite in Ussü's stomach and soul whenever his thoughts turned to it. He had failed his superiors, each commander in turn, failed in attaining his one assigned task: achieving Malazan domination in this theatre. Decades ago, before the invasion fleet left Unta, Kellanved himself had set the task upon him.

He remembered his surprise and terror that day, so long ago now, when the old ogre had taken his arm and walked him out along Unta's harbour mole. Dancer had followed; how the man's gaze had tracked their every move! 'Ussü,' Kellanved had said, 'I will tell you this: in the end conquering is not about what territory or resources you control . . . it is about recasting the deck entirely.'

And he had mouthed something insipid about certainly meaning to and the Emperor had pulled his arm free to jab his walking stick impatiently to the south. 'Everywhere, for every region – for every person – hands are dealt from the Dragons deck. To create true fundamental change you must force a complete reshuffling and recasting of all hands. Turn your thoughts to that.' And the man had smiled slyly then, leaning on the silver hound's head walking stick, staring out over the water and Ussü remembered thinking: *As you have, wherever you have gone.*

They reached the lowest levels of construction. A locked iron door barred entrance to deeper tunnels carved from the native rock. Here Ussü used a key from his own belt to unlock the portal; no guards remained. Beyond, Borun and Yeull lit torches from lanterns and continued; Ussü locked the door behind them.

He believed these rough winding ways dated back to before the establishment of Paliss itself as a state capital, or even as a settlement. It seemed to him the dust their footfalls kicked up carried with it a tang of smoke and sulphur. Perhaps a remnant of the immense crater lake that dominated the big island.

The torch Yeull carried spluttered and hissed as the man shivered ahead of Ussü, muttering beneath his breath as if in conversation with himself. Ussü wondered, not for the first time, just when a new overlord might be necessary. Not he or Borun; both had found their place. One of the remaining division commanders perhaps, Genarin, or Tesh kel. Yeull had never been popular with the men, given as he was to brooding. But he'd been getting less and less *reliable* of late.

Borun led the way into a chamber carved from stone. Along one side stood a row of smaller alcoves, each barred. *Cells.* And around the main room instruments of . . . *punishment and persuasion.*

Just as Ussü had found them so long ago when the fortress fell. Very bloodthirsty, that last Roolian dynasty. And forgotten in the most distant pit, enduring, perhaps older even than that generation itself, the last occupant. Had he been overlooked during those last days of panic as the Malazan fist closed? Or had he already been forgotten – slipping from the living memory of humanity as dynasty followed dynasty in their cycles of rebellion and decline? Who was to say? He himself refused to enlighten them.

Borun stopped at a great iron sarcophagus some three paces in length lying within a metal framework upon the bare stone. He set his torch in a brazier, then took hold of a tall iron wheel next to the frame. This he ratcheted, his breath harsh with effort. As the wheel turned long iron spikes slowly withdrew from holes set all down the sides of the sarcophagus, and in rows across its front.

When the ends of these countless iron spikes emerged from within the stained openings a thick black fluid, blood of a kind, dripped viscous and thick from their needle tips. A slow rumbling exhalation of breath sounded then. It stirred the dust surrounding the sarcophagus.

Ussü bent over the coffin. 'Cherghem? You can hear me?'

A voice no more substantial than that breath sounded from within. *I hear you.*

'You say you have information for us? You sense something?'

Food. Water.

'Not until you speak.'

Water.

Ussü took a ladle from a nearby bucket and dashed its contents across the spike holes in the iron masking the head of the casket. 'There. You have water. Now speak!'

And the Overlord? He is here?

'Yes.' Ussü gestured Yeull forward.

But the Overlord would not move; he stood immobile, staring, one hand clenching the fur hide at his neck, the other white upon the haft of a torch held so close as to nearly set his hair aflame. His face appeared drained of all blood, its skein of scars livid.

'High Fist . . .' Ussü began, coaxing, 'you must speak.'

The mouth opened but no sound emerged.

I sense him there, his heart pounding like a star in the night. Overlord, I have news for you.

'Yes? News?' the man croaked, stricken. 'What news?'

They are coming for you, Yeull.

'What's that? Who?'

Ussü cast an uncertain glance across the sarcophagus to Borun who had cocked his armoured head aside, gauntlets clenching.

You did not think they would allow you your own personal fiefdom, did you? Your superiors, far to the north, they are coming to reassert control of their territory. No doubt you will hang as a usurper.

'How can you know this?' Ussü demanded.

I sense their approach.

'From whence will they come? The west or the east?'

The east.

Ussü did not think it possible for the High Fist to pale any further, yet he did. 'High Fist . . . we cannot be sure . . .'

But Yeull was backing away, shaking his head in terrified denial, his eyes huge dark pits. 'No, they are coming . . . they will never stop. Never leave me alone.'

Ussü moved to follow. 'High Fist . . .'

And can you guess who leads them?

Though Ussü knew this ancient being was laughing within, savouring his power over them, he turned to regard the impassive scarred iron mask, had to ask, 'Who?'

Your old friend, Overlord . . . the one some name Stonewielder.

Yeull leapt to the wheel, torch falling. 'How do you know this?' he demanded.

I sense what he carries at his side – an artefact unique in all existence, but for one other.

The ratcheting of the mechanism shocked Ussü as it spun under Yeull's hand.

The spikes thrust their way irresistibly into Cherghem's flesh – such as it was – much deeper than ever, as far as they could, and the prisoner groaned, convulsing in a shudder that shook the stone beneath their feet. Then, silence. Ussü listened for an intake of breath, heard none.

'That's enough from you,' Yeull ground out, snarling. He retrieved his torch, motioned to the stairs. As they walked the Moranth commander fell back to join Ussü. 'Think you he was lying?'

'No. It was inevitable . . . just sooner than I had hoped.'

'What must we do?'

Ussü eyed the back of the Overlord, almost invisible in the gloom. 'More germane to my mind is the question . . . what will *you* do?'

The Moranth's chitinous armour plates grated in an indifferent shrug. 'I am pledged to Yeull, my commander. He orders, I obey.'

'I see.' Ussü did not bother disguising his relief. *Over a thousand Black Moranth – our iron core. We may yet have a chance.* 'Through my contacts I will warn Mare, let them know another invasion fleet will be approaching.' They reached the locked iron door and Overlord Yeull, waiting, jaws clenched rigid in irritation and frustrated rage. 'With any luck,' Ussü finished, 'not one ship will escape them as before.'

* * *

No less than five times Tal, First of the Chase, promised her war band blood. Each time the trespassers slipped their grasp. No ambush succeeded. Not even the gathering cold slowed the passage of these foreigners across the icefields. Now the Chase, the premiere Jhek war party, must content itself with a protracted hunt across the crevasses of the Great Northern Agal.

Tal signalled a halt, pulled off her bulky fur and hide mitts. Her breath clouded the air. Hemtl, her second, stopped next to her. His furred hood and ivory eye-shield obscured his face, but she could well imagine his boyish sulk. He motioned to the tracks scuffing the snow. 'Still they remain ahead. They must be of the demons of old, the Forkul.'

'The Forkul would not run,' said a third voice and Tal suppressed a jerked start of surprise – Ruk had done it again. She turned: there he stood, arms and legs all crooked, in his hides of white, hair whiter still, the pale silver of frost. 'At least not from us,' he finished.

'What would you know of the Forkul?' Hemtl demanded. Wincing, Tal turned away. *You are second, Hemtl. Ruk did not seek the position. No need to remind anyone – except yourself.*

Ruk was silent, allowing the wind to whisper his answer to each: *More than you.*

The rest of the hunt had halted a distance back and crouched, indistinguishable among the wind-blown drifts. 'This is a waste,' Tal said to the blinding white horizon. 'I have lost count of the spoor we've passed.'

'Five snow bear and stragglers of the Ice River herd,' supplied Ruk.

'The insult must be answered!' Hemtl snarled.

Still facing away, Tal let out a long pluming breath. 'What does the land say?'

'Stone and rock are far away, Tal,' said Ruk. 'The Jaghut ice smothers all other voices.'

'Yet?'

'Yet there are whispers . . .'

She turned to the old man. Why the reluctance? His shielded gaze was turned aside. His hair blew free. *Did the man not feel their old enemy's biting cold?* For the first time in the hunt Tal felt the tightening in her throat that comes with the cornering of a snow bear or a giant tusker. Who were these strangers? 'Whispers of what?' she breathed.

'Of the ancestral Hold. Tellann.'

'Impossible!' burst out Hemtl. 'That cannot be.'

'Not impossible,' answered Tal, thoughtful. 'The Elders still walk the land. Logros, Kron, Ifayle. The path is still open – we have just lost the way.'

'The Jag curse of ice has smothered it,' Ruk agreed.

'There *are* other ways . . .' Hemtl said, his voice sullen. 'The Broken God beckons.'

'He is not of the land,' Ruk answered, his dismissal complete.

Tal raised a hand to sign for a halt. 'Ruk and I will go ahead, see if they will speak to us.'

'Speak?' said Hemtl. 'To what end?'

'Who knows?' And she laughed to chide Hemtl. 'Perhaps they will surrender, hey?'

Tal and Ruk jogged onward. They picked up their pace from their normal league-sustaining trot of pursuit, closing the distance between them and their quarry. After a time the change in tactics was discovered and the party of four ahead slowed then stopped, awaiting them far across the ice. Closing, she and Ruk slowed as well, came to a halt themselves. Tal held out her gloved hands. 'Do you understand me?' she called in Korelri.

'We do,' an accented voice answered from over the windswept field. 'What is there for us to talk of?'

What was there for them to talk of? Where could she possibly start? 'By what right do you so arrogantly cross our lands?'

The four spoke among themselves. One raised his hands to his mouth. 'Your lands? We thought these wastes empty. Why do you chase us?'

Why? What fools these foreigners were! 'Why? Because these are *our* lands! You are trespassers. You eat caribou – that is food taken from our families.'

The four spoke again. 'We offer our apologies. But there are so many. That herd numbered thousands!'

Tal and Ruk could not help but exchange looks of exasperation. *Foreigners!* Elder Gods deliver them from the uncomprehending fools. Tal called across the ice, 'Yes, so it would seem. Yet every one of those spoken for, and that all our families have! What of the herds of your lords? What if they were kept all together and someone, seeing all their number, helped himself to one seeing as they numbered so? What would then happen to him?'

'He would be imprisoned, or maimed,' admitted the foreign trespasser, his voice now sounding tired. 'Very well. Come forward. Perhaps we should speak.'

Tal looked to Ruk, who nodded his assent. They found three men and one woman, all four ill dressed for the cold, shivering, the leathers under their cloaks soaked in sweat that froze into frost and ice before Tal's eyes. *How could these ill-prepared wretches have forestalled them time and again?* But the spokesman, a muscular squat fellow, dark-skinned, was sitting on his haunches calmly awaiting them. Tal squatted down with him. 'Greetings.'

'Greetings. It would seem we owe you our apologies and reparation of some kind. That is acceptable to us if it is acceptable to you. What repayment would you require?'

Astonished, Tal glanced up at Ruk but found the man grinning at one of the strangers, a skinny youth bearing an unruly thatch of thick black hair. This one wore a brooch on his wool cloak, a silver snake or dragon over a red field. The sight of that insignia triggered a distant recognition within Tal. Thinking of that vague impression, she asked, 'Your names, first.'

The four exchanged uncertain glances. Why the uneasiness? What could they possibly have to hide? But then the spokesman shrugged. 'Fair enough. I am Blues. This is Fingers, Lazar, Shell. We are of the Crimson Guard.'

Tal rocked back on her heels. That name she knew. Crimson Guard – they had ruled Stratem to the south in her grandfather's time. Warriors and mages, her grandfather had told her. War is for them as is the hunt for us. Examining the four, Tal now wondered who had let who escape back there so many times on the trail.

The two named Fingers and Shell straightened then, their gazes roving about. Blues frowned. 'What . . . ?'

'It's a trap,' Fingers said. 'We're surrounded.'

Ruk thrust himself to his feet, cursing. 'The young fool!'

Tal straightened as well, knowing what she would see. Hemtl had cast the Chase out in a broad encirclement and they closed now, he coming forward. He pointed his spear, calling, 'Harm our two and you all die!'

None of the four had made any move to defend themselves or restrain Tal and Ruk. Tal raised her hands to Blues. 'We had no knowledge of this.'

Blues gave his gentle assent. 'I know – you wouldn't have delivered yourselves otherwise.'

'Let me speak to him.'

'You'd better,' the man answered quietly.

That gentle warning moved Tal to run to Hemtl. Ruk remained, as if offering himself out of shame as hostage.

'*You fool!*' she snarled, closing.

The young man was panting, his face flushed. 'We have them. Your trick stopped them.'

'It wasn't a *trick*. This isn't a *game*. I was close to terms. Now, thanks to you, I doubt I'll be able to salvage this . . .'

But Hemtl wasn't facing her. Spear levelled, he shouted, 'Release our man or you will all die!'

Tal slapped him. The blow sent his visor flying, loosed his mane of long kinked hair to blow in the wind. His eyes went huge. 'I see it now,' he breathed. 'You would betray us – allow them to escape for payment. You are a *whore* . . .'

She raised her arm to slap him again but he was quicker and it was as if instantly the man's spear was through her stomach. She felt the broad flint head glance from the bone of her pelvis. *How easy it is to die*, she thought, amazed, before a sea of pain erased all else. To her shame she screamed but over that she heard the roar of Ruk's bull outrage.

Tal did not expect to ever awaken again, yet she did. It was night. The lights of the Holds shimmered pink and green in the black starry sky. A fire burned nearby. A woman's face loomed close. The foreigner, Shell. Then Ruk, face wet with tears. 'What . . . what . . .' she murmured before sleep took her once more.

When she awoke again it was light and she was strapped in a travois. The men and women of her hunt all gathered around. Ruk pushed his way forward. He took her head in his rough hands. 'I thought we'd lost you.'

'What happened?'

'You were healed. The foreigners healed you. It was far beyond our skills. We're taking you home now.'

'Ruk!' she snarled, then gasped her pain. 'What *happened*?'

The old man glanced away. The wind threw his long snow-bright hair about. 'I killed him.'

She'd thought so. Good – in that he'd managed to keep it among themselves. No new blood feud. Now Ruk would present himself at the Guth-Ull, the council of chiefs, and hear their judgement. They should be lenient, considering.

'And the foreigners?'

'Gone.'

'*Gone*? I can't even *thank* them?'

Ruk shook his head in wonderment at the strange ways of all those not blessed enough to be of the Jhek. 'They left as soon as they knew you were mended. Would not wait. Said they'd been in a rush because they were in a hurry to rescue a friend. Damned odd these strangers, yes?'

No. Perhaps not so odd, old friend.

* * *

'So where, in the name of all the buggering Faladah, are we?'

Kiska eyed the man. Her . . . *what*? Protector? She'd frankly rather die. Guide? Obviously not. Partner? Hardly. Ally? . . . Perhaps. To be generous – perhaps. She knew nothing of the man, though she'd like to think that the Enchantress was no fool. He was wrapping a cloth about his face and neck in a manner that spoke of long practice and easy familiarity. She scanned the horizon: league after league of desolate near-desert prostrate beneath a dull slate sky. She knew this place. It had been a long time, yet how could anyone ever forget?

'Shadow. We are in the Shadow Realm.'

The man grunted his distaste. 'The Kingdom of the Deceiver? He is reviled in my lands.'

Kneeling, Kiska laid her roll on the ground. She took articles from her pockets and waist, including a water skin, wrapped dried meat and the sack, and folded them tightly into the roll, which she then tied off with rope. This went on to her back. She pulled a grey cloth from beneath her leather hauberk, and, like Jheval, wrapped it round her head and face. Thin leather gloves finished the change; she yanked them tight, then checked the ties of the two long-knives she carried towards the back of each hip.

Jheval looked her up and down, from her now dusty knee-high boots up her trousers to her full-sleeved hauberk and the headscarf she was tucking in. 'You're too lightly armoured,' he observed.

'Have to do.'

'It won't.'

'That's my problem.'

'Not if I have to carry you.'

'You won't.'

The Seven Cities native had half turned away, scanning the surroundings. Now he eyed her sidelong, bemused. 'How did you know that?'

Arsehole. She gestured to one side. 'Let's take a look from that rise,' she said, and headed off. After a moment she heard him follow. *At least he hasn't tried to take charge. That's something. And he had the grace, or the confidence, to admit he had no idea where they were. Nothing too insufferable yet.*

The yielding sands pulled at her feet; already she felt tired. From the modest rise she now saw what she presumed to be the hills the Enchantress spoke of. They were no more than lumps on the distant horizon – or what she assumed must be distant; there was no way of knowing here in Shadow. Beside her Jheval grunted upon spotting the feature, and in that single vocalization Kiska read his frustration and disgust at the sight.

Smiling behind her headscarf, she headed down the slope.

Some time later – and she had no way of knowing how long that might've been – as they walked more or less side by side, yet apart, she grew tired of squinting into the distances, searching for a hint of the geography she'd encountered during earlier visits to this realm. She saw nothing familiar, and decided it was ridiculous to search for it; Shadow must be vast, and any traveller in Genabackis may as well hope for a glimpse of the Fenn Mountains.

During all this time she hadn't spoken. But then, neither had Jheval. Clearing her throat, her gaze fixed ahead, she began, 'So. Strictly speaking, should we be enemies?'

A silent pause; perhaps long enough for a shrug. 'Not at all. Are you some sort of Imperial fanatic?'

'No! I withdrew from service.' She glared to see his eyes amused above what must be a smile hidden by his scarf. 'I was a private bodyguard.'

It was hard to tell, but she thought the smile disappeared. 'Not so unalike after all, then.'

'We are quite unalike, thank you,' she sniffed, and regretted it instantly – that priggish superior tone. He just gave a low knowing chuckle and Kiska was then very glad of her scarf for it hid her flushed embarrassment.

For all their walking the range of hills appeared no closer. The dune fields interspersed by flats of hardpan passed monotonously. They passed occasional ruins of canted pillars and shattered stone walls half buried in the sands. The emptiness struck Kiska as odd; her memories were of a much more crowded place.

'We were enemies once, I suppose,' the man said after a time, perhaps only to hear a human voice in all this silence. 'For you were a Claw.'

Kiska turned on him, about to demand who said so, and to deny it utterly, but then the absurdity of it all came to her and she deflated, her shoulders falling. She gave a dismissive wave and continued on. 'How did you know? Did the Enchantress tell you?'

'No. It's in your walk. The way you move.'

'Seen many, have you, up there in Seven Cities?'

'I was stalked by a number of them,' he answered, without any note of boasting.

She glanced over, attempting to penetrate the layers of his armour, his face-masking headscarf. 'I'm impressed.'

It was his turn to wave the issue aside. 'Don't be. My friend killed most of them. He's very good at killing. I'm not.'

Kiska was caught off guard by this surprising claim, or confession. 'Really? What *are* you good at then?'

Now came an unmistakable broad smile behind the scarf. 'Living.'

Kiska almost shared the contagious smile before quickly turning away. After walking again for a while, she began, 'Yes. I was a Claw. I trained as one. Was offered command of a Hand. But I refused. I withdrew.'

'I thought they wouldn't allow that,' he said. 'That they'd just kill you.'

'Sometimes. If you go independent. Not if you join the regular ranks. Or, as I did, serve as a bodyguard within the Imperium.'

'It must have been hard . . . walking away from all that . . .'

'Not at all. It was simplicity—' She stopped, peering aside. 'What's that?'

The undulating terrain had brought a hollow into view where a large dark shape lay twisted among broken ground. Jumbled tracks led from it off to their right.

'It's not moving,' said Jheval.

Kiska gestured onward. 'Let's just keep going.'

'We should at least take a look.'

She shook her head. 'No. This is Shadow – we mustn't involve ourselves.'

But Jheval was already heading down the slope. 'Aren't you even curious?'

'This is no place for curiosity . . . *or stupidity*,' she added under her breath, peering warily about. Yet follow she did. It was the fresh corpse of a titanic lizard beast. Upright, it would have stood twice her height. Its forearms ended in curved blades, battered and stained. Jheval was crouched by its great head. He had pulled down his face scarf.

'So . . . this is K'Chain Che'Malle,' he said, musing.

'Yes. A warrior. One of their Kell Hunters.'

'What is it doing here, I wonder.'

'I have no idea.' Whatever had happened, the beast's death had not been easy. Great savage wounds gouged its sides and legs. Dried blood sheathed its scaled skin. Kiska noted a track close by and she knelt: an enormous paw-print wider across than the span of her hand. She straightened, rigid. 'Jheval . . .'

The sandpaper hiss of the tail shifting warned them and one forelimb scythed through the air where Jheval had been crouching. His morningstars appeared almost instantly as blurs. The beast twisted, lumbered to its clawed feet. A kind of harness of leather and metal hung from it in tattered ruins. Kiska saw there was no point in running: the thing's stride was greater than her height. Jheval desperately gave ground in a series of clashing parries, somehow deflecting each of the Kell Hunter's ponderous slashes. Kiska was appalled; it seemed to her that any one of those blows could have levelled a building.

Since they could not outrun it she had to slow it down. And it seemed to be ignoring her. She lunged after the beast, long-knives drawn. A forward roll brought her within reach of its trailing leg and she slashed. A bellow of pain rewarded her, together with a blow from its tail that crushed the breath from her and sent her tumbling across the sands.

She awoke coughing and gagging. Jheval was crouched over her, water skin raised. She wiped her face and peered about. Off in the distance a trumpet roar of pain and frustration blasted the air.

'You carried me.'

He sat heavily, out of breath. 'No. I dragged you.'

'Thank you *so* much.'

'You're welcome.'

She suddenly remembered what she'd found next to the fallen Kell Hunter and struggled to rise. 'We have to move.'

He pressed her down gently. 'No, no. You crippled it. And it was too stupid to know it was dead anyway.'

She batted his hand aside. 'No, you fool.' Then, failing to stand, she grabbed the hand. 'Oh, help me up.'

He pulled her to her feet and she hissed, cradling her side. It felt as if someone had swung a tree at her. 'We have to go,' she gasped. 'They might return.'

The man was eyeing her, suspicious. 'Who?'

Clutching his shoulder, she tried a step. 'The creatures that tore that Kell Hunter apart. The hounds. The Hounds of Shadow.'

'Even they could not—'

'Trust me,' she said, impatient. 'I've seen them.' She took a tentative step all on her own. 'Now, we have to go.'

The man was scanning the surroundings, scowling, clearly dubious. But at length he shrugged, acquiescing. 'If you insist.' He took her elbow to help her along.

* * *

The corpses may have been fishermen unlucky enough to have had their boat sink, or overturn. Perhaps. They were found tangled on the shore of the tiny Isle of Skytower, a rocky outcropping at the centre of Tower Sea. Yet since the sea, and the isle, were forbidden to all by order of the Korelri Chosen, it was unlikely they had arrived by choice.

Summoned by the watch, Tower Marshal Colberant, commander of the garrison, reluctantly climbed his way down the bare jumbled rocks of the isle's steep shore. He was old, and frankly cared nothing for the world beyond his life's duty overseeing this, the most isolated and secure fortress of the Korelri Chosen. Living fishermen or sailors from nearby Jasston or Dourkan barely interested him; their dead remains could hardly be worthy of his attention. But Javus, their youngest recruit to this, the most demanding and important posting achievable for all Chosen, had been very insistent. Such keenness ought to be encouraged.

So Colberant hiked up his long cloak and steadied himself with the haft of his spear as he carefully tested each foothold among the jagged black rocks that led down to the island's desolate shore. Desolate because within Tower Sea no fish swam, no bird nested, and no plant spread its green leaves. For here against Skytower ages ago the full fury of the demon Riders smashed winter after winter while Colberant's ancestors fought to complete the final sections of the great Stormwall. And here even now, after so many thousands of years, the land had yet to heal and find its life again.

Downslope, Javus waited a good man-height above the tallest of the high-water marks. At least, Colberant mused, the lad knew better than to extend an arm to help his ageing commander. Planting his spear, Colberant made a show of peering about. 'So where are these bodies that have so spooked you, young Javus?'

The youth smiled, already familiar with his commander's teasing manner. He slipped an arm from his wrapped cloak. 'Just there, Marshal. And it is not the corpses that are unsettling – rather the manner of their passing.'

Colberant arched a sharp brow. 'Oh?' But the young Chosen, his gaze lowered, would say no more. The marshal probed the rocks and continued on a few more paces. Here he halted, then lowered himself to his haunches, both fists tight on the spear haft.

He would not have thought them corpses had he come across them alone. Tangled lengths of sun-dried driftwood, perhaps. More than ten individuals certainly, deposited high above the highest of all the tide lines. Yet each was as browned and desiccated as if found within a cave.

It had been many years since he, an elder among the Order of the Chosen, had heard of such things. Squatting on his aching haunches he glanced up at the heights of the black volcanic rock tower looming above them. *They say the Blessed Lady spurns many and that few achieve permission to sit at her right hand. Is this a warning? Have we angered her with our weakness of late?* Who was to know? Not even he, considered the most ardent in his devotion, dared guess her moods. He straightened, returned to the waiting Javus.

He smiled his reassurance. 'Drowned fishermen. Their boat must have overturned. No matter how many times we tell them not to enter Tower Sea, still they come.'

The young man remained troubled. 'With all respect, Marshal, I've seen drowned bodies. Those men and women have not been in the sea.'

Colberant shrugged his indifference, began searching for a way up. 'The sun, then, has dried them since.'

'I only say, Marshal, because I am from Skolati originally . . .'

'Oh?'

'Yes . . . and in Fist is a similar inland sea, Fist Sea. And there on its shores we sometimes find similar . . . things.'

Colberant turned to face the recruit squarely. 'I do not find it surprising, Javus, that people should drown in either sea.'

'But as I said, none of—'

The marshal had raised a hand for silence. 'Your diligence is to be commended . . . but this is a matter for the Order now. You will speak to no one regarding this.'

Drawing himself up taut, the youth bowed curtly. 'As you say, Marshal.'

'Thank you. Now, perhaps you could show an old man the easiest path back up to the tower, yes?'

Another stiff bow. 'Of course, Marshal.'

Colberant had asked for Javus' guidance but he did not need it; he had been walking these rocks for decades. His sandalled feet sought purchase on their own as his thoughts flew far ahead. *I must send word to Hiam immediately. The supply launch must be readied. Javus will wonder . . . but to be honoured with this posting his loyalty must already stand beyond reproach. For here in this tower, secluded from the Stormwall, guarded by four hundred most dedicated of the Chosen, are sequestered the Order's holiest of relics. Including, so our ancient lore has it, the gift responsible for the founding of our Order, given from the hand of the Blessed Lady herself.*

* * *

All that day Ivanr knew of the army's approach. He said nothing about it to the boy. Smoke and dust was a distant haze obscuring the higher valley. The hint of cook fires and the miasmic pong of stale human sweat and poorly cured leather made him wince; he had been a long time away from any human settlement.

He set camp in the evening, hobbled the mounts. The boy sat, arms tight around his shins, watching, silent still.

Not a word since leaving that pathetic village. Seeing one's family butchered before one's eyes might put a halt to discussion.

Yet look at me . . .

'Hungry?'

No response, chin on knees, eyes big and hair unkempt.

Ivanr cleared his throat. 'We have bread. Meat. Preserves. Care for some cheese?'

Nothing. A shudder from the gathering cool.

Ivanr sighed.

I have been alone in the mountains for a month and the one human being I choose to travel with won't say a damned word. Serves me right, I suppose.

He set to gathering firewood.

While he collected the dry bracken and sticks, he called, 'A man has only two hands, you know. Be nice to have a warm fire going by now . . .'

He paused, glanced over his shoulder. The boy was watching him over his. 'Never mind. Tricky business this, stalking twigs. Maybe when you're older . . .'

He sat facing the camp fire, finishing off the bread; the boy stared back, the tear of dried meat that Ivanr had placed in his hand still there. Ivanr was waiting for the advance scouts of the force up-valley to decide they were harmless.

'Am I evil?' the boy asked, so sudden, so unbidden, that Ivanr thought someone else had spoken from the dark.

'I'm sorry, lad. What was that?'

The earnestness of the boy's gaze was a needle to Ivanr's chest. 'Am I evil?'

'By all the gods true or false – *no!* Of course not. Who would say such a thing?'

'My father did. When he gathered us all together. Ma and the little 'uns. Said we were evil in the sight of the Lady and had to die for it.'

Ivanr stared through the fire between them. He felt his face darkening and a heart-squeezing pain. *All the unholy gods. What can anyone say to that?* 'No, lad,' he managed, fighting to keep his voice light. 'That's wrong. Your father was . . . led wrongly.'

He heard them approaching then through the rough chaparral. Encircling – at least they got that right. As the scouts emerged from the dark – two men and two women – the boy jolted upright mouthing an inarticulate yelp. Ivanr quickly crossed to set a hand on his shoulder. Beneath his palm the lad was shivering like a colt. 'Who are you?' Ivanr demanded, if only because they had said nothing.

'Where are you from, Thel?' one of the women demanded.

'I've been farming. There's a village beneath the slope here. They're killing everyone. We fled.'

She studied him while the other three collected his gear and unhobbled his mount. 'Hey! That's my horse.'

'Not any longer,' said the woman. She was hardly older than a girl. 'Why did you flee?'

'I've had enough of killing.'

That struck the woman as funny and she gave a derisive snort. 'Then you should've kept to your fields, because you are now part of the Army of Reform.'

'Reform? Who came up with that?'

The woman pressed the tip of her Jourilan longsword to his chest. 'Careful, recruit.' The lad's eyes were huge on the woman's sword.

'You don't kill your recruits, do you?'

'Just the spies and infiltrators.'

'I'm not the type.'

'No? Then what are you?'

'I'm a pacifist. I've renounced killing.'

Another derisive snort and the woman lowered her blade, sheathing it. She shook her head in disbelief. 'A damned Thel pacifist. Now I've seen everything.' She scanned the others. 'We ready?'

'Aye.'

'Okay. Back to camp.' She waved Ivanr onward. 'Beneth might want a word with you.'

Walking through the night, a comforting arm over the lad's shoulders, Ivanr wondered on that name, Beneth. Could it really be the same he'd heard so much of over the years? The heretic mystic of the mountains, hunted for so long. Had he now gathered to himself an army of followers? Or had refugees merely coaleesced naturally around him? The appearance of these scouts supported that theory: scruffy mismatched armour, no uniform. The possibility was troubling; he did not relish being pressed into an army of religious fanatics. He knew his history. There had been uprisings in the past, millennial movements, charismatics, schismatics, peasant rebellions. All crushed beneath the hooves of the Jourilan Imperial cavalry and the banner of the Blessed Lady.

Late in the night they passed between pickets and reached the army encampment. Here the woman stopped him. 'Just you.'

The boy peered up, his brows troubled. Ivanr patted his shoulders. 'He's with me.'

The woman's sour scowl, apparently her normal expression, eased into something like mild distaste. 'We have a large train of followers. Refugees. Families. He can join the camp.'

It occurred to Ivanr that from all he'd seen so far this assemblage was nothing more than one bloated congregation of refugees, but he thought it imprudent to say so at the moment. He crouched before the lad. 'Go with this girl here. She'll take you to a family. They'll feed you. Take you in. Okay?'

The boy just stared back, the crusted dried blood Ivanr couldn't remove black in the dim torchlight. The eyes remained just as empty as before. *Show* something, *damn you! Anything. Even fear.*

He straightened, nodded to the woman. She took the lad's hand. 'Is he . . .' and she gestured to her head.

Ivanr almost slapped the young scout. 'No!' He softened his voice. 'He's seen some terrible things.'

She grunted, dubious, pulled him away. The lad went without a sound. He looked back once over a shoulder, his eyes big and gleaming in the dark. It somehow saddened Ivanr that he should go so easily and he felt a stab of pain as he wondered if perhaps he'd been forgotten already. One of the remaining scouts gestured. 'This way.'

The tent was large but no different from any of the others surrounding it. Guards stood before the closed flap. They searched him then waved him in. When he ducked within, the first thing that struck Ivanr was the heat, that and the bright light of a fire and numerous lamps. He stood blinking, hunched beneath the low roof.

'Take a seat,' said someone, a man. 'You're making me uncomfortable just looking at you.'

Squinting, he made out scattered blankets and cushions. He sat. 'My thanks.'

'So, you are just up from the lowlands.'

'More or less.'

'And what awaits us there?'

'Chaos and bloodshed.'

A barked laugh. 'You *were* just there, weren't you?'

His vision adjusting, Ivanr made out three occupants. The speaker was middle-aged, bearded, well dressed in a tailored shirt and jacket of the kind once fashionable in the Jourilan courts. That and his accent placed him as a Jourilan aristocrat. The second occupant was a woman, thick-boned, dressed in a battered plain coat such as might also serve as underpadding for heavy armour. Her hair was hacked short, touched with grey, and her nose was flattened and canted aside, crushed long ago by some fearsome blow. He could not place her background – Katakan, perhaps. The last occupant was farther into shadows, a hump of piled blankets topped by an old man's bald gleaming head, a cloth wrapped round the eyes. 'What do you want with me?' Ivanr asked. 'I'm just a refugee.'

The old man's face drew up in a wrinkled smile. 'Greetings, refugee.' He cocked his head to one side and raised it as if looking off just above Ivanr. 'My name is Beneth. Describe him, Hegil.'

'He's the closest to a full-breed Thel that I've ever seen,' said the bearded man. 'Was once better fed but has lost weight recently. Carries himself like a soldier – is probably a veteran. And rides a horse recently stolen from the army.'

'What do you say to that, Thel?'

'I'd say your friend's right – and that he's been in the army too.'

The old man – blind for some time, Ivanr decided – seemed to wink behind the cloth wrap. 'You are both correct, of course. I would hazard the guess that you are Ivanr. Welcome to our camp.'

Ivanr couldn't help starting, amazed. 'How did—'

'Ivanr the Grand Champion?' said Hegil, equally amazed.

The blind old man's expression was unchanged, maddeningly secretive, almost mischievous. 'As a soothsayer might say, I saw it in a dream. Now come. We have tea, and meat.'

Ivanr did not object when trenchers of food were passed round: goat on skewers, yoghurt, and freshly baked flatbread.

'So someone here knows me,' he said to the old man.

Beneth was chewing thoughtfully on his bread. 'Not that I know of. Do you know him, Hegil?'

Hegil, obviously once a Jourilan officer, was now eyeing Ivanr with open hostility. 'Only by reputation.'

Beneth nodded. 'There you are. But let us not get ahead of ourselves. I guessed correctly because I was forewarned you might come to us.'

'Forewarned by whom?'

'By the Priestess.'

Ivanr almost choked on the goat. 'Is *she* here?'

Again the knowing smile. 'I hear in your voice that you've met her. No, she is not, but many of those gathered here are adherents of hers. They passed along the information. In any case, as I said, let us not get ahead of ourselves. Introductions first.' He motioned to his left, where the woman in the functional-looking coat sat. 'This is Martal, of Katakan.' She inclined her chin in wary greeting. 'Martal is in charge of organizing our forces.'

Best of luck to you, Martal.

'Hegil is the commander of our cavalry.'

Ivanr nodded to the aristocrat. An odd arrangement – just who was in charge then? Hegil or the woman? He shifted uncomfortably and stretched a leg that threatened to seize in a knot. 'Well, thank you for the meal and I wish you well, but I must be getting on. I'm sure you have better intelligence than I can provide.'

Beneth again cocked his head in thought, as if listening to distant voices only he could hear. 'May I ask where you might be getting on to, Ivanr? Have you given any thought to where you might be headed?'

Ivanr chewed a mouthful of flatbread. He shrugged. 'Well, no offence, but I would hardly tell you that, would I?'

The old man nodded at such prudence. 'True. But let me guess. You were thinking of heading across the inland sea to the Blight Plains, and perhaps continuing east to the coast to take ship to other lands where the name of Ivanr is not known.'

Ivanr coughed on his flatbread, washed it down with a mouthful of goat's milk. He glowered at the innocently beaming fellow. 'Your point, old man?'

'My point is that everyone here was drawn to this place for a reason. We are assembled here and in other locations for a purpose. What that purpose is I cannot say exactly. I can only perceive its vague outlines. But I do assure you this – it is a far greater end than that which any of us could achieve in the pursuit of our own individual goals.'

Ivanr stared at the blind old fellow. *Delusional. And a demagogue.* The two tended to go hand in hand. Prosecute someone, chase them into the wasteland, and they can't help but be driven to the conclusion that it's all for some sort of higher good – after all, the alternative would just be too crushing. It takes an unusually philosophic mind to accept that all one's suffering might be to no end, really, in the larger scheme of things.

After a long thoughtful sip of goat's milk, Ivanr raised and lowered his shoulders. 'I can assure you that I was not *drawn* here.'

Beneth appeared untroubled. He waved a quavering, age-spotted hand. 'A poor analogy maybe. Guided. Spurred along by events, perhaps.'

Scowling at his own foolishness in actually attempting to debate with the old hermit, Ivanr shrugged. He would get nowhere in this. 'Well, again, thank you for the meal. Am I to assume that I am your prisoner? After all, you could hardly allow me to leave and possibly reveal your presence here in the hills.'

'They know we're here,' said Hegil.

'They've placed spies among us,' added Martal, speaking for the first time.

Ivanr found it hard to penetrate her accent. 'Really? Why don't you get rid of them?'

The old man's mouth crooked up. 'Better that we know who the spies are than not. And we can use them to send along the information we want sent.'

Not quite so otherworldly, are you, holy man? Ivanr could not deny feeling a certain degree of admiration for such subtlety in thinking and tactics.

'In any case,' Beneth continued, 'we could hardly deter Grand Champion Ivanr from leaving our modest camp, should he choose to. Yes?'

Ivanr merely raised an eyebrow. *You damned well know you could should you choose to. About ten spearmen who knew what they were doing ought to take care of that.*

'But before we retire why don't I tell you a story? My story, to be exact. One that I hope might shed some light on why we are here, and what we hope to accomplish. I am old, as you see. Very old. I was born long before the Malazans came to our shores with their foreign ways and foreign gods. I was also born different. All my life I could *see* things other people could not. Shadows of other things. These shadows spoke to me, showed me strange visions. When I spoke of these things to my parents, I was beaten and told never to entertain such evil again. For such is how all those born *different* are treated here among the Korelri and Roolians – all those you Thel name invaders.

'Foolishly though, or stubbornly, I persisted in indulging my gifts, for they were my solace, my company, the only thing I had left after I had been named *touched*. And so one day representatives of the priesthood, the Lady's examiners, came for me. Since you persist in your evil visions, they said, we will put a permanent end to your perverted ways. And they heated irons and put out my eyes. I was but fourteen years of age at the time.'

The old man cleared his throat. Martal pressed a skin of water into one of his hands, which he took and drank. 'I was left to starve, blind, in the foothills of the mountains south of Stygg. The Ebon range. But I did not die. When I awoke I found that I possessed another kind of vision. The vision of a land like this but subtly different – a kind of shadow version. I wandered the wilderness, the ice wastes, the snow-topped Iceback range. There I was shown images of the past and present that lacerated my spirit, horrified me beyond recounting. I was shown that these lands are in the grip of a great evil, a monstrous deformation of life that has persisted, entwining itself into our ways here in these lands for thousands of years. One that must be rooted out and cleansed. And to that end we are all of us gathered here.'

Ivanr glanced from face to face searching for scepticism or ridicule, but saw only a kind of gentle affection for the old man. Hegil was nodding, his gaze downcast. Even Martal – who appeared the most hardened veteran Ivanr had met in a long time – was affected: her flat broad face twisted in a ferocious scowl. *Lady preserve him, this was far worse than he'd imagined. Crusaders.* The Priestess had infected all these people with her madness. Right then he saw that he had to confront her. Visions came of this refugee rabble marching to be mowed down by Jourilan Imperials. Mass murder. All in *her* name. Someone had to make her see her responsibility for all these deaths. To make her stop this hopeless cause. And it surely would not be any of them.

He cleared his throat and raised his hands, gesturing helplessly. 'I'm sorry for all that you have suffered, Beneth. But again, none of this has anything to do with me. I wish you luck. Though I have to say that I do not think you will fare well against the Jourilan Army.'

'We are not fighting the Jourilan Army. Or even the Jourilan Emperor himself. But that aside, I am surprised to hear you say that none of this has anything to do with you.'

He could not suppress a shiver of unease. 'What do you mean?' He could have sworn the old man cocked a brow behind the bandage across his eyes.

'Why . . . she sought you out, of course. And now you have found your way here among us. Surely you do not think this mere coincidence?'

And why did the tree fall on my house? Because the hundred other ones that fell did not, old man. We invent patterns when we look back on what has brought us to wherever we happen to be. This particular choice, or that particular turn. All in hindsight . . . when in truth all was mere chance. This is where people go to flee the carnage below and so – wonders of wonders – here we have all congregated. That is all there is to it, old man. Nothing more. Ivanr finished his goat's milk. 'Well, we simply disagree there.'

Again, the knowing, indulgent smile. 'So you say. But it is late. I must sleep. A guard will show you a billet. Good night.'

Ivanr nodded his assent. 'Good night. It *is* an honour to meet you, none the less.'

'The honour is mine, Ivanr.'

Once the Thel had quit the tent, the Jourilan aristocrat cleared his throat.

'Yes, Hegil,' Beneth said, somehow conveying an exact knowledge of what the man would say.

'You did not tell him.'

The old man shook his head. 'That would have been too cruel.'

'He will find out eventually – perhaps in a worse way,' Martal warned, her voice rough and flat, perhaps from her mashed nose.

'Perhaps,' the old man allowed. 'Yet he will hardly bandy his name about, nor will we. And few of the cult have reached us as yet.'

Hegil snorted. 'The cult of Ivanr. A pacifist cult in the name of a bloodthirsty Grand Champion! Surely things have gone too far in this proliferation of schisms and sects, Beneth.'

'Hundreds have been inspired to refuse service. How many more have been imprisoned, or tortured to death? All in his name.' The old man shook his head in rigid finality. 'No. I would spare him that burden. At least for as long as we dare.'

* * *

When frost glittered on the hinges of his cell door, Corlo knew it was time for them to come for him. This season the wait was not long. He was meditating. Though the otataral torc at his neck precluded all access to the Warrens, as did the malign watchful presence of the Lady, he could still practise the mental disciplines that facilitated and deepened his reach.

The lock clattered and the door grated open to reveal the usual Chosen guard, backed by crossbowmen. The man motioned him up. 'Time to go.'

Corlo eased himself from the cold stone floor, straightened his jerkin. 'Time to move him?'

As usual, the Korelri did not answer. They marched him through the rambling tunnels of cells and storerooms; this time they passed many open doors, doors normally shut and locked at any other time of the year. What he saw puzzled him greatly: *empty . . . so many empty rooms!*

Outside, the cold clasped his throat like an enemy and Corlo gasped. *Hood take them, but the Riders were upon them with a vengeance.* His guards pushed him on to the stone stairs up to the barracks behind the jumbled rock slope at the wall's base. It was a familiar path, the way to Bars' chambers, and Corlo dragged his heels to enjoy the too brief period of relative freedom.

A troop of impressed guardsmen – shackled veterans of the wall – was coming down. A man came abreast and Corlo's breath caught in recognition even as the man's mouth opened in shocked mute surprise. *Halfpeck!* Corlo craned his neck to watch the man descend. Shackled at the ankles, the fellow Crimson Guardsman thrust up a fist, defiant, waving.

Corlo answered that fist with his own. The stock of a crossbow struck his head, sending him stumbling on. *Halfpeck living! How many more might there still be?* Last he'd been sure there were seven including him and Bars. All of the Blade alone. Of the fate of the crew, he knew little. Bars insisted on treating the surviving crew of their ship, the *Ardent*, as part of his command. But for his part, Corlo really only counted the Blade. Perhaps Halfpeck knew of others . . . *where was that contingent headed?*

Corlo climbed the stairs, his mind seething. And where might each survivor be? Where among the thousands of bodies and leagues of wall could they be hidden? Should he slip free of the otataral he might know in an instant – but so too would the Lady become aware of him. And he'd seen too much of the cruel insanity that resulted from her touch to risk that.

At the door to Bars' quarters the Chosen ordered the crossbow be pressed against Corlo's head, then banged the pommel of his sword to the boards. No one answered.

After a time the Chosen motioned for Corlo to speak. 'It's me, Corlo. They're here to move you.'

Nothing from the other side. The Chosen unlatched the bar that crossed the door, lowered it, and stepped back. The door swung open, pushed from within.

Corlo stared, appalled. His commander's hair hung in a ropy unwashed tangle. His eyes glared beneath, red-rimmed and bleary. A grey beard added decades to his appearance, not to mention the stained and torn linen shirt hanging loose. He held an earthenware jug in one fist. This he threw over a shoulder to fall somewhere with a crash. 'Off to winter quarters, are we?'

The crossbow rammed its warning hard against the back of Corlo's head. Corlo raised his hands. 'Take it easy, Commander. Just a short walk.'

Weaving, Bars waved his reassurances. 'Yes, yes. A nice ocean view for me, hey?'

The Chosen pointed the way with his naked blade.

The entire march up to the main walk of the wall Corlo wrestled with the decision whether to tell or not. *He'd seen Halfpeck! How many more survivors might there be? Yet how much of a favour would the news be?*

They walked a stretch of the main marshalling pavement, the top of the wall proper, just behind the raised walkways of the outer machicolations. Corlo felt the waves pounding up through his boots and icy drops burned his cheeks. Pennants hung heavy and stiff, already sheathed in frozen spray. Soldiers from all parts of the subcontinent came and went: Jourilan, Dourkan, Styggian, and others. These were honoured veterans, but not true Korelri Chosen of the Stormguard. Those could be seen up on the walls. Every twenty paces stood an erect figure wrapped in its deep-blue cloak, tall silver-chased spear held upright, facing the sea.

The Chosen assigned to lead their party directed them along the curve of the curtain wall to the nearby tower, the Tower of Stars, the main garrison of this section of the Stormwall.

As they entered its narrow stone passages and stairways, again Corlo was stricken. Should he tell? Opportunities were rapidly dwindling. Soon they would reach Bars' holding cell. Indeed, it was not long before the Chosen called a halt and unlatched an iron-bound door.

Bars stood eyeing the man, a crooked, almost fey grin on his lips. Corlo's breath caught. *Gods, no – don't do it!* The Chosen stepped away, gestured him in with his blade. Bars' glacier-blue eyes shifted to Corlo and the mage winced to see seething rage, yes, and a bright fevered tinge of madness, but no despair. No flat resignation. He made his decision then.

Bars entered and the door was pushed shut behind him.

Corlo would wait for despair.

* * *

As he and Captain Peles rode through Unta's yawning north gate, Rillish had to admit that the capital's rebuilding was coming along well. One had to give this new Emperor his due. In the wake of the emergencies and chaos of the Insurrection – as it had come to be known – the plenipotentiary authorities the man so generously granted himself had allowed him to brush aside any resistance to his plans. He probably now had more personal authority than the old Emperor ever did.

And the capital's old attitude of arrogant superiority was, if anything, even greater now. Captain Peles and he at the van of their troop had to press their way forward through an indifferent – even dismissive – mass of foot traffic and general cartage. It was an experience of the capital new to Rillish, who most recently had been a member of the Wickan delegation to the throne. Then, he had travelled with an honour guard of the Clans. Then, much scowling and moustache-brushing from his escort had met the harsh stares and glowers of the citizens. The veterans assigned as his bodyguard had savoured it. But Rillish had been disheartened. Was there to be no accord between these mistrusting neighbours?

Now, he couldn't even urge aside a runny-nosed youth yanking a bow-legged donkey. He hunched forward to rest his leather and bronze vambraces on the pommel of his saddle and cast an ironic glance to Captain Peles. The woman held her helm under one arm, her long snow-white hair pulled back in a single tight braid. Sweat shone on her neck and she was scanning the crowd, her pale eyes narrowed. A large silver earring caught Rillish's eye, a wolf, rampant, paws outstretched, loping, tongue lolling. He recalled the twin silver wolfheads, jaws interlocking, that was the clip of her weapon belt.

'You are an adherent of the Wolves of War, Captain?'

Her head snapped around, startled, then she smiled shyly. 'Yes, sir. "The Wolves of Winter", we name them. I am sworn.'

Rillish waved aside a bundle of scented sticks a spice hawker thrust at him. 'Sworn, Captain?'

The smile faltered and the woman looked away. 'Our local faith.'

Much more there, of course – but any business of his?

'Fist Rillish?' a voice called from the press. 'Rillish Jal Keth?'

He scanned the crowd, caught a face upturned, arm raised, straining. 'Yes?'

It was a young woman, a servant. She offered a folded slip of paper. 'For you, sir.'

'My thanks.' He opened the missive and found himself confronting runes – the written glyphs of the Wickan tongue. *Dear Mowri spare him!* Hours spent cracking his skull over these as a member of the Wickan delegation returned to him. He frowned over the symbols.

Come. Su.

Ah. One did not refuse the imperative form issued by the shaman Su. Especially when that elder was so respected – or feared – that she ordered about the most potent and famed Wickan witch and warlock, the twins Nil and Nether, as if they were her own children. A relationship not too far from the truth, Rillish mused, in a culture that named all elders 'father' and 'mother'.

And that message conveyed in a manner assuring secrecy as well. He imagined no one else in the entire Imperial capital, other than a Wickan, could parse their runes. He tucked the slip into his glove, regarded Captain Peles. 'We part ways here, Captain. I have an errand.'

She frowned, disapproving.

A worrier this one, always earnest.

'My orders . . .'

'Were to convey me to the capital. You have done so. Now I have business to attend to.'

A cool inclination of the head: 'Very good, Fist.'

Rillish reined his mount aside. *Not happy, this one, that I should wander off on my own. Perhaps to some tryst . . .* He stopped, turned back on his saddle. 'Captain, perhaps you would like to accompany me. Have an officer lead the troop to the garrison.'

The woman saluted, the surprise and confusion obvious on her broad open face.

Always wrong-foot them – keeps them on their toes.

Rillish led the captain to the east quarter of the city, a rich estate district. Just last year during the days of the Insurrection the mercenary army the Crimson Guard, an old enemy of the Empire, had attempted to destroy the capital by blowing up the Imperial arsenal. The firestorms that arose after that great blast had raged for days through several of the great family holdings: D'Arl, Isuneth, Harad 'Ul, Paran, and his own, Jal Keth. The devastation had been so widespread because, frankly, the general populace had not been particularly motivated to help out.

And so we reap what we sow.

He hooked a leg around the high pommel of his saddle, easing into a Wickan sitting style – though with a twinge as an old wound cramped his thigh. 'My family is from here, you know, Captain.'

'Is that so, Fist.'

'Yes.' *Not too loquacious this one, either.* 'And what of you? Where are your people from?'

The broad jaws clenched, bunching. Then, reluctantly, 'A land west of the region you name Seven Cities. A mountainous land of steep coasts.'

'And does this land have a name?'

The woman actually appeared to blush. *Or was it the heat beneath all that armour?* 'Perish, Fist.'

Perish? Don't know it – though, somehow familiar. 'Not an Imperial holding, then.'

Now a confident, amused smile curled the lips, almost wolfish.

'No. And I would counsel against the Empire ever making the attempt.'

'It seems we may get along well after all, Captain. The Wickans feel the same way – Imperial claims to the contrary.' Rillish pulled up before the remains of a fire-eaten gateway. 'And here we are.'

The woman wrinkled her nose at the lingering stink of old fire damage. 'Are you sure, sir?'

Two figures straightened from the waist-tall weeds choking the gateway: two old veteran Wickans. One was missing an arm, the other an eye. Both offered Rillish savage grins and waved him in. He urged his mount up the bricked approach.

'They seemed to know you well, sir,' Peles noted.

'We shared a long difficult ride once.'

Ahead, the fire-gutted stone walls of a manor house loomed in the deepening afternoon light. Already vines had climbed some galleries. In his mind's eye Rillish saw those empty gaping windows glowing lantern-lit, carriages arriving up this very approach bearing guests for evening fêtes. He could almost hear the clack of wooden swords in the countless wars he and his cousins had fought through these once manicured grounds. He shook his head to clear it of all the old echoes. Now weeds tangled the blackened brick. Fountains stood silent, the water scummed. Outbuildings, guesthouses, stables, stood as empty stone hulks. And in the midst of it all, smoke rising from cook fires, like conquerors amid the ruins, lay an encampment of Wickan yurts.

Rillish swung a leg over his saddle to slide easily down. The captain struggled with her mount, which seemed disgusted by her inexperience and just as determined to let her know it. Wickan youths ran up to yank its bit. 'What is this?' she asked, amazed.

'Welcome to the Wickan delegation. This estate is now the property of the throne. I suggested that perhaps they could be housed here.' *Not that anyone else would take them*. 'Wan ma Su?' he asked a girl.

She pointed. 'Othre.'

'This way, Captain.' He led Peles across the grounds to the base of a towering ironwood tree, the only survivor of the firestorm that had raged through the district. The Wickan Elder and shaman, Su, seemed to live here, tucked in amid its exposed roots. The giant had been a favourite of his youth, though its limbs stood too tall for climbing. Rillish wondered whether the tree owed its continuing survival to her presence, or, judging from the woman's extraordinary age, perhaps it was the other way round.

In either case he found the old woman's gaze as sharp as ever, following their approach with a hawk-like measure. 'And who is this great giant of a woman?' she demanded, displaying all her usual tact.

But Rillish only smiled. He remembered achieving certain difficult clauses in the Wickan treaty of alliance merely by bringing Su into the chambers – how Mallick squirmed under her gaze! Whereas the Emperor still made his skin crawl. 'Su, may I introduce Captain Peles of Perish.'

Su cocked her head, her black eyes sharpening even further. 'Perish, you say? Interesting . . . Come here, child.'

Rillish wondered whether Su had ever heard of Perish; the woman had an annoying way of acting as if her every utterance or act was pregnant with meaning. Yet he'd learned to keep his doubts to himself as any questioning earned a terrifying tongue-lashing. And Peles, to her credit, knelt obediently.

'Yes,' Su murmured, peering up at the woman. 'I see the wolves running in your eyes. Whatever you do, Peleshar Arkoveneth, you must not abandon hope. Hold to it! Do not give in to despair.' She waved the captain off. 'That is my warning for you. Now go.' Peles straightened, bowing. She appeared, if anything, even more pale than before. Those sharp eyes now dug into Rillish. 'And what of you? How many children have you now?'

'Another on the way.'

The old shaman sniffed. 'Very well. At least you are good for something still.'

'You have some news then? Or did you ask me here just for the pleasantries?'

A crooked finger rose. 'Careful, friend of my people. You remind me of a fellow I know from Li Heng. My patience is not boundless. You are off for Korel, that tortured land. Here is my warning. You Malazans go to fight a war in the name of the Emperor, but you go to fight the wrong war. Swords *cannot* win this war. Though the Empire sends many swords, perhaps even the most potent of all its swords, peace can never be brought to that land through force of arms. As the Sixth has discovered to its own shamed failure.'

She gestured to one side, snapping her fingers. 'I have arranged to have attached to your command this woman as cadre mage . . .'

A figure emerged from a nearby yurt, a woman, middle-aged, thick-waisted, her hair a mousy brown tangle. 'This is Devaleth. She is of Korel. From Fist, actually.'

Rillish was surprised. 'A Korel mage? How can we possibly—'

'Trust her? Rillish Jal Keth! As an Untan noble who negotiated a treaty for the Wickans I am disappointed in you. No, we have spoken long and she is concerned, Rillish. Concerned for her people and for her land. She will not betray you.'

He offered the woman a guarded nod.

'So this is the fellow,' the woman said to Su, her accent thick.

'Yes. The best that could be arranged. Time was short, after all.'

Rillish glanced between them. 'Now wait a moment . . .'

'He has been apprised?'

'Yes. To the extent that he is capable of understanding.'

'Su!' Rillish looked to Peles to find the woman hiding a grin behind her hand. He gave the Wickan shaman a curt nod and turned away. 'It would seem I am outnumbered.'

'A prudent withdrawal, sir?' Peles offered, following.

'Indeed, Captain. Indeed.'

At Imperial Command, Rillish's honorary Fist rank could not even win him an audience with the secretary to the High Fist D'Ebbin. Instead, a clerk lieutenant studied the packet of orders supplied by Captain Peles and pursed his lips in disbelief. 'You should have been through here weeks ago.'

Already Rillish's teeth ached from clenching them. 'That's *Fist*, Lieutenant.'

'Yes, *Fist*.' The lieutenant's stress made it clear that such a commonplace rank could not possibly impress anyone here at Command. He flipped shut the leather satchel and held it out. 'Report to the West Tower.'

'The Tower of Dust? Hasn't that been given over to the mage cadre?' The clerk's tired look told Rillish that he had just been demoted to village idiot. He took the packet from the man's limp hand.

'The tower is—'

'I know the way, *Lieutenant*.'

Rillish turned to Captain Peles, who had been standing a discreet distance off, helm under her arm.

'It seems I am for the West Tower.'

Peles saluted, her bright blue eyes puzzled. 'You are not to accompany us? We embark with the tide. We and some last elements are to catch up with the fleet.'

'It looks as though they have something else in mind for me.'

Peles bowed, accepting the capriciousness of orders. Rillish answered the bow. Very much at ease with the chain of command, this one, he reflected.

Rillish had not even passed through the main entrance to the West Tower when his papers elicited shocked disbelief from the officious-looking woman challenging all comers. 'You're late,' she accused. Knowing the army, Rillish didn't bother pointing out that he had only accepted the reactivation a few days ago.

'This way.' Her tone allowed no doubt just how much trouble his existence was causing her.

She led him down a circular stairway. Rillish had never before been within the Tower of Dust, or beneath the old palace, and the sensation troubled him. *Yet this is my birth city. Is it the taint of the old Emperor that seems to hang over these dusty passages?*

They entered a round chamber floored by set stones. Rillish noted graven wards and symbols in silver encircling the floor's circumference. Black gritty dust lay in heaps kicked aside here and there. Within waited two nondescript cadre mages, a man and a woman, their robes discoloured by the dust. Also waiting was the Fistian mage, Devaleth.

Rillish bowed to the woman. 'Why did you not mention . . .'

'I didn't know myself,' she ground out. Clearly she was even more put out than Rillish; her pale round face glistened with sweat even in this cool air, and her hands were clamped to her sides. 'I have a horror of this,' she hissed.

'Of what?'

'Warren travel.'

Now Rillish understood and he felt his mouth crook up in dry irony. 'I have no fond memories of it myself.'

The two cadre mages clapped their hands and motioned them aside. Facing one another, they began tracing an intricate series of gestures and motions. While Rillish watched, the space between them darkened. Streaks of grey appeared behind each gesture, as if the mages were painting or slashing the air. Presently, the slashes broadened, thickened, and connected. A great gust of warm dusty air burst into the chamber. Rillish, blinking, hand raised before his face, saw a ragged gap opening on to a dark lifeless plain.

The two mages stepped within. One impatiently beckoned Rillish and Devaleth to follow. He gingerly stepped through. Almost immediately a gust of air pushed him forward. He peered round to find the four of them all alone in the midst of an ugly landscape of ash and gritty dead soil.

The two mages headed off without comment. Rillish let Devaleth go ahead. 'Where are we?' he asked.

'The Imperial Warren,' the male cadre mage called back over his shoulder, disgusted.

Devaleth barked a cutting laugh. The man glared, but said nothing. Presently he turned away, shoulders hunched.

'Pray, what amuses?' Rillish asked as they walked along. The sandals of the mages and his own riding boots raised small clouds of dust that hung lifeless in the heavy air.

'The *Imperial* Warren?' the woman sneered. 'What arrogance. So may the fleas of a dog name the dog the Fleas' Dog.'

The mage's shoulders flinched even higher.

'You say we are trespassers here?'

Clearing her throat of the dust, the woman spat. 'Less than that. Cockroaches invading the abandoned house of a lost god. Maggots wiggling across a corpse and claiming it as theirs . . .'

'I get the idea,' Rillish offered, turning away to clear his own throat of the itching dust. *Gods, what pleasant companionship. This was to be his cadre mage?* 'So, you are of Fist?'

'Yes. From Mare.'

Rillish eyed her anew. Mare! A sea-witch of Mare, adept of Ruse! What could possibly have turned her against her own people? 'I am a veteran of the invasion, you know.'

'Yes. Su told me.'

'And . . . if I may be so indelicate . . .'

The woman eyed him sidelong. 'Why am I here now with you Malazans?'

'Yes.'

She shrugged her rounded shoulders. 'Travel broadens the mind, my Fist.'

Rillish was about to prod for further clarification but she was staring off into the distance, her mouth tight. He decided to wait, thereby granting the time for her to work through what appeared a natural – and to him understandable – reluctance to speak.

'Having all you know or have ever been taught overturned as a deep pit of lies is a humbling experience,' she eventually said, still staring away. 'It is no wonder no one is allowed to travel from our homelands.' The thick lips turned upwards in a humourless smile. 'We were told it was because ours was the happiest and richest of all lands, and that anyone leaving would return to corrupt it with inferior ideologies and ways.' She eyed the dull leaden sky, pensive. 'And I suppose that is true – at least the half of it.'

'I see.' The woman's views agreed with what little intelligence Rillish had gathered from interviewing natives of the archipelago. He hoped he could count on her. She would be an invaluable asset. Though she would not last long once exposed as a traitor. She would be marked for death, just as Greymane was for his heresies against their local cult.

He glanced to her as she walked along: head down as if studying the dust, hands clasped at her back.

She knows this far better than I.

Arrival was an anticlimax, even after the dull monotonous walk. The cadre mages merely re-enacted their ritual then curtly waved them through. *No doubt in a hurry themselves to quit this unnerving, enervating realm.* They stepped into an empty stone-flagged room, torchlit, disconcertingly similar to the one they'd just left. Rillish's perplexity was eased by the entrance of an unfamiliar Malazan cadre mage, this one a cadaverous old man.

'Welcome to Kartool, sir,' the fellow wheezed. 'The fleet is assembling. You are just in time.'

'My thanks.' *Kartool. Vile place. Never did like it.* 'By any chance, would you know who is commanding the force?'

The old mage blinked his rheumy eyes, surprised. 'Why, yes, Fist. Have you not heard? It is all the talk.'

Rillish waited for the man to continue, then cleared his throat. 'Yes? Who?'

'Why, the Emperor has pardoned the old High Fist, Greymane. Reinstated him. Is that not amazing news?'

Rillish was stunned, but he forgot his shock at the grunt of surprise and alarm from Devaleth. The woman had gone white and staggered as if about to faint. Despite his own reeling amazement – his old commander! *Whom he had turned his back on!* – Rillish caught the woman's arm, steadying her.

Devaleth shook him off. 'My apologies. It is one thing to join the enemy. But it is quite another to find oneself serving under a man condemned as the greatest fiend of the age. The Betrayer, they named him, the Korelri. The Great Betrayer.'

Betrayer? Gods! Wouldn't the man regard him, Rillish, as just that? Didn't they know at Command? No. They couldn't have, could they? How the Twins must be helpless with laughter. For was it not his own silence that damned him now?

A mad laugh almost burst from him then as he contemplated the utter ruin he had prepared for himself.

* * *

No sooner did one of Bakune's clerks appear at the door of his office to hurriedly announce, 'Karien'el, Captain of the Watch,' than the man himself entered and closed the door gently, but firmly, behind him.

Bakune sat staring, quill upraised, his surprise painfully obvious. Recovering, the Assessor returned the quill to the inkwell and opened his mouth to invite the man to sit, but the Watch captain thumped down heavily before Bakune could speak.

Clamping his mouth shut, Bakune nodded a neutral greeting, which the newcomer ignored, peering about the office, studying the many shelves groaning beneath their burdens of scrolls and heaped files.

'Might I offer some Styggian wine?' Bakune suggested, motioning to a side table.

'No.' The man still hadn't glanced at him. 'Have anything stronger?'

'No.'

'Pity.' The small hard eyes swung to Bakune. 'How long have we known each other, Assessor?'

Oh dear, very *bad news*. 'A long time, Captain.'

Karien'el nodded, his neck bulging. Studying the man, it occurred to Bakune that all those intervening years had not been good to him. He'd put on weight, was unshaven, and generally looked unhealthy, with red-shot narrowed eyes, grey teeth, and a pasty complexion. *Drank far too much as well.* He, on the other hand, was wasting away with his thinning hair, constant stomach pains, and stiffening of the joints.

'What can I do for you?'

An amused snort followed by a one-eyed calculating gaze. 'Ever wonder why you've been here at Banith all this time . . . not one promotion while so many others went on from Homdo or Thol to the capital?'

Bakune pushed himself back from his desk. 'I suppose I'm just not one to curry favour or agitate for consideration.'

'Obviously.'

Bakune could not keep his irritation from tightening his face. 'What is it you want, Captain?'

'And your wife left you, didn't she?'

'*Captain!* I consider this interview finished. Please leave.'

But the man did not move; he just sat there, his wide blunt hands tucked into his belt at his stomach. He cocked his head aside as if evaluating the effects of his comments. Bakune had a flash of insight that raised the hair on his neck: *just as he must when interrogating a suspect.*

Swallowing, Bakune steadied his voice to ask, cautiously, 'What is this about?'

A satisfied nod from the captain. 'Truth be told, Assessor, I really shouldn't be here at all. I'm here as a favour because of all the years we've worked together. It's about your investigation.'

'And which investigation would that be?'

The man cocked his gaze to the locked cabinet.

Dizzied, Bakune felt the blood draining from his face. 'Your men have searched my office.'

An indifferent shrug from the captain. 'Just doing my job.'

'Your *job* is to enforce the law.'

The unshaven, pale moon face moved from side to side. 'No, Assessor. Here is where you have failed to question far enough. I enforce the will of those who decide what is the law.'

So, there it was. The brutal truth of power. Was this why I failed to question further? A selective self-serving blindness? An inability, or a reluctance, to admit to this unflattering truth behind everything I stood for, or believed in? Or was it simply the everyday pedestrian distaste of peeling back the mask and revealing the ugliness behind?

'In any case,' Karien'el said, 'we have our suspect.'

'You do?'

A slow firm nod. 'Oh yes. We've had our eye on him for some time now. A foreigner, and a priest of one of those degenerate foreign gods as well.'

Bakune pressed his hands to his cluttered desk. 'And how long has the man been in the city?'

Again the man hunched his shoulders in an uncaring shrug. 'A few years now.'

Bakune did not have to say that the killings went back decades.

Sighing, Karien'el straightened, pushed himself to his feet. 'So, Assessor. You need not continue your investigation. We have our man. As soon as he makes a mistake we'll bring him in.'

Meaning when the next body surfaces you'll arrest him, trot out a few paid witnesses, then execute the man before anyone can pause to think.

And it occurred to Bakune that for that execution to be enacted he would have to draw up and sign the papers. *My name will be the authority behind this execution.*

Bakune hardly noticed Karien'el bow and leave the office, quietly shutting the door behind him. He sat unmoving, staring into the now empty space above the chair, silent.

And if I refuse? Who would write my name into that blank?

Would Karien?

Yes, he would.

But he does not have the authority.

Bakune rose, went to the tiny glass-paned window of his office, stared out at the pebbled rippling view of the Banith rooftops to the tall spires and gables of the Cloister beyond. But there was one other in the city who did.

You, dear Abbot. And you have sent your message by way of Karien. It seems that perhaps I have *questioned enough. Come close enough for you to finally act.*

The Assessor's gaze shifted to the tall locked cabinet and a cold dread coiled in his stomach – that all too familiar pain sank its teeth into his middle. He crossed to the cabinet, the sturdiest piece of furniture in his office, and examined its doors. Unmarred, as far as he could tell. He drew the key from the set at his waist, pushed it in and gave it two turns.

He swung the doors open and stared within.

Swirling dust. Torn scraps. Empty shelves.

Failure.

A decades-long career of sifted evidence, signed statements, maps, birth certificates, and so many – too many – certificates of death. Affidavits, registries, and witnessed accounts.

Gone. All gone.

Bakune fell back into his chair. He hugged himself as the pain in his stomach doubled him over, retching and dry-heaving.

He wiped his mouth, leaving a smear of blood down his sleeve.

Damn them. Damn everyone. Damn the Abbot and his damned precious damned Lady.

* * *

The soldier was most definitely dead. Limp, looking boneless on the deck of the *Lasana*, he – and most definitely a *he*, being naked and such – had died a most ugly and agonizing death.

'Take a good look, soldiers of the 4th!' Captain Betteries shouted.

Not that he had to shout. Suth noted how the fish-pale corpse dumped on the decking silenced the constant chatter more surely than any sergeant's bellow.

'This soldier chose to desert . . . a crime punishable by death.'

The soldiers of 4th Company craned their necks, peering round their companions. Betteries, hailing from the archipelago region of Falar, shook his head disgusted, scowling behind his rust-red goatee and moustache.

'But the real mistake this soldier made was trying to desert here and now on the island of Kartool.' Suth, and everyone else on board, glanced towards the beckoning, oh-so-near, treed and shaded shore of Kartool. 'Terrible mistake! And why?'

'The spiders,' everyone repeated on cue, halfheartedly.

'That's right, boys and girls. The yellow-banded paralt spiders to be exact. You've been repeatedly warned! The island's overrun with them. Look how the poison attacks the nerves and muscles. I'm told the unbearable agony alone can kill.'

The man's face *was* hideously contorted; so much so it was painful just to look at it. Suth didn't think anyone could even recognize the fellow. And his limbs were twisted as if someone had broken the joints.

'. . . look at the crotch and neck where the nodes of your clear humours are gathered. They have swollen and burst . . .'

Suth's gaze skittered away from the crotch where – yes – the flesh was horribly mangled by exploded pustules.

'. . . poor fellow. I almost feel sorry for the bugger. Better a clean sword-thrust, yes? Anyone care for a closer look?'

No one volunteered. Captain Betteries ordered the corpse be left lying on the boards. In less than one ship's bell under the glaring sun its stink drove everyone to the stern decking behind the mast. Lard,

Suth knew, was on punishment detail for the day. That detail would have to dispose of the body and scour the deck come sundown. Suth could only shake his head; the fool might mutiny.

Grisly though it was, opinion on board the *Lasana* was that the company captain's display had been the highlight of the month, a welcome relief from the cloying boredom of weeks of confinement waiting like prisoners on board a flotilla of assembled hulks. Shore leave came in rotation once every five days and then strictly within the grounds of the Imperial garrison in Kartool city. And that was a full day of close-order drilling that left everyone wrung out like wet leather.

Other than more drilling and cleaning details on board the crowded ships, there was little else to do but engage in the soldier's favourite pastime of out-strategizing Command. Suth was crouched on his haunches next to the ship's side with his squadmates Dim, Len, Keri, Yana, Pyke and Wess. The two squad saboteurs, Len and Keri, had a line over the side; Dim could sit content to stare at nothing all day; Yana was inspecting her armour; Wess was apparently asleep; and Pyke was holding forth as he usually did.

'Gonna get us all killed, the officers running this circus.'

Dim roused himself to shade his eyes. 'Why's that?'

The squad corporal gave the big Bloorian recruit a sneer of lazy contempt. 'Don't got us any squad mages, do we? Or healers or priests worth the name.'

'Maybe they're aware of that,' Yana drawled without looking up from rubbing the rust from the mail of one sleeve.

A spasm of irritation twisted the man's face and he glared down from the duffels and crates he reclined on. 'Then maybe they should do something about it!'

'Maybe they have – why should they tell you?' she said distractedly, and scoured the mail with a handful of sand she kept in a pouch.

Pyke just made a face; he narrowed his gaze on Len, who was peering out over the gunwale, line in hand. 'And what about you, Len? Still think we're headed for Korel?'

'It's a good bet,' the saboteur answered, his voice hushed, as if a fish were close to his bait of old rotting leather.

'Ha! A pail of shit, that's what that is! Korel! Might as well jump over the side with a stone tied round your neck right now. Save the

Marese the trouble of doing it for you later. You lot are fools. No one's gotten through that blockade.'

'Some have,' Len answered, still hushed.

Pyke again pulled a mocking face and this time his gaze settled on Suth. 'What about you, Dal Hon? What's your name again? Sooth? Hello? You speak Talian?'

A number of responses occurred to Suth as he crouched, testing his balance against the motions of the ship, and alternately tensing one arm, then the other. The traditional jamya dagger sheathed at his side thrown into the man's neck was one. But murdering a fellow soldier – no matter how irritating – would get in the way of his testing himself against whichever enemy they were to face. And so he exhaled, easing the muscles of his shoulders, and said without looking up: 'There is much running of vomit and faeces on board this ship. Please stop adding to it.'

Pyke, a native of Tali, just gaped a moment, uncomprehending. Then Dim chortled, having sorted his way through the comment, and the corporal leapt from the piled equipment, drawing a fighting knife from the rear of his belt. 'Ignorant Dal Hon! I'll teach you respect.'

Suth straightened as well. His curved jamya blade slipped easily from its oiled ironwood sheath. 'Your constant chatter bores me.'

'Give them room!' Yana bellowed, straightening and using her armour to push back the crowd.

Word spread like an alarm through the hundreds of men and women gathered on the deck and they jostled for a view, climbing the piled crates and bales and lining the upper decking. So far no one had managed to force his or her way through to put a stop to the confrontation.

Pyke made a show of pointing the straight blade. His dark eyes were wide with a silky love of violence. 'Talk? How 'bout if I cut your tongue out?'

Suth just bent his knees, arms spread. So far Pyke had squirmed out of every drill, ducked any practice, and shirked all work details. But he was a tall fellow, solidly built, a veteran of combat. And he gave every appearance of being experienced in killing – but so was Suth. This sort of one-on-one challenge was his specialty; he'd grown up practising it with his friends – and rivals – every day. What was new to him was all this Malazan organized soldiering.

'Put them away!' a new voice bellowed.

Suth edged sideways. Sergeant Goss had pushed his way into the cleared circle. Since the corporal gave no indication of complying, Suth chose not to as well. Goss pointed to Pyke. 'Do I have to say that twice?'

Scowling, Pyke straightened, let his arms fall. 'This *recruit* needs a lesson, sergeant.'

'Knifing him won't give it.' Goss turned on Suth. 'Put that away, trooper.'

Suth complied.

Goss raised his chin to the some three hundred infantry crowded on deck. 'I know tempers are short. I know we're all jammed in here like sheep with nothing to do. But the waiting's near done. Remember, discipline is what will keep you alive! And . . .' here the burly man lowered his voice, 'on board ship naval punishment is the rule. And believe me . . . you don't want to be whipped by the barbs of the daemon fish. You'll wish you were dead. That's all. Fall out.'

As the crowd turned away the sergeant motioned his squad to him. 'Pyke,' he said, his voice even softer, 'you are hereby stripped of rank—'

'*What!*'

Goss merely watched the taller man, his eyes almost lazy in their nests of wrinkles. He cocked his head ever so slightly. Pyke hunched, grumbling under his breath, '. . . better off on my own . . .'

'Yana—'

'No.'

'No?'

'I'm not going to mother these apes.'

Goss grunted his understanding. 'Len, you have it.'

'Many thanks,' the older saboteur answered, sounding far from pleased.

'That's all.' Suth and the others saluted; Pyke merely flicked his hand as he turned away.

After a lunch of fish, hot grain porridge, and fruit fresh from the island, Suth sought out Len. At least, he reflected, these Malazans were making sure they ate well before being thrust into whatever in the Abyss awaited them . . .

He found that the saboteur had returned to his fishing. 'Catch anything?'

'Nothing edible. All the fish off the coast of this D'rek-damned island are poisonous – just like the spiders.'

'What do you know of the sergeant?'

'Goss?'

'Yes. Everyone's wary of him. We're more crowded here on board this ship than a herd of thanu at a river crossing. I have to fight my way to get anywhere. I've watched him walk the deck here – everyone gets out of his way.'

Len turned to face him, set his elbows on the gunwale. Gulls and other seabirds swooped and dived over the waves between the anchored troop transports, squabbling over the trash and leavings cast overboard. Though it was nearing winter the sun's heat prickled Suth's back and chest. Growing up he'd rarely worn any sort of shirting; now Malazan military standardization had him and everyone in thick long-sleeved jerkins of wool, felt, leather or layered linen – the undergarments of their heavy armour.

'Goss, hey?' the old saboteur repeated thoughtfully, and he rubbed the crushed and uneven left side of his throat and jaw responsible for his hoarseness. 'All I know is talk. Rumour. You know how it is. All kinds of stories get bandied about but no one really knows anything. Anyway, he's served all his life and now he's pushing fifty. Thing is, he's new to the regulars. So, question is . . . what outfit was he with all that time?' The man offered Suth a wink. 'Some think maybe the Claw.'

The Claw. Imperial assassins. Trained slayers. These soldiers spoke of them with awe and fear. For his part Suth yearned to test himself against one. He nodded his understanding. 'That saboteur lieutenant, Urfa. She called him "Hunter".'

'That's right. The old hands, that's their code for a Claw.'

Suth scanned the crowded deck; amidships room had been cleared for close-order drills and shield work. A detail was checking for rot in the sails of the three-masted vessel.

Len yawned expansively. 'But it's all talk. No one knows for sure. And he's not saying.'

Across the way Suth caught Pyke watching. The man pointed as if still gripping his blade, and smiled a promise. Suth just looked away; it was his experience that those who made the most show and bluster were the least dangerous.

'Listen,' Len tapped him on the chest and raised his chin in the direction Suth was staring, 'don't worry about Pyke. He would've ridden you until you broke. Now he knows he can't.'

Too bad. I've been too long without practice. 'And the little mean-looking one, Faro?'

'Faro?' Len waved his disgust. 'Faugh! The man's wanted for murder in more cities and provinces than I can name. He just loves to pick fights and knife people. You stay out of his way.'

'Yet he listens to Goss.'

'Yeah . . . strange, that.' And the saboteur offered a sly sidelong glance before returning to his fishing.

That night their squad had the last watch. Pyke didn't even report. Wess showed up but promptly lay down among the piled equipment and went back to sleep. Lard was still on punishment detail for brawling. Suth had arrived on deck to find Len already fishing; best time of day for it, the saboteur had whispered hoarsely. That left him, Keri, Yana and Dim. Faro, of course, was nowhere to be seen. Suth didn't mind standing alongside Keri and Yana, both veterans. But Dim – well, it wasn't his fault, but the man was just painfully *dim*.

The water with its moods was alien to him, growing up as he had on the plains of Dal Hon. There, one's ears were as important as one's eyes – more so of course in the night. Dawn came differently as well, a distant flame-orange glow gathering across the sea's clouded east and a diffuse bluish light all around. The bay was calm, as was the slate-grey expanse of Reacher's Ocean beyond. A mild wind brought the surge of the heavier surf out beyond the bay. Cordage shifting and the planking of the ship's hull creaking sounded unnaturally loud in the stillness. From another of the anchored vessels five bells rang.

Suth stopped his slow pacing to face east. The wind brought something else. Another noise rose and fell behind it. He cocked his head to one side, listening. A distant call? Horns? At sea?

'Did you hear that?' Keri had come to his side, whispering.

'Something . . . There!' Far out in the open waters a ship nosed into view beyond the bay's headland. One far larger than any of the cargo vessels and coastal raiders Suth had seen so far. While he and Keri watched, another slid into view, identical in silhouette, three banks of oars flashing in the sunrise. And another.

'Moranth Blue warships.' Len now stood with them. 'See the towers on the forecastles?'

Suth nodded, eyes slitted. Horns brayed all around, the assembled fleet welcoming the newcomers.

'Our escort.'

Suth turned to Len. 'How so?'

'Built for naval warfare only, those ships. Not raiders. Not transports. Deepwater only. Hood, they draw too much even to enter a harbour.' The old saboteur spat over the side. 'No question where we're headed.' Suth, Keri, Dim and Yana now all studied the saboteur. 'A naval battle such as hasn't been seen since the crushing of the Falar fleets. The Empire never forgets a thing. It finally means to respond to these Marese defeats. So it's Korel.'

Yana and Keri were clearly shaken. Suth's reaction was merely relief. It was good that the waiting was finally over.

That morning the troop vessels were unnaturally quiet as the recruits and veterans of the 4th lined the sides, watching the fleet assemble. Even Wess found the interest, or the energy, to rouse himself from the folds of his cloak to join the crowd at the gunwale. Suth was surprised to see that the man was far older and more grizzled than he'd thought, and he wondered just how many campaigns the veteran had slept through.

Len pointed out Falar vessels, sleek and swift; broad Seven Cities galleys; and three-masted Quon men-of-war. But the Moranth Blue warships held everyone's interest. They lumbered over all like the tusked behemoths of Suth's native Dal Hon savannah. Armoured towers at the bows rose some three storeys tall.

Through the day, as their transports manoeuvred to join the convoy, talk turned to their presumed destination. Many still held out hope for Genabackis; perhaps a new southern front cutting across to join Black Coral. But Len just shook his head. The old saboteur gathered a great many dark looks, as if his broaching Korel had doomed them all to it.

'What about these Korelri Chosen, the Stormguard?' Yana asked Len as they sat in the shade of a reefed sail.

The veteran frowned. 'I haven't faced them, but they say they're the best soldiers out there, man for man.'

Yana looked affronted. 'Then it's up to us women – as usual.'

Keri nodded her fierce support. But Len raised a hand. 'I mean among them. They say there're damn few women in their ranks, for some reason or 'nother.'

Pyke had been listening, clearly unimpressed. 'I hear these Genabackan Seguleh are far more dangerous.'

'The Seguleh aren't soldiers,' Len answered. He eyed the man directly. 'Never forget that. If it came to war with them – we'd win.'

Pyke laughed, waved Len's claim aside like nonsense.

'The Korelri fight only one enemy,' Wess announced from under the folds of his cloak, surprising everyone.

Suth took a bite of fruit fresh from shore and watched Len nod his assent. 'True enough. You face a wall o' water thirty feet high comin' at you every winter and that breeds some discipline. It's the other soldiers we'll face, the Dourkan, Roolian and Jourilan. They fight because they know the Korelri are right there behind them and they won't yield. They never yield. They can't.'

'If we even reach them,' added the disembodied voice of Wess.

Len just pursed his lips, obviously displeased by Wess' comment. Looking troubled, Yana said nothing as well. Suth searched their faces; there was something here. Something he was missing.

It was Pyke who broke the silence. Laughing, he pointed at Suth. 'Dumbass Dal Hon! Better learn to swim before we get there. 'Cause none of you are even going to see the shore. No Malazan ship has reached Korelri in over twenty years.'

'Shut the Hood up, Pyke,' Len snarled. But he didn't deny the man's claim. No one did.

* * *

The snow was slashing almost diagonal in the chill wind streaming over the forward crenellations of the Stormwall here next to the Tower of Stars. Lord Protector Hiam watched the fat flakes stick like ash to his cloak. They glowed against the dark blue weave then melted with an almost audible hiss. Below, the heavy waves coming in from the strait heaved sullenly against the base of the wall. Their scum of slush and ice grated like the massed teeth of a thousand demons of the deep. *Which was a poetic image not too far from the truth, if a touch overused by all the singers and bards.* The numbness in his fingertips told Hiam what this weather presaged. The season of storms was upon them. From this evening onward the iron braziers and torchpoles all along the curtain walls and watchtowers would stay lit day and night against the arrival of the enemy, the alien wave-borne demon Riders.

But not their only *enemy.*

They were coming. The mindless expansionists from the north. Hiam stamped the iron heel of his spear to the stone flagging and continued his informal tour of the wall. Word had come from the Roolian priesthood of the Lady: a marshalling of all troops, the nation lumbering to a war footing. Columns marching east to the Skolati frontier. And word from their agents among the Mare ports: all available vessels being stocked and readied. *What could these invaders possibly want here in this – and it had to be said – rather impoverished and frankly out-of-the-way region?*

As Chosen officers and regular soldiers appeared out of the driven snow before the Lord Protector each hastily saluted, spear crossing chest. Hiam answered, offering a reassuring word, or a chiding joke where his instincts told him it would not be taken ill. *Could the priests have been right all along? They said there was only one thing here in these lands that could attract any foreign power: the faith of the Blessed Lady. That these Malazans had come to crush the true religion.*

It seemed inconceivable. But why else come? He could think of no other explanation. Surely these Malazans had lands enough all over the world. All that blood and treasure expended. And for what? One measly island the inhabitants of which were so self-centred, so self-deluded, that they actually named their island a continent?

A great dark knot of men and equipment loomed ahead through the blizzard. Though it was morning, clouds as low and thick as smoke lent the day the twilight pall of evening. Next to a wall-mounted giant crossbow scorpion, a work crew stood gathered, blowing on hands and stamping feet and peering out over the lip of the most outward machicolations. The cart of a movable winch rested with them, rope extending out and down.

Hiam waited while word of his presence spread through nudges and glances. Their blue jupons over leathers marked them as sworn apprentice engineers, not a compulsory work crew. They saluted, arm across chest. Hiam acknowledged then indicated the rope. 'Fishing for Riders already?'

Grins all around. 'It's Master Stimins, sir,' one answered. 'We've been checking repairs all up and down the wall these last days.'

Hiam peered over the edge; the rope disappeared into bottomless swirling white. 'Rather late in the season . . .'

Another salute. 'Yes, sir. 'Tis.'

Hiam set a wry grin at his lips. 'Our Master Stimins is afraid of nothing, hey? He'd push aside the Riders themselves to inspect a crack, yes?'

A few chuckles of appreciation answered, all of which Hiam thought a touch forced. He motioned to the winch. 'Let him know he has to come up.'

'Aye, sir.'

Hiam set his gaze northward into the churning slate grey where sky and sea melded into one brooding curtain. What could be so pressing? The time for repairs had long passed . . . though, Lady knew, they never had enough. Each summer it seemed all they could manage was to shore up the worst of the damage, let alone begin a course of rebuilding. His thoughts touched upon, but refused to pursue, the logical consequences of years of such makeshift repair: degradation, decay. Creeping structural weakness—

The clatter of the winch's iron teeth interrupted the Lord Protector's reverie. He watched the rope as it played in. It continued for some time. By all the false infernal gods, that was a *lot* of yardage. Was the man testing the water? The fool! Didn't he know advance scouts had sometimes been spotted this early?

One particularly ugly snarl in the rope caught Hiam's eye. Was that a *splice*? The man was trusting his life to a spliced rope? He could only shake his head. For all the man's many faults, a lack of courage was not one.

Eventually a great yelling and spluttering reached them from below the machicolations. 'I said I'm not done yet, you damned whoresons! Listen to me! Would you – oh, just help me up!'

A hand in fingerless gloves appeared, scrabbled at the stone ledge. The crew leaned over the edge to drag the man up. 'Lady damn you all!' he snarled, straightening, and pushing them away. He was shuddering with cold. 'I'll let *you* know—' He caught sight of Hiam, clamped shut his lips.

'A word please, Master Engineer.'

Mouth still set, the old man fumbled with the buckles of his harness. His hands were too numb and an apprentice untied them for him. He shouldered himself out of the leather strapping. 'Take the winch to th' fourteenth tower,' he told the crew. 'Wai' for me there.'

The crew began packing the equipment. Hiam motioned for Stimins to follow him aside. When they were a distance off he asked: 'Why are you still carrying out inspections, Toral? You've got that crew wondering.'

The old man was kneading and blowing on his hands. A shudder took his spider-like frame. Behind his grey beard his lips were blue. He was looking off into the distance, his mind clearly elsewhere. 'We're just behind, tha's all.'

'We're behind every year. That's no excuse. You're checking something. What is it?'

'Just . . . some old research.'

'Does it have to do with what we spoke of . . .' Hiam stepped closer, lowered his voice despite the moan of surf and wind. 'The degradation?'

The Master Engineer was staring off into the middle distance once more, his lined face almost wistful. 'Yes . . . That is, no. It bears upon it.'

Hiam fought down the urge to take hold of the man. What had so shaken him? 'What is it? Tell me. I order you to tell me.'

But Stimins just glanced over, studying him, his rheumy eyes swimming, and then his lips twisted up into a grotesque attempt at a reassuring smile. Hiam was shocked to see in that expression the same face he turned to his own subordinates when they asked about undermanned patrols and empty seats at the messes. 'Do not worry, sir,' the old man said. 'You've enough to concern yourself with.'

And he walked away to disappear into the driving snow, leaving Hiam alone to stare into that churning white that seemed to be consuming the wall while he spun on his own small island of stone and all he could think was . . . the fourteenth tower. Ice Tower. The lowest point in all the leagues of Stormwall.

CHAPTER IV

It is said that the Priestess came alone out of the icy fastness of the Southern Emptiness, wearing only rags, her feet bare, leaving behind a path of blood. Yet all whom she met, priest and lay alike, bowed to the fire of her gaze. It has also been said that with the wave of a hand she flattened a Jourilan keep outside Pon-Ruo where the local priest of Our Lady the Saviour denounced her. This last rumour is not true. For she demands nothing, not even recognition; asks not a thing of anyone. All who would follow her must do so of their own volition. And do not be deluded. They do so. In their scores.

Prison Writings
Dust Ebbed, apostate
Dourkan

On a rocky shore just east of the city of Ebon the camp fires of the city's outcasts and destitute flicker like the myriad lights of that great fortress and urban sprawl itself. At one such driftwood fire sit two old men and three old women, the women layered in threadbare shawls and skirts, the men in old finery, much patched and frayed.

One of the women rocked and sang tunelessly under her breath as she knitted. She cast a sly glance aside from beneath her ropy grey hair. 'I see you there, Carfin,' she crooned. 'No sneaking up on ol' Nebras!'

A shadow detached itself from the surrounding gloom, straightened long and tall. 'I was not sneaking,' a voice answered, as deep and slow as the surf licking almost to the fire's edge. 'I merely walk quietly.' This fellow emerged from the night as a tall narrow-limbed man in dark shirt and trousers, both a patchwork of mending. He sat far back from the fire.

'We are six,' the second woman announced, and she jerked back a quick drink from a silver flask that then disappeared into her shawl.

'We are indeed, Sister Gosh . . .' one of the men answered, standing. He raised his gaze to the night sky, a hand going to his patchy goatee. Nebras rolled her eyes; the other man hung his head. 'The stars are in alignment to allow our convening. The Goddess Below waits yet, breath held. Master of Chains searches without success. We, the High and Mighty Synod of Stygg Theurgists, Witches and Warlocks—'

'Such as we are . . .' muttered Nebras, not pausing in her knitting.

'—are hereby come to order. Totsin Jurth the Third presiding as senior member. Now, first item of business. Sister Gosh, will you bless our assemblage?'

The silver flask disappeared once again into the shawl. Sister Gosh sat straighter, rearranged the folds of her layered wraps. She raised one crooked finger and squinted an eye. 'Let's see. Yes. May the Lady not track us down or sniff us out. May she not catch us in her grasping hands to stuff us down her greedy throat. May she not suck the marrow from our bones, nor boil our blood in the heat of her eternal hunger until our eyeballs pop and our tongues burst aflame.' She eyed Totsin. 'How was that?'

Totsin's grey brows had risen quite high. 'Well . . . yes. Thank you, Sister Gosh. Quite adequate, if rather visceral.' He cleared his throat. 'Now, second order of business. Absent members. What news of Sister Prentall?'

'Caught by the witch-hunters and delivered to the Lady,' announced the third woman.

'Ah.' Totsin glared at Sister Gosh, who mouthed *I didn't know!* 'Thank you, Sister Esa. Any other news? What of Brother Blackleg?'

'Dead,' said the other man, now staring deep into the fire, his chin in his hands.

'Ah. Not . . . the Lady . . . ?'

'No. His liver.'

'Ah. I'd thought him indestructible.'

'As did he, obviously,' the man observed laconically.

Totsin nodded, wiped his hands on his greasy trousers. 'Very well.

Sad news. We are diminished greatly. Yet night turns inexorably, and winter comes. We needs must consider the future and what is to be our course of action given the proliferation of signs and portents confronting us . . .' Nebras had drawn up her shawls tightly and raised a hand. Totsin blinked at her. 'Ah, yes . . . Sister Nebras?'

'As you say, Totsin. The wanderings of the Holds wait for no one – like the tide. And it is strangely high this night. Let us be on our way then.'

'But . . . we have yet to decide . . .'

'Very good, Totsin,' cut in Sister Gosh. 'I vote we decide. Carfin?'

The lanky man far from the fire pushed back his hanging black hair, clasped his frayed jerkin. 'I abstain.'

'Abstain?' Sister Gosh snapped. 'You came all this way just to abstain? Why didn't you just stay in your mouldy cave?'

'It is not a cave – it is a subterranean domicile.'

'Perhaps we could—' began Totsin.

'And you're an obtuse ingrate.'

'Hag.'

'Eunuch.'

'If we could just—'

'Actually, eunuch isn't the technically correct word—'

'I see something!' the fellow staring into the fire announced.

Sister Gosh sat up, as did Totsin. Even Carfin drew closer. 'What is it, Jool?' Sister Esa whispered.

The man thrust out a clawed hand. 'The tiles!'

Sister Nebras drew a pouch from her quilts, upended it into the man's hand. He slashed his other hand through the fire, casting burning embers aside to reveal the steaming sands beneath. 'Fire, Night, Earth, Light, Seas, Life, Death. All are gathered now for this coming season at the Stormwall.' Jool cast the tiles across the steaming sands. 'I see conflagration.'

'Well . . . it is a fire,' Totsin whispered to Carfin.

A glare from Sister Nebras silenced him.

Jool studied the spread of the small wood and ivory tablets. 'All paths lead to destruction now. There is no escape for anyone. This season will see the grasp of the Lady tightened beyond all release. Or shattered beyond repair.'

'Who opposes?' Sister Esa hissed.

The man reached down to gingerly pluck one tile from the sprawl. He held it up to the light of the remnant embers and examined it, puzzled. 'Where is this one from?' he asked Sister Nebras.

She set it in her palm. Everyone crowded close. 'It's the oldest of all my dearies,' Sister Nebras said, breathless. Her brows rose in wonder. 'And yet my most recently gained.'

'Bloodwood,' Carfin observed.

'Inscribed with a House,' said Totsin.

'The House of Death,' Sister Nebras said, hushed.

'It's from Jakatakan,' said Jool, certain.

Sister Esa let out a small yelp. 'Jakatakan! Then . . . it's *them*.'

Sister Gosh straightened, nodding. She took a fortifying nip from her flask and sucked her teeth. All waited, tense, while she gathered herself. 'Jakatakan. Ancient isle. The mythical island beyond the Riders.' She addressed the others. 'But not so mythical, yes?'

'Until *they* came,' breathed Sister Esa.

'And what name did they come bearing?' Sister Gosh demanded.

'The name of the Island of the House of Death,' said Totsin.

'*Malaz*,' said Carfin, facing outward to the night.

'They are coming,' affirmed Sister Gosh. 'All contend now. The Lady. The Stormriders. The Invaders. And whosoever shall prevail this season, this land shall see their grip so tightened, their power so increased, that never shall we escape.'

Totsin pulled at his beard. 'Yet what of *their* domination? Foreigners . . .'

'We are all foreigners here,' Sister Nebras sneered.

Jool drew a surprised breath. 'Bloodwood . . .'

'Of course!' Sister Esa answered. 'The Elders. The First. They never capitulated.'

'*Blood*,' Carfin droned into the night, morose. 'I like it not.'

Sister Nebras crouched to gather up the tiles. 'So the time for flight and hiding is past. We must join our hands on to this casting. *Aya!*'

Jool knelt. 'What is it?'

The old woman held up a gnarled hand, joints swollen and crooked. 'Did you not see this one?' Cradled in her palm was a tile that glimmered mother-of-pearl, carved from shell. On it was inscribed a stylized warrior armed with a long spear.

Jool examined it yet dared not reach out. 'The tile of the Riders hidden there, deep within the heart of the fire.'

'And yet even now deathly cold to my touch.'

The two locked gazes, saying no more. Sister Nebras drew an awed breath. 'The Riders. The Lady and the Invaders shall bleed each other dry and *they* will finally prevail.'

'The casting is . . . suggestive,' Jool allowed.

'Perhaps we should reconsider—' Totsin began.

'No,' Sister Nebras said. 'I've had my fill of her *protection*.'

'Enough talk,' Sister Esa agreed, adding, 'she is always listening.'

With that the six separated, five walking off separately in different directions. The one remaining stared silently off into the night for a time. He kicked through the sands of the reading then drew himself up stiffly. All alone, he adjusted his tattered cuffs and smoothed his goatee. 'Very good,' he announced. 'Very good. We are decided then. By my authority as senior member this assembly is adjourned.'

* * *

'Biggest damned dogs I have ever seen . . .' breathed Jheval, clearing his throat and spitting.

He and Kiska were hunched down in a narrow crevasse that split a rock face. Though the two Hounds of Shadow had withdrawn, Kiska glimpsed the occasional blur of dun brown and shaggy tan. *Ye gods, what monsters these guardians of the Shadow Realm!* Even more terrifying now than when she'd seen them in her youth. She still heard the occasional skitter of kicked stones, and sometimes she could feel the growls of the great beasts vibrating the stone against her back. Even when the silence lengthened she was not fooled. She knew they were still out there, waiting. *Canny beasts*. Sucking in great breaths, she lowered her head between her knees to fight the gathering darkness of utter exhaustion. She held her side. That had been close. So close, she had the impression that the hounds had been playing with them, allowing them the illusion of escape. It was only chance they'd come across this tiny retreat. *But they hadn't really escaped at all, had they? Only delayed the inevitable.*

At least she was with someone who could keep his head. Even while she watched, Jheval took one sip from his water skin, just enough to wet his mouth. He knew how to survive in a desert – even if this really wasn't a desert. A different kind of one, she supposed. A desert of eternity.

'How long do we have?' he asked, undoing his headscarf.

'You mean – how long can we last?'

He used the scarf to rub his short sweat-soaked hair. 'Yes, I suppose.'

'Good question . . . This is Shadow. From what I've overheard it may be that in principle we have for ever. We will be slow to hunger and thirst. Eventually, I suppose one of us will be driven mad by our position and the other will be forced to kill that one . . .'

'Or vice versa.'

She blinked at the man, then nodded her appreciation of the point. 'Exactly so – by that time, who could say?'

He leaned his head back, staring up at the vault of the narrowing roof. 'So, a waiting game.' He offered her a sideways grin. 'Luckily, I'm especially good at those.' He edged himself down into a more comfortable position, giving every impression of a man completely at ease. 'I have all the time in the world. What of you?'

Kiska considered the question. Could she definitively argue that time was of the essence? No one could know. Yet prudence would dictate that she not delay. 'Unfortunately, I cannot say the same.'

A shrug. 'Well then. Let us hope conditions change. As for myself – I care not.'

'Truly? You really couldn't care either way?'

'No.' He was tossing small stones out on to the cracked dirt before the opening. Kiska's first reaction was irritation, but now she saw the reasoning behind the seemingly insignificant tic, and smiled. *Teasing. The man was actually teasing them.* And perhaps, eventually, they would tire of investigating these constant false alarms, and would come to ignore them. *Then . . .*

'When I . . . *left* . . . Seven Cities,' he began, musing, 'I was with a woman. We had much in common. I thought that I'd finally met a woman I could come to think of as a partner.' He let out a long breath, a wistful sigh. 'But . . . she too couldn't believe that the future held no fascination for me. It interested her, though. Greatly. *She* had ambitions. I, apparently, did *not.* And so we parted ways, and there was much shouting and many broken pots. An ugly domestic scene – the sort I swore never to find myself involved in.' He looked over, his dark eyes narrow in what she imagined must be a habitual squint. 'What of you?'

Kiska stretched her arms up over her head. She leaned her head back to stare at the dark crack above. 'You asked of the Claw. Well . . . have you ever joined something because you thought it was a shining perfect example of what could be right in the world? Only, in time, to discover that it was just as corrupt and petty and, frankly, as stupid as everywhere else?' She glanced over to catch him eyeing her with a strange intensity. He lowered his gaze. 'So it was with the Claw. I was very young when I joined. I'd grown up sheltered – and a touch spoiled. Like anyone, I suppose.'

She shifted to find a more comfortable seat on the rock, began kneading her side. 'I knew nothing. But then, that is the definition of being young, yes? So how can you possibly fault anyone for it? In any case, I began to see and hear around me how promotions went to those from certain families, or to those who knew certain people in the organization. The success and advance of incompetents is a universal mystery, yes? Some would say it is because those above prefer subordinates who do not threaten them. I do not agree. I would say such reasoning only reveals that person's *own* preferences. Myself, I would want only the most skilled and accomplished around me – how else might one be more assured of success?'

'Not everyone feels that way,' Jheval muttered darkly, his gaze inward.

'No,' Kiska agreed. 'So I found it to be in the Claw. I came to see that many were only concerned with their own advancement and avoiding responsibility for mistakes, and I saw how this directly threatened the lives of those below and around them. Including myself. And so I walked away rather than be a casualty of someone's self-seeking.'

She glanced over and was startled to see the man studying her once more. He became aware of her regard and quickly looked away.

'We haven't heard anything for a time, have we?' he asked. 'Perhaps they've given up.' And he smiled, knowing full well the answer.

'And what of you?' Kiska asked.

Jheval kept his gaze lowered, his eyes averted. After a long pause he murmured, 'Another time, perhaps.' A rather awkward silence followed that, into which Jheval clapped his hands and rose to his feet, bent over. 'Right. Let's have a look then.'

'Don't be a fool.'

He gave her a mad grin. 'Have to test the waters occasionally, don't we?'

'Don't—'

But he'd jumped out, rolling, and stood, knees bent. 'Hey, y'shaggy lapdogs! Where are you?'

The answer came with stunning swiftness. A great dun mountain of muscled hide and flashing teeth pounced exactly where Jheval stood – or would have been standing had he not launched himself backwards to land scrambling and kicking his way back into their narrow hole. Kiska helped yank him in while a great blow struck shards of rock from the fissure and the enraged snarling was an avalanche. Jheval lay on top of her, gasping. He sent her a grin over his shoulder. 'Your turn next time,' he said, and rolled off.

Kiska just shook her head. *The lunatic! He was actually enjoying himself! Still, that grin – so damned boyish.*

* * *

Every jolt of the narrow launch sent lightning flashes of pain across Rillish's sight. Wincing, he squeezed his brow while the eighteen-marine crew rowed him and Devaleth across the intervening sea to Admiral Nok's flagship, the *Star of Unta*. He'd been drinking far too much Kartoolian spirit these last few days while trying to make sense out of this new posting.

Greymane, reinstated. Who would have thought it possible? He'd heard that the man's own troops had tried to kill him; that Korelri assassins had cut his heart out; that he'd fled condemned by Malazan High Command. Now he was back after having served for a time in the ranks of the Empire's most enduring enemy, the mercenary Crimson Guard. Mallick Rel obviously cared nothing for the man's record under prior rulers – which dovetailed nicely with Rillish's own evaluation of the Emperor: there was someone who cared nothing for old accepted ways, who would do whatever it took to win. Perhaps Mallick saw something of that quality in Greymane. Who knew? With the grim overcast dawn of this day he'd thrown the last empty bottle out of the window and come to the final conclusion that the best he could hope for was that the man would fail to remember him.

That would be the absolute best possibility. Otherwise . . . gods, how could he bear to face him?

Devaleth sat across the bows, utterly at ease in the pitching craft; she was, after all, a mage of Ruse, the Warren of Sea-magics. She sent him a narrowed glance, not supportive – nor, thank Burn, pitying – but watchful, coolly evaluating. She knew there was something between him and their High Fist, but either it was not her way to push herself forward, or she simply did not care the least. And, after all, she was in no hurry to meet the man herself, damned as a walking anathema in her own land.

In the end, it was that seeming indifference that brought Rillish to wave her to him. He rested a hand on the gunwale, steadying himself against the rough seas while the marines struggled to make headway. Devaleth merely crouched before him, somehow able to adjust to each pitch and roll. Cold spray splashed his arm and the shock further cleared his head.

'It was my second command,' he said, holding his voice low. At least here, unlike on board any crowded troopship, he could be assured of the necessary secrecy. 'I was part of a contingent of reinforcements. Mare war galleys caught us short of Fist. Hardly a fifth of us made it to shore.' He shuddered at the memory: the icy waters; the cries of the drowning. His words did not do justice to the hopelessness of seeing one's command shattered before one's eyes. 'We were folded into the Sixth. Soon after, as a noble, I was called in to bear witness to the judgement of Governor Hemel and the court martial against Greymane.' He could not stop his throat from tightening at the memory. 'I was new, a mere lieutenant. I knew procedures had been rushed. Testimony was thin, if not fabricated. But I also knew the campaign had fallen apart and that Command was looking for someone to hang it on. I chose not to interfere.' He glanced up and found her eyes hard and dark and fully on him, studying him rather mercilessly, and he looked away. 'So that is it. That one time I put my career first. And now, it would seem, I'm to pay for it.'

Her gaze slid aside, to where the tall masts of the *Star* could be glimpsed beyond the rise and fall of the steel-blue crests and troughs. The wind dashed her unkempt hair. 'You were young and new to the situation – perhaps that's precisely why you were chosen. In any case, we shall see what sort of man this Greymane is by how he acts. I will watch – but remember I can be of little use. I am, after all, a traitor.'

As, it seems, am I.

The cabin was warm with the breath and presence of too many bodies in too small a space. He and Devaleth were the last to arrive. Nok, whom Rillish had never met, made the introductions; Rillish's counterpart, Fist Khemet Shul of the Eighth Army, his bald scarred head resembling a lead sling bullet. The man gave a guarded nod. The Moranth Blue commander, Swirl. His armoured plates shone with the deep blue of open ocean. Kyle, a dark moustached youth resembling a Wickan warrior, though much broader and longer-limbed, who was Greymane's adjunct. And the High Fist himself, who – thought Rillish – had watched him all this time with a brooding cold gleam in his eyes.

'High Fist,' Rillish said, bowing.

The man ignored him to study Devaleth. 'You are most welcome, mage. As you know, we are short of cadre.'

'With reason, High Fist. The, ah . . . *influence* . . . of the Blessed Lady will render them useless.'

'But not you, nor your fellows?' Nok put in, and he smiled behind his moustache to reassure her that this was no cross-examination.

'No, Admiral. We in Mare have turned our eyes to the sea, and the mysteries of Ruse. Which, I imagine, brings us to the matter before us.'

The Admiral inclined his head. 'Indeed.' He turned to a small table and a map drawn on vellum. With one long pale finger he sketched the line of advance. 'We anticipate contact in three weeks' time, off the coast near Gost—'

'Forgive me,' Devaleth interrupted, 'but you will be lucky to reach Falt.'

Nok's snowy white brows rose, but it was the Moranth Blue commander Swirl who spoke: 'You are so certain?'

All eyes shifted to Devaleth; Rillish felt like a spectator at his own briefing. The heavy-set woman was in no way intimidated by the weight of both Greymane's and Nok's regard and Rillish wondered whether it was because they were currently in the woman's element.

She merely shrugged her rounded shoulders. 'The moment your bows turned south, the murmur of those waves reached Mare. Even as we speak their warships are setting out as quickly as they can be readied. The goal will be to reach you as far north as possible.'

The High Fist and the Admiral exchanged glances. 'Thank you, Devaleth,' said Greymane. 'You have been most forthcoming.'

'We can anticipate, then, some sort of massing of forces, north of Fist?' Nok asked.

Another shrug. 'As best can be managed . . . yes.'

Nok smoothed his moustache. 'I see. Thank you. Now, Fist Rillish, I have read your debriefing from when you returned from Korel, but I wonder if you might enlighten everyone as to conditions on Fist when you were sent out.'

Rillish acknowledged the request, but he was puzzled. 'That was nearly ten years ago, Admiral. Surely you have more recent intelligence?'

'Nothing reliable. Rumours, hearsay. No eyewitnesses, such as yourself.'

Ye gods. A decade of silence? What had been going on all this time? Rillish cleared his throat. 'Well, Admiral, High Fist. I was under Captain Jalass, 11th Company—'

Greymane grunted, causing Rillish to stop. As all eyes turned to him, the High Fist appeared embarrassed. He cleared his throat, rumbled, 'I remember her. *She* was a good officer.'

'Yes,' Rillish agreed, 'she was.' The High Fist's emphasis on that *she* shook him, but he continued: 'She stocked four Skolati traders and sent them out under my command. We were to await her off False Point just north of Aamil. We waited five days but she never appeared. On the fifth day I opened our orders and saw that our mission was to reach Malazan High Command and deliver a sealed packet of communications . . .' Rillish's gaze rose to the wooden ceiling beams and he took a steadying breath. 'Because the northern route was so perilous, I elected to set a course due east, hoping to rendezvous with a Genabackan contingent and to return via the secure Falar trade route . . .'

Devaleth spoke up, disbelieving. 'Am I to understand that you crossed the entire ocean, what we call the Bloodmare Ocean, in a Skolati tub?'

Rillish nodded.

The woman shook her head, appalled. 'God of the Waters . . . I thought *I* was a sailor.'

Nok raised a hand to speak. 'The report of the journey itself would make an amazing tale. Two vessels finally reached an island off the coast of Genabackis. There he landed for sweet water. Then, that night, the ship burst aflame and an attack by a band of black-masked children slaughtered a contingent of thirty marines in the time it took to draw breath . . .'

'The Seguleh,' Swirl grunted. 'You set foot on the island of the Seguleh . . .'

'So we discovered, yes. That was where we sighted land. We barely escaped.'

Swirl inclined his helmed head in salute. 'That you escaped at all is remarkable.'

'In the interests of time I must move ahead to that packet itself,' Nok continued. 'It was delivered. And its contents have remained one of the most closely guarded secrets of the Empire ever since. Laseen had me apprised. Possibly Dujek. But other than we few I do not know who else may be aware . . . Topper perhaps. Under the new Emperor's orders you are all to be briefed now.'

Across the cabin Greymane's gaze had narrowed and his thick

lips drew down in disapproval. It seemed obvious to Rillish that the High Fist must be wondering why he had not been briefed beforehand. Yet Nok must have his reasons: perhaps it was to engender a kind of cohesion. After all, they were heading for Korel, and history showed that any force sent there found itself completely on its own.

The Admiral took a steadying breath, pausing as if searching for the right words. 'In brief, within the orders and communiqués contained in the packet was evidence that Command of the Sixth had named itself Overlord of Fist – not in the name of the Empire, but in pursuit of its own ambitions. That it had thrown off all fidelity to the Empire and considered itself sovereign.' The Admiral's pale gaze went to Greymane. 'In short, High Fist, the Sixth has mutinied.'

Rillish felt gut-thrust. *Hood preserve them. It's official. Judgement has been levelled from the throne. The Sixth has gone too far.* And how far did the conspiracy go back? Had the governor, and the Fists, had this in mind all along? And Greymane! Was this why he was thrust aside? Rillish studied the man: his old commander. *What must he be feeling?*

The big man had drawn a shaky breath and closed his eyes. In the weak light of the cabin he appeared to have paled.

Devaleth spoke into the silence: 'This expedition . . . I take it then that it is less an invasion force . . .'

Nok nodded, his lips pursed. 'You are correct, mage. We are invading, yes. But we are doing so to bring the Sixth to heel.'

And so, Rillish compiled to himself, *we fight not only an entire subcontinent, Marese, Korelri, Theftian and Dourkan, but Malazans as well. Traitorous Malazans. Gods below – are we enough for even one of these enemies?*

* * *

Horses were few in the Korel subcontinent and so the Army of Reform walked. What dray animals had been gathered – oxen, mules, and a few cast-off half-dead horses – went to hauling the large high-sided wagons that were under construction day and night. 'For supplies,' Ivanr had been told when he'd asked about the non-stop building. He was dubious: who needed such sturdy wagons to haul materiel? But it was none of his business and so he returned to searching for word of the boy among the mass of camp-followers, craftspeople, cooks, butchers, metalsmiths and petty merchants.

A quiet lad. Head wound. Might not have spoken at all. Came

into camp a few days ago. On the fifth day a woman pulling a cart among the train of refugees got a thoughtful look in her eyes.

'May have seen him. What's he to you?'

'I brought him in. Who's he with? Do you know?'

'Who's he with?' The woman laughed. 'He's with all the lads and lasses with two arms what can walk. Taken into the ranks he was.'

'*Into the*— He's just a child.'

Her gaze slitted and she spat to one side. 'Tall as my Jenny he was, and as hale.' She eyed him again. 'Everyone must do their part. No place for layabouts . . . or cowards.'

Ivanr stopped walking alongside her. 'My thanks.'

She just snorted and continued on, back hunched, hands wrapped in the leads of the two-wheeled cart in which rattled her few remaining possessions. An infant sat in the rear, legs kicking, thumb in mouth. Ivanr headed for the van of this great snaking mass of humanity.

Army of Reform? What army? He could find no army here in the traditional definition of the word. A mob of displaced farmers and city refugees clinging together out of fear and being issued cumbersome pikes and spears was all he could see. It was suicide. The Jourilan cavalry would sweep them from the field.

And yet . . . he had to admit *some* order lay beneath surface appearances. Far down the valley squads of men and women could be glimpsed scavenging and scouting the route; he'd seen the rags they used to mark the best paths. Dust obscured the main body where the files of infantry marched amid the great swaying hulks that were the wagons. Infantry! If you could call them that: youths in nothing more than cloth gambesons, if as much. Their only weapon these tall unwieldy spears. Not a sword to be shared among them. And riding with her staff up and down the course of the march, Martal all in black: dark dusty hauberk, leggings, boots and gloves. Some had even taken to calling her the 'Black Queen'.

Martal . . . Ivanr wondered, seeing her ride past. Katakan, Beneth had said. He couldn't recall hearing of any such military commander out of Katakan. He headed for the training grounds: trampled fields of relatively level land downslope where squads of recruits were massed. *Stepping on each other's feet and jabbing each other with their pointy sticks.*

Looking back, he realized he was not alone. He was being followed by a Jourilan officer complete with a rounded iron helmet, a jack of boiled leather, and a thick green winter cloak. Ivanr stopped and waited to see what the fellow would do. The refugees filed by, some carrying great bundles of possessions; two barefoot children pulled an old man along by his rags.

Instead of stopping dead, or sidling guiltily past, as Ivanr expected, the man returned his glare with a ready smile, and saluted. 'Lieutenant Carr, at your service, sir.'

Ivanr sighed inwardly and continued on. '*My* service? You are just passing by, I should think . . .'

The man kept pace, hands at his belt. 'Respectfully, no, sir. I've been asked to escort you.'

'Escort me? Escort me where?'

'Why, wherever you should wish, sir.'

'Don't call me "sir".'

'I feel that I must, sir. Based upon your accomplishments.'

'Accomplishments?' Ivanr eyed the man sidelong. *Young.* 'What accomplishments? Bashing people with a piece of metal is no accomplishment.'

But the man was not nonplussed; he grinned, cocking his head. 'Well, if you put it that way . . .'

They passed behind a particularly long train of the tall wagons swaying like the great behemoths of the icefields to the south, and Ivanr waved the dust from his face, coughing. 'Gods all around us! Why is Beneth burdening himself with these monstrous contraptions? They must halve his rate of march.'

'For supplies, I understand,' Carr said, sounding as convinced as Ivanr. 'As to their speed . . . they are no slower than the refugee train.'

'I'd drop that lot as well.'

'Oh no, sir! They're why we're here.'

Ivanr now examined the officer directly. *Just a lad – barely into his shaving.* 'Sounds backwards to me.'

Carr clasped his hands behind his back. 'Traditionally speaking, I suppose so. But this is no traditional situation. At least, as far as these lands are concerned.'

Ivanr grunted and continued walking. Something in the lad's mannerisms made him ask: 'What were you doing before you joined?'

'I was a scholar. An acolyte priest.'

Ivanr grunted again; he'd thought so. 'And because you could write you were given a commission . . .'

'A commission in a nonexistent military organization – just so, sir. And, I must admit, my family name is known. But all of us here are fleeing, or seeking, something, yes? Myself, I was fleeing . . . dogmatic rigidity, let us say.' A self-deprecating shrug. 'The army formed itself out of the disaffected, the apostate, or plain refugees of the fighting. It exists to protect and escort *them*.'

'Escort them? Escort them where?'

'Why, to Blight, of course.'

'Blight? And what will happen when you get there, may I ask?'

'The gates will be thrown open and we shall be welcomed as liberators.'

Ivanr halted; Carr peered up at him in mild surprise, blinking. 'You are joking, I hope.'

The youth almost blushed and coughed into a fist to cover his reaction. 'Only partially. We have reason to believe that a great proportion of the population is sympathetic to our aims. And that our arrival will be all that is needed to ignite them.'

Ivanr continued on. *Fanatics. All of them. On both sides.* 'That may be so, Lieutenant. But when last I saw them the walls of Blight were tall. And I have the feeling that this army is not the only one on the move.'

He pushed through to the marching grounds where a knot of trainees – *gods, could they even be called that?* – milled into each other, their tall spears clattering. They squinted like befuddled children at a fellow red-faced from cursing them. Ivanr pulled a hand down his sweat-grimed face as if to wipe the vision from his sight. *Gods protect us all. This will not do. They ought to be given* some *chance.*

He cupped his hands to his mouth. 'Halt!'

A great banging of hafts as half the trainees stopped.

The red-faced fellow gaped, then gathered himself. 'Who in the name of the Lady of Lies are you?'

'Temporary replacement.' He jerked a thumb over his shoulder. 'Talk to the lieutenant here.'

From then on Ivanr kept his back to the man and addressed the gathered infantry. *Some hundred young lads and lasses, gap-toothed oldsters. The lad could be among them. Still, most are here because they want to be; not the impressed near-prisoners of the Imperial infantry. Well, first things first.* 'Who here knows his or her right hand?' he bellowed, taking full advantage of his great Thel lung capacity and presence.

A few right arms rose timorously.

'Very good! Some of you actually got that correct! Now, take that arm and extend it out straight from your shoulder – that's right, move over! I want an arm's length between everyone. Let's go.'

The majority of the crowd just stared back, uncomprehending.

He took a great breath and roared: '*Now!*'

A forest of rattling as everyone ran into everyone else.

Ivanr turned to the lieutenant, who quickly swapped his stifled laughter for a look of sombre attention. The red-faced would-be drillmaster was nowhere in evidence. 'Lieutenant Carr.'

'Sir?'

'I will have need of a drum, or some sort of drummer lad.'

'Aye, sir.'

* * *

The identity of the man strapped and immobilized on the table was irrelevant to Ussü. A serum distilled from oil of durhang rendered the subject insensate while, most important, in no way inhibiting the fleshly systems. The body may as well be that of a dog or a sheep. Indeed, he had begun his experimentation with such animals. But – as he had discovered – for his purposes the human essence provided by far the greatest efficacy. He rested a hand upon the naked chest, felt the pounding of the heart. Strong. Excellent. Not the usual sickened or starved prisoner. Perhaps this one will last long enough . . .

He nodded to his apprentices. One, Yurgen, made a last circuit of the tower chamber, checking the iron shutters, the barred iron door, then drew his sword and readied his shield. Such experimentation can summon the most alarming manifestations. Ussü once almost lost an arm to an entity that took possession of the corpse of a great boarhound. His two other apprentices, Temeth and Seel, stood at his elbows.

He extended a hand and Seel gave over a knife of keen knapped obsidian, the handle leather-wrapped. Ussü felt down along the ribs of the subject – yes, just between these – and made an incision up over the barrel of the torso, beginning at the side and ending at the sternum.

Before he came to Korel none of these elaborate preparations would have been necessary. Indeed, he would have been repulsed by the idea. One merely had to reach out and there would be the Warren at one's fingertips. Yet here he and all the other lesser Malazan practitioners had been rendered impotent. Some had been driven mad; others had killed themselves, directly or indirectly, through concoctions or drugs meant to facilitate access.

He held out the knife and Temeth took it away and another instrument was placed in his hand: a tool of wooden wedges and metal screws. Ussü eased the slim leading tips of the wooden wedges into the incision between the ribs. Seel daubed at the blood welling up.

'Gently here,' he warned the two, who nodded and leaned forward to peer more closely. He began working the screws, one by one. The wedges parted. Turn by turn, a hair's-breadth at a time, Ussü created a cavity at the body's side where the ribs curved.

He, however, had chosen a different path . . .

Power existed here in the Korelri subcontinent. The followers of the Lady had access. And the source of that potential, he had discovered, lay in . . . *sacrifice.*

When he judged the opening large enough he nodded and Seel took hold of the spacer. Leaning forward over the subject, almost hugging him, Ussü slipped his hand into the gap at the side. Gently, reverently almost, he eased inward, fingers straight. He felt his way around organs, slipped past ligaments, parted layers of fat, until the tips of his fingers brushed the vibrating, quivering, seat of life. With one last push he cradled the heart and with his other hand he reached out for his Warren.

Steady pressure on the heart brought to his summoning a tenuous ghost-image of Mockra. He eased his grip tighter; the heart laboured, pulsed in his fist like a terrified animal. He sought out a vision at the limits of the Warren's divinatory potential – *of prescience.*

Grant me a vision of what is to come!

And he saw – he saw . . . desolation. Shores scoured clean by a tidal wave invasion of the sea-borne demon Riders. The land poisoned, lifeless. Cities inundated, corpses lolling in the surf in numbers beyond comprehension.

Annihilation.

No! How could this be?

A mere hand's breadth from his face the eyes of the subject snapped open. The apprentices flinched away, yelping their terror. Yurgen charged forward.

'Halt!' Ussü returned the corpse's dead stare, for dead it was, the organ immobile in his hand. 'Greetings, Lady.'

A smile, the eyes rolling all white. 'I have tolerated your heresies, Ussü,' the corpse barely mouthed, 'because I sense in you a great potential. Set aside your disbelief. Cleave to the True Path.'

'They are coming, Blessed Lady. New Imperial forces are on their way. We must . . .' he wet his lips, 'join forces.'

'You have seen this? How strong you are, Ussü. Stand at my side.'

She knows nothing of our prisoner. She is not omniscient.

Again the dead smile. 'I allowed you Malazans to land because you brought a renewed vitality to the true faith. You have strengthened me in so many ways. There is nothing like a challenge to inspire and confirm a faith. And so I welcome you again.'

'Yet the true enemy awaits. What of the Riders?'

The lips twisted, snarling. 'I have no vision of them. *She* stymies me yet. That Queen bitch has ever stood in my way!' The body eased beneath Ussü, the fit seeming to pass. 'Kneel before me, Ussü. Embrace me as your Goddess.'

The corpse raised its head to whisper at his ear, intimately close: 'Let me touch *your* heart.'

Revolted, Ussü threw himself from the body. Yurgen swung, the blade passing through the neck to slam into the table. Ussü pushed aside Seel and Temeth to stand swaying, his heart hammering as if brushed by ghostly fingers. *Hood preserve them!* What were they dealing with here? He crossed to a washbasin and rubbed the gore from his arms. Temeth passed him a towel and he dried himself then rolled down his sleeves.

He eyed the three. 'A gag will be the order of the day, next time, Yurgen.'

All nodded, faces pale as snow.

* * *

They had been at sea for two weeks when Sergeant Goss came down to the jammed quarters below decks and crouched amid the hammocks. It was the beginning of their squad's sleeping shift and some were bedding down while others were watching games of troughs and dice. Len gestured the squad close. Suth was lying in his hammock and he folded an arm under his head. Wess was snoring above him.

'Guess you been hearing the rumours,' Goss said when most had gathered round.

'Which rumours? There's been nothin' but all this time,' Pyke said.

Suth agreed. There was a plague of rumours aboard: that they would yet strike east for Genabackis; that they were headed for

Stratem to pursue some mercenary company; that the expedition could not possibly succeed because the Empire had run out of cadre mages; that Greymane was commanding and he was bad luck; that the Emperor had struck a pact with the Stormriders; that Mare vessels had been sighted shadowing them and the sea would take them all. For his part Suth was unperturbed. To him this was just a particularly obvious example of how all talk was, in point of fact, useless.

'First, it's about Greymane. It's official. He has command.'

'Oponn's luck!' said Pyke. 'Where'd they dig him up? I heard the man was so incompetent his own officers got rid of him. We're better off without *him*.'

'That's not what I heard,' Len growled. 'The old veterans spoke well of him.'

'Nothing we can do about it,' Yana said from where she knelt, steadying herself on a hammock.

That observation struck Suth as extraordinarily wise and he nodded his sombre agreement.

'The other's about fighting alongside the Blues,' Goss went on.

'Yeah, we heard,' Pyke said. 'Some damn thing about volunteering to fight with them. Volunteer? What for? Not for damned honour 'n' glory or any damned shit like that, I hope.'

'Shut that anus you call a mouth,' Yana murmured – she had less and less time for the man as the days wore on.

Unperturbed, Goss raised and let fall his shoulders. 'There's some as see it that way. But, no. This is for places on the Blues' vessels that will lead the shore assault. So, you could say it's a chance for some loot.'

'Loot,' Pyke snorted, scornful. 'A gut full of iron more like.'

Fighting on land. To Suth that sounded preferable to fighting at sea. 'How are they choosing? Do you just ask?'

Goss nodded, accepting the question. He leaned aside, clearing his throat into his fist. 'Well, there's to be what you might call tryouts. Them Blues is mighty selective. They won't let just anybody on board.'

Lard looked up from juggling his dice. One eye was still black and his bald head still bruised from his last fit of brawling. 'What's that? Fighting?'

Pyke rolled his eyes. Goss rubbed the bristles at his cheeks, smiling. 'Yeah. 'Gainst the Blues themselves.'

Blowing out a breath, Lard sat back down. Pyke's laugh was a sneer. 'Hard lumps. And for what? A chance to get yourself killed? No, the rule is don't volunteer for nothin'.'

But Kyle leaned back to stare at the sweat-stained canvas hammock above. He'd been watching these armoured Moranth. Clearly worthy opponents. And he'd been too long without testing himself against anyone.

Far too long.

When the *Lasana*'s turn came and the volunteering squads were called to ready themselves for the next morning, the 17th was one of five named. Pyke was furious. Below decks he first pinned Lard: 'Was you, wasn't it? You Hood-damned fat fool.' Lard waved the man away. He turned on Dim next: 'Or you – dimwit?'

Dim just looked confused.

'Shut up,' said Yana from nearby. 'Look to your kit.'

'My kit? *My* kit! There's no way I'm turning out for this! No way. *You* lot are the fools.' And he stormed off.

'Good riddance,' Lard called after him, and aside, to Dim: 'Was it you?'

Dim blinked at the man. 'Was it me what?'

Lard caught Suth's eye and raised his glance to the timbers above. 'Never mind.'

Every soul on board the *Lasana* jammed the decks that morning. The sailors hung in the rigging, arms crossed under their chins. It was overcast, and a strong cold wind was blowing off the Strait of Storms. Two squads of Moranth Blue marines had come over by launch. The five Malazan squads had the stern deck to ready themselves while amidships was being cleared. The sergeants huddled together to draw lots to determine order. The 17th picked second. When Goss came back with the news Suth leaned close to his ear.

'Swap for last.'

Goss eyed him. 'What if they don't want no swap?'

'Tell them we need time, we're short, whatever you must.'

The sergeant grunted his agreement; you could say they *were* short. Faro, Pyke and Wess hadn't shown. And it was clear from their usual plain leather jerkins that Len and Keri weren't planning on fighting.

Yana joined them. She stood even taller and broader in her full shirt of thick padded scale, boots, broadsword at her wide leather belt, full helm under one arm. 'Minimum is five,' Goss said, as he rubbed his jaw and eyed the squads readying their arms. 'If we can't field five, we're out.'

'Where's Pyke?' Suth asked.

Goss' jaws clenched. 'Out. Says he fell down a companionway ladder. Twisted his knee.'

'Dead-weight useless shit,' Yana snarled. 'We don't need him. We have five with you anyway.'

'No sergeants. Just regulars.'

'Shit.'

'And Wess?' Suth asked.

'I think *he's* around here somewhere,' Yana answered.

'Dig him up – I'll see what I can swing.'

Suth searched the crowds nearby. When he returned Goss was back. The sun was warming the decking and the wind had picked up. The sailors were busy trimming the canvas to steady the ship. 'We're fourth,' Goss said.

'Good.'

The sergeant eyed him; he brushed his fingers over his greying bristles. 'You want to watch them fight . . .'

'And they'll be tired.'

Goss laughed. 'Don't count on that.' He watched Suth again, a small tight smile pulling at his lips. 'It was you, hey? Put our name in. I thought maybe Yana did it just to get Pyke's goat.'

'I'm bored.'

The sergeant leaned his elbows on the railing. 'Well, you won't be real soon.'

Suth motioned to the two squads of Moranth marines waiting amidships. The plates of their head-to-toe armour had taken on the iron-blue of the clouds, or were reflecting it. They were readying large oval shields and the weapons they'd brought: some sort of wooden shortswords. 'They're that good?'

'These could be among their best. Veterans of years of warfare. I've even heard it said that alone among the Genabackan peoples the Moranth will fight the Seguleh. And it's the Blues who meet them at sea. They're good all right.'

Dim pushed through the crowd, shepherding along a mussed and irritated-looking Wess. 'Here he is.'

'Where'd you find him?' Suth asked.

Dim's thick brows clenched in their usual expression of befuddlement. 'In a hammock, of course.'

Wess stuck his hands into his belt and lifted his chin amidships. 'What's all this?'

Goss shook his head in awed disbelief. 'Just get kitted up,' he said.

The 11th was first up. Everyone had to use the wooden weapons the Moranth provided. While they were no doubt dull-edged Suth imagined you could still easily maim someone with the vicious things. He, Yana, Lard and Dim watched; Wess lay down on his jack of banded armour and promptly went back to sleep, or pretended to. Len stood with Goss next to Suth. One of the Moranth squads squared off against the 11th's picked troopers, three male and three female heavy infantry. The captain of the *Lasana* ordered the start by giving the nod to a trumpeter.

It was over far more swiftly than Suth's worst fears. Not because of any weakness in the 11th. Rather, it was because of a terrible tactical choice: they decided to take the fight to the Moranth. When the trumpeter blew his blast the troopers charged.

Their rush was magnificent. A great shattering roar went up from the assembled men and women of the 4th Company and the *Lasana* seemed to shudder. Even Suth felt the hair on his neck rise and he mouthed his encouragement: *Yes! Get 'em!*

But they charged as individuals, shields unlocked. The Blues held easily and picked them off one by one. It was a brutal and efficient lesson in what a disciplined wall of shields can accomplish. Suth was especially sobered; less than six months ago that individual bellowing all-out attack would have been his. And he would have gone down just as swiftly. Having had the discipline of holding the line beaten into him, he now understood something neither he nor his brothers and sisters growing up on the Dal Honese plains could puzzle out. How was it that man for man, or woman for woman, no Kanese or Talian was a match for the Dal Hon warrior, yet years ago their tribal armies crashed like surf against the Malazan legion? How could that be? Poor generalship had been the judgement against the chieftains of their grandfather's time.

Now he knew better. For the warrior fights as one, while the soldier fights all as one. No single warrior, no matter how skilled, can defeat ten, or fifty. Or in this case, five. But he, Suth, could defeat two . . . if he could just count on his fellows to hold long enough. Yana and Lard would hold, he believed. But Dim – the big man was just too good-natured, nothing ever seemed to rouse him. While Wess . . . all the gods of the plains . . . how many campaigns had the man slept through?

The 6th was up next. No dash and thrust for them. Seven rectangular Malazan-issue heavy-infantry shields lined and locked. The Moranth squads traded out. The trumpeter loosed a blast. Two shieldwalls carefully edged towards one other across the decking. Shouting went up; running odds on the match – three to one against the 6th.

'A good lesson here,' said Len at Suth's side.

'A good many,' Suth answered absently, a finger brushing his lips, intent on the Blues' swordplay, the shields grating and sliding along each other.

'Including the hardest of all . . .' Puzzled, Suth glanced to the man, who lifted his chin to the other selected four from the squad. 'Trust.'

Suth almost snorted, dismissing the ridiculous claim, but caught himself. *Trust. Yes, he could see that . . . yes, he could trust Yana. But a useless fool like Wess, or Dim? How could he possibly trust them? That would take . . .* And his shoulders slumped. *Mocking gods . . . it would take trust.*

So. He was stuck with them. Was this the canny old saboteur's lesson? He caught the man's eye and nodded, then turned to his squadmates. *If I am stuck with them, then if I just complain or am sullen or resentful I am no better than Pyke. The obvious step, then, is if I want the squad to work, it is up to me to do everything I can to make it work.*

'I want an edge,' Lard demanded, his gaze fixed on the fight below. A groan sounded from all around as a trooper fell, screaming and clutching at his gut.

Suth considered. At least if Lard broke the centre wouldn't be compromised. He shrugged. 'Fine with me.'

Yana nodded.

'What about me?' asked Dim.

'Yana and I will flank you.'

The big man brightened like a child. 'That's great!'

Suth and Yana shared a look: either she or he would have the best chance of recovering when he went down.

'Wess!' Yana bellowed. 'You have one edge!'

A muted grumble answered her.

Soon after the first trooper fell the Malazan line disintegrated and the infantrymen lowered their arms as it was clear they'd been overborne. The Moranth disengaged and saluted.

The 20th was next. If the 4th Company had a heavy elite the 20th was the closest thing to it. The men and women were all veterans, none unblooded recruits. They formed up and waited, silent. The trumpet blew and they charged, taking everyone, including the Moranth, by utter surprise.

This was no disorganized rush. Shields remained locked and smashed as a line into the unprepared Blues. The Moranth fell back nearly to the ship's side. A roar erupted such as never before. Troopers of the 4th jumped up and down, buffeting one another; the sailors shook the rigging.

Even Goss managed a full smile and muttered, 'Nicely done.' But he added aside to Suth, 'They won't fall for that again.'

After some fierce swordplay the Blues righted themselves, leaning away from being pressed into the side. Step by step they began edging round to circle back to the mid-deck. Cannily, the 20th matched the sidelong shift of shieldwall to abut against the mainmast. Both squads chose to use the mainmast to anchor their flank and now the fight shifted to the opposite flank. Whoever could turn that would win.

Though the weapons were blunted wood, blood now flowed on to the decking. Suth winced at the thought of the force it would take to break skin. With a great heave the Blues turned the open flank, bringing down that trooper. Unlike the 6th, however, the 20th formed a square of four and grimly fought on. The men and women of the 4th Company, quietened by the turning of the flank, now gained their voices, shouting their encouragement.

But the engagement was long past any question; it was just a matter of time. The 20th shrank to a triangle of three, then the remaining two back to back, and finally the last cut down by thrusts from all sides.

'Well, we're up,' said Goss into the silence following that brutal demonstration. Sailors came out and wiped the decking. The Moranth squads changed out. Suth and his squad pushed their way down to the midships.

They broke through to the cleared decking and though Suth had faced uncounted duels and matches, he found his mouth dry, his heart racing. He saw Wess tuck a ball of something into his cheek. 'What's that?'

'Resin of d'bayang poppy, and kaff leaves. Deadens pain. Want some?'

Suth didn't bother hiding his distaste. 'Gods, no. I don't want to be doped.'

'You'll want some later. Believe me, we're in for some pain.'

Suth just grunted; he couldn't dispute that. He turned to the rest of the squad. 'If it looks like we're going to lose a flank, form square.'

Lard laughed at that. 'Yeah. A square of five. Ha!'

'Just do it.'

'Who made you—'

'Do it,' cut in Yana.

Lard subsided, looked to tightening his shield strap. Suth adjusted his helmet.

'Ready?' Ship's Captain Rafall called down.

Yana pulled on her tall full helm, clashed her wood sword against her broad infantry shield. 'Ready!'

The Blues squad readied their shields.

Five, Suth saw. One for one. And an idea came to him. 'Yana, Lard – concentrate on your man on the end. We'll take up the slack.'

'Two against one, aye,' Yana answered.

The trumpet blew.

There was no time for strategy after that. Suth could only focus on hammering his right, hoping to cover for Dim, who should be covering for Yana. He only hoped Wess wouldn't go down right away. The hardened tip of a wood shortsword jabbed for him like a viper. The Blue opposite bashed his shield like an anvil, hoping to overbear him. And he nearly succeeded, for this type of fighting was new to Suth. A great shout went up over the pounding of blood in his ears, the gasping breaths. He caught out of the corner of his eye the sight of Wess calmly and methodically edging aside the Blue's thrusting shortsword, his moves precise and efficient, almost lazy. *He's conserving his strength! Gods! To think he'd doubted the man.*

Dim, on his right, was too slow and awkward with his shield and was absorbing terrible punishment from the blunt-edged thrusts. But he didn't go down. *Too dumb to fall! It probably didn't even occur to the man as a possibility.* A starry hammer-blow to his head was Suth's last clear impression and chagrin came with the realization that it was *he* who had lost his focus.

An uncertain amount of time later his surroundings unblurred and stopped spinning. He was standing; someone had his arm. He shook his head. 'Okay . . . I'm okay.'

Goss's face appeared close, squinting into his. 'You took quite a shot.'

Suth touched a gloved hand to his forehead, hissed at the pain. The fingers came away wet with blood. 'What happened?'

'Lard and Yana teamed up. Took down two Blues.'

'So we won!'

'Naw. You lost. But you did better than most of the others. Congratulations.'

Troopers of the 4th came now, clapping him on the back and shoulders. Lard's coarse laugh sounded above everyone's voices. The Blues, Suth saw, were calmly readying for the next fight. All unharmed? And then, after this, off to the next ship and the next set of duels? By the Great Witch! It was inhuman.

He looked over and almost groaned: Wess was steadying him. Wess, of all people! The man let him go while giving him a sceptical eye, gauging his stability. 'Told you so,' he said, and spat out the ball of leaves and resin. Then he crossed his arms over his shield and leaned against it, apparently not even winded.

Oponn's laughter! It just went to show you never could tell.

The 2nd went last. They acquitted themselves well, forming square immediately and offering a stubborn defence that held out the longest against the Blues' steady pressure. Over the next few days word came of what squads were tapped to ship over to the Blues' vessels. Of the five on the *Lasana*, three were asked: the 20th, the 2nd, and their own 17th. Of the two passed over, it occurred to Suth that each displayed one possible unforgivable failing: one did not fight as a unit, while the other did not fight to the end. It was a worrying lesson. It suggested to Suth that the Blues were expecting a ferocious confrontation where quarter would not be asked for, or given.

* * *

Banging at the front entrance to his house woke Bakune. It was past the mid-night. His housekeeper came to his bedroom door sobbing about ruffians and thieves. He ordered her to the kitchen. He felt quite calm, which was a surprise. He'd known he'd been living on borrowed time since all his files and records had been confiscated.

Would it be treason or heresy? Or did it really matter? Of course it didn't.

Steeling himself, he left his rooms and descended the stairs to the front. He opened the door and blinked, uncertain. No troop of the Watch; no Guardians of the Faith from the Abbey; just one dumpy figure in a cloak dripping with wet snow who pushed him aside and slammed the door.

The figure threw back his hood to reveal himself as Karien'el.

Bakune could not keep from arching a brow. 'I knew you'd be coming for me, but I didn't think you'd come yourself.'

Weaving, Karien'el waved the comment aside. 'Screw that.' He was drunk, perhaps gloriously so, his nose a bulbous wreck of broken vessels, a web of flushed angry veins across his cheeks. 'I've come to say my goodbyes, my friend. Do you have any wine or something stronger in this wretched house?'

'So, someone *is* coming to take me, then?'

Karien looked confused for a moment, then chuckled. 'Lady, no, my friend. *I* am the one going away. My just rewards, I suppose. Now, let's have a toast to the old days.' He headed for the parlour like an old visitor, when in fact Bakune could not remember ever allowing the man into his home.

Sighing, Karien'el thumped into a chair, glass of Styggian wine in hand, while Bakune teased the embers of the banked fire back to life. What could the Watch captain want here? Hadn't he already destroyed his life? Perhaps he'd come to ask him to do the honourable thing.

'You are going away then?' he asked stiffly.

'Yes. Haven't you heard? No, I suppose you wouldn't have.'

Bakune eyed him, uncertain.

'The Lady and all these foreign gods as well, man!' Karien growled. He tossed back the wine. 'You remain a fool. But an honest one – which is why I'm here.'

Bakune did not answer. Pursing his lips, he prodded the wood with a poker; it seemed the man had come to talk and he had best allow him to unburden himself then send him on his way.

'The Malazans, man. They're leaving. Marching away tomorrow. All the garrison.'

Bakune almost dropped the poker. 'Lady— That is . . . that's unbelievable.'

Karien'el slyly tapped the side of his nose. 'Part of my job is to know things, Assessor. And I've been hearing rumours of the massing of troops in the east, and a summoning of the Mare fleet.'

'The Skolati . . . ?'

'No, man! Not the useless Skolati.' He struggled to lever himself from the chair, gave up, and waved the empty glass. Bakune brought the carafe and poured.

'No, not the Skolati. Mare doesn't push out every hull that will float for the Lady-damned Skolati!'

Kneeling, Bakune returned to the strengthening fire. The house was freezing; it was an early winter. 'Then . . . who?'

'Exactly. So . . . who?'

Examining the fire, Bakune shrugged. 'I assure you, Karien – I have no idea.'

The man cradled the glass against the round expanse of his gut like a sacred chalice. He hung his head and rolled it slowly from side to side. 'All the gods real or unreal, cursed or blessed . . . Must I do everything for you, Assessor? I have wrapped it all up nice and tidy. Can you not make the leap?'

'I am sorry, Karien. It is late. And really, I do not deal in supposition.'

Sitting back, the Watch captain rubbed his eyes and sighed his exhaustion, defeated.

'No, I suppose not. I should have known better.' He took a sip and smacked his lips. 'Very well. I will do all the work for you – as usual. A second invasion. A new wave of Malazan legions.'

Bakune forgot the fire. He straightened. 'But that is incredible . . .'

'Credible. Quite credible.'

'Mare will—'

'Mare failed the first time, don't forget.'

'Then the garrison, the Malazan Overlord, is marching on Mare?'

The captain made a disgusted face. 'No he's not marching on Mare! He's marching to repulse the Malazans should any of them succeed in landing!'

'But he's Malazan . . .'

Karien'el stared at Bakune for a time then downed his remaining wine and pushed himself to his feet. 'I don't know why I bother. I think perhaps I pitied you, Assessor. All these years not taking one coin to drop a charge, or decide a case favourably.' He gestured to the tiny parlour. 'Look at this place. Here you are in a cramped walk-up in town when other Assessors hold estates and manor houses. I know what your pension will be, Bakune, and believe me – it won't be enough.' He headed for the foyer. 'Yeull named himself Overlord of Fist for life, my friend. All these decades of tribute and taxation to our rulers the Malazans. The sales of slaves and prisoners to the

Korelri . . . all that gold. Has any of it reached the Imperial throne in far-off Quon?' He shook the melt from his cloak. 'Not one Styggian penny! The throne wants its due in territory and taxation. They'll hang Yeull as a usurper. And he knows it.'

'But you say *you* are leaving . . .'

Karien snorted and drew on his cloak, throwing up its broad hood. 'The Malazans aren't going alone. They're taking all the militia with them – and you are looking at the captain of the local militia.'

'The Watch is marching with them?'

'Yes. Not that we have a choice. I'm here now to give the lads the time to desert. If anyone's left when I get back I'll be surprised.'

Bakune stood in something of a daze; he couldn't believe what he was hearing. 'Who will keep the peace? Enforce the laws?'

'Ah! Now we get to the nub of the matter. The Abbot, my friend. The Guardians of the Faith will be the new authority.'

'The Guardians? But they are nothing more than religious enforcers.'

'Exactly. So be careful, man.' He rested a hand on the door latch. 'Which brings us to my final message. I've always been a betting man, Bakune, with an eye on the main chance and all my options. I've made no pretence about it all these years. Well, I've placed a number of bets. And in case I should not come back and the Malazans win through – as I believe they shall – then I want you to know that your files still exist. I was ordered to destroy them but I salted them away instead . . . just in case.

'So, there you are. Those two lads who've been shadowing you? I transferred them to your office. They're reliable. That's it. The best I could do. Good luck. And farewell.'

Karien'el went out, pulling the door shut behind him. Bakune stared at the closed portal. *And farewell to you, Karien. It would seem I never really knew you. But then, I suppose we are both hard men to know. Best of luck to you as well.*

* * *

Winter is more than a bitter time on the Stormwall. The wind blows keen from the north. It cuts more than the breath or exposed flesh. The sight of an entire sea of hate charging down upon you does more than bruise the vision. It tests the spirit. One either breaks beneath the weight of all that unrelenting enmity, or one's spirit is annealed into something stronger, something almost inhuman.

So it was with a calm detachment that Hiam opened his eyes to the dark of night and a knock at his door. He sat up, noted the grip of the cold on his arms, his breath misting the room. 'Enter.'

His aid, Staff Marshal Shool, opened the door, helm under an arm. 'Apologies, Lord Protector. Thought you would want to know. Riders sighting coming in via the communication towers.'

'Very good, Shool.' Hiam went to the hearth, where a pot of tea was kept hot night and day, poured a thimble. 'Where?'

'The Great Tower, Ruel's Tears, and Wind Tower.'

'A broad front.'

'Yes, lord.'

'Contact?'

'Light skirmishing reported.'

'Wall Marshal Quint?'

'Tower Nine, I believe, lord.'

'Very good, Shool. I will move command to the Great Tower.'

'Yes, lord.'

Hiam inclined his head. 'I will be down shortly.'

Shool bowed. 'Very good, lord.' He withdrew, pulling shut the door.

For the first time that season Hiam dressed for war. Over thick fleece insulating shirts and vesting he strapped on a boiled leather cuirass faced in iron rings and chased in silver, leather vambraces and leg greaves, and pulled on thick leather gauntlets backed in iron mail. Last was his layered felt cloak. He tucked his helm under an arm and went to the north window. Here iron shutters rimed in ice sealed the opening. He unbolted the shutters and yanked one open, sending a shower of ice clattering to the floor. A great gust of searingly cold air blasted into the chamber, buffeting the fire. The season's cloud front hung like a dark ceiling, lashed by lightning. To the north, a bluish-green glow lit the horizon: the aura of the risen Stormriders. Below, waves crashed over the lowland rocks of the dead shore to pound the wall's base like a hammer of demons. Hiam felt the report of each blow rising through his sandalled feet as a murmur of vibration.

So, a westerly launch. Were they hoping to draw attention from the centre? Too early to tell yet. And broad. A broad opening front. Could they know? No – how could they? Some claimed they spied from the shallows, counted men. He did not think so. Still, tradition dictated a constant showing of strength at each section. Even if it meant marching the same men up and down its length.

Hiam pulled on his helm, its forward-sweeping cheek guards allowing a tight slit for vision. He swung shut the iron leaf. Behind him the wind had snuffed the fire in its hearth. He struggled to dismiss attributing any significance to this sign. *Lady strengthen them now. For now was the time of their greatest testing.* He descended the stairs.

Upon the ramparts Chosen saluted as he passed. He was flanked by Shool and a picked troop of guards. 'The Champion?' Shool asked over the buffeting wind.

'Have him moved out.'

'Yes, lord.' Shool waved for a runner.

Though the waves crashed, spume lashing, and the wind was a constant punishing roar, the iron nails set for traction in the sandals of the Chosen clashed loudest in the rhythm of their marching. Hiam took great satisfaction from that steady beat. Ahead, Tower Twelve jutted outwards, taking full advantage of a higher rocky headland. There Chosen and mixed guards pointed east, shouting, their words lost. Hiam stopped, leaned outward over crenellations for a look. Far back across the sweep of some four curtain walls – contact.

Immense breakers pounded, their weight cast back by the curved slope of the wall in broad wind-lashed swaths of spray. Within flowed the opalescent glow of Stormriders, speeding back and forth, seeking weaknesses in the defence. Hiam raised his spear, shaking it. 'For the Lady!'

A great answering shout went up from the Chosen – though the regulars seemed far from eager, eyeing one another and shifting the grips on their spears.

'Let us hurry,' Hiam called to Shool. 'This may be a full assault.'

* * *

The muted booming of waves reached Corlo through the uncounted tons of rock of the wall. He sat, arms crossed over his knees, shackled in a holding cell in line with other impressed and prisoner 'defenders' of the wall. So it was no surprise to him when the barred door rattled open and Chosen warders entered, unlocking chains.

'Stand at attention!'

It took some effort to straighten, Corlo having been enclosed in the unheated cell for weeks so that his legs were numb and weak.

Beside him rose a great giant who he thought carried Thelomen or Tarthinoe blood. 'Looks like we may see some action,' he murmured to the man.

'No talking in the ranks!' a Chosen yelled.

'If I should fall,' the huge fellow rumbled, 'I am Hagen of the Blackrock, Toblakai.'

Corlo's legs felt weaker and he slid down the cold slick wall. '*You are Toblakai?*'

'Yes. What of it?'

'But the guards call you "Thel".'

Hagen snorted his contempt. 'Here in these lands – what do they know?'

'You're not of here?'

'No. I am of the south. A land of mountain forests, cold rushing streams.'

Corlo gaped at the giant. 'The south? You mean the Ice Wastes?'

'No – beyond that.'

A Chosen warder stopped in front of Corlo, kicked his feet. 'Stand!' Corlo could only stare uncomprehending at the guard. *South? But that was Stratem!* Thinking furiously, he clutched a leg. 'Ah! I cannot. My legs are numb. Frozen.'

The Chosen Stormguard scowled his disgust. 'You're coming whether you can walk or not.' He gestured to the Toblakai. 'You. Thel. Carry him.'

Behind his great mane of tangled hair and beard the giant gave Corlo such a grin.

Hagen cradled Corlo in his arms like a child. When they stepped out on to the ramparts and the cutting wind sawed at their flesh he hunched, protecting Corlo from the worst.

'You are from Stratem, then?' Corlo asked, his voice low.

'I know of no Stratem.'

'That is the land south of the Ice Wastes.'

'My friend,' Hagen rumbled, 'the land south of the Ice Wastes is Toblakai land.'

Corlo thought it best not to press the matter. The giant's shackles clattered and scraped across the ice-rimed stones of the walk. He glanced behind, then frowned down at Corlo. 'Eight crossbowmen follow us. I usually only warrant four.'

'I always have eight.'

'You are a most dangerous fellow, are you?'

'I'm a mage.'

The huge fellow grunted again. 'A mage? Always I hear how these Korelri are so frightened of magi. You do not look so fearsome to me.'

A stave cracked against Hagen's back. 'No talking!'

'Is that rain?' Hagen asked airily. 'I thought I felt a drop.'

'Perhaps it was just the wind.'

'Yes. The wind as from a baby's rear.'

'Far enough!' the Stormguard shouted. 'Stop here. You, Thel. Set him down. You, Malazan, stand or sit. It is up to you.'

Hagen set Corlo down. 'You are a *Malazan* mage?'

Corlo winced at the phrasing, but nodded just the same.

The iron-bound door to a nearby tower swung open and out shambled a fettered and shackled figure in a torn linen shirt, his hair and beard tangled and matted.

'Who is this unfortunate?' Hagen asked.

Corlo took a deep breath, appalled – but not surprised – by Bars' deterioration. 'You are looking at the current Champion of the Stormwall, my friend.'

'Great Mother protect us.'

'Yes indeed,' Corlo agreed softly.

The Chosen took a cocked crossbow from a guard and pressed it to Corlo's head. 'Talk to your friend, Malazan. Impress upon him the nearness of his death. He shall stand the wall whether he holds iron or not.'

A clout of the stock urged Corlo forward. He stopped before his friend and commander, Iron Bars. The man did not look up. Did not even seem aware that someone stood before him. A great wave crashed against the nearby curtain wall, sending a wind-driven lash of icy spray that drove everyone to hunch – all but Bars, who did not flinch. Corlo waved a hand before the man's staring pale eyes. Not a glimmer of recognition. Lunacy? Withdrawn beyond all touch? No, he could not believe it. The vow he swore would not allow it. The Vow of the Crimson Guard: undying, unyielding resistance to the Malazan Empire so long as it should endure. This vow had sustained the original Guard, who swore it for some one hundred years, made them virtually immortal, able to defy even evidently mortal wounds. Such a vow would not allow defeat.

But he was torn – should he speak of Halfpeck? Would it make a difference? He raised a hand, 'Bars . . . I have news . . .'

'Enough, Malazan!' The Stormguard shoved Corlo aside. 'I have seen this pose before. A cold dash of the Storm Sea brings them all round right quick!'

Crossbowmen urged Bars forward. Chains clunked as he shuffled along.

Corlo and Hagen were forced to follow at a distance. 'Your friend, I fear, has the look of a jumper,' said Hagen.

'I don't believe he'll jump.'

The Toblakai had the sensitivity not to answer.

The detail marched them about another league east, well past the Wind Tower. Here, they watched while Bars was unshackled. 'I know why I am here, Hagen,' Corlo said. 'Why are you? Why were we chained together?'

'I wondered that too, Malazan. But now I know.'

'You do?' Covered by crossbowmen, the Chosen led Bars by a single chain down on to the lowest defences, the outermost machicolations of this section of the wall. The way was treacherous; already ice layered the stone in a thick blue-green blanket. Hammering reached Corlo as the Chosen banged at an iron ring encased in ice. 'So . . . why?'

The giant's jaws worked and he let go a long heavy sigh. 'Before your friend arrived, Malazan, *I* was the Champion of the wall.'

Corlo blinked, staring, then comprehension dawned, and he swallowed hard, kneading his hands. 'I see.'

A great wave, a tall comber, came rolling up this curtain section of the wall, breaking at the crenellations. Chosen and regulars stood hunched behind shields, spears ready, watchful and tense. A half-section away what they waited for appeared in the shape of a Stormrider. It reared from the spume, scaled armour glittering hues of mother-of-pearl and opal. A long jagged ice-lance darted at the nearest guard, who took the blow upon his shield. Immediately, nearby guards closed, spears thrusting. The second rank, crossbowmen and archers, loosed upon the figure who turned away, shield raised, to submerge with the receding wave.

Corlo unclenched his teeth and let out a breath that plumed before him. He'd never get used to the way they just appeared like that. Who were these beings? The Korelri named them demons come to destroy the land. Malazan scholars thought them just another race – if a mindlessly hostile one.

Hagen flinched then, fists rising, as a Rider breasted the crenellations directly in front of Bars and the Chosen. The Stormguard spun, sword out blindingly fast to parry a lance-thrust, then rolled backwards out of range. Say what you would about these Chosen, Corlo reflected; they were damned good. The Rider thrust at Bars, who merely twisted sideways, the lance scything the air exactly where he had stood. A storm of crossbow bolts sent the Rider curving down behind the wall.

'That one will be back next wave,' Hagen murmured. 'Certain.'

The Chosen drew an extra blade, dropped it at Bars' feet and backed away. Around Corlo the crossbowmen quickly reloaded, using goatsfoot hooks to pull down the twisted sinew cords.

At the defences Bars made no move for the blade.

'Take it, fool!' Hagen bellowed, hands cupped to his mouth.

'Take it, Bars!' Corlo yelled.

Hagen tapped Corlo's shoulder, motioned to the east. 'Here it comes . . .'

A great swelling comber struck like an avalanche as it rolled down the curtain wall. All along its length, amid the spray, defenders thrust at glimmering phosphorescent figures that lunged, rearing.

'Take it!' Corlo roared with all his strength, into the rushing thunder of the wave. Bars seemed insensate, a bedraggled figure in a soaked linen shirt, long matted hair dripping, rags wrapped at loins and feet.

As the wave reached opposite, bulging and breaking, two Riders lunged, both thrusting jagged lances. Bars seemed merely to brush one thrust aside while grasping the other lance and pulling it from the hands of the Rider. The crossbowmen and archers fired volleys, driving the two helmed figures back. They regarded Bars steadily as they sank from view. Bars threw away the lance, which burst into fragments upon the flagged ramparts.

'I will admit to being impressed,' Hagen said.

The Chosen closed on Corlo. Steam plumed from the Stormguard. He yanked off his helmet and pushed back his sodden hair. 'Your friend must defend the wall!' he roared. 'If he doesn't – the next volley takes him! Then you're next!'

'I must get closer.'

'No closer. I'll not lose two men to this position.'

'Time is running out,' Hagen warned. 'The next wave gathers.'

Corlo cupped his numb hands to his mouth. 'Blade Commander! Commander! Avowed!'

At the defences, Bars' head slowly turned their way. Corlo could make out no expression behind the wind-lashed hair and beard. This could be it – he may give himself up. Corlo's last resort came to him and his stomach twisted at the thought. *No! That would be terrible!* Yet he had to save him . . . Sickened, he held up his hands, forcing insensate fingers straight. 'Seven! Seven of the Blade!'

It appeared to Corlo that the eyes widened, the mouth opened as if in disbelief. Corlo thrust his hands higher, fingers extended. Bars raised his own hands, stared at them, then held them up with seven fingers out as well.

'The wave . . .' Hagen warned.

'Yes! Seven!'

The hands dropped and the dishevelled figure stared about as if coming to himself. The wave struck in a shuddering impact, driving a lash of spume that obliterated the sight of Bars at the crenellations. When the sheet fell Bars remained, sodden, dodging the thrusts of two Riders then lashing out an arm to knock one down behind the wall. The other he punched, helm shattering like cracked shell to reveal, briefly, a head much like that of any man, if pale and thin. That Rider sank as well.

Bars picked up the blade still at his feet, turned, and pointed at Corlo.

Rather than thrilling Corlo the gesture terrified him. *I am a dead man. If not the Riders, then my own commander. I am so sorry, Bars.*

The Chosen grunted his relief. 'Good. I was worried there, for a moment. Threat of death always brings them round. Half-detachment stand down! Warm your bones! You two as well,' he added, indicating Corlo and Hagen.

As they shuffled to the nearest tower, Hagen leaned down to Corlo, who dragged along behind. 'Very impressive. Your man reminds me of the fellow who was Champion before me – though he has not the man's elegance. He was Malazan too. They called him Traveller. Do you know him?'

Corlo shook his head, hardly listening, feeling that he would vomit with self-loathing. 'No. I don't know anyone named Traveller.'

'No? Too bad. If anyone deserved fame, he did. I would face anyone with sword, axe, or spear, but not that fellow.' The Toblakai leaned closer, glancing left and right. 'He escaped, you know,' he whispered hoarsely, and winked.

Corlo could not muster any interest in the man's hints. *From what I have done, Hagen of the Toblakai, there is no escaping.*

*

Closer to the wall's centre sections, the door to a minor tower crashed open to admit two Chosen Stormguard aiding Hiam, the Lord Protector. They sat him next to a roaring fire. One pulled off the man's helm, poured a glass of steaming tea. The other yanked off ice-layered gauntlets to rub the pale clawed hands.

'He stood two shifts in the thick of it,' said Shool, crouched, rubbing the man's hands.

'Come and get me next time!' Wall Marshal Quint snarled.

'I had his back!'

'Quit bickering,' Hiam slurred through numb lips. 'I am fine.'

Gaze slitted, Quint canted his head to the door. Shool nodded. Aside, Quint rounded on the younger man. 'You do *not* allow this to happen,' he hissed, outraged.

'I cannot *order* him—'

'Then get me! Send word! Anything.'

'He's determined—'

'I know. But standing to the end is my job right now, not his. We can't afford to lose him. Understood?'

'Yes.'

The older man's scarred face softened, and he brushed melting ice and rime from Shool's cloak. 'It's too early for this, yes? Wait for the midseason bonfires and the high-water bore. Let's not all call for the Lady's Grace yet, hey?'

A curt nod from Shool, who was hardly able to stand himself.

'Very good. That's the extent of it, you know – my sympathetic side. From now on it's the butt of my spear for you lot and the business end for the Riders, yes?'

The lad managed a half-smile. 'Aye, Wall Marshal.'

'Good. We're done here.' Quint pulled on his helm then yanked open the door, admitting a blast of frigid wind and a swirl of snow, and stamped off to the ramparts.

Shool heaved the thick door shut behind him. *Yes, old spear, there will no doubt be time for the Lady's Grace. I can see it in the eyes of all the brothers and sisters. We may yet all be calling on the Lady before this season's end.*

CHAPTER V

> And so the people came to the land promised and set aside for them by the Blessed Lady from time immemorial. And they found it empty, virgin, and unspoilt, but for the wild peoples who lived like animals upon it and knew not Her name. And so the people brought to these wild folk Her name with flame and with sword. And they were enlightened.
>
> Excerpt from *The Glorious History of Fist*
> Compiled in the Cloister of Banith

DEVALETH STOOD PEERING OUT OF ONE OF THE LARGE GLAZED windows of Nok's cabin on board the *Star of Unta*. Rain lashed the glazing, obscuring her view of the dim evening light and the vessels rising and falling out amid the great iron-blue rollers. Yet they called to her, the gathered mages of Ruse out there. How the Warren beckoned! She just had to reach out . . . they would all know then, of course. And they would mass against her and she would not last an instant.

For the last three days and nights Greymane's expeditionary force had been losing ships to Marese predation. It had become a continuous running engagement of sudden ramming and retreat into the heaving waves.

Greymane's divisional Fists, Shul and the nobleman Rillish, had withdrawn to their own vessels. Greymane had asked her – his 'sea-witch', he called her – to remain with him and the Adjunct, Kyle, on board the flagship. Reports streamed in of these darting Marese attacks, and every dawn the list of lost vessels mounted. 'Morale?' Nok had asked one Malazan captain come in from the convoy rear. The woman shook her head. 'We understand orders not to pursue or engage, Admiral. But . . . it's hard to just sit there and wait for them to take us like ripe fruit.'

This evening Nok leaned over his desk, charts flat beneath his palms. His long white hair hung down, obscuring his lined face. 'Prevailing winds will remain out of the north-west?' he asked her.

'Yes.'

'By now, I presume,' he continued, straightening, and pushing back his hair, 'any fleet would have bunched up, ready for slaughter, or been torn apart in countless minor engagements.'

Devaleth glanced to Greymane, a dark shape hunched in a chair, leaning forward, thick forearms on his knees. 'Yes.' She remained fascinated by the man, unable to take her eyes from him.

'Then,' Nok gestured to an aide, 'let us not disappoint.' To the aide: 'Send my compliments to Admiral Swirl. Have him direct the Blues' warships to begin forming up.'

'Yes, Admiral.' The aide departed.

She'd been leaning against a wall, her arms across her wide chest. She watched the aide go, frowned her disquiet. 'Admiral . . . with all due respect . . . no one has ever defeated we Marese at sea.'

'That was never our intent,' Greymane said from his dark corner seat.

The young Adjunct's face echoed Devaleth's own confusion – this was news to him as well. Greymane sat forward, the chair creaking ominously beneath his bulk. 'Nok and I are in accord on this. Only a fool attacks an enemy where he or she is strong. Such a fool deserves to fail.'

'But the battle order . . .'

'The Blues will form a wedge between the Marese and us,' Nok explained. 'A skirmish line, or flying chevron, call it what you will. They will engage.'

'While you . . .'

'The transports, with a few Blue vessels, will punch through and head for the coast.'

Devaleth was shaking her head, horrified. 'The losses . . .'

'I am charged to secure this front for the Empire,' rumbled Greymane. 'And I intend to do that. One way. Or another.'

But she was not convinced. 'You don't understand what you are facing, High Fist. To you Malazans the "Warren of Ruse" is a forgotten mystery. We of Mare have never forgotten it. And it is more than a Warren of power to us. It is our religion. Every Mare vessel is sanctified to Ruse. Every vessel carries a priest-mage sworn to Ruse. The rowers and crew are all initiates. Every board and rope is bound by ward and ritual to the will of the captain. High Fist . . . *our vessels cannot be sunk*.'

'If *we* are going to sink, Devaleth,' Greymane said, low and precise, 'then why are you with us?'

'High Fist . . .' Nok objected.

But she raised a hand, accepting the blunt question. 'Fair enough. You have been to the region, High Fist. You know why I am returning.'

'I may. But I want to hear it from you.'

She felt a tight grimace twisting her face. 'The cult of the Lady. It must be confronted. It is a sickness upon us.' In the gloom, Greymane was nodding his agreement. 'Do you know, High Fist,' Devaleth continued, musing, 'why your Malazan invasion failed in the first place?'

'No.'

Almost hoarse with the strength of her emotion, she ground out: 'It is because our lands have already been conquered. We just don't realize it.'

Kyle, she saw, shared a look with the High Fist and something eased within her chest. *They know. Somehow, they understand.*

'Devaleth . . .' Greymane began.

'Yes?'

'Remain with the Admiral. Give him all the help you can for the coming battle.'

She flinched, considered explaining how outnumbered she was – thought better of it – bowed curtly. 'Yes, High Fist.'

Greymane gestured to Kyle. 'And you . . .'

'Yes?'

'The assault. I want you with them in case there's trouble.'

'Me? What of you?'

'I will be with the last transport.'

'*What?* The Marese will pick you off!'

'Kyle . . . consider the men. It won't look like flight if my banner is with the rearguard.'

'Admiral, talk some sense into him.'

Carefully pouring himself some wine while the vessel rolled and heaved, Greymane was almost chuckling. 'The Admiral, Kyle, agrees.'

The youth sent a wordless appeal to Devaleth but she shook

her head; she agreed as well. The least hopeless of all the hopeless options, it seemed to her.

Kyle stared from man to man, unable to find the words. The two commanders exchanged amused looks. Finally Kyle waved his disgust. 'Lunatics – both of you!' He stormed out.

Bowing, Devaleth followed.

Alone, the two were quiet for a time; Nok accepted a glass from Greymane. 'Your Adjunct,' Nok said, savouring the drink. 'Are you sure the lad is up to the job?'

Greymane swallowed, then frowned over his answer, considering how to reply. Eventually he cleared his throat. 'Nok . . . I tell you this in all trust. Kyle is from Assail.'

The old Admiral straightened, his eyes widening. 'That is impossible.'

'I was with the Crimson Guard when it slunk its way wide south of Assail lands. Kyle was recruited then. He'd come down from the north.'

'There's so much I would ask . . . What of the Imass?'

But the High Fist was shaking his head. 'No. He's just a tribesman. He knows nothing of wars or fighting further north. Although . . .' and here the High Fist looked away, thoughtful, 'there were three lads – friends of his – I believe they knew more of what was going on up north. They kept damned mum about it all, understandably.'

Nok raised his glass. 'One mystery at a time then.'

Greymane answered the salute. 'Yes. A slow fighting retreat, yes? Give us all the time you can, Admiral.'

The old man smoothed his white moustache, grinning. His eyes, deep in their nest of wrinkles, flashed an almost fey anticipation. He extended a hand. 'Until we meet again on the west coast.'

Laughing, Greymane took the hand as hard and dry as wood. 'Until then, Admiral.'

*

A shake of his foot woke Suth. The hold was almost completely black.

'Collect your kit,' Goss's voice whispered from the dark. 'We're shipping out.'

Suth grunted his acknowledgement. He swung from his hammock, began pulling his gear together. Around him the 17th stirred to life.

He'd been thrown around below and so he knew what to expect

when he climbed up on to the deck. Tall waves crashed into the *Lasana*, sending a biting spray across his face. Beside him a sailor was ordering a coil of rope. 'There would be a storm, wouldn't there?' he said to the fellow.

The sailor looked up. He was chewing a great wad of something that he spat out. He glanced around at the low slate-grey clouds, the heaving rough seas. 'Call this a storm?'

Smart arse. The 20th was gathered at the port rail. Suth carefully edged his way over. Next to the tall *Lasana* a small launch was struggling to come alongside. The waves alternately threw it up then dropped it suddenly and the waters threatened to suck it under the *Lasana*'s hull. On board, Blue marines used poles to fend it away from the giant transport. Sailors from the *Lasana* threw down rope ladders. 'After you!' one shouted gaily to the gathered heavies, laughing.

A trooper sent the man an evil eye.

'Hey, Yana!' a woman from the 20th yelled: Coral, its sergeant. Suth glanced back to see Yana running up. 'This is stupid! We want a cradle.'

'What's the hold-up?' Yana asked, her eyes puffy with sleep.

'Ha! Very funny. We should have a cradle for this.'

'Fuck, I hate all this fucking water,' someone said next to Suth. Surprised, he glanced down to see Faro. Though the small man wore heeled boots, he barely came up to Suth's shoulder. He held his pipe in his teeth, unlit, and wore a loose dark jacket over a vest and shirt. 'Let's get going,' he said mostly to himself, set both gloved hands on the rail, and promptly vaulted over.

A horrified shout went up from everyone crowding the rail. Suth threw himself forward to peer down. The man was hanging from a rope ladder, being knocked about, swinging wildly.

'Who in Hood's name is that?' someone said.

'One of Goss' boys.'

'His pet knife.'

'Get hisself killed.'

The Blue marines allowed the launch to lurch closer. Faro let go and flew, landing and rolling in the broad belly of the launch.

'Blast it!' Coral snarled. 'Bring rope! Tie your gear to ropes.'

One by one the squads lowered bundled gear until the wide belly of the launch was fairly covered. Then they descended by rope ladder. By the end, the launch was riding insanely low in the rough seas. The Blues pushed off and set long sweeps. They gestured that everyone should lend a hand. Some thirty men and women scrambled to help, displaying more eagerness than they had the entire journey.

They crossed to a Blue vessel waiting nearby. Troopers were climbing netting hung at its sides while launches bobbed like insects and empty ones were being raised. Despite his fear of either drowning or being dashed to pieces, Suth was curious to see the inside of one of these ships. Eventually their turn came, but not soon enough for some of the men and women, who had thrown themselves to the sides, heaving up their guts.

Suth waited in line for the dangerous task of climbing the netting. When he finally pulled himself up on to the decking he lay soaked and exhausted. Their gear followed, heaved up on ropes. They collected their kits then were directed below decks to quarters. Rain lashed down now, as cold as ice. A Blue marine directed them to the companionway. On the way Len, next to Suth, touched his shoulder then brought a finger to his eye, glancing aside. Suth followed the man's gaze to where a soldier leaned against the side, arms crossed. He was a young fellow, broad with a long moustache, in a sheepskin jacket under thick cloaks.

'The Adjunct,' Len murmured. It was the first Suth had seen of him. 'Some say he's Greymane's hatchet-man.' Suth merely grunted, knowing nothing of him. 'Maybe he'll lead the landing.'

'Or maybe he's here to execute anyone who holds back,' said Pyke, who'd come abreast of them.

'Then I guess that would be you,' said Len, aside.

Suth laughed out loud as they took the stairs.

* * *

Like a curtain of night a dust storm hung in the distance, cutting the horizon in half. It was, Kiska finally decided, strangely beautiful in its own stark way. She had no idea how much time she'd spent watching the front's grave, stately advance across the far plain. An afternoon? A day? Two days? Who was to know here in Shadow? Or were these even the right questions to ask?

Her companion in their unofficial captivity lay curled up asleep, or at least pretending. He was good at both: relaxing and pretending. She saw him as a natural hunter, with that ability to wait indefinitely for prey to wander by, while the pretending part was all the camouflage necessary. Indeed, so far he had learned much more about her than the reverse.

And on that note . . . Kiska turned from the narrow gap, adjusted her sore back on the jagged rock seating. She cleared her throat. 'So . . . you fought against the invasion, then . . .'

Jheval grunted the affirmative, stretched.

The man is like a cat.

Blinking, he gave her a questioning look.

'Did you face the Imass?'

'Am I dead?'

'Sorry. Silly question. Did you—'

The man had raised a hand for silence. He rubbed his face, yawning. 'No, an understandable question. Your Imass hold such a grip on your Malazan imagination. There was only Aren, really.'

Kiska understood. It was shortly after the massacre at Aren that the dreaded undead army of Imass abandoned Imperial service to march off into the deserts west of the Seven Cities region. Everyone assumed it had to do with the transition from Kellanved, the Emperor, to Laseen, his successor. 'But you fought . . .'

'Oh, yes. I fought against you invaders.' Jheval gestured vaguely, agreeing. 'I was young, foolish. I thought I was so fast and skilled and smart that nothing could touch me.'

He stopped there, staring off at the rock wall; perhaps reliving old memories. 'And?' Kiska prompted after a time.

A shrug. 'War taught me otherwise.'

'You ran into someone smarter and more skilled than you?'

He looked to her, quite startled. 'Oh no. I haven't met anyone smarter or more skilled than I.'

Ye gods! Queen deliver me from this man's overweening vanity! 'So what did happen, then?' she asked, rather drily.

'I saw that such qualities were mostly irrelevant in war. Chance. It all just comes down to dumb chance. Whether you live or die. Chance. The tossed siege boulder crushing the man next to you. The arrow shot high into the sky coming down through your shoulder armour without breaking your skin. The half-strength patrol running into a party even smaller than it.' Jheval made a wave through the air as if tossing something away. 'So it goes. Some fall, some are spared. But not for any good reason.'

Such a cold and futile view of life made Kiska shudder. 'Surely the gods decide . . .'

'. . . who lives and who dies?' Jheval canted his head, looking pensive. 'We are trapped here, so it would be best not to argue . . .

But from what I have seen the gods do not decide anything. Oh, certainly they intervene occasionally, when it suits their purposes, but otherwise I think they are as bound by happenstance as we. And you know what?' He looked to her, knitted his fingers across his waist. 'I find that endlessly reassuring.'

Kiska decided that she did not understand, nor possibly like, this man at all. Something in his words – the ideas behind them – instilled a nameless panic in her chest. Now she felt trapped, while all this time the possibility hadn't really been a worry. She knew she had to act; she had to *do* something or be driven insane. She climbed to her feet, crouched over double in their cramped cave. 'Time to test the waters . . . don't you think?'

Jheval was surprised once again, his brows rising. 'Really? I was only joking, you know. About taking turns. I'll go.'

'No. You're right. We should share the risk. What weapon, do you think?'

'What weapon?' He laughed. 'One of your Malazan Moranth munitions, I should think.'

Kiska held out her empty hands. 'Barring one of those. A stave, I think, to hold them off.'

'You've already gone mad if you think you could hold one of them off.'

Kiska began pulling lengths of blackened metal pipe from slim pockets in her cloak and at her belt and vest. She spoke while she worked: 'I've seen them before, you know. These hounds. They're strong, but they have their limitations.' The sections screwed together and latched, locking.

Jheval watched closely without saying a thing. Finally, he cleared his throat. 'Their limitations, I think, have nothing to do with us poor mortals. And that toy . . . it's of no use. Let me go.'

'This toy is as strong as, if not stronger than, any staff. It was custom built for me by the Moranth.'

'I'm sure the hounds will pause to admire it.'

Kiska gave what she hoped was a carefree smile. 'We shall see.' And she edged out of the crack. She heard behind her a stifled call and was relieved. *Good. At least he knew enough not to shout.* Straightening to a fighting stance, she peered about, listened, and then sensed outwards with an awareness now long attuned to these surroundings. The bare rocky slope appeared empty, as did the sandy hillsides to either flank. *Nothing so far. No swift ambush. Now comes, as they say, the weighing of the gold. How far dare I venture from our bolthole? Surely they are watching, waiting tensed for that one step too many.*

Kiska bounded out three steps then immediately spun and raced back as fast as she could then spun again, crouched, stave ready. *Nothing. Seen that one before perhaps.*

A slight scrape snapped her attention to the rear. Jheval was there, edging out to the far side of the crack. His hands were clasped at the morningstars tied to his waist, ready to pull them free.

What was the fool doing? Offering himself up? Didn't he trust her to do this right? She waved him back. *All for naught, probably. Surely these hounds have better things—*

'Kiska!'

She spun and there one was: bounding in the air, almost upon her. She had the impression of a tawny blur, the red maw, wet fangs, then she yanked her stave between them and the blow knocked her backwards. Sharp rocks slammed into her back, taking the breath from her. She lay dazed for what she was sure was her last moment.

Her awareness cleared and she saw Jheval fending off the hound. The morningstars spun almost invisible from his hands. The hound's every effort to bull forward or lunge was met by a smashing blow from the flanged iron heads that sent it flinching, snarling and rumbling like the very stones grinding. Kiska put off her amazement at what she was seeing and jumped to her feet. Then it was a chaotic blur of images: her stave thumping the beast's broad chest, Jheval's feet clawed from beneath him in a red spray; the stave, twisted, sliding a blade and slashing beneath an eye, buying the time for the man to leap upright. The two retreated, scrambling, alive only because they could cover each other. Then a stumbling collapse backwards into the slim gap to fall over one another.

The beast howled an ecstasy of rage, sprayed froth and blood. Blows shuddered the rock face. Only then could Kiska relax her chest enough to draw a full breath. They lay immobile, limbs entwined, both watching the opening.

Low rumbling as the beast eyed them through the gap; its bulk almost completely occluded the dim half-light. It padded off.

Jheval started laughing. It began as a low chuckle but built to a loud full release of unreserved relief, exhilaration, and frank amazement. Kiska could smile and share an embrace but that was all.

Now she understood that this narrow cave could very well become her tomb. She sat with her knees tight to her chest and covered her face to wipe away hot tears that she could not stop.

* * *

Devaleth went to a side of the *Star of Unta*'s deck, grasped hold of the cold wet wood. Greymane had left for the final troop vessel while his Adjunct, the young Kyle, had taken a launch out to the Blue transport that would lead the shore assault, there to represent the High Fist. She wondered if the lad was up to it; he appeared to be a savage warrior, but could one so young command the respect of these hardened troops?

There on deck she might have thought of herself as alone when in truth she was far from it: sailors dashed back and forth setting out leather buckets of sand and water, readying ropes and repelling poles. Marines assembled the ship's armoury of weapons, checked the crossbows, and oiled the large stone-throwing onager at the bows. Amid all this chaos and preparation Devaleth felt at home. She'd grown up spending more time at sea than on land. Her school had been sitting cross-legged next to a ship's mage, old canny Parell, where she learned her trade through storms, battles, and calm nights when the sea became so still one could see all the way down to Ruse's infinite gateways.

Nok was at the tall sterncastle, where he would oversee the coming battle. Next to him a Blue liaison coordinated with Swirl by way of a fire in a tall brazier that could be made to flare differing colours, sometimes intense orange, or a brilliant blood red, or green, or even sea blue.

'The coming battle' – *listen to yourself, woman. As if what is to come can in any way be termed a battle. What is to come will be a slaughter. I may reach land by way of my Ruse talents, but for most of this force it will be the ancient sea god's cold welcome below.*

So why am I here, as this Betrayer so rightly challenged? Because something has to be done. I must make some effort, no matter how feeble it may prove to be.

I, too, am a betrayer.

A marine stopped at her side. 'High Mage, the Admiral wishes your counsel.'

She nodded. 'Of course.'

Ever courtly, the Admiral bowed as she joined him. Devaleth was grateful though she knew herself to be a far from courtly figure. Nok waved a long wing-like arm to encompass the night. 'I would have your impressions, Devaleth. What's going on?'

'They have been waiting for a sufficient number of vessels.'

'To do what?'

'Attack en masse.'

'And have they achieved this threshold?'

She shrugged. 'I have no way of telling. Though I will know it when the order is given.'

He cocked a greying brow. 'Oh?'

'It will be given through Ruse,' she said dully. 'I will sense it.'

The Admiral glanced at her sharply then smiled behind his thick silver moustache. 'You do not think much of our chances, do you?'

'I'm sorry, Admiral. I do not see how this expedition can end any differently from its predecessors.'

He accepted that. His gaze scanned the distant low shapes of the Mare war galleys just visible in the gathering night. An aide came to his side, murmured something. He responded, 'In a moment'; then, addressing Devaleth, said, 'You in Korel do not really know the Moranth, do you?'

Uncertain of the Admiral's tack, the High Mage was slow to respond. 'No. Not really.'

'We have been allies for decades now. We've achieved great things with what minor alchemies they were willing to trade with us.'

'I have heard that the Malaz–Moranth alliance has cooled, of late.'

The flagship struck a particularly large wave, the bows rising very tall. Everyone on the sterncastle braced for the pitch forward. The vessel slammed down into the trough, the bows disappearing in spray. Nok had taken hold of the ship's tiller. Devaleth alone stood with her hands held behind her back. Amazingly, the charcoal fire still burned in its brazier. A kind of foreign magic? And what *was* everyone waiting for? This time her Mare compatriots seemed slow to the attack, while the Moranth–Malaz expedition held back as well. She sensed her brethren's uncertainty. These alien Moranth vessels . . . what hidden menace was deployed here? They were wary.

'It is true that our alliance seems to be paper-thin these days,' Nok said, resuming their conversation. 'We've been unable to get any further soldiers out of them. It may be internal for all we know.' He gestured to the Blue liaison with him. 'But our deal with the Blue here is very different. A contract, cut and dried. Nothing political. So now we shall see what the Moranth themselves can accomplish when a task is given over to them wholly.' He nodded to his liaison. 'Give the order.'

'Aye, sir.' The Moranth Blue dropped a packet on to the brazier. It took a moment to catch, but then it flared, sizzling and popping, to send up a tall silvery-white flame that cast the sterncastle into fierce relief and flashed from the surrounding waters.

Devaleth was forced to turn away, shielding her eyes. *Order for what? Engagement? Surely not!*

After the blinding actinic-bright flare died down, she straightened, blinking, willing back her night vision. At first she saw nothing, heard only the ship groaning in the high seas. *Of course, fool! It will take time for these two unwieldy giants to embrace.*

'Order the transports to move,' Nok told the liaison.

'Aye, sir.' The Blue reached for another packet.

This time Devaleth was ready; she flinched away, an arm across her eyes. As it was, a brilliant gold glow dazzled her vision, fading to leave afterimages of dancing stars.

She straightened, temporarily blind. *This was it. Now would be the clash. How many of Greymane's transports would push through to reach the shore? All you foreign gods, please not the pitiful few of before.*

*

Crammed into the hold of the Blue vessel, his knees drawn up to his chest, Suth was pressed in thigh to thigh with his fellow Malazan infantry. It was hot, clammy and damp, and the least comfortable he'd been all journey – especially with Wess asleep on his shoulder. The sergeants stood at small openings in the sides, peering out and passing on information. Other than the greater roominess and general cleanliness, the main difference between the Blue vessel and the one they had left was that the former didn't stink nearly as foully as the Malazans'. In fact, it was nearly odourless. Ignoring the vile sour sweat of the men and women crowded in the hold, the main scents Suth could detect were very strange. One Len told him was sulphur, while another reminded him of honey, and another of pine sap. It was all very unnerving. *And these Korelri think their Stormriders are alien.*

A flash of brilliant white light cast a clear image of the hold, the troops sitting jammed together like firewood, their eyes and sweaty faces gleaming. Darkness returned just as instantly. Everyone clamoured to know what it was.

'Some kind of signal,' came the rather unhelpful explanation.

Then Moranth armoured boots tramped the decking, trapdoors

crashed open. Orders to climb. Waiting in line, frigid seawater pouring down the steep stairs. Up on the pitching deck, ordered to sit alongside Blue marines. Suth steadied himself with a ratline to gaze out over the night-dark waters. Ahead, a line of Blue dromonds parting. Low dark Marese war galleys swarmed around them like dogs worrying tired Thanu. The strikes of ramming reached Suth like the reports of distant explosions.

A golden-amber flash lit the night like a reflection of the sun, searing the vessels into silhouettes against the dark waters, only to snap away instantly. The Blue marines surged to their feet. Orders were bellowed from the after-deck. Suth found Len amid the crowd of troopers. 'What is it?' he shouted over the thumping of boots and the crash of the sea.

'We're off the leash,' the saboteur answered. 'Now we'll see if we came all this way to any purpose,' he added grimly.

Suth gave his private agreement. He wore only his padded gambeson, trousers and helmet, sword at his side. His armour lay wrapped below. The order seemed a useless precaution given the freezing waters and distance from shore. Still, perhaps it served to reassure some. He saw the Adjunct at the rail, his long dark hair blowing loose. He too wore only hide pants and sheepskin jacket; the ivory or bone grip and pommel of his sword shone with a near unnatural brightness.

Fire lit the night, flickering out of the distance ahead. Everyone gaped, staring. Even the Adjunct turned, his dark eyes narrowed. Another burst of flame illuminated a scene out of the Harrower's realm: a Blue man-of-war, rammed, and down from the tall tower at its bows poured not arrows or javelins, but a stream of liquid fire. While Suth watched, dark shapes on board the Mare vessel writhed amid the flames. Some threw themselves overboard. He thought he could almost hear their screams of agony.

'Sorcery!' rose a shout from nearby.

'No,' murmured someone – Len. 'Alchemy. Moranth incendiary. It even burns on water – see!' He pointed, urgent. Indeed, the flames were spreading across the waters, pooling and wave-tossed, to engulf yet another Mare war galley. 'So this is their answer,' the saboteur continued, awed. 'Come close all you like . . . ram, and burn.'

*

As more fires burst to life in the darkness all around, Devaleth stared, horrified. *Her countrymen!* She lurched to the side of the sterncastle, clenched the wood to keep from falling. *Torched like vermin! This was outrageous!* She turned on Nok. 'You knew . . .'

The Admiral had the grace to appear pained. 'I knew their intent, yes. But whether it will be enough . . .' He shrugged.

'This is barbaric! You Malazans claim to be civilized.'

His gaze sharpened. 'Is leaving a man to drown any more civilized? Dead is dead.'

She turned from him. *So, will it be enough?* All around she felt Ruse stirring. Flames died, steam misting into a suppressing fog. Yet through the waters, even submerged, the foreign alchemies of the Moranth burned on, sizzling and bubbling.

'Give the order to advance with the transports,' Nok told the liaison.

Moments later a verdant green brilliance threw Devaleth's shadow out across the water, flashing from the sides of vessels locked together, sails burning, dark shapes flailing amid the waves. A light rain, Ruse-summoned, began to fall.

They passed a Blue dromond assaulted by three Mare war galleys. Two had stove it in, rams entangled in broken wood. Grapnels shot like quarrels from crossbows mounted on the side of the Moranth vessel. They trailed rope that entangled the enemy ship. Staccato eruptions reached Devaleth as the Blues tossed munitions of some sort down on to one war galley; shattered wood flew, bodies spun over the sides, and the vessel lurched like a kicked toy.

Yet the battle was not all one-way. The Marese streaked like greyhounds, ramming at will. Many Blue vessels reared stern high, or wallowed, dead in the water. These the Marese ignored; in the shifting action of a naval engagement, to lose mobility was to be useless. That Blue man-of-war, rammed twice – even if it remained afloat, it was now so cumbersome it was for all purposes sunk.

A war galley emerged from the smoke, the swirling flames and the spume-topped waves, and charged the flagship. Its sides were scorched and smoke poured from its decking, yet the crew rowed no slower. Devaleth glanced back to the Admiral, who was watching its approach, a hand raised. The temptation to summon her Warren pulled at her. The fleshly demands of plain self-preservation. Yet to do so would announce herself to every ship's mage present and invite a storm of reprisals.

It was close now; the oars had hit that unmistakable frantic ramming pace. The mage at the stern was a scarecrow figure in burned robes streaming smoke. They must have fought through the Lady's own fury to reach them. At the last instant Nok gave the order and the flagship swung over with a swiftness startling for a vessel of its size. Bows turning, the *Star* now threatened to run over the war galley's bank of oars, but a barked order from that ship's master brought the sweeps high and the two vessels passed within an arm's span of one another. Devaleth saw Nok salute the ship's master at the tiller, who watched the Malazan vessel, his face unreadable. The war galley sped off into the night, its fate unknown. Did it engage another vessel? Did it at last, burned to the waterline, put her vaunted claims to the test?

That master's face had been unreadable because, like myself, he probably had no reference for what was happening all around him. Things simply did not happen this way when the Marese went to sea. It was more than humbling. It was shattering.

*

Having been rammed and sunk on his first run to Korel lands, Rillish Jal Keth watched Mare war galleys manoeuvre out amid the dark ocean waves and felt a bowel-tightening sense of having seen all this before.

That the great ungainly transport still floated was something of a miracle. It had been a day of dodging and running, hiding behind the screen of Blue men-of-war. But the order had been given to break out. The fence was down and the wolves were in the fold. Now two war galleys cooperated in cornering the tall Quon three-master carrying over four hundred souls.

He turned to the transport's master next to the ship's tiller. 'Not long, I think, Captain.'

'Aye. It's every man for himself out here now,' the man grumbled.

Rillish crossed his arms, eyed the low sleek vessels cutting through the waves under oar and sail as swift as arrows. A light rain had started up, obscuring everything in a chilling grey haze. 'I've heard they are unsinkable,' he mused.

'So they say.'

Rillish cocked his head to one side, wiped his face with the back of a hand, thought of the ramming he'd experienced before. 'We have near four hundred Malazan heavy infantry on board this vessel, Captain. Their ships might be better than ours, but I'm willing to wager that our marines are more ferocious than theirs. How would you like a vessel that can't sink under your feet?'

The ship's master stroked his whiskered chin. His slit gaze shifted over to one Mare war galley sliding past, forcing a port turn from the sailing master. Then his gaze shifted back to Rillish. A broad smile split the man's whiskers. He leaned over the railing of the sterncastle. 'Ready all grapnels! Ready all boathooks! All troops on deck! Ready for boarding!'

'Aye, aye, sir!' the mate shouted from amidships. 'Ready for boarding!'

Rillish saluted the captain and went to his cabin. His aide helped him strap on his cuirass of banded iron, his vambraces and greaves. Last, he tied on his weapon belt and twinned Untan duelling swords. His helmet he tucked under an arm. Then he returned to the sterncastle. He found the ship's captain and the sailing master both struggling with the long arm of the tiller.

'Took your time,' the captain called over the worsening weather. 'Can't hold them off any longer.'

'Offer them a fat broadside target, Captain.'

The man spat with the wind. 'Don't tell me my business, landsman.'

'I'll be at the side.'

The captain waved him on. 'Give them my sharp regards, yes?'

'That's *my* business, Captain.' He descended to amidships and pushed his way through the crowd of heavies. He thrust his helmet at a nearby soldier, then climbed up into the ratlines. The spray of a wave crashing into the transport slashed over him. He regarded the crowded deck. 'Soldiers of Malaz!' he bellowed with all his strength. 'We're about to be rammed! There's nothing to be done for it. But I'm glad!' He pointed over the slate-grey waves. 'Out there is a much better ship than this damned tub and they're about to offer it to us! Now . . . what say you!'

Fists and swords thrust to the sky. A great answering roar momentarily drowned out the gusting wind, the booming sails. Rillish added his own raised fist. 'Aye! Now – ready grapnels! Ready ropes! Ready boathooks!'

'For the Fourth!' rose a shout.

'Eighth!' came an answering call.

'For the Empire!' Rillish shouted.

A great roar answered that: 'Aye!'

In no way did Rillish consider himself a sailor but even he could see the attack coming. One war galley threatened their port side, so the sailing master and the captain obligingly pressed their weight upon the arm to show the enemy their stern-plate and in so doing exposed their starboard to the second war galley, which was already lunging in upon them. Its bronze-capped ram thrust down into the dark green of a trough only to leap upwards again, throwing a crest of water high above the sleek vessel's freeboard.

One more wave. 'Brace for ramming!' Rillish wrapped an arm and a leg in the ratlines.

The blow came as an enormous shudder, but such was the mass of the transport that it failed even to lurch sideways. Rillish was thrown yet managed to keep his grip on the ropes. Grapnels flew. The Marese crew back-oared powerfully. Canny Malazan marines used the boathooks to snare oars, throwing the banks into confusion. Shattered wood snarled as the master threw the tiller aside, bringing the vessels together. Marese oars snapped or were thrust down as the two ships swung to clash together. Rillish could imagine the carnage that must be occurring within the war galley.

'Board!' Rillish roared. Men swung down on ropes or jumped. One fell short and grasped an oar, only to disappear with a shriek as the sides pounded together. A rope ladder was tossed, unrolling, and Rillish grasped hold of it. Marese marines waited below in dark leathers. A volley of arrows slashed the side of the Malazan transport. Men and women fell, striking the deck with leaden thumps.

Rillish crashed heavily to the deck, righted himself. Around him marines pushed forward to the stern. The Marese had raised a shieldwall amidships and from behind this bow-fire raked the boarders. Rillish drew his two slim duelling blades. 'Forward!'

More of the heavy infantry reached the deck, adding their weight to the surge against the shieldwall. Rillish clawed his way to the front rank. He danced high, stabbing down over a shield to feel the blade flense cheek, grate from teeth. The man screamed, gurgled, fell. Rillish tumbled down on top of him. In the cramped confines of the narrow vessel a marine fell across Rillish and as she did so a gout of water shot from her mouth and even from her ears. Her dead eyes rolled blood-red, their vessels burst.

Sea-magics! The ship's mage! Rillish straightened, wiped the foul water from his face. There! At the stern, hair wild in the wind, gold torcs at his arms, gesturing, and with each wave a swath of marines falling, clutching their throats. Rillish gulped for air. 'Take the stern, heavies! For the Empire!'

The press heaved against the shieldwall, but the Marese held. The ship's mage wreaked murder through the marines. His powers seemed unlimited here in his element. Then a great bull of a trooper in bright mail broke through the wall and, wielding a two-handed blade that he chopped up and down more like an axe, reached the sterncastle stairs. The shieldwall was shattered, disintegrating. The trooper reached the stairway and marines poured up with him. The ship's mage threw some magery that levelled many, but the trooper in the bright mail coat, the helm cast to resemble a snarling wolf's head, shook it off to reach the man with a great two-handed blow that severed him from collarbone to sternum.

Rillish came clambering up to the stern to see the marine pull off the helm to show what he'd suspected: the matted silver hair and flushed sweaty face of Captain Peles. Rillish clapped her on the shoulder. 'Well fought, Captain.'

She inclined her head to Rillish. 'And not many Fists lead a charge against a shieldwall.'

Rillish waved that aside. 'The mage – he didn't slow you down . . .'

Panting, the woman gave a modest shrug. 'The Wolves were with me this day, sir.'

'Well, thank them for that.'

A sailor saluted Rillish. 'Captain's regards, Fist. The transport is stove through, irretrievable.'

'Have all personnel transferred over. Cut the lines.'

'All, sir? That's far too much weight for a vessel this size. We'll wallow in these high waves, take on water . . .'

Rillish just laughed. 'Haven't you heard, man? These vessels are unsinkable.'

After the sailor left, shaking his head, Peles regarded Rillish. She pushed back her sodden hair. 'Now what, sir?'

'Well, as the man said. We're overcrowded.' He gave Peles a grin. 'I think we could use another ship.'

Peles was cleaning her two-handed blade on the robes of the dead mage. 'Aye, sir. That we could.'

*

Suth's Blue transport was secured side by side with a twin as a kind of gigantic catamaran. They carried suspended between them some sort of beam construction as long as the ships themselves. Despite this awkward arrangement they made good time, had bulled through swaths of burning sea, knocked aside rudderless hulks, submerged countless souls shouting and begging from the waves, and looked to be keeping place as the standard-bearer for the charge to the Fist coast. Dawn was nearing and in the half-light more Marese war galleys could be glimpsed cutting across their bows. 'Too many,' Len said, his elbows on the railing. 'Don't know how we'll make it.'

Orders rang out and Blue sailors, indistinguishable from their marine brethren, climbed the rigging. More sail unfurled, billowed and bellied, taking the wind aslant. Suth watched the tall mainmast, amazed by the sight.

'Still too slow,' Len grumbled.

A Moranth sailor in the crow's nest gave a warning shout.

'Here they come,' said Len.

The sleek black war galleys closed from either side, lunging like tossed javelins. As they closed the Blue captain found an extra ounce of speed from somewhere to slip just ahead. The troops sent up a great cheer as the Marese coursed across the transport's broad foaming wake.

'We won't surprise them like that—' Len was beginning when twin reports as of siege arbalests sounded from the Marese galleys and missiles came hissing through the air to crash into the transport's stern. The vessel lurched almost to a standstill and everyone's feet were cut from beneath them while barrels tumbled overboard and ropes snapped, singing.

Recovering, Suth clambered to the rear. Here among the wreckage of broken wood and twisted iron Blue marines were hacking at what appeared to be giant grapnels that had gouged hold of the stern.

'Cut them!' someone shouted.

'They're chain!'

'We're dragging!'

A Blue officer appeared, yelled orders. Axes emerged. Out amid the brightening waves Suth saw more Mare vessels closing. The grapnels led via lengths of chain to thick ropes that stretched to the two war galleys. Both were backing oars, sending up a great churning froth of water.

'Cut them!'

'Chop the wood!'

Then the young Adjunct was there. He brushed aside the Blue axemen. 'Room,' he shouted, and drew his blade. Sunlight blinded Suth, flashing from the curved ivory blade. The Adjunct swung it overhead two-handed, hacking, raising high piercing shrieks of metal. The transport lurched forward. A marine almost fell overboard but was pulled back. The Adjunct swung again and the ship sprang free, surging ahead. Suth stared where the chains swung, severed cleanly just back from the grapnel.

The Adjunct sheathed his blade.

'It cut,' someone whispered. 'Cut iron . . .'

'Did you ever see the like . . .'

The Adjunct glared with his dark eyes as if expecting some sort of challenge, then turned away without a word.

Later, Suth, like many, went to examine the severed links. He found the iron mirror-bright and clean. Its edge was so sharp it cut one of his fingers.

They had pushed on through the greatest concentration of Mare vessels. Behind, bursts of orange glare and a banner of thick black smoke hanging low over the water obscured dawn. A final war galley rammed them on the port forward of the mainmast, but a volley of lobbed munitions from the Moranth left the ship so devastated that it drifted away, seemingly unmanned. As for the transport, while Suth was bent over the gunwale inspecting the great hole punched into the side, a Blue marine just said: 'Our ships are also hard to sink.'

Orders came later that day to return to the hold to get some sleep. The assault would come tomorrow. The marines filed back down. Talk now lingered on this Adjunct. Who was he? Where was he from? One crazy rumour had him once serving among the mercenary company the Crimson Guard.

'I hope he's with us tomorrow,' Dim said.

For once, Pyke had nothing to say.

*

Their captured Mare war galley rocked dead in the water as it was too jammed with marines to row effectively. Rillish and the Malazan captain, a mariner named Sketh out of the Seven Cities region, argued over everything in their new overcrowded vessel. The captain berated Rillish for heaping everyone into the war galley; Rillish responded by inviting him to rejoin his crippled former command. The captain told him to keep his mouth shut, as *he* was the captain; Rillish pointed out that Seven Cities was a desert.

In the midst of another heated exchange, Captain Peles tapped Rillish's shoulder and gestured aside. 'We're not alone.'

Another Marese war galley was oaring up slowly. It rose and fell with the waves. The crew looked to be curious. Rillish immediately ordered everyone down. 'Flat!' he hissed. 'Lie on top of each other, damn you!'

Rillish left Sketh standing at the stern with its slim centre-set tiller arm. 'What am I to do?' the man whispered, fierce. 'I am to stand here all alone?'

'Wave them closer.'

Sketh waved. 'I will report this to the Admiral, you fool. He will see you in chains.'

'Just get them close.'

'How? I am no foreigner like them.'

'Yell in your Seven Cities dialect.'

Sketh gaped at Rillish, but kept waving. '*What?*'

'Go ahead!'

'Very well, fool!' And he shouted something that sounded unpleasant.

A trooper near Rillish guffawed. 'Yes?' Rillish said.

The man looked uncomfortable, cleared his throat. 'Ah, well. He said that he could smell their unwashed backsides from here and that he wished they would come no closer.'

Rillish turned to Peles. 'That should confuse the Abyss out of them.'

Sketh yelled some more. This time the trooper almost blushed. Rillish eyed him expectantly.

'Goats . . . and mothers,' the man mumbled.

The Marese war galley was now so close Rillish could hear the crew talking. Someone in the vessel was shouting. Sketh answered in Seven Cities. Rillish heard oars knocking oars.

'They've spotted you!' Sketh shouted.

Rillish jumped up. 'Now! Fire!'

The vessel was frustratingly just beyond a leap away, now backing oars. Malazan marines sprang up to fire crossbows point-blank across the deck and into the oarlocks. 'Next rank!' Rillish yelled.

Those who had fired fell back or squatted to reload. The next rank surged forward, firing almost immediately. 'Bring us alongside!' Rillish bellowed to Sketh.

'We have no headway!' Sketh answered, furious.

Fortunately the marines' fire had raked the stern decking clear and the tiller of the galley swung loose. Anyone who raised a head was the target of a swath of crossbow bolts while wounded oarsmen encumbered their banks. The bronze-sheathed ram was swinging their way. The Malazan marines continued their merciless fusillade.

The ram bumped their side, slid, gouging the planking with a screech of wet wood. 'Board!' Rillish yelled a war cry and jumped with all his strength.

He didn't make it. His heart lurched as he realized in mid-leap that he'd fall short. He grasped the gunwale, his face slamming into the wood. Stars burst across his vision and hot blood gushed over his mouth. A sailor reared up over him, sword raised, only to disappear as a Malazan trooper crashed down on to him. Dazed, Rillish struggled to pull himself over the side. Fighting raged across the vessel. Rillish tumbled gasping on to the decking amid the fallen. He straightened, wiped the back of a gauntlet across his wet mouth, clumsily drew one blade, and peered about, blinking. The fight was over. They had their second ship.

The rest of the morning did not go as satisfactorily. They had to fashion a rough kind of Malazan standard to fly over their captured vessels just to stop the Moranth from shooting fire at them whenever they drew close. Rillish peered up at the black cloth, squinted in the strengthening light, and shook his head. 'Might as well call ourselves pirates and be done with it, hey, Captain Peles?'

She was offended. 'Oh, no, sir. This is a fine ship. Our boatwrights could learn a few things from it, I think.'

So damned literal. He shrugged. The night and morning had been exhilarating yet disappointing and he was in a poor mood. Exhilarating because they were alive and the engagement was over and they were victorious. Disappointing because they were now spending the majority of the time in a futile chase of other Marese war galleys that always outpaced them. The Malazan sailors were unfamiliar with the rigging, Sketh didn't have a feel for the vessel's handling, and they were still overburdened.

Good enough. He sat, tucked his gauntlets into his belt, and dabbed a wet corner of his surcoat to the dried blood smearing his face. Sketh had command of the other captured vessel while his sailing master was with them. The man had sent them off with a storm of Seven Cities curses.

Rillish didn't ask for a translation.

Now they trailed the transports heading to the coast. Marese war galleys shadowed them, keeping their distance. Somewhere ahead Greymane's banner marked the straggling tail of the invasion force while behind the majority of the Blue dromonds maintained a screen sweeping southward. *Onward to Mare itself* . . . he wished them luck with that.

For now it was the landing that preoccupied him. How many transports had broken through? Would they succeed in taking Aamil? He knew he'd arrive too late for the first assault. Yet at least he'd arrive; there were too many as couldn't boast that.

* * *

The day after the Malazan garrison and the city militia marched away inland, Bakune rose, put on his best robes as he had every day, and headed out for his offices close to the centre of town. He'd decided to face things squarely; to find out, for better or worse, where and how things stood. Was he to be arrested? And if not, what of his authority? Was he to be merely closely watched by the Abbot and his self-styled Guardians of the Faith? Or dragged in chains before the holy courts? He did not consider himself a brave man; the anxiety of not knowing was simply burning a hole in his guts.

His housekeeper wept as she shut and locked the door behind him.

The streets were unnaturally deserted for this early hour. Indeed, an air of uncertainty hung over the entire city. The harbour was almost empty; news of the renewed Marese blockade had stopped the pilgrim vessels from running; and Yeull, the Malazan Overlord, had ordered all naval and merchant vessels north to Lallit up the coast. To make things worse a bitterly cold front had swept over the Fall Strait to leave remnants of snow in the shaded edges of the streets and roofs. The only institution bustling with energy was the Blessed Cloister and Hospice, as hordes of citizens crowded its halls to pray and seek the intervention of the Lady.

Two Guardians of the Faith stood before the closed double doors of the city courts. Like all of these self-appointed morality police, they were bearded, wore heavy robes, and carried iron-bound staves. Bakune stopped short, drew a deep breath, and asked more bravely than he felt: 'Why are these doors closed?' A scornful superior look from both men sent a cold shiver down his back.

'The civil courts are closed until further notice, petitioner.'

Bakune forced himself to ask, 'By whose authority?'

The Guardians shared a surprised glance. 'By order of Abbot Starvann, of course.'

Bakune swallowed hard, but pressed on: 'And by what authority does the Abbot intervene in civil affairs?'

One Guardian stepped down from the threshold. He held his stave sideways across his body. 'You are Assessor Bakune?'

Bakune managed a faint, 'Yes.' His hands were damp, cold, useless things at his sides.

'You will come with me.'

The Guardian started down the street. Bakune hesitated. Why should he cooperate? But then, what else could he possibly do? Should he run? Where? Be dragged kicking and blubbering down the street? How undignified. The Guardian stopped, turned back to peer at him. He set his stave to the cobbles with a sharp rap of its iron-bound heel. To cover his panic, Bakune drew out his lined gloves and took his time pulling them on. When he had finally finished tugging each finger, his heart had slowed and he had reconciled himself to what was to come. As he approached the Guardian he even managed to say evenly, 'Cold this morning, yes?'

The man turned away without replying.

After two turns the Guardian's destination became clear to Bakune and his panic took hold of him once more. The Carceral Quarters. Of course. Where else for an undesirable such as himself? Despite the biting wind out of the west, sweat pricked his brow and he dabbed at it with the back of a glove. More Guardians at the thick armoured doors to the Carceral Quarters. The City Watch was no longer in charge of maintaining order. Bakune's heart sank; not for himself, but for his city, his country. They were sliding back into the ancient age of superstition and religious rule. All the strides of civilization over the last few hundred years were being swept away by this crisis.

In the halls Bakune was handed over to a priest, who, with obvious distaste, looked him up and down. 'You are Assessor Bakune?'

'Yes.'

The priest gestured him on. Two Guardians walked behind, staves stamping the stone flags in time. He was led past many galleries of cells to one far beneath the holding areas reserved for common thieves and murderers. Bakune's stomach tore a bite out of his innards with every turn and every staircase down. What a fool he'd been! Karien'el had as much as urged him to run! Looking back now, it seemed as usual that Karien'el had done all the work to lead him to the obvious, self-serving decision, which he had then mulishly refused. The priest opened the door to the cell and stood by it. The Assessor could not move; was this it then? The end for him? Would he obligingly walk in like a calf to the slaughter? A Guardian stepped close behind, set his stave down hard in a stamp that echoed harshly within the narrow passage. Almost unable to breathe, Bakune wiped a gloved hand down his face, and then straightened. No! No weakness! He would show these fanatics how a civilized man, a man of true ethical principles, behaved. He stepped up next to the priest, met his eyes and nodded. 'Very well. Since you leave me no choice.'

The priest slammed the door shut behind him.

Facing what he had thought was to be his prison for perhaps the rest of his – presumably short – life, Bakune halted, startled, because it was not a cell. It was a courtroom. His heart clenched and his innards twisted; the Lady was not done with him. She was not content that he should quietly disappear in the confusion of all this upheaval and panic.

It was to be a trial. Signed confession. Public disapprobation. The courts divine would legitimize themselves by discrediting the courts civil. Very well. The good opinion of the public had never been his obsession. Quite the opposite, in fact.

A long table ran along one wall, and behind it sat three tall chairs. *My judges.* A single, much poorer chair faced the table from the other side. Bakune sat in this, crossed one leg over the other and carefully folded and smoothed his robes. He pulled off his gloves, clasped his hands on his lap. And waited.

Shortly thereafter many men came marching up the passage. The door clattered open. In walked another priest, this one much fatter and older, wearing the starburst symbol of Our Lady. He was vaguely familiar. The priest's brows rose upon seeing Bakune. 'My dear Assessor! Not *there*!' Bakune placed him: Arten, Chief Divine of the Order of the Guardians of the Faith. Abbot Starvann's second. This court was to have a seal of the highest authority. Chuckling, Arten invited Bakune to move to the other side of the table. 'Here, if you would. On my right.'

Bakune could only stare up at the man. *The* other *side of the table?*

Arten repeated his invitation. Guardians now stood waiting at the door, someone in chains between them: a short, extremely stocky figure. Bakune rose shakily to his feet. Arten shepherded him round the table. 'There you are. Very good.' He nodded to the Guardians, who entered.

Bakune sat, blinking, quite shocked, while the prisoner was seated opposite, armed Guardians flanking him. Bakune took the time to study him. He was well past middle age yet still quite powerful, with burly shoulders and chest. But the man's most striking feature was the faded blue facial tattooing of some sort of animal. *A boar – so the man was, or had been, sworn to that foreign god . . . the boar . . . Fener! Lady, no. Could this be he? That foreign priest Karien'el had mentioned?*

The priest who had first escorted Bakune now sat on Arten's left. 'Brother Kureh,' Arten addressed him, 'would you read the charges?'

Kureh drew a sheaf of parchments from within his robes, sorted through them, and then cleared his throat. 'Defendant . . . would you state your given name?'

The man smiled, revealing surprisingly large canines. 'As of now,' he ground out in a rough voice, 'I take the name Prophet.'

'Prophet,' Kureh repeated. 'Prophet of what?'

'A new faith.'

'And does this new faith have a name?' Arten asked.

The man regarded Arten through low heavy lids. 'Not yet.'

'And which degenerate foreign god does it serve?'

'None . . . and all.'

Kureh threw down the parchments. 'Come, come. You make no sense.'

The man lifted and let fall his shoulders, his chains clattering. 'Not to your blinkered minds.'

Kureh glared his rage. Arten raised a hand for a pause. 'Pray, please educate us.'

The man sighed heavily. 'All paths that arise from within partake of the divine.'

Arten nodded, smiling. 'True. And Our Lady is that divine source.'

Here the man revealed his first burst of emotion as his mouth drew down in disgust. 'She is not.'

It seemed to Bakune that the man could not be trying harder to commit suicide.

Kureh slammed his hands to the table. 'I for one have heard enough!'

Arten sadly shook his head. 'Yes, brother. A disturbing case. There is almost nothing we can do for such delusion. We can only pray the Lady grant him peace.' He regarded the man for a time, drew a breath as if reluctant to continue. 'You give me no choice but to broach the distasteful subject of your implication in the murder of a young girl last week. Possessions of yours were found with the body—'

'Convenient,' the man sneered.

'And witnesses . . .' Arten gestured to Kureh, who raised papers, 'have attested under oath to seeing you with the girl that evening. How do you plead?'

'Disgusted.'

'You remain defiant? Very well. The papers, Kureh.' Brother Kureh slid a few sheets and a quill and inkpot to Arten, who signed the papers then slid them along to Bakune. 'Assessor, if you would please . . .'

Bakune examined the sheets. As he suspected: a death sentence calling for public execution. The charge, murder. He set them back on the table. 'I cannot sign these.'

Arten slowly swung his head to look at him. 'Assessor Bakune . . . I urge you to give due consideration to your position. And sign.'

Knowing full well what he was about to do to his own future, Bakune drew a weak breath and managed, 'I see no compelling evidence of guilt.'

'No evidence!' Kureh exploded. 'Have you not been sitting here? Have you not heard him self-confessed from his own mouth? His utter lack of seemly repentance?'

'Sign, Assessor,' the Prophet urged. 'Do not sacrifice yourself on my account.'

'The accused is dismissed!' Arten roared, and pointed to the door.

The Guardians marched the man out. Arten rose to stand over Bakune. 'I am disappointed, Assessor. Surely it must be clear to you that what we require is merely your cooperation in these few small matters. Give us this and you may return to your insignificant civil affairs of stolen apples and wandering cows.'

Bakune blinked up at the man. He clasped his hands to stop their shaking. 'I do not consider the life of a man a small matter.'

'Then I suggest, Assessor, that you spend your remaining time considering your own.' He snapped his fingers and a Guardian entered. 'Escort this man to his cell.'

'Yes, Divine.' The Guardian grasped hold of Bakune's robes and pulled him to his feet, then marched him out. In the hall he glanced back to see the strange man, this Prophet, peering back at him as he was dragged off. And it was odd, but the man appeared completely unruffled. Bakune could not shake the impression that the fellow was allowing himself to be taken away.

* * *

'That smoke in the distance there,' Ivanr asked, gesturing to the northern horizon. 'That all part of your big plan for deliverance?'

Lieutenant Carr had also been watching the north as they walked amid the dust of the main column, his expression troubled. Beneth's rag-tag Army of Reform had reached the plains, which fell away, rolling gently to northern farmlands and the coast. To the east, they had passed the River White where it charged down out of the foothills bearing its meltwater to the bay. Burned cottages, the rotting carcasses of dead animals, and the blackened stubble of scorched fields was all that had greeted them so far. It seemed to Ivanr that the Jourilans would rather destroy their own country than see it given over to any other creed or rule.

They also met corpses. Impaled, crucified, eviscerated. Some hung from scorched trees. Many bore signs or had carved into their flesh the condemnation *Heretic*.

Ivanr knew that the advance scouts had passed these grim markers days ago, but Martal must have ordered them to remain untouched. At first the sight of the bodies and the vicious torture their torn flesh betrayed had horrified the untested volunteers of the army; many of the younger had actually fainted. As the days passed and the endless count of blackened, hacked bodies mounted, Ivanr saw that fear burn away, leaving behind a seething anger and outrage. His respect for this female general's ruthlessness grew. It seemed odd to him that he'd never heard of her before. Where had Beneth found her? Katakan? He couldn't think of any mercenary or military leader hailing from that backwater there in the shadow of Korel.

Carr waved the dust from his face. 'There must be fighting in Blight.'

'You think so?'

More Reform cavalry charged past, heading for the front of the straggling column. A small detail, only some forty horses. The sight reminded Ivanr of the Jourilan nobleman, Hegil, supposed commander of the army. So far all the man commanded was the cavalry. He seemed to share the Jourilan nobility's contempt for infantry, judging the peasantry beneath his notice. But the vast majority of the Army of Reform was just those peasants – farmers and displaced burghers – and to them, if the army had any leader, it was Martal.

The potential for confusion or outright argument troubled him. An army was like a snake; it should not have two heads.

Ivanr and Carr's place in the column reached a curve in a hillside offering a view east of the city of Blight and the Bay of Blight beyond. The city's stone walls were tall. But now smoke wreathed them, billowing in plumes from almost everywhere within. It drifted inland, a great dark pall, driven by the prevailing wind that held from the north-east during this season of storms. The south gate gaped open, a dark invitation. The Army of Reform was ordering ranks before it. Seeing this, Ivanr cursed and pushed ahead. Carr followed.

Ivanr tracked Martal simply by keeping an eye on all the messengers coming and going. He found the woman mounted, surrounded by staff and bodyguards, dressed as always in her blackened armour, black boots and blackened gauntlets, her short night-dark hair touched with grey. Such martial imagery was all in keeping with some kind of legendary warrior-princess, until one saw her face: the lips full, yes, but habitually grim, drawn down as if constantly displeased; the eyes dark, but sharp and dismissive, not mysterious or alluring; and the nose what one would expect to see sported by some grizzled campaigner, canted and flattened. The Black Queen indeed.

A queen of war.

The guards allowed Ivanr and Carr through. When Martal finished with a messenger Ivanr cleared his throat. She nodded distractedly for him to speak.

'You're not going in there,' his said, his disapproval clear.

A faint near-smile, her gaze scanning the broad columns of infantry. 'No, Ivanr. We're forming up. I'm told the adherents of the Lady are withdrawing to the north.' She spared him a quick glance. 'They need time to complete their flight.'

Ivanr grunted his appreciation. 'You would burden the Jourilan Imperials with them.'

'Yes. Why should we be the only force herding civilians along? The difference being *ours* fight.'

'Once they withdraw the city will be ours,' Carr said, triumphant.

'So we'll own a burned-out ruin,' Ivanr added, sour.

Martal was reading a scrap of vellum brought in by a messenger. Its contents twisted her lips into an ugly scowl. 'For Hegil,' she told the messenger, who snapped his reins and charged off. She blinked now at Carr as if seeing him for the first time. 'If we own it already, Lieutenant, then we can ignore it.'

'You mean to just go round,' Ivanr breathed, impressed.

'In conquering a nation, squatting in the towns and cities is the surest route to failure.'

Ivanr's breath caught. He eyed the woman anew, her heavy outland armour of iron bands over mail, black-lacquered, battered by years of service. That opinion had the sound of quoted text. 'What would you know of conquering nations?'

The woman merely smiled. But it was not a reassuring smile; it spoke of secrets and a dark humour. She pointed a gauntleted hand to the west. 'Jourilan lancers are harassing our flank. That would be the 10th Company, the Green Wall. Your lads and lasses, yes, Carr, Ivanr?'

The two exchanged alarmed looks. 'Gods beyond, Martal,' Ivanr exploded. 'Why didn't you say so?' They pushed their way out of the ring of guards.

Tenth Company, which had selected the nickname the Green Wall, was formed up in a wide front, pikes and spears facing west. Beyond their ranks skirmishing Jourilan cavalry raced back and forth across open ground of burned fields. Edging his way through, Ivanr reached the front rank. He'd already collected a spear. 'Lights,' Carr said, drawing his sword. 'They won't press a charge.'

'They're pinning us down, though. Can't advance. Where's Hegil's cav?'

Carr shrugged. 'Occupied elsewhere, perhaps. We've few enough.'

'Can't just sit here. Martal's damned wagons are about to roll up our backsides.'

Carr glanced behind: the entire mass of the Army of Reform was lurching west, groping its way round the city, about to run them over.

Ivanr straightened, taking a great breath. 'Company! Broaden line! On my mark! Now!' He watched to the right and left while the rows adjusted their spacing to allow an extra pace between them. It was one of the most difficult manoeuvres he'd covered with them. He'd never dare attempt it facing a body of heavies awaiting a chance for a charge. As it was, the movement caught the eye of the lights and they raced over, forming a chase line, swinging close, lances still held tall. Ivanr bellowed: 'Company, brace!' Carr raised his sword.

The flying chevron of lights charged obliquely across the line of the levelled pikes and spearheads. Lances and javelins flew. Men and women screamed, impaled. The clean line of bristling pikeheads shook, rattling. A second charge was swinging in behind the first. Ivanr fumed. Archers! Where was their support? They needed archers to drive these skirmishers off. 'Steady, company! Brace!'

The second charge circled past. Another flight of javelins and lances drove ferocious punishment into the column. Ivanr saw the wall of pikes waver like wind-tossed grasses. 'Steady, Lady damn you all! Break and you're trampled!'

Then a wall of smoke came streaming down from the plumes overhead, obscuring everything. The thick greasy fumes stank of awful things. Things Ivanr didn't want to imagine burning. He covered his mouth. Soot darkened his hands. Everyone was coughing and cursing. Blind to everything, he heard dropped pikes clattering to the ground. Somewhere in the dark horses shrieked their terror. He glimpsed a smudged light off to his right and staggered to it. Here in a small depression he found an old woman hunched over a smoking fire, blowing on the glowing brands.

'What are you doing here?' he demanded.

The old woman blinked up at him. She wore the tattered remains of layered wraps over frayed skirts. 'Making lunch.' She dropped handfuls of freshly cut green grass and green leaves on the fire. A great gout of white smoke billowed up.

'Would you stop that!'

'Stop it? I'm hungry.'

'You're making all this smoke!'

'Don't be ridiculous. All this smoke is from the city.'

Carr came running up, waving the fumes from his face and coughing. 'The cavalry has fled. The field is clear.'

Ivanr eyed the old woman crouched before the fire like a penitent, bony elbows sticking out like wings. She gave Ivanr a wink. 'Horses, they say, are in a terrible fear of fire.'

'What is your name?'

'Sister Gosh.'

'Well, Sister Gosh. If the Lady knew there was magery here on this field, you'd be a dead woman.'

'Then it's a good thing there was none o' that. Just an errant gust of wind and smoke from the city, hey?'

'You play a dangerous game, Sister.'

'Now's the time for it.'

Ivanr grunted his agreement. He faced Carr. 'Have the company form up for advance. Martal wants us past the city.'

Carr saluted. 'Aye, sir.'

Sir? When did that happen? And what did that make him? Ivanr frankly had no idea and he decided he didn't care.

* * *

Those veterans who managed to doze off below decks were woken in the late afternoon just before evening. Some twenty Malazan squads and a horde of Blue marines crowded the two dromonds that constituted the ungainly catamaran. A meal of watery soup came around in pots and ladles. Sails were trimmed. The bow-crest eased to almost nothing. Suth nudged Len while they ate their flat hardbread. 'We've slowed, yes?'

'Yeah. Have to give the others time to catch up, hey? And the sun's setting – can't have that in our eyes.'

Suth returned to the grainy bread. He hadn't thought of that. To the west the shore passed as distant green hills, wooded, with few signs of habitation. Beyond rose a crest of tall misted mountains, dark and snow-peaked. Goss came round, gripping shoulders and making a last equipment check. He and Len grasped forearms. 'We're sixth in line. Form up along the port side.'

'Any munitions to share out?'

Goss snorted. 'I suspect these Blues will be supplying more to the fight than any of us would like.'

Len waved that off. 'Had to ask. And that thing between the ships. What is it?'

'Don't know. Blues are all mum about it. May be a catapult.'

After Goss moved on Keri sat with them. 'That's no catapult.'

'Been checking it out, have you?' Len rumbled with a sly smile.

'Yeah. And it ain't no catapult.'

'What is it then?'

She hunched, peering round. 'I got a theory . . . too crazy to say, though.' She drew her weapon, what Suth had learned the Malazans called a 'long-knife'. She checked its edge.

Suth frowned. 'You're not coming with us on the assault, are you?'

Keri's gaze narrowed on him and her thin lined face lost all expression. 'Why?' she asked, her voice flat.

''Cause you're only wearing leathers.'

She relaxed, slapped her weapon home in its wooden sheath. 'Listen, kid . . . this is your first engagement, so maybe *you* should stay behind *me* . . .'

Len laid a hand on her shoulder. 'Take it easy, Kerr. He's green.' To Suth: 'Just remember, in battle, we saboteurs tell you to do something – you do it. Okay?'

Len was the corporal so Suth said nothing, though he saw no reason why he should do whatever the saboteurs told him. They weren't even armoured heavily enough to last the first exchange. It was useless bringing them along on what he assumed would be a plain frontal assault.

As the afternoon gave way to the evening more Blue and Malazan vessels gathered. The ships manoeuvred into battle groups. Messages passed as brilliant flaring colours, while Malazan vessels exchanged coded signals by flags. Suth heard from the talk going around that the Blue Admiral, Swirl, was in charge and that the sergeants weren't particularly happy about it. They'd have preferred to have Greymane here. No one mentioned the young Adjunct.

The fleet rounded the headland of a bay and there before them was the harbour of Aamil. It had the look of a fortress stronghold built specifically to resist any assault from the sea. Suth thought of Mare nearby to the south. Twin curving moles met at a narrow harbour entrance flanked by stout guard towers. The main fortress rose straight from the water in a tall featureless curtain wall of salt-stained grey limestone blocks. Access from the harbour was limited to the narrow inlet between the fortified towers.

Voicing Suth's thoughts, Len let go a long low whistle. 'Now *that's* a stronghold.'

'These Blues better know what they're doin',' Keri grumbled.

'They have so far.'

Yana squeezed by, cuffed Suth. 'Let's go. Form up.'

Distantly, the ringing of bells echoed from across the bay. The Skolati were readying themselves.

Four Blue men-of-war led the attack. As the ships closed on the harbour entrance, what appeared to be a dark flight of birds erupted from each of the broad squat towers. The flights resolved themselves into twin showers of arrows. The bow-fire scoured the decks of the men-of-war. Suth could just make out the oval shapes of raised shields lining those decks. Then twin thumps echoed and two great rocks, both trailing flames, came flying from atop the towers. The rocks screamed down to scatter immense showers of spray between the ships.

Suth was kneeling with his squad next to the portside railing, in line with the other marines. 'Damned big onagers on those towers,' Len mused.

'Have to sneak by close,' Keri said.

'Why?' Suth asked.

'With them machines,' Keri said, 'their aim's worse the closer you are.'

The voices of the squad sergeants rang out: 'Ready shields!'

Ahead, two of the men-of-war rocked on the water as another pair of fiery boulders crashed into the sea between them, while the remaining two swung wide, one to each side, drawing close to the tumbled rock shore of the mole and out of sight. Len chuckled at that.

'What?' Suth asked.

'There's a nasty choice. Shoot at the ship whose crew's about to besiege you, or keep firing at the rest?'

Suth bit down and resorted to pleading with his insane collection of Dal Hon gods that the gigantic target he currently rode – two dromonds side by side! – would somehow fail to be hit.

A third volley of stones, now no longer flaming, arced skyward. One came hurtling down on a Blue transport, cleanly smashing the vessel in half in a terrific shattering of wood. The other sent a wash of spume over the lumbering catamaran.

'Can we even fit through?' Len shouted to a nearby Blue marine.

The Moranth peered ahead. 'It will be . . . how do you Malazans say . . . a close thing.'

Bellows rose from all sides: '*Raise shields!*'

Suth quickly huddled beneath his. Everyone likewise hunched. He heard a hissing as of sleet or heavy rain and he tensed his arm. Then came a hammering all around as a forest of arrows slammed into the hardwood decking and the layered wood, leather, and lacquer of the shields. A few men and women cried out as arrows punched through to impale arms, or found unprotected flesh. A marine next to Suth snarled his pain and outrage as an arrow nailed his foot to the deck.

A warning shout went up from the stern and Suth twisted to see the helmsman down and Blue sailors scrambling to right the tiller arm. The awkward behemoth lost headway, began edging sideways in the narrow harbour inlet. Everyone started yelling warnings.

'Stay under cover!' the sergeants warned.

An immense explosion from the port tower punched the catamaran. Rocks tumbled down the mole. A cloud of dust and smoke engulfed the guard tower on that side. Just visible above the smoke, the roof platform canted, tilting in slow motion, to fall backwards away from the harbour inlet. Keri jumped to her feet, shield held over her head. 'Yeah! Hood take you! That's the way to do it!' She was hopping up and down. Everyone was cheering as the tower disappeared into the cloud of debris and rocks that came churning the water and even clattering on to the decking.

'Get down!' Goss yelled.

Keri, and many others, tumbled forward as one dromond, the other half of the catamaran, grated against submerged rock. 'Ready poles!' a Blue officer called. Blue sailors and marines dropped shields to obey. 'Push off!'

From beneath his shield Suth watched as the marines and sailors strove to free the catamaran. Meanwhile, the withering bow-fire had not diminished from the other tower. Many fell, clutching at arrows that seemed to sprout from nowhere. Troopers clamoured to be allowed to lend a hand. 'Stay where you are!' the sergeants yelled.

The catamaran rocked again as another explosion took the tower on the opposite side. This one sprayed stones and debris out over the harbour so close as to pluck Blue sailors from the bow of one of the dromonds. The tower tilted, settling, and slowly slid down the mole in an avalanche of rubble that crashed into the harbour.

Everyone jumped up cheering. Suth noted that as it fell the tower buried the Blue man-of-war anchored at its feet. He wondered how many, if any, had remained on board.

With all hands contributing, the catamaran grated free of the rocks and edged its way through the harbour mouth. Peering behind, Suth saw practically the entire invasion fleet bunched up behind them. Not the brightest decision, it seemed to him, to send them through so early. Perhaps they ought to have been last. Or maybe he was just thinking of his self-preservation.

Now the fleet poured in practically bow to stern, one after the other. A fresh round of bells sounded from Aamil. Smaller onagers and catapults on the walls fired, most falling short as they tested their reach. Suth's catamaran headed straight for the centre of the curtain wall. The other vessels fanned out to either side.

Fishing boats and cargo vessels now rose into flames all about the harbour. The Skolati sailors sent them coasting out to meet the invaders, then abandoned them. The Blue vessels appeared to ignore the much smaller fireships, knocking them aside, though they did furl all their canvas – the most flammable part of them, Suth imagined.

A great thrumming brought his attention to the main stronghold wall where it climbed straight up from the water. A black cloud rose, arcing up into the darkening night-blue sky. 'Raise shields!' the sergeants bellowed once more. Already sick of the threat of arrows, Suth hunched again.

The swath the fortress bow-fire raked across the vessel was astonishing. The deck appeared almost furred in arrows. So intense was the missile fire, no counter-barrage could even be attempted. Everyone tightened into balls and hid for their lives beneath their shields. Sneaking a glance from under his, Suth saw transports thumping against wharves, lowering wide gangplanks, and emptying their cargoes of marines in great surging hordes that charged up the stone piers.

Arbalests and scorpions on nearby men-of-war cracked, firing, and Keri stood again. 'This I gotta see!'

'Will you get down!' Goss yelled.

A fusillade of explosions engulfed the top of the curtain wall in smoke and bursting fragments of stone. The rubble fell in long arcs to sleet the waters or punch through vessels. Keri sat, disappointed. 'Mostly sharpers, those.'

Len shook his head. 'What'd you expect? We're right under the damned wall!'

An order went up from the Blue sterncastle: 'Raise the tower!'

Keri jumped to her feet again, punching the air. 'I knew it! Did you hear that? It's a tower. A Hood-damned siege tower!'

All the while the withering barrage of arrow-fire continued to rake the decking. Suth began to wonder how this woman managed to survive *any* engagement. Near the bow sailors struggled with circular mechanisms while Blue marines protected them with raised shields. The ratcheting of iron vibrated the dromond as the sailors worked what appeared to be some kind of immense winch.

The tall construction, as long as the vessels themselves, began to swing upwards from the stern. Suth stared, genuinely amazed. Overlapping shields layered the front and sides. The open rear exposed a plain scaling ladder. A shielded walled and roofed box topped it.

Everyone watched its agonizingly slow climb to the vertical. Water poured from the thing, some crashing down to the decks. Len was stroking his chin, quite impressed. Keri hopped from foot to foot, hardly able to contain her excitement. 'I read about one of these in *Gatan's Compendium*. We've never been able to build one.'

But Len was frowning now, troubled by something.

It was too short. Too short by far. The curtain wall rose nearly twice its height. Just as Suth opened his mouth to ask about this the ratcheting changed timbre to a deeper, more laboured, slower turning. And the tower began to rise. Not the entire thing; it became obvious that the tower was in fact built of two segments, one snug inside the other. It was the inner one that now rose.

The Skolati had reorganized the battlement defences and rocks pelted down, smashing to the decking, flattening troopers. The arrow-fire returned to its unrelenting stream. Suth adjusted his helmet strap one-handed, the other supporting his shield up over his head.

'*Move forward!*' sergeants bellowed. 'Ready to climb!'

The men-of-war and flanking support ships fired another salvo from their arbalests, scorpions and bow onagers and Suth flinched, knowing now what was to come. Staccato explosions atop the wall obscured it in smoke and dust. Rubble came showering down upon them in pebbles and stones large enough to knock a hole in the deck. A marine in line disappeared as a stone smashed her flat. Everyone cursed the Blues to Hood. Suth agreed, wondering what was worse: the defending arrow-fire, or their own supporting counter-barrage. Now he understood Len's cryptic remark about the Blues supplying more munitions to the fight than they would want.

'*Forward!*'

The troopers readied themselves, shields overhead. Suth peered under his to the bows. He caught a glimpse of the Adjunct, now in a red cloth-wrapped helmet and a heavy banded hauberk with mail sleeves. The young officer leaned in to take the ladder first. Two squads of what looked like elite Blue marines followed him. Soon after that the line edged forward.

Arrow-fire returned, scattered, but gathering in density, clattering like hail. A roar shook the dimming evening as the marines, Blue and Malazan, clamoured before the west gatehouse. A much heavier defence faced them there. Suth's mouth had gone as dry as dirt yet his palms were wet. Action was what'd he wanted all this time but now that it was here it was not what he'd been expecting at all.

This was no testing of individual prowess of the sort boasted by his brothers and sisters back in Dal Hon. Yet, bizarrely, the courage it demanded was perhaps even greater: one had to abandon all personal control, release one's fate to the greater effort. It was terrifying, yet intoxicating. He felt helpless, yet part of an unstoppable force.

His squad, Goss leading, reached the bow decking. Here a section of the railing had been removed and a gangway led to the rear of the tower. A solid line of men and women slowly worked their way up the ladder above, shields swinging at their backs.

'Keep moving,' a Blue officer told everyone who passed, a hand on his or her shoulder. 'Do not stop at the top. Push forward. Make room for more.' Pyke took a grip of the ladder ahead of Suth, while Wess was behind. Len and Keri brought up the rear.

Though water still poured down the construction, Suth found the climbing easy. Some sort of sand or grit coated the rungs of the ladder. Arrows and rocks rattled from the layered shields, striking at poor angles.

'Move your fat arse,' Pyke yelled at Dim, above.

The tower shook then, rocking back and forth, and a crash sounded above. Suth hugged the rungs for his life. But no one came tumbling down and the tower remained upright. A beast-like roar from the top told the story. Enough troopers had reached the platform to lower the gangway and charge. Iron rang from iron and now bodies fell tumbling past to hit the water with a splash, or strike the decking with a sickening thump. Suth fixed his concentration on each rung before him and just climbed.

He dared not look down; he'd never been much for climbing. His arms ached already and he hadn't even reached the fighting yet. Then from either side hands grasped his shoulders and pulled him upright. 'Go! Go! Go!' someone yelled, propelling him forward. He charged after Pyke, drawing his sword and readying his shield. The gangway sagged and swayed beneath him. He reached the wall battlements and stepped down amid shattered stone and a carpet of fallen bodies. The noise that buffeted him from behind the curtain wall almost knocked him back. Fighting clashed from either side. Explosions lit the evening across the port city as Moranth incendiaries came arcing in overhead to fall blossoming in orange and gold flame. Suth stood transfixed by the sight of such chaos. This was not fighting as he knew it; this was war. Two arrows hammering into his shield shook the trance from him and he charged to the right after Pyke.

His squad was bunched up at the rear of a line of marines choking an open walkway leading to a tower. 'What's the hold-up?' Yana called.

'Who knows?' someone shouted back.

Arrows clattered from the stones around them, fired from rooftops behind the wall. 'Let's move!' Lard bellowed. 'Our backsides are hanging out here!'

'I'm sure they're working on it!' another voice called back.

An explosion shot smoke and debris on to the broad street below. In the fitful light Suth glimpsed fallen bodies, broken rock and equipment. Marines appeared, charging after retreating defenders. A great shout went up from within the tower and the line began advancing.

'Who do you think that was?' Keri asked Len as they shuffled down the tight passage.

'Thumbs, maybe. Or Slowburn.'

'Naw. Tight work like that? Musta been Squeaky.'

Len made a noise. 'She's overrated.'

'Cap it!' Goss barked from below.

They charged through a guardroom and hall cluttered by fallen Skolati defenders and marines. A barrier of furniture had been blasted aside, and the stone was slick underfoot with blood and fluids. The tower door had been demolished. The squads piled up behind pushed them out like a great vomit of rage, confusion and frustration. Squads peeled off down narrow streets. Goss was there and he yanked Suth aside to send him over to where Yana, Lard and Dim stood together in a triangle watching the darkened doorways and windows. Suth joined them, followed by the rest. Goss addressed them, hands raised. 'Okay. This is where it gets hairy. The Skolati have fallen back but they'll re-form. Where, we don't know. We're to push to the east gate tower to hit them from behind. Follow me. Stay close. And keep your eyes open.' They formed two columns, Len and Keri in the middle, Goss leading, and headed up one of the narrow cobbled streets.

'How do we know this is the right way?' Pyke said, his voice low.

'We don't, okay?' Yana growled. 'So shut the Hood up.'

Once they entered the canyon-like street the light disappeared. Only a pale shifting glow from the fires in the city offered any details. Echoes of fierce fighting elsewhere came and went. Jogging down the street, Suth felt more exposed than if he were out on the savannah at night blindfolded. Despite the chaos the city seemed to be holding its breath.

'Where is everyone?' Pyke hissed. 'This is stupid. We should all be together.'

'Everyone just kinda took off,' Wess said absently, chewing something, and he spat out a stream of brown.

Ahead, Goss stopped, raised a fist. The street dead-ended at a small courtyard. He gave a 'turn round' signal.

'Shit,' Wess mouthed, and he eased one of the two long-knives he carried.

'I think—'

'No one gives a shit what you think, okay, Pyke?' Yana cut in. 'Now be quiet. I'm trying to listen.'

'Listen? Listen to what?'

Yana tilted her head. 'Something . . .'

'*Form up!*' Goss bellowed.

Above, all round the square, windows crashed open. Arrow-fire raked the cobbles. The squad hunched, backs to each other, shields out. Goss kicked open a door only to have someone charge out and strike him in the chest with a woodsman's axe.

It surprised Goss more than damaged him as he was wearing a heavy brigandine. He stabbed the man, pushed him aside, and then urged the squad to follow him in. A horde of Skolati burst from the surrounding doorways. The squad stabbed and thrust from behind their shields as they retreated into the building.

'Lard, Yana, hold the door,' Goss yelled.

'Aye!'

While Lard jabbed, cursing, and Yana shield-bashed, Suth edged to a rear stairway. He watched Goss and Len crouch together in the middle of what were someone's living quarters. 'Can't stay here,' Len said and he picked up a pot and peered into it, sniffing.

Goss nodded heavily. 'I know. I know. But there's too damned many.' He cocked his head, eyed Len speculatively. 'You carrying?'

Len pursed his lips, considering, then nodded.

Goss stood. 'Togg's teats! Why didn't you say so, dammit!' He turned to where Lard and Yana hammered back with their shields, stabbing at those of the clamouring crowd who could push up to the door. He waved his disgust. 'Clear the street.'

Len stood. 'Keri! We're on.'

Steps sounded on the stairs. Goss snapped his fingers at Suth, who was nearest. Suth charged up the stairway. He met a line of bearded men in boiled leather armour. The lead man swung a curved sword in a clumsy panicked arc. Suth let it pass then thrust straight through the man's inner thigh. The fellow screamed and fell from the stairs into the room, where the rest finished him. The second leapt for Suth but he shifted sideways to let him fall past. The third swung for his head. He ducked, climbed higher and stabbed, severing the fellow's ankle tendon. This one lost his footing and tumbled into Suth, who shrugged him off the stairs to fall and be finished.

'Secure those rooms!' Goss shouted.

'Aye!' Suth charged, shield high. He saw no one until he entered one room to find an open trapdoor, a ladder, and four Skolati soldiers. He charged. His shield-bash knocked three off balance. The fourth swung for his head, the blade cracking off his iron helmet, making his head ring and stars burst in his vision. He stabbed this one in the shoulder before spinning to put his back to a wall. They all closed at once, crowding one another. Suth trusted in his shield and concentrated on the one on his right. He parried a swing, sliding his shorter blade along the sword, and thrust low beneath the hauberk. The blade grated along the pelvis bone as it slid in.

Suth turned from that man without waiting to see him fall – the thrust had to be fatal. A blade skittered along the top of his shield; another hit his shoulder, numbing his shield-arm but not piercing the armour. Then the three were down and Len and Keri were there, long-knives bloodied.

'That was stupid,' Len told him, his voice low. 'You tryin' to win this war all by yourself? Next time you call for support, yes?'

Suth nodded, surprised to find his heart hammering, his throat parched and arms shaking. Keri was kneeling to clean her blade on the headscarf of one man; that casual gesture made Suth re-evaluate the woman.

Len cuffed his shoulder. 'Now come with us.'

'Yessir.'

They went to a room overlooking the street. Suth peered out. The street was jammed with Skolati citizens. Their screaming and cursing was an unintelligible roar. Soldiers fought to force their way through the mob, weapons held high. Len and Keri shrugged off their shoulder bags and knelt. They straightened, holding small dark green orbs in each hand.

Len used his elbow to nudge Suth back from the window. 'Munitions!' he yelled back towards the interior of the building.

'Aye,' came Goss' answering shout.

Len leaned out to throw his, one to each side of the doorway, and ducked away from the window. Twin explosions shocked Suth, popping his ears and knocking him backwards. Dust streamed down from the roof. Keri leaned out, tossed her munitions farther, one after the other, and then went to one knee. Those eruptions echoed like hammer-strokes in the courtyard.

Len faced the interior, hands cupped to his mouth: 'Clear!' He scooped up his bag, grabbed Suth's shoulder to propel him to the stairs. 'Go!'

Downstairs the squad was formed up at the smoke-shrouded doorway, ready. 'Go!' Yana shouted, and they charged. Suth brought up the rear, covering Len and Keri. Outside he nearly tripped on men and women lying cut down on the street, or hobbling, soaked in blood from the countless minor slashing wounds of the munitions Keri called 'sharpers'. A low moaning rose from countless wounded and dying. They escaped the courtyard, charged back up the way they'd come. After a few turns Keri shouted, pointing up a side alley, 'This way!'

Goss signed a halt then came to her. 'What is it?'

'This should lead to a main way.'

Pyke waved his dismissal. 'How would she know?'

'Shut up,' Suth told the man. Pyke glared his rage.

'Okay.' Goss pointed up the alley. 'Let's go.'

Suth kept to the rear behind the saboteurs. As they jogged along the narrow twisting way, he asked Keri, his voice low, 'How *do* you know?'

She smiled, her teeth bright in the gloom. 'Acoustics.'

'What?'

'Sounds. These sounds belong to a big space.'

All he could hear was the distorted clash and snarl of countless engagements all melded together into one rumbling as of a midnight thunderstorm. He shook his head – he was not used to cities. Ahead the squad was crouched where the alley opened on to a broad, treed boulevard that appeared to lead up from the waterfront. In the moonlight and shifting yellow glow of fires Suth glimpsed citizens running across the way carrying bundled possessions in their arms. Len tapped him, pointed up the boulevard. A squad of Moranth Blue marines. Goss waved an advance. They jogged up to the Blues.

As they went someone straightened among the Moranth: the young Adjunct. He'd been kneeling to examine dark shapes that resolved into a number of fallen Malazan soldiers. Goss offered the Adjunct a very truncated salute that he answered with a nod.

A gasp from Dim brought Suth's attention to the fallen. They looked strange, skeletal, flesh drawn in and wrinkled, pulled back from grinning teeth. It was as if they were desiccated.

'What is it, sir?' Goss asked.

'Looks like magery.'

'We were told to expect none.'

'That's true, Sergeant.' The Adjunct's gauntleted hand went to the bright ivory grip of his sword, as if the movement were an unconscious habit of his while thinking. 'I'm told there's only one kind here.' He was gazing up the boulevard to a tall building, spired, its arched roof silver in the moonlight.

'*Shit*,' Keri murmured, aside.

'What is it?' Suth asked, low.

'Their Hood-spawned local cult.'

'You're with me,' the Adjunct told Goss. He signed to the Blue commander, who jerked a nod and waved to his marines. They spread out, advancing. Goss motioned for his squad to take the centre behind the Adjunct.

More Malazan dead littered the stairs leading up to the building's open door. It looked as though a squad had come to investigate something and been cut down by magery. Not one corpse of a defender could be seen. The Adjunct drew his blade and entered first. Half the Blue squad followed, then Goss motioned his in, and the remaining Blues brought up the rear. Within, braziers on tripods and lamps hanging from the distant ceiling lit a broad open chamber. Pillars ran in double rows along a centre aisle. Some sort of bright ornament, shaped like a starburst, hung on the far wall. Dark tapestries hinted at scenes of storm-racked waters and a woman in white flowing robes.

Four men stepped out from behind pillars to meet the Adjunct. They wore long priestly robes, were bearded, and carried stout staves. 'You are a fool to have entered here,' said one.

'Surrender, and you can keep your religion,' the Adjunct answered.

'Fool! You cannot *take* our faith! The Lady is with us now. All those who dare to invade are doomed.'

The four struck their staves to the polished stone floor. Suth felt something strike him like a hand at his chest, or a gust of wind. Blue marines on either side clutched at their throats and helms, gagging. They fell to their knees. All those near the Adjunct, including Goss's squad, remained standing. The four priests gaped at them, astonished. It might have been a trick of the uncertain light but the young Adjunct's blade seemed to shine more brightly then. The Adjunct stepped up and swung. The priest raised his stave and the sword sliced right through the iron-braced dark wood. The priest staggered back, then his eyes blazed with an inner light and his lips twisted back from his teeth. 'I see you now,' he grated, his voice changed, somehow torn from his throat. 'The Bitch Queen would send her soldier. But it will take more than you. I will drink your heart-blood.'

The Adjunct swung again and the man's head spun from his neck. At that the spell seemed to shatter and everyone charged, cutting down the priests in a frenzy of loathing. They hacked the corpses long after they'd fallen, then Suth crossed to where the Adjunct was on his haunches, his blunt tribesman features drawn down in a frown. The youth was examining the decapitated corpse. Not one drop of blood could be seen pooled at the severed neck. Suth's heart lurched in his chest and his gorge rose sour in his mouth. He turned away, staggered outside the temple to suck deep the warm smoke-tinged air. Wess emerged, clapped him on the back. 'Fucking butcher's work, hey? Not proper soldiering.'

'You've – seen – things like that before?'

He gave a curt nod. 'Yeah. There's nothing you can do. Either it gets you or you get it.'

Suth drew in a deep breath. Distant fighting still rumbled from the waterfront. 'What now?'

'What now?' Wess adjusted his helmet. 'Now the real fighting starts. We're headed to one of the gate towers!' and he laughed, spitting.

Goss came out, followed by the rest of the squad. 'Form up. We're for the east gate. Double-time.'

The Adjunct emerged as well. The remaining Blue marines took up positions around him. He signed to Goss, who shouted, '*Move out!*'

*

It was long past mid-night when Rillish's two captured Marese galleys, one rammed and listing, limped down the coast. He was certain they must be the last vessels and would arrive too late for the assault. That they still floated at all was enough, of course, but still, he was disappointed.

A Skolati merchant caravel, fat and slow, crossed ahead of them, bows to the south. The Skolati were not alarmed; for all they knew they were crippled Marese struggling home. Rillish was willing to let them go. It had been a night of alarms and excursions, flight and chase, and they were all exhausted. A figure walked to the stern of the distant cargo vessel, set a foot on the low rail to peer back at them. He was armoured, and the orange pre-dawn light caught at bright silver filigree adorning his cuirass and headgear, and tracing the longsword sheath.

Rillish's breath caught in his throat. *Burn deliver them!* He ran back to the sailing master. 'Take that ship!'

The man blinked sleepily. 'What?'

'Come aside of it! Take it! Now!'

The sailing master squinted at the vessel. 'It isn't even a warship!'

'Do it!' Rillish gripped his sword. 'Or I'll force you.'

The man scowled behind his beard. 'Very well!' He leaned on the tiller arm and the galley began to heave to. Rillish faced the crowded vessel and shouted: 'Row! Row now with all your strength! One last charge!'

The troopers groaned, protesting, but the galley picked up speed. The Malazan sailors with them adjusted the sail to cut closer to the weak wind. Rillish watched for a time then turned on the sailing master. 'We're barely gaining. Can't you do more?'

'Your soldiers row like retards. They are not in time. It takes years of training. Still,' and he shrugged, 'we are gaining.'

Rillish shaded his gaze to look behind. The other captured galley was following, but at a great distance. The sailing master saw his gaze. 'He is cursing you very much right now, I think.'

'Yes. I expect so.'

He found Captain Peles at the bows. She eyed him, puzzled. 'A prize of war, Fist?'

'A hunch. We're going to board. Do *not* charge ahead. Form a line, shields out. Yes?'

She saluted. 'As you order, sir.'

'Very good.'

Their progress was agonizing. A pale pre-dawn glow gathered to the east. Arrow-fire flew from the cargo ship but it was thin and uninspired. As they drew aside, Rillish saw that he'd been right. Three men in dark armour, silver-detailed, awaited them at mid-deck. *Three Korelri Chosen – veterans of the wall.* He was glad to have more than a hundred heavy infantry backing him up.

Eventually, the sailing master was content with their relative positions and the bow of the galley swung over towards the bow of the cargo vessel, cutting it off. 'Toss grapnels,' he called. 'Ship oars!'

Marines threw the pronged iron grapnels, heaved on the ropes. The vessels swung together. Oars that were slow to be drawn were snapped. Their ends swung, hammering troopers flat.

'Board!' Rillish yelled, stepping up on to the railing and leaping. The troopers followed, shields at their backs. Rillish fell, rolling, then jumped up to retreat to the infantry now lining the ship's side. The sailors of the cargo vessel stood empty-handed, surrendering. The three armoured men calmly faced them alone, weapons undrawn. 'Ready shields,' Rillish ordered. The troopers complied, forming line. He drew his duelling swords, pointed to one of the Korelri Stormguard. 'Surrender and you will be spared.'

'Do you know who we are?' the man asked from behind the narrow slit of his chased blue-black helm.

'Yes. I know.'

'Then you know our answer.'

'Yes.'

'We cannot allow you to boast of our defeat, invader. You will not have our swords or armour to spit upon as spoils of war. It would be an insult to Our Lady. That cannot be permitted. And so—'

Rillish took a breath to shout, lurched forward. 'NO!'

The three turned and vaulted over the side. Rillish threw himself to the rail, staring down. Three dark shapes sinking from sight, blades drawn, glinting in the slanting light, held upright before their helms. *Gods! It was inconceivable. Such fervour. Such dedication. Such waste.* He found tears starting from his eyes and he turned away.

Captain Peles was there, peering down, troubled. 'So those were Korelri, yes?'

Rillish cleared his throat. 'Yes,' he said, his voice thick.

'And we are to invade their lands?'

Rillish almost laughed at the thought. 'Yes.'

The woman said nothing; her sceptical look was enough.

'Captives, sir!' A trooper ran up, saluted. 'The cargo – human captives. Hundreds jammed in down there.'

Rillish answered the salute. 'Thank you, soldier.'

'Slaves?' Peles said, surprised. 'They are slavers?'

'Of a kind, Captain. Bodies. Hundreds of bodies destined for the wall. Warm bodies to man it and defend it against the Stormriders.' Rillish could see that the woman was shaken. 'We'll sail the vessel for Aamil. We'll free them there – if we have the port. Have the master send over what sailors he can spare.'

Captain Peles saluted. 'Aye, sir.'

*

Just after the sun cleared the horizon Rillish's captured Skolati vessel bumped up against the stone pier at Aamil in one of the last available berths. Malazan sailors threw down ropes. The mage of Ruse, Devaleth, was there waiting to greet him. After last orders to the ship's master, he went to the gangway and found Captain Peles there with a detachment of Malazan heavies. 'No need, Captain.'

'Every need, sir.' She saluted. 'You are an Imperial Fist. You should be treated as such.'

Rillish answered the salute, nodded his exhausted acquiescence. 'Very well, Captain.' He climbed the gangway to bow to Devaleth, who gave wry, but pleased, acknowledgement.

'Good to see you made it,' he said.

'And you.' She gestured up the pier. 'This way.'

She led him to a tall thick gateway. Peles followed with his guard. The detritus of war was piled high here and teams came and went, still pulling bodies from the heaped wreckage and carting them off to be buried or burned. Rillish was surprised that the broad stone archway was still intact. As they walked beneath it, the stones marred by dark stains, Rillish observed, 'Why didn't the Blues just blow the gate?'

Devaleth walked with her hands clasped at her back. She was frowning at the ground, her face drawn, her eyes bruised. 'Yes, why not? They've burned and blown up everything else.'

Rillish cleared his throat. 'I'm . . . sorry for your countrymen, Devaleth.'

She nodded absently as they walked. 'I never thought I'd see it happen. The blockade broken. Do not get me wrong – I am glad, of course. It is necessary. Still . . .' she gave him a wintry smile, 'a shock to one's pride.'

A squad posted at an intersection straightened, saluting. Rillish answered the salute. Devaleth led him round the corner. 'I understand,' she said, 'the Blues fear a counter-assault from Mare. And so they left the defences as intact as possible.'

'Ah. I see. How are the Skolati?'

'Quiet. Just as shocked, perhaps. Staying indoors. No doubt they hope we will just go away.'

'You were here for the attack?'

'No. I was with the Admiral. After we broke through the blockade he sent me on with some last messages for the High Fist.'

Rillish felt his chest tighten. 'Ah. Yes. Of course.' The stink of smoke that hung over the city now made Rillish sick. He'd known, of course, that he would be reporting to the man, but he'd somehow managed to keep it all out of mind.

Devaleth gestured up the narrow cobbled road to an inn where Malazan troopers stood guard. 'Here we are.'

As Rillish entered, two squads lounging in the common room straightened to their feet, saluted. Rillish answered, nodding to them. He motioned for Captain Peles to wait here with his guard, then followed Devaleth up the stairs.

Two troopers stood guard at a door on the third floor. Devaleth knocked and it was opened by the young Adjunct, Kyle. His thick black hair was a mess, his wide dark face smudged with soot, and he still wore his armoured hauberk – he'd not even cleaned up from the fight yet. He inclined his head in greeting. 'Fist Rillish,' he called out, opening the door wide.

The High Fist was within, facing a man in rich-looking robes, bearded and sweating, flanked by Malazan troopers. Greymane waved the man away. 'That's all for now, Patriarch Thurell. I want everything gathered at the main square. Supplies, all mounts, cartage.'

'Yes, yes. Certainly.' The man bowed jerkily, hands clasped at his front. He seemed terrified. The troopers marched him past Rillish and out of the door.

Greymane peered down at Rillish. His eyes seemed a brighter blue than usual, glittering from under the wide shelf of his brow. Rillish bowed. 'Congratulations upon your victory, High Fist.'

Greymane leaned against a table, crossed his arms. 'Here at last, Fist Rillish Jal Keth. Now that the fighting is over.'

Rillish clamped his teeth against the urge to laugh the comment off, cleared his throat. 'We saw much action at sea.'

'No doubt.'

Swallowing, Rillish squeezed a gloved hand until it ached. He felt Devaleth there at his side, her own stiffness, but he dared not look to her. 'You have orders, sir?'

Perhaps it was the room's poor lighting, but Rillish thought the man was glowering as if trying to think of what to do with him. His wide mouth drew down and he heaved a heavy breath. 'It just so happens that a number of squads from the 4th have struck on ahead inland – my very intent, as it happens. You are to lead the rest of the

4th after them. Push, Fist. Push on westward. I will follow with Fist Shul and the main body. Adjunct Kyle here will accompany you. As will the High Mage.'

Rillish jerked an assent. 'Certainly, High Fist. I understand. You wish to break out before the Skolati can organize a counter-strike.' He nodded to the Adjunct, who stood watching from the door, his face emotionless, hands at his belt. 'You are most welcome.' The young man just nodded, utterly self-contained. *So, my minder. Greymane is to take no chances with his subordinates this time.*

'You will leave immediately. I understand we can even offer some few mounts.'

'That would be welcome as well.'

The High Fist grimaced again as if uncomfortable, rubbed his unshaven jaw. Rillish hoped it was because the man was as ill at ease with this interview as he. Then Greymane merely waved to the door. 'That is all.'

Rillish drew himself up stiffly, saluted. 'High Fist.'

The Adjunct opened the door.

Reaching the street, Rillish said nothing. Ranks of infantry marched past. Smoke plumed up from still-burning buildings. Broken rubble choked a side street. None of it registered clearly with him; everything spun as his pulse throbbed in his chest and temple. As they walked side by side, Devaleth and he, the Adjunct having remained behind for now, Devaleth said quietly, 'You show great forbearance, Fist.'

Rillish glanced behind to Captain Peles and his guard, gave a curt wave as if to cut the memory away. 'Whether I bellow and bluster, he remains my commanding officer. There is nothing I can do. Therefore, I'd rather cultivate equanimity. For my peace of mind.'

'His paranoia threatens to incite the very actions he suspects.'

Rillish shot her a hard stare. 'I'll thank you not to talk of such things again, High Mage.'

She inclined her head. 'As you prefer, Fist.'

'For now let us get the 4th organized. I will hold a staff meeting at noon.'

'Very good, sir.'

* * *

Orzu had fished the inland seas of Korel and its archipelagos all his life. He'd been born on a boat, part of no nation or state, had grown up knowing loyalty to no land or lands. Lately he and his clan had been living in a tiny fishing hamlet so small it appeared on no map. It was a collection of slate-roofed stone huts on the shores of the Plains of Blight. And if one climbed the tallest hill within a day's walk and squinted hard to the south one could just make out the snowy peaks of the Iceback range. So it was quite a surprise to him when three men and a woman came tramping down the barren shore of black wave-smoothed stones to where he sat mending his nets in the lee of his boat.

He watched them approach, making no secret of his open examination. Seen hard travel. A shipwreck further up the coast, maybe? Armed and armoured. Soldiers. But whose? Stygg? Jasston? None had the look. The shortest was distinctly foreign-looking with his dark, almost bluish hue.

If they were raiders they were the sorriest-arsed brigands Orzu had ever seen. Thieves did come through occasionally: outlaws from Jasston, thugs from Stygg. He and his fellow villagers had no particular weapons or armour to oppose them; their main defence was in appearing to have nothing. And so he just eyed the four while they walked up and the foremost, the bluish-hued fellow, rested a hand on the side of his boat drawn up on the strand and addressed him in mangled Katakan: 'You sell boat?'

Orzu took the pipe from his mouth. 'No, I no sell boat.'

'We pay much gold, many coin.'

'Fish don't want coin.'

The four talked then, their language foreign, but with a very familiar lilt to it. Orzu thought he could almost catch the odd word or two. Closer now, he also noticed how the tip of one's nose was black, the edges of another's ears. The skin of all four was cracked and bloodied, flaking. Frostbite. Damned severe, too. They couldn't have come down from the Ice Barrens, could they? But that was a desolate emptiness.

'We pay you to take us. To Korelri. Yes?'

Orzu thought about that. 'How much coin?'

The spokesman gestured to the tallest of them, a great thick warrior in a mail shirt that hung to his ankles, a wide shield on his back, and a helm tied to his belt. His long black hair was a great mane. This one handed over a fat leather sack. The spokesman gave it to Orzu. It was amazingly hefty. Orzu peered in, took out a coin. Gold. More fortune than he'd ever dreamed to touch. He cinched the bag up tight. 'I take you. But must bring wife, children.'

The four eyed one another, confused. 'Take your . . . family?' said the spokesman.

'Yes. My price. Bring wife, children. Go tomorrow morning. Yes?'

'Why . . .'

'My price. Not so high, yes?'

'Well . . .'

'My name Orzu. We have deal, yes?'

'Blues. We have a deal.'

Blues? What an odd name. Must be for the hue of his skin. Orzu shrugged inwardly. No matter. He set down his mending and stood. 'First we eat. My wife make you fish stew. Is good, you see.'

That caught their interest. All four perked up at the mention of hot food.

Shipwrecked. Must be. What other possible explanation could there be? This was good. They would eat well, meet the family.

And he had such a very large family.

The stench was the hardest thing for Shell to endure. She sat near the doorway – nothing more than a gaping hole in the piled stones of the walls of the hut – and held the clay bowl down away from her face. All the while the fat woman, this fellow's wife, grinned toothlessly at her, the only other woman present. At their feet a great gang of children cried, fought among themselves, gaped at her so close she could smell their stale breath, and gobbled down the rotten stew. Whose were they? Not this old couple, surely.

'Blues,' she called, edging aside a youth who seemed determined to find something hidden far up his nose. 'Let's just take a boat and go. We're wasting time.'

From where he sat next to the gabbling old fellow, apparently the patriarch of this horde, Blues shook his head. 'It's their livelihood, Shell. They'd starve.'

Lazar stuck his head in. 'There's more coming outside. Two more boats are pulled up.'

'Thanks.' More of them! A damned family reunion.

At least Fingers seemed in his element: fascinating the kids with tricks of sleight of hand. They squealed when he made stones appear from their noses and mouths. She called to Blues: 'There's more of them outside.'

He spoke to the old man, listened, cocked his head in concentration. In-laws. His daughters' and sons' spouses' brothers and sisters and their children.

On the subcontinent known to some as Korel, to others as Fist, the Chosen who defend the Stormwall against the attacks of the ocean-borne 'Riders' foretell that should these Riders broach the wall they shall sweep on to engulf the world entire in an eternal reign of ice and storm.

Despite these claims, the Malazan Emperor Kellanved ordered his armies to invade Korel lands. This confronted the Stormguard with a horrifying choice: defend the wall or defend their lands. Skilfully, Kellanved swiftly withdrew the necessity for said choice by offering to limit his holdings to territory currently occupied. The Chosen readily agreed to these terms. In this, and many other pacts, it may be said that Kellanved manoeuvred and negotiated his way to Empire. Few in these times appreciate this distinction.

Sketches of History
Ordren Stennist
Academe, Kartool

'Well, who in the Queen's name are *these* kids?'

Blues looked surprised. 'Haven't you been listening? Grandchildren, of course.'

'Blues . . .'

'How do you like the food?'

'It's vile. Why?'

A laugh. 'Just wondering, because it looks like we're in for a lot more.'

'What do you mean?'

Blues waved to encompass the kids, the men and women sitting outside on the bare smoothed stones, watching and waiting. 'Because it looks like we just hired the entire clan.'

'*Blues!*'

The next morning twelve broad fishing boats, longboats Shell imagined you might call them, lay pulled up on the strand. Orzu's clan of fisherfolk was busy piling them up with their meagre smelly possessions. Now that she'd had time to reflect upon it, she couldn't blame them. This was their chance to escape this desolate shore. Others had now found the courage to speak; a girl, fat with child and carrying yet another, seemed to have attached herself to Shell.

'What is your name?' she asked the girl.

'Ena.' The child she carried in her arm was fighting to open her blouse to reach a swollen teat. She brushed the small hands aside. 'You?'

'Shell. Where will you go?'

She shrugged. 'We go to Theft.'

'What will you do there?'

Again the indifferent shrug. 'Same as here.'

You are wiser than you know, young woman-child. For you, things are sadly unlikely to change.

Ena was eyeing her soft leathers under her thick travelling cloak, her leather gloves and tall boots. 'Where you come from?'

'The south. Far to the south. Before that, far to the north.'

An older woman, exact relationship uncertain, came and took the child from Ena, then the two argued back and forth for a time until the old woman marched off enraged.

'What is it?' Shell asked.

A smile. 'Mother says I am lazy. Work to be done. But I tell her I am no longer a child to be ordered about. The . . . Blessed Lady . . . she is known where you are from?'

Shell was surprised by the non-sequitur. It was a moment before she could reply. 'No. She is not known. She is only known here.'

Ena tucked a hand under the swell of her belly. Her many relations tramped back and forth readying the boats. Blues was arguing with Orzu next to one particularly overloaded skiff; he appeared to be miming sinking.

'Yes. We thought so, no matter the words of her priests.'

'Her priests? You have heard them?'

Ena nodded with child-like earnestness. 'Oh yes. They come here. Half-starved wanderers. They stay and preach to us. Lady this and Lady that. They try to convert us.'

'*Convert* you? You do not worship the Lady?'

She nodded, so serious. 'Oh no. We are the Sea-Folk. We follow the old ways. Oh, the last of the priests seemed harmless enough until he tried to use the boys to satisfy himself. So we bound him and threw him to the Sea-Father.'

'The Sea-Father? Oh, yes. The old ways.'

'Yes. The Sea-Father. The Sky-Father. The Dark-Taker. The fertile Mother. And the Enchantress. The priests spoke against her the most. But we do not listen. We know the Lady by her ancient name. Shrikasmil – the Destroyer.'

Shell studied the child-woman while she stared out to sea. She was pretty despite her greasy hair, the grimed unwashed face. Pretty perhaps only because of her youth and her pregnancy. 'Why travel to Theft, then? Surely you will not be welcome.'

Again the uncaring shrug, though tinged by a wry smile. 'Nowhere are we welcome. We are the Sea-Folk. We come and go as we please. We choose to harbour at Theft till they chase us off. It was strange, you know . . .' and she cocked her head, her brows wrinkling, 'he was glad when we threw him in. Happy. He wanted to be martyr to the Lady. They all want to die for her. It is perverse. Shouldn't faith seek life?'

Shell said nothing. Ena answered her own question with what seemed her response to everything: a shrug of dismissal. Then, rousing herself, she walked off to lend her family a hand. Shell remained, facing the sea, troubled. Something the girl had said. Dying for her. *They all want to die for her.* Something in that clawed at her instincts. She did not know what it was, yet. But there was something there. She could feel it the way she could feel the Lady's own baleful hot gaze glaring from the north. From this point onward none of them should dare summon their Warrens.

BOOK II

The Land

CHAPTER VI

History consists of nothing more than the lies we tell ourselves to justify the present.

Book of Forbidden Knowledge
Odwin Innist, condemned scholar

After the tenth wave of the night Lord Protector Hiam discovered his endurance was failing him. Times were he could stand two watches of back-to-back fighting without feeling the strain. But in the weakened parry of a Rider's lance-thrust, his spear nearly wrenched from his grasp, he saw instantly that he would not last to the dawn.

He abandoned the counter-strike, readying instead, content to let that Rider slide past. The men of his bodyguard urged it on. Yet there was no time to recuperate as the next wave came crashing in far higher than he could ever remember this early in the season. It inundated the lowest defences. Hiam charged down where Chosen wallowed in the knee-deep, frigid water. Riders now walked the outer machicolations. Their shell-like scaled armour hung as ragged skirting all the way down to the waters. They dropped their lances and drew saw-bladed longswords.

He and his six bodyguards crashed into the Riders like their own wave. Hiam faced one, lunging high to draw his parry while his bodyguard thrust low to impale the demon, who grunted and grasped the spear, only to have his hand slashed as the guard yanked free the broad leaf-shaped blade. This one fell into the shallow water to dissolve like ice rotting. Another Rider shook off the attacks of two Chosen to charge Hiam. He parried the Rider's swing but the ice-blade caught at the haft of his spear like a gripping fist to heave it aside.

A kind of calm acceptance took Hiam then. The Rider was inside his guard – this was how it should end for him. The fiend's sword swung, but a spear from a guard deflected the blade enough for it to clash from Hiam's full helm like a bell. The blow brought him to one knee.

His guards pressed close, defending. Hiam regained his footing, launched his spear at the Rider then shrugged his broad round shield from his back and drew his thrusting blade. By this time his guards had finished the last Rider.

So be it. The spirit is willing but age has wrought its betrayal. Imagine, to have survived nearly thirty seasons upon the wall only to fall to so pedestrian an enemy – the snail's crawl of the years.

Out amid the chop of the surging breakers the Riders did not press their advantage. The nearest reined in its horse-like mount of glowing sapphire ice and pearl-like spume to sink beneath the surface. As it went Hiam believed he saw it raise its lance in salute. *Lady damn them for this façade of honour and courtesy. They fool no one.*

The attack upon this section of the wall was over for now. A tap on his shoulder let the Lord Protector know his shift might as well end. He rotated out, accompanied by his guard of six, back to the marshalling walk behind the layered walltop defences. Shaking, he drew off his lined gauntlets to warm his hands over a nearby brazier. He told himself the shaking was the cold . . . only the cold.

I'm slowing. Twice the age of these men around me. Might not last the season. All it takes is one mistake, or the mounting sluggishness of exhaustion. Better this way, though. Better to fall now on the ramparts than perhaps to live to see . . . No! That is unworthy – Lady forgive me! Now is my trial of weakness.

He pushed down his steaming hands until the heat seared them and he groaned, yanking them away. Tears started from his eyes. *How I will miss these men!* He felt as if his heart were squeezing to a knot in his chest. *That is my regret. That I will share no more time with my brothers. These are the best of men. Our cause is just and our hearts are pure.*

Other hands extended over the charcoal embers and Hiam glanced up to see Wall Marshal Quint eyeing him with narrowed gaze.

'A close one,' Quint murmured.

Hiam cleared his throat. 'Shouldn't have been. I just lost my footing.'

Not even deigning to honour that with a response, Quint watched him from over the embers.

'You have a report?' Hiam asked, rather testily.

A slow nod. 'Trouble in the west. Out near the Wind Tower. Seven fell in one shift – a run of bad luck.'

Hiam straightened, alarmed. 'And?'

'Marshal Real was there. He called for the Lady's grace – and was answered. He held until relief arrived.'

Grunting his understanding, Hiam relaxed. 'I see. Bless him then. The Lady has gathered him to her. May he sit as one of the Holy Martyrs.'

Quint nodded again. 'She judged him worthy.'

'And our champion. How is he doing?'

'He has roused himself. We should squeeze another season out of him after all.'

'Excellent. That frees up a lot of men.'

'Yes. And you – just what did you think you were doing down there?'

Hiam drew his cloak more tightly about his shoulders. 'Helping out.'

'Damn foolishness is what that was. Throwing yourself away. Don't do that. We *all* need you. The men need to know you're here watching over them. That alone is worth a thousand spears.'

Hiam was quite impressed by his old friend's burst of loquaciousness. It was the most he'd heard out of him in years. He smiled chidingly at the scowling Wall Marshal. 'Why, Quint . . . if I didn't know better I'd think you were worried.'

'Ha! I want you out of the action. Am I going to have to post a guard on you?'

'You wouldn't do that.'

'You know I would and you know it's within my rights.'

It is at that. The Wall Marshal was meant as a counter-weight to the Lord Protector – and his judge also, if need be.

To change the subject Hiam asked, 'Any word from Master Stimins?'

Quint snorted his contempt. 'Came across him on the Rampart of the Stars. Lying prostrate he was, ear to the stones. Says he was listening to the wall. Mad as a barking cat.'

Hiam smiled, imagining the confrontation. Quint's outrage. Stimins' complete confusion in the face of it.

Quint turned his head aside, drawing Hiam's gaze to an

approaching runner. The man jogged straight up, extending a folded slip. Hiam thanked him and took the missive.

Emissary from Overlord of Fist. Must talk. Shool.

Hiam nodded to the runner. 'I will accompany you back.' To Quint: 'You have the wall, Marshal.'

Quint's scarred face twisted even further. 'It's about damned time.'

It was after dawn when Hiam and the messenger reached the Great Tower. The Lord Protector was clenching his teeth against the sour bile of exhaustion and he managed the last few trotting leagues on blind will alone. Reaching the door he nodded stiffly to the messenger, dismissing him without daring to risk a word. Within, he leaned back upon the door to suck in great lungfuls of the warmer air and tried to swallow to wet his parched throat. A guard approached and he knelt, adjusting the studded leather wraps and his greaves. Seeing him, the guard, a Chosen veteran, stood to attention. 'Sir!'

Hiam straightened, nodded to acknowledge the man then edged back the folds of his cloak and drew off his full helm. He pushed a hand through his icy sweat-soaked hair. 'Hot out there tonight, Chenal.'

'And me stuck in here.'

'No matter – more than enough for all of us. Tomorrow, yes?'

'Aye. Tomorrow.'

'Guests?'

Chenal raised his gaze to the ceiling. 'Claims to be Roolian. But he's one o' them invaders from way back. Plain as the nose on his face.'

'Thank you, Chenal. Give them my regards tomorrow.'

'That I will, doubly.' He saluted, fist to heart. 'Lord Protector!'

Hiam answered the salute, headed to the circular stairs. He took his time. He wiped his face on his cloak as he climbed, steadied his breath. Outside the door he paused, then slowly pushed it open. Within, Marshal Shool leapt to his feet, saluting. 'Lord Protector!' Another man wheeled, startled from where he stood warming himself at the fireplace. The moment he turned Hiam knew him as Malazan, as his skin ran to a far darker hue than the coffee brown common among many of this region. He was wrapped in furred cloaks and wore thick boots, and a fur hat rested on a chair nearby.

Hiam acknowledged Shool, who extended a hand to the guest: 'Lord Hurback, emissary of the Overlord of Fist.'

Hiam bowed, placed his helm on the narrow table next to the door, set his shield on a stand, then hung his cloak. 'Lord Hurback. You are most welcome.'

Hurback bowed also, then his thick black brows wrinkled in confusion. 'You have seen fighting, Lord Protector?'

Hiam went to a sideboard, poured himself a cup of tea, picked up a slice of black bread. 'Of course. Every brother – and sister – of the Stormguard fights. During the season none is away from the wall for more than a day.'

'Of course,' the emissary echoed weakly. 'How commendable.'

Hiam invited him to sit before his plain wooden desk and slid in behind. He tried not to show the relief he felt as he eased his weight from his aching legs. Shool bowed and moved to leave; Hiam gestured that he should remain.

'To what do we owe the honour of your visit, m'lord?'

The man sat, taking care to straighten his fur-trimmed robes. Ermine and wolf, so it appeared to Hiam. His curly black hair was greased to a bright shine and rings set with red stones glittered at his fingers. Hiam reflected that this was perhaps the first of these invader Malazans he'd met who wasn't in chains at the wall. *They sell their own as readily as they sell any other – remember that, Hiam.*

'I bear a personal missive direct from Overlord Yeull. I have been entrusted with its contents and have been instructed to offer any further clarification as needed.'

Full of his intimacy with this self-styled Overlord, isn't this one . . . Hiam eyed his cot waiting for him across the room. *Why didn't he just hand over the damned thing?* 'He is well, I hope? Any word from our Mare allies regarding these renewed Malazan aggressions?'

The emissary goggled at him, clearly startled beyond words. *What do they think we are here? Brainless brutes? Our intelligence service is vastly superior to theirs. Across these lands every adherent of the Lady knows where their loyalties ought to lie. With us. Those whose blood defends them.*

'The Lord Protector is eminently well informed,' the emissary managed. 'Reports are that they have broken the invading fleet and that only a few stray vessels managed to land on Skolati shores.'

That is not what our sources in Mare are reporting. So, landings are confirmed. A thought struck the Lord Protector and he almost glared at the hapless emissary: *Lady forgive them! He hasn't come to request troops to help defend Rool, surely!*

Struggling to keep his voice level, he asked, 'And what can we in Korel do for the Overlord?'

An expression flitted across Lord Hurback's broad flat face, one Hiam was unaccustomed to seeing opposite him: a kind of vain smugness. The emissary extended the sealed vellum missive. 'You shall see, Lord Protector.'

Vaguely troubled by the man's manner, Hiam broke the seal, opened the folds, and read. It was some time before he looked up again. 'Is this true?' he breathed, stunned and perplexed. 'The Overlord pledges ten thousand fighting men for the wall? Even now? Facing invasion? This does not make sense . . .'

In the face of the Lord Protector's amazement, the emissary's self-satisfaction returned. He shrugged as if to dismiss the offer as inconsequential between friends. 'It makes perfect sense, Lord Protector. As you know, we in Rool cleave tightly to the Blessed Lady – more so than many of our erstwhile allies, yes? We know this land's true enemy. And we are concerned. This pledge is a measure of that concern.'

And what, dear Lady, does Yeull expect in return? Yet . . . ten thousand! Half again our entire remaining complement. It was as if they knew! Our Lady, as Lord Protector, defender of your lands, this is an offer I simply cannot *reject.*

Hiam took a slow sip of the now cold tea and regarded the emissary, who answered his look with half-lidded satisfaction. *However much I may dislike the messenger or dread the answer, I must ask.* He cleared his throat. 'And what, if anything, does the Overlord request in answer to such extraordinary generosity?'

Knowing he had won, Lord Hurback smiled broadly. He raised his hands, open and palm up. 'The smallest of requests, Lord Protector. Nothing you could possibly object to given the measure of his offer. Indeed, you should even welcome his proposal . . .'

Listening, Hiam could not dismiss the suspicion that nothing this man might propose would be welcome. Yet listen he did. His commitment to the defence of the wall gave him no choice – this was perhaps what men like this emissary, or Overlord Yeull, could never understand. They could ask for twenty galleys full of gold, or all the jewels of the mines of Jasston. Such worldly treasure was as nothing to the Stormguard, who were ready to give over everything they possessed – which was in truth only the armour on their backs and the weapons in their hands, and of course their lives – to defend their faith.

* * *

Most mornings Ivanr awoke shortly after dawn. As an officer he had the privilege of a private tent, which servants attached to the brigade raised and struck each day. It was framed with poles set into the ground and others laid atop as crosspieces. Felt cloth wrapped it against the cold of the region's winter. The bedding was of woven blankets over sheep hides. Rising, he straddled the honeypot and eased his taut bladder, then pulled on a long tunic of linen and quilted wool that hung down to the thighs of his buckskin pants. He rewrapped the rags round his feet and strapped on sandals that tied up just beneath his knees.

A cup of tea and a flatbread lay on a board set just inside the flap. Taking them up, he thrust aside the cloth to find a crowd of men and women sitting in a semicircle before his tent. He stared. They stared back. Steam from his tea plumed in the frigid dawn air.

'Yes? What?'

One old fellow raised a staff to lever himself upright; the others followed his lead. He looked familiar but Ivanr couldn't quite place him.

'Hail, Ivanr. I bring the word of the Priestess.'

Now he knew him: the old pilgrim he'd met months ago. He eyed the crowd, uneasy. 'Yes? What of it?'

The pilgrim inclined his head as if in prayer. 'I bring her last instructions, given just as she was taken from us.'

'She's . . . dead?'

'We do not know. She was imprisoned at Abor.'

Ivanr grunted his understanding. 'I'm sorry. She was . . . something special.'

'Yes, she was. Is. And her last words speak of you.'

Now his empty stomach twisted, and to fortify himself he took most of the tea and a bite of the bread. *Now what? Just when he'd kicked the brigade into shape. Couldn't she – they – just leave him alone?* He looked over their heads to the stirring camp. *Maybe he could just ignore them.* They would be marching today, as usual. Keeping their pikes at the ready against the ranging Jourilan Imperial lights who relentlessly dogged them, harrying, darting in, skirmishing.

The old pilgrim drew himself up straight. The wind tossed his thin grey hair and his robes licked about his staff. 'The Priestess has spoken, Ivanr of Antr. Before she was taken away she named you her disciple, her true heir in the Path.'

At these words the crowd reverently bowed their heads.

Ivanr was struck speechless. Had they gone mad? Him? Heir to the Priestess's mission? What did he know of this 'Path' of hers? He was a ridiculous choice. He shook his head, scowling. 'No. Not me. Find someone else to follow around – or, better yet, don't follow anyone. Following people only leads to trouble.'

He dismissed them with a wave of his flatbread and walked off to find Lieutenant Carr.

'As I warned you before, Ivanr,' the old pilgrim called after him, 'it is too late. Already many deny the Lady in your name. With or without you, it has begun. Your life these last few years has been nothing but denial and flight. Are you not tired of fleeing?'

That last comment stopped him; but he did not turn round. After a pause, he continued on. *No matter. Let the religion-mad fool rant. Faiths! Name one other thing that has brought more misery and murder into the world!*

That day they continued the long march north. Farmlands gave way to rolling pasture, copses of woods, and tracts of land given over to aristocratic estates and managed forests. Their pace had improved as the army now openly followed the roads laid down decades ago by the Imperial engineers. And always, hiding in the edges of copses, or walking the ridges of distant hills, the Jourilan light cavalry, watching, raiding pickets and falling upon smaller foraging parties.

This incessant raiding drove Martal to order the baggage train moved to the interior of the column. The pike brigades marched ahead, behind, and to the sides. Archers ranged within their perimeter, ready to contribute to driving off the cavalry.

Ivanr was sceptical of these bands of roving archers. Short-bows so cheaply made he could break them in his hands. He complained of them to Carr: 'I could throw rocks farther than these can reach.'

The lieutenant laughed as they walked along. It had rained the previous day, the winter season in Jourilan a time of dark skies and rainstorms, though this season had so far proved remarkably dry. Mud of the churned line of march weighted their feet and spattered their cloaks. 'This is a peasant army, Ivanr. There are only a handful of professionally trained warriors with us. These farmers and burghers aren't trained to pull a real bow. You know that takes years. Martal has to work with what she has at hand. And hence these bands of archers with short-bows. All those too young or old or weak to hoist the pikes.'

Ivanr thought of the boy. He'd yet to find him among the regulars. Perhaps he'd been sent to pull a bow. He supposed that would make more sense. 'And these hulking carriages?'

Carr shrugged his ignorance. 'That is Martal's project entirely. I'm not sure what she has planned for them.'

Ivanr didn't believe a word of that. *You know, Carr. You've been with Beneth for years. This army's lousy with spies and you're just keeping quiet. Very well. No doubt we'll see sooner than we'd like.*

Over the next few days of marching, Ivanr managed to push the old man's words from his thoughts. Among the men and women of his command he noted nothing more troubling than stares, hushed murmurs, and an unusual alacrity in obeying his orders. What disturbed him far more was the constant presence of Jourilan cavalry on the surrounding hillsides and always ranging ahead, just out of reach. Every passing day seemed to bring more, and as far as he could see Martal was content to do nothing about it. Poor Hegil Lesour 'an 'al, the Jourilan aristocrat commander of the Reform cavalry, was run ragged day and night ranging against the Imperial lights. Making it worse was the lack of winter rain; normally the fields and roads would be almost impassable this time of year.

Eventually, Ivanr was fed up enough to put aside his determination to avoid Martal and any hint of his participating in the command structure, and fell back to where she rode with her staff at the head of the spine of the army, the long winding column of carriages. He waited until she rode abreast of him, her mount keeping an easy walking pace, then stepped up alongside her.

Her blackened armour was covered by dust and mud kicked up in the march and a light misting spotted it in dark dots. She brushed a hand back through her short hair and nodded to him. 'Ivanr. To what do we owe the honour?'

'Honour? What do you mean, honour?'

Martal's smile was tight and wry. 'Just the talk of everyone. How the Army of Reform is privileged to have with it the spiritual heir to the Priestess.'

Ivanr was not amused; he eyed the woman thinly. 'That would be Beneth, I'm sure.'

'Beneth, I understand, sees himself as a prophet of the movement only. While *she* was its arrival . . . but all that is not my area of expertise.' As she smiled down at him he thought she was deriving far too much amusement from his predicament. 'Perhaps you should speak to him about it.'

I'd rather stand the wall, Martal. 'That's not why I'm here.'

Now the lips crooked up. Her gaze roamed, scanning the ranks, or the surrounding copses and farmland. 'No? Then what can I do for you?'

Where *was* this woman from? Closer now, he thought her no native of the region. Her complexion was smooth, the hue of dark honey, her black hair thick and bristly. From some distant land like Genabackis? Or perhaps Quon Tali? Why not the lands south of the Great Ice Wastes? What of them? Ivanr almost asked but thought it too public here, surrounded by her staff and guards. In fact, the idea of a private conversation with this woman was suddenly very desirable. Realizing he was staring, he looked away, cleared his throat. 'I'm here about horses.'

She nodded appreciatively. 'Really? I had no idea you were interested in horseflesh.'

'Only when there's more of it than I could possibly spear.'

'Ah. You are concerned.'

'Extremely.'

'You are wondering what is going on.'

'Very much so.'

'I see.' She drew off her black leather gloves, slapped them into a palm while looking ahead. 'Now, let me understand this. You haven't come to any staff briefings. You will not dine in Beneth's tent. You refuse to participate in any of the command discussions. Yet now you come to me demanding to know what's going on . . .' She peered down at him and a mocking arched brow took the sting from her words. 'Is that an accurate appraisal, Ivanr of Antr?'

Ivanr lowered his gaze, grimacing. *Aye, he deserved that. Can't have it both ways. Either you're in or you're out.* He looked up, acknowledging her point. 'I suppose that's about right.' Somehow, he did not mind being teased by this woman.

She was smiling quite openly now, looking ahead, and he studied the blunt profile of her flattened nose. 'They're all around us now,' she said. 'Massing for an attack. The traditional cavalry lancer charge that has scattered every tradesman rebellion, peasant army, and religious uprising before.'

'What are they waiting for?'

'Better terrain. North of us the land opens up. Broad pasturage, smooth hillsides. They'll form up there and wait for us to arrive.'

He swallowed, thinking: Now comes my question. 'And you? What are you waiting for?'

The dark eyes captured his gaze for an instant, unreadable, searching, then she looked skyward. 'Rain, Ivanr. I'm waiting for more rain.'

* * *

At first Bakune refused to number the days of his imprisonment. He judged it irrelevant and frankly rather clichéd. But being imprisoned in a cell so narrow he could touch a hand to either side, and so short it was less than two of his paces, he almost immediately came to the realization that, in point of fact, there was little else for him to do.

Those first few days he sat on his straw-padded cot attempting to calm himself to the point where he would not embarrass himself when they came to execute him. Each day that then passed, in his opinion, made that outcome less and less likely. After the first week he decided that he would be down here for some time; they must be planning to let him work upon himself in the solitude and the dark and the damp. So he attempted to cultivate a more distanced, even ironic, attitude. It simplified matters that he saw his predicament as so very rich in irony.

Just how many men and women had he condemned to these very Carceral Quarters? More than he could easily quantify. What did he think of his country's law enforcement regime now that he was the object – nay, perhaps *victim* – of it? Far less sanguine, he had to admit. These stone walls were scouring from his skin a certain insulating layer of smugness, a certain armouring of self-righteousness.

By the second week he began to worry. Perhaps they really *did* have no intention of returning to him. Every passing day made that possibility ever more likely as well. What need had they of his endorsement now that their control grew ever more firm? Perhaps through his own stiff-necked pride he had succeeded only in making himself superfluous. Yet a part of him could not help but note: *So this is the process . . . how many convicted had he himself condemned to rot for months before being dragged out to reconsider their stories?*

The mind . . . gnaws at itself. Certainties become probabilities, become doubts. Whilst doubts become certainties. And nothing is as it was.

What will become of me? Will I even I recognize me?

On the seventeenth night strange noises awoke him. It was utterly dark, of course; even darker than during the working day as all torches and lamps had been taken away or extinguished. But he believed that what jerked him awake was a definite crash as of wood smashing. He went to his door and listened at the small metal grate.

Whispers. Heated whispers. Angry muffled argument. *Whatever was going on?* He was tempted to shout a question – then, steps outside his door. Two sets: one light, the other heavy and flat-footed. The dim glow of a flame shone through the door's timbers. He backed away to the not-so-far wall.

A faint tap on the door. A low growled voice: 'Hello? Anyone there? Are you the Assessor, Bakune?'

This did not sound like a midnight execution squad. He made an effort to steady his voice, said: 'Who are you?'

'A friend. You are the Assessor?'

'Yes,' he answered faintly, then, stronger, 'Yes – I am.'

'Very good. I'm going to get you out.'

What? Lady's dread, no! An escape? Escape to where? 'Wait a moment—'

'I'll be right back.'

'I will get him out!' boomed a new voice.

'*Will you shut up!*' hissed the first. 'You will do no such thing. You've already done enough.'

'But this is my specialty,' the second voice bellowed out again cheerily. 'I will pick the lock!'

'*No!* Don't . . . stand back, Assessor!'

Bakune already had his back to the opposite wall. He had to straddle the vile hole that served as the privy to do so. He jumped as the door crashed with a great blow that made his ears ring. Dust and broken slivers dropped from the aged hand-adzed planks. It seemed as if a giant's fist had struck it.

'Would you stop doing that!' the gravelly voice shouted.

'One last delicate touch!'

The door jumped inward to reverberate against the wall. A bald head gleaming with sweat peered in – the defendant, the priest. Bakune couldn't recall his name. Next to him stood a giant. So tall was he that the opening only came up to his shoulders, and so wide Bakune did not think he was capable of entering the cell.

'There!' the giant announced. 'The lock is picked!'

The priest rolled his eyes to the ceiling. 'We're leaving,' he growled, then glared at the giant. 'It seems we have no choice!'

The giant bent his head down to peer in. 'Using my unparalleled skills in stealth and deception I have effected your escape, good Assessor.'

Bakune shared an incredulous look with the priest. 'How very . . . discreet . . . it has been, too.'

Beneath an enormous bushy heap of curly hair bound up on top of his head, the man beamed. The two would-be rescuers appeared to share a Theftian background by their accent and their blunt features. 'But I am not going.'

The giant's gaze narrowed and he peered left and right as if confused. The priest sighed. 'Yes, I understand. But there's no choice now . . . they'll just kill you out of hand. Or torture you to death. Come, time is short.'

'I can't—' Bakune stopped himself. *Can't break the law? Whose law? These Guardians have no legitimacy.* He felt his shoulders fall. 'Yes. Very well.'

'Good. This way.'

The priest led. The giant, who gave his name as Manask, followed him. Bakune was last. Up the hall they came to a guard station – or the remains of one. The door had been smashed open and guards lay bashed into unconsciousness. Bakune eyed Manask, who gestured proudly to encompass the scene. 'I snuck up upon them.'

'Yes . . . I see.'

'They did not suspect a thing!'

The priest lit an oil lamp then urged them forward. Speaking as quietly as possible, Bakune demanded, 'And just where are we going?'

'We will flee into the wilds,' announced Manask. 'Live off berries and mushrooms. Slay animals with our bare hands and wear their hides.' Bakune and the priest both wordlessly studied the man, who looked back at them, eager. 'Yes?'

'I've a boat waiting,' the priest growled.

Bakune felt infinite relief. 'Where are we going?'

The priest rubbed the grey bristles at his jaw and cheeks as if surprised by the question. 'Going? Don't know. Maybe we'll just hide,' and he shrugged. 'Now, c'mon. We've wasted enough time.'

Bakune was surprised when the priest led them a different route from the way most prisoners were brought in. As Assessor he'd visited the Carceral Quarters a number of times, but always by the main way. The route the priest took brought them to narrower, winding halls. After a time he realized that they walked the passages of the old fort that the carcery had been built upon. A lifetime of enquiry and assessing prompted him to wonder about this.

At one point, while they waited for Manask to edge his huge bulk round a particularly tight corner, he murmured to the priest, 'You know these ways well.'

The priest's frog mouth widened even further into a tight smile that suggested he knew exactly what Bakune was up to. 'I've been through here before. Long ago.'

'In similar circumstances, perhaps?'

But the man just smiled. Gasping, Manask yanked himself free, his armour scraping the walls. 'Free!' he announced. 'Slippery as an eel! Able to wriggle through the tightest of corners!'

The priest just shook his head; it seemed the pair knew each other well. Old friends. Old conspirators and criminal partners too? It seemed probable. There was something familiar there; something he could not quite recall. This couple must be well known. It also occurred to him that there was something strange about Manask's armour: it appeared to consist of a great deal of layered padding. And he walked strangely upon his boots, which apparently comprised no more than tall heels and thick soles. While upon closer examination a significant portion of the man's height was really nothing more than his immensely thick nest of hair.

After many twists and turns, the halls becoming ever narrower and more neglected, the priest stopped before a door. He whispered: 'This should lead to the kitchens. From here we can make our way out, then down to the waterfront—'

Manask lurched forward. 'I will sneak ahead!'

Like a moving wall he pushed Bakune ahead of him. 'Wait! There's not enough room! Please . . .'

The priest threw open the door and the three burst through like peas from a pod to crash into shelves of pots and hanging pans. Bakune bumped a table and stacked bowls came crashing down. 'Quiet as mice now!' Manask yelled.

A man – one of the prison cooks, obviously – bolted up from his cot to gape at them. Manask heaved a long oaken table on to the fellow, sending crockery flying in an explosion of shattering. 'Let us creep right past this one's nose!' The giant charged on, upending tables in his path. 'I will spy the way!'

Bakune and the priest remained standing amid the wreckage. The priest hung his head, sighing. He motioned Bakune onward. They picked their way through the broken crockery.

* * *

Shell was surprised that it was only a few days before she became acclimatized to the stink and the shocking lack of hygiene on board the boats of the Sea-Folk. Her gorge no longer rose. She even became rather casual about squeezing the ubiquitous fleas, all the while trying not to think about where they'd been biting her. The boats were open to the elements and so the sun roasted her during the day while the wind sucked all the warmth from her through the night. The flotilla kept to the south shore, putting in every other night at secluded coves and beaches. As they travelled the Sea-Folk caught fish and other creatures that they sometimes gutted over the sides and ate raw – a practice Shell could not bring herself to share despite their constant pressing upon her of the limp and tentacled delicacies.

Some lines should not be crossed.

These Sea-Folk also practised the revolting custom of rubbing animal fat over themselves; they lived perpetually in the same coarsely sewn hides, which they never took off or washed; their hair they never cut or washed but oiled instead into thick ropes. She felt as if all this filth were a contagion she would never rid herself of. Yet none of the huge extended family was ever obviously sick as far as she could tell.

Travelling on another of the boats, Blues and Fingers appeared to share none of her qualms. Closet barbarians, they happily rubbed fat upon themselves and ate raw things that had more eyes than was proper for any animal. Only Lazar shared her reserve; the huge fellow, taller and broader even than Skinner, his Sea-Folk hides bursting at the seams, sat with arms crossed, frowning at the family as they scampered over the boat and just shook his head as if perpetually amazed.

The young girl-mother, Ena, who seemed to have adopted her,

came to her side carrying a bowl of that rancid fat. 'Cold, yes?' she asked. Shell, arms crossed, shivering, shook a negative.

'No. Fine.'

The girl got a vexed look as if she were dealing with a stubborn child. 'You are cold. This will keep you warm.'

Some privations are better endured. If only as the lesser of two evils. 'No. Thank you.'

Ena set a hand on her broad hip. 'You foreign people are crazy.' And she moved off, taking wide squatting steps over the heaped gear and belongings.

We're not the ones rubbing animal fat on ourselves.

Shell threw herself down next to Lazar at the pointed stern. She looked him up and down. 'You're dirty, but at least you're not all greased up.'

He raised then lowered his shoulders. 'I layered.'

'Can you believe this? Some people are willing to live in absolute filth.'

The hazel eyes shifted to her. 'Seems to me we coulda used some of that grease out on the ice.'

'You think it works?'

The look he gave her echoed Ena's. He raised his chin to the nearest of the clan, an elderly uncle on the boat's tiller arm. 'See that outer hide jacket, the leather pants, the boots?'

Shell studied the gleaming greasy leathers. 'Yes. What of it? Other than they've never been washed for longer than I've been alive.'

'You raised on the coast, Shell? I forget.'

'No.'

Lazar grunted. 'Ah. Well, all that oil makes his clothes practically waterproof. No spray or rain can get through that, so he's toasty warm. I'm thinking these lot know what they're doing.'

Fine. But there's gotta be a cleaner way to do it.

Later that day Shell was roused from a doze when all at once the Sea-Folk jumped into action. The men and women went to work rearranging the gear, giving tense quiet orders. Shading her eyes, she peered around and spotted a vessel closing: two-masted, long and narrow, no merchant boat.

Ena came to her and Lazar. 'Say nothing, yes? No matter what.'

'What is it?' Shell asked.

'These navy ships, they stop us whenever they wish. Steal what they like. Call it fees and taxes.'

'What country are they from?' Shell asked.

Ena blinked her incomprehension. 'How does that matter?'

Lazar barked a laugh. 'She's got that right, Shell.'

Shell waved her reassurance. 'We won't interfere – unless we have to.'

'Good. Our thanks.'

The girl waddled away, awkward in her pregnancy.

Shell and Lazar watched while the warship trimmed its sails. Boats of the flotilla were ordered to come alongside. Marines climbed down rope ladders and 'inspected' the cargo. Studying the worn and begrimed gear of her own boat, Shell didn't think the pickings very rich. Something did startle her though: a gleaming brass teapot now rested amid the blackened cooking pots, and a roll of bright yellow cloth peeped from beneath a frayed and stained burlap covering. And a tall female figurehead, painted white, now graced the boat's prow. When had that appeared? She nudged Lazar and indicated the figurehead.

He nodded. 'Like I said.'

Two more inspections proceeded as the first: the marines ransacking the boats, tossing goods up into their ship. The afternoon waned. A cold wind blew though the sun was hot. Thankfully so far neither their boat, nor the one carrying Blues and Fingers, had been waved over. As the third inspection finished, Shell half rose from her seat: the marines were dragging someone with them. A young man or woman. Elders on board clutched at them, only to be thrust aside. 'Lazar! Do you see that? What're they doing?'

'Looks like a head tax.'

Shell clambered to where Ena sat beneath a wind-rippled awning. 'What's this? What's going on?'

Her gaze shaded, the girl said grimly, 'It happens sometimes.'

'*Happens?* What're you going to do about it?'

The girl's voice tightened even more. 'What would you have us do? There is nothing we can do. The strong prey upon the weak – that is how it has always been.'

Shell spun away. If only they could get Blues or Lazar on board that ship, then these Sea-Folk would see the strong preying upon the weak! And then – she let go her held breath . . . and then she would only have proved Ena's point.

And what would these Sea-Folk do with such a ship anyway? How would they explain it? They just *found* it? No. Distasteful as it was, Ena was right. There was nothing they could do. Being what she was, Shell was used to being on the taking end of such exchanges. How much harder and galling it was to be on the giving!

The youth had been urged on board at sword-point. Sailors climbed the warship's spars to give out more canvas. The vessel pulled away.

'Now what?' she snapped, unable to hide her anger and frustration.

'Now we wait.'

'Wait? Wait for what?'

'We shall see.'

'Shell!' a voice called across the waves; it was Blues. The Sea-Folk were oaring his boat closer through the tall slate-grey waves.

'Yes?'

'Did you see that?'

'Yes.'

'A tough one to swallow.'

'You did nothing?'

'Almost did. Orzu and the others here begged us not to interfere.'

'Same here. What now?'

'Orzu says we have to wait a time.'

'What in Hood's name for?'

'Don't know. No choice.'

The boats bumped sides and the Sea-Folk lashed them together. Supplies were handed back and forth. Shell waved to Fingers, who was a miserable shape at the stern, near prostrate from seasickness. Poor fellow; she had at least found her sea-legs.

'So who were they?' she asked Blues.

'Some country called Jasston.' He pointed south. 'That's their shore.'

'And the north?' The coast to the north was dark, and not once had she seen a fire or a settlement.

'Some land called Remnant Isle. No one lives there. Supposed to be haunted.'

Shell saw that the figurehead of the white woman was now gone, as was the gleaming brass teapot: secreted away for the next 'inspection'. She frowned then and wiped her hands on her thighs, but the problem was her trousers were as dirty as her hands. 'And the youth? What will happen?'

Blues' face seemed even darker than usual. 'Orzu says almost everyone taken prisoner in all these lands ends up on the wall, sold to the Korelri.'

The wall and its insatiable thirst for blood. And Bars was on it. Had he fallen? No. Not him. Yet they could die – all of them. They were of the Avowed, yes, but they could still drown or be hacked to pieces. Could he be dead already? Their mission a failure?

A hardening in her chest told Shell that should that be the case, these Korelri Stormguard might find themselves swept from their own Hood-damned wall.

The Sea-Folk untied the lines securing the boats. Blues waved farewell. The flotilla idled, tillers and oars used only to hold steady. Yet they were moving. She'd heard they were in a narrow stretch of water called Flow Strait. The coast to the south was crawling ever so slowly past.

The sun was approaching the horizon almost due west. Shell shaded her gaze from its glare. The wind picked up; it would be a damned cold night. Then shouts from ahead – excited yells. Everyone in her boat stood to scan the waters. Shell likewise clambered up, her feet well apart. What was this?

The lead boat was under oar, moving south with stunning speed. Shell stared. So far this journey all she'd seen was a lackadaisical nudging of the oars. Seemed these Sea-Folk could really charge when they needed to. Of course – why exert yourself unless necessary?

The lead boat back-oared now, slowing. Shell squinted, and as the intervening waves rose and fell, she thought she glimpsed a dark shape and splashing amid them. A fish?

Figures leaned over the side of the boat, gesturing, waving. Shell flinched as someone jumped overboard. Queen preserve them! They'll drown!

She turned to Ena and was surprised to see her amid her kin, everyone hugging and kissing one another. Seeing her confusion, Ena came to her. She waved ahead, laughing. 'It is Turo. He found us.' She cupped her hands to her mouth, shouting, 'Finished playing in the water, Turo?'

Shell felt her brow crimping as her gaze narrowed. 'I do not understand, Ena.'

The girl-woman giggled, covering her mouth. 'You do not know, do you? Why, everyone in these lands knows the Sea-Folk hate to be captive. We throw ourselves into the sea rather than be prisoner.' And she grinned like an imp. 'So many of us taken away disappear like that.'

Shell felt her brows rising as understanding dawned. She looked at Lazar, who was smiling crookedly in silent laughter.

High praise indeed, coming from him.

Beneath the setting sun a dark line caught Shell's eye and she shaded her gaze. 'What's that ahead to the west?' she asked, her eyes slitted almost closed.

Ena's smile was torn away and a hand rose in a gesture against evil. 'The Ring!' she hissed. Turning, she yelled orders at her kinsmen and women. All were galvanized into action. Hands went to mouths and piercing whistles flew like birdcalls between the boats. Gear was shifted and a mast appeared, dragged out from beneath everything to be stepped in place. Tarps covering equipment and possessions were whipped free, rolled and mounted as shrouds. The speed and competence of the transformation dazzled Shell. She tried to find Ena to ask what was going on, but was brushed aside as everyone on board seemed to be holding a line or adjusting stowage. She finally reached the girl towards the bow, where she was twisting a sheet affixed to the sail.

'What's going on? What is it?'

She shot a glance ahead. 'You do not know? No, of course not.' She sighed, searching for words. 'It is, how do you say . . . a cursed place. A haunt of the Lady herself. The Ring. A great circle ridge around a deep hole. Some say bottomless. And it is guarded. Korelri Stormguard are there. None dare approach. It is very bad luck we come to it so late. Those thieving landsmen delayed us half the day!'

Shell nodded, allowing her to return to her work. She found a place where she could sit out of the way at the bow and peered ahead, trying to separate some detail from the sunset. Stormguard here! Just within reach. What would these Sea-Folk say if they knew they were carrying four outlanders intent upon challenging this military order that so dominated the region? They would probably think us insane. All these generations *they* have survived beneath the very gaze of the Lady through strategies of trickery and deception.

Perhaps, she thought, hugging herself for warmth, they would be wise to follow suit.

* * *

Kiska dreamt of her youth on Malaz Island. She was walking its storm-racked rocky coast, with its litter and treasure and corpses of wrecks from three seas. And she was reviewing the ruin that was her life. *My childishness and wilfulness. Yet who isn't when young? My foolish decisions. Yet how else does one learn?* Her loss on the field at the plains. *I failed him!* She picked her way through the bleached timbers and crab-picked bones while all around her the island appeared to be shrinking. Eventually she could complete a full circuit in a mere few strides.

And it was closing even tighter.

A sharp pain such as stepping on a nail woke her. Groggy, she blinked up at jagged stone above. Her cave. Her prison. She was still here.

'Hist! Kiska! Are you still with me?'

She raised her head. Jheval was there, silhouetted against the slightly lighter cave mouth. 'Yes,' she croaked. Her mouth felt as dusty and dry as the cave floor itself. 'Regrettably.'

'I'm hearing something new,' he murmured, keeping his voice as low as possible.

There is nothing new in Shadow, Kiska pronounced to herself. Now where had she heard something like that?

'And I haven't seen our friends for some time now.'

Meaningless. Without significance. Empty. Futile.

'Kiska!'

She blinked, startled. She'd dropped off again. She levered herself up by the elbows. 'Yes?'

He gestured her to him. 'Come here. Listen. What do you make of this?'

Crawling to the cave mouth was one of the hardest things Kiska had ever forced herself to do. She thought she could hear her every sinew and ligament creaking and stretching as she moved. She fancied she could see the bones of her hands through her dusty cracked skin. She planted herself next to Jheval, who appeared to be watching her carefully. 'Yes?' she demanded.

He glanced away and seemed to crook a smile as he turned to the silvery monochrome landscape beyond. 'Listen.'

Listen? Listen to what? Our flesh rotting? The sighing of sands? There's nothing—

She heard something. Creaking. Loud abrasive squeaking and creaking like wood on wood. What in the world? Or – in Shadow?

'Perhaps we should have a look, yes?'

'It does sound . . . close.'

The man was grinning now through the caked-on dirt of his face. How pale the son of the desert looked now, dust-covered. Like a ghost. Though a lively one. She felt a kind of resentful admiration: he seemed to not know how to give up.

'Very good. The both of us, yes? Side by side.'

She nodded, swallowed to sluice the grit from her mouth. 'Yes. Let's go. I have to get out of here.'

'Yes. I feel it too.' He edged forward, hunched, then straightened outside the narrow crack. Kiska picked up her staff and followed. Out on the sand slope she expected the air to be fresher and cooler, different somehow. Yet the lifeless atmosphere seemed no better. It was as if all Shadow was stale, somehow suspended.

They climbed a nearby bare hill. Kiska tried to be watchful. She knew they should expect an attack at any instant. But she could not muster the necessary focus; she just felt exhausted by all the waiting and almost wanted to have it over with. And no hound appeared. When they reached the crest and looked beyond, they saw why.

It was a migration. Across the plain before them stretched columns of large creatures. Through the plumes of dust it appeared as if many of them marched in teams, heaving on ropes drawing gigantic boats lashed to wheeled platforms. It was the ear-splitting screeching of these wooden wheels that assaulted them, even from this great distance.

'Locals on the move,' Jheval said, and started down the hillside.

Kiska followed, reluctant. Walking out upon them in the open? How could he know they weren't hostile? They didn't look even vaguely human.

Before they reached the lowest hill a figure veered towards them, a picket, or outlier of some sort. As they neared, he – or she, or it – reared ever taller until it became clear to Kiska that it was nearly twice their height. It was, clearly, a daemon, a Shadow creature. Dull black, furred in parts, carrying on its back a brace of spears twice again its own height. It looked insectile: multiple-faceted eyes, a mouthful of oversized fangs, out-of-proportion skinny limbs that appeared armoured. Jheval hailed it, waving. Kiska gripped her staff and winced. She almost shouted: *How do you know it speaks our language? How do you know it won't eat you?*

It stopped, peered down to regard the two of them. Jheval stood with arms crossed, examining the creature in turn. Kiska kept her staff at the ready.

'Do you understand this language?' Jheval asked.

'Yes, I know this tongue,' it replied in a startlingly high piping voice.

Jheval was clearly surprised. 'You do? Why?'
'This is the language of the pretenders.'
Pretenders? Ah! Cotillion and Shadowthrone.
'Greetings. I am Jheval. This is Kiska.'
'My name would translate as Least Branch.'
Jheval gestured beyond, to the columns of its brethren. 'You are on some sort of migration?'
'Yes. Though not one of our choice. We have been forced to move. Our home has been destroyed.'
Destroyed? Queen forfend! What force could possibly overcome an entire race of Shadow daemons? And here, in their own homeland.
Jheval was studying the columns. 'You are sea-people?'
'Yes. We fished the giant bottom-feeders. We gathered among the shallow wetlands. But the great lake that has supported my people since before yours rose up on your hind legs has been taken from us. Great Ixpcotlet! How we mourn its passing.'
An entire lake gone? 'What happened?' Kiska asked, astonished. This went against all her impressions of a timeless Shadow realm.
She imagined that many expressions must be flitting across Least Branch's face, but she and Jheval could not read them. 'A Chaos Whorl has eaten into this realm you call Emurlahn. It has swallowed Ixpcotlet. It grows even as we flee.'
Kiska almost dropped her staff. 'A Whorl? Like a Void? Touching Chaos?'
Some sort of membrane shuttered across Least Branch's eyes – an expression of surprise? 'Yes. Just so. We go to find another body of water, and to warn others. Perhaps we may even find the Guardian.'
Kiska stared anew. 'A guardian? Gaunt, ancient? Carries a sword?'
The creature took a step backwards, obviously stunned. 'You know of him?'
'Yes. I've met him. He calls himself Edgewalker.'
'He spoke to you? That is . . . unusual. We name him the Guardian.'
Jheval was eyeing her, clearly surprised himself.
Least Branch gestured, inviting them to accompany him. 'Come, won't you? Don't you know it is dangerous out here? The Hounds are about.'
All the way down the hill Kiska wondered if Least Branch was

tempted to ask why the two of them laughed so much. How they chuckled uncontrollably, then, catching one another's gaze, burst out anew. *Don't you know the Hounds are about?*

Least Branch led them to the rear of the migration. They passed two of the boats. Each towered over them, scaled to their gigantic makers. They rumbled on their immense platforms pulled by teams of hundred of the daemons. The dust blinded and choked them and Kiska glimpsed Jheval untying the cloth wrapped about his helmet to wind it over his mouth and face. She imitated him, winding a scarf over her face and leaving only a slit for her vision. The noise was the worst, as wooden wheels shrieked against wooden axles. The daemons did not seem to mind the cacophony but it almost drove Kiska mad.

Behind the horde, among the churned-up dirt, the shin-deep ruts and tossed rubbish, the gnawed bones, broken pots and excrement, Least Branch stopped to point back along the trail of broken earth. 'Just follow our path. You cannot miss it. But you do not really seek this Whorl, do you? It opens on to the shores of Chaos. And we sense behind it an unhinged intelligence. We flee it. As you should, too.'

Kiska was staring up the trail all the way to the flat horizon, which to her eyes appeared bruised, darker. 'Yes,' she said. 'I believe it's what we're here for.'

'Then I must say farewell, though I confess I am tempted to accompany you.'

'Why?' she asked.

'Because I believe there is a chance you will meet the Guardian. I say this because he has spoken to you once and so may again, for he seldom does anything without a reason. And so, should you meet him, ask him this for myself and for my people, the fishers of Ixpcotlet – why did he do nothing? Why did he not intervene? We are very confused and disappointed by this.'

Kiska faced Least Branch directly, gazing almost straight up. 'If I meet him I will ask. This I swear.'

The daemon waved its thin armoured limbs, the meaning of the gesture unknown to Kiska. 'I will have to be satisfied with your vow. My thanks. Safe journeying to you.'

'Goodbye. And our thanks.'

'Fare you well,' Jheval added.

They watched the great daemon lumber away. The spears clattered and swung on its back as it went. Alone now, free of their huge guide, Kiska felt exposed once more, though the plains that surrounded them lay utterly flat and featureless.

Jheval cleared his throat. 'Well, I suppose we'd best get on our way.'

Kiska eyed him: his fingers were tucked into the lacing securing his morningstars; a habit of his while walking. Thinking of her behaviour during their imprisonment, Kiska said nothing, nodding and starting off. Perhaps they would discuss those days – perhaps even weeks, who knew? – of cramped involuntary companionship some time in the future. Right now it was too close and too raw.

Perhaps, as she suspected, neither of them would ever mention it again.

* * *

They had assembled forty thousand regulars supported by a backbone of six thousand Malazan veterans of the Sixth. The force was known officially as the Army of Rool. Envoy Enesh-jer commanded, representative of Overlord Yeull. Ussü served as adviser, while Borun commanded his detachment of a thousand Black Moranth. The Overlord remained at the capital, Paliss.

Ussü was mounted, out of consideration if not for his age, then for his rank. Most of the officers and all of the Envoy's staff were mounted. However, there was no organized cavalry force large enough to play a major part in any engagement, save harassment, scouting and serving as messengers. The Jourilan and Dourkan might pride themselves on their cavalry, but it had never been cultivated in Rool, or Mare. Possibly the peoples of Fist followed the model of the Korelri – who of course considered horses particularly useless.

Ussü wished they had many more mounts; the crawling progress of the army chafed him. They had yet to reach the Ancy valley, let alone the Ancy itself. Perhaps it was pure nostalgia, but he was sure the old Sixth could have managed a far better pace. Riding by, he shared many a jaundiced gaze with the veterans, sergeants and officers, as together they scanned the trudging, bhederin-like Roolian troops. He pulled his cloak tighter against the freezing wind cutting down from the Trembling range and stretched his back, grimacing. *Gods, when was the last time he rode for more than pleasure? Yes, we're all older now. And perhaps the past glows brighter as it recedes ever further. But what we face is not the past – it is the present Malazan army. What of their standards? Who is to say? We know just as much of them as they of us.*

And so two blind armies grope towards each other.

Where lies the advantage? Intelligence.

He spurred his mount to the van, and the coterie of officers and staffers clustered around the Envoy. *Like flies. Yet is that fair? This Enesh-jer was selected by Yeull. Though it seems as if the choice was based more on the fervency of the man's devotion to the Lady than on any command competence or experience. Like those of his staff and inner circle: more like priests in their pursuit of rank and prestige than interested in field command. And so similarly am I suspect to them. Magicker, they whisper. Dabbler in the forbidden arts.*

Ussü eased up to catch the Envoy's gaze as he rode past, but the man was engaged in conversation with an aide, his lean hound's head averted – stiffly, it seemed to Ussü. The staffers and other lackeys were not so circumspect. Some eyed him coolly, others with open disapproval, while the worst offered open enjoyment of what could be taken as a deliberate, calculated insult.

Ussü revealed no discomfort. He bowed respectfully in his saddle, urged his mount on. In advance of the van, he kneed the mare into a gallop. What lay ahead? Three days ago word had reached their column by way of refugees of the fall of Aamil. The stories were wild, even given a penchant for panicked exaggeration. The city levelled; citizens slaughtered; a demon army in blue armour, which from their description Ussü quickly understood to be Blue Moranth. The invaders marching west. Things became rather fanciful after that. Flash floods tearing down from the Trembling range carrying off hundreds of the invaders; roads washed out; murderous hailstorms, landslides and earthquakes.

The literal end of the world. Absurd. Though, nights ago, a shaking of the ground and yells of horror and alarm throughout the camp woke everyone. Such manifestations were thought to represent the displeasure of the Lady.

The landings would have been more than ten days ago now. Just where were these invading Malazans, their new rivals? Had scouts reached the bridge? Had their commander – could it really be Greymane? – ordered a spear-like dash for control of this single crossing over the Ancy?

And why was Yeull so reluctant to destroy it?

Climbing a rise he came to a small contingent of Roolian horse halted at its crest. In their midst sat Borun, looking rather uncomfortable atop a broad, muscular stallion. Ussü walked his mount ahead until he shared their view down into the Ancy valley stretched out below, the broad river flowing south towards Mirror Lake at the foot of the Black range. Mid-valley it broadened over a course of shallow rapids spanned by the long slim timber and stone bridge raised by Malazan engineers of the Sixth what seemed so long ago. Beside it, on the west shore, the bailey and stone keep of the fortress of the Three Sisters, named for the rapids. Surrounding the fortress sprawled a small town of farmers and businesses catering to travellers of this main trader road.

Borun dismounted and joined him. 'Any sign of them?' Ussü asked.

'None. We seem to have beaten them here.'

'I'm surprised. They must be aware of the bridge's importance.'

'Perhaps,' the Black Moranth commander mused, 'they assume it already destroyed.'

Ussü eyed the blunt side of the commander's helm. Yes. If it were up to them it would have been blown immediately. 'You still have munitions?'

The helm tilted an assent. 'We yet have some crates we salvaged from our wrecked vessels.'

'I suggest you put them to use.'

Borun faced him direct; Ussü could discern no detail behind the narrow vision slits of his helm. 'The Overlord has not given his permission to mine the bridge.'

Ussü smiled faintly. 'We can always blame the Malazans. Their saboteurs can't leave any bridge unblown.'

A sound escaped Borun's helm as he rocked slightly. It took a moment for Ussü to recognize the gravelly hoarse rasping as laughter. It was the first time he'd ever heard it. 'Let us go down and examine this fortress, then. Shall we?'

'Yes, High Mage.'

To Ussü's critical eye, the fortress of the Three Sisters was more a glorified tax hut than a defensible fortification. Its walls were thin, single-layered. It possessed a ditch, yes, but the causeway leading up to the gate was far too wide for his liking. And streaming up this causeway came a steady line of refugees carrying their few worldly goods wrapped in rags, heaped in donkeys, or pulled in carts. To

Ussü's surprise they were also allowed to drive cattle, goats, and sheep up into the bailey. Where would the fodder come from to feed all these animals? Flanked by Borun, he urged his mount ahead through the press. He reflected that, if the worst came to the worst, at least they could eat the animals.

Within, makeshift huts crowded what should be an open marshalling field. Smoke rose from a blacksmith's hut across the way. A long barracks of a sort ran down one side. Across rose the motte, topped by a square stone tower keep. A slimmer inner causeway led up to its gate. Ussü directed his mount to that dirt ramp and to the black-robed figures standing upon it, each bearing a staff.

Upon reaching the base, Ussü bowed in his saddle. The four bearded priests remained unmoving. 'Greetings. I am Ussü, adviser to our Overlord. This is Commander Borun.'

One of the priests gave a slight nod. 'Greetings, Ussü, Borun. I am Abbot Nerra. I command this fortress.'

Ussü blinked his surprise. 'What of Captain Hender?'

'He has been relieved.'

Ussü strove to keep his face blank. Hender was a veteran of the Sixth. He would have sent these refugees onward, not allowed them to clog up a military outpost. The disarray, the admission of all these civilians – so many mouths to feed! – now made sense.

'And where is the Envoy?' Nerra demanded.

Turning in his saddle, Ussü saw that indeed the Envoy, surrounded by his entourage, was just now entering the bailey. He gestured to the gate. As the Envoy drew near, the priests of Our Lady descended the ramp until their heads were close to level with those mounted. Abbot Nerra bowed to Enesh-jer, who received the obeisance as if it were no less than his due. 'My lord Envoy,' Nerra began, 'the fate of this flock, all those loyal to Our Blessed Lady, is in your hands.'

The Envoy's lean features drew back in a skull-like grin. 'We will stop these invaders. Heretics and unbelievers all.'

Ussü glanced from face to face. Could these men really be in earnest? When Enesh-jer arrived with the Sixth he knew nothing of this local cult. Still, it was said that there was no fanatic like the converted. He looked to Borun then wondered why he bothered: it was impossible to read the armoured Moranth. If he could distinguish anything from the man's posture, it was disengagement and boredom.

'Do not concern yourself, Abbot,' Enesh-jer was saying. 'We

will establish a bridgehead across the Ancy. No invaders will reach Roolian lands.'

'Excuse me, m'lord.' Ussü spoke up, astonished. 'Surely you do not plan to march forces across the bridge. They will be isolated upon the far side. If the bridge is not to be blown we must remain on this shore, defend here.'

Something like a hissed sigh escaped the Envoy's slit lips and his eyes bulged in his skull face. 'No doubt,' he enunciated, nearly strangled by his passion, 'our Overlord sees some value in your opinions on *esoteric* topics, Adviser. But in matters of tactics and disposition of forces I suggest you remain silent.'

Inwardly Ussü fumed, but he also felt a distinct chill as all eyes studied him – many with open enmity. Keeping his face flat, he bowed.

Enesh-jer nodded stiffly, accepting Ussü's apparent deference. 'I will remain to command the fortress with, ah, your permission, Abbot.' Nerra bowed. 'Very good. There remains, then, the matter of the near shore . . .'

Ussü kicked Borun's armoured boot. The Moranth commander loudly cleared his throat. 'I would ask for the honour, Envoy. With your permission.'

The Envoy gave a wave to signal his granting of said honour.

Ussü bowed again to take his leave and reined his mount round. He was ignored. As he crossed the bailey Borun joined him. 'This fortress is a death trap,' Ussü murmured to the Moranth commander. They urged their way forward through the press of wide-eyed civilians and complaining animals. As they reached the ramp across the ditch, he studied the narrow wall of set stones and shook his head. 'There will be no siege. It will be a sacking.'

'Perhaps they will hold them on the far shore,' Borun answered, his voice even more hoarse than usual as he tried to keep it low.

Ussü sighed. 'Perhaps. But if I were Greymane – if he survived to land – then I would send marines ahead to cross to the north and south to make a lunge for the bridge while the main forces closed. And if they succeed in that, we must withdraw swiftly. I suggest to the south, then west.'

'Then that recourse of which you spoke. Just in case.'

'Yes. I would also require a tent in your camp, Borun. Where I can work unmolested. And prisoners.'

'Prisoners? Who?'

'Any. It does not matter. So long as they are strong. I mean to do some scrying.'

Borun inclined his helmed head. 'As you request, High Mage.'

*

For the night watch Suth crept down with Len and Yana to the forward nook of rocks where a viewpoint was kept on the bridge over the Ancy far down the valley below. They relieved a team from the 11th, three women. Suth tried to meet the gaze of one as she was of Dal Hon. But she looked through him as if he wasn't there and he knew why: she was a veteran while he had yet to truly prove himself.

Yana peered out over the rocks. 'Nice of them to mark out their lines with torches like that for us.'

Len, lying flat with his chin on his folded forearms, said, 'They're working day and night. Digging ditches, making stake rows, traps, burning all the brush cover. Digging in.'

'Damn fools.'

Suth looked to Yana. 'Why?'

'The river splits their forces in two.'

'So? They can retreat over the bridge.'

Len and Yana just shared a glance.

'What I can't figure,' Len said, 'is why that bridge is standing at all.'

'Maybe it's a trap,' Suth offered.

'Not worth the risk. You'd only get a few hundred troops.' He was shaking his head. 'Hard to believe ex-Malazans are in charge down there.'

Yana snorted. 'They're outlaws. Deserters. Good for nothing.'

But Len was unconvinced. He kept shaking his head, lips pursed.

Suth sat back to wrap his cloak more tightly about his shoulders. It was winter season here in Fist. A chill wind blew out of the north. Locals named it cursed. Not that he'd met that many locals. They tended to run away; thought them some sort of demons come to eat their young. Through their entire advance west across Skolati all they found were deserted hamlets, abandoned farmsteads. Everyone had fled to the hills or taken to the cities in the south. Suth found it incomprehensible. But then he came from a land that had known countless sweeping conquests and changes of rulership while this one was so insular they'd even forgotten their current rulers had invaded a generation ago.

All three stiffened as someone hissed from their rear. It was Keri. 'Officers coming – pull your pants up.' She scrambled away into the dark.

The three eyed one another. *Officers?* Yana mouthed, annoyed.

Then footsteps descending among the rocks, three sets. Len just raised his eyes to the night sky, turned away. Suth watched, saw who it was emerging from the dark and reflexively straightened, then forced himself to relax as he remembered the battle rules against identifying officers. It was their captain, Betteries, their Fist, Rillish Jal Keth, and the representative of their overall commander, the Adjunct.

Yana straightened as well while Len, exercising the code of complete indifference affected by saboteurs, ignored the newcomers. Captain Betteries signed for Suth and Yana to stand down, invited the Fist and the Adjunct to a lookout some distance off. Suth pretended to return to the watch but studied the three out of the corner of his eye. Betteries was gesturing to the valley below as if explaining tactics; the Fist was also adding comments, and nodding. The Adjunct just listened, his dark sun- and wind-burnished face revealing nothing. Suth's gaze strayed to the twinned swords sheathed at the Fist's belt. Untan duelling blades. Formidable weapons. Long, narrow, twin-edged and needle-pointed. Able to both cut and thrust. Once polished perhaps, but now battered, the leather sheaths hacked and worn. As for the Adjunct's weapon; Suth pulled his gaze from the curved sword whose ivory pommel and grip seemed to glow with an inner light.

'Now we're in for it,' Len murmured.

'You think this is it?' Suth answered, low.

'Yeah. The main force must be in striking distance.'

'So – when?'

The saboteur frowned his uncertainty. 'Sooner than we'd like, no doubt.'

The Adjunct gestured then, suddenly, catching all their eyes. The young man was pointing off to the dark. Then he crooked a finger. Out from a slim shadow between rocks straightened Faro. He inclined his head in acknowledgement. The three officers spoke briefly then picked their way back. Captain Betteries lingered long enough to give Faro a snarled dressing-down before heading off. Their squad 'scout' leaned back against a rock, pulled out his short-stemmed pipe, and began packing it.

Suth cast Len and Yana a questioning look: both shrugged, so he headed over. Faro ignored him while he worked on his pipe. 'Well?' Suth asked after a time. The man didn't answer. 'What do you want? A damned bag of Imperial suns?'

The man glanced up, bared his bright pointed teeth. 'A little wet behind the ears to be makin' demands, don't you think?'

'I'd say we're squadmates now and it would help the squad to know the plan.'

Faro snorted, looked past Suth to Len and Yana, both of whom were now standing, shrugged. He clenched the pipe in his teeth, unlit. 'Tomorrow night. The main columns are gonna dash in.'

'And us?' Len asked, stepping up next to Suth.

Faro smiled again, this time evilly, Suth thought. 'You boys have to make sure that bridge is still there when it's time for Greymane to cross it. That or get blown up with it.'

'Blown up?'

Faro nodded, grinning his pointy grin. 'Oh yeah. There've been rumours of Moranth Black forces among these Roolians and Sixth veterans. Now it's confirmed. Odds are they got their munitions too.' He raised his chin in a question to Len. 'How do you like that? Bein' on the receivin' end for a change, hey?'

The old saboteur kept his face carefully blank. 'Let's not start a panic,' he drawled. 'How'd you get spotted anyway? Thought you were better than that.'

Faro just pulled his lips back even more. 'That Adjunct. Talk is he was Crimson Guard. They say the ghosts of their own dead watch over them.'

For some reason the idea of that sent a cold shiver down Suth's back. It seemed to him that that would be the last thing he'd want.

*

Ussü had to bring all his waning influence to bear just to be allowed entrance into the main keep of the Three Sisters. Once within he was kept waiting through half the night while he knew not what was discussed in the Envoy's hall. How to reconquer Skolati, perhaps. Or such premature nonsense.

Finally, past the mid-night ring on the candles, he was *summoned* into the Envoy's presence. Members of the Lady's militant religious order, these Guardians of the Faith, stood watch at the door to his quarters. Escorted in, Ussü bowed. He blinked in the glare of many more candles and lamps, then found the Envoy warming his hands at a brazier. The man was surrounded by sumptuousness: woven hangings depicted scenes from the Lady's ages-long war against the enemy, the demon Stormriders. Thick rugs and cushions lay strewn about. Bright icons of the Lady gleamed on tables, on the walls, each with its own cluster of slim white candles representing the purity of faith. The Envoy wore a heavy wrap of dark wool though the room was stifling. Two Guardians of the Faith stood within to either side of the doors. 'This is my devotional time, *High Mage*,' the man said. 'So please be quick.'

Ussü decided to try compliance first and therefore set aside all complaints or cutting remarks. 'I have been busy, m'lord . . .' for an instant the chilling vision of five pale corpses piled haphazardly near the wall of a tent flashed before his vision but this he also thrust aside and continued, 'scrying, m'lord. Scrying our surroundings. Attempting to divine what is to come. I have glimpsed the enemy. They are close. I believe an attack is imminent.' He took a cautious breath, and in the Envoy's silence, plunged on: 'M'lord, you must withdraw from the east shore. Any retreat, or rout, will press our forces into the river. Only a handful will make it across the bridge—'

Envoy Enesh-jer had shot up a hand for silence. He faced Ussü, glaring what the mage could only name hatred. 'You have *scried*, have you?' Taking a step closer, he studied Ussü as if he were an object of disgust. 'Why Our Lady tolerates your perverted dabbling in these demon-arts is beyond my understanding. However, her tolerance and compassion is infinite. And so I must honour it. As to the deployment of our forces, mage . . . you have far overstepped your authority. You have no say in this *at all*.'

Ussü almost gaped his amazement. Did the Envoy actually believe what he was saying? He'd thought all these airs mere calculation for advancement. Had the man in truth found faith? It *could* happen, Ussü supposed. But 'dabbling in arts'? What nonsense was this? Clenching his teeth to keep his voice low, Ussü grated, 'Enesh-jer . . . stop pretending to be a local. You were born in Gris. I knew you as a young lieutenant in the Sixth. *What insanity is this you are talking*?'

The Envoy flinched away as if struck. He waved to the guards. 'Leave us!'

As the Guardians closed the door behind them Enesh-jer lurched to a table, poured himself a glass of wine and downed it. This seemed to calm him. 'Ussü – you are a mystery to me. Where are all our other cadre mages, hm? Where have they gone?' And he laughed.

'Oh, yes! I remember. I was there. The Lady's power, Ussü! She has crushed them all. She is paramount here. No one can touch her. She is *real*! What are these other so-called gods? Hood? A bony face on the merely inevitable. Burn? Nothing more than lip service to an ancient hearth-spirit. And Shadowthrone?' He laughed. 'Well, I need not even comment. Ussü, what are all these other gods but rivals angered by her supremacy?' He thrust an arm to the east. 'And them! Out there! They too will fall to her. No one can defeat her in these lands. Over all these ages everyone who has tried has fallen! Even *he* . . . even Greymane was thrust aside.' The Envoy opened his arms as if to say none of this mattered anyway. 'And even if we should lose Rool to this new invasion force, the Korelri remain. You know what the Stormguard are like. What they can do. They cannot be defeated!'

Ussü could only shake his head. *So, not so much faith as a bowing in submission to a greater power. Yet is there any distinction? Is not worship no more than a prettified effort at cringing ingratiation? Perhaps now is not the time for the philosophical question. No matter. These arguments I know and understand.* 'Enesh . . . the Stormguard only defend the wall. They will not fight your war for you.'

The Envoy now smiled with a kind of animal slyness. He stepped close. Sweat gleamed on his narrow hatchet face. His eyes were wide, the pupils huge. He took Ussü's hands in his. 'Poor fool! How you cling to your delusions. Yet you too have adapted to these new truths.' He raised Ussü's arms to reveal the blood staining the sleeves of his robes. The stigmata of his latest . . . efforts. 'You too are *implicated*, friend. You too are with us. Up to your bloody elbows.'

And in the man's glazed eyes, Ussü thought he saw the Lady there, laughing at him.

*

Rillish leaned back against a sun-warmed rock and stretched out his leg to rub the thigh. A cold clear night was before them. He was more exhausted than he could ever remember – day after day of continuous riding back and forth, joking, cajoling, outright browbeating – whatever it took to get the troops moving again. And his leg had never really recovered from that old wound. It was so numb he knew he couldn't stand even if he wanted to.

How he longed for a fire! A hot meal, something to warm his hands over. But some bastard had forbidden all fires. That bastard being he. But they'd arrived. They'd made it. And though tired, wrung out, he judged his men and women angry and damned irritated enough to still look forward to a fight.

And the entire time young Kyle, the Adjunct, had ridden with him, though usually keeping to the extreme lead elements. He was an awkward rider, clearly not used to horses, but freakishly hardy, able to ride all day then walk the perimeter through the night. In his opinion the youth may not have the tactical experience to command, but what he did have could not be learned: that certain something that made men and women willing to follow his orders. Rillish saw how the troopers regarded him, the deference, the way their eyes tracked that weapon at his hip. It was similar to the way they acted in Greymane's presence.

It was a regard that were he, Rillish, a lesser man would drive him to a petty and galling resentment. He pulled a boot off and wriggled his toes. Good thing he wasn't so inclined. He was just a gentleman trooper, here to do his people right, then retire and get contentedly fat. He may not like the Adjunct's choosing to accompany the squads tasked with preserving the bridge, but he could hardly stop him. Another commander might have taken the action as some sort of personal affront, or dismissed the youth as a glory-chaser. But the truth was that the contingent had a low chance for survival, and the Adjunct's presence could help greatly. He would have gone himself but for Greymane's orders placing him in command of the attack meant to draw attention from the bridge teams. He would lead the probe against the extreme easterly lines while the majority of his forces waited in the north for a drive to the bridge. Ahead of everyone, though, five squads would float down the Ancy to the bridge and once there act to preserve it from any possible demolition. Captain Betteries had outlined what he had in mind and he was satisfied with the man's choices. It would be a small force counting on secrecy, but should something arise signals had been established.

Rillish rummaged in a saddlebag and unwrapped an old bruised pear. Biting into it reverently, he held the sweet flesh of the fruit in his mouth, tried to ease the tension from his shoulders. Nectar. Absolute nectar. He could look forward to four hours or so of sleep before the night attack. And he would sleep; the troops knew their jobs. He was now in that enviable, but difficult, command position of seeming irrelevancy. The challenge for him was to refrain from interfering and to trust the men and women to do the right thing.

Another problem was that on paper he commanded all the Fourth's elements. But in truth his charging advance had spread his command over several days' march. Flash floods had cut off sections of the columns, delaying their advance for days. Tremors had sent landslides across paths down steep valley sides, mangling and stranding units. It was as if the very land were battling them – at least here in the north. The result was that he currently had with him at the leading edge of his spear-like dash less than three thousand soldiers of the Fourth. Indeed, had the Skolati mustered the will and coordination for a counter-offensive, they could have found him embarrassingly exposed.

But they hadn't. That had been Greymane's throw. He had judged the Skolati shattered and proceeded upon the assumption. And privately Rillish agreed. Not that he had to – it just made his job a little bit easier to bear.

Communiqués from the main body under Greymane put the van of his forces still two days' march away – a distance the High Fist intended to cross in one day and night of continuous forced march beginning immediately. Thus Rillish's orders. Hold until the High Fist arrived with the van. If they were to choose to destroy the bridge, they would do so tomorrow. Every hour thereafter strengthened Greymane's position as more and more of the Fourth and the Eighth dribbled in.

These messengers also talked among the men before returning, and it appeared that Greymane's reputation among the troops had gained an even greater burnishing. Soldiers, being the inveterate superstitious lot they were, attributed their good luck in avoiding the worst of these strange manifestations of flood and earth tremors to Greymane's, and his High Mage's, protection. A comparison Rillish might also choose to resent. But he was of the mind that anything that strengthened the morale of the troops was to be encouraged, even if he personally came out the worse for it.

He finished the pear, said goodnight to his aides, then rolled up in his blanket and promptly fell asleep.

*

At their camp among the rocks Suth sat with the rest of the 17th and thought about what to do before the night wake-up call. They and four other squads had been selected to make for the bridge. Some fifty or so men and women, give or take. He doubted, for example, that Faro would show, though Pyke was still with them –

to everyone's disgust. Should he try to sleep? Why bother when he knew he wouldn't? He eyed Wess, who was taking his time preparing a long-stemmed pipe. The herbs going into that bowl might help him sleep but he couldn't face the river half numb. To one side Dim was already asleep, while Lard was steadily working through his remaining stash of food. Sergeant Goss sat in low conversation with Len and Keri; discussing the bridge no doubt.

Then Pyke sent up a low laugh, pointing aside. 'Look who's here, Yana. It's your boyfriend! Dragging his sorry arse back for a grab at yours.'

It was a stoop-shouldered hulking trooper from the 5th, shaggy-headed like the great horned cattle of the Dal Hon savannah. Suth couldn't remember the fellow's name. Gipe, something like that. Yana stood, flicked Pyke a gesture, faced the fellow hands on hips.

'What have you got to say, then?' she demanded.

The fellow hung his head, kicked at the ground. 'Sorry. I guess.'

'Sorry,' Yana echoed. She crossed her arms. 'You're sorry?'

'Yeah!' He looked up all sullen; then, eyeing Yana, his expression melted away to a kind of hurt mope. 'Yeah.'

Shaking her head, Yana stepped up to take his head in her hands and planted a great kiss on his lips. 'Silly fool! You just had to say so!'

The consternation mixed with delight that played across the man's unguarded face almost made Suth laugh out loud. Helpless. Utterly helpless in her hands.

They linked arms and Yana scooped up her bedroll as they walked off.

'Brainless oaf,' Pyke said. 'Probably doesn't even remember what he's supposed to be sorry for.'

'It ain't the *what* of it that matters,' Wess commented from where he lay on his side, eyes closed, pipe cradled gently in one hand.

Pyke wrinkled his face. 'What in Hood's name is that supposed to mean?'

Keri walked up holding a blanket at her shoulders. She was eyeing the retreating couple and stopped before Suth. 'They make up again?'

Suth nodded. 'Yeah. Again?'

The woman had a strange sort of half-smile on her lips as she looked down at him. 'Yeah. They always make up before every standing battle then have a big ol' fight afterwards and break up.'

Suth snorted. These Malazan soldiers – the oddest lot of misfits all jammed together.

'Me, I get all tense. Can't sleep. What about you?'

Shrugging, Suth had almost said no, not really, when he looked up at the woman standing over him in the blanket, her shirt untucked and untied, and the words died in his mouth. He swallowed and stammered, 'Yeah. Me too. Tense.'

The smile broadened and as she reached down he reached up and they entwined arms. 'Come on then,' she said. 'I know a way to work off all that tension. And bring your blanket – I don't want to freeze my arse off.'

*

A knock on the front pole of his tent woke Ussü. He rose, threw on his thick outer robes over his shirt and trousers, and called out, 'Yes?'

'Word from Borun, High Mage. A disturbance in the east.'

He raised the flaps; a Black Moranth trooper bowed. 'Take me to him.'

Borun occupied a slight rise in the valley slope below the Three Sisters fort along the descent to the Ancy. The vantage offered a view of Three Sisters town, the bridge, and a slice of the far shore where the Roolian forces were dug in. Since it was night all Ussü could see were the dancing shadows and dots of light of torches moving far from the shore. 'What is it?' he asked the Moranth Commander.

'Listen.'

Ussü slowed his breathing, worked on calming his pulse. He reached out to the east with his senses, though careful not to draw upon his Warren. Not yet, in any case. Then over the churning of the river as it charged south he heard it: the definite muted roar of contact. 'I thought them at least a day away yet,' he breathed, the air pluming in the chill night.

'Could be an advance force sent ahead to probe us,' Borun offered.

'Why announce their presence before they're fully assembled?'

The Moranth commander said nothing. It was his way of letting Ussü know that he had no idea.

'The . . . ah . . . packets? They are in place?'

Borun nodded. 'All set.'

'Very good. You have sent someone, I assume?'

'To ascertain the character of the contact, yes. She should be returning soon.'

'Ah – of course.'

The matt-black helm turned to him. 'High Mage, the Envoy has committed nearly fifteen thousand troops to the far shore. We cannot abandon them.'

Yet, Ussü added. 'Very good, Commander.' He peered round the position; Borun's tent stood nearby. 'You wouldn't have a stool, would you?'

'Of course, High Mage.'

Shortly afterwards a Moranth Black trooper came jogging up. He – she, Ussü corrected himself – saluted. 'It appears to be a small force of no more than a few thousand probing the road defences, Commander. The Roolians are holding them off.'

'Or are the Malazans not pressing as hard as they might?' Ussü cut in.

The scout turned her helm to Borun, who gave a small wave, granting permission for the woman to answer. Why the permission, Ussü wondered. Ah, yes! He'd asked for an *opinion*.

'Hard to say, High Mage,' she began, slowly, 'but if I must offer an interpretation, I would say that no, the invaders are not pressing as hard as they might. Though their small number would rule out advancing as they would be overwhelmed,' she added.

Invaders. How odd to hear that from our mouths when we ourselves are invaders. Yet he nodded at the Moranth scout's words. To Borun, he said, 'Then why attack at all? A waste of men and women when they have no chance for reinforcements.'

The blunt bullet helm cocked slightly as Borun thought. 'Could be an impetuous officer, or one hungering to make a mark for him or herself. New to combat.'

'If I were Greymane I'd cashier the fool.'

'Let us hope this officer's uncle is far too important for that,' Borun suggested, with the closest thing to humour Ussü had yet heard from the man.

'You don't know Greymane,' Ussü said darkly.

*

They were given logs to grip for the trip downriver. As it was the winter season the Ancy was low. Great boulders thrust up amid its wide length and intermittent rapids foamed its surface. Suth was told he should be able to touch bottom most of the way down – if he reached for it. Their equipment they stashed in rolls and tied to the logs. In teams of three they slogged out through the shallows to the deeper, swift-flowing centre channel. The cold mountain water took his breath away and stung as if burning. The river stretched before him like churning night beneath the stars. It humped and hissed where rocks lurked just beneath its surface. It pulled at him as if eager to pin him under them.

One by one they lifted their legs and allowed the current to draw them along. Slowly at first, Suth was pulled around submerged boulders; then more swiftly, as if down a slick chute, he picked up speed. He tried to hold his feet out before him and the trick worked a number of times as hidden rocks merely drove his knees into his chest and barked his shins. He clenched his teeth against the pain and raised his head for a glimpse ahead of the dark span of the bridge: nothing yet. A curl turned him, and as he sped along backwards he used one hand to pull himself back round. As he did so he caught a glimpse of the timber undersides of the bridge almost overhead and the sight nearly made him let go of the log in shock. A small island of boulders lay ahead, the water cresting around them, and he reached down for bottom here to slow himself. The water slammed him into the rocks, crushing the breath from him. He hugged the log, mouth open and head down as water foamed over him. He hoped to all his Dal Hon gods that anyone peering over the side of the bridge would merely see a length of driftwood jammed among the rocks.

Now what? He was pressed here as tight as if strapped in. He tried to edge himself out but the current kept pushing him back into his hollow. Come sun-up he would be sure to be spotted – if he wasn't dead from exposure by then!

Something struck him a blow and for an instant he thought he'd been hit by a crossbow bolt from the bridge. But it was a length of rope, pitifully thin, pressed up against him. Struggling, he wrapped the rope round one arm as many times as he could then gripped the log again.

A yank almost dislocated his shoulder. *Ye gods, have a care!* The pressure was steady and agonizing. The rope cut into the flesh and muscle of his arm. He felt a tingling as its circulation was cut off. Slowly, the excruciating pull overcame the water's pressure and he popped free of the trap like a cork. He could only float limply, hardly able to keep a grip of the log one-handed. Hands drew him out of the water.

'Who's this guy?' a voice whispered.

'He's with Goss' bunch.'

'Hunh.' A cuff on his cheek. 'Well, welcome to the 6th.'

Through numb lips Suth slurred, 'Have to get to my squad.'

A dark shape over him snorted. 'No way. You sit tight. We're on the job now 'cause this bridge is mined to blow.'

*

Ussü jerked awake at a touch on his shoulder; he'd fallen asleep leaning forward against his staff. *Those efforts earlier must have taken more out of me than I suspected. And I'm not getting any younger.* It was nearly dawn; the eastern horizon held that same pink you could find inside a seashell. Ussü felt the chill of the winter night painfully in his hands and feet. He nodded to the Moranth trooper, and crossed to where Borun was in conversation with others of his command.

'No sortie?' Borun was asking.

'None ordered. Just repair of the lines and retrenchment.'

Borun bowed to Ussü. 'The day's regards, High Mage.'

'The engagement is over?'

'Yes, some time ago. A slow withdrawal of the invaders.'

'A slow withdrawal? And the Envoy did not press them, maintain contact?'

'No. Orders forbade it.'

Ussü was astonished. '*Why?*'

'Perhaps he fears an ambush or a counterattack.'

'And so he hides behind his lines.' The foolishness of it was dismaying. 'We've abandoned all initiative. *Given* it to them.'

'True,' Borun granted. 'But they do have to come to us. Perhaps you could say time is on our side.'

It was dawning upon Ussü that the Black commander had the annoying capacity of being able to see all sides of any tactical situation. 'Let us hope so,' he eventually replied. Then he cleared his throat; he was fading without his morning herbal infusion and hot spiced tea. 'In the meantime, I will be in my tent. Send word of any development.'

Borun inclined his helmed head. 'Very good, High Mage.'

* * *

Devaleth knew she was no veteran of land campaigns, but it appeared to her that Greymane, in his dash to reach the Roolian border and the advance element under Rillish, was making excellent time.

They had a lot of ground to make up. The High Fist had lingered for over a week to sort out the new Malazan military rulership and accept the surrender of Skolati elements that came trickling in. Then he waited, jaws bunched impatiently, while the remaining Skolati commanders scattered throughout the countryside bickered and undermined each other until finally, disheartened and demoralized, the army failed to field an organized resistance.

Once it became clear that no pending threat remained, Greymane assembled ten thousand soldiers from the Fourth and Eighth and immediately set out for the Roolian border. Fist Khemet Shul remained behind with orders to consolidate, assign garrisons, and follow as soon as prudent.

And at what a pace! As horses were rare everyone walked – and walked – and walked. Greymane rose with the dawn and did not stop walking until after nightfall. Meals – a crust of stale bread scavenged from an abandoned village, or a scrap of dried meat – were taken on the stride. The man was utterly relentless; those who could not keep up were left behind. Soon for the soldiers it became a matter of pride to see to it that that would not happen to them. More than one trooper limped past Devaleth leaving a trail of bloody prints.

Devaleth was one of the handful mounted – albeit on a donkey. Some no doubt thought her lucky, but she knew the truth: it was a kind of torture. The animal's spine was like a knife and the beast would deliberately stop suddenly and dip its head in an effort to tumble her upside down. Whenever this happened soldiers nearby suggested a knife to the hindquarters, or a sharp stick to one ear, but for some reason she could not bring herself to beat the animal and so it had its way. She became resigned to it, thinking herself still far better off than the poor footslogging regulars.

In deference to her position as mage she also had one of the two tents; the other served the mobile infirmary, which followed along the route of march drawn by a team of oxen. All other logistical support and followers – the blacksmiths, armourers and cooks – Greymane had left behind in his utter determination to catch up. For the rankers, it was scavenge on the march or starve. Devaleth saw abandoned overgrown garden plots pillaged, roaming livestock claimed, and even a wild ubek doe brought down by javelins and butchered on the spot, haunches carried off over shoulders for the cook fires.

Each night she had to track down Greymane. She'd eventually find him wrapped in his muddied travelling cloak, lying among the troopers next to some fire or other. His long ash-grey hair would be almost luminous in the night, and likewise the beard he was growing. Devaleth would ease herself down near the fire and from the edge of her gaze usually spend the evening studying the puzzle that was this man.

It seemed to her that he was in his element. Here, in the field, sharing the company of the regulars. Clearly, this was where he was most comfortable. No wonder he'd been so eager to get away. Yet what of the men and women of his command? She knew some officers liked to fancy themselves as being of the common people, with a common touch and able to rub shoulders with the average rankers, when they clearly actually lacked all such gifts. From the glances and bearing of all those the High Fist talked to or sat among Devaleth saw that he had their hearts. In this manner he fit the mould of the old Malazan commanders she'd heard of: the legendary Dujek, the gruff Urko, or the revered Whiskeyjack.

Yet on this subcontinent he was the most reviled criminal in history. Here was the man who, when she was a student at the Mare academy, dared to approach the enemy, the Riders, who would wipe them all from the face of the earth. Was he an utter solipsist? No, he did not strike her as such. Heartless sociopath? Again, no. Or to be pitied as a pathetic gullible fool? No, not that.

Then . . . what?

He was a mystery. A man who went his own way and be damned to the consequences. She didn't know whether to admire the fellow, or to be profoundly terrified of him.

That dilemma took a new twist when, on the fifth day of marching, the ground shook. It was a common tremor; Devaleth was used to them. Local folk superstition attributed them to the Lady's struggle against the Riders. This one appeared to have been centred nearby as the ground opened up beneath the rear elements and many tumbled into a gaping sinkhole. Soon after this the van was crossing a stream when a flash flood stormed down with stunning fury and swept some fifty soldiers away. It was the first of many more disasters: ravines collapsing, rockslides down steep valley sides. It was as if the very ground were revolting against them.

Yet none of these manifestations struck near where Greymane marched. A region of peace and calm seemed to encircle him. No tremor could be felt. No twisting ridgeback descent was suddenly swept out from beneath his feet. Sensibly, as the days passed, and the tremors intensified, the column came to constrict around wherever

Greymane happened to be walking. And since Devaleth accompanied the High Fist, she was always caught up in the crush.

The ninth night of the march she sat at a fire with the High Fist. She had wrapped her robes and blankets around her, arms tight about her knees; the cold had intensified as they approached the windward side of the island. During a moment of relative privacy she cleared her throat and ventured, low: 'She reaches for you but she cannot catch hold. Why is that?'

The man's ice-cold eyes slid to her and the wide jaws slowly unbunched. 'Don't know what you're talking about.'

'We both know what I'm talking about.'

The lips pulled down, granting acknowledgement. 'Do you know what the troopers think?'

'What does that have to do with it?'

He smiled as if having achieved some sort of victory. 'What have you noticed recently? How have the boys and girls been treating you?'

Devaleth frowned. What insanity was this? Certainly they were talking to her now, offering advice on how to ride. And she'd noticed she was never alone. A number of them now flanked her all through the day. And they offered bowls of berries and hot strips of meat from whatever animal happened to be on the fire at night.

He leaned close to lower his voice. 'They think *you're* the one defending them.'

She stared at the High Fist, appalled. 'But that's not true!'

He raised a hand for silence. 'That doesn't matter.' He eased back; his gaze returned to the fire where it usually rested, studying the flames. 'I've come to understand that the truth isn't really what's important.' He cocked his head, his cold blue gaze edging back to her. 'What really matters is what people come to agree *is* the truth.'

Devaleth found she could not hold his gaze and glanced away. Was that a message for her? For everyone? Was everything, then, a lie? Yet he had not denied that he did approach the Riders.

'Get some sleep now,' he said, rolling over and wrapping himself in his thick cloak. 'We'll reach the Ancy valley tomorrow or the next day. There'll be no sleep then.'

* * *

Suth was freezing on his perch under the bridge. The wind whipped unimpeded through the wooden girders he and members of the 6th squad sat among like miserable monkeys. It had dried him but sucked all the warmth from him in doing so. Constant traffic rattled and groaned overhead across the squared timbers of the bridge bedding. Dust and gravel rained down, threatening to make him cough. He hugged himself, adjusted his numb buttocks, and tried to pull some slack from the rope securing him to his seat. Beneath his feet the blue-grey waters of the Ancy churned past.

They'd climbed what the saboteurs named 'piers': timber frames filled with rocks and rubble. The bridge rested atop five of them. They hid high among the braces and joists of the underframing, safe from the eyes of those up and down the shores. Still, it made Suth twitch to see the enemy collecting water and urinating just a stone's throw from the most shoreward pier.

He and the 6th occupied the top of one of the central piers standing in the deepest water. Elsewhere, the second pier eastward, the rest of the 17th had taken up a similar position. He'd tried slithering out to rejoin them but the 6th's sergeant, Twofoot, had signed an enraged no.

And so they waited, hidden, while the saboteurs did whatever it was they were supposed to do. Which so far looked to Suth like absolutely nothing. The 6th's, Thumbs and Lorr, had pulled themselves out to a bundle roped to the bridge's supports midway between two piers and there they'd remained all morning, pointing to various parts of it and whispering.

Bored and numb with cold, Suth turned to the nearest trooper and whispered, 'What're they up to?'

This heavy infantryman kept some kind of leaf-and-nut concoction jammed in one cheek. 'Checkin' it out,' came the laconic reply between chews.

No kidding. They've been doing that all morning. 'Yeah. But what're they gonna *do*?'

A shrug. 'Gotta check for boobytraps.'

'Then what?' Suth whispered again.

'I dunno. Disarm 'em, I suppose.'

Suth sat back, defeated by the soldier's denseness – or at least his unrelenting pose of it. 'What's your name, anyway?'

The man chewed for a time as if giving the question some thought, then said, 'Fish.'

Fish. Suth eyed the fellow, the thick arm slung through a triangular gap between timbers, the wide bovine jaws working. *Fish?* 'Why Fish?'

'I dunno. The drill sergeant asked about my family so I said, "We fish." So he says, okay. You Fish.'

Suth stared. *Remarkable. All without the slightest inflection.* He would've liked to have pressed the fellow to see how far he could carry it; but perhaps that was enough talk as Twofoot glared murder at him whenever he opened his mouth. He sat back again in an attempt to find a more comfortable position. 'Right.'

Something moved over his head and he jerked a flinch that nearly dropped him from his perch to hang over the river like a piece of idiotic fruit. It was a saboteur, a woman, pulling herself along a timber, skinny in muddy leathers. She let herself down next to him to take up a squatting pose, arms over her head gripping the wood. She winked. He nodded back, uncertain. He'd seen her before: damned ugly with snaggled teeth, bulbous eyes that looked able to peer in two directions at once. Long hair pulled back and tied so tight as to make her eyes bulge even more. *Urfa. The saboteur lieutenant.*

'What's up?' he barely mouthed.

'Time to start the show.' And she bared her yellow uneven teeth.

'You going to drop the munitions into the river?'

The woman looked absolutely horrified. She eyed him as if he were crazy. 'Hood no! We're gonna keep them.' Then she swung out under the horizontal timber, hand over hand, nothing beneath her but river, shaking her head at his stupidity.

Well how was I supposed to know? He watched while Urfa joined the short, rotund Thumbs and the equally lanky Lorr on their crowded perch. The three of them began pulling out tools from various pockets all about their trousers, vests and jerkins. Elsewhere, Len and Keri would be starting this very process. The idea of Keri leaning over a munition and being blown to bits made him squirm. *Still, the woman had a gentle deft touch – if that counted for anything. And if things went awry with Thumbs here he'd be just as dead as well.*

*

Ussü was washing his hands at a basin when Borun ducked into his tent. The Moranth commander looked at the sheet-covered body on the central table, then at Ussü. 'Any news?'

Ussü frowned his disappointment. 'No. None. This one died immediately. Shock. Sometimes the heart just gives out. Have you anyone else?'

'We do have a captive . . .'

'Yes? Bring him. I must see what's going on.'

The Moranth Black officer gripped his belt in both gauntleted hands and was quiet for a time, his gaze on the body. Ussü knew his friend well enough to read reluctance and a kind of vague unease. 'Yes?'

'She is . . . Malazan.'

'Ah. I see.' *Unease on two fronts.* 'Do not worry, my friend. We are at war. We must do what we must.'

The matt-dark helm inclined a slow acquiescence. 'Very good, High Mage. She will be sent.' Borun ducked from the tent.

Ussü turned to his aides, pointed to the body. 'Get rid of that. Prepare the table.'

Yurgen bowed. 'Yes, High Mage.'

When the captive was delivered Ussü was disappointed by how tiny she was. *Not much room in the chest cavity to reach the heart.* He gestured for his apprentices to prepare her. She was gagged, her arms stretched out to either side and strapped, legs bound straight. Ussü found himself studying her face much more closely than he had any prior subject. Hazel eyes bored into his, full of animal fury. *Spirit. And tawny. Were you of Tali perhaps? A soldier? But so gracile! A scout, possibly. Yes, probably so. Still, there is hope. This conceit some have of males being stronger than females – not borne out by the evidence. Women always endure longer than men. Through privation, stress, even wounds. And so perhaps my efforts will bear fruit.*

Taking his sharpest instrument, an obsidian-bladed scalpel, he cut open her ragged shirt, exposing her side. Then, feeling his way with his fingers, he slit down vertically between the ridges of two ribs. He held out a hand: 'Spacer.'

The wood and brass instrument was set into his palm. Probing with his fingers he found purchase on the ribs. The subject convulsed, gurgling an agonized scream; Ussü flinched away. *Damn. Have to start all over again.* 'Stop her from moving!'

'Yes, High Mage.' Yurgen and Temeth leaned on the slight woman, using their weight to steady her torso.

'Very good. Let's begin again, shall we . . .'

At the first turn of the spacing screws the subject let out a lacerating incoherent howl of anguish then slumped, unconscious. *Thank the Lady! Now I can concentrate.* He pressed ahead with the procedure while he could. When his questing fingertips brushed the woman's heart he felt his Warren come to him with a power he hadn't felt in decades. Head down close to the subject's naked shoulder, eyes shut, his inner sight pierced the edges of Mockra and flew free.

And almost immediately the Lady was there to greet him. It was as if a cat had taken him by the nape of his neck. Her voice seemed to stroke as if searching for the perfect place to clench.

Ussü. My loyal servant. What blasphemy is this you practise in my name? Abandon these false delusions and join me!

He could not speak; was utterly helpless. And she knew it.

You trust too much to my affection and forbearance. It is only . . .

The voice broke off. He sensed a swirling shift as crushing pressures built around him. He glimpsed something bright amid mist. A blade. A bright blade.

Another is here . . . An interloper! She *is here. This is intolerable! How dare she!*

Something snapped round his neck like a vice. Blinking, he forced open his eyes to see that the subject had somehow slipped an arm free of the strapping and was now strangling him with an inhuman strength. *Yurgen! Temeth! Where are you!*

I will destroy the bitch!

The subject's head rolled over to face him, the eyes open but empty of life. Something fell free round the neck, a leather strap and pendant. The simple stone bore an engraved image: an open hand. *Emblem of the Queen of Dreams!* An image flickered in those staring glassy eyes, a presence. And Ussü felt soul-crushing shame.

You have betrayed me, Ussü, another voice whispered to him. The sadness and regret borne in those words brought tears to his eyes. He felt himself fading from consciousness but behind the voice came faintly the rush of running water.

No! This one's mine!

A blow and the iron band at his neck was yanked away. Someone supporting him. He clasped his throat, gasping for air. Borun, arm round him, sword bared and bloody. Ussü looked down: the woman's torso, headless.

'Speak,' the Moranth commander demanded.

Ussü was massaging his throat. His apprentices all lay fallen round the table as if slain where they stood. Stiffly, he knelt beside Yurgen, turned the youth's head to peer into his eyes. *Not lifeless. Alive.*

But blank. The mind wiped clean. Perhaps, as they say, Mockra is a child of High Thyr. Perhaps, as they whisper, the Enchantress knows no boundaries. 'The bridge, Commander,' he said, still kneeling. 'I heard . . . water.'

'Guards!' the Moranth bellowed, storming from the tent.

Ussü could not look away from those empty orbs. *What was your last sight, Yurgen? Who did this? Was it truly the Enchantress? Perilous indeed is my . . . research. Yet I am helpless without it. What am I to do? Betrayer to both sides? In the end, is there to be no sanctuary, no refuge, for me?*

*

The first Suth knew of any trouble was a change in tone within the general noise of the Roolian forces. Traffic over the bridge grated to a halt. Then a great many footsteps came thumping over the bed. Along the river's shores a crowd of soldiers pressed down to the silt and gravel bars. He noted with a sick feeling that they all carried bows.

Then pointing, yells, bows raised, fired. A storm of arrows flew to the tops of the most shoreward piers. 'We're spotted, lads and lasses,' Twofoot called – just to make it official.

No fucking kidding. Suth felt that his backside was now very exposed and very fat.

'We gonna go for a dive?' Fish called.

Twofoot frowned a negative. 'Naw – we'd all just get shot.'

Scraping sounded once more high among the timber bracings and a black-armoured figure appeared, sword out, rope snaking up from its shoulders. Everyone stared, amazed. *A Black Moranth*?

'Get the fucker!' Twofoot bellowed.

Suth launched himself up, only to be yanked backwards by the rope at his waist. He flailed like an upturned beetle, almost falling off the timber. Fish and the others of the 6th made for the Moranth while he, or she, scrambled hunched among the crossbeams for the saboteurs.

Before any of the 6th could close, a crossbow bolt took the Moranth in the chest and it slipped from its perch to fall swinging and spinning from its rope. Lorr raised his crossbow from his shoulder, regarded the emptied weapon, then, with a shrug, dropped it to the milky-blue water below.

'Ain't you two finished yet?' one of the 6th yelled.

'Shut your Hood-damned mouth,' Thumbs answered.

Suth slit the rope at his waist, readied his weapon. Arrows pecked at the timbers around them. They were hiding amid the understructure and it was a difficult shot for the archers as they had to aim high to make the distance. 'Now what?' he shouted to Twofoot. The 6th's sergeant ignored him.

Someone was yanking on the Black Moranth's rope, attempting to raise it. But the body just kept banging upwards into a horizontal beam. After a few goes whoever was trying must've given up as the rope suddenly slithered hissing through the maze of timbers and the body plunged to disappear into the Ancy.

'Boats,' Fish noted laconically, and he raised his chin upriver.

Suth shifted his seat. Sure enough, a whole flotilla of boats was being readied upriver on both shores. Archers were pouring into them. *All my homeland gods damn them! Now what? They were completely trapped! Couldn't go up. Couldn't go down. Couldn't stay. Whose bloody plan was this anyway?*

Thumbs swung free of the timber he'd been lying prone upon. A fat sack hung from his waist and a big grin was pasted on his broad face. 'We'd better—' An arrow appeared at his side, driven all the way up to the fletching. He grunted, peered at it amazed. 'Just my friggin' luck.'

Lorr lunged for him but he let go and fell, looking up at them all, his face a pale oval. He disappeared into the opaque turbulence around the pier's base.

'Damn!' Twofoot snarled. 'Things are gettin' discomfortable.'

There's an understatement. 'Should we just jump?' Suth called.

Twofoot chewed on that. 'You could jump on to one of the boats an' sink it like the big sack of shit you are. Now keep your mouth shut!'

Funny bastard. Wait till we get out of this. I'll find you. And to think I didn't even bring my shield!

Everyone tried to scramble even higher into the crossbeams to find cover from the bow-fire. Suth was shifting sideways to another bracing when the entire bridge jumped. The blast knocked him from the top of the timber. He clung on, swinging. Through the roaring in his ears he just made out a scream as someone fell. Pieces of shattered equipment and timber splashed into the river below.

After a brief stunned silence Twofoot bellowed: 'Up and at 'em!'

Up! Up? A charge? What about me? Suth managed to hook a foot over the brace. The 6th was climbing to the edges of the underframing, headed over the top. *Wait for me, damn you!*

*

From the hillside Rillish saw as well as everyone the surge of black figures charging the bridge; the wave of archers darkening the shores on both sides of the Ancy. The flight of bow-fire merely confirmed it. He straightened and beckoned an aide to him. 'Last report on Greymane?'

'Sometime tonight is the best estimate, Fist,' the woman answered. Her eyes remained fixed on the distant bright ribbon of river. Then she swung her gaze to him, entreating. *I was once so young; so eager. Now it is only the costs I think of. Would it be worth it? The maths is unforgiving: there are only some fifty of them, after all.*

But – as always – there is so much more than mere numbers at stake.

Turning, he nodded to Captain Peles at his side. Then, to the aide: 'Order the charge. We strike straight to the shore, cut south to the bridge.'

The woman was already dashing off.

'We'll hold,' Peles said, securing her wolf-visored helm.

'We have no choice now.'

*

From his tent Ussü was watching the attack while sipping a restorative glass of hot tea boiled from a rare poppy found on the foothills of the Ebon range. He dropped the glass in shock when a blast shot smoke and debris blossoming over the bridge. Human figures, carts and equipment flew pinwheeling to splash soundlessly into the river.

Damn the Lady! Was that them or us? Deliberate, or accidental?

As the smoke cleared he could see that the explosion hadn't completely severed that length of the bridge: a few thick braces still spanned the section. *Accidental perhaps – not where it was meant. That, or we Malazans built damned well.* Borun came jogging up. Beyond him, fighting had broken out all over the bridge. *The rats driven up from cover. Can't be too many of them.*

'Not us,' the Moranth commander announced.

'Unintentional.'

'For those holding it – undoubtedly.'

Hooves shook the ground as one of the Envoy's entourage came thundering over to them and brought his mount to a savage halt. It was one of the self-styled Roolian noblemen: a Duke Kurran, or

Kherran. The man pointed to Borun. 'What treachery is this? You had your orders!'

'We are not the only ones with munitions,' Borun pointed out, his hoarse voice bland.

'It is hardly in their interests to demolish the bridge!'

'They would strand the forces on the far shore,' Ussü observed. 'With their retreat cut off they may surrender and we will have lost a third of our army.'

The Duke glared as if Ussü had suggested that very plan to the enemy. Through clenched teeth he ground out: 'The Overlord will deal with you.' He yanked the horse's reins around.

'We shall be blamed no matter what,' Borun said, his gaze on the retreating noble.

A Black Moranth runner sped to Borun, spoke to him. The commander turned to Ussü, who was straining another glass of tea. 'The advance force on the far shore is attacking.'

This time Ussü managed not to spill his tea.

*

Suth pulled himself up and over the bridge railing to roll amid scattered equipment and splayed corpses. Smoke still plumed from the east end where for all he knew the bridge had collapsed. To the west lines had formed amid turned-up wagons. He threw himself into cover next to a cart, shouted to the nearest trooper, a woman binding her own arm: 'What's going on?'

'We're holding this side,' she answered; then, eyeing him, added, 'The 17th?'

'Yeah.'

She motioned ahead. 'You're further on.'

He thanked her and crawled forward. Arrow-fire fell thick and indiscriminate. *What do these archers think they're doing? There's more of them than us!* Ahead, an empty length of bridge swept by bow-fire stood between him and the squads defending the barrier of wagons. He spotted Yana, Goss and Wess amid the fighting. *Thank the Hearth-Goddess! It hadn't been Keri . . . What to do? No shield! Oh well. Nothing for it!* He hunched and bolted out across the open length of bridge.

Arrows peppered the adze-hewn planks as he ran. He didn't bother dodging; these were all just sent high in the hopes of hitting something. Close to the barrier white fire clamped its teeth into his right thigh and he fell rolling into cover.

'That was foolish,' someone said, righting him. It was the young Adjunct; he peered at Suth's leg, frowned beneath his moustache. 'You've broken the shaft.' Suth couldn't answer, the pain was so all-consuming. He thought he was going to throw up. 'Urfa!' The Adjunct stood. 'She'll take care of you.'

The saboteur lieutenant threw herself down next to him. She pushed him flat none too gently. 'Why am I doin' this?' she grumbled. 'I'm no Hood-damned nurse!' Suth was on his stomach with her lying on him, her elbow on his neck; he could hardly breathe let alone speak. A cold blade slashed the back of his trousers. 'I see it!' she announced. 'Just because I've done a few amputations!' She added, lower: 'I bet our Adjunct boy can sew too! This'll hurt.' A blade stabbed the back of his leg. He screamed, adding his voice to the roar of battle surrounding them. She was digging in the meat at the rear of his thigh. Stars appeared in his sight. The clash of fighting receded to a mute hollow murmur. His vision darkened.

*

They fought their way down the riverside. They trampled the camp, kicked over tents and cook fires, kept their backs to the muddy shore. Rillish fought with both swords; Captain Peles and other guards covered his flanks. It seemed to him that this force didn't particularly want to dispute their route to the bridge.

He didn't blame them now that it was useless. The blast had surprised everyone. Stones and litter had rained down all around. It seemed to him that the Roolian forces hadn't really recovered from that explosion. Their officers urged them on but he could imagine the average foot soldier wondering why he should die for a useless piece of wood and stone.

Especially now that they were utterly cut off.

Still, they were more than willing to allow Rillish's force to rush in to be encircled; that suited their officers. Once their archers began taking shots at him Rillish retreated to the Fourth's shield wall and ordered everyone to hold ground defending this end of the bridge.

He just hoped Greymane wouldn't judge him too harshly for delivering damaged goods.

Then a man appeared, escorted by Peles. He was scorched, sleeves burned away, skin blistered and black. Rillish recognized him as Cresh, sergeant of the 11th, one of the teams sent to secure the bridge. The man saluted.

Rillish answered the salute. 'Good to see you, Sergeant. I'm glad you survived. Too bad they got to it anyway.'

'No, sir, they didn't.'

Rillish studied the man; didn't he have a full beard last he'd seen him? 'What was that?'

'Was an accident. Us. Lit off above the bed. We've beat down the fires an' taken a squint. My boy Slowburn says there's enough of the frame left. Give us time and we'll have it patched up.'

Rillish stared at the sergeant, then turned to the Roolian lines. *Damn. How soon before* they *see that?*

*

Ussü judged it half an hour's glass and so he turned to Borun while the commander fielded messages and enquired mildly, 'Why is there still fighting on the bridge?'

The Moranth commander did not even look up. 'You I will tell the truth – I have been husbanding my own people. This is one battle and we have a war to fight.'

'I see.'

'Also, there are reports of one among them anchoring their lines. He carries a weapon . . . witnesses call it white or yellow, like ivory. None is willing to face him.'

Ussü's gaze snapped to the distant bridge where a horde of soldiers pressed, pikes and spears waving like a small forest. *White or yellow . . . bright . . . the weapon he saw? No doubt. Did this one deserve his attention? But he was exhausted from being caught like a fly in the confrontation between the Lady and the Enchantress. He simply was not up to it.*

A grunt from Borun pulled his attention to the slope. There a band of black-clad priests descended, staves striking the ground as they paced. Soldiers flinched from their advance. Ah! Abbot Nerra and his three assistants. This fellow on the bridge had also drawn the Lady's attention. She would now take a hand. He should get closer; this could prove quite instructive.

'I would witness this,' he told Borun.

The Black Moranth commander grunted his disinterest. 'If you must. I will remain.' He waved one of his aides to accompany him.

Ussü descended. Or rather, he attempted to; the soldiers did not cooperatively part for him as they had for the priests. And it was a terrible press as thousands jammed in towards the bridge to reach the enemy. In the end he settled for following in the wake of the Moranth as he – or she? – forced a way through.

*

Suth could stand; if he gritted his teeth hard enough and concentrated. Urfa's binding was as tight as a winding-sheet and she'd wrapped with it a poultice that stank of fat and urine and other things he didn't want to think about. But it was supposed to be proof against the wound's suppurating.

He was reserve now, of course. Rear rank. Bending over stiffly, he picked up a spear. The front lines had all scavenged shields and now fought a stubborn defence. All except the Adjunct, who watched from behind, ever ready to push in where needed. No archer could reach them now, unless he dared step out from the enemy's front lines. In which case they still had their crossbows.

When the Adjunct happened to be standing near him, Suth asked, 'Do we retreat?'

The young man smiled behind his moustache. 'Not unless we can take our wagons with us.'

This close Suth wondered why he had ever considered the officer young. He was no younger than himself, surely, nor a good portion of the entire army. This was a young person's calling. Probably it was the rank: the fellow was slim in years to be second in command to a High Fist.

The Adjunct's gaze narrowed, the cross-hatching of wrinkles all around almost hiding the eyes – a plainsman's gaze. 'Trouble,' he breathed, then, gesturing, 'Goss, Twofoot, to me.'

Suth strained to look: men in dark robes advancing. Pressure eased along the twelve-foot width as the Roolian soldiers backed off. Four more priests of the Lady, just as at the temple in Aamil. He remembered his throat constricting then, his stolen breath. Would that happen again? And would the Adjunct be able to counter it as before?

The four stamped their iron-shod staves to the timbers and stood waiting. Flanked by his sergeants the Adjunct stepped out to meet them.

'I am Abbot Nerra,' one of the priests announced. He did not wait for the Adjunct to reply; indeed, it was clear that he did not want any response. 'You are trespassing. Retreat from this valley and you will be unmolested. You have the word of the Lady. Such is her infinite leniency and forbearance.'

'Generous of the Lady to offer territory we already hold,' the Adjunct answered.

The Abbot appeared to have expected such an answer. 'Surrender now or be driven before the Lady's wrath like ash before the wind.'

'Is this the leniency or the forbearance?'

The Abbot was untroubled. '*Her* patience is without end. Mine is not.' He signalled to his fellows.

At the same instant the sergeants signed as well and from behind the upturned wagons saboteurs jumped up to fire crossbows. Multiple bolts slammed into the priests, some passing through entirely to speed on and strike soldiers behind.

The four staggered but none fell. The Abbot raised his eyes and something more seemed to glare from their depths that fixed them all with their rage. 'Blasphemers! Your essences will writhe in agony!'

Energy detonated between the priests in crackling arcs and filaments. The timbers shuddered as if pounded by a charge of cavalry. Everyone flinched: the Adjunct, the sergeants, even the Roolian troops. The robes of the priests began to smoulder and smoke. A chain of the energy lashed out, striking one wagon in an explosion of shards sending men and women flying. Suth remembered the spear in his hand and took one step to launch it. The leaf-blade disappeared into the torso of a priest while the haft immediately burst to ash. The priest seemed unaffected by what was certainly a mortal wound.

The four advanced a step, staves held horizontal before them. The wagon Suth hid behind slid backwards, almost knocking him from his feet. He staggered, yelling his pain with every hop of his injured leg. Another chain of energy lashed the lines and soldiers fell, smouldering, charred and withered.

Then the Adjunct lunged forward, rolling. A priest fell, his leg severed at the knee. Another swung his stave and the Adjunct caught the blow on his sword, two-handed. The stave was severed in a blast that sent the youth spinning to slam into the bridge's side. The eruption flattened a score of the nearest Roolian soldiers as well. That priest fell, his arms and chest in bloody ruins, his hands gone. The remaining two pushed onward, seemingly uncaring and unaffected. The wagon slammed backwards into Suth once more.

'Drop!' Urfa called, and she straightened to throw a fist-sized orb. Suth hunched behind the wagon. Normally the crack of the munition would have made him flinch, but now the blast was lost in the maelstrom of wrath unleashed before them. When the woman peered up again she gaped, snarling, '*Shit!*'

He peered, an arm shielding his eyes, to see the two still advancing despite countless slashing wounds – one's face a bloom of blood from a mortal head wound. The Adjunct appeared to be unconscious. Suth hobbled over to him, and found Goss examining him. 'What do we do?' Suth shouted.

'Don't know!'

The pale yellow blade lay on the timbers. Both Suth and Goss eyed it. 'Should I touch it?' Suth asked.

'Don't know!'

'Oh, to the Witches with it!' Suth picked it up; it was warm in his hand and not quite as heavy as an iron weapon. Nothing seemed to happen to him. The curved blade looked more golden than pale yellow, translucent at its edge. He turned to the remaining priests. They were ignoring them, intent upon forcing everyone back up the bridge. He glanced at Goss, who wore a thoughtful frown.

'Maybe I should . . .' the sergeant offered.

Well, he *was* wounded. A great yell snapped their attention to the priests. A soldier had leapt from cover swinging a two-handed sword. The trooper wore a long mail coat and a helm whose visor was hammered into the likeness of a snarling beast. Suth recognized her as an officer he often saw with Fist Rillish. Her heavy blade crashed into a blocking stave, triggering an eruption of energy that crackled and lashed all about the bridge. *But she hadn't come with them! What was she doing here?*

A second arcing blow slipped under the stave and slit one priest across the gut almost to the spine. A spin and she brought the weapon swinging up to catch the second at the groin, tearing a gash up to his sternum. Even then neither priest fell. Smoke now plumed from them as if driven by a ferocious wind; it appeared to Suth that they'd been dead for some time. Enraged, her mail blackened and scoured by the energies, the woman kicked one of the priests. He fell corpse-stiff in a clatter of dry limbs.

The crackling power snapped out of existence; the staves lay consumed to blackened sticks, iron fittings melted. A crowd of troopers from the Fourth washed over them all. They came dragging carts and equipment that they heaved up into a barricade. Suth and Goss helped the groggy Adjunct up.

Goss offered a wink. 'Have to be the hero another time, hey?'

Suth examined the pale blade. 'I guess it takes more than just a sword.' He picked up a torn cloak and used it wrap the weapon.

The sergeant was nodding his serious agreement. 'Yeah. Looks more like a question of timing to me.'

The Adjunct was standing on his own now. He rolled one shoulder, wincing and hissing his pain. Suth offered him the sword. He took it and shook his head. 'Fat lot of good it did me.'

'You're still alive, sir,' Goss pointed out.

The Adjunct nodded thoughtfully, accepting the point. 'True enough, Sergeant.'

Goss straightened, offering an abbreviated battlefield salute, and Suth turned to see Fist Rillish approaching. 'Just in time,' the Adjunct called.

Fist Rillish bowed. 'Let's hope Greymane is as prompt.'

The Adjunct was massaging his shoulder. 'When do you expect him?'

'Tonight – Burn speed him.'

The Adjunct grunted his acknowledgement. 'We should be able to hold till then. I leave you to it.'

Fist Rillish bowed again, turned to Sergeant Goss; he pinched his chin between his thumb and forefinger as he studied the man. 'Your captain is on the east shore, Sergeant.'

'Yes, sir.' Goss took Suth's arm. 'On our way.'

*

Within the pressing mass of Roolian soldiers Ussü tapped the shoulder of his Moranth escort. He had seen enough. It was now plain to him that this second wave of invasion brought more than mere soldiers. Other powers, it seemed, deemed the timing right to challenge the Lady's long dominance. Head down, he walked back up the slope, hands clasped behind his back. If it was equally evident to *her* by now . . . then he may be able to strike a bargain, of a kind.

Head down, lost in thought, he failed to note the row raging around Borun's command position. If he had seen it he would have turned right round; as it was, he walked right into it. 'You! Mage,' someone demanded. 'Talk some sense into your companion.' Ussü looked up, blinking: a crowd of the Envoy's officer and aristocratic entourage surrounded Borun. The Duke had spoken. *Kherran, that was his name.*

'Yes, my Duke?' Ussü asked mildly.

'Remind him of his duty!'

Ussü turned to Borun. 'Well, Commander? Whatever is the matter?'

'It is now Envoy Enesh's wish that the bridge be blown.'

Ussü raised an eyebrow. *Rather late for that.* 'I see. And?'

A shrug. 'We do not possess sufficient munitions for the task.'

'I see.' Ussü turned to Duke Kherran. 'You heard the man. You had your chance. Now it can't be done.'

The Duke advanced upon him, his round face darkening with rage. For a moment Ussü thought he would strike. Through clenched teeth he snarled, 'We note you had sufficient munitions to mine the bridge earlier!'

'That was earlier,' Borun said, his voice flat. 'Now, more importantly, what we do not possess is the bridge itself.'

The Duke was almost beyond words in his frustration. He pointed to the structure. 'Well . . . do it here! This end!'

Borun waved the suggestion aside. 'Inconsequential. The damage would be no more than that incurred on the far side. It could be repaired in a day. No, our only hope would be to seize the nearest shoreward pier and demolish it.'

'Well? Do it!'

'We do not possess sufficient munitions for the task.'

The man went for his weapon. He froze in the act, his chest heaving, gulping down air. 'You two . . . You are deliberately frustrating our efforts! You wish us to fail! Overlord Yeull will deal with you!' He gestured to the entourage. 'Come!'

'I strongly urge that all boats be pressed into a general withdrawal from the east shore,' Borun called after the Duke.

'Let it be on your head!'

The Moranth commander watched them march off. 'We will be blamed no matter what,' he mused aloud.

'Yes. But not to worry.'

The matt-dark helm turned to him. Ussü could almost imagine the arched brow. 'No?'

'No. I have a feeling that we may count on the intervention of a higher authority.'

The helm cocked sideways in thought. 'Indeed.'

Ussü entered the opened front of his tent. He searched among his herbs, touched a hand to his teapot: cold. 'Hot water!' he shouted. At the fire a servant youth leapt up to do his bidding. 'So much for the imponderables, Borun. What of the practicalities? Do we withdraw?'

And Ussü glanced out of the tent. The Moranth commander was facing the river, armoured hands brushing his belt at his hips.

'No.'

Ussü was quite surprised. 'Really? We relinquish one bank just to keep the other?'

The commander entered the tent. He picked up a twist of dried leaves and brought them to his visor, took an experimental sniff. 'Haste, High Mage. Speed. This quick dash to take the bridge. The forced march across Skolati. All these speak of a strategy for a swift victory. Yes?'

From a meal set out for him Ussü tore a pinch of cold smoked meat. 'Granted.' The dirt, he noted, had been raked clean. Poor Yurgen, Temeth and Seel. Able apprentices, but all without even the slightest *talent*. What would he do for assistants now? He sighed. Ham-handed soldiers no doubt.

Borun crossed his arms, leaned against the central table. 'Then it is my duty to frustrate this strategy, no? I must impede, slow, delay. Disputing the crossing will effect that.' He began pacing. 'Oh, he may cross downstream, or upstream, but that would add weeks to his march. Not to his liking, I think.'

'Very well. So we remain.'

'Yes. And thus the question, High Mage . . . What can you contribute?'

Ussü popped the meat into his mouth, both brows rising. *Ah. Good question.* He cleared his throat. 'I will need new assistants.'

* * *

Bakune sat hunched forward on his elbows over his small table next to the kitchen entrance at the back of a crowded tavern. He was dressed in old tattered clothes, his dirty hair hung forward over his face and he kept one hand tight round the shot glass of clear Styggian grain alcohol. He studied that hand, the blackened broken nails. When was the last time he had been so dirty? If ever at all? Perhaps once, as a child, running pell-mell through these very waterfront streets.

That night of the escape the Theftian priest might have had a boat waiting but neither he nor Bakune had anticipated the harbour's being closed. No vessels allowed in or out. The gates of the city had been sealed as well. They might have escaped their cells, but they effectively remained imprisoned within Banith. Bakune was under no illusions; he was certainly not important enough to warrant these precautions, nor did he think the priest so. No, the posted notices revealed that these prohibitions against travel had been levelled more than ten days ago.

The giant Manask, about whom Bakune had his doubts – after all, the man's features betrayed none of the telltale markers of Elder blood, such as pronounced jaw, jutting brow, or deep-set eyes – had then bent down for a whispered conference with the priest. It was yet some time to dawn and the three occupied a narrow trash-choked alley close to the waterfront. While Bakune kept watch, the whispering behind him escalated into a full-blown shouting match with the two almost coming to blows. Only his intervention brought silence. The priest glowered, face flushed, while the cheerfulness the giant usually displayed was now clouded, almost occluded.

Manask had turned to him, set a hand on his shoulder, and winked broadly. 'You will wait here a time, then Ip— the priest will lead you to our agreed hiding hole. I myself must travel ahead by stealth and secrecy to make arrangements for our disappearance. Do not fear! These clod-footed Guardians will not track us down. For am I not the most amazing thief in all these lands? Come now, admit it, have you never seen anything like me?'

'No, Manask. I admit that I have never seen anything like you.'

The giant cuffed the priest. 'There. You see?' The priest just rolled his eyes. 'And now . . . I must away into the gloom . . .' and the giant backed down the alley, hunched low. 'Disappear like smoke . . . like the very mist . . .' He waved his hands before his face as if he were a conjuror, hopped round a corner. 'There! And I am gone! Ha!'

'Like a fart in the wind,' the priest growled.

Bakune never did find out just what the giant's 'arrangements' constituted. The priest had merely slid down one dirty wall and sat for a time, arms hung over his knees. Then, after a while, he had stood, sighing, and motioned for the Assessor to follow. They walked the back alleys. It struck Bakune that the city was astonishingly quiet, the streets empty; there must be a curfew in place. Eventually the priest stopped at one slop-stained door. The alley was appallingly filthy here, littered with rotting food and stinking of urine. Cats scattered at their intrusion. The door scraped open and an old woman eyed them as if they themselves were no better than the rubbish they stood among. She pulled the door open a crack more and beckoned them in with a desultory wave.

It was the kitchen of some sort of public house. The old cook kicked a bundle of rags in a corner and a child sat up, rubbed the sleep from her eyes and blinked at them. The woman picked up a butcher's knife and motioned curtly. The girl nodded, and urged them to follow her. Behind them the heavy blade slammed into the chopping block.

Bakune had since learned the girl's name was Soon. Her plight pulled at his heart. To see her cuffed and kicked, forced to perform the dirtiest, most degrading tasks in the tavern, made him wince. True, she was half-blood, of the old indigenous tribes, but still it grated. The child was forced to do this work simply because she was small and weak and could not defend herself. It had never before occurred to him to be bothered by such a pedestrian truth. Such was the normal way of the world: the powerful got their way – it was their prerogative.

Perhaps seeing this principle demonstrated by a fist applied vigorously to the head of a child put a different perspective on it. A perspective that had not been available from his seat of office, or any courtroom.

He spent his days here in the tavern, named the Sailor's Roost, retreating at night to the room he shared with the priest and attempting to sleep through the shouts, the drunken brawls, and the shrieks of real pain and faked pleasure. As for the priest, the man hadn't left the room since they first entered it. Of Manask he had seen no sign.

Of course, if they wanted to sneak away, they could. The gates might be officially closed, vessels prohibited from sailing, the streets patrolled by the Guardians of the Faith, but the human urge to profit cannot so easily be suppressed. Already this night Bakune had overheard several arrangements for illegal shipments and deals to smuggle individuals in and out of the city. This tavern seemed a regular hotbed of black-market activities. He wondered why no cases involving it had ever come before him.

Early on the priest had made it clear he had no intention of leaving. He would stay for reasons of his own that he would not discuss. He also told Bakune that he and Manask would do whatever they could to help him escape.

Immediately his Assessor's mind was suspicious of such generosity. 'And why would you do so?' he had asked.

Sitting on his mattress of straw the priest had smiled his wide frog-like grin. 'And why did you refuse to sign my death certificate? Who was I to you? A stranger. Nothing. Yet you helped me.'

'I was merely following the dictates of my calling. It would not have been just.'

The smile was swallowed by a sour glower. 'Just,' he grunted. 'You are a man of principle and no hypocrite, and you have my respect . . . but it seems to me that your notion, and practice, of justice has been rather narrow and blinkered.'

Bakune had no idea what the man meant. His brows crimped and he was silent for some time. *Narrow? Had he not known – and enforced – the laws of the land all his life?*

'Manask and I can arrange to have you on a boat tonight.'

Silent, Bakune shook his head in a negative.

'No? You won't go?'

'I cannot leave.'

'Why not?'

Bakune smiled. 'For reasons *I'd* rather not discuss.'

The priest cocked a brow. 'I see. So you will remain.'

'Yes.'

'Very well. Suit yourself. Who am I to tell you what to do?'

Bakune eyed the man, uncertain. 'So . . . I may stay?'

'Yes. Certainly. You should be safe here.'

'Well . . . my thanks.'

Now, Bakune turned the shot glass in his hand and thought again about his reason for remaining. That he was free now to act as never before. More free even than when he was the city magistrate, its Assessor. Then, he'd been constrained on all sides. Now, yes, he was a fugitive, hunted, but he could do as he wished. He could pursue lines of inquiry and take actions he'd only dreamed of months ago. What consequences could he possibly be threatened with now? The Abbot and his Guardians through their actions had only escalated matters. As, of course, all confrontation does.

From beneath his unwashed hair he watched the crowded room. Yes, he was safe here. The tavern catered to sailors and petty merchants – all now stranded and waiting for the Guardians to relax the curfew and the injunctions against movement.

Men and women from all nations of the subcontinent mingled here; even some who might be hiding origins from beyond the Ocean of Storms. Surely, then, such a concentration of foreigners deserved the close scrutiny of the Guardians. Yet he saw no signs of their surveillance. Unless, of course, they were somehow even more subtle and discreet in their methods than Karien'el.

Which, from what he'd seen so far, he very much doubted.

He sipped the fiery near-pure alcohol and winced. *Lady be damned! Why were there no laws against serving such poison?* He was about to rise when two men thumped down at his tiny round table. At first he flinched, thinking: *Invoke the Riders and they appear.* Then he recognized the two slouched, stoop-shouldered, lazy-eyed men as the guards Karien'el had tapped to shadow him. His composure regained, he regarded them narrowly. 'Yes?'

The one with the darkest brows and a fat moustache pointed to his glass. 'You gonna drink that?'

'What do you two want?'

'I want one of those,' said the other.

'Well you can't have it 'cause it's mine,' said the first.

'Neither of you—'

'Just 'cause you asked first,' the second pouted.

'That's right. I showed 'nitiative. That's why I'm the captain.'

'What do you two think . . .' Bakune tailed off as the first guard took the shot glass between his thumb and forefinger and downed the entire drink. Then he carefully brushed back his ridiculous moustache to the right and left using the back of his hand, and sighed.

Like a cat. And so, to Bakune's mind, the man became Cat.

The other, who was regarding his companion with a kind of sour resentment, Bakune couldn't tag with a name. The fellow was pulling at his thick lower lip, his eyes on the now empty glass, and at last he offered, 'You ain't the captain of me.'

'I'll just be going then,' Bakune said, half rising.

'Don'tcha have orders?' Cat said. Then, to his partner, he added, 'Course I'm captain. Chain of command! Chaos otherwise.'

'Orders?' Bakune asked. Then he remembered: Karien had placed these two under his command. *Lady, no!* He *was the commander of these cretins!* He sat back down.

Cat shrugged. 'Just thought maybe you might on account of all the bodies.'

'Bodies?'

Stroking his moustache, Cat directed Bakune's gaze to the empty glass. Giving a sigh of defeat, Bakune raised a hand to the tavern-keeper. The other fellow's hand shot up as well. Bakune signed for two. He sat with arms crossed until the shot glasses arrived. The two raised the glasses. 'Your health, ah, sir,' said Cat.

Bakune leaned forward. 'Listen . . . what are your names anyway?'

'Puller,' said the junior partner, wiping his wet lips.

'Captain Hyuke at your service, sir,' said Cat, his voice suddenly low and conspiratorial.

'You're no captain,' Puller complained.

Bakune used his thumb and forefinger to massage his brow. *Blessed Lady! Puller and Hyuke? He preferred Cat and, what, Mole?* 'Listen . . . you two. No one's captain until Karien gets back.' The two exchanged knowing, sceptical looks. 'So, how about sergeant, Hyuke . . . if you must?'

Hyuke sat back grinning while he brushed his moustache. Then he cuffed his partner. 'Hear that, Pull? I just made sergeant.'

Bakune felt his shoulders sag.

''Nitiative,' Hyuke added, nodding profoundly.

Puller pouted into his glass.

'So what was that about bodies then, Sergeant?'

'Ah!' Hyuke touched a finger to the side of his bulbous nose. 'Been turning up at an awful rate. Used to be no more than one every few months, hey? Now it's two a week.'

Bakune felt himself clenching tight. A hot sourness bubbled up in his stomach. 'Where?' he said, his voice faint.

'All over. Both male and female. All young, though.'

Damn this monster, whoever he was! Taking advantage of the upheaval. 'Thank you, Sergeant.' He swallowed to wet his throat. Something took a bite out of his stomach.

Hyuke was frowning at him. 'You okay, Ass— ah, sir?'

He waved a hand. 'Yes. Now, are we safe here? Can we use this place?'

Both nodded. 'Oh, yes,' Hyuke said. 'Safe as the baker's wife in the morning.'

Bakune felt his suspicions stirring once more. 'Why?' he asked slowly.

The partners exchanged uncertain looks. Hyuke opened his hands. 'Because he's busy baking . . .'

Bakune just glared. Hyuke's thick brows rose. 'Ah! I see. On account this is Boneyman's place.'

'Boneyman . . . ?'

The two watchmen shared another glance; it seemed they could communicate solely by looks alone. Hyuke shook his head. 'Really, sir. You bein' the Ass— ah . . . I'm surprised.'

Bakune struggled to keep his face flat. 'Please inform me. If you would be so kind.'

'Boneyman runs the smuggling and the night market here in town, now that—' Puller loudly cleared his throat, glaring, and Hyuke frowned, confused. Puller tilted his head to glance significantly to Bakune. Hyuke's brows rose even higher. 'Ah! Well . . . now that things have . . . changed . . .' he finished, flustered.

Bakune felt his gaze narrowing. *Things have changed now, have they? Now that Karien'el has been marched off to war. So that was why so very few black-market cases ever came to me. So be it. All that is the past. The question is what to do now.*

'Things'll be really bad next week,' Puller complained.

'How so?' Bakune asked.

The big stoop-shouldered fellow blushed, looking to his partner for help. Hyuke cleared his throat. 'On account of the Festival of Renewal.'

Of course! He'd lost all track of the time. The winter festival celebrating the Lady's arising and our deliverance from the Stormriders! Banith will be crushed beneath pilgrims as usual – surely the Guardians will allow the shiploads of worshippers to dock! And the Cloister will be open to all devout as well. This monster will think he has a free hand that night. That's when we will act! He nodded to his two men. 'We'll lie low until then.'

Hyuke touched his finger to his nose. 'Wise as a mouse in a kennel, sir.'

Puller was frowning. 'A kennel?'

Hyuke leaned to him. 'No cats.'

The man's round face lit up. 'Oh yeah. Course!'

Hyuke stood, brushed his moustache. 'Thanks for the drink.' He motioned to Puller, who remained slouched in his seat, unhappy again. 'What?'

'I still don't see why you get to be sergeant.'

Hyuke cuffed his partner. 'Tell you what. You show some command qualities like me an' maybe you can make corporal.'

Puller straightened, his eyes widening. 'Really? Me? Corporal?' He stood and the two pushed their way through the crowd. 'You think so?'

'If you're the best candidate.'

Bakune watched them go. *All the foreign gods help him. What did he think he could possibly accomplish? Still, he had to try, didn't he? Yes. That's all one could do. Follow the dictates of one's conscience.*

He got up to return to his room, where the priest would no doubt be sound asleep despite the raucous crowd of the night.

* * *

They followed the track of the daemon migration. The carnage it wrought across the rolling Shadow landscape was unmistakable. *So much for my fears of wandering lost*, Kiska thought wryly. How long they walked she had no idea. Time seemed suspended here in the Shadow Realm. Or so it had seemed to her. But now change had struck. What the daemons described as a 'Whorl' had opened on to Shadow and drained an entire lake, obliterating their aeons-old way of life. That Whorl sounded suspiciously like the rift that had swallowed Tayschrenn. It even touched on to Chaos, or so Least Branch claimed.

They'd been walking in a protracted silence. Neither, it seemed, knew what to say. She thought of asking about his past, but comments from him suggested that that was a sensitive, if not closed, subject.

Then something moved beneath her clothes.

Kiska shrieked her surprise; she dropped her staff, tore off her cloak, her equipment, her jacket. Jheval watched, tense, hands going to his morningstars. 'What is it?'

Kiska retrieved her stave, pointed to her heaped clothes and equipment. 'There!'

Jheval regarded the pile, frowned his puzzlement. 'You were bitten? A scorpion perhaps?'

Something beneath the clothes shifted. 'Did you see that?'

One of Jheval's morningstars whirred to life. 'I'll finish it.'

'No!' Gently, she prised apart the layers until she revealed her blanket and the few odds and ends wrapped in it. Kiska felt an uneasy sourness in her stomach. *The sack! Some* thing *inside?*

Kneeling, she untied the blanket and gingerly unrolled it. The dirty burlap sack was exposed. Something small squirmed within.

'Do we let it out?' Jheval asked.

Kiska rocked on her haunches. 'I don't think so. I don't think we should yet.'

'Well I'm not carrying it.'

She gave him a hard stare. 'You haven't been, have you?'

The man had the grace to look chastened. He brushed his moustache. 'I was just saying . . .'

'Never mind.' Raising it gently, she tied the sack to her belt. Perhaps there it wouldn't get crushed – if it could be. She drew on her jacket, her bandolier of gear, shoulder bags and cloak and started off again. 'Come on.'

After walking for a time she regarded the man who was pacing along beside her, hands clasped behind his back. 'So you participated in the Seven Cities uprising.'

'Yes.'

'And now you are here hoping to buy some sort of pardon.'

Jheval waved a hand deprecatingly. 'Oh, not a *full* pardon. I don't think I will ever be granted that . . . but it would be good not to have to worry about my back for the rest of my life.'

Now Kiska wondered just what crimes the man had committed against the Empire. Or, in a case of bloated vanity, he may just *fancy* himself an infamous wanted criminal. Or he was just plain lying to impress . . . her. She cleared her throat. 'So. You served in the army of this Sha'ik?'

The man stopped dead. '*Served*? I? I . . .'

'Yes?'

A cunning smile crept up his lips and he waved a finger. 'Now, now. You see a mystery and you thrust a stick in – what will emerge? A lion or a goose?' He walked on. 'You thought you'd found a weakness, yes?'

Thought?

'But all that is over,' he said, waving a hand again. 'For a time I was a true believer. Now, I'm just embarrassed.' He slowed suddenly, shading his gaze. 'What is that?'

Kiska peered ahead: a dark shape in the midst of the daemons' wide migration track. Some sort of abandoned trash? A corpse?

Jheval picked up his pace. Kiska clasped her staff in both hands, horizontal across her waist. Then the stink struck them. She almost gagged. Rotten fish; an entire shack of rotting fish. A shoreline of putrescence. 'Gods!' she said, turning her head and wincing. 'What is *that*?'

Jheval pressed a hand under his nose. 'Perhaps we should go round.'

The dark shape moved. It seemed to heave itself. Jheval growled some Seven Cities curse, started off again. Kiska followed.

Closer, the shape resolved itself into the disintegrating, putrid remains of a very large fish. A fish that at one time might have been as large as a full-grown bull. Two extraordinarily large ravens stood atop the corpse – both looking very glossy and well fed. But that was not what captured Kiska's and her companion's attention. What they stared at was the scrawny old man in rags attempting to drag it.

He was yanking on a rope tied to a grapnel stuck in the fish's enormous bony jaw. Kiska and Jheval stopped and watched. The man was making no progress at all that Kiska could see, though a track did extend off behind the carcass.

Jheval cleared his throat.

The man leapt as if stabbed in the rear. The ravens let out loud squawks of surprise and protest, launching themselves to whirl overhead. The old man spun round, glaring. He was dark, his frizzy hair mostly grey. 'What are you looking at?' he demanded.

Kiska did not know where to begin. Jheval pointed. 'That's a big fish.'

The old fellow hunched, peering suspiciously about. He held his arms out as if trying to hide the huge corpse. 'It's mine.'

'Okay.'

'You can't have it.'

'I assure you—'

'Get your own.'

'I don't want your damned fish!' Jheval shouted.

The old man put a finger to one eye, nodding. 'Oh, yes. That's what they all say . . . but they're *lying*!'

Jheval caught Kiska's gaze. He tapped a finger to his head. 'Let's go.'

Kiska followed, reluctant; it seemed to her that there was more here, that none of this was an accident. In her earlier visits to Shadow she'd had the impression that the Realm had been trying to tell her things. That everything was a lesson, if she could only understand the language.

The old man straightened, astonished. 'You would go?' He waved both hands at the fish. 'How could you abandon such a prize? Surely you would not turn your backs on such an opportunity?'

'It is of no use to us,' Jheval said.

'Use?' The man shouted, outraged. 'Use! Is that your measure? Utility? Have you not longed all your life to catch the big one?'

Overhead, the ravens' raucous cawing sounded almost like laughter.

Kiska glanced back. The man was staring after them. As it became clear they would not stop he ran round the carcass to follow but something yanked him back to fall on his rear and he let out a startled squawk. The rope, she saw, was tied round his waist.

'Wait,' she called to Jheval.

The Seven Cities warrior halted. He hung his head. 'Kiska. He's a mage lost in Shadow and gone insane.' He faced her, hands apart. 'I've heard of such things.'

'We can't just leave him . . .'

The man shrugged, unperturbed. 'Why not?'

'Well *I'm* not going to just walk away.'

She found him lying on his stomach, kicking and punching the dirt, crying, 'It's not fair! Not fair!'

'What's not fair?'

He stilled, turned his head to look up at her, smiled crazily. 'Nothing.' He sat up, brushed the dirt from his tattered grimed robes.

Peering down at him, Kiska sighed. She pointed to the huge fish, its exposed ribs, saucer-sized eyes milky and half pecked out. The two midnight-black ravens had resettled on its back and now paced about searching for morsels. 'It's dead. Putrid. Useless. Drop the rope and come away.'

The old man gestured helplessly. 'But I can't.'

'You can't? You mean you won't.'

He shook his head, bared his grey uneven teeth in what might have been meant as a cringe of embarrassment. 'No, I mean I can't. I can't untie the rope. Could you . . . maybe . . .'

'Oh, for the love of Burn!' She turned the handle of her stave and its blade snicked free. She stabbed the rope, slitting it.

The old man sprang up. 'I'm free! *Free!*' And he giggled.

Kiska backed away, uneasy. It occurred to her that she might just have made a serious mistake. But then the old man threw himself down on the slimy putrescent carcass, hugging its jaws. 'I don't mean *you*, my lovely one. No, no, no. Not you! I won't go far. I promise. There could never be another like you!'

The ravens cawed again, protesting.

Her stomach clenching and rising with bile, Kiska continued backing away. 'Well . . . good luck.'

She rejoined Jheval, who'd been watching, arms crossed. As they walked he jerked a thumb backwards. 'You see? What did I say? Crazy as a sun-stroked rat.'

Walking with her staff across her shoulders, arms draped over it,

Kiska reflected that that may be so, but at least the crazy mage was free of the trap he'd made for himself. *Not that he might not blunder into something worse, here in Shadow.*

The track had become soft underfoot. The surface was brittle, dried in patterns of cracks; the wheel-tracks deep slit ruts. Ahead, the flat horizon was one dark front of churning black and grey clouds. Lightning glowed within.

'You are looking for the lake?'

Kiska and Jheval jumped, spinning. It was the old man. Jheval glared at Kiska as if to say, *Now look what you've done!*

'What are you doing?' Kiska demanded.

He peered up at her, his beady yellow eyes narrowing. 'I should think that's obvious. I'm following you.'

'Look,' Jheval said. 'What do you want?'

He tilted his head, considered the question for a time. 'I want to be left alone.'

Jheval gaped, spread his arms to the vast emptiness around. 'You want to be alone yet you follow us?'

A scowl of annoyance. 'Not you two.' He pointed to his head. 'The voices. They won't leave me alone. Do this. Do that. Give me this, give me that. Will they never stop?' He dug his hands into his thin hair. 'They're driving me crazy!'

Jheval eyed Kiska then rolled his gaze to the sky. 'Okay. The voices. Listen, I've heard that if you dig a hole in the ground and stick your head in it makes the voices go away.'

'*Jheval!*' Kiska cuffed his shoulder. She turned to the man. 'What's your name?'

His brows furrowed in thought. Kiska flinched away when a waft of fish-rot struck her. She glimpsed two dark shapes wheeling far overhead – the giant ravens?

'Warbin al Blooth?' the old man muttered. 'No, no. Horos Spitten the Fifth? No. That's not right. Crethin Spoogle?' He yanked frantically at his hair again. 'I can't remember my name!'

Kiska held out her hands. 'It's all right. Never mind. But we have to call you something – just pick one.'

'I can't! You pick one.'

'I have some suggestions,' Jheval muttered.

Kiska waved Jheval onward. She tried to think of inoffensive names. 'Okay. How about Grajath?'

'No.'

'Frecell?'

'No.'

She clenched down on her irritation. 'Warran?'

'Warran,' he echoed. As they walked along he repeated the name, trying it out. 'Okay. I suppose that will do.'

And thank you too! She gestured ahead. 'You came this way?'

'No. Yes. Maybe. Once. Long ago.'

Jheval snorted, shaking his head.

'And the lake?'

The old man shot her a narrowed glare. 'Why? The fish?' He pointed. 'I knew it! You're after an even bigger one! Well, you're too late! It's gone.' He laughed hoarsely, cleared his throat, and spat something up.

'Not the fish!' Kiska snapped. 'The Whorl – the Rift – the thing that drained the lake.'

Warran waved dismissively. 'Oh, that. No fish there.' He gestured aside. 'Best to go that way.'

Now Jheval was eyeing the old man. 'Why?'

'Shorter. No crabs.'

'Crabs?'

'You think that fish was big? Wait till you see the crabs that eat *them*.'

'Ah.' They stopped. Jheval looked at Kiska. She squeezed her hands on her staff. She squinted to the storm on the horizon.

'Is that it?'

Warran nodded. 'Yes.'

'You'll show us the way round the lake?'

'Yes – but then we're through! No more favours! I mean, fair's fair.'

She let out a long breath. 'All right. Show us.'

He rubbed his chin, clearly taken aback. 'Really? Okay. Ah, this way – I think.'

Jheval hung back next to Kiska, opened his mouth. 'I know!' she cut in. 'I know. We'll see. Time doesn't seem to matter, does it? We'll just backtrack if we must.'

He frowned, considering this, then shrugged. 'Very well.'

After a time they came to a field of tall sand dunes. A miasmic wind hardly stirred them. Tufts of sharp brittle grass grew on their slopes and in the troughs between. Kiska found the going very tiring as her sandalled feet sank into the shifting sands. Occasionally she would peer around for the two dark shapes; eventually she would find two dark dots on a distant rise, or black angular shapes cruising far above. She almost spoke of them to Jheval but decided not to raise the subject in front of their companion.

'After I caught my prize I was struck by many regrets,' the odd fellow announced suddenly as they slogged up one slope.

'That you didn't have the strength to pull it?' she offered.

'Oh, no. I was making progress . . . slow . . . but progress. No, my biggest regret was in not thinking ahead.'

'Oh?' she said drily.

'Yes. Because it is one thing to catch what you've always sought. After that it is quite another matter. The question really should be: what do you do with it once you've caught it?'

Kiska could only frown, uncertain. There seemed almost to be something there. It was almost as if it applied to her – a tangential lesson? Homey aphorism? Or insane babble? The problem was she had no idea how to take anything this crazy old man came out with.

CHAPTER VII

Be not too rigid,
For you will shatter;
Be not too yielding,
For you will be bowed.

Wisdom of the Ancients
Kreshen Reel, Compiler

SHELL THOUGHT THE STRAIT OF WATER THAT RAN ALONG THE SOUTH side of the long narrow island of Korel very calm given the constant storm raging just to the north. It had been snowing for the last three days and nights. She couldn't recall when she last saw the sky. Thick dark clouds hung so low she thought the masts would scour them. It was dark and bitterly cold. Snow flurries gusted over the boats constantly – an improvement, however, on the numbing sleet that had left her wet and chilled to the bone. So cold was she that she found herself wondering about that rendered fat Ena had been offering.

As their small flotilla approached the Korel shore the Sea-Folk brought her and Lazar over to the boat carrying Blues and Fingers. If anything, Fingers was even more miserable than she. His seasickness had left him weak and now he complained of chills, aches, a racking cough, and a constantly running nose. He spent all his time hunched under blankets at the bows, where they sat with him now.

'Orzu hasn't said so,' Blues began, 'but if they land there's a good chance the Korelri will just grab the lot of them.'

'They must've known that from the start,' Fingers objected, and coughed wetly.

'That's why we're paying them,' Lazar said.

'Since we're talking problems anyway,' Fingers said, sniffing and hawking something up over the side, 'maybe Shell should 'fess up about ours.'

Blues sat back against the side as the boat rocked in the rolling waves. It was evening and the Korel shore was a jagged dark line dominating the north. Shell watched his gaze move between them. 'You mean about this "Lady".'

'Un-huh. Look, I know the plan was for us to get hold of Bars then the five of us blast through to a Warren to escape. But you must feel her strength. This is way more than we bargained for back in Stratem. There's a good chance she could slap us down . . .' He coughed, holding his chest and grimacing in pain.

Blues was nodding, eyeing the distant shore. 'So maybe something more . . . mundane.'

'In which case' – Fingers pressed shut one nostril and blew heroically, emptying the other over the side in a blast of stringy wetness – 'we'll need a boat. And a crew.'

Lazar raised his dark brows in silent appreciation. Shell inclined her head to the suffering little man. *God's grin, Fingers. You may be as sick as a dog, but you are your usual cunning self.*

Blues turned away, gestured amidships, and called: 'Get Orzu.' Then he looked Lazar up and down. 'You look the part more than any of us. How would you like to be the next Champion of the wall?'

The big man considered, frowning, then spat over the side. 'I hear the pay is the shits.'

Orzu at first refused. What else could the man do? Shell mused. After all, when four armed and dangerous passengers ask you to sell them into slavery it would be prudent to show *some* reluctance. Only their continual assurances of their seriousness half convinced him. Then Fingers pointed out that in any case they intended to be let off on the Korel shore, and so he, Orzu, and his clan of Sea-Folk might as well profit from it. The old man finally bowed to that logic.

The deal struck was their bounty in return for one boat, with a minimal volunteer crew, to remain behind until the spring's turn, celebrated here by bonfires lit in the name of the Lady's Blessing. For the rendezvous, if any, Orzu suggested a maze of isthmuses, saltwater swamps, and narrows south of the city of Elri. Blues agreed.

Then the man said he had to go ahead to make the arrangements.

He peered at them all for a time, a hand pressed to the side of his face, shaking his head, then gave a heavy sigh. 'You are crazy, you foreigners. But fare you well. May the Old Ones guide you.'

'You too,' said Shell.

'Take care of your family,' Blues said.

The old man pressed his hand atop his head. 'Aya! They are so many! Such a burden. It is heavy indeed.'

They took shelter in an isolated cove on the uninhabited south shore of Korel. It seemed the Korelri had no interest in what they named Crack, or sometimes Crooked, Strait. All their attention was reserved for the north, and the threat beyond.

In the morning Ena accosted Shell while she ate a breakfast of fish stew. 'What foolishness is this I hear?'

'Foolishness?' Shell answered mildly.

'You giving yourselves over to the Korelri? In truth?'

'Yes.'

The girl-woman made an angry gesture. 'Stupidity! You will be killed.'

'Not necessarily.'

'Look at you. You are no warrior.'

'Ena . . . I've served in a mercenary company for a very long time. You'd be surprised.'

'The Riders . . .'

'An enemy like any other. Listen, Ena. You would do whatever you must for your family, yes?' A guarded angry nod answered that. 'Very good. And so would I. At least grant me that dignity.'

Again, a slow nod. 'You do this for your people?'

'Yes.'

The young woman sat and cradled her broad stomach. 'I will stay with the boat.'

Now it was Shell's turn for anger. 'You most certainly will not.'

'The Korelri will not harm me.'

'When are you due?'

An indifferent shrug. 'Soon.'

'Can't have that kind of complication.'

'Babies are born all the time everywhere. It is not a complication.'

'It is if it's not necessary.'

Ena smiled mockingly. 'Babies are not necessary? You have been too long in your mercenary company, I think.'

That stopped Shell. She could not maintain her anger in the face of chiding from someone certainly younger in years, but perhaps older in other ways, than her. *True. There is no stricture. It would not seem to be against the Vow. Why not, then? Time away from duties, I guess. Always something else to do. And now I am too old. Yet, am I? I took the Vow in my twenties . . . Strange how this had not occurred to me before. Change in company, I suppose.*

She studied the girl's blunt profile while she looked out to sea. Straggly dirty hair, grimed face; yet sharp intelligent dark eyes. 'Don't stay with the boat, Ena.'

She smiled wistfully, agreeing. 'The Elders wouldn't allow it anyway.'

'Good luck with your life and your child, Ena.'

'And you, Shell. May the Old Ones guide you.'

Old Ones? Shell thought about that. Which Old Ones might that be? Burn, she imagined. The Elder Gods. Hood. Mael. D'rek. Osserc? K'rul? Sister Night? That sea-cult that was probably another face of Mael, Chem'esh'el? Who knew? Something chthonic, certainly. Perhaps they should accept all the help they could get, but with the proviso this cult of the Lady presented: one should be careful of whom one accepts help from.

*

The exchange took place on a military pier at the Korelri fortress named Shelter. Shell, Blues, Lazar and Fingers were led up, hands securely tied. It was overcast as usual, a grim dark day. Snow blew about them in flurries. The flat grey fortress walls and the stone pier all had a military look to them. No colour, starkly functional. A troop of guards accepted them. From his dark blue cloak and silver-chased armour, the one leading the detachment was the lone Korelri Stormguard. And he was old, grey-bearded.

He looked them up and down, each in turn, while Orzu watched, clasping and reclasping his hands. Blues and Lazar the Chosen accepted immediately. He stopped in front of Shell.

'You can fight?' His accent reminded Shell of the rural Malazan Isle twang.

She raised her bound wrists. 'Untie me and find out.'

The man ran a hand through her blonde hair, longer now than she usually kept it. 'Perhaps you could contribute more in one of the brothels.'

Twins' laughter! I didn't even think of that! Maybe I have *spent too long in a mercenary company.*

And so she head-butted him.

He lurched away, gasping his pain, a hand to his nose. Blood gushed over his mouth. The guards leapt forward, weapons sliding from sheaths. But the Stormguard raised his other hand. His eyes were black with rage, yet that rage slipped away and the mouth twisted into a grin revealing blood-stained teeth. 'Show the Riders your spirit, woman.'

Next he turned to Fingers. He regarded him carefully, his thin shivering frame, pale drawn face, cracked lips, sick watery eyes and running nose, and was not impressed.

'I don't want to be in the brothel either,' Fingers said.

'Show me your hands,' the man growled.

Fingers held them up. The Stormguard turned them over, felt the palms. Then there was a metallic click and Fingers yanked his hands away: a dull metal bracelet encircled one wrist.

'That's otataral, mage. Don't try any of your daemon tricks.'

Fingers' shoulders sagged. He glared at Orzu. 'Did you tell him? Bastard!' He went for Orzu but the Stormguard kicked him down. Lazar lashed out, but somehow the Chosen slipped the blow.

Shell was impressed. And he was probably assigned this duty because he was too old to stand the wall. For the first time she wondered just what they had gotten themselves into.

The Stormguard pushed them along. 'Pay the man, Gellin. Standard bounty.'

'Standard?' Orzu yelped. 'But they are skilled fighters. Champion material.'

'Oh yes? Then how is it you got the better of them?'

Orzu held up his open hands. 'Come now, Chosen sir. You are too old for such naivety. Even the greatest fighter must eat and drink. And it is so very easy for d'bayang or white nectar to find its way into such things. And as for the rest . . . well, then it is all so very easy.'

The old Chosen stomped over to the guard called Gellin and took the bag of coin from him. He threw it down before Orzu, where it split amid the slush and footprints on the stone pier. The coins clattered, some sliding into the water. 'You disgust me. Take your money and go before I run you through here and now.'

Orzu fell to his knees, bowing and scooping up the coins. 'Yes, honoured sir. Certainly. Yes.'

Shell wanted to say something, but of course she couldn't. She allowed herself one glance back: the old man was still on his knees, pocketing the coins, peering up through his hanging grey hair. He did not so much as wink.

She remembered some of her conversations with Ena; thought of deception and false fronts. For generations this was how the Sea-Folk survived. *And now we, too, have elected for that same strategy. I can only hope our own subterfuge will prove as successful.*

* * *

Devaleth found the nightly staff gatherings increasingly uncomfortable. The remaining Roolian force had held them at the bridge for four days now. Each time a push gathered yardage, or established a foothold on the opposite shore, a counterattack from elite forces, mainly the Black Moranth, pushed them back. The narrow width of the bridge was now their bottleneck. And they were stuck in it.

Greymane's van had arrived near dawn of the night they took the bridge, scattering the remaining Roolian forces on the east shore. Unfortunately, the forced marching had taken its toll and his troops could not break through.

It was winter, and food was scarce. What meagre supplies Greymane's forces had carried with them were exhausted. Foraging parties ranged everywhere. Any effort to harvest fish from the Ancy was met with bow-fire from the opposite shore. Not one horse or mule remained. Some troops now boiled leather, moss and grasses. Fist Khemet's relief column, escorting all their logistics, was still a week away.

They had to break through soon, before they were too weak to fight at all.

The stalemate was taking its toll on the High Fist. He obviously felt the suffering of his troops. His temper was hair-thin and increasingly it sharpened itself on one target: the Untan aristocrat, Fist Rillish. Greymane stood leaning forward on to the field table, arms out, long hair hanging down obscuring his face. Kyle sat beside him, legs out straight. Devaleth hung back close to the tent flap as if waiting for an excuse to flee. Fist Rillish stood rigid, back straight, helmet under one arm.

'One more assault . . .' Greymane ground out, as he had these last days.

'With respect, the troops are too weak, sir,' Rillish countered, again.

Greymane raised his head just enough to glare at the Fist. 'The more time passes, the weaker they are!'

The nobleman did not flinch. 'Yes, High Fist.'

'Then what do *you* suggest?'

Rillish drew a deep breath, pushed on. 'That we defend.'

'Defend? *Defend!* Defence has not gotten us this far! If we could just break through there is nothing between us and Paliss!'

'Yes, High Fist. But we cannot. Therefore we should dig in, defend. Wait for Fist Khemet's column.'

Greymane's bright blue gaze, almost feverish in the tent's gloom, shifted to Kyle. 'What do you say?'

The Adjunct shifted uncomfortably, the chair leather creaking beneath him. He cleared his throat. 'I am no trained officer, of course . . . But I have to agree with the Fist.'

'It is sound, High Fist,' Devaleth cut in.

Without turning his head to acknowledge her, he grated, 'I did not ask you.'

'Sir!' Rillish objected.

The High Fist pushed himself from the table, scattering maps. He went to a sideboard and poured a drink. Tossing it back, he slammed down the glass. 'Very well. Fist Rillish, order the troops to raise defences across the west approach to the bridge and to hunker down.'

Rillish bowed. 'Yes, High Fist.' He nodded to Kyle and Devaleth, pushed aside the flap. Greymane watched him go, his mouth sour.

Kyle stood. 'Greymane . . .'

But the High Fist threw himself into a chair, his chin sinking to his chest, arms hanging loose at his sides. 'Not now, Kyle.'

Devaleth edged her head to the flap; Kyle nodded reluctantly. 'Goodnight,' he offered.

Greymane did not answer.

They walked side by side in silence for a time and then Devaleth cleared her throat. 'You have seen him like this before?' she asked.

Kyle's first reaction was to deny it, but he paused, acknowledging it. 'Yes. He can be very . . . emotional.'

Devaleth nodded her agreement. 'I believe your friend is very frightened.'

'*Frightened?* What do you mean?'

'I mean just what I said, frightened. Kyle, you were not here for the first invasion. I was in training in Mare. I heard first-hand accounts. I've read histories of the campaign. Kyle, I think he sees it all happening to him again. That first time they were held up in Rool. Delay followed delay. Eventually, they never made it out. I think he fears it will be the same this time, like some sort of awful recurring nightmare.'

The young plainsman turned away. To the west the Ancy flowed like a dark banner beneath overcast skies. Camp fires dotted the valley across the river. Devaleth knew that *they* had food and supplies. Here, the troopers hoped for snow so that they could eat it.

'But it won't happen again,' he said, certain. 'This time it's different.'

'Yes. We may not even make it to Rool.'

He spun to her. 'No. I don't accept that. The army facing us is fragile, pressed to its limit. I can sense it.'

She crossed her arms. Her tangled hair blew in the frigid wind and she pushed it aside. 'So are we.'

'So what are you saying, woman? Come, out with it.' His tone almost said the word *traitor*.

She held her face flat. 'It is early yet. And speaking of fragility, is it not fragile to fall apart at the first sign of resilience in the enemy?'

She arched one brow and turned away.

Kyle did not answer, but looking back, Devaleth saw him still standing there, peering out over the river, presumably reflecting on her words. She was fairly confident she'd made her point, and that this young man would make the same point to his friend.

* * *

The Army of Reform now straggled like an immense snake over the southern Jourilan plains. Ivanr no longer marched with his brigade; Lieutenant Carr had that in hand. The overcast winter skies continued to threaten rain that rarely came. Jourilan cavalry utterly surrounded them, harrying and probing, though not yet massed for a sustained charge. Ivanr didn't think it would be long before that day came.

In all his searching he still hadn't found the nameless lad he had rescued. What he did find was that he was accreting a bodyguard. Slowly, day by day, more and more fighters, men and women, surrounded him in the lines or marched nearby. It annoyed him that ranks of guards should stand between him and the regular troopers, but nothing he said would deter these self-selected bodyguards. They wore plain armour and for weapons favoured either the sword or a spear haft set with a long curved single-edged blade named, simply enough, a sword-spear. Most, Ivanr noted, were sworn to the cult of Dessembrae.

They even claimed to have frustrated two assassination attempts. 'Frustrated?' he'd demanded, disbelieving. 'How?' Their stubborn gazes sliding aside to one another told him his answer. 'No more killing!' he ordered and they bowed.

This morning, just after the long train had roused itself enough to begin moving, a few of their remaining mounted scouts came galloping from the far advance. Something ahead. Ivanr scanned the horizon; hardly any Imperial cavalry in sight. Not good. If they were not here, they were all somewhere else.

Later, during the march, word came via that soldiers' gossip-train of word of mouth that the Jourilan cavalry had been spotted ahead. They were pulling together to the west of the army's line of march. If the cavalry were finally forming up, then it seemed to Ivanr that Martal would have to respond – though just how she could respond still remained a mystery to him. This was the crux where most of the past uprisings and peasant rebellions had been smashed: the impact of horseflesh and the trampling and lancing of panicked civilians.

The march continued as usual that day, however, until late afternoon, when the order came to make camp. All through the evening, bivouacking, hovering around fires, the men and women of the Army of Reform could not help gazing to the distant hillside where the bright pennants of the Imperial cavalry flew in the wind; where tall tents of white linen glowed warm and bright from within, and the occasional nicker of a horse reached them through the night.

This façade of normality as if nothing had changed, the calm ordering of the camp, all of it infuriated Ivanr. Meeting the cavalry in open battle was exactly what the Imperials wanted; that was their game. Martal should not play it. Yet try as he might, he could not see any alternative to the failed old tactics of forming up obligingly to meet the enemy. It never worked for any of the past uprisings and peasant movements, and he could not imagine it working now.

He could not help snorting and chuffing his frustration. He would eye the distant encampment then turn away to prowl before his tent, rubbing his jaw, thinking, the eyes of his bodyguards following him, until finally he could stand it no more and he stalked off to talk to Beneth.

He found the old man ensconced in his tent as he always was, heaped in blankets next to a travelling hearth, his eyes covered. Even as he entered Beneth spoke. 'Greetings, Ivanr.'

Ivanr froze. 'How did you—' The man was blind!

Beneth gave his wry smile. 'Who else could shake the camp with his fury?'

'I have good reason, Beneth. What is the plan—'

'Of course you believe yourself fully justified,' Beneth cut in. 'Doesn't certitude stand behind *both* sides in almost all confrontations?'

'The situation doesn't call for philosophy, old man.'

'No? Then just what does it call for?'

Ivanr thrust a hand out to the north. 'Withdrawal! We should keep moving as we have been. Cooperating like this only plays into their hands. And you'll have dragged all these people to their deaths.'

The tent flap was thrown aside and Martal came in. She wore her dark travel-stained leathers. Her hair was unkempt and sweaty from her helm. She regarded Ivanr thinly. 'Your lack of faith is troubling, Grand Champion.'

Again, he could not read the woman's guarded angular face: was she serious? Or mocking? More than ever he was certain she was from foreign lands. 'Faith? Faith in what? It's faith that has brought us all these troubles.'

'In that at least we are agreed.' She crossed to a table, pulled off her gloves and began washing her hands in a basin.

'Ivanr is worried about the morrow,' Beneth offered.

'I do not have the time to reassure every jumpy trooper,' she said into the basin, and splashed her face.

Reassure! Ivanr gaped, absolutely furious. *How dare she!* 'I demand—'

She turned on him. 'You are in no position to demand anything! And your little show of pique has only unnerved everyone further. I am not used to being questioned by my subordinates, Brigade Commander. I suggest that if everyone does their job tomorrow we will have a good chance of victory. More than that, no responsible commander can promise her people.'

'I can hardly do my job if I do not even know what it is.'

The woman was drying her hands on a cloth. 'Ivanr . . . you have been a champion, not a soldier. Whereas I have been a soldier all my life. Your job is now that of the soldier – to follow orders. The simplest, and the hardest, of jobs. If there is secrecy regarding plans and tactics, remember that our camp is rotten with spies. We dare not reveal anything yet.'

A long exhaled breath took much of Ivanr's tension with it; he found himself agreeing with this demanding woman. Secrecy for secrecy's sake he scorned. Spies he could understand. So, the best she was willing to offer at this time was the indirect promise that *something* was in the works. Very well. He inclined his head in assent. 'I'm only worried for the safety of my people.'

'I know, Ivanr. Otherwise I would not even be talking to you.'

He snorted at that. 'Well. Thank you for your condescension.'

Her smile was utterly cold. 'Of course.'

He bowed to Beneth. 'Tomorrow, then.'

'Good luck, Ivanr.'

'My thanks.'

After the tent flap fell the two within were silent for a time. Beneth inhaled to speak, but Martal forestalled him. 'I know!'

'You are too harsh.'

'If he wilts then he is hardly worthy, is he?'

'*She* chose him.'

'I certainly didn't,' she muttered, taking a mouthful of bread.

The old man's expression softened. 'You've been spoiled, Martal.'

The woman was nodding her agreement as she sat among the piled blankets, sighing her exhaustion. 'There was only ever one champion worthy of the name.'

'You must let all that go. This one is no longer a champion, nor will he be required to serve as one again.'

'Then why is he here?'

The old man was silent for a time in the dark. He brought a wavering hand up to touch the cloth across his eyes. 'I am tiring, Martal . . . the pressure she is bringing to bear upon us is almost unsupportable. She knows what might be coming and she is desperate—'

The woman sprang to her feet. 'No! No more such talk.'

'Martal . . .'

'No.' She snatched up her gloves and a goatskin of water. '*You* are why we are here.' She stormed out, leaving the old man alone in the gloom. He winced, pressing his fingertips into his brow.

'I'm sorry, child. It has all come so late. So damned late.'

*

Ivanr sat on a collapsible camp stool, glowering into the fire. He couldn't sleep. All that had been said, that could have been said, that wasn't said, tramped in maddening circles in his mind. Was he a good commander? He thought he was. He believed he had the best interests of his people at heart. What more could be asked? But was he a commander of *this* army? What had been his own opinion not so long ago? That an army was like a snake – it shouldn't have two heads. Had he been agitating to become that extra head? Surely not! He hadn't asked the Priestess to name him her successor! Was it his fault then that many looked to him? No, of course not.

Was Martal threatened? Did she see him as a rival? No. That was not worthy. She'd given him the brigade for the sake of all these opportunistic gods! No, that was not it. It was him. He'd expected the treatment he'd been given as a Grand Champion, but here he was merely a new face. That was it.

He lowered his head and clenched it in his hands. Damn the Lady! He'd behaved like some sort of aristocrat demanding privileges! He groaned. *Foreign gods! Just the sort of behaviour that made him sick.*

'Ivanr,' a woman said nearby. 'Ivanr?'

Head squeezed in both hands he croaked, 'Leave me alone.'

'Poor Grand Champion! Having a pout, are we?'

'Who the—' Ivanr peered up to see ragged shapeless skirts rising to the wide midriff and layered shawls of the old woman, Sister Gosh. She held a long-stemmed clay pipe in her blackened teeth, and her hair was a wild mess of grey curls. He lowered his head. 'What do you want?'

'Need your help. Gotta run an errand.'

'Go away.'

'No. Has to be you. In the blood, you could say.'

He straightened, frowning. All about the camp fire his self-appointed guards lay asleep. He eyed the woman narrowly. 'What's going on?'

She drew a slim wooden box from her shawl, shook it. Something rattled within. 'Martal wants rain. We're gonna get her some.' She shook the box again. 'Skystones to bring it.'

He snorted. 'You don't believe those old stories and superstitions. Stones from the sky!'

The woman's lips drew down, sour. She sucked heavily on the pipe, exhaling twin plumes from her nose. ''Struth! Like to like.

Once touching, always so. These are the old truths. Long before anything. Houses or such.'

'What do you need me for?'

'They'll recognize you.'

'Who—'

A tall shape emerged from the gloom: a pale fellow in ragged black clothes, hands clasped behind his back. 'Time, Sister,' he called.

'Yes, yes!' She urged Ivanr up. 'Come.'

Still he did not rise. 'Who's this?'

'A compatriot.'

'What have you done to my guards?'

Sister Gosh waved a hand impatiently. 'Nothing. They sleep. If they awoke they would see you gone. Now come.'

He stood, peered around at the darkness. 'Gone? Where?'

She headed off. 'The land here sleeps, Ivanr. We have entered its memories. Come.'

He followed, if only to ask more questions. 'Memories? The past?'

She took the pipe from her mouth, spat. 'Not the true past, the real past. Only a memory of it. See ahead?' She pointed the pipe.

It was a shallow bowl in the countryside far to the east of the encampment. There, two figures awaited them, another man and a woman. The woman was petite, perhaps even older than Sister Gosh, her face as dark as ironwood, hair pulled back in a tight bun; the man was a short skinny fellow, his hair and beard a tangled mess. The man was digging at something. He called, 'Here! Hurry!'

It was some sort of smooth domed stone. As the fellow wiped it clean Ivanr realized it was a fisted knot of dirty ice. 'What is this?'

'Look behind you,' the other woman invited.

He turned, saw a distant wall of ice white and emerald blue. Horizon to horizon it stretched, shot by refractions of light. 'What is it?' he breathed, awed.

'Do you not recognize the Great Ice Barrier?' Sister Gosh asked, having come to his side. 'Or the Barrier as it was, ages ago?'

'Time!' the tall one insisted again.

'Yes, Carfin.' Sister Gosh indicated the other woman: 'Sister Esa.' The bearded man: 'Brother Jool.'

With an effort, Ivanr kept his gaze from the distant icefield. *So it's true. The Barrier once covered all these lands.*

'The stones?' Jool asked. Sister Gosh raised the box and it seemed to fly to him on its own. It struck his hand with a loud slap.

'What is this?' a new voice called and everyone turned, then relaxed. Another older man emerged from the gloom, bearded, in tattered finery. 'The Synod has not convened! This has not been agreed!'

'We agreed to act, Totsin,' Sister Esa snapped.

The newcomer drew himself up straight. 'Ritual magic? Consorting with Elders? This exceeds all Synod procedural conventions.'

'What conventions?' Jool asked, frowning.

'Time is wasting!' Carfin called out, rising panic in his voice.

Totsin opened his hands. 'Well . . . obviously it's understood that anything *extreme* would endanger us all . . .'

'We're pretty much all here,' Sister Gosh observed tartly.

'This will draw her!' Totsin hissed.

'That tends to happen when you actually *do* something.'

'I want no part of it.'

Sister Gosh peered round at everyone. 'Ah – we didn't invite you.'

Totsin took hold of his chin. His brows rose high in shocked surprise. 'I see. Well . . . I'll go then.'

'Yes. Go then.'

Bowing, the man turned and walked off to disappear into the night as if stepping behind shadows.

'I sense her attention!' Brother Carfin called. 'Prepare him!'

'This place is of your kind, Ivanr,' Sister Gosh said, facing him. 'Toblakai is one name. Your ancestors came here to make propitiations, offerings. Like to like. Power to power. It is the old way.' She drew a wicked-looking thin curved blade from within her shawls. 'Give me your hand.'

He resisted the urge to hide his hands behind his back. 'For what?'

'A small cut. Then you rub that hand over the ice. We will do the rest.'

'That is it?' he asked, dubious.

'Yes.'

He held out his left hand. She slit his palm in a swift – rather practised – flick. 'On the ice, now!'

'She comes,' Carfin intoned, his voice catching.

Ivanr knelt and ran his hand over the knotted lump. At first it was cold under his palm but quickly it warmed. He was shaken to see no trace of blood left behind. Something shook the ground to the north and Sister Gosh growled in her throat like a beast. He glanced over but saw nothing in the dark.

'She should not have found us so easily,' Jool said.

'The tiles,' Sister Gosh barked to him, then, 'Carfin, Esa. Do something.'

Something halfway between a sob and a groan escaped the tall fellow, Carfin, as he walked stiffly off. 'Madness!' he said to the night, his voice choking. 'Madness.' It seemed to Ivanr that wisps of utter darkness now spun about the man like fluttering scarves. Sister Esa knelt to gather handfuls of mud, then followed.

Jool pressed a thin wooden tile to the ice, which hissed, steaming.

'Now call your gods,' Sister Gosh told Ivanr.

He peered up at her, frowning. 'What?'

'Call them. Hurry!'

'How?'

'*How?*' She gaped at him, almost dropping her pipe. 'What do you mean, *how*?'

'I've never . . . that is . . . our old gods and ways are gone. Listen – you never said anything about praying or anything like that!'

She and Jool shared a strained look. In the dark, something shook the ground again and a high-pitched keening started up. 'Cowled one help us now,' she muttered. 'Look. In your mind call to your ancestors. All the way back – as far as you can reach. Do it!'

Feeling like an utter fool, Ivanr strove to comply. He imagined his ancestors, generation before generation, all serried off into the past like an infinite regression, back as far as possible. And he called to them.

'Sister Esa and Carfin have fled,' Jool announced.

'Then it's up to me,' Sister Gosh answered.

'Good luck.'

Ivanr opened his eyes, straightened. Jool was backing away, box held high, shaking it like a musical instrument. Sister Gosh threw the pipe away; it streamed an arc of embers as it went. She took a quick nip from a silver flask that disappeared just as swiftly into her shawls. 'Are you with me?' she asked Ivanr, her gaze fixed to the north.

From the dark, a soft crying-like keening started up again.

'What is it?' Ivanr asked.

'If flesh – our flesh – can be blasphemed . . . this would be it.'

He grasped at his belt: he was unarmed. 'What can I do?'

'Stop it from reaching the shrine. Or me. Or Jool.'

Ivanr raised a brow. 'Right . . .'

Behind, Jool shook the box ever faster until its rattling seemed a continuous hissing. Ivanr had no idea what he was to do. 'How do I—'

A shape lumbered out of the dark. Its appearance almost sent Ivanr running. Very large, fully as tall as he, humanoid, yes, but more like a sculpture of flesh: pale fish-white, so obese as to seem poured of fat. And atop the heap of bulging flesh, a tiny baby's head, hairless, mouth wet with drool, babbling and crying.

'Gods!' Ivanr cursed, wincing his disgust, his stomach rising to sour his mouth.

Sister Gosh threw her hands down as if pushing at the ground before the thing. The topsoil beneath it was gouged apart as if by a scythe. The thing rocked backwards, keening and gibbering – in pain or fear, Ivanr could not tell. The naked ground under its feet heaved and roiled like mud. Heat coursed so intensely from the old woman that Ivanr had to step away. The thing pushed ahead once more. A colossal leg sucked free of the dirt to swing forward.

'Damn the gods, she's strong,' Sister Gosh snarled through clenched teeth. 'Do something!'

'Do *what*?'

'Stop it!'

'All right!' He edged up to the gash of mud. He noted that the water that fed it was melting from the knob of ancient ice. The monstrosity seemed to be ignoring him as it fought to make headway. Gingerly, he stepped into the mud. It was warm, but not uncomfortably so. He crouched, arms out, and launched himself forward to take the thing at its huge belly. Striking it was like sinking into a vat of blubber. He heaved, legs bent, straining.

The creature did not even seem to notice him. It continued lumbering ungainly, attempting to advance. One swinging great tree trunk of an arm gave him a fearful blow to the back but he didn't think it deliberate. All the while the creature kept up a babble that sounded eerily like an infant's mouthings.

Another blow cracked against Ivanr's head, sending him face down into the mud. He rolled aside before the thing could trample him, deliberately or not. Heavy with the clinging dirt, he rose and threw himself on its back. He hooked an elbow beneath its tiny chin and squeezed as tightly as he could. So far the thing's rolling empty eyes seemed not to have even rested upon him. But now that he had a choking grip, the head turned and wide-open eyes found him. Ivanr believed that he could have held on, could have finished the monstrosity, but at that moment words emerged from within its baby-like babble and a child's voice begged, '*Help me.*'

Shocked and horrified, he lost his grip and slid down the thing's mud-slick back.

Jool let out a shout then, the rattling of the box deafening. There was an eruption like a thunder blast directly overhead, accompanied by a blinding flash and the sound of multiple impacts thudding into the creature like sling bullets. It tottered, mewling and whimpering, and fell face forward. Ivanr lay in the mud, staring. *All the gods forgive them. Had that been a child*?

He tried to sit up and realized that he was sinking. Panic seized him. The mud had his legs and arms in a grip of iron. He almost laughed hysterically as all he could think to shout was, 'Help me!'

Sister Gosh called something but he couldn't make it out as the mud had his ears. He saw her pointing, her mouth moving. '*Do something!*' was all he managed before the wet choking glop filled his mouth, stopping his breath, and the fire of complete terror burned all conscious thoughts from his mind. His last impression was of something even more crushing taking hold of him like an immense fist round his middle, and squeezing him.

He awoke on the floor of his tent, a scream of terror echoing in his ears. The flap shot open and two of his guards bolted in, weapons bared. Ivanr peered around, blinking; the guards stared at him. He noted that water ran from them. In fact, the deafening drumming of a downpour hammered the tent's roof. He stood to push past them and look out: sheets of rain were coursing down like a lake upended.

He turned to the guards, who were still eyeing him, uncertain. 'I thought I was drowning.'

They laughed, sheathed their swords. He let them out then stood for a time at the open flap watching the rain hammer down. Wet and muddy tomorrow. So Martal had her rain as she wished. Yet surely she couldn't have been counting on it. It was all so uncertain – she must have more than this pulled together. Or so he hoped.

Tomorrow then. They'd all find out tomorrow. He lay back down to try to get some sleep.

The downpour lasted all through the night. A cloudburst. As if all the month's rain had been stopped up only to come blasting out in a single night. It was still falling so heavily in the morning that Ivanr could not make out the distant Jourilan Imperial cavalry. He pulled his cloak tighter about his shoulders and squinted against the sheets of water as he made his rounds. Cold drops ran from his helmet to his neck and he kept his hands tucked inside his belt to warm them. The ground had become sodden and pulled at his sandals as he walked. It seemed to him that Martal had placed her cohorts too deeply, on too narrow a front. What if the lancers wheeled round them? It looked as if there was room to edge past on the right flank where the ground fell off slightly towards a copse. True, the ranks had been trained to fend off in more than one direction, but they were untested, and there could be a panic if the enemy appeared from another quarter. Or the cavalry could ignore the infantry entirely to scour the train where it had been gathered together in a camp on the far side of the trunk road. This time, however, he kept his misgivings to himself and hoped that Martal was holding Hegil Lesour 'an 'al and his remaining cavalry in reserve for just such a danger.

He walked the lines, trailed by his bodyguard. Men and women in the ranks called to him and it took some time before he understood the shout: 'Deliverer.' *Deliverer? When had that started?* He sensed the cynical hand of Martal behind the word. He scanned the hillside where it dissolved into the grey misted rain. It seemed the deluge had delayed the Imperials. They were no doubt waiting for the worst to pass. Very well. What to do? The truth was he felt completely useless. What would be his role now? Carr had the brigade in hand; lingering there would only undermine the man's authority. Foreign gods, where even to stand? To the rear with Martal? No, that would only make both of them uncomfortable. He should go where he could do the most good. That meant the lines; his presence might save lives among the troops, harden the unit against breaking.

He went to find Carr.

Scarves of fog traced their way across the field and between the cohorts, making the silent men and women seem an army of ghosts. His cloak hung heavy and sodden, though warmed now by his body heat; his feet, however, in soaked swathings and leather sandals, were clotted in mud and chilled numb.

He found the lieutenant to the rear of the brigade, flanked by messengers. Carr bowed. 'Ivanr.'

Ivanr answered the salute. 'Permission to join the front line, Lieutenant.'

The man's brows wrinkled. 'I thought you took a vow against killing . . .'

'True. But I never said anything about horses.'

The lieutenant seemed to be taken by a coughing fit. 'Ah! Well, then, by all means . . .'

Saluting, Ivanr chose a pike from the weapons standing in reserve and joined the lines. He took a kind of cruel satisfaction seeing the five men and three women of his guard likewise take up pikes to join him. *Good! If they really are skilled, then maybe we've just strengthened this unit more than our presence disturbs it.*

The heat of the climbing sun thinned the clouds, though they did not disperse entirely. The fog clung to the lowest hollows and coursed over the neighbouring cohorts, leaving only the tops of the pikes pointing up like a forest of markers. The hillsides drifted into view, revealing rank after rank of horsemen, each as still as a statue. The only movement was the occasional shake of a horse's head, the only noise the faint jingle of harness. Ivanr studied the lines. *Lady's curse, there were a lot of them.* More must have arrived in the night. He saw few of the heaviest of the heavies: the mailed Jourilan aristocrat on a fully caparisoned warhorse. The vast majority were Imperial lancers supported by light cavalry.

Then horns sounded from the hillsides: the Imperial call to readiness. Ivanr wiped the cold mist from his face, raised an arm. 'Stay firm! They'll break if you stay firm!' Another blast of the horns and the front ranks started forward. The low rumbling of the thousands of hooves reached him as a distant shudder in the ground. 'Crowd up! Brace yourselves!'

The enemy's pace quickened, reaching a gallop. Lances came levering down to be tucked firmly under arms. Even Ivanr, who had faced countless opponents over a lifetime of training and combat, felt the almost overwhelming urge to run, to flinch away, to be anywhere but in front of this mountain of horseflesh about to crush him. That these men and women, ex-villagers, farmers, burgher craftsmen and women, should somehow find the determination and courage to stand firm shamed and awed him. *All gods, true and false, where do people find such resolve? Where does it come from?* Ivanr was the closest he'd yet come to conversion to some idea of divine inspiration.

Then the landslide struck.

He'd deliberately aimed low, meaning to take a horse in the chest. But despite their training and the rough spurring of their lancer masters, the mounts could not be forced to wade straight into the solid wall of unmoving humans. They sawed aside at the last instant, or reared. Ivanr's pike took one low in the shoulder and was almost torn from his grasp as the horse continued on aslant of the formation. Elsewhere, the formation was uneven in places where a horse tumbled into the lines, kicking and thrashing, screaming amid the cohort. But the majority of the charge milled ineffectually at the rear of the first wave, only to edge on round, picking up speed once more, aiming for another unit.

'Form up!' Ivanr bellowed, panting, his blood thrumming within him. He strained to watch the manoeuvring. *Would they take on another cohort? Or would they make for the train? Where were the blasted skirmishers?* He realized they couldn't take charge of the field without breaking formation. There was no way to stop the charges. *Where were all those blasted archers Martal was training?*

He watched with tightening dread as a second charge formed up unmolested, the horses nickering and stamping.

Damn the gods! They could keep this up all day. All they needed was one solid strike. A bit of luck. He and the troopers were safe in their cohorts – but they were also just as effectively trapped.

*

From a wooded hillock overlooking the camp of the Army of Reform, Sister Nebras sat next to her smouldering fire and knitted. She pulled her layered shawls tighter, keeping one eye on the gathered camp, the assembled carriages, the corralled horses, staked dray animals, carts and tents. Somewhere within that train the heart of the movement against the Lady, its voice and rallying point for nearly half a century, lay dying.

And she did what she could to help him hang on.

The uproar of warfare reached her as animal screams, the commingled roaring of thousands of throats and the rumbling of massed hooves somewhere beyond the misted rain where slanting shafts of sunlight broke through here and there. But all that commotion was no business of hers. She was embroiled in the real battle; the true duel of wills and intent that would guide these lands for the next century. She and her sisters and brothers had committed themselves, finally stepped out into the open to declare their opposition.

And it was about damned time, too.

Yet Beneth was dying. He'd directly resisted the Lady for decades. She had no idea how he'd done it. Sister Nebras was a witch, a manipulator of chthonic spirits and the lingering wells of power at ancient shrines, cairns and ritual sites. And she had no illusions regarding her strength. In her youth she'd travelled abroad, sensed the aura of true magi – in Malaz she knew she'd be regarded as no more than a hedge-witch. Yet Beneth delved into none of these sources. He merely set his will against the Lady, whom Sister Nebras regarded not as the goddess she claimed to be, but rather as a sort of force of nature, if not a natural one. How did he do it? His very success unfortunately undermined her own personal thesis that one need not resort to the divine to explain any of this. She knitted with greater fury, the wooden needles a blur.

It was most irksome.

A presence nearby, and she tilted her head to peer aside through her thick pewter-grey hair. 'I see you there, Totsin. No sneaking up on ol' Nebras.'

Totsin bowed, a hand at his ragged beard. 'Sister Nebras.' He stepped up out of the woods.

'What are you doing here? The Lady's gaze is near.'

Totsin nodded gravely. 'Yes. That's why I've come.' He sighed, rueful. 'I've come to lend a hand.'

'Ha! There's a turn to startle everyone! Well, though damned late, you're welcome. I would be lying if I said I did not need the help. The burden is—'

Sister Nebras froze, needles poised. Glaring off to the woods she leapt to her feet. 'By all the— She's here! She slipped in behind you!'

Totsin spun, mouth open. 'I sensed nothing . . .'

'Idiot! Well, too late now.' She dropped her knitting to raise her hands. 'Ready yourself – we must fight.'

'Yes, Sister Nebras. We must fight,' he answered, his voice pained.

She glanced aside, unsure at his tone. 'What . . . ?'

Totsin unleashed a blast of force that threw Sister Nebras from her feet to fly crashing into a thick birch trunk that quivered from the blow. She fell in a heap, back broken, staring up at the sky. He stood over her, peering down.

'Any last insults?' he asked.

'You will die . . .' she breathed.

He shrugged. 'Undoubtedly – but long after you.'

She mouthed: '. . . why . . . ?'

A shining light was approaching, casting stark shadows of light and dark among the trees. Totsin bowed to the source somewhere out of her vision then returned to her. 'Why, you ask? Surely that ought to be clear. You and the others pay me no deference. You mock me. Defy my wishes. I have *seniority.* I am a founding member. I am *in charge*! I will recruit a new Synod. One where it will be absolutely clear that *I* am the ranking member and no one will dare challenge me!'

'Totsin . . .'

'Yes?'

'You couldn't be in charge of a privy.' And Sister Nebras laughed, coughing, to heave up a mouthful of blood that drenched her chin and shirt-front.

Totsin frowned his disgust and turned away. He bowed down on one knee before a floating brightness that held the wavering outline of a robed woman.

'Well done, Totsin Jurth the Third,' came a woman's soft voice, filling the clearing. 'The Synod is yours to mould as you wish. For is that not your right? Your obligation? As founding member and most senior practitioner?'

'I am yours, Most Blessed Lady.'

'And now I must go,' said the vision, regret tingeing its voice. 'I am so very late for a much overdue visit. Until later, most loyal servant.'

Totsin bowed his head to the ground. When he raised it she was gone and the clearing was dark once more. He straightened his vest, brushed his sleeves, then walked off into the woods already thinking ahead, wondering which minor – *very* minor – talents he might approach once all this unpleasantness was behind him.

*

Ivanr held the broken haft of his pike in one hand while waving back the line. 'One step back!' Twice already he'd nearly tripped over the fallen – theirs and the enemy's. He also limped where a wounded Imperial had stabbed him in the foot. That was the problem with twelve-foot pikes . . . useless for infighting. Panting, he regripped the broken haft, squinted into the thinning mist. Was it another rush? Disembodied horns sounded a recall across the slope. Somewhere to the east a cohort had shattered and the Imperials had descended like kites on meat to run down the fleeing refugees. Now the cavalry were re-forming higher on the hillside, readying for another rush and choosing their targets at will. Damn Martal! Had she placed *all* the skirmishers with the train? Where were they? He was of half a mind to find her. But of course he wouldn't: not because of the likelihood of being trampled, but because of what the men and women would think seeing him run off.

A great mass of lancers, the largest remaining body of them, came thundering down to the west, thinning across their front as they went. Ivanr watched them pass – damn them! Bored with taking runs at us they're off for the train!

Troops of about fifty lancers coursed among the cohorts to keep them pinned. They swung about, charging, but mostly sawing off at the last instant to avoid the pikes. At least they too had no archers, Ivanr thought ruefully. The men and women of the cohort peered about, blinking. 'Keep formation!' Ivanr bellowed. 'They'll be back!'

He swallowed, parched, glancing down to the south, waiting for the telltale plume of smoke, the screams, the refugees fleeing the wreckage of the train.

But nothing appeared. Silence. Occasionally the smaller troops thundered past, threatening them, but by now the cohorts mostly ignored them – they hadn't the mass to press any attack. Then, from the west, one by one, and in larger squads, bowmen and women appeared – theirs. They halted to pull back their child-like short-bows to loose in unison then retreated back to the distant woods.

The lancers curved in upon them, charging across the field, only to suddenly rein up as a great dark cloud came arcing overhead, descending in a hissing swath, smacking into chests, limbs, shoulders. Horses screamed, rearing. Men fell unhorsed or dead already. The nearest cohort roared and charged. Pikes took mounts and men in ghastly impaling slashing wounds to heave them over. Ivanr felt his own cohort quivering to join the melee and he raised an arm: 'Steady! Keep formation!'

To the west a deep roar sounded from the misted lowlands and out charged muddy waves of archers numbering in the thousands. Ivanr felt the knotted tension of battle uncoil in his stomach. He straightened, resting his weight on the shattered pike haft, letting out a long low breath.

'At ease!' came Lieutenant Carr's command from the rear. The waves of archers overran them, searching for more cavalry. Men and women among the cohort cheered them as they dashed past, some grinning. Ivanr noted muddy Imperial cavalry helmets bouncing from the belts of some of those who ran by. He turned to congratulate the men and women around him, squeezing shoulders and murmuring a few compliments. Then he limped off to find Carr.

The lieutenant was still at the rear, and he saluted. Responding, Ivanr saw a sabre cut across the man's shoulder. He knew the rear had been charged a number of times; he'd felt it in the animal-like flinching of the cohort as the impact reverberated through the tightly packed ranks. It seemed the lieutenant had been fighting outside the lines the entire time. 'Permission to leave formation.'

Grinning, Carr nodded, wiped his face. 'Of course. And thank you. You steadied the front enormously . . . no one wanted to be seen giving way.'

Ivanr waved that aside. 'Congratulations, Lieutenant. Well done.'

He limped off across the churned slope, heading west. His bodyguard, the remaining two men and two women, followed closely.

As he walked the gentle slope the dark bodies of fallen horses and riders emerged from the mist. The grisly humps gathered in numbers until a swath of butchered cavalry choked the landscape. Ivanr flinched back as one sandal sank into oozing yielding mush. *A marsh?* There had been no such feature here yesterday. Horses thrashed weakly, exhausted and mud-smeared, disturbing the ghostly scene. Every lancer had been cut down by bow-fire right where they'd stuck. A merciless slaughter. Tracing the route, Ivanr saw it all in his mind's eye: the swooping charge, the sudden lurching massing, the milling confusion. Then from the woods archers emerging to fire at will. And this boggy lowland; Sister Gosh's skystones abetted by his own blood?

A horse nickered nearby; he turned to see Martal herself coming, followed by a coterie of officers and aides. She stopped her mount next to him. Kicked-up mud dotted her black armour. She drew off her helmet, leaned forward on the pommel of the saddle and peered down at him. He thought she looked pale, her eyes bruised and puffy with exhaustion, her hair matted with sweat.

'Congratulations,' he ground out, his voice a croak.

Her gaze flicked to the killing-fields. 'You disapprove.'

'They were trapped, helpless. You murdered them all without mercy.' He eyed her: 'You're proud of it?'

The woman visibly controlled herself – bit down a curt retort. 'This is no duel in some fencing school, Ivanr. This is war. They were prepared to cut down all of us – you included.'

'Enough died there. We had no support!'

'It had to be convincing. They had to have control of the field.'

He shook his head, appalled by the chances she'd taken. 'An awful gamble.'

'Every battle is.'

Shaking his head he felt hot tears rush to his eyes and wiped them away. 'I know. That's why I swore off it all.' He laughed. 'Imagine that, yes? Ridiculous.'

Martal cleared her throat, drew off one gauntlet to rub her own sweaty face. 'Ivanr . . .'

'Yes?'

'Beneth is dead.'

He stared. '*What?* When?'

'During the battle.'

He turned to the forces coming together on the field, troopers embracing, cheering, and he felt desolate. 'This will break them.'

'*No it will not*,' Martal forced through clenched teeth.

He eyed her, unsure. 'You can't hope to withhold it . . .'

Her lips tightened once more against an angry response. 'I wouldn't do something like that. And besides, word has already gotten out. No, it won't break them because they have you.'

He regarded her warily. 'What do you mean?'

'I mean his last wish – his last command to me. That you take his place.'

'*Me?* That's ridiculous.' It seemed to him that Martal privately agreed with the evaluation. He considered her words: 'his last *command* to me'. *She's only doing this because of her extraordinary faith in and devotion to that man.*

And what of him? Had he no faith in anything? Anyone?

He examined his hands: bloodied, torn and blistered. He squeezed them together. 'Well, perhaps I shouldn't be in the lines now anyway . . . rather awkward place for someone who's sworn a vow against killing.'

The foreign woman peered down at him with something new in her gaze. 'Yes. About that . . . a rare thing to have done. Beneth did not mention it, but did you know that some fifty years ago he swore the same vow?'

Ivanr could only stare, struck speechless. Martal pulled her helmet back on, twisted a fist in her reins. 'No matter. You have me to spill the blood. The Black Queen will be the murderess, the scourge.'

He watched her ride off and he wondered: had he also heard in her tone . . . *the scapegoat*? A mystery there, for certain, that feyness. It occurred to him that perhaps she was no more relishing her role than he. *And just what is my role? What was it Beneth did? I've no idea at all. All the foreign gods . . . I have to find Sister Gosh.*

* * *

The Shadow priest, Warran, led Kiska and Jheval across the dune field out on to a kind of flat desert of shattered black rocks over hardpan. The lightning-lanced storm of the Whorl coursed ahead, seemingly so close Kiska thought she could reach out and touch it.

The two great ravens kept with them. They coursed high overhead, occasionally stooping over the priest, cawing their mocking calls. Warran ignored them, or tried his best to, back taut, shoulders high and tight as if he could wish the birds away.

After a time Jheval finally let out an impatient breath and gestured ahead. 'All right, priest. There it is. You've guided us to a horizon-to-horizon front that we could hardly have missed. You've done your job. Now you can go.'

The priest squinted as if seeing the mountain-tall front for the first time. 'I think I will come along,' he said.

'Come along?' Jheval motioned for Kiska to say something.

'You don't have to,' she offered.

Warran gave a deprecating wave. 'Oh, it's quite all right. I want to.'

'You do?'

'Oh yes. I'm curious.'

Jheval sent Kiska a this-is-all-your-fault glare.

'Curious?' she asked.

'Oh yes.' He stroked his unshaven cheeks, his beady eyes narrowed. 'For one thing – where did all the fish go?'

Jheval made a move as if to cuff the fellow. Kiska glared at the Seven Cities native. 'I think,' she said, slowly and gently, 'they're probably all dead.'

Warran examined Kiska closely as if gauging her intelligence. 'Of course they are, you crazy woman! What does that have to do with anything?'

Kiska fell back next to Jheval. They shared a look; Kiska irritated and Jheval knowing.

Curl by curl, mounting clouds over clouds, the Whorl rose higher in the dull sky of the Warren until it was as if it were leaning over them. The closer they came the more it resembled the front of a churning sandstorm, though seeming immobile. It cut across the landscape as a curtain of hissing, shimmering dust and dirt.

'Can we cross it?' Kiska yelled, having to raise her voice to be heard over the waterfall-roar.

'How should I know?' the priest answered, annoyed.

The ravens swooped past them then to land to one side where something pale lay half buried in the sands. They pecked at it, scavenging, and Kiska charged. Waving her arms, yelling, she drove them from their perches atop what appeared to be the body of a huge hound.

Jheval ran up, morningstars in his fists. 'Careful!'

Kiska knelt next to the beast, stroked its head; it was alive, and pale, as white as snow beneath the dirt and dust.

'A white hound,' Jheval mused. 'I've never heard of the like.' He beckoned the priest to them but the man refused to come any closer. He stood alone, hunched and bedraggled, looking like the survivor of a shipwreck. The hound was panting, mouth agape, lips pulled back from black gums, its fearsome finger-long teeth exposed. 'Is it wounded?'

Kiska was running her hands down its sides. 'I don't see any wound. Perhaps it is exhausted.'

'Well, there's nothing we can do.'

'No.' She stroked its head. 'I suppose not. A handsome beast.'

Jheval snorted. 'Deadly.'

The thing in the bag at Kiska's side was squirming now, as though impatient. She rose. 'We should pass through.'

Jheval gestured helplessly to the storm. 'And what is on the other side? Is anything? We'll be lost in this front, just like at home.'

Kiska freed the cloth from her helmet, wrapped it round her face. 'There must be something. The hound came from there.'

'Yes, fleeing!'

A shrug was all she would give to such an unknown.

Glaring his irritation, Jheval undid his sash – it proved to be a very long rope of woven red silk. He offered an end to Kiska and she tied it to her belt, asking, 'What of the priest?'

The warrior made a face. 'If we lose him, we lose him. Something tells me, though,' he added, sour, 'we won't be so lucky.'

'Very well.' Kiska hunched, raising one arm to her face and clamping her staff under the other like a lance.

Before the wall of churning dust took her, Kiska cast one last glance to the priest. He was motionless, as if torn, peering back into

Shadow, then at them. She urged him on with a wave of the staff and then she had to clench her eyes against the storm of dust.

The passage through the barrier, or front, or whatever it was, took far less time than Kiska anticipated. Within, she was tense, readied for an attack, though none came. All she noticed were voices or notes within the rampaging wind. Calling, or wailing, or just plain gibbering. She did not know what to make of it. At one point she thought she was seeing things as, in the seeming distance, immense shapes grappled: one a rearing amorphous shape with multiple limbs, the two others dark as night. It appeared to her that the two night-black shapes ate the larger monstrosity. Quite soon she stumbled out into clear still air to find herself on naked rock.

She pulled the scarf from her face. Dust sifted from her cloak and armour to drift almost straight down in the dead air.

She flinched as Jheval began untying the rope at her belt, but then she relaxed and allowed him the intimacy. 'Where are we?' she breathed, wondering.

The man peered round, narrow-eyed. 'I don't know. But I don't like it.'

'Is it the Abyss?'

'No,' answered a third voice and they turned to see the priest. Dirt layered his robes and grey kinky hair. He shook himself like a dog, raising a cloud of dust. 'Though it is close, now. Closer than we would like. This is still Emurlahn, now a border region of Chaos. Half unformed, sloughing back into the inchoate.' The priest's eyes tightened in anger, almost to closed slits. 'Lost now to Shadow.'

For an instant Kiska believed she'd seen him somewhere before. Then the man peered about, confused. 'I see no fish . . .'

The thing at her side wriggled and pushed at the sides of the burlap bag. She knelt. 'I suppose now is as good as any time.' Jheval stepped close – a hand, she noted, on the dagger at his belt. She laid the bag down, now bulging and shifting from whatever was within. She undid the string and straightened up. The thing worked its way free of the coarse cloth. It looked like a sculpture of twigs and cloth, bat-shaped, winged, somehow animate. It launched itself in the air, the wings of tattered cloth flapping.

It flittered about them as agile as a bat or a moth. Then suddenly the two ravens were among them, stooping, black beaks snapping. Kiska raised her arms. '*No!*'

The thing pounced on Warran's head, clutching his hair with its little twig fingers, chirping angrily. The priest bellowed and leapt into the air. He ran in a blind panic, batting at the thing while the two ravens whirled overhead, harrying him. Kiska and Jheval watched him go, arms waving, to disappear amid the rocks.

She eyed Jheval, uncertain. 'Sometimes I think that fellow is much more than he seems . . . at other times, far less.'

'I think he's lost his mind,' Jheval muttered. He scanned the horizon then pointed. 'There's something.'

Kiska shaded her eyes though the light was diffuse. There was a smear in the distance, a dark spot low on the horizon like a storm cloud. 'Well . . . Warran did run in that direction, more or less.'

Jheval shrugged and started off. She followed, arms draped over the stave across her shoulders.

After a time the bat-thing returned to circle Kiska then flew off again in the general direction of the smear on the horizon. They came across Warran fanning himself on a rock. Of the ravens, she saw no sign. Jheval peered down at the winded sweaty priest for a moment and then said, 'Perhaps we should rest here.'

'I'm not tired,' Kiska said.

'Perhaps not. But who knows how long it has been. Or,' and he caught her eye, 'when we may get another chance.'

She grunted at that, acquiescing. 'Our guide . . .'

'No doubt it will return.'

'Yes. Sleep,' Warran enthused, brightening. 'I will keep watch.'

Jheval and Kiska shared a look. 'I'll go first,' said Jheval.

Kiska arranged her cloak, set her staff and knives on their belt next to her. Then she rolled on to her side and attempted to rest.

It seemed the next instant that someone was shaking her booted foot and she raised her head to see Jheval wave her up. It was darker now – not as night proper, as the light of 'day' was not proper either. She sat up as he sat down. There was something in his expression as their gazes met. Wonder? Apprehension? She couldn't quite tell. In any case with a nod he directed her attention to one side then lay down. She rose, collected her weapons.

She found Warran standing off to that side, but he was obviously not what Jheval meant with his nod – it was certainly what Warran himself was staring at in the far distance.

For a moment the bizarre horizon line confused her until she remembered that this was Chaos and so need not make sense to her. The darkened sky was dominated by rippling curtains of light such as those she'd seen over the Strait of Storms in her youth. But these lights circled and danced around an empty black spot in the sky close to the horizon. And it may be that she was mistaken, but it also seemed as if the land itself curved up to meet the thing.

'Is that it?' she asked Warran, hushed. 'The Whorl?'

He nodded. 'Yes. That is it. And it looks as if it does not end in Chaos. It looks as if it touches upon the Abyss. Upon nonexistence itself.'

'What do you mean?'

'I mean that hole is eating everything. Chaos included.'

At first she rejected the man's melodramatic pronouncement. Ridiculous! Yet, Chaos *was* stuff. Just unformed or differently organized stuff that *she* would call chaotic. Not nothingness. That was Outside. Beyond. The Infinite Abyss.

Gods above and below. *Infinite*. Did that mean unquenchable? Would it perhaps never stop? Was Tayschrenn somehow involved in such a . . . such a flaw in existence?

Or was he its first victim?

'Yes, everything,' Warran continued, eyeing the distant bruise as if personally affronted. 'Even all the fish.'

* * *

Bakune did not think his time wasted while he waited for the eve of the new year, the Festival of Renewal. He haunted the common room of the Sailor's Roost – or Boneyman's, as everyone called it – and listened to the bustle and murmur of illegal commerce surrounding him. Then slowly, as he became a familiar face, he started asking questions. And in less than a week he learned more about the habits, preferences and operations of the Roolian black market and smuggling than he'd pieced together in a lifetime administering justice from the civil courts. At first he fumed at Karien'el. It seemed he'd been the man's pet; fed only what the captain wanted pursued. But then, as he had more time to reflect, he realized that as much of the blame lay with him.

This deeper understanding came one night while he sat with the Jasstonese captain of a scow that plied the main pilgrim way of the Curl, from Dourkan to Mare. The man, Sadeer, was rude, a glutton, and smelled like a goat, but he loved to talk – especially if the audience was appreciative of his wisdom.

'These pilgrims,' Sadeer announced, belching and wiping his fingers on his sleeves, 'we feed on them. They are our food.'

Bakune cocked a brow. 'Oh? How so?'

The fat captain gestured as if encompassing the town and beyond. 'Why, our entire economy depends upon them, my friend. What would this town be but a wretched fishing village were it not for your famous Cloister and Hospice? And what demand would there be for my poor vessel, such as it is? We feed upon them, you see?'

'Their gold is much needed, yes,' Bakune admitted, sipping his drink.

Sadeer choked on a mouthful of spice-rubbed fish. He waved furiously. 'No, no,' he finally managed, and gulped down a glass of wine. 'That is not really what I mean. Gold is just one measure – you see? The meaningless transfer of coin from one bag to another is just a mutually agreed-upon measure of exchange. The important value lies elsewhere . . .'

Bakune dutifully rose to the bait: 'And where is that?'

Sadeer wagged a sausage-like finger. 'Ah-ha, my friend! You have hit upon it. The true value, the deeper measure, is attention. Attention and relevance. That is what really matters in the end. The lack of gold, the condition of poverty, that can be remedied. But the lack of attention? Irrelevance? These are much harder to overcome. They are in fact terminal.'

'I see . . . I think.'

The Jasstonese captain was picking his teeth with a sliver of ivory. 'Exactly. The true economy is relevance. Once you are judged irrelevant – you are out.'

Later that night, after Sadeer had risen, belching, and lumbered off to find a brothel, Bakune sat at his small round table thinking. Attention. He'd not paid attention. Or had turned a convenient blind eye to what he did not want to pursue. That was his fault. A narrowed vision – and wasn't that precisely what the priest had accused him of?

Two days later came the Festival of Renewal. Boneyman's was crowded. It was not a day, nor a night, to be a foreigner on the streets of Banith, or in all of Rool for that matter. Unless one wore the loincloth of the penitent. From the door, Bakune watched while the holy icons were paraded through the streets on their cumbersome platforms held aloft by hordes of the devout all competing for the privilege – some trampled underfoot in an ecstasy of fervour. A number of the platforms carried young girls or boys draped in the white silk of purity, dusted with the red petals of sacrifice. Drops of blood spotted the silks of some, dripping from the stipulated woundings at wrists and neck.

Bakune now winced at the sight. How could he not have seen it before? The children, the red petals symbolizing blood, the woundings. All prescribed. All handed down as ancient ritual. What was all this but a more sophisticated playing out of what in earlier times had been done in truth? Ranks of the penitents came next, marching in step, naked but for their loincloths, each wielding flail or whip or chain, each lashing their backs in step after slow measured step up the devotional way to the Cloister doors.

Blood now flowed in truth. No stand-in. No delicate inferential symbolism. Flesh was torn. A carmine sheen smeared the backs of these men. It ran down their legs to paint their footsteps red. Bakune flinched as cold drops struck his cheek. He raised a hand and examined the traces on his fingers.

I am implicated. Marked as accomplice and abettor. Sentenced. My hands are just as red.

Unable to stand the sight of it all, he went inside.

He stood at the bar of the low-ceilinged common room and glimpsed Boneyman himself sitting in a far corner: bald, gleaming in sweat, nothing but hollow skin and bones; hence the name.

'Not a good night to be out,' growled a voice next to Bakune and he turned: the priest had emerged from their room.

Bakune signed for a glass of wine. 'Does everyone know my plans?'

'Not so hard to guess.'

'You would dissuade me?'

A slow shake of the head. 'No. I'll come along.'

'You will? Why?'

'You'll need me.'

'Whatever for?'

'In case you succeed.'

Bakune studied the man: the squat toad-like posture that instead of conveying weakness or sluggishness somehow gave the impression of great power held in check. 'And if you are along, then so too your companion, Manask, yes?'

The man grimaced his irritation. 'Yes. But on a night like this . . . he would hardly be noticed.'

But Bakune was not listening; he was plucking at half-memories. Something about two men, a priest and a giant. Something about the first invasion . . . 'Did you fight in the first invasions?'

The man's gaze slid to the open door where hordes still lined the way and the occasional icon or statue of the Lady tottered past over the heads of the crowd. 'You are Roolian,' he said. 'What do you think of your quaint local festival now?'

So, a change of topic. Very well . . . for now. 'It disgusts me,' Bakune answered curtly, and he downed his wine.

The narrow weighing gaze slid back to Bakune. 'Disgust . . . Is that all?'

Bakune considered. He examined his empty glass. No. There was more than that. Far more. 'It terrifies me,' he admitted.

The priest was nodding his slow profound agreement.

At dusk Hyuke and Puller thumped down at Bakune's table. 'What's the plan?' the sergeant asked. He was tossing nuts into his mouth one by one and spitting the shells to the floor. The nuts stained his mouth red.

'Surveillance,' Bakune said, and he grimaced his distaste at the sight of the man's carmine lips, teeth, and tongue.

'Is that all? What if we get a bite?'

'Then capture.'

The ex-Watchmen nudged one another, winking.

'Alive!' Bakune said.

The two lost their smirks.

'You have your truncheons?'

'Yeah. Got 'em.'

'And the priest will be along as well.'

'Hunh,' grunted Hyuke. 'That means the big guy.'

'You've seen him?'

Hyuke gave a look that asked how stupid he could be.

Bakune coughed into a fist. Right. How could anyone *not* see that thief?

Puller had been pinching his lower lip. 'Where?' he suddenly asked.

'Where what?' Hyuke said, annoyed. 'Where'd we see him? When he escaped. That's when. *Eluding pursuit*, he called it. Throwing a guy off a roof! That's eluding pursuit all right.'

'No, no. Not that. And anyway, you weren't hurt so bad. No, what I mean is where are we going?'

Hyuke glared at his partner. 'Fine. Right.' He looked to Bakune.

The Assessor envisioned his map. How useless that they should have taken it, he realized, when he had every detail impressed upon his mind. 'We'll keep watch on the South Way.'

Hyuke grunted his ill-tempered agreement and spat more shells on to the floor.

The priest was waiting for him in the kitchen. The old cook – whose name Bakune had yet to discover – eyed the two of them like chickens ready for dismemberment. Bakune bowed a wary farewell to her and they hurried out into the alley. They kept to the lesser side streets, but even here the noise was inescapable, a constant low roar punctuated by cheering and chants.

As the dusk deepened, bonfires lit the night at major crossroads. Crowds circled them, chanting prayers to invoke the renewal and return of the Lady. Bakune saw the flaw in his plan then. Tradition dictated that these fires be kept alight all through the night. The most devoted would circle them continuously in a slow shuffle till dawn. The Cloister would be jammed with pilgrims and the priests would all be pressed into performing cleansings and blessings.

The night was just too damned busy. Still, was that not cover enough for anyone who could slip away or go unnoticed among the hordes and the tumult? What to do? He leaned to the priest. 'We can't see anything from here.'

The priest was nodding. He slipped a hood up over his head and motioned Bakune onward. They joined the throngs pushing and shoving their way up and down the street. Hawkers waved roasted meats on sticks and all the usual amulets, beads, blessed healing salves, and other trinkets.

The crowd thickened, pulling them along. Not even the priest's none so gentle thrusts could free them. Bakune heard chanting ahead, and as the words uttered from hundreds of throats clarified in his mind the hair on the nape of his neck rose.

Burn her! they chanted. *Burn her!*

He caught the priest's gaze, horrified. The man pushed ahead, drawing Bakune in his wake. At a tall heap of bracken and firewood two Guardians of the Faith held a girl wearing a torn white slip. Her hair was frizzy and wild, a Malazan half-breed. She was weeping, her hands tied at the wrist.

'*No!*' Bakune heard torn from the priest in a muffled grunt.

'This one is known to many of you!' one of the Guardians was shouting. 'Long has she preached against the Lady! She espouses foreign gods! In our fathers' time she would have been cleansed long ago . . . but we have been wayward in our fidelity!' The man gestured to the east. 'And look how we are rewarded. Fresh invasions. The insult of foreign occupation!'

He raised both hands over the now silent crowd. 'My friends – we are being punished! Yes, punished! For we have been lacking. Negligent. Too many of us give lip service only to our guardian, our deliverer, our one and only protector! The Lady is turning her face from us, and rightly so . . .'

He took a torch from a man next to him. 'We must rededicate ourselves. Prove our devotion with blood . . . and with sacrifice . . .' He pushed the girl down on to the piled bundled branches. She lay weeping, perhaps crazed with fear. He thrust the torch into the kindling.

Bakune stared, horrified, paralysed with disbelief. How could such an appalling barbaric thing be occurring before his eyes? Were they not all beyond such things? Would no one stop this?

The flames leapt up then almost immediately fell away. It was almost as if they were sucked down and snuffed. At Bakune's side the priest had simultaneously smacked his hands together in a loud slap. Bakune stared at the man, as did many others nearby.

Oh no. More than a mere priest?

The two Guardians shared a bewildered look, then they peered out over the crowd. 'Who is here?' one called. 'Reveal yourself!'

A woman who had been next to the priest suddenly pointed, shouting: 'It was this one! I saw!' She made a sign against evil at her chest. Bakune thought it prudent to join the crowd flinching away from the man.

One Guardian pushed forward. 'Hold him!'

'Ha ha!' a great voice bellowed and a giant figure straightened from among the press, throwing off a cloak. 'My diversion worked!' Manask took one long step up on to the heaped bracken. 'Now, while all eyes are elsewhere I shall snatch this innocent away!'

Everyone stared at the bizarre apparition. 'Who in the Lady's name are you?' the remaining Guardian demanded. In answer Manask kicked the man down into the crowd. He threw the girl over his shoulder and followed. Pilgrims swung at him with staffs and sticks but all rebounded from the man's rotund figure. He bulled forward. People fell like dry grass before him.

'And now I make my furtive escape! Where has that phantom gone, the crowd gasps!' He kicked down a door and ducked inside.

The priest pressed a hand to his forehead as if to blot the sight from his eyes.

The Guardians arrived at the doorway. 'After him!' one shouted, pushing another fellow to the door. But none appeared willing to chase so gigantic a quarry. Snarling, the two dived within.

'Disperse now!' the priest suddenly yelled in a surprisingly strong voice. 'Go home and examine your consciences, each and every one of you! What if that were your daughter, your wife, or yourself upon that blaze? What then?'

The nearest pilgrims turned on him. Those carrying staves held them in white-knuckled grips. The priest returned their furious stares calmly, almost haughtily. He crossed his thick arms. One by one the press thinned until all had drifted away. Bakune and the priest were left alone in the darkened midnight square. Alone but for two figures across the way sitting on the stone steps of a bakery, heads back as if asleep: Hyuke and Puller.

The priest sighed and waved to invite Bakune to accompany him to the gaping doorway. On the second floor they found the two Guardians unconscious and bound. Manask was standing at a window, eating a wedge of cheese. The girl lay on a child's pallet. Bakune joined Manask to peer nervously over the streets. 'More will come,' he warned.

'They are too busy, I think,' the priest answered. He sat on the pallet, brushed the girl's hair from her face. 'Ella,' he whispered gently. 'Come to me.'

The eyelids fluttered. A gasp, chest heaving. The eyes opened wild, white all round, then found the priest. The trembling limbs eased, relaxing. 'I'm so sorry,' she whispered. 'I tried. Really I did. After you disappeared I took up your message. They came for me – but I am not as strong as you.'

He brushed her brow. 'You shouldn't have taken up the burden, Ella. That was not my intent . . . I am the one who should be sorry. I should have realized.'

She sat up then, gripping his arm. 'They have seen you! You must hide!'

Gently, he removed her hand, stood. 'No. No more hiding or running. In fact, I think it is long past the time when I should have acted. Yes.' He pressed a hand to her cheek. 'I go now to confront the demon in her den. *You* are the one who must hide. Go to the settlement just outside the town. You'll find sympathizers there. Continue the mission. In secret for a time. Do I have your word?'

'She will destroy you!'

His frog smile was reassuring, and unconcerned. 'They have you now, Ella. I am not required.'

Clearly the girl wanted to argue but clearly she also respected his wishes, and so she was silent, tears coursing down her cheeks. The priest went to the window where Manask stood tapping the wedge of cheese against his chin, frowning. 'I am not so clear on this plan, my friend,' Manask said. 'As I see it, your delivering yourself gains us entry to the Cloister. Once there, while they are busy prodding you with red-hot pokers and eviscerating your bowels, I clean out the treasury. Is this the plan?'

'Something like that,' the priest growled, glaring.

'Ah!' Manask nibbled the cheese. 'Well, I like my half of it.'

Bakune eyed the priest, uncertain. 'You're not really going to walk into the Cloister, are you?'

The priest appeared distracted, his head cocked as if listening to some distant sound. 'No, not the Cloister,' he said, his brows furrowing. 'That's not where she is . . . What is that noise?'

Bakune heard it as well. Roaring, yelling. A mob – a riot. 'Things have gotten out of control,' he murmured.

'No. Worse than that. That's real terror. Come.' He started to head for the stairs, but stopped and turned to the girl. 'Leave town now. Speak to no one. Farewell, and may the gods overlook you.'

'Farewell,' she managed huskily, barely able to speak.

At the street Hyuke and Puller were waiting for them. 'Somethin's up,' Hyuke drawled. The two ex-Watchmen were eyeing Manask, their truncheons in their hands.

Townsfolk ran past, coming up the street from the waterfront in an ever-thickening torrent. Screaming was clearer now, rising from downslope. 'What's going on?' the priest asked.

Hyuke thrust out a leg, tripping a man, who fell without a sound. He lay on his back struggling to rise while Hyuke held him down with his foot. 'What's going on!' Hyuke demanded.

'I like your way of tricking information out of people,' Manask said. 'Reminds me of my own techniques.'

'They're coming!' the man gasped, his eyes fixed downslope.

'Who?'

'The Stormriders! They're here! In the harbour! Run! *It's the end of the world!*' And the man brushed Hyuke's foot aside to scramble away.

'Riders here?' the priest muttered. 'Absurd.'

The crowd thickened; all rushed past, ignoring them. Bakune heard more shouts warning of Stormriders. The priest headed down against the rising tide of humanity. Bakune followed. Manask clomped away into a side street. A number of distracted townsfolk ran into the priest, only to rebound as if having encountered an iron post; Bakune kept in his wake. Several shops were aflame on the waterfront – perhaps from abandoned bonfires. And out past the pilgrim ships at anchor, further out on the dark azure blue of the bay, rested a score of far larger vessels.

They were nothing like any ships Bakune had ever seen before, and he'd grown up next to the sea. Three-masted, extraordinarily large, with dark-painted hulls and tall castles at the fore. 'What are they?' he asked of the priest.

For the first time Bakune heard awe in the man's voice as he answered, 'I've never seen them myself, but they match descriptions I've heard. Moranth vessels. Moranth Blue.' The priest faced him, his expression amazed. 'The Malazans are here, Bakune. This means they've completely broken Mare. Passed through Black Water Strait.'

Bakune could only stare at the man while townsfolk pushed past. Some carried snatched precious goods wrapped in cloths or in baskets. He knew where all were fleeing; where the entirety of Banith's population plus thousands of pilgrims would end up: clamouring before the doors to the Cloister. The very place he had to go. 'I must speak to the Abbot.'

'I imagine the man's rather busy right now.'

Bakune pointed to the harbour. 'We must decide how to respond to this. We don't even have a militia!'

'No doubt the Guardians will order everyone to fight to the death.'

Bakune turned away to head with the tide. 'Don't be foolish.'

He just caught the priest's dark: 'I wasn't.'

Long before they were far enough up the Way of Obtestation to glimpse the tall copper doors of the Cloister it became clear that the night's panic and confusion had degenerated into open terror and riot. Looting had begun, citizens breaking into shops to snatch what provisions or supplies they could before heading for the presumed safety of the Cloister, or striking inland to flee the coast.

Bakune's two guards now walked at his sides, truncheons at the ready, which they swung at the slightest provocation. The priest went ahead; so far no one had become so drunk on panic as to attack him. Of the giant Manask, he'd seen no sign. *This must be his night – the night the thief dreamed of all his life. Law and order shattered. All households and shops open to plunder. This must be what a sacking is like. Something we in Rool hadn't witnessed in generations.*

Pushing round a turn in the Way, they saw ahead a milling press of humanity filling the narrow path like a solid wedge that ran fully up to the distant torchlit – and now firmly closed – copper doors. Before the entrance massed Guardians fought to keep back the mob. Staves rose and fell like scythes. Everyone begged for entry, arms raised, hands beseeching. Bakune leaned to the priest to shout: 'This is impossible! I know another way!'

Nodding, the priest forced a path through the press to a side alley. Once within he turned to Bakune and invited him to lead. Bakune caught Hyuke's eye. 'The gardens.'

'That low wall?'

Bakune nodded.

Hyuke heaved Puller forward by his soft leather hauberk. 'Let's go.'

Bakune and the priest hurried side by side behind. 'Where are we headed?' the priest asked.

'There's a large garden within the grounds. Parts of it touch upon an exterior wall. We'll try there. And your friend,' Bakune added. 'Where is he?'

'He's with us.'

'Really? On a night like this? Any building would be open to him. Gem merchants, goldsmiths.'

'He's convinced the Cloister sits on a mountain of riches. Nothing will keep him from it.'

Bakune could not resist asking the question that had been on his mind since first encountering the astonishing fellow: 'So – he really is a thief?'

The priest eyed him, one brow raised. 'He takes money from others. Does that make him a thief? So too then are most advocates and bankers.'

Bakune did not think that explanation entirely convincing but he said nothing. Personally, he thought the fellow would come away empty-handed from any search of the Cloister. Still, all those contributions from so many thousands of pilgrims and devout over all these generations . . . but no, the operating costs of such a huge establishment no doubt consumed all of it.

Once they reached the length of street where one wall ran alongside the Cloister gardens it became clear that Bakune was not the only resident to think of this alternative route. Makeshift ladders leaned against the brick wall; abandoned possessions cluttered the street. The foreign pilgrims might come bashing against the main gates, but the Banith residents had headed for the back entrance. Hyuke took hold of a ladder and shook it to test its solidity.

'Don't go in,' a hoarse voice warned from nearby.

Everyone turned; an old woman sat in the shadow of the wall.

'Why not?' Hyuke asked.

The woman pointed up. 'No one's come back. I've called and called. And there were screams. Terrible, they were.'

'There's panic all over,' Hyuke said dismissively.

'Where is everyone, mother?' Bakune asked.

'Run off. Fled when the screaming started.'

Bakune caught the priest nodding. 'Stay here, mother,' the man said gently. 'Warn everyone away.'

Then a great voice boomed from an alleyway: 'Touch nothing! It may be a trap!'

The priest flinched as if he'd been stabbed and he cursed beneath his breath. Manask came lumbering from the darkness. The two ex-Watchmen smacked their truncheons in their palms, jaws clenched.

'Silence now, everyone!' he shouted. 'This is my particular specialty. I will climb the wall!' The huge man took hold of the ladder, and with much grunting and fumbling dragged himself up its length. The wooden poles bent like bows under his weight. From beneath, Bakune saw that the man's boots were thick platforms, perhaps solid wood or iron. No wonder he could kick down doors! They must weigh as much as mattocks.

Gasping and grunting, the man levered himself up on top of the wall and sat panting. In this awkward position his thick padded armour puffed up around him like a globe. 'Ha ha! I have ascended the wall! From here I will secretly scout ahead!'

'No!' the priest hissed. 'Wait, damn you!'

But Manask had swung his feet over and dropped from view. A great thump sounded from the far side. Followed, shortly, by a bellowed: '*Hello?* Anyone there? *Hello?*'

Puller was scratching his head. Hyuke thrust his truncheon through its loop on his belt. 'Well I'm not usin' that ladder – the guy wrecked it.'

They selected another and the four of them climbed over. Hyuke went first, and Puller last. The gardens were extremely dark and quiet considering the tumult churning the night just beyond its walls. Only Manask's hollered hellos broke the relative silence. Bakune led the way to the Cloister.

It was here on the path that he came across the first body. He tripped over it and fell into a low evergreen shrub. Hyuke helped him up. The priest examined the body. It was a middle-aged man, a citizen. 'No wound,' he said.

'So what happened?' Hyuke asked.

'His life was taken from him.'

'Taken? How? By who?'

The priest did not answer. He gestured ahead to the dark shadow of the large building ahead. 'The Cloister?'

'Yes,' Bakune said.

The priest started ahead. 'Only I should enter.'

Bakune followed. '*What?* After all this? I have to see the Abbot.'

The priest glanced back, his gaze sympathetic. 'He may not see you,' he growled, enigmatic.

Bodies now lay thick upon the gravel paths and across the manicured beds of flowers. They lay where they'd fallen, undisturbed, as if asleep. Across the grounds pounding could be heard from the direction of the main gate. The tall iron-studded doors of the Cloister itself hung agape. A few low lamps glowed within. The priest turned to the ex-Watchmen. 'Guard the doors. Don't let anyone in.'

Puller was yanking on his lower lip; Hyuke's doubtful gaze slid to Bakune. The Assessor nodded. They shrugged. Puller leaned against one door. The priest headed in, Bakune following. 'And Manask?' he whispered.

The priest took hold of Bakune's sleeve and the Assessor was astonished by the man's strength as he easily yanked him back. 'Never mind him. You shouldn't come.'

'I have to. The answer to a mystery is here. I must have it.'

'It's no mystery,' the priest growled. 'You already know the answer. You just refuse to see it.'

A great acid bite was taken from his stomach then and Bakune grimaced, clenching his jaws against it. The priest steadied him. 'You look pale, Assessor. Are you well?'

Bakune nodded, curtly, gestured the priest on. 'I have to know,' he gasped through his teeth. 'Please.'

Obviously against his better judgement the priest relented. He released Bakune. 'If you must. Stay behind me.'

Together they walked the halls and rooms of the Cloister. The priest's path seemed to be taking him unerringly towards the inner chapel of Our Blessed Lady. Early on they came to more bodies. 'These are all priests and acolytes of the Lady!' Bakune exclaimed, shocked.

The corpses lay like twisted dolls amid dropped boxes and chests, bundled clothes and even silver icons all tumbled together. 'Looks like they were packing,' the priest observed drily. Bakune winced, seeing blood pooled and caked around mouths, nostrils, glazed eyes, and even ears. He swallowed, tasting iron in his own throat.

As they neared the inner chapel, the corpses lay even more thickly. Heaped, even. Picking his way between them Bakune imagined he was seeing most of the hierarchy of the entire abbey. 'Who could have done this?' he whispered, awed. Again the priest did not answer.

They came to the chapel doors, which stood slightly open. The priest pulled one leaf aside, revealing a scene of devastation. Heavy stone pews lay scattered like toys. Dark stains marked swaths across the gleaming polished granite floor. Mangled bodies lay pushed up against walls as if flattened by the blows of a giant. The stink of blood and voided body fluids drove Bakune to cover his nose and mouth with a sleeve. After a few moments, the priest entered. His sandals slapped noisily on the tacky smeared stone floor. Bakune followed even though he did not wish to – he feared being separated from the priest even more.

Ahead, sitting on the white marble altar stone beneath a broad shimmering starburst tapestry of gold and silver thread, waited a tiny figure. A child. A young girl with long black hair wearing a plain orphan's smock.

She smiled, brightening, and slid off the altar. 'Ipshank!' she piped, delighted. 'You've come!'

The priest gave a slight bow. 'M'lady.'

Bakune stared at the man. *Ipshank? Where had he heard that name before? Of course! Renegade! One of the highest of the Lady's hierarchy to throw off her worship. That was during the first invasion. The animal tattooing . . . turned to one of the foreign gods then. Now I begin to understand.*

Ipshank inclined his head to indicate the tossed bodies crumpled amid the broken stonework. 'Still as impatient as ever, I see.'

The child stamped her foot and the entire edifice shuddered around them. Dust came sifting from the hidden ceiling and enormous blocks of stone grated and shifted. Candelabra hung on long chains from the darkness above swung overhead, moaning. '*They would flee! Flee!*' Bakune clamped his hands to his ears in agony. He fell to his knees. Warmth made him pull his hands away – blood smeared his palms. A pink mist swam before his vision.

'And this one?' the child's voice asked.

'He had to see with his own eyes what no one could convince him of.'

'Well, he has seen enough.' A blow like the slap of a battering ram batted Bakune aside. He struck a fallen stone pew, heard bones crack. The agony blackened his vision for a time. But he fought to retain his consciousness: he *had* to see! Had to witness!

'You have reconsidered my offer?' the child was saying.

'You know the answer to that,' came the man's coarse gravelly voice.

'A pity. Now you are bereft. You betray me, and then that god you clove to . . . the one your grunting ancestors squirmed before . . . the beast . . . you rejected him as well! Such an honour he offered you! Destriant! Arch-priest! And now he is cast down. Who could possibly be next for you? Truly, I am curious. Who will you run to next?'

'None. I've made up my own.'

A very un-girlish laugh echoed through the chapel. 'Your *own*? You cannot do that!'

'I have done so. And I have sent it out into the world to make its own way.'

'Enough foolishness, Ipshank. I renew my offer. Be my Destriant. The power you will wield will be unlimited. Join me! I have found my High Mage. And my Mortal Sword – or should I say Spear? He awaits my enemies on the Stormwall. Together we will sweep these invaders from our shores.'

'I am sorry, m'lady, but it is too late for that. They are here now. Banith is defenceless. You must withdraw.'

'*Withdraw?* Leave? This is *mine*!'

The building shook beneath another blow. The floor bounced, shifting the strewn wreckage, and glass shattered all along the walls. A candelabrum fell to explode in shards. Something wet struck Bakune and he turned his head, blinking and squinting. It was an arm. The arm led to the robed body of the Abbot Starvann Arl. The priest had been right: he would not see Bakune. For no legs emerged from beneath those wet stained robes, and upon his bearded face, frozen surprise. Stunned astonishment. *You thought you could control her, didn't you? And perhaps, over time, you came to think you* were *in charge. You came to think that she truly* was *just a child. You poor deluded fool.*

'No? You will not go? Very well.' Sandals slapped the wet sticky floor. Gentle arms lifted Bakune. 'Stay then, if you must. Those inhuman Moranth are coming. I leave you to them. Best of luck . . . I hear they have no blood within their armour.'

'No! How *dare* you! I order you to stop!'

Bakune watched the chapel swing around him as he was carried to the doors. 'Goodbye. I can't imagine what they'll do to you.'

'Come back!' the child shrieked. 'I *demand* that you return! Do not leave me!'

Past the doors, they were halfway down the hall when a great scream tore the air around them. The almost inhuman noise was like a spike penetrating Bakune's skull and he yelled his agony, bashing the heels of his hands to his forehead as if he could force the needle points from behind his eyes. The priest, Ipshank, paused, shaking his head to clear it, then set Bakune down. 'Wait here.'

Bakune could not even speak to answer. He lay propped up against the wall, panting in agony.

Shortly, Ipshank returned; he carried the young girl slack in his arms.

'Is she . . . dead?' Bakune mumbled, and he spat out a mouthful of blood.

Ipshank shook a negative. 'No. Unconscious. She will awaken remembering nothing.' He extended an arm and pulled Bakune upright. The Assessor clutched hold of the man's shoulder to take one limping step. 'So . . . who is she?'

'Just a vessel. A body used and cast aside. An avatar, some might say.'

'Then . . . what of the Lady?'

They were approaching the entrance hall and the priest was peering ahead, frowning in puzzlement. 'She is elsewhere, as I said.'

Bakune squinted as well: the outer doors were closed and barred. With Hyuke and Puller was Manask. But Bakune frowned, for it looked as if both ex-Watchmen were struggling to stab the giant with a spear. Then the scene reversed itself in Bakune's rattled mind and it became clear that both men were struggling to yank out a spear stuck in the huge man's chest. Hyuke had one foot up against

Manask's stomach and was heaving while Puller was jerking the haft up and down. Manask himself had his back to a wall, both fists on the haft, his face crimson with effort.

'Ah ha!' he called, noticing them. 'The holy man comes descending from the mount! What wisdom for us mere mortals?'

'Find anything, Manask?'

The giant's eyes flicked left and right. 'Why . . . no. Nothing. Nothing at all. Not a thing. No sacks of pretty gems set aside in secret hordes. No jewel-encrusted gold icons. Odd that, a cloister without icons! No stone chest of gold coins so large I could not move it hidden in the foundations. A shame that. In short, I come away empty-handed.' And he let go the spear.

'And this?' Ipshank flicked the end of the spear haft.

'A mere token of affection from the thousands of devout surrounding us.'

Ipshank's brows rose. 'Ah. I see.'

Hyuke peered at the girl. 'Who's this?'

'A survivor,' Bakune quickly said. 'Everyone else is dead.'

Ipshank eyed him for a moment, saying nothing. He looked to Hyuke. 'Find me somewhere she can sleep.'

'Sure. There's lots of rooms.'

Bakune eased himself down one wall. His left arm ached ferociously and he couldn't move it. He suspected it was broken. At last Manask managed to pull the spear from his thick armour; he eyed its bright razor tip, impressed. 'This one almost tickled me.'

Bakune had been studying the man's face – one quite thin and long for someone supposedly fat. 'You're Boneyman, aren't you?'

The man grabbed at his great mane of bushy hair, patting it. 'What's that? Boneyman? Ridiculous!' He cleared his throat and peered around. Lowering his voice, he asked, 'You wouldn't happen to have a hammer and chisel, would you?'

'No. Why?'

'No reason! None at all.' He examined the long spear, its wide thick blade, and rubbed his chin. 'Hmm. Well, while no one is looking, I shall sneak away unnoticed! Here I go, stealthily, like a very shadow.' And the man clumped off down the hall.

Farewell, Manask. Best of luck with whatever mad plan it is you've concocted.

Bakune gathered a handful of sleeve and wiped at the blood drying on his face. 'What are they doing out there?' he asked Puller.

The man frowned, thinking about that. 'Sitting. Praying.'

Bakune slowly nodded at the news. 'Right.' *No more challenging questions for that one . . .*

Ipshank returned. Bakune raised a questioning brow.

'She's sleeping.'

'What now?'

The priest looked off towards the front, his wide mouth turned down. 'Wait till dawn then get you out of here.'

Bakune paused in wiping the flakes of blood from inside his ears. 'I'm sorry? I can't hear so well right now. Did you say . . . me?'

'Yes. You.'

'Whatever for?'

The priest found a carved stone fount in which he splashed his face. 'What for? Hasn't it occurred to you, Assessor, that you are now the senior authority here in Banith? Who else must negotiate with the Moranth?'

Bakune stared. 'Me? Negotiate?'

'Yes, and soon.'

'Soon? . . . Why?'

Ipshank pressed his fingers to his brow, sighed. 'Before someone else does.'

'Someone else? But whoever would do that?'

The priest peered down at him as if to see whether he was serious. 'Boneyman, for example. He just might decide to take himself down to the wharf.'

Bakune lurched to his feet. 'No! All the gods – not *him*! We must go.'

Ipshank was nodding steadily.

From the doors Hyuke spoke up: 'If you're in charge now can I be captain? I mean . . . you have to have more'n a *sergeant* guarding you. Gotta impress these backwoods Moranth, an' all.'

Smiling evilly at Bakune's discomfort, the priest gestured up the hall.

CHAPTER VIII

The Holies of the Lady's worship are a triumvirate: the Three Gems. The first is the Lady Herself, She Who Protects. The second is the Chest, That Which Abides Within. The third is the Priesthood, Those Who Serve.

Thus are we protected, sustained, and guided. It is a perfect system and the envy of all.

School Primer
Damos, Jourilan

At first Ussü was merely irritated by the late night summons from the Envoy, Enesh-jer. Hands at his back, he tramped up the shallow hillside of the Ancy river valley. A servant preceded him, lantern raised, while two Moranth Black guards followed.

The bodyguard was a recent precaution Borun had forced upon him since the assassination attempt a week ago. Only his sudden recourse to the Warrens, a reflex action, had saved his life that night. The unleashing of power that came with that summons had surprised even him. The assassin had been pulverized instantly, organs burst, fluid gushing from all orifices. The man's slim keen blade had only brushed the surface of his neck – no more than a shaving cut. Later, he and Borun kicked through the wreckage of his tent. Neither spoke; Ussü imagined both their thoughts ran to suspecting a Claw. How many, he wondered, had Greymane arrived with . . . the openly self-declared plus the covert, salted away to remain hidden, watchful.

And the Lady had not intervened. She'd allowed him this – teasing? – access to his Warren. Perhaps even abetted his effort. Never had such raw puissance come at his call. It was, to be frank . . . *seductive.*

Pausing, he turned to peer back over the valley. Numerous fires glittered here on this west side of the Ancy while on the eastern shore hardly a one lit the pure dark of the night. *False and true gods: they've even run out of firewood.* The stories they'd been hearing of the privations endured on that far shore almost moved him to pity. Almost. Starvation, boiling leather to gnaw upon. Sickness. Countless soldiers cut down by bow-fire as they desperately attempted to fish the river. A number had even been caught here on this side having swum across. And were they spying? No – they carried panniers crammed with stolen food.

Ussü drew his thick winter cloak tighter about himself and continued on. A childish display, this summons. An attempt by the Envoy to remind everyone he was still in command, while succeeding only in demonstrating his pettiness.

Guardians posted at the iron-bound door allowed Ussü entrance to the keep proper. Within, he hung up his thick wool cloak. His Moranth guards bowed, halting, knowing they were not allowed in the private quarters. At the inner chamber doors two more Guardians of the Faith stood watch. These pulled open the heavy oaken leaves. Within, Ussü was surprised to see quite a crowd. Most of Enesh-jer's coterie of minor Roolian aristocrats and army officers stood jammed almost shoulder to shoulder in the smallish meeting hall. More Guardians of the Faith lined the walls, fists on their iron-heeled staffs.

The entourage parted for him – and not with their usual sullen arrogance either; many carried knowing grins, some even let go soft laughs as he passed. Hands at his back, Ussü pursed his lips; so, some new form of torture thought up by Enesh-jer. What would it be now? Had he finally become reckless enough to follow through on his threat to arrest him for witchery?

He found Borun standing at the front and Ussü's frown turned to a scowl. *Lady look away! He's not going to demand that Borun attack again, is he? He'll only force the commander to refuse in front of everyone.* The man's instability was verging on dangerous, but Ussü said nothing. He took a deep breath and clamped his lips tight. This night the Envoy wore his full official uniform of rich fur cloak, gold rings at fingers, and thin silver circlet. He held a roll of vellum that he tapped in the palm of a hand. Ussü eyed the scroll. Word from the Overlord? If so, the night's atmosphere just took on a far more dangerous tenor.

Enesh-jer briefly inclined his hound's head to Ussü. He raised his hands for silence. 'Commander Borun, Ussü. Thank you for attending. As many of you know, a messenger arrived a little while ago having ridden through the night from his posting to the west. He has brought word from our Overlord in Paliss.' Enesh-jer motioned for silence again though hardly anyone had spoken. 'My lords, the messenger's credentials are confirmed, the missive's seals are authentic and unquestionable. This is no fraud, no effort to sow confusion.'

The Envoy took hold of the scroll in both hands, regarded Ussü. A smile bared his sharp teeth. 'Commander Borun, Ussü. It seems that my many justified complaints and communiqués regarding your behaviour and performance have finally been answered. Your insubordination, your intransigence in the face of my orders, all is well known to everyone here. Now, the Overlord has heard of it and he has answered. You, Commander Borun, and you, *Adviser* Ussü, are hereby summoned to Paliss.' And he extended the scroll.

Borun bowed, accepting the vellum. For a time he studied it through the visor of his helm, then silently handed it to Ussü. The mage read quickly – the wording was definitely Yeull's . . . yet the missive cited no reason for the recall, just that he should travel with all dispatch and speed for Paliss.

Lady's revenge! Was this a summons to execution? Enesh-jer obviously believed so. He thought himself vindicated and Ussü could see no reason why he should not. 'M'lord,' he ventured, 'may I ask—'

'No you may not! Enough talk from you. Enough words.' The Envoy swallowed, forcing himself to stillness. 'You have been pulled from the front . . . which was my request all along. Go! Now. This night.'

Teeth clenched so hard they hurt, Ussü managed a very curt bow. Turning, he saw that the entourage had remained parted. *They all knew already. This was just a pantomime, a public humiliation and a show of power. Let all others considering dissent beware! This could happen to you too!*

Pulling on his cloak to leave, Ussü discovered his robes were wet where a number of the hangers-on had spat upon him.

On the way back down the valley Borun summoned messengers to give quick commands in the clipped foreign Moranth tongue. Ussü was silent for a time. There was nothing to say. Finally, he sighed, and asked: 'Will we ride together?'

'Yes. We will go ahead with an advance force. It will take time for the full withdrawal.'

Ussü stopped short. 'Withdrawal?'

'Yes.'

'You mean you are leaving with all your Moranth?'

'Of course.'

Ussü's voice rose with his amazement: 'Does *he* know that?'

'Yes.' Borun's tone remained maddeningly flat.

'And he . . . *approves* . . . ?'

'Of course. You know he has long regarded me as an impediment to his overall command. He considers my removal a victory.'

'Borun – you and your Moranth are the only reason this command remains. Only your heavy infantry is holding these Malaz—' Ussü corrected himself, 'Greymane back.'

'Envoy Enesh-jer is not of that opinion.'

'Dammit, man. They'll all be dead within a week!'

'Perhaps.'

'Then Greymane will dog any retreat all the way to Paliss.'

The Black commander halted at the entrance to the tent he'd set aside for Ussü's use. 'I do not believe so, High Mage. Regardless, I suggest you redirect your energy and concern to what might lie in your own future. Have you not wondered what might stand behind this summons?'

'No, not yet. I don't know. Yeull has been convinced by Enesh-jer's lies, perhaps.'

Borun clasped his gauntleted hands at his back, regarded the dark river. Ussü thought his mood reflective. 'My reading of Yeull is that he is many things, but no fool. High Mage, he is a frightened man. Something has happened. Something that terrifies him. And he has called us to him.'

Ussü sighed. 'I only wish I could share your . . . faith.'

'Faith?' The Black commander sounded bemused. 'It is an estimation. A bet, if you will. Everything is a gamble.'

Ussü smiled now. 'Really? Everything? What of those who do not gamble?'

'Those who do not gamble do so betting that terrible things will eventually happen to those who do.' And he bowed to leave. 'High Mage. We both have a busy night ahead of us. Until then.'

Ussü bowed as well. He watched the commander march off. Messengers who had been keeping a respectful distance now crowded the man. *Gods above and below, Yeull. What have you done to deserve the loyalty of such a man? It's a mystery.* Shaking his head, Ussü turned to packing his equipment.

* * *

The ground had been scoured naked here in what the Shadow priest, Warran, claimed was Emurlahn dissolving into the 'between-ness' of Chaos. Humped bare granite, resembling bedrock, gave way to pools of sand in dips and hollows that churned like water as if containing *things* just beneath their surface. Curtains of ash swept over them like gauzy blankets, only to drift on. A brief rainstorm out of the empty sky left them soaked in black dust.

Their bat-like guide led them steadily on towards the dark hole that lay on the horizon like a great unblinking eye, or an opening on to nothingness. The ravens took turns harassing the little flier, making half-serious attempts to snatch it from the air – at least when they were not hopping ahead of Warran and cawing their derisive calls.

Kiska had no idea how long they had been walking, or how much time had passed. Or even if such a consideration as 'time' was relevant here – wherever *here* was. In any case, it seemed that nothing had happened for a very long time when something heaved itself out of one of the pools of dust.

Warran charged ahead eagerly, only to stop suddenly. Good gods, Kiska thought, was the man hoping it was a fish?

But it was not. It was a twin to the daemon who had helped them earlier, Little Branch. It pulled itself free of the clinging quicksand then straightened to a similar height – twice Jheval's – and carried the familiar brace of terrifyingly sharp spears on his back.

'Greetings, Azalan,' Warran called, raising his hands.

'*Murderer!*' the daemon bellowed, and in one swift motion drew a spear and thrust it through the priest until it splintered against the bare stone behind. Warran toppled. The huge length of the spear bobbed from him like an enormous quill.

Jheval's morningstars whirred to life in his hands. Kiska leapt aside to give the lethal weapons room then struck a ready stance, staff extended.

It advanced on them, pulling free another spear. '*Slayers!*'

'What do you mean?' Kiska tried. 'Slayed who? We've killed no one!'

'It's Chaos-maddened,' was all Jheval had a chance to yell before the daemon was upon him, thrusting. He parried, knocking the deceptively slim and fragile spear aside, but found himself still a good two paces distant from the fiend. '*Shit*,' he snarled as they both realized that neither could get close enough to strike.

The thin haft twisted then, whipping, and caught one of Jheval's morningstars, sending it flying off into the sky. '*Shit!*' Kiska agreed, and charged. The butt end of the spear flashed toward her; she parried, but the strength of the blow drove her sideways to land painfully on naked rock.

Jheval parried with his remaining morningstar, standing edge-on, retreating, as the daemon thrust again and again. Backpedalling far too swiftly he stumbled, and the spear whipped again, slapping him across the face to send him down with an arc of blood jetting from his nose.

Kiska glanced round in a panic for her staff but the creature was right there, rearing over her, spear raised. 'Die, killers!' it yelled.

Killed who? What? For this I die?

The daemon looked away, turned its spear to bear upon another, too late. A white blur struck it in the chest and the two fell rolling and tumbling over the broken rocks. Kiska levered herself on to her elbows to watch a great white hound, almost as large as a horse, clamp its jaws on the shoulder and neck of the daemon and bear down. Black ichor shot; the fiend shrieked, pounded a fist on the hound's back. A great snapping and popping of cartilage sounded then, and the daemon's head flopped loose, the body spasming. Hunched over the corpse the beast growled at Kiska. Its eyes glowed the deep red of heart's blood.

She raised her open empty hands to whisper, 'It's okay, boy. Okay.'

Rumbling, gaze fixed on Kiska, the hound slowly dragged off its prize, leaving a smear of black over the rocks. Kiska let it disappear among the larger stones before heaving herself upright. She rolled a shoulder, wincing, rubbed her bruised back. *Gods, what a blow!*

She limped over to Jheval, found him sitting up, a fold of cloth pressed to his face dripping blood in his lap. She helped him up. He bent his head back and groaned. 'Fucking broke my face! Shame about the old guy,' he added.

Kiska nodded. 'Yes. Poor fellow. He was harmless enough. Did you see the hound?'

He nodded behind the cloth pressed to his face. 'Yes. I know a fellow who'd love to tackle that thing.'

Kiska decided that perhaps the man had taken too hard a blow to the head. 'That was the beast we saw before we entered.'

'Could've been.'

She looked down at the fallen priest – and frowned. Something was wrong. Then the man lifted his head and took a squinted, one-eyed look round. 'Is it gone?' The spear fell with a clatter.

Jheval let go a savage curse, blood exploding from under the cloth. 'I *saw* you impaled!'

'Not at all! It passed through my shirt,' and he pushed a hand through the slash, waving it.

Jheval stalked off, cursing afresh. Kiska studied the old man while he dusted himself. 'He's right,' she said. 'It could not have missed you.'

The old man waved deprecatingly. 'It was nothing. I merely edged aside.' And he turned sideways, mimicking a dodge, and laughed.

That laugh raised Kiska's hair; she'd heard it before, she was sure. It held an undercurrent of mockery that she found unnerving. Just who or what was the man deriding? She couldn't be sure it wasn't herself. In any case, she was far from satisfied. She watched while the old fellow picked up the long spear and held it out before him, bobbing it up and down. He glanced at her. 'You wouldn't by chance have any string, would you?'

Once Jheval returned, morningstars retrieved, they continued on, albeit at a slower pace. Kiska kept watch for the hound: was it following? Or had it fed its fill? Peering back she saw Jheval watching her and she cocked a questioning brow.

The man touched gingerly at his nose where a rolled-up bit of cloth blocked one nostril. 'It's there,' he said, his voice pained.

'How do you know?'

'I've spent a lifetime hunting and being hunted. I know.'

Kiska was only half convinced: more of the man's bluster? He raised his chin to indicate Warran, who walked ahead carrying the spear jauntily over a shoulder. 'That one. He's up to something . . .'

'Who isn't?' she answered, eyeing him sidelong, smiling to take the sting from it.

'Yes. Well. I mean it. He's playing his own game and at some time it may not include us. Just a warning.'

'I will keep it in mind.' Yet not so long ago the Seven Cities native had dismissed the old man as useless. In any case he was only affirming her own intuition; the priest was dangerous – but if he was so dangerous then why travel with them? Safety in numbers would hardly be a concern of his.

They continued on under the unchanging sky, where sinuous writhing lights glowed both in the dimness of night and in the only slightly brighter diffuseness of day. Their bat guide flitted about them, apparently tireless. A band of bruising developed across Jheval's face as black as tattooing; his dark eyes peered out of shiny swollen circles. The hound still followed, keeping its distance. Or so at least Kiska believed, as she caught occasional glimpses of snowy white on the edge of her vision. The two huge ravens, she noticed, went nowhere near the beast.

Ahead, the priest Warran suddenly stopped. He knelt to examine some long black shards lying on the scoured granite. Kiska and Jheval came abreast of him and halted as well. Jheval stooped to pick up a piece but the priest batted his hand aside. 'Do not touch it.' Jheval glared at the man's hunched back. The priest held his hands over the shards as if sensing or testing for a time; then he gently lifted one of the longer shards and examined it closely.

To all appearances it might as well have been black glass. Kiska thought that if you were to reconstruct the pieces they would form a crystal-like length of about an arm's span.

The priest let the shard fall. 'This is very bad.'

Jheval snorted, straightening. Kiska asked, 'What is it?'

'A kind of prison. Very ancient. Perhaps from before the shattering of this Realm. It was forged to contain some *thing* for all eternity. But Chaos has eaten at it, weakened it, and the entity contained within has burst free.'

Jheval snorted again, scornfully.

Warran eased himself up. He peered about, squinting. 'Shadow is something of the rubbish heap of time. Over the ages whatever others want hidden, or buried away, into Shadow it goes . . .'

'Enough of your charlatan mumblings,' Jheval growled. He waved to Kiska. 'Let's go.'

'I believe him.'

Jheval gestured helplessly. 'Fine. It matters not. We must keep going regardless.'

Nodding, Kiska tore her gaze from the seemingly infinite refraction of crystalline light and shadow. She forced herself to walk away; something deep within her shuddered at the fascination those broken slivers of night cast upon her.

After a time the priest sidled up next to her as they walked. He still carried the spear over one shoulder. 'You said you believed me,' he said, peering up at her with his age-yellowed eyes.

'Yes.'

He was glancing about; he'd been doing that a lot since they found the shards. Even suddenly darting looks behind – perhaps only because it so obviously drove Jheval to distraction. 'Why?'

She shrugged. 'Because it sounded a lot like something someone I met in Shadow would have said.'

The man's greying brows rose as he walked along. The extraordinarily long spear bounced on his shoulder. 'Oh? Shadow? Who?'

'A strange being named Edgewalker.'

The priest stopped dead. Kiska walked for a time then stopped, peering back. The man was studying her narrowly, his eyes pinched almost shut. 'Met him, have you?' he asked, something tight, almost waspish, in his voice.

'Yes. Once. Long ago.'

Now the priest snorted his disbelief. 'An unlikely claim.' He continued on past her. 'He doesn't talk to just anyone, you know.'

Kiska watched the man's stiff back as he marched off. She had to stifle a laugh. *Was this jealousy? Is the man put out that I've met and spoken with this strange haunt of Shadow? A kind of . . . what? . . . rivalry?* She walked on, shaking her head.

Later she caught Warran watching her, only to quickly glance away. *Good. About time I gave someone something to think about. I'm tired of being the only one here without some kind of cloak of mystery. The old man has his past; Jheval has his. Even the ridiculous ravens are enigmas. Maybe now he – and Jheval! – will take me more seriously.*

Some time later all three suddenly stopped. Even the two ravens, exploring forward, came wheeling back squawking their alarm before flying off into the distance.

A figure stood ahead, midnight black from its rounded half-formed head to its feet. Sensing them, it turned. It held something in one hand close to its face, studying it. A tiny, frantic, flapping thing.

Oh, damn. As Warran said: this is bad. Kiska felt her insides tighten at the aura she sensed surrounding the thing. Intensity. Incredible potential. *What use staff or morningstars against this foe? It would laugh at such toys.*

'Let me play this one,' Warran murmured beneath his breath. Then he rushed up to the figure and clapped his hands as if in pleasure.

'Ah! There it is! We've been searching everywhere. My thanks, sir, for catching it.'

Kiska and Jheval arrived to flank Warran. Fear coursed through Kiska more strongly than it had in years. She decided that at any sign from the entity she'd drop the staff and try her two throwing knives first – for all the good that would do. Jheval, she noted, kept his hands on the grips of his morningstars. She glanced about for the hound but prudently the beast appeared to be keeping its distance. *No fool it.*

The disturbingly blank moulded head edged down to regard the short priest. Ripples crossed the night-black visage and Kiska was unnerved to see a mouth appear and eyes blink open. 'This construct is yours?' The words sounded unlike any language Kiska knew, but she understood them just the same.

Warran was rubbing his hands together. 'Well . . . not *ours*, of course, so much as our master's . . .'

'Your master?' The bat flier flittered in its hand like a trapped moth.

'Yes. Shadowthrone . . . the ruler of Emurlahn.'

The matt-dark head cocked sideways. 'An unlikely conceit. Emurlahn has no ruler. Not a true ruler. Not since the beginning.'

The priest jerked upright, intrigued. 'Really? Fascinating. But as you can sense – it is linked to power.'

'Yes. There is a surprising weight to it. I am . . . piqued.' It held the flier close, examining it. 'There is something hidden within. Tucked away.' It reached with its other hand.

'Perhaps I may be permitted . . . ?' the priest asked quickly.

The entity regarded him for a time. 'Very well.' It held out the flier. 'Do it.'

Warran bowed as he accepted the flier from the entity's hand. He examined it. 'Ah yes. All one need do is—'

The flier whipped from his hands and shot straight up into the air. Everyone watched it diminish to a dot among the flickering curtains of light. When Kiska looked back the entity's gaze was fixed upon Warran in enraged disbelief, as if it could not comprehend that anyone would dare disobey it.

The priest covered his mouth with his hands. 'Oh dear. It appears to have gotten away from me.'

'*You* . . .' the entity breathed.

Warran raised a finger. 'Wait! To make up for that I have something that belongs to you.'

'There is nothing you—'

From his sleeve Warran drew a length of black crystal. The entity flinched back a step, seeming to draw in upon itself. Kiska stared, amazed. She could've sworn the man hadn't pocketed any of the shards.

'That is of no use,' the thing breathed. 'You do not know the ritual.'

'True. *But*, if you balance the symmetries . . .' Warran broke off a section and threw it aside. He was left with a square facet about the size of a jewel which he held up for examination. 'Then the remaining forces should be in equilibrium – don't you think?' And he tossed it to the entity.

The bright black jewel struck the being on its chest, like a drop of ink, and stuck there. It batted at it, turning in circles. '*No!* Impossible! How could you? *No!*' It looked to Kiska as if it was now shorter than it had been, thinner. Yes, she was sure that as it flailed, staggering, it was diminishing in size. As if it was disappearing bit by bit.

Kiska winced, feeling ill at the sight. What an awful thing to witness. The entity was now no higher than her waist, the jewel an ugly growth on its chest. 'Please!' it begged in a squeaking voice. Kiska turned her face away. When she looked back the jewel lay alone on the bare stone ground.

Warran stooped to pick it up then tossed it high and snatched it from the air. 'Ha-ha! Caught one!'

She glanced to Jheval, and though his face was ashen and sheathed in sweat, he rolled his eyes, letting out a long breath and rubbing his palms along his robes. *Yes, a close one. And yet, given what they had witnessed, were they now any safer alone with this increasingly unnerving priest of Shadow?*

* * *

Bakune was the most nervous he could ever recall being in his entire life. He stood on the pier, awaiting the invader launch that would take him out to meet the de facto new ruler of Banith – at least until a counter-offensive drove these Moranth daemons from their shores. His two bodyguards, Hyuke and Puller, he ordered to remain on the pier; he simply could not bear the idea of having the two imbeciles with him while he negotiated with this foreign Admiral. The priest had gone his own way, saying that for the time being Bakune could always find him at Boneyman's.

The launch bumped up against the stone steps below and the Blue marine escort beckoned him down. Stiff, his heart almost strangling him so uneven and powerful was its lurching, Bakune edged his way down the slippery, seaweed-slick stones. He seated himself dead centre athwart the launch and drew his robes about him, one arm bound tight, hand tucked into his sash. The Moranth marines rowed.

Glancing back, Bakune thought that the city was quiet this morning – perhaps it had exhausted itself in its panic through the night. A few tendrils of smoke rose where fires yet smouldered. The waterfront was empty; usually it would be bustling with fishermen and customers at this early morning hour. He drew his collar higher against a cutting wind that blew in from Sender's Sea, and perhaps had its origins in the Ocean of Storms itself.

The Moranth expertly and swiftly negotiated their way through the harbour mouth and out to the gigantic Blue vessels anchored far beyond, where, not coincidentally, they effectively blockaded the town. Bakune took the opportunity to examine these invaders more closely. Though the Overlord commanded a detachment of Black Moranth infantry, Bakune himself had never seen any of them close up. Like their black brethren, these Blue Moranth were encased head to foot in an armour of the most alien manufacture. Scaled, articulating, almost insectile in its appearance. And Bakune could now understand the terror of his fellow citizens: for all anyone knew these could be the Stormriders themselves come to take possession of the surface. They were that shockingly foreign, especially to a historically closed land.

None spoke to him, and he addressed no one. The launch came up against a particular vessel where steps of wood and rope had been lowered over the side. As he extended a foot to take the stairs one Moranth Blue reached out a gauntleted hand to steady him and Bakune flinched away, almost dunking himself in the bay. Recovering, he gingerly set a foot on to the wet staircase, and, catching the ropes in his one good hand, hauled himself on to the contraption.

More Moranth Blue soldiers – sailors perhaps, or marines, he had no way of knowing – waited on the stairs to aid him. While he could not help but avoid their touch, he had to admit they were damned solicitous. On deck, he found the vessel clean and well ordered, but betraying obvious signs of battle damage: scorching from fires, savaged gunwales where grapnels might have taken hold, ragged sails. The Marese had obviously fought hard. A Blue sailor invited him aft to the cabin. Up a narrow hall he came to a room that appeared to serve as reception chamber, office, and private bedroom all in one. Wide glassed windows let in sunlight and showed a rippling view of the open sea to the east.

A tall and very thin man stood from behind a table and offered a brief bow. Bakune responded, mystified. Who was this? A secretary of some sort? Where was the Blue commander?

'You understand Quon Talian?' the man asked, sitting, and inviting Bakune to do the same.

Bakune bowed again. 'Yes. It is the language of the ruling class here.'

'You are the local magistrate . . . "Assessor", I understand?'

Bakune sat. He eyed the man more closely: quite old but well preserved. A shock of pale white hair, white moustache and goatee; face and arms sun- and wind-darkened to the hue of ironwood. Bright sharp eyes that appeared . . . amused. 'I am Assessor Bakune.'

'Excellent. I am Admiral Nok. I command this Malazan naval unit.'

Nok? Now where had he heard that name before? And a regular Malazan in command? Not some Blue Admiral? Well . . . that was something at least.

'First of all,' the Admiral continued, 'let me reassure you that the last thing we wish to do is interfere with day-to-day life here in Banith. I want that to be the message you will pass on to your people . . . that they should simply return to their normal routines and merely . . . ignore us.'

Ignore the enormous vessels blockading our harbour? You ask a lot, Admiral.

'Secondly, I also want to reassure you and the people of Banith that we in no way wish to interfere with your local religious practices. You may continue to worship as you choose.'

Bakune struggled not to quirk a sceptical brow. *Really? That flew in the face of everything he knew regarding these Imperials. Everyone agreed their goal was eradication of the Lady's cult. A goal he himself had given no thought to prior to last night.* He tried to keep all inflection from his voice as he murmured, 'How very generous of you.'

The reply seemed to disappoint the Admiral, but he continued, hands clasped on the table before him, 'We of course will require some small supplies and refitting: food, potable water, lumber, rope and such. You will supply a list of merchants and we will reimburse in Imperial script.'

That would make me popular . . . but I don't have to tell anyone who supplied the list . . . would that count as collaboration? Bakune stirred uncomfortably, cleared his throat. 'And your troops, sir? A billeting list?'

The Admiral waved the consideration aside. 'The troops will remain on board our vessels for a time – to avoid any unnecessary tensions. However, there will be patrols.'

'Of course.'

'Very good. Then, we have reached an understanding. Our goal is to interfere as little as possible. The populace may even forget we're here.'

I doubt that very much, Admiral. But we can always hope.

The Admiral stood, came round the table and invited Bakune to precede him out. Straightening, Bakune bowed and entered the hall. The Admiral, he noticed, had to hunch to avoid bashing his head in the companionway. On deck, Bakune was shown to the set of stairs hung over the side. Blue sailors moved about, handling gear, adjusting the sheets. Bakune passed an opening on to the hold and saw for an instant how empty it was. *Where were these troops? Was this not a transport?*

The Blues sailors with him urged him on and he stepped out on to the stairs. He bowed to the Admiral one last time, then firmly grasped hold of the rope guides and started down.

On deck Admiral Swirl came to Admiral Nok's side at the gunwale. Together they watched the launch return to shore. 'What do you think?' Swirl asked.

Nok rolled his neck, easing the muscles. 'Hard to say. Very guarded, that one.'

'At least he was not overtly hostile.'

'But no fool, either. I just hope we've bought enough time.'

'How far away do you think he is?'

'I don't know.' Nok scratched his moustache. 'Frankly, I was half expecting him to be here already.'

The Blue Admiral nodded his helmed head, perhaps agreeing. 'And the patrols?'

'Four at first, let's say. Two four-hour shifts.'

'Reserve?'

'A hundred marines at the pier.'

The Blue Admiral was nodding again. 'That's about all we can field . . . Let's hope they don't test us.'

Nok grasped hold of the gunwale, eyed the townscape. 'They will. But let's hope we're out of here before then.' He leaned his elbows on the wood and let out a long low breath into the icy wind. 'We're here, Greymane . . . but where are you?'

* * *

'Well – would you look at that,' Wess drawled while hunched behind his wide heavy-infantry shield. Kneeling behind his own shield, Suth ignored him. Len, whom they both covered, shushed the man as he untangled his line. A pink and gold dawn was brightening beyond the eastern hills. The three stood at the Ancy's muddy shore.

It was their turn to go fishing.

For his part, Suth silently prayed to his entire inbred menagerie of Dal Hon gods that they get a bite right away. Any moment now the archers would catch sight of them and the torrent would begin. He reached down to select a water-polished stone from the shallows and stuck it in a cheek to suck on. It was an old trick to stave off hunger and thirst. Being of the Dal Hon, he was no stranger to want. He'd grown up through a number of droughts and lean times, so these last weeks of privation hadn't hit him as hard as some. Likewise Wess, who never seemed to eat anyway; the man would just jam a ball of some resin or leaf into a cheek and he'd be good for the day. Lard, however, could hardly muster the strength to stand, while Pyke had disappeared – deserted, probably. Dim they'd lost in the defence of the bridge. Keri had taken an arrow in the side and lay in the infirmary tents. Yana was sick with the epidemic of the runny shits, which afflicted almost everyone in camp and added terribly to the general indignity of dying by degrees. Goss seemed unaffected, though his eyes were sunken and his cheeks behind the salt and pepper bristles were as hollow as caves.

'You guys really should take a peek,' Wess said.

'Quiet,' Len hissed, sotto voce.

Suth watched the water, seeking any slim darting shape. If only he held a sharp fishing stick now instead of this bulky shield.

'Okay, but I gotta tell you—'

'What?' Suth cut in, glaring. Wess inclined his head towards the far shore. Suth scanned the slope; the lightening dawn was revealing the enemy – and themselves as well to the archers keeping watch on the shore. Smoke hung like mist, slowly drifting. Suth's own breath plumed in the chill morning air. He examined the ranks. Something strange there . . . he couldn't quite put his finger on it. 'Something,' he breathed.

'Un-huh. No Moranth. Them Black bastards is gone. Their whole encampment's picked up 'n' flown.'

Len straightened. '*What?*'

Wess was right. Where the Moranth encampment had stood now stretched an empty field of churned-up mud.

Len started rolling up his gut fishing line. 'Let's go.'

'They'll all see in a minute,' Wess objected.

An arrow hissed past them. 'Now *everyone* can see,' Suth cursed.

'We haven't caught a thing,' Wess pointed out. 'Unless we bring something to the pot we don't get a share . . .'

Len shoved the line into a shoulder bag. 'This is important.'

An arrow slammed into Wess' shield, throwing him back a step. Len started backing away and Suth moved to cover him. Sighing, Wess followed. Outside bow range they met a crowd gathered along the shore, pointing and talking, and pushed their way through. Suth heaved the heavy shield on to his back. 'We should report,' Len said. Wess just rolled his eyes.

They crossed to where their squad had set up camp. Yana lay under an awning made from a tattered blanket. Goss sat before the blackened pit where they used to cook their meals when they had food and firewood.

'The Moranth look to be gone,' Len told Goss.

Goss nodded at the news. 'So I heard.'

'Good report there, Len,' Wess said, lying down.

'Now what?' Suth asked Goss.

A slow shrug from the man where he sat in his threadbare padded aketon. 'Guess we'll attack.'

'Attack? Half of us couldn't drag our backsides across the bridge.'

Goss pondered that for a time. 'I hear they got lotsa provisions over on that side . . .'

'If we controlled the river we could build weirs,' Len added.

Suth was suddenly maddeningly hungry. It was as if the mere mention of a solid meal was enough to set his juices flowing. He almost said aloud how desperately famished he was, but refrained: those who mentioned that forbidden subject were looked on as if they were idiots. *Who in the name of Togg and Fanderay isn't, you horse's arse?* was the usual comment. He lay down to sleep, mumbling, 'Let's just get it over with.'

*

An aide summoned Devaleth to the command tent. It was still quite early; she hadn't even broken her fast yet with a glass of thin tea. She finished dressing hurriedly and headed across camp, which was seething with the most commotion she'd seen in weeks. Was there to be a fresh assault? Or an attack? The bridge was quiet; rather, everyone was studying the far shore. Glancing over as well, she tried to see what was of such interest but couldn't identify it.

She found Greymane and the Adjunct, Kyle, standing before the tent, scanning the west shore. The High Fist appeared more animated than she'd seen in a long time. The man had frankly been deteriorating; losing weight, becoming withdrawn and sullen. Only Kyle seemed able to rouse him from his dark moods. Now a faint smile, or eagerness, kept pulling at his mouth behind the iron-grey beard he'd been growing. Kyle bowed, greeting Devaleth. Even Greymane offered a smile – though one tinged with irony. 'What do you think, water-witch? What are we to make of this?'

'Make of what?'

Kyle raised his chin to the west. 'It seems the Moranth Black have decamped.'

'Really? Whatever for?'

The High Fist nodded. 'That's what everyone's wondering.'

Fist Rillish appeared, walking stiffly and carefully towards the tent. Devaleth fought an urge to help the man – that he was even on his feet was painful to see. The dysentery ravaging the troops had drained pounds from the man: his face was ashen and greasy with sweat, and his shirt hung loose on him. He saluted and the High Fist curtly responded.

'I understand the Blacks have marched off,' he said weakly.

'So it would seem,' Greymane rumbled.

'Then we will be attacking?' Devaleth asked.

'Not quite yet . . .' Greymane answered, his shaded gaze on the far shore.

'Oh?'

'It could be a ploy,' Rillish explained. 'A fake withdrawal to draw us into committing ourselves. The remaining troops would fall back, then the Moranth would counterattack, catching us exposed.'

Devaleth knew she was no strategist, but she was dubious. 'Sounds very risky.'

The High Fist was nodding his agreement. 'Yes. And unlikely – but best be sure.' He looked to the Adjunct. 'Kyle, take some scouts north, cross the river, and follow them till nightfall.'

Devaleth felt a stab of empathetic pain for Fist Rillish: strictly speaking, the Adjunct was not currently in the hierarchy of command. Greymane should have addressed the Fist. Yet the nobleman's taut strained face revealed nothing. Kyle invited the Fist to accompany him, saying, 'Perhaps you can recommend some names . . .' Kyle at least seemed aware of the awkwardness.

The High Fist watched the two leave, his mouth turning sour once more, and ducked back into the tent. Devaleth was left alone to ponder the news, and she wondered whether this was the opportunity Greymane had been waiting for, or just another false hope. The gods knew some relief was desperately needed. Fist Shul remained bogged down with the rest of the invasion force, stymied by landslides, floods, downpours and two Skolati uprisings. It seemed the supplies the High Fist had counted on sat rotting in the rain and snow along some nameless track.

*

Around noon, while Suth dozed, someone came to camp. He thought he heard his name mentioned, then someone shook him. He sat up, blinking in the harsh light, to see Captain Betteries scowling down at him the way someone might regard a dog turd he'd just stepped in. Suth saluted.

The captain returned the salute; he was bareheaded, his red hair a mess. His eyes were bruised, and he wore only a dirty linen shirt hanging down over wool trousers. 'You Suth?' he asked, his voice hoarse.

'Aye, Captain.'

'You can scout?'

Suth thought about saying no, then decided he'd probably already been volunteered for whatever it was so nodded. 'Aye.'

'Come with me.'

Suth dragged himself upright, grabbed his armour. 'Leave that,' Betteries ordered. Shrugging, Suth complied.

Sergeant Goss eased forward. 'I'll go, sir.'

'No, not you. Just the young bloods.' The sergeant's face clouded, but he said nothing. 'Let's go, trooper.' Goss saluted and the captain acknowledged it. 'Sorry, Goss.'

The captain collected three others, two squat Wickan plainsmen and a tall girl recruit, coarse-featured, wearing thick leathers, with a wild tangled mane of hair tied off with beads, bits of ribbon and leather braces. 'Barghast,' one of the Wickans mouthed to Suth.

The Adjunct was waiting for them. He wore plain leathers. Tall moccasins climbed all the way to his knees. His sword was sheathed high under his shoulder, wrapped in leather. Suth had seen a good deal of the young man, but he was struck anew by how rangy the fellow was, squat but long-limbed, his face seemingly brutal with its long moustache and broad heavy chin. He motioned to piled equipment. 'Kit yourselves out.'

Suth picked up a shoulder bag and found a stash of food. A strip of smoked meat went straight into his mouth while he searched through the rest. Belted long-knives went to his waist, a bow and bag of arrows on his back.

The Adjunct spoke while they readied themselves. 'We'll head north then cross the river. We're to shadow the Moranth. If you're spotted, cut away – no leading back to anyone.' All three nodded, stuffing their mouths. 'All right. Let's go.'

They jogged off. The Adjunct led them east at first, off behind a hillock until out of sight of the far shore, then cut north. Suth was wincing for the first few leagues: gods he was weak! But then his legs loosened up and he found his rhythm.

The Barghast girl jogged along beside him. 'You are Dal Hon?' she asked, grinning.

'Yes.'

'They say you are good warriors, you Dal Hon. We must fight sometime.'

Fight? Ahh – *fight*. He eyed her sidelong: heavier than he usually liked, but that was a promising grin. 'What's your name?'

'Tolat, of the Yellow Clay clan.'

'Suth.' He flicked his head to the two Wickans following, their eyes on the western skyline. 'What about those two?'

'Them?' Tolat shook her head. Her tangled mane swung in the wind. 'Too much like my brothers. But you . . . you are different. I like different.'

Wonderful. Some Barghast gal out to taste the world. Well . . . who was he to complain? The same could be said of him. 'Any time you want lessons, you just let me know.'

She let out a very unladylike braying laugh and punched his arm. 'Ha! I knew I would like you!'

'Quiet back there,' breathed the Adjunct.

Tolat made a face, but Suth did not. He remembered the solid iron grapnels clutching the stern of the Blue war galley, and the Adjunct swinging, severing each cleanly. And on the bridge, shields parted like cloth by that bright blade wrapped now in leather. He also recalled overhearing Goss mutter something while eyeing the young man: 'Damned Crimson Guard,' he'd said, as if it were a curse.

Crimson Guard? Some here claimed seeing them at the Battle of the Crossroads, where the new Emperor was victorious, but Suth wasn't sure he credited stories like that. Surely they were long gone by now . . . In any case, he was fully prepared to follow *this* one's orders.

Mid-morning they crossed the river. The Wickan youths held their bows and arrow bags high out of the water as they half drifted, half paddled across. Tolat and Suth followed suit. On the far shore they ran anew, now picking up the pace, eating as they went.

Night fell and still they hadn't caught sight of the Moranth column. They'd found the main west trader road and seen signs of a large force's passing; but still the Adjunct wanted confirmation, and so he pressed on into the dusk. Even the two Wickans, Loi and Newhorse, grimaced their pain when he'd signed for them to start off west anew.

Suth was beyond grimacing: his chest burned as if aflame, his legs were numb dead weights, even his vision swam. All his gods forgive him. Not one decent meal in weeks and now this? *Neethal Looru – the god that comes in the night whom no one has seen. Take me away from this!*

Tolat cuffed Suth on the back, grinning. 'Come now, Dal Hon. Show me what you can do!'

He was beginning to dislike that grin.

It was near the middle of the night before they sighted the Moranth. The reason became instantly obvious as they saw that the damned Blacks hadn't stopped. They obviously intended to march through till dawn and then probably through the next day as well – otherwise why bother stealing the night march? They meant to get as much room between themselves and Greymane's forces as they possibly could.

Suth and his fellow scouts were crouched in the dark amid the brittle brown stalks of a harvested field. Snow lay in patches.

The frozen ground numbed Suth's hands. The Adjunct gestured a withdrawal back behind the ridge of the hill.

Inside a crude shack, a harvest shelter, they sat together, watching the darkened surrounding fields. 'They aren't stopping,' the Adjunct said, blowing on his hands. No one disagreed. 'We'll rest here, then return.'

'I'd rather rest in that farmstead we passed,' Newhorse said.

'No – no distractions.'

Suth sympathized completely with Newhorse. In this run, more than a full day's march for any army, they'd come across occupied farmsteads, corralled cattle, a herd of sheep, even orchards. No scorching tactics of withdrawal and burn here. This country was rich and unspoiled.

'I smelled cooked meat . . .' the lean Wickan continued.

'I only smell your foul breath,' Tolat said.

The Adjunct raised a hand. 'Save it. Rest. I'll take first watch.'

Suth could barely hold himself erect; he lay down immediately, wondering what this Adjunct was made of to have run him into the ground – and then stand watch!

He was nudged awake what seemed the next instant. It was still dark, though close to dawn. Everyone was tense; Tolat was readying her bow while keeping the weapon down amid the grass. 'Something's up,' she breathed. Suth did not move because he immediately saw the Adjunct standing at the edge of the field.

'What is it?'

'Don't know. He just woke us, walked off.' She continued readying her gear. 'It's like he's listening.'

Squinting, he saw how the man clutched his blade, head cocked, before he came jogging back.

'I shouldn't have come. I've attracted . . . attention. We have to go.'

'What is it?' Newhorse asked.

'Just run.'

Suth set off as best he could but he hadn't recovered from yesterday's exertions. None of them had; their pace was much reduced. Only the Adjunct seemed unaffected. He often ran ahead, scanning the hillsides while the day brightened around them. A few farmers and herdsmen worked the fields. All fled when they caught sight of them. It appeared that some sort of evacuation had been imposed upon the population, but not all had complied.

Then Suth caught sight of shapes shadowing them through the fields: low, loping. Hounds. A great pack of beasts. Even as Suth saw them the Adjunct shouted, pointing to an outcrop of rock. They swerved, making for it. Charging the formation, the five set their backs to the thrusting rock face. The hounds burst from the fields all about them, closing. They came snarling, and Suth saw how foam lathered their mouths, their eyes rolling, white all round.

'Rabid!' he yelled, certain.

'Ancients take them!' Tolat answered and she snapped out her bedroll, wrapping it round an arm.

Suth had no time; he'd lost the chance to follow suit. He and the Wickans drew their long-knives. The Adjunct unwrapped his bright curved blade. The animals leapt upon them. Suth used his blades to parry slashing claws. Loi went down almost right away, missing a lunge and falling screaming. The hounds closed over him at once and his cries were cut off instantly. They flinched in, closing upon each other, pressed their backs to the cliff wall. Tolat chanted some sort of war song as she stabbed, rammed her blanketed arm into open maws. Newhorse stabbed as well, using the point to force the hounds away. Suth followed suit. The Adjunct waded in using the tulwar blade one-handed, a long-knife in the other, taking the fight to the hounds. They lunged but he met them full-on, severing heads, limbs, torsos. Two clamped their teeth into him, an arm and a leg; he swung the gleaming tulwar to sever their heads.

Then the animals suddenly ran, yelping, skittering and falling in their desperation to flee. The four stood still, listening, only their harsh breaths sounding in the night. Suth felt his limbs quivering their anticipation . . . some *thing* was coming. They could all feel it.

Argent flame burst to life in a pillar of roaring, blinding, coruscating power. Suth flinched away. He covered his eyes with an arm, squinting. He could just make out a shape within the searing brilliance, a woman's outline.

The Adjunct struck a ready stance, weapons raised.

'Greetings, Outlander,' a woman's voice whispered, jarringly sweet in tone, yet coiling with venom. 'The stink of that sorceress bitch is upon you. Where came you by this blade of yours? Was it a gift . . . from *her*?'

Suth could barely stand: the voice itself hammered at him like blows. It gnawed at his thoughts like acid.

The lashing flames drew closer yet the Adjunct did not retreat. 'Who are you, man? What land are you from? There is a strangeness in your blood. I smell it. Perhaps . . . I should taste it . . .' Suth shouted a useless warning as high above a lash of flames whipped up to come slashing down. The Adjunct did not wait for it. He rolled forward into the pillar, swinging his bright blade two-handed across the maelstrom.

A blast like an eruption of Moranth munitions blew Suth backwards off his feet. He rolled tumbling to strike the stones at the base of the outcrop and lay dazed.

Suth did not think he'd lost consciousness. He remembered staring at the overcast sky watching snowflakes come floating down to tangle in his eyelashes. He blinked his eyes, rubbed an ear where ringing deafened him. Groaning, he levered himself to his feet. Gods, that reminded him of the blasts that took the wall of Aamil. He staggered forward to find the Adjunct. He found Tolat with him, his head on her lap.

'Is he alive?' Suth asked, or thought he did; he couldn't hear his own voice.

She shrugged, mouthed something.

'We have to get out of here!'

She stared up at him, uncomprehending. He mimicked picking up the Adjunct and moving. She nodded, then pointed behind him. He turned, alarmed, but it was Newhorse limping up. Blood gleamed down his torn shirt. Suth motioned to the man's wound; Newhorse pointed to Suth's head. He touched gingerly at his numb temple and came away with a smear of blood. *Damn stones!*

The Adjunct's scabbard was empty. Suth cast about and eventually found the blade lying amid burned stalks. It still smoked. Using a fold of leather, he picked it up and shoved it back into its scabbard. *Had he killed this 'Lady' they were all going on about? Probably not.*

He and Tolat carried the Adjunct while Newhorse scouted ahead as best he could. It took them a day and a night to reach the Ancy, and there they were defeated. They could not cross. All they could do was stay hidden and keep watch for any foraging or scouting parties on the far side of the river whose attention they could attract.

The Adjunct never really recovered. He babbled in a foreign tongue, sweated and shivered in some sort of fever. Eventually Tolat, who could at least claim to have swum before, argued she should go ahead for help. Suth and Newhorse agreed that was better than waiting to be seen. So before dawn Tolat waded out into the frigid Ancy and pushed off, disappearing from sight amid the chop and froth of the swift current. Suth collected some water and returned to the copse where they hid from any Roolian patrols.

*

It just so happened that Devaleth was up already when word reached her that one – *one!* – of the Adjunct's party had finally returned. She went as swiftly as she could to the High Fist's tent. Had it been an ambush by Roolian scouts? Had they been detected by the Moranth? Or was it this new mage she'd been sensing? Somehow the man could act without raising the Lady's ire. All along something had bothered her about sending Kyle; the prospect had troubled her but she hadn't spoken up during the meeting. Now she wondered.

A guard raised the opened flap and she saw the female scout, soaked to the bone, standing before the High Fist. Fist Rillish sat to one side, pale but intent.

'By the gods, let the woman sit!' Devaleth burst out before thinking.

'I'd rather stand, thank you, High Mage,' the woman managed, her voice a croak.

'As you choose, Tolat,' said Greymane. Aside, to an aide, he said, 'You have that?'

'Yes, sir. A copse a few hours north. They should see us.'

'Only one squad should approach the river,' Greymane warned. 'We don't want to attract any attention.'

'Sir!' gasped the scout Tolat, wavering on her feet.

'Yes?'

'That's just what the Adjunct said, sir. Attracting attention . . . that he did . . . attract . . .'

Devaleth took the woman's arm; she peered at her confused, her eyes glazed. Her weight shifted on to Devaleth, who grunted, suddenly having to support her. Two other aides took Tolat from the mage and carried her out.

'Of course,' breathed Rillish from his chair. 'I should have seen it . . . that sword of his. It must have attracted the— *Her* attention.'

Greymane turned on the man. 'So only now you think of that, Fist Rillish *Jal Keth*.'

'Sir!' Devaleth called out, dragging the High Fist's attention from Rillish. 'We *all* missed that. If anyone is to blame, it is me. I should have foreseen it.'

For the first time Devaleth felt the full force of the High Fist's furious ice-blue gaze and she was shaken by the feyness churning there just below the surface. Then the man somehow mastered himself, swallowing, drawing a great shuddering breath, and nodded at her words. 'Yes . . . you are right. Yes.' He turned away, drew a hand across his face. 'I missed it too.' And he laughed. 'I! Of anyone, I should have thought of that!'

She thought then of the grey blade the man had once carried. Said to have been a weapon of great power. It was responsible for his name in these lands: *Stonewielder.* And that name a curse. What had happened to it? No one spoke of it, and she'd yet to see anything more than a common blade at the man's side. He must have lost it during all the intervening years.

'Kyle is wounded – attacked by the Lady,' Greymane told Devaleth. 'Can you heal him?'

She thought little of her chances but she nodded. 'I'll get ready. Send him to my tent.'

The High Fist nodded and Devaleth bowed, exiting.

Greymane turned to a staff officer. 'Spread the word. We attack at dawn.'

The woman's brows climbed her forehead. 'But it *is* dawn . . . sir.'

'Exactly.' He gestured to the tent flap. The woman almost fell in her scramble to leave.

Rillish pushed himself to his feet. 'I'll ready my armour then, High Fist.'

Greymane had gone to the rear of the tent, thrown open a travelling chest. He studied the Fist as if seeing him there for the first time. 'No. You stay here.'

Rillish's face twisted as he fought to control his reaction. 'Then . . . who will lead the assault?' he asked, his voice as brittle as glass.

The High Fist slammed an iron barrel helm on to the table. He set a hand atop it, and his eyes burned with a bright blue flame. '*I will.*'

*

Rillish went to Devaleth's tent to await delivery of the Adjunct. He eased himself down into a chair and said to the Marese water-witch, 'Thank you for your support.'

The woman was readying pots and cloths. 'Certainly,' she replied, distracted. 'The man is too harsh. Too unforgiving.'

'He is a storied commander . . .' he began.

'With much to prove?' she suggested, peering over a shoulder.

'. . . for whom men and women will fight. But, yes, there is a history there. A history I was a part of.'

Turning, wiping her hands on a cloth, the stocky woman eyed him. 'You need not wait here. There's nothing you can do. As,' and she sighed, 'I suspect there will be nothing I can do, either.' She waved to the open flaps. 'Go on.'

He offered her an ironic courtier's bow, then, straightening, he waved to a guard. 'Bring my armour.'

Too weak to walk steadily, Rillish ordered a horse. Armoured, with the help of two grooms, he mounted. He felt much better sitting well supported between the tall cantle and the pommel. He hooked his helmet on the latter and eased on his gauntlets. The day was overcast and cool. Good weather for a protracted engagement – though he doubted Greymane had any patience for such. He regarded the bridge and the column of heavies jamming it, all eager to press forward, and frowned. He signed to a messenger. 'Bring me the saboteur lieutenant.'

'Aye, Fist.'

He kneed his mount to start it walking down to the bridge. Not much later a mud-spattered gangly woman jogged up to his guards and pushed her way through. She gaped up at him, grinning with snaggled discoloured teeth, and her bulging eyes appeared to stare in two directions at once. 'You asked f'r me, Fist?'

Oh yes, Lieutenant Urfa – once met, never forgotten. 'Yes, Lieutenant. The bridge . . . should it be so . . . burdened?'

The woman squinted at the structure. She turned her head to stare first with one eye, then the other. Then she burst out with a string of the most unladylike curses Rillish had ever heard and charged off down the slope without even saluting. Rillish watched her go, and leaned forward on his pommel, sighing. 'Send word to Captain Betteries – no more than four abreast across the bridge.'

'Aye, Fist.' Another staffer charged away.

Gods! Did he have to tell them not to jump up and down too? Just what they needed, collapsing the bridge now after all this time. He saw an unattached lieutenant, a messenger. 'Where is the High Fist?'

'At the barriers, sir, organizing the assault.'

'I see. He's waiting for sufficient troops, I suppose?'

'Yes. I believe so, Fist. You have a communiqué?'

'No. We shan't bother him.'

He and his guards had reached the jam of infantry choking the bridge mouth. Swearing under his breath, Rillish kneed his mount forward, shouldering the armoured men and women aside. 'Captain Betteries!' he shouted.

'On the bridge, sir,' a sergeant answered from the press, saluting. 'Held up a touch.'

Rillish sawed his reins ruthlessly to stand his mount across the bridge mouth, blocking it. 'You! Sergeant . . . ?'

'Ah. Sergeant Tight, sir.'

Tight? Oh well . . . Rillish pointed to his horse. 'Form up your squad here – four abreast!'

'Aye, sir.'

Tensing his legs, Rillish rose up high in his saddle to bellow so loud and with such force that his vision momentarily blackened: 'Next squad form up behind!' Weaving, he grasped hold of the pommel.

A hand steadied him from behind – Captain Betteries. Rillish nodded to the officer, who acknowledged the thanks and then turned to the soldiers. 'Scouts we sent across report they have livestock on the other side!' he shouted. 'Full larders. Even beer.'

Sergeant Tight rubbed at his tearing eyes. 'Bless 'em.'

'But no one advances until we're all formed up right and proper!'

'Aye, sir!' came the shouted response. The captain turned back to Rillish.

'My apologies, Fist,' he murmured, his face pale.

'Quite all right. Something of a whim this . . . deciding to cross today.'

A fierce smile from the company commander. 'Yes. Good day for a walk.'

'Sergeant,' Rillish called over the shouting and barked orders.

'Aye, Fist?'

'A word of advice. If you ever make Fist grade, change your name.' And he kneed his mount out of the way, leaving the man behind frowning and scratching his head.

Captain Betteries held back the press with his bared sword. He waited until the mass that already jammed the length of the bridge had filed across, then allowed on one squad at a time. Rillish scanned the far shore. The Roolians had raised barricades – overturned wagons, heaped logs and stones. Greymane had his forces forming up short of the barriers, waiting.

The Roolians were also forming up. More and more of their forces were converging. This assault held the promise of eventually embroiling all combatants from both sides. Greymane, he imagined, would not withdraw or let up until he'd broken through – perhaps even if it meant fighting on into the night. Rillish cast about and found a messenger. 'For Captain Betteries. Have a quarter of our forces held back.'

The messenger saluted and ran off.

Shortly later the man returned, saluting. 'Compliments of Captain Betteries, Fist. He responds – a quarter of our forces? That would be the sick-list.'

Damn Soliel! True enough. They don't have the resources. It's today, or never.

A great thundering animal roar of rage swelled then from the barriers and the Fourth Army arose at the command of a giant of a man in banded iron armour raising two swords, and charged.

*

Suth could not believe his eyes and ears as he stumbled along the east shore of the Ancy, far behind his rescuers. Columns crowded the bridge, horns sounded orders, and already there was clashing at the barriers on the west shore. They were attacking! And it was happening without him!

Once they'd been helped across the Ancy, Suth had waved the squad on: they were burdened enough carrying the still unconscious Adjunct and Newhorse, who was too weak to walk. He could make it on his own. Waving good luck, the rescuers had jogged off, leaving him to follow as best he could.

Now they were attacking without him! And he exhausted and without his armour. He was never going to live this down. Footsore, his head throbbing, he went to find his gear.

*

Devaleth thanked the squad that had carried in the Adjunct, yet wasted no time in hurrying them out. Closing the flaps, she turned to the young man lying on the pallet. It was far worse than she'd imagined. She cut away the leather and cloth around savage bites in thigh and arm – already they festered. A compound of leaves steeped in a tincture that cleaned wounds went on those. As to his mind – she pressed a hand to his hot brow and reached out, ever so tentatively, to his thoughts, then yanked her hand away as if stung.

Chaos and confusion, yes, but not shattered. Astounding. His mind ought to be irrevocably crushed – so much so that it would be a mercy to let him slip away. Perhaps it was because the man was no mage. No *talent*, as they said among these Malazans. Not *cursed*, as she'd say herself.

Yet . . . something else. Something deeper, more troubling. Her brow furrowing, she bent closer to the man's eyes. Reaching, she lifted one lid with a finger then flinched away. *Ancient One protect her! For an instant . . . but no. Impossible. It must have been the light. That could* not *have been an amber glow.*

*

They'd left his gear at their camp. Wincing and hissing his pain, he pulled on his long padded gambeson then laced up his hauberk and grieves. Helmet high on his head, he limped down to the bridge. A mounted officer, an unattached lieutenant acting for Command, thundered past then reared, halting.

'What are you doing here?' he demanded.

Suth saluted. 'Just returned from scouting up north, sir.'

The officer grunted, accepting this. 'You're wounded.'

Suth wiped his face, finding a layer of flaking dried blood. 'It's nothing, sir. I can fight . . .'

'Report to the infirmary.'

'Sir, no. I—'

'*No?*' The officer wheeled his mount to face him directly. 'I *order* you to the infirmary!'

Suth bit his tongue. *Fuck! Should've just saluted, dumbass!* 'Yes . . . sir.'

Nodding a warning, the officer kicked his mount and raced off, dirt flying. Suth glared at the ash-grey overcast sky then headed for the infirmary tents.

*

Envoy Enesh-jer watched the engagement from a narrow window in the top floor of the Three Sisters stone tower. Some time ago he'd summoned the field commander, Duke Kherran, and now impatiently awaited the man's arrival.

Far later than he expected, the man appeared, helmet in hand, cloak dragging in dirt behind. His round moon face gleamed with sweat. Mud spattered his fine mail and Roolian brown surcoat. 'With all due respect, Envoy, it is unadvisable to summon me from the—'

'*Duke Kherran!*' Enesh-jer cut in. 'Last I knew I was the Overlord's chosen and so you shall treat me as such.'

Stiffening, the Duke clamped his lips shut. He knelt on one knee, bowed, then straightened.

Enesh-jer nodded. 'That is better. Now . . . I have been watching the engagement and I am rather surprised to see that our lines have in fact retreated. Why is that, Duke, when I gave strict orders that these invaders were to be swept from the bridge?'

The Duke blinked at Enesh-jer, utterly at a loss. At last he cleared his throat and said, 'Of course, Envoy. I will see to it myself.'

'Good. Do so. And Duke . . .' Enesh-jer bent closely to him. 'If you cannot fulfil my expectations then remember – there are many others here awaiting their chance.'

Duke Kherran bowed again, his face held rigid. 'Envoy.' He marched out. Enesh-jer eyed the mud the man had tramped into the room, his mouth sour, then returned to the window.

Behind him the thick doors swung closed and the lock rattled shut. The Envoy whirled round. 'Hello? Is someone there?'

A man all in black stepped out from behind a display of carved ivory icons of the Lady. He was quite short and he smiled with small pointed teeth. The Envoy backed away. The man plucked an icon from a shelf, studied it. 'You remember enough, don't you, Enesh-jer, to know who I am.'

The Envoy reached behind him to touch a wall, pressed his back to it. 'I will call for the guards.'

The man waved the icon towards the entrance. 'Those doors are built to resist a siege.'

The Envoy raised his chin, ran a hand down the front of his robes, straightening their folds. 'I am not afraid to die. The Lady will welcome me.'

'A true believer.' The man tossed the icon over a shoulder to shatter on the flagstones. The Envoy winced. 'You come across them . . . now and then.' The man walked to one of the slit windows, peered out. 'Ah! He's broken through. Took him longer than I thought.' He offered a wink. 'Guess he's out of practice.'

Enesh-jer slid along the wall to a window, glanced out. His face paled even further. It was the invaders who had broken through. Leading the charge came an armoured giant. Even as the Envoy watched, the man heaved aside an overturned cart, knocked soldiers from their feet with raking blows.

'In a rare fury, he is,' the assassin commented.

'Both his swords are broken,' Enesh-jer said, wonder in his voice.

'Breaks all his swords, he does.' The man glanced at him again and bared his pointed teeth. 'All 'cept one.'

The Envoy raised a hand to clutch at his throat. 'No. I refuse to believe it. *Lies*.'

The little man's smile was a leer. 'Yes, it's him. Your old friend, Greymane. I hear he carries a grudge for all you betrayers. Voted to oust him, didn't you?'

Enesh-jer was shaking his head in denial. 'Yeull would have told me.'

'Or not.' The man leaned back against the window slit. 'Question is then . . . do I kill you or not? Who's it going to be? Me or him?'

The Envoy straightened, adjusted his rich silver-threaded robes yet again, jerked his chin to the assassin. 'You.'

The man smiled. Long thin daggers slid into his hands. 'Good.'

*

Devaleth reached the end of her options quite quickly with the wounded Adjunct. She'd cleaned the wounds as best she could and studied the man to diagnose what afflicted him. The problem was that what had happened to him was far beyond her own quite minor expertise. Some sort of fever coursed through his blood, probably inflicted by the animal bites. As to what his contact with the apparition of the Lady might have done to his mind – she had no hope of ameliorating that.

Someone spoke from the front of the tent. 'Mage of Ruse. May I enter?'

She straightened, reached out to her Warren. 'Who are you?'

'I am Carfin, of the Synod of Stygg.'

The Synod of Stygg? She'd thought that mere legend, stories. An association of mages who met despite the Lady's best efforts to stamp them out. She relaxed, slightly, calling out, 'You may enter.'

'My thanks.'

Devaleth flinched, spinning: the mage had spoken behind her.

He was tall and skeletally thin, wearing tattered dark finery: trousers, vest and shirt. Arms clasped behind his back, he was studying the Adjunct. 'You seek to heal him.'

'Yes.'

'We in the Synod agree that he must be healed. Certain of us foresee a role for him.'

'A role? In what?'

His gaze had not left the Adjunct. He pursed his lips distastefully. 'This one is foreign indeed.'

'What do you mean? Foreign – how?'

'Unfortunately . . . what ails him cannot be treated in any mundane way.'

She let out a long breath. 'I see.'

He lowered his head to study her from under his stringy black hair. 'Yes. One or both of us must access our Warren.'

'Ah.' And bring down the Lady upon them. They may heal the Adjunct, but then one or both of them would be dead or no better off than the Adjunct was now. 'I don't know if I'm ready for that.'

'No one is,' said someone from the flaps and both Carfin and Devaleth jumped sideways to regard the newcomer. He was an older man, bearded, in battered, travel-stained clothes.

'Totsin?' Carfin said, his gaze narrowed. 'What in the name of the ancients are you doing here?'

The man entered, pulling the flaps closed behind him. 'I've come to see what I can do here.'

Carfin returned his gaze to the Adjunct. 'Well. Damned late, but welcome, I suppose.'

The man, Totsin, bowed to Devaleth. 'Mage of Ruse. Not many of the Marese have joined the invaders, I presume?'

Devaleth offered him a thin smile. 'Not many. You are with this Synod?'

'From very far back, yes.' He gestured to the Adjunct. 'What do you intend?'

'He must be healed by Warren.'

'Ah . . .'

Devaleth nodded. 'Yes.'

'Who?' Totsin asked.

'We are . . . considering,' Carfin answered. He sniffed the Adjunct and wrinkled his nose. 'Terribly foreign.'

Totsin smoothed his greying beard. 'If it must be done, then, well, no option to flee exists for me. As to our host, well, we are not at sea . . .'

Carfin cocked his head, looking like a tall emaciated crow. 'You are suggesting . . . ?'

The older man raised his hands in a helpless shrug. 'Well – if now is the time to commit fully, as the Synod appears to have voted . . .'

The tall mage ran a hand down the edge of the pallet, the other going to his chest. 'True enough, Totsin. Though coming from you that is a surprise.'

Devaleth cast a look between the two. 'What are you getting at?' she demanded.

Totsin bowed. 'Carfin here is a mage of Darkness – Rashan, I believe the Malazans name it.'

'I see.' So, Carfin could heal the Adjunct then flee into the Warren of Rashan, hoping to shake off the Lady. Seemed straightforward enough. 'Yet . . . you are reluctant . . . you fear the Lady's attack, of course . . .'

Carfin was shaking his head, almost blushing. *The man's not afraid – he actually looks embarrassed!* He cleared his throat. 'Unlike Ruse, madam, we here under the thumb of the Lady rarely dare to exercise our, ah, talent. The truth is – though I know how to do it – I have never actually *entered* Rashan . . .'

Oh. Oh dear.

'And so having entered . . .' Carfin continued, 'I have no way of knowing whether I'll ever be able to *return* – if you see the dilemma.'

'Yes,' Devaleth breathed. She touched his arm. 'I understand fully.' She regarded Totsin. 'What of you? You seem ready enough to push others forward.'

He raised his hands apologetically. 'My talents run in, ah, other directions.'

The tall pale mage took Devaleth's hand, kissed the back of it. 'Madam, it is of no concern. I will do this. It is something I should have done long ago, in any case.' He looked to the older man. 'Totsin. My thanks. You, of all of us, stepping forward has emboldened me. My thanks.'

The older mage was dragging his fingers through his ragged beard, his gaze fixed on the Adjunct. 'Yes. Now is certainly the time to act.'

'You should both wait outside.'

Devaleth nodded. She clasped the man's hands in hers. 'My thanks.' He bowed very formally.

Outside, Devaleth focused on emptying her mind of all concern for what was going on within. She turned her back to watch the engagement on the far shore. It appeared that the infantry, even with the aid of Greymane, had yet to break through. Just as before. Too narrow a front to assault. And they were all so weak – famished, sick.

Totsin had walked off to one side and was kicking at the dirt, hands clasped at his front.

Though Devaleth was prepared for it subconsciously, the sudden levelling of the Lady's awareness and ferocity left her staggered. Behind her the tent cloth billowed and tore as if a silent explosion of munitions had been unleashed within. One pole yanked free, falling crooked. She sent an alarmed glance to Totsin, who had turned, his gaze hooded. He raised his thin shoulders in a shrug.

She closed on the tent while making a strong effort to withhold any sensing outwards. 'Carfin?' she called. No one answered. She edged aside the cloth, peered into the darkness. 'Carfin?' Totsin entered after her. She found the Adjunct as before: lying supine, undisturbed. But he was alone and her possessions had been reduced to wreckage. Either the Lady had snapped up the mage of Darkness, or he had escaped. Made his own leap of faith.

She quickly laid a hand upon the young Adjunct's brow, let out a long breath of relief. 'The fever has lessened. His mind is . . . calm. He sleeps.'

'He actually did it,' Totsin mused from the entrance. 'I am astonished.'

Something in the mage's manner irked Devaleth. 'You should be grateful.'

'And . . . he is gone.' The man studied her now, hands loose at his sides. 'What of you, mage of Ruse? It must be hard – being so far from the open sea, from the source of your power.'

Searching for a clean cloth and water, Devaleth said, distracted, 'I do not have to be on the sea to call upon it.'

'Ah. Yet you are weakened, yes? By such separation?'

She looked up from digging among the scattered pots and boxes to where he stood at the entrance, his eyes oddly bright in the gloom. 'Whatever do you mean?'

The man appeared about to say something. He raised his hands to her.

Then someone threw open the tent flap behind him.

*

Suth sat in the grass outside a tent in the infirmary area waiting to be seen by one of the bonecutters who had been sent along with the expeditionary force. Personally, he had no faith in them, though he understood the use of herbs and poultices and such to cure sicknesses and fever and cleanse wound-rot. He also accepted the need to drain the black-blood that can sometimes come to even the smallest cuts. All these mundane healings and procedures he would grudgingly go along with – all except head wounds. From what he'd seen growing up on the Dal Hon plains, head wounds were a mystery to everyone, even these self-professed healers. They'd prescribe the strangest things, from temple-bashings to drilling holes in the skull to remove 'pressure'.

He swore that if they tried anything like that he'd be out of the tent quicker than shit from one of these gut-sick soldiers around him. From the fighting across the river a great roar reached him and he bolted upright. There appeared to be movement at the front; a break-through? Dammit! And he was stuck here!

A man joined him. His shirt-front was sodden, blood dripping to the ground, and he was wiping his hands on a dirty rag. 'What is it?' the fellow asked.

'Might be an advance.'

A grunt and the man eyed him up and down. 'What in Togg's name are you doing here?'

Suth pointed to his head. 'Fell on a rock.'

'You can walk, talk – you're fine. Bugger off. There's enough to handle.'

Suth jerked a salute. 'Yes, sir!' He dashed down the slope.

On his way to the bridge he noticed the High Mage's tent. It leaned drunkenly aside, the cloth torn in places as if it had been attacked. *Where they said they were taking the Adjunct!* He ran for the tent.

He threw open the flap and an old man he'd never seen before turned upon him. The fellow gestured, his mouth opening. Suth reacted automatically and his sword leapt to the man's throat.

The man snapped his mouth shut. 'It's all right, trooper!' a woman called from within. 'Relax.' The High Mage came forward, pushing the sagging cloth out of her way.

Suth inclined his head. 'High Mage.' He sheathed his sword.

'*High Mage* . . .' the man breathed, something catching in his voice.

'Honorary only,' she told him.

He touched a quavering hand to his throat, said, 'Perhaps I had best be going.'

'If you must,' the High Mage answered, her gaze narrow.

'Yes. In case *she* should return. Until we meet again, then,' and he bowed.

The High Mage lowered her head ever so slightly. 'Until then.'

The man gave Suth a wide berth and walked off down the slope. Suth watched him go, then remembered why he'd come. 'The Adjunct – how is he?'

The High Mage pulled her gaze from the retreating figure. A frown turned into a smile, her plump cheeks dimpling. 'I believe he is well, trooper. I do believe he will recover.'

Suth let out a great breath. 'My thanks, High Mage.'

'Don't thank me. Though perhaps I should thank you,' she added musingly.

'I'm sorry, High Mage?'

'Nothing. Now, no doubt you wish to return to the fighting, yes?'

'Yes.'

'Very well.' She shooed him away. 'Go, go.'

Bowing, Suth turned and ran down the slope as best he could. He jogged, hand on his helmet, wincing where it dug into his wound, and he wondered whether he should have told the High Mage that for an instant he could have sworn he'd seen murder in that fellow's eyes. But that was not something you would mention to a High Mage based upon a fleeting impression, was it? Not if you didn't want to make a lot of trouble for yourself. And he'd already missed enough of the damned fighting.

*

The Malazan guards posted at the doors to the Envoy's chambers saluted and stood aside for Greymane. He entered, pulling off his helm, which he slammed down on a convenient table, scattering icons and small reliquary boxes. He pulled off his bloodied gauntlets and scanned the room. A man dressed all in black – black trousers, black cotton shirt, and black vest – sat in a plush chair, smoking. Something that might be a body lay on the floor, hidden under a rich silk bedsheet.

Greymane slapped the gauntlet into his helm, then pulled a white scarf draped over a tall statue of the Lady and wiped away the sweat sheathing his face and the blood smearing his hands. 'How many more of you are there, hidden away like lice?' he asked.

The man smiled, revealing tiny white teeth. 'I'm more of a freelance.'

The High Fist only exhaled noisily through his nostrils. He raised his chin to the body. 'Is this him?'

'In the flesh.'

Still wiping his hands, Greymane used a muddied boot to pull the cloth away. He stared at the pale face for some time. 'Enesh-jer,' he breathed.

'You knew him?'

The High Fist scowled at the question. 'Yes. I knew him well enough.'

The man was studying his thin kaolin pipe. 'What do you want done with him?'

Greymane stared down at the body for a time. 'I used to want that head on a pike. Now, I don't care. Burn him with the rest.'

The man coughed slightly, covering his mouth. He eyed the High Fist anew. 'These Roolians don't burn their dead. They bury them.'

'We don't have the time.' He tossed the bloodied scarf on to the body. 'See to it.'

The man offered a vague bow as the High Fist picked up his helm and stalked out. He sat for a time, tapping the pipe in a palm, frowning.

* * *

Ivanr chose to walk rather than riding in the large two-wheeled cart that had carried Beneth. The conveyance was his now, holding the tent and brazier and few simple goods belonging to the spiritual leader of the Army of Reform. He'd set aside his sword and armour, wearing instead layered plain clothes and a cloak against the winter. He used a walking stick, yes, but other than a shortsword hidden under his cloak he appeared weaponless. His self-appointed bodyguard surrounded him as before, but at a greater, more respectful – and less visible – distance.

Walking in this manner he felt he now had a much better feel for the army. Infantry, men and women, would call out or bow for his attention and he would listen to their comments. Often they were only looking for reassurance that they were doing the right thing – a reassurance he had no reservations in providing. As the days passed he saw an ever greater need for such comfort . . . or, dare he say, *hope*. Was this the great secret of leading any revolution? That really all anyone needed was the assurance, the *faith*, that they were doing the right thing? At least Ivanr felt in his heart that their goal was desirable. Perhaps that was all *he* needed.

At night Martal, and sometimes the cavalry commander Hegil, visited after the evening meal. These informal command meetings were quiet and uncomfortable, the memory of Beneth still too raw. Mainly Ivanr asked Martal questions about the strategic aim of the campaign. Apparently this amounted to marching on Ring and defeating the Imperial Army before its walls.

'Very . . . ambitious,' was Ivanr's comment. 'You know you will be facing the flower of the Jourilan aristocracy. Hundreds of heavy cavalry who fight with lance and sword. They will mow down these pike formations just by weight and shock.'

'They may,' Martal allowed.

'What of you, Hegil? You know what we'll be facing.'

The aristocrat leaned back on the cushions, sipped his cup of honeyed tea. The man was nearly bald, his hair all rubbed off from wearing his helmet for most of his adult life. 'Yes, Ivanr. These won't be lights, or lancers. But we've known what it would come down to. From the beginning Beneth knew. He and Martal worked up a strategy to support the pike squares.'

'And that is?' He regarded Martal.

Her short black hair gleamed with sweat and oil. She shrugged, her mouth turned down. 'We'll be bringing our own fortress.'

He eyed her, waiting for more, but she would not raise her gaze. Was this all he was to get? Should he push now, in front of Hegil? She may think nothing of outright refusing him . . . Very well. He'd wait. Push again tomorrow.

Soon after that Hegil cleared his throat, and, bowing to Ivanr, left for his own tent. Martal rose as well. 'Please,' Ivanr invited. 'Won't you stay a little longer?'

She nodded stiffly, but sat. He studied her more closely now while she kept her gaze averted: her smashed nose, the scars of sword cuts on her forearms and the marks of heavy blunt blows to her cheek. Where had this woman gained her military training? Surely not in any Jourilan school, nor among the Dourkans. Yet she had obviously seen fighting all her life.

'You are not of Fist, or Jasston, or Katakan. Where are you from?'

A smile of nostalgia touched her mouth, but she was still looking away when she spoke. 'I was born in a minor city named Netor on the Bloorian plains.'

'Bloor . . . ?'

'I am Quon Talian by birth. What you would call Malazan.'

Ivanr did not know how to react. All the gods! Should this get out . . . No wonder the distance. The air of mystery surrounding this Black Queen served a good purpose. 'I'm . . . amazed,' he managed.

She was the enemy. The grasping foreigners who would steal this land from them – or so ran the common wisdom.

'How came you . . .' But of course.

She was nodding. 'Yes. The invasion. I grew up the daughter of a minor landholder on the border with a neighbouring country. There were always raids and clashes for control of territory. I experienced my first battle – seven of them against five of us – when I was thirteen. Shortly after that I ran away to join the Imperial Army. I was a captain with the Sixth Army when we landed on Fist.'

'And you . . . deserted?'

If the woman was offended, she did not show it. Her expression turned more grim as she studied the far tent wall. 'You've heard the stories, haven't you? Greymane, Stonewielder, denounced by Malazan Command. Betraying the army, or some such nonsense.'

Or consorting with the Stormriders to undermine the Korelri.

She shrugged. 'In any case, I was too vocal in my support for him. When he was ousted I had to flee, or face the knife.' She shrugged again. 'That's about it. I wandered, was unable to find transport out of the subcontinent. An attempt to travel south overland brought me to Beneth. And he saved my life.'

'I see,' Ivanr breathed. What more could one say to such a tale? *Dear gods, are you no more than manipulators of chance and fate?* No wonder so far her tactics had defeated the Jourilan. Ivanr knew his own land was too tradition-bound in its methods, too tied to known ways of doing things. This woman came trained in a tradition infamous for its pragmatic embrace of the unconventional. These Malazans would adapt whatever worked; and in Ivanr's eyes that was to be admired, even though such flexibility and adaptation served them ill here in these lands – leaving them Malazan in name and no more.

Martal bowed and left soon after, and Ivanr let her go. He set the revelation far back in his mind – no hint could be given to anyone – and part of him, the tactician, couldn't help but admire how in a single stroke the admission, the intimacy of the secret, had entirely bought his trust.

And he tried not to dwell on the conversation until word came to the Army of Reform of a second Malazan invasion.

Some days later a runner summoned Ivanr to the command tent. There he found Martal and lesser officers, including Carr, now a captain, cross-examining a sweaty and exhausted citizen.

'What evidence was there?' Martal was asking.

The man, dressed like a common labourer, blinked, uncertain. 'No evidence, Commander. Everyone agreed, though. The entire ship's company was alive with the news. Malazan vessels had broken the Mare blockade.'

Ivanr looked sharply at Martal. The woman did not glance at him.

'Ship's company? How many?' another officer asked.

'Over two hundred, sir.'

'And they were all in agreement?'

The man blushed. 'I did not question all. But everyone was talking at once on the pier and none contradicted or disagreed with the others. All carried the same news.'

'And this vessel came from Stygg?' Carr asked.

'Yes, sir. From Shroud. Everyone said they saw signs of Stygg readying for invasion.'

Someone else entered behind Ivanr and all the officers stared, quietening. Ivanr turned: it was the mage, Sister Gosh, in her layered muddied skirts, shawls and stringy iron-grey hair. Martal raised a hand. 'It is all right. She is welcome.'

'The news is true,' Sister Gosh said. 'A second Malazan invasion.'

Martal glared at the old woman. 'Everyone out,' she grated. The officers filed out. Sister Gosh and Ivanr remained. Once they were alone, Martal ground out, 'You knew.'

'Oh, yes. But you wouldn't have believed me. Yeull, the Overlord, has managed to keep it quiet. But Malazan forces are marching upon him and a foreign fleet has entered Black Water Strait.'

Martal crossed to a table kept stocked with bread and cheese, meat, wine and tea, but she touched none of it, her back to them. 'That man, one of Beneth's agents in Dourkan, also mentioned certain – hardly credible – *rumours* about who was leading this invasion . . .'

'Yes,' Sister Gosh said softly, her expression softening. 'They are true as well.'

The woman's head sank forward and she leaned much of her weight upon the table. Ivanr looked to the mage. 'Who? Who is it?'

Sister Gosh eased herself down on some cushions. 'I think we really could use some tea.' She looked to Ivanr, cocked a brow.

Ah. He went to the table and poured three small glasses. One he left with Martal, who had not moved, had not even acknowledged him. One he gave to Sister Gosh, and the last he sat with.

'The second invasion is led by the man who led the first,' Sister Gosh told him.

Ivanr's gaze snapped to Martal's rigid back. But that would mean . . . 'No. He was discredited, denounced. How could they reinstate him?' The very man Martal refused to condemn – at the cost of her career, almost her life. Stonewielder. The Betrayer, as the Korelri named him.

Still facing the tent wall, Martal spoke, her voice almost fey. 'The worship has been stamped out here in these lands, but we Malazans pay homage to chance, or fate, in the persona of twins. Oponn, the two-faced god of luck.' She shook her head. 'Who would have thought . . .'

'I believe Beneth did,' said Sister Gosh.

Martal turned and for a fleeting instant Ivanr caught something in her gaze, something like hope, or a desperate yearning, before the woman's usual cool hard mask reasserted itself and he felt a pang of disappointment. *I am no Beneth. To this woman there can be no other Beneth. Like her loyalty to her previous commander, this woman's devotion is hard won, but once given is never withdrawn.*

'How so?' she asked, crossing her arms and leaning back against the table.

Unlike so many others, Sister Gosh did not flinch under the commander's hard stare. 'Think of the timing. Beneth has been hiding in the mountains for decades, receiving pilgrims, freethinkers, all the disenfranchised and disenchanted, and sending them back out as his agents and missionaries all over the land, into every city, founding sects and congregations of brethren. Laying the groundwork, in short, for a society-wide revolution. Then, out of nowhere, unbidden, inconceivably, his priestess arrives to ignite firestorms of uprisings and outright insurrections all over Jourilan. Yet still Beneth does not act. He waits years. Why?'

Her gaze narrowed, Martal almost sneered, 'You are suggesting he was awaiting this second invasion?'

The old woman raised her shawl-wrapped shoulders. 'Think of it. Suddenly, this year, he descends from the safety of his mountain to bring a central organizing presence to this war and reform in Jourilan. Why this year? Perhaps in his visions he saw it.'

'Coincidence,' Martal scoffed.

'Coincidence?' Sister Gosh answered, a note of scolding in her voice. 'You who invoke Oponn?'

'Someone had to act,' Ivanr mused, almost to himself. 'The Priestess so much as told me she would not fight.'

A long silence followed that comment and Ivanr looked up, blinking. 'Yes?'

Both women were staring at him. 'You've *met* her?' they said in unison.

'Well, yes.'

'When—' began Sister Gosh.

'What did she say?' Martal demanded.

'She . . .' *Gods, she asked that I sit at her side . . . and I refused her!* He swallowed, shaken. 'She . . . told me . . . that is, she said she believed I was on the right path . . .' He rubbed at his suddenly hot and sweaty brow. 'She seemed to be . . .'

She believed I'd come to the path intuitively, she'd said. Laughing gods! She was trying to give me *reassurance!* He pressed a fold of cloth to his brow, cleared his throat.

'What was she like?' Sister Gosh asked.

Gods! What was she like? He daubed the cloth to his face, struggled to speak. 'She was young. Too young for what she'd experienced. On her hands, her thin arms, and body, there were scars of beatings. Of a life of hard manual labour. Of starvation. And there was blood, too, in her past. She'd done things that tormented her. I saw all this in her eyes. Heard it in her words . . .' His voice trailed away into nothing – he could bear no more.

'I didn't know,' he heard Martal say, quietly.

When he looked up they were gone and he was alone. He sat staring at nothing, suddenly desolate. How could he possibly . . . He was nothing! Wretched! Any comparison was laughable! A mockery! How *dare* he parade himself as her . . . as some sort of . . . no. Impossible. He should slink off into a hole.

And yet . . . she had come to him. She *chose* him. Should he not have faith – *faith! Gods, do not laugh!* – in her judgement? If he had confidence in her – and he did! He felt it – should he not then honour her choices?

But it was hard. Looking ahead he saw that embracing her path would be the most challenging, the most difficult calling he could ever take on. In its light everything he had done to date could only be seen as preparatory. So be it. Whether he was worthy or not was beside the point. Only in the doing can the measure be made, and then only in hindsight.

That task he would leave to others.

* * *

The storm was as violent as any Hiam had ever witnessed. Through driving sheets of sleet he watched rolling combers the size of mountains come crashing in like landslides. The reverberations of their impact shook even these stones here in the upper reaches of the Great Tower. The clouds massed so low it seemed the very Stormwall itself was blocking their passage, while above all the sapphire and emerald glow of the Riders rippled and danced. *It was as if they somehow knew. Could somehow sense this was their moment.*

The closest they might ever come.

But not victory. Never that. He would not allow that. She *might choose to test her instruments to their very limit . . . but they would not break.*

They would endure.

The heavy plank door to his apartments rattled and Hiam closed and barred the shutter on the storm. Quint entered, cloak wrapped tight about him, spear in one hand, helm in the other. He'd just come from the wall and Hiam noted how the lingering energies of the enemy sorcerers, the Wandwielders, glowed like an aura about the spear's keen tip. 'Wall Marshal. What brings you here this ill-favoured night?'

Quint pressed up close against the desk. His scarred face was clenched, the eyes darkened slits against the light of the chambers. 'Where is Alton?' he whispered. Hiam winced; he'd dreaded this moment, knowing it was unavoidable. He drew breath to speak but the Wall Marshal continued: 'Where is Gall? Longspear? Went?' Hiam raised a hand, nodding for silence, but the man ground on, his voice cracking: 'I can find them *nowhere.* No one knows where they've gone.' He set his helm on the desk and gripped the spear in tight, scarred fists, the knuckles white.

'I can answer that, Quint—' Hiam began, but was interrupted again.

'Section Marshal Courval is missing. A fifteen-season veteran on the wall. One of our best. He, too, has been *reassigned.* Lord Protector . . . *what have you done!*'

Hiam raised both hands. 'Calm yourself, Quint. I knew you would not agree and so I did not inform you. I acted on my own authority.'

'To do what?' He raised his chin to the window, the storm, and the sea, beyond. 'To weaken us *now*? In our time of greatest need?'

Hiam watched, fascinated, while that keen spear-tip edged down towards his chest. Strangely, he felt no fear. *I let the Lady decide – as she chooses.* 'You are right, Quint. They have all been pulled from the wall.'

'Where?' the man gasped, sounding close to weeping.

'An exchange, Quint. Overlord Yeull of Rool has promised ten thousand troops for one hundred Stormguard. Soldiers, Quint! Not starving, cringing prisoners or bullied conscripts. Trained fighting men.'

The man was shaking his head, his eyes swimming in tears. 'Ten . . . You fool . . . he is laughing at you right now. They've been invaded – *he'll never send any of them!*'

The spear was almost level now. *So, it is to be the blade for me, is it, Quint?* Hiam fought to keep his voice level. 'Then Courval will return. Do you really think those Roolians could stop a hundred Stormguard?'

The Wall Marshal took a shuddering breath. His arms quivered; and Hiam knew it was not with exhaustion. The blade tilted up a notch. 'No. No one in this entire region could stop them. Section Marshal Courval will see the impossibility of this exchange and he will return. And when he does . . .' The spear's butt slammed to the stones. 'We will have an assembly on your leadership, Hiam. I swear to that.'

Hiam inclined his head in assent. 'I agree, Wall Marshal. Until then.' He waited until Quint reached for the door, then spoke again. 'I have before me entries from your quartermaster clerks, Quint. Were you aware of Master Engineer Stimins' many requisitions?'

From the door the man grimaced his impatience. '*What?*'

'Monies for labourers. For tools, stone, chain, rope, and other such equipment?'

'What do I care for the man's stones and rope?'

'You should, Quint. If I were you I would be far more concerned about Stimins' continuing construction work than my, ah, *unorthodox* efforts to bolster our numbers.'

The Wall Marshal dismissed Hiam's words with a curt wave and slammed the door shut behind him.

Hiam sat for a time in the dim office. Beyond the shutters the wind howled and battered like a fiend struggling to break through. *You kept quiet about it, Stimins. I wouldn't have found out but for oh-so-conscientious Shool. Pray let it not be the foundation behind*

Wind Tower. What had been his words? We may have one hundred years – or one.

Poor Quint. Did he not see that should these desperate clutchings at straws fail, we will all be far too busy for a leadership review. Perhaps I should step down? Save him the trouble. It would be good to be facing them spear in hand again when . . .

But no. That is an unworthy thought. Forgive me, Blessed Lady! I mustn't give in to weakness. We will prevail as we always have. Too much rests upon our shoulders. The lives of every man, woman, and child of this region even unto the Ice Wastes rely upon us!

Hiam pressed his hands to his hot face and felt the wetness there at his eyes. *Forgive my weakness, Lady. Yea, though the shadow of doubt is upon me, I shall not waver . . .*

* * *

For some reason Shell hadn't anticipated that they would be split up. It was done expertly, with a brutal efficiency born of centuries of handling captives. Lazar had led their manacled file – either by chance or by design – while Shell followed, then Blues, and lastly Fingers. Their escort chivvied them up along a steep climb through a town whose bundled inhabitants hardly looked up from their daily tasks: just one more file of condemned on their way to an anonymous death upon the wall. They climbed to a fortress that squatted half sheltered under a rocky slope that rose even higher. Once inside the fortress they were pulled and pushed into a series of underground corridors. After much marching Shell was thoroughly lost and they had passed far into what seemed a great sprawling underground complex. Heavy bronze-bound doors led off the halls into tiny rooms, cells perhaps, and further corridors.

Without warning barred gates thrust across the narrow corridor they walked, separating Lazar at the front and Fingers at the rear. Lazar tensed to fight but a sharp sign from Blues stood him down, and he relaxed, reluctantly. The guards unlatched the big fighter from the chain gang and led him off down another corridor; the same was done to Fingers, who called after them: 'See you around!' Shell and Blues were left together for the moment until a Chosen soldier in his silvered blue-black armour and dark blue cloak unhitched Blues and led him off.

She was alone. After the Chosen escorting Blues up another corridor had disappeared, a regular local guard pulled at her blonde hair. 'You're for the wall, then,' he said, so close she could smell his foul breath. 'What a waste. How 'bout a last screw before you die? Hmm?'

She kneed him in the groin and he fell gasping. Before the rest of the escort could react she stomped on his upturned face, spraying blood all down his chest. Only then did they grab her arms and she allowed them to pull her away – that had been enough of a demonstration. Two of her escort remained behind to walk the injured guard to an infirmary, leaving only three to restrain her. She realized she could easily overpower these, but that was not her intent. She could hardly find Bars as a fugitive on the run. And so she meekly submitted to their amateurish cuffs and prodding.

Now she sat in a holding pen, fettered at the ankles, legs drawn up tight to her chest to help conserve her warmth. Lining both walls of the long narrow chamber were her putative co-combatants: a more surly and unimpressive lot she couldn't have imagined. Prisoners all, unwilling, uncooperative, more like those condemned to die by execution than fighting men and women who believed they possessed any chance for survival. Shell was mystified. With these tools the Chosen expected to defend the wall? They might as well throw these people off the top for all the difference it would make.

'Who here is a veteran?' she called out to the entire chamber. 'Anyone stood before?'

In the torchlit gloom eyes glittered as they shifted to her. A brazier in the centre of the room crackled and hissed in the silence. 'Who in the Lady's name are you?' someone shouted.

'Foreign bitch!'

'Malazan whore!'

A man who had been ladling out stew up and down the line knelt before her. 'There's no point,' he murmured as he dropped a portion of stew into a bowl at her feet.

'We'd have a better chance if we—'

'Chance? What chance is it you think most here have?' On his haunches he studied her, his gaze sympathetic. 'You are Malazan, yes?' She nodded. 'Already then they hate you. What's worse, you are a veteran, yes?' She nodded again, but puzzled now. 'So most here hate you even more. And why? Because already you stand a much greater chance of surviving than they – you see?'

'If we worked together we'd *all* stand a much greater chance.'

He shook his head. 'No. It does not work that way.'

His accent was strange to her. 'You're not from round here either.'

'No. I'm from south Genabackis.' He stood, motioned to a man apparently asleep two places down, older, with a touch of grey in his hair. 'Ask him how it works.'

'Thank you – what's your name?'

He paused, looking back. 'Jemain.'

'Shell.'

'Good luck, Shell.'

She squinted over at the older fellow, ignored the continuing insults regarding her person and what she might do with a spear. 'Hey, you – old man!'

The fellow did not stir. He must be awake; no one could sleep amid all this uproar. She found a piece of stone and threw it at him. He cracked open an eye, rubbed his unshaven jaw.

'What's the routine?' she demanded.

He sighed as if already exhausted by her, said, 'It's in pairs. One shieldman. One spearman – or woman,' he added, nodding to her.

'That's stupid. We should mass together, fend them off.'

He was shaking his head. 'That's not the Stormguard's priority. Their priority is to cover the wall. There's a good stone's throw between you and the next pair.'

'That's stupid,' she repeated. This entire exercise struck her as stupid. An utter waste.

The older fellow shrugged. He was eyeing her now, narrowly. 'You're not Sixth Army.'

'No. I'm not.'

'What're you doing here then?'

'Shipwrecked on the west coast.'

'What in Hood's name you doin' there?'

It was her turn to shrug. He bared his yellowed teeth in answer to his own question. 'Reconnaissance, hey?'

She didn't reply and he leaned his head back against the stone wall. 'Don't matter. We're not goin' anywhere.'

Two days later the Chosen came for them.

The bronze-bound door slammed open and a detail entered to unlatch the chain securing their ankle fetters. Covered by crossbowmen, the lines along both walls stood. At an order one file, Shell's, began shuffling along out of the door. The line walked corridors, ever upwards, the air getting colder and steadily more damp. They came out into a night-time snowstorm. Guards pushed them up steep ice-slick stairs cut from naked stone. The cold snatched Shell's breath away and bit at her hands and feet. To left and right lay slopes of heaped boulders rising up to disappear into the driven snow that came blasting from the darkness. The guards urged them on with blows from the flat of their blades. As she walked she tore a strip of cloth from her inner shirt and wrapped it round her hands.

From down beneath the rock came a great shudder that struck Shell like a blow. Stones tumbled and grated amid the boulders. A roar sounded above, a waterfall thundering, which slowly passed. The file of prisoners exchanged wide-eyed, terrified glances.

The Stormwall. She was to stand it. Only now did the certitude of such an unreal and outrageous fate strike home. Who would've imagined it? The stairs led up into a tower and a circular staircase. In a chamber within the tower two Chosen Stormguard awaited them at the only other exit, a portal leading to narrow ascending stairs. A single brazier cast a weak circle of warmth in the centre of the room. 'Sit,' one of the Stormguard told them.

While they waited, regular guards distributed sets of battered armour, mostly studded leathers, some boiled cuirasses, a few leather caps. All the equipment bore the gouges and scars of terrible blows – many obviously mortal. Just for the warmth, Shell grabbed a cap and strapped it on tight. No one spoke. Two men vomited where they sat. One shuffled to the piss-hole in a corner at least five times. The vomit froze solid on the stone-flagged floor.

Shell saw piled rags and took a bunch to wrap round her head, neck and hands. The old veteran, she noticed, had unwound a scarf from his waist and wrapped it round his head and neck.

A shout echoed from the stairway and the Stormguard closed on the front of the line. While one watched, the other struck the chain from the fetters. The first two, the first 'pair', were pushed up the stairs.

Counting off, Shell looked at the man next to her, her partner to be. He was skinny and shuddering uncontrollably – either from the cold or from terror. 'What's your name?'

The man flinched as if she'd struck him. 'What?'

'Your name . . . what is it?'

'What does that matter? We're dead, aren't we?'

'Quiet,' one of the Stormguard warned.

'We're planning!' she answered, glaring. The man scowled but didn't answer. 'Have you used a spear?'

The fellow looked on the verge of tears. 'What? A spear? You think it matters? You think we have a chance?'

'This is your last warning,' the Stormguard said quietly.

Shell muttered a response. *Shit! I'm going to be chained to this fool? I'd be better off on my own.* She leaned forward, trying to pull more warmth from the brazier. Well . . . it may just come to that . . .

The wait lengthened. Everyone sat in an agony of tense anticipation. After what seemed half the night one of the Stormguard squinted up the narrow chute of stairs and then back at them. 'Sleep,' he said.

Shell did not sleep. She sat back, eyes slitted, while the man next to her nodded off – though perhaps he simply passed out in an utter exhaustion of dread. At intervals, one Stormguard paced the chamber. She watched him when he passed. Who were these soldiers? Their manner struck her as one of a military order, one dedicated to their Blessed Lady. She'd heard of them all her life, of course; they were always cited in admiration. And she could admit to having once shared that awe for what seemed – from far away – an honourable calling. Once.

Now, they'd rather fallen in her regard.

Eventually, inevitably, their turn came. The Stormguard struck them from the chain and pushed them up the narrow stone stairway. Her partner went first, and when he reached the top someone passed him a spear, which he flinched from before shakily taking.

Fanderay help us. The shield was thrust at her. It was a broad curved rectangle of layered wood, bone and bronze. The narrow chute of the stairway opened on to a small frigid room with one door; that door was lined in rime, its threshold wet with melted ice and slush. She knew where that door led.

While she fought with the shield's old strapping the entire structure around and beneath her shuddered, jerking, and a great booming burst through the room like a thunderclap. She rocked, taking a step. Ice fell like glass shards from the walls. The regular guards holding cocked crossbows on her and her partner grinned at them over the stocks of their weapons.

The outer door slammed open and in came a Stormguard. Sleet and wind-tossed salt spume coated his cloak. His longsword was drawn and he gestured to them with it. Her partner, to whom she was linked by a few arms' length of chain, gaped at the Chosen, frozen in terror, or disbelief. His eyes blazing within his narrow vision slit, the Stormguard snatched the spear close to its wide leaf-shaped blade and yanked the man forward.

In this undignified manner they stumbled out on to the marshalling walk of the Stormwall. A brutal wind cut at Shell while sleet slashed almost level. The coming dawn brightened the east behind massed heavy clouds. The Stormguard urged them along, now tugging on the chain linking them. As he force-marched them he was yelling: 'You will face the enemy. You will fight! If you flinch or cringe I will kill you myself! And believe me . . . you have a better chance against them than against me!'

He led them up stairs that were no more than flows of ice cascading down from a higher wall, a machicolation perhaps. Here the cut stones sloped downward, no doubt to cast the wash of the crashing waves back over the face of the wall.

Shell reached the top and had her breath stolen from her. The sea raged beneath a horizon-wide ceiling of black cloud. White caps tossed up scarves of spume while overhead curtains of blue-green bands shimmered and danced.

The Stormguard was hammering their chain to a pin close to the lip of the wall. Shell's partner stared at her, horror and despair in his eyes. Past him, through a gap in the blowing snow, she caught two figures crouched in the middle distance.

Straightening, the Stormguard faced them. 'Fight, and there's a good chance you'll live. Refuse to fight and I'll slit you like a dog. Remember that.' And he jogged away down the stairs.

The man with her threw down his spear.

'What are you *doing*?'

'Give me the shield!' he demanded, shivering as if palsied.

'What?'

'Give me the shield!'

She considered breaking his neck right then and there, but couldn't bring herself to do it. She thrust the shield at him and retrieved the spear. 'You cover me with that blasted thing,' she told him, but he didn't seem to be listening.

They didn't have long to wait. From the east came a distant rumbling as of a roll of thunder. *A wave's coming. The Riders come with the crest, probing for weaknesses.* She readied the spear, opted for a broad stance, the haft extended out as far ahead as possible. *Best then not appear weak.*

The sea appeared to swell as a great rolling comber heaved itself shoreward. It came at an angle, striking to the east first, rumbling down the wall like an avalanche. Phosphorescent light gleamed within, shimmering and winking. The Riders.

As the wave drew abreast it crested the wall to send a wash over her numb feet and legs up to her knees. Some *thing* flowed past, a shape, gleaming in oily rainbow shades of mother-of-pearl. Her partner recoiled, bumping her – for a moment she was afraid he was going to try to clutch her.

'You saw it!' he stammered. 'They are daemons!' He threw down the shield to claw at the ring and pin imprisoning them.

'Pick up the shield,' she told him, fighting to keep her voice calm. A secondary swell grew following the main crest. 'Hurry.'

He yanked, sobbing. Blood from his frozen, torn fingers smeared the naked iron.

'Pick it up.'

The swell rolled abreast of them. The man reached out to her. 'Use the spear! Lever—'

A slim jagged weapon thrust from the face of the water to burst through the man's chest. It withdrew before Shell could respond. Something reared, lunging, a humanoid figure, armoured, helmed. Steam plumed from it as it thrust at her. Despite her shock Shell parried, then the Rider's own momentum carried it off and away with the receding wave.

Shell was left alone, chained to a corpse in the blowing snow. To the west she watched another pair engage the wave as it passed their station, then all was quiet as the sea withdrew. It seemed to be readying itself as lesser waves hammered and clashed. She shivered; her feet were now far beyond any feeling whatsoever. She wondered whether she could walk even if she had the chance.

It seemed she would have to wait. She considered the body hardening at her feet, the chain linked to its ankle fetter, the razor edge of the spear. A lever, he had suggested . . . but no. He wasn't impeding her. Not yet.

No relief came. Shell knelt down on her haunches, blew on her fingers while hugging her frigid legs to her. *Damn the shield; she'd use the spear two-handed.*

The temptation to reach out to her Warren was almost irresistible. Just the quickest summoning of power and she would be free – but then where would she go? And the Lady would sear her mind more surely than these Riders might skewer her. She might be a mage foremost . . . but she was also an Avowed of the Crimson Guard, and she would show these Riders what that meant.

The huge cut stones of the wall shuddering beneath her feet announced the arrival of another wave. She watched its ice-skeined bulge as it came rolling in from the north-east. Flashes of lightning accompanied it, and greenish light danced above. Like mast-fire it was . . . the brilliance that sometimes possessed a vessel.

Shell readied herself, searched for purchase over the treacherous ice-sheathed stone. Her hands, she noticed, alarmed, were now frozen to the spear's haft. The wave rolled along the fortifications, cresting over the top as it came. When it swelled abreast of her a figure seemed to lift itself from the water, carrying lance and shield. It reared, heaved the lance at her. She parried. As it went for the sword sheathed at its side she thrust with her spear, taking him, or it, on the shield. In a practised move the Rider took hold of her spear haft then threw itself backwards into the water, taking the weapon with it. Her hands flamed as skin was torn in strips.

She cursed in a blind white fury worse than any she had known before. *Damn these scum! I will not die here! The vow I swore was against the Malazans!* A second Rider reared before her on whatever it was they rode – water animate as half wave, half beast-like mount. Weaponless, there was nothing for it but to hammer an arm across the front of the attacker, unhorsing him. As he fell she grabbed the pommel of his sheathed sword but the touch burned her hand as if she'd sunk it into embers and she cried out, recoiling.

Thankfully, the wave subsided, rolling on. She sank to her knees, cradling her numb hand to her chest. *Damn them all! Stupid fucking waste!*

Still no relief came. She knelt, panting; blood froze in a sheath on her hands. She felt so sluggish, utterly numb. Strangely, there was no pain. It was as if she were floating. *Maybe if I just lie down for a moment . . .*

Rattling shook her to wakefulness. Someone was hammering at the ice-encrusted ring and pin imprisoning her. Her chains came free and he reached for her. Standing, she straight-armed the man from her. She swore at him but her lips were numb and she could only mumble. He seemed to study her for a time through the narrow vision slit of his helm, then he grasped the chains and dragged them, pulling her and the corpse off the wall.

They knocked the fetters from her in the tiny marshalling room, then she was prodded back down the stairs. A guard kept her moving, a bared blade levelled against her. In the prison chamber she was reattached to the main gang-chain and she allowed herself to slide down the wall in what felt like the most luxurious warmth imaginable.

Almost immediately she fell asleep. Some time later she awoke to a touch on her foot. It was the prisoner who'd fed them earlier, Jemain. He knelt to rub a greasy unguent on her face, arms, legs and hands. 'It will prevent infection and aid healing,' he told her.

She saw his bare ankles. 'You're not chained,' she noted belatedly.

'I'm a trustee.' Lowering his voice, he added, 'That was quite a show you put on. Be careful or they will move you to a hot spot.'

She laughed, hurting her cracked lips. 'That wasn't hot?'

He smiled. 'Oh no. First they put you on a slow station – see what you can do.'

A new Chosen entered the chamber, blue cloak wrapped tight about him. He spoke in low tones with the two Stormguard. Jemain lowered his head to mutter, 'Too late.'

The two posted guards marched down the line to Shell. While one watched, hand on swordgrip, the other struck her from the chain. This one then freed the older Malazan soldier as well, and linked her and him together.

'She needs time to heal,' Jemain told them. 'Her hands—'

The nearest Stormguard struck him a blow that sent him tumbling. Shell lashed out but the Chosen slipped the blow, drawing his weapon to strike her in the gut with the pommel. She grunted without falling and the man fell back one step, his eyes widening behind the narrow vision slit. The old Malazan veteran threw an arm across Shell to draw her back as well.

She knocked his arm aside. 'Don't you dare touch me, Malazan scum.'

The veteran let his arm fall to look her up and down, wonder on his face. 'Togg take me . . .' he breathed. The trustee, Jemain, also stared up at her – he looked about to say something. The Stormguard drew his blade, gestured to the exit.

Glaring her fury, Shell gave the faintest of nods. She edged her way through the narrow chamber. The eyes of all those chained along both walls watched her pass. As she came to Jemain he raised an arm and she helped him up. Hugging her close, he whispered, 'Do you know Bars?' Then he gasped as her grip tightened convulsively.

'Where is he?' she grated.

'I know.'

'Come to me.'

'Get a move on,' the Stormguard ordered.

Pulling away, he murmured, 'I'll try.'

She let him go, forcing her burning hands to open, then shuffled on. The Malazan veteran, she noted, also gave the trustee a long hard stare as he passed.

So this Jemain knew Bars. But then, here on the wall, who did not? Perhaps it was nothing. But the Malazan appeared close to guessing her identity as well. And she was now paired with him. Well, as before . . . she may be better off alone . . .

BOOK III

And All the Shores Between

He stands watching the Chosen on the wall
Gripping the stone in both hands
Staring down into the blur of sickle blades,
Clouds of spray and snow blow behind
And all to the horizon, to the curve
Of wall that marks the shore,
Nothing but men swinging.
When the sea fills the gap
His cousins raise their spears.
For twelve hours the sun strives
And the reaper reaps.
The boy stares down into that sweep
Of hot oiled blade and tempered ice,
And I hope he will not fall.

Epic lay, *The Wall*
Derak Ranathaj

CHAPTER IX

Looking back
is a flame in the eyes.
Best not to linger like flies
on the refuse we have made.

No, I know nothing of what came before.
Nor do I care.

It is much easier to worship the future
that will never come.

Occasional Rhymes
Jhen Karen'ul of Stygg

Bakune sat in the high chair of the Banith Courts Civil and listened to the advocate for the aggrieved finish his argument. It was all he could do to force himself to pay attention. Outside, an occupying army patrolled the streets and blockaded the harbour, while here within these walls advocates and agents connived and conspired with as much unashamed greed as before.

Something within the Assessor wanted to scream. Under his robes he pinched his fingers into his palms to force himself to follow the advocate's unlikely, and contrived, line of reasoning. After the summing up Bakune quickly hammered his desk. 'Advocate, I see no clear and compelling evidence here to support your claims of collaboration and war profiteering.'

The advocate rose anew, swept his robes back from his arms. 'Assessor . . . it is clear from this merchant's sale of goods to the enemy . . .'

'Sir, if I were to prosecute every merchant who has dealt with these Moranth then the Carceral Quarters would be full to bursting. That alone is no evidence of collusion or traitorous behaviour as your client contends. Meanwhile the accused, your client's main rival in the timber concession, I understand, suffers under this cloud of doubt, his reputation stained, his business eviscerated. I suggest you work towards assembling compelling and material evidence to support your charges. Until then – case dismissed.' Bakune hammered the desk again, and the foremost of the crowd jamming the court rose, half of them relieved, the other half muttering their dissatisfaction.

The Assessor turned to the next packet of documents, but somehow he could not muster the energy to face them. He hammered the desk a third time. 'Court closed for the morning.'

An eruption of protest, shouting, papers waved in fists, the court bailiffs struggling to hold back the mob. Bakune swept out of the court; he simply no longer gave a damn. Where were these urgent calls to action, the public outrage, when youths were disappearing from the streets? He frankly had no sympathy for this sudden new passion for litigation. *Our country is invaded by a foreign power, alien troops walk our streets, and our reaction? We attempt to sue them and each other.* Bakune was ashamed that his countrymen would see in all this nothing more than an opportunity to make a quick profit.

He gathered up a few files then headed out to return to his offices. His guards took up positions around him – a precaution pressed upon him by Hyuke, now Captain Hyuke of the City Watch. The surviving members of the Lady's priesthood had damned him for meeting with the enemy – as if they could just ignore them and hope they'd go away.

It was so frustrating *he* was tempted to walk away. Damn them all for their sudden newfound concern for 'justice' and the self-righteous aggrieved umbrage only the selfish can muster. At least no new murder following the characteristics of all those that had come before had yet surfaced. Certainly there had been killings: drunken stabbings, crimes of passion, spousal murders – oddly enough from those most vocally concerned with 'traditional Roolian values', it seemed. But no bodies of youths turning up in the tide. For that Bakune was grateful, and chose to take some small measure of credit. He'd even had a word with Boneyman, and Soon, the young servant girl, now worked as an apprentice cook in the kitchens.

He found Hyuke awaiting him outside his office, looking no different from before with his ridiculous fat moustache and lazy manner. Only his uniform had changed; Bakune did not think much of the epaulettes. He opened the door and waved him in. 'What is it?'

The new Watch captain slumped in a chair, his eyes sleepy. 'Them Blues want a warehouse and grounds to set up quarters on the waterfront. No one's volunteering.'

'Surely that's a matter for the Lord Mayor's office.'

A tired nod. 'True enough. Except the Lord Mayor's scarpered.'

'What?'

'Last night. Run off. City treasury's empty too.'

'You're implying a connection?'

The man rolled his eyes. 'What're we gonna do?'

'What do you mean "we"? The Vice-Mayor must step in.'

A shake of the head.

'The Lieutenant-Mayor?'

A disappointed pursing of the lips.

'The city treasurer?'

'Arrested. A person of interest.'

'Ah. That leaves . . . ?'

'You.'

'*Me?* Lady forfend, no.'

'Sorry, but we've 'bout run out of all other contenders. The Abbot's dead, the Lord Mayor's gone. That leaves you. Congratulations – this mess is yours.'

Bastard Mayor Gorlings. Never did like the pompous ass. Now he's run off and left me to clean up. And I don't want any of it. Bakune eyed his Watch captain. At least the fellow seemed willing to do whatever he told him. He supposed it was time one of the deputy assessors sat the bench. 'Confiscate the necessary property. Tell them they'll be paid in script.'

Hyuke's long face lit up in a grin and he stroked his moustache. 'That I like to hear.' He stood. 'They'll hate you.'

'They'll hate me anyway.'

'That they will.' The man gave a brief bow. 'Lord Mayor.'

Late that night as he was walking home, he was struck once more by how quiet the city was. The seemingly endless tide of pilgrims had ebbed. Countless citizens had fled the coast for the dubious safety of the inland towns. The capital, Paliss, was apparently choked with refugees. And the Overlord? Strange rumours circulated concerning him and his seeming non-response to this invasion.

Bakune's housekeeper opened the door for him, curtsying – this too was new. Everyone treated him with either far more respect or far more hostility, depending upon where their particular interests happened to lie. His guards took up positions before his door. His cook was in the kitchen preparing an evening meal – another new addition. He hung his cloak then poured a drink. Entering his parlour he found the priest, Ipshank, sitting in his most comfortable chair.

Bakune nodded and sat, reminding himself to have a word with the housekeeper, who, apparently, was a convert to this priest's strange new religion.

'Nice place,' the priest said.

'A previous visitor called it wretchedly small.'

'How our perceptions can change.'

'Ipshank . . . perhaps you shouldn't . . .'

'No one knows I'm here.'

Bakune rubbed his pained brow. 'It's just that I'm already being labelled a traitor . . .'

The priest sat forward. The beast tattoos on his face darkened in the dim light. 'I'm here to let you know things are going to get much worse.'

'Wonderful.'

'You've heard the rumours regarding our Overlord, Yeull? The Roolian Army?'

'Which? I've heard twenty contrary stories.'

The man sat back. 'Well, there's to be no counter-offensive. No effort to free Banith.'

Bakune nodded. Already he'd come to that reluctant conclusion. It had been more than ten days and still no Roolian forces had arrived. What's more, he'd heard some very alarming rumours regarding the disposition of that army. He sipped his liqueur. 'I'd heard a rumour that Paliss was being abandoned.'

The priest nodded. 'The official word is that the Overlord will hold the north then retake the south.'

'What do you think?'

The man didn't answer for a time. He looked down as if studying his wide spade-like hands. 'I was going to leave, you know. Days ago.'

'Oh?'

'Yes. I said it was time I confronted the Lady . . . and I was on my way.'

'And something stopped you.'

'Yes. One of those rumours. One that made too much sense.'

Bakune lifted his glass then stopped himself and set it down. He didn't know if he wanted to hear anything that could possibly trouble *this* man. 'Must I hear this?'

'Yes. Bakune, I believe that the Malazans . . . Greymane . . . is coming here.'

Bakune waved away the possibility. 'That's absurd. He'll march on Paliss, of course.'

The priest was shaking his head. Light from the fire gleamed from his bald pate. 'No. This is his fleet. It's awaiting him.'

'Awaiting him? To take him where? They've only just got here! No, once he is close the Moranth troops will disembark and join him to march on Paliss. And if he is victorious, we will have a new overlord.' Bakune shrugged his helplessness. 'Simple as that.'

The priest stood. 'No. It's not so simple. Chaotic times are coming, Bakune. It may be that there will be no overlord. Then there will be a need for people who can see ahead. Think on that. That is all I suggest.' He peered down at Bakune. 'I do not know if we will see each other again. But if not – best of luck, and my blessing.' He set a hand on Bakune's shoulder. 'I'll see myself out the back.'

Long after the man had gone Bakune sat on into the night. The fire died away to embers. He reached out and swallowed the rest of his liqueur. He'd never been much of a religious man though he'd attended services all his life – as a matter of course as a civic official. Strangely enough, only now did he have the feeling of having been in the presence of a true priest, one less concerned with the welfare of the gods than with the real welfare of the people. It was a strange, discomforting sensation that made him feel that somehow he too ought to be concerned. All his adult life he'd lived under the Malazan yoke. He couldn't imagine how things would be otherwise.

Yet it was worth thinking about, as the man said. For what if in the course of this coming confrontation no clear victor arose? Or what if Yeull died and the Malazan forces were crippled? What then? Regional warlords would arise. Disintegration of the state. Chaos. Who would guard the interests of Banith?

Well, he supposed that would be him.

* * *

Kiska was surprised to find this nether-Chaos Realm flush with life. Lizard-like things scuttled from their path to disappear amid the broken rock and shifting sands of the region. Tough thorny bushes choked depressions. Even things you might call blind albino fish swam in shallow rock pools. She'd wondered what the white hound had been surviving on. Now she believed she had her answer. She also thought the prospect of fish would excite the priest, Warran, but the man showed no interest. 'Too small,' he'd complained. This did not stop him from eating his share, though, after Jheval filleted a few. Their tiny bat-guide led them on, apparently tireless, and though their ultimate goal was obvious it led them true, avoiding defiles, gorges and a swampy lowland Kiska was glad to skirt.

Ever present in the sky loomed their destination, the immense bruise, or blotch, of the Whorl. At night it took the appearance of a circle of pitch black surrounded by a gyre of brilliance as curtains of light rippled and swirled. 'The energy of destruction,' the priest called the light.

The only strange or disturbing event that occurred for some time concerned Warran. During the relative gloom of one night Kiska got up to relieve her bladder and in doing so she passed behind the priest where he sat cross-legged facing the Whorl.

For an instant it seemed to Kiska that she could see the brilliance of the stars and the rippling banners of energy *through* the body of the priest. As if he were translucent, or wasn't really there at all. She blinked, pausing, and stared again, but the impression was gone and the man was glaring over his shoulder.

'I'm trying to meditate – if you don't mind!'

And she'd retreated, apologizing. But the vision would not leave her and she found herself watching him much more closely than she had before.

Then, after an unknowable passage of time, a sandstorm blew in upon them. It came from ahead, the direction of the Whorl, a great wall of obscuring sand or dust boiling over the land towards them. First, the ravens, which had been hopping amid the rocks – searching for insects, Kiska wondered – let out great warning caws and swept up into the air. Jheval pointed to a clump of boulders and they ran to hunch in its lee. Kiska yelped as something latched itself on to her, but it was their guide, returned to wriggle under her cloak.

Warran straightened then, his brows rising in amazement. 'This is no storm.'

'Of course it is,' Jheval snapped from behind his scarf. 'Now get down!'

The priest raised a warning hand to Jheval. 'No. This is something much worse. Do not move.' And he stepped out into the open.

'Fool! Come back!' Jheval moved to follow but Kiska stopped him.

'Wait. Perhaps he knows what he's doing.' She had time for one glance around for the hound – had it found cover? – before the cloud engulfed them. The diffuse light of the day darkened beyond the murkiness of night. The noise was almost too loud to hear: it hammered her ears with its reverberation. Something bit her hand – a sharp nip – and she looked down to see some sort of fly feeding upon her. She squashed it. Jheval pressed his head to hers, shouting: 'Bloodflies! Flesh-eating flies! They'll flense the meat from our bones! Do something!'

But Kiska flinched away. She cuffed at her head where they crawled in her hair. She thumped her armour where they'd wormed their way beneath. The bites were an agony; they dotted her hands like a pox. When a nip lanced far within her ear she screamed, her howl inaudible even to her, and fell curling into a fetal ball.

She didn't think she'd passed out but slowly she became aware that the ocean of pain was diminishing, fading to a lingering searing agony that no longer threatened to push her into unconsciousness. She rose and wiped her face, feeling a warm smear – her forearm was sheathed in fresh wet blood. Peering around through narrowed eyes she saw that the cloud of flies had receded. It circled them now at a distance: a churning wall of a million ravenous mouths.

The priest was there and he passed her a cloth. She took it to dab at her face and arms, wincing as the weave rubbed the raw wounds. Jheval rose, hissing and groaning. If she looked anything like him right now she was a mess: his face ran with blood, as did his hands and forearms.

She saw that not one wound scarred Warran. 'You're not bitten!' *Damn the man! How was it he escaped?* 'What's going on?'

'We had something of a negotiation, he and I.'

'He?'

Warran held up his opened hands. 'Well . . . *it.*'

'What is . . . it?'

'It is D'ivers. It appears to have haunted these shores of Chaos for some time. It has grown quite powerful, as you see.'

'Negotiation, you said?' asked Jheval, his voice clenched with pain.

'It flees the Whorl,' Warran explained. Raising his voice, he called: 'Is that not so?'

As the horde circled, hissing and thrumming, the massed whisperings of the millions of wings changed timbre. The tone rose and fell and incredibly Kiska found she could understand:

The Hole hungers more than I . . .

'What name should I call you?' Warran asked.

We do not remember such things. We are many. No one name can encompass us.

'Been here *too* long . . .' Jheval muttered.

Kiska stepped forward. 'We are travelling to solve the mysteries of this Whorl.'

So this Cloaked One with you claims. Beware, then. Many are gathered on its verge, intent upon capturing its power. Dangerous beings. Ones even I *choose not to consume.*

'Our thanks.'

It is nothing. This Whorl troubles me. Remember, all you meet need not be hostile. But beware the Army of Light.

The cloud peeled away, churning and spinning, rising like smoke. It drifted off the way it had been flying – away from the blot of the Whorl. The three watched it go. Kiska jumped then as the twig- and cloth-guide stirred to life under her cloak and leapt high into the eerie non-sky.

Jheval was dabbing at his face. 'That *thing* is fleeing exactly what we are headed for.'

'It can't eat a hole,' said Warran.

Kiska eyed the priest. 'What is this Army of Light?'

Warran cocked his head, indifferent. 'I assure you I have no idea.'

Jheval muttered something sour. They continued walking. The Seven Cities warrior paced along next to Kiska. 'I don't know why you try,' he said.

'Try what?'

He jerked his head at the priest. 'Him. Asking him questions. He's done nothing but lie to us. He's hiding something, I'm sure of it. Did you hear what that thing called him? "Cloaked"? He's a scorpion disguising himself with us.'

'You have not been so forthcoming yourself,' the priest called loudly from where he walked some distance off, and Jheval growled his anger. 'Who is not hiding things, hey, Jheval? Why is it, I wonder, that it is always those with the most to hide who accuse others? Why do you think that is . . . Jheval?'

Kiska cocked a brow to the Seven Cities native, who glowered, jaws clenched, saying nothing. There was no more talk that day and as the dimness of night gathered they found another of the small pools where pale transparent fish lazed. She and Jheval took turns washing and treating their wounds. Returning from the pool, Jheval was clean of his blood, but the angry red dots of the countless bites on his face and hands made him look like the victim of a particularly virulent pox. She supposed she looked no better.

Lying down on her spread cloak, her rolled gear under her head, she thought of the words of the D'ivers creature. Powerful beings had gathered to the Whorl. Beings even *it* chose not to attack.

And it had chosen not to attack them. Or rather, perhaps she should say that it had chosen not to attack Warran. There it was again. Cloaked. She agreed with Jheval, of course. Yet maddeningly there was nothing she, or he, could do about it.

The next day they continued on after breaking fast on the raw flesh of the fish. Oddly enough, it was Jheval and she who did all the catching – Warran wouldn't go near them. Their usual walking order was she and Jheval leading, Warran bringing up the rear. This was how they were when, from beneath disguising layers of sand, armoured figures leapt up to bar their way.

There were more than twenty of them: some sort of patrol or guard, similarly clad in pale enamelled armour of cuirasses with scaled sleeves and leggings and white enamelled helmets. They carried pale shields, cracked and yellowed now, and the blades of their bared curved swords gleamed yellow.

Warran came up to stop beside Kiska. 'The Army of Light,' he announced.

Thank you very much.

One called something in a language Kiska did not know. The man tried several more until finally speaking in Talian. 'Drop your weapons.'

'Who are you to threaten us?' Kiska shouted back.

'Your companion also,' the man answered.

'We can take them,' Jheval murmured, hardly moving his lips.

'You do not really think this is all of them, do you?' Warran said. 'Best comply. Let's not make a scene.'

'Easy for you,' Kiska answered under her breath. Louder, she called, 'Very well. But this is hardly the way for civilized folk to behave.' She knelt to set down her staff. Snarling his disgust, Jheval threw down his morningstars.

The party surrounded them, marched them on. The ground became more and more uneven. Their path wended round rocky outcroppings, boulders the size of buildings. At one point their escort stopped and spoke among themselves, their tone surprised. Then the white hound appeared, pushing its way through them to come to Kiska's side. It paced there for a time with her; dried blood flecked its white and streaked-yellow hair.

'Not far off enough, were you, hey?' she told him – though she still dared not reach out to actually pet him.

They climbed a tall slope of loose bare broken stones, winding back and forth across its face until they reached the crest and saw an army spread out before them in a valley of black rock. Kiska was stunned; it was one of the largest gatherings of forces she'd ever seen. Tents dotted away into the distance. Smoke rose from countless fires. Their escort urged them on down the valley slope. As they descended the hound loped off – it seemed he had no interest in entering the encampment. Kiska watched it disappear among the rocks, feeling suddenly alone and vulnerable; for some reason she felt she could count on that beast more than she could trust the two men she travelled with. *And what of this force? The Army of Light? Was this one of those gathered to claim the Whorl? One of those the D'ivers would not attack – a hesitation she could well understand. Yet what could they hope to achieve? You couldn't attack this manifestation. There was nothing there!*

They were led down and into the camp. Kiska saw that the force was composed entirely, as far as she could see, of heavily armoured infantry. All were alike with their pale narrow features, white or streaked fair hair. *And just who were they anyway?* Kiska was urged into a tent, separated from Jheval and the priest. She was alarmed by this but there was nothing she could do.

Within she found a pallet and a small table containing a jug of water, a washbasin, and a platter of food: dried meat of some sort, thin unleavened bread, fruit and cheese. All very plain and austere. *Like a goddamned monastery.*

A guard entered, helmet under an arm revealing long loose dirty-blonde hair: female. 'Take off your armour and all your equipment.'

'Is this how you treat all your visitors?'

'We are within the shores of Chaos, not the concourses of the Glimmering Commons. Your equipment?'

Sighing, Kiska complied. Each piece of armour, each weapon, the guard took and tossed outside the tent, leaving Kiska in boots, trousers, shirt, vest, and cloak.

'Boots,' the woman said.

Kiska set her hands on her hips. 'Really?'

The woman merely gestured to the opening. 'Shall I call in my companions and strip you entirely?'

Kiska almost invited her to do so. Almost. She kicked off the boots. Searching them, the guard found the two throwing blades slipped down the lining of each.

'Cloak.'

Kiska stared, then she laughed. *Hood-damned humourless methodical military order. Must be.*

She was reduced to the stained silk chemise and shorts she wore for comfort beneath everything. Only then did the woman relent and allow her to dress. When she finished the woman's only comment was a curt, 'Follow me.'

Two more guards fell in behind as the woman led her through the camp. It was very well ordered, almost ruthlessly so. Off-duty soldiers sat before their tents repairing equipment or eating. All were quiet; their demeanour surprised Kiska, who was used to the noise and complaints and banter of Malazan troops. She also reflected that she hadn't seen their tiny guide for some time. *Good. The little thing was showing better judgement than they.*

She was escorted to a tent and the flap was tossed open to reveal Jheval and the priest. Her guide urged her in. 'Wait here.'

'Hurry up and wait,' Kiska muttered as she entered. She nodded to the other two.

'You're all right?' Jheval asked.

'Yes. Who are these people?'

'The Army of Light,' Warran repeated blandly. 'I should have thought that was obvious.'

'And what does that mean?'

'Tiste Liosan.'

Jheval cursed under his breath. The label meant something to him, that was clear, but it meant nothing to her. She knew of the Tiste Andii, of course, the Children of Night. She'd even heard of the Tiste Edur, the Children of Shadow. Now the Tiste Liosan? The Children of . . . Light? 'What do they want?'

The priest shrugged his bony shoulders. 'I should think they are here to investigate the Whorl.'

'In such force?'

Again the maddening shrug. She was about to ask another question when the flap slid open and in walked several of their captors. Four had blades bared while the lead one, the fifth, stood with hands clasped behind his, or her, back. Other than the manner of assured command, there was no way to tell this one apart from the others.

'What are you doing here?' the commander asked, the voice revealing her as a woman.

'We are here to investigate this manifestation, the Whorl.'

'Whorl? We name him the Devourer.'

'Him?' Kiska echoed. 'Him – someone? But how can it be sentient?'

The commander pulled off her visored helmet and shook out sweaty matted blonde hair. Her features were blunt and heavy, her jaw square, her brow-ridges thick. The eyes captured Kiska's attention: gold flecked the irises, which shone almost mauve. 'It is summoned and sustained by a powerful magus,' she said. 'And it has broached the borders of Kurald Liosan – among many others.'

Kiska hoped her face betrayed no reaction. *A powerful mage. Tayschrenn. Yet . . . malevolent? Perhaps he has been driven mad . . .* She missed what the woman said next and realized that they were introducing themselves. 'Kiska,' she blurted out.

The woman nodded. 'My name and titles happen to be rather long. I go by Jayashul. Commander Jayashul. I hear you were accompanied by a Hound of Light and that speaks well of you. Please be our guests. Abide by the rules of our camp and you are welcome. Obviously you represent organizations or political entities which are likewise troubled by the Devourer. Rightly so.' She nodded to Warran. 'I see from your presence that Shadow, too, is concerned. No doubt your patron resents the loss of any of what little Realm he has left.'

'Shadow is everywhere,' Warran replied, rather smugly.

The woman's gaze narrowed at that, but she offered a shallow bow. 'Until later.' They each answered the bow. The commander swept from the tent followed by her guards, leaving behind one man to watch them.

'Would her highness allow us to walk through the camp, do you think?' Warran asked the guard.

The guard's gauntleted fist went to his sword. 'You will show respect. She chose not to honour you with her titles but you should know she is Jayashul 'Od Lossica. She Who Brings the Dawn. Daughter of our Lord Liossercal.'

Kiska stared at the tent flap. *Burn's own blood.* The daughter of Osserc, Lord of the Sky. Never did she think she would ever be in such company. Jheval, she noted, had gone almost green at the news; the name meant a great deal to him. Exactly what, she wondered if she would ever discover. For his part, Warran clasped his chin in one hand and mused aloud: 'The fellow does seem to have a lot of daughters.'

* * *

On the eighth day of their unopposed advance across Rool, Suth reflected that life was good. No one was trying to eviscerate him; no one was taking potshots at his head; he was even eating better than when growing up on the Dal Hon plains – meat every day! Unheard-of luxury. His only complaint was that no one was greasing the wheels of all the wagons and carts the army commandeered as it advanced across the countryside.

This day it was their turn to rest in those vehicles. Suth sat with most of his squad in the back of a wagon, huddled amid cloaks and blankets. Keri was back with them, but so was Pyke: the man had simply appeared at their camp one morning looking far too well fed for Suth's liking. Yana was of the opinion that he'd deserted to the Roolians during the stand-off and had been stuffing himself while the rest of them starved – and that now that the Roolians had been scattered to the winds he'd come slinking back. Suth was inclined to agree. It galled him no end that good-natured comrades whom he'd trusted with his life such as Dim and others would die in the fighting, while the shirkers like Pyke coasted on without harm. It was enough to tempt him to murder. He calmed himself with the thought that it wasn't all over yet.

While they lazed, the winter sun warming them, Suth stretched his leg, massaging the wound, then looked over to Sergeant Goss, head back, apparently asleep. 'Sergeant . . . what's this about you and the Claw?'

Yana gave him a glare. Keri and Len perked up, eyeing the man, who hadn't moved yet. Suth waited. The wheels squealed, columns tramped on either side. At least there was no dust as a cold sleet fell almost daily. Eventually Goss cracked open one eye to weigh him with a hard stare. Then the sergeant took a long breath, exhaled as if letting something go. 'This is just for inside the squad, understand. Yeah, I was in the Claw.'

Yana's brows climbed almost comically. Lard let out a whistle. 'I knew it!'

'Don't mean a damned thing,' Goss growled at Lard. 'I quit.'

'Why?' Suth asked, deciding that he might as well push while he could.

A dark glower answered that and the man leaned his head back again. 'Politics. Had a bellyful. Quit for some honest fighting.'

Suth thought there was more to it than that, but knew that was all he was going to get. 'And Faro?' he asked. 'What about him?'

Goss' gaze slid to him and lay there for some time, flat and hard. 'We don't talk about him.'

Well . . . some progress, at any rate.

Everyone was silent for a time, rocking as the wagon trundled over the rough road. Suth was grateful to Goss for opening up. He felt privileged. Part of a special brotherhood. Looking back, he could hardly remember the brash youth who'd joined up so many months ago. Then his goal had been to challenge everyone he met; to test himself against all comers. Now the last thing he wanted was to draw his sword in anger. He'd be happy if he saw no more action till the end of the campaign. And frankly, the way things were shaping up, it looked as though that may be the case. The Roolian forces were scattered over the countryside. Rumours of counter-offensives swept through the column occasionally, but nothing ever came of them. It seemed the Roolians were on the run, retreating north.

'Where are we headed, anyway?' Lard asked after a time, dreamily, as if half asleep.

'The capital, of course!' said Pyke, sneering.

Len appeared about to say something but he pursed his lips, deciding against it. Idly, Suth wondered why the man would keep his opinion to himself.

'Right. The capital, Paliss,' Goss said, his eyes closed.

'Of course,' Pyke said again, glancing round. 'Where else?'

No one spoke and Pyke just snorted, waving his dismissal of Lard. Uncertain of the silences surrounding him, Suth cast a look to Yana, who gave the slightest head shake. Suth took the sign and eased back, closing his eyes.

Towards noon a mounted junior officer came up alongside the

wagon; he looked them up and down, making no effort to hide his distaste. 'You 2nd Division, 4th Company, the 17th?'

Goss straightened, saluting. 'Yes, sir!'

'New orders. You've been transferred to a cohort attached to Fist Rillish. Report to his banner.'

Goss saluted again. 'Yes, sir.'

The officer answered the salute. 'That's all.' He kneed his mount on.

Lard groaned, 'Just when I was enjoying myself.'

'Rillish!' Pyke spat. 'A useless eunuch. What're we doing with him?'

'What you got against him?' Yana demanded, taking the opposite corner as she always did.

'Everyone knows Greymane has no time for the man. Why do we need him when we have the High Fist?'

'Muzzle it,' Goss said, his tone conveying his utter boredom with their bickering.

Stretching and grumbling, they collected their gear and went in search of the Fist's banner. They found it standing south of the trader road that the united Fourth and Eighth Armies travelled westward. Assembled around it were four other squads from the Fourth: the 20th, the 11th, the 6th, and the 9th. Suth spotted the Barghast girl, Tolat, among the crowd. She blew him a kiss and he, turning away, ran into Keri.

'So who's the big gal?' she asked, a brow arched.

'We were scouting together.'

'Is that what you call it now?'

He had no idea what to say but Goss saved him by bellowing, 'Stake out some ground and set up camp!' Then he and the other sergeants reported to the Fist.

While they ordered their bivouac Suth hunched down next to Len. 'What's with you 'n' Pyke?'

The man said, low, 'I'm pretty damn sure he crossed the river.'

'So?'

The old saboteur grimaced his disappointment. 'So . . . was he caught? Did he cut a deal?'

'What d'you mean, a deal?'

Len glanced about to make doubly sure they weren't being overheard. He needn't have worried: as usual when there was work to be done Pyke was nowhere around. 'Handing over intelligence.'

Suth found that incredibly hard to credit. 'C'mon. On us? Who's got foot-rot or the clap? Who cares?'

Len nodded thoughtfully while hammering pegs. 'General health – good point. But no, what I mean is deployments, strategic goals, all the rumours that run through the ranks.'

'All that talk is nothing but horseshit.'

'Not at all. Some is pretty damned shrewd.'

'But who would he talk to? There's no one around.'

Len frowned. 'Well, where's the bastard off to right now?'

Startled, Suth looked round. It was true: Pyke was nowhere in sight. Just what *was* the prick doing all the time? 'I'll fucking kill the bastard.'

'No you won't. We'll just watch and wait. It's Goss' call.'

Suth knelt back down. 'Hood-spawned bastard. I can't believe we have to put up with him.'

'It's like family,' Len told him, smiling lopsidedly. 'You can't pick your squadmates. Goss has his eye on him.'

The next morning, while the very tail of the expeditionary force rumbled past, they assembled for orders. Pyke was once again in line and Suth glared; when had he come sneaking back? Then he remembered Len's warning and forced himself to look away.

The Fist was talking to the sergeants and Suth was pleased to see the Adjunct, Kyle, with the man. He looked as good as new, if a little more battered. Aha! This could be interesting. Then he thought of the last special mission and decided that maybe that wasn't what he wanted after all.

Orders were given and, accompanied by a few wagons, they headed off south, down nothing more than a rutted mud cart track across open country while the rest of the army carried on west.

No, Suth decided. This was not what he really wanted at all.

They marched the full day south, following a farmers' trail. Mixed snow and rain soaked Suth all the way through his layered aketon down to his linen. Only the marching kept him warm. From what he'd heard it was maybe another day's march to the Mare border. He wondered if they were off to check that frontier. Yet with only fifty or so soldiers?

They pushed on into dusk. The Fist's escort led, the Adjunct accompanying him. Twilight swiftly deepened beneath the cloud cover. Scouts appeared from the shadows, Tolat among them. They conferred with the Fist's party. Orders came back for heightened readiness. Goss signed for shields to be unslung.

A further march through dusk into night proper brought their party to the smooth grassy crest of a dry valley and there, across the way along the far crest, torches flickered. In the valley a single tent glowed, lit from within. Dark pennants hung limp before it. There was too little light to tell, but those pennants might be the brown of Rool.

Wess spat a mouthful of brown spittle and set his heavy shield on the ground to lean over it. 'Parley,' he said, nodding his certainty.

Parley? Suth thought, studying the far torches. Whatever for? They had the Roolian forces on the run. Why would they waste time talking to them? Unless, unlikely as it seemed, this was surrender? No. It couldn't be this easy. Could it? Suth was surprised to find part of him hoping such was the case, while another part was offended by the idea. He wondered which half would be rewarded come tomorrow.

Goss' voice cut through the night. 'Stand down! Bivouac here!'

Suth shared an unenthusiastic look with Wess. Setting up after dark. Gods, how he hated it.

*

Rillish sipped hot tea while he eyed the waiting tent in the golden light of dawn. Figures moved about it; only about five of them that he could see. The rest of the party remained on the distant crest. *Some commander of the Roolian forces has asked for a meeting,* Greymane had said. *See what they want and if it's of any interest to us.*

And I agreed – then Greymane sent the Adjunct as well and again I said nothing though there was no need for both. One or the other. Kyle could negotiate for the High Fist; indeed, that was almost what the role of Adjunct was designed for. Why both of us is now painfully obvious even to the men: Greymane has no confidence in his Fist.

Kyle joined him, head bare, wearing just his padded and stained gambeson and soft leather trousers. Rillish knew that almost any other Fist in his place would resent and hate this young usurper of his or her authority, but older now, and a father, certain this was his last command, he could not muster the energy for seething bitterness. Quite the opposite: he always found himself wanting to offer the young man advice.

Which, surprisingly enough, this young Adjunct seemed to listen to, or at least he could hide his own resentment and contempt.

An aide offered Kyle tea, which he accepted. 'How many should we take?' he asked.

'About five, perhaps.'

The Adjunct raised his glass to the far crest. 'And how many hiding beyond that high land?'

'Good question. Do we really have to talk to them, hey?'

The Adjunct picked up a hardtack biscuit, dipped it in the tea. 'I think so.'

'I agree. And the High Fist did not say who he'd be sending.'

Kyle grunted his understanding: hard to set a trap when you don't know who's coming. 'Who do we take?'

'A couple of sergeants, I suppose.'

'If you don't mind . . . there're some hands with us I've been out with before.'

Rillish nodded his agreement. 'And that sergeant – Goss. I'll find them.'

Kyle set down his glass. 'Don't bother yourself, Fist. I'll hunt them up.'

'I—' Rillish bit down the rest of his objection. The Adjunct turned back to him, frowning behind his long moustache.

'Yes?'

'Nothing.'

Inclining his head in an informal salute, the young man left.

There it was again. Interference or consideration? What would the men and women of the cohort see now? The Adjunct active, giving orders, in command, while I stand aside apparently useless? Was this how the Adjunct wished it? Or had the youth interpreted such message duties as beneath the Fist? Did he not mind them seeing him acting as an aide? Or was he one not to give any thought to that at all?

He didn't know enough of the man to be sure either way. So far, however, it appeared that the foreign plains youth really didn't give a damn about any of these issues of rank or prerogatives of command. If true, it would be a relief to Rillish not to have to worry about such trivial things.

*

In the morning the Adjunct came by and spoke to Goss. The squad watched sidelong from their places hunched round the fire, warming their hands and stamping their feet. Len ladled out a broth from their cookpot. Blowing into his fists, Goss approached, gestured to Suth. 'Kit up. You 'n' me are goin' for a walk.' Suth nodded. 'The rest of you . . . gear up and keep watch. We don't know how many of the bastards there are.' He gave Len a hard stare. 'Corporal. You're in charge till I get back.'

Len saluted. Yana, Suth saw, was eyeing Pyke, who seemed to be ignoring everyone.

Goss glanced at Suth. 'What're you doing still here?'

Suth downed his broth and went to get ready.

Six of them came walking down the overgrown farmers' trail into the valley. The Adjunct and the Fist led, followed by Sergeant Coral of the 20th and Goss, then Suth and Tolat. While a small woman, Coral was rumoured to be lethally quick with her longsword, which she could wield in one or both hands.

The pennants were Roolian brown. The tent front was wide open to reveal a carpeted floor, a brazier with a tea service, and some foodstuffs. Four guards stood outside. Inside sat three men, waiting. Two were obviously guards while the third wore thick rich sleeveless robes over leather armour set with rings and studs.

The three stood and the fat one came forward. 'Greetings. Thank you for answering my invitation. I am Baron Karien'el.'

Rillish bowed. 'Fist Rillish Jal Keth.' Turning to the Adjunct he paused, said, 'My aide, Kyle.'

Suth was surprised to hear that bit of misdirection, but decided that there was no point in letting the man know just who was with him. And the Adjunct made no objection.

The Baron bowed and invited them in. 'Sit, please.'

Goss and Coral motioned that they four should remain outside. They spread out in a broad arc. Suth tried not to overhear but he couldn't help it – the Baron had a very loud voice.

'I am honoured, Fist, and . . . encouraged . . . that the High Fist would send such a high-ranking officer.'

'It is nothing,' answered Rillish. 'The High Fist is keen to see an end to hostilities.'

'Would you like some tea?' the Baron asked.

'Thank you, yes.' One of the guards readied the tea. Rillish continued, his voice uncertain: '*Baron* Karien'el, did you say? I do not recall hearing of you before – you are Roolian, yes?'

The man waved to himself, his swarthy face, black beard. 'Yes, I am Roolian, as you see. Not Malazan stock. I am recently come into my title.'

'Congratulations. But it was my understanding that the aristocracy were of Malazan descent, as a rule.'

'Only among you foreign invaders.'

The Fist was quiet for some time. He sipped his tea. Tolat, Suth noted, was watching the field of tall grass surrounding the tent and that reminded Suth that he too ought to be keeping a lookout. Rillish cleared his throat. 'Am I to understand then, that I am not addressing a representative of Overlord Yeull?'

The fellow stroked his thick rich beard, smiling. 'Correct, Fist.'

Suth glanced about, alarmed. *Thesorma Raadil! An insurgency! These Roolians see the chance to rid themselves of all of us!* But why announce this?

'And you have a proposal?' Rillish asked, his tone expressing dry disinterest.

The Baron held up his open hands. 'I will be frank. We Roolians wish to see the last of all of you Malazans—' The man waved a hand at some reaction from Rillish. 'Now, now. If I said otherwise you would know me for a liar, yes?'

'Fair enough.'

'Very good. On these grounds of candour let me offer a gesture of our neutrality. May I?'

Rillish nodded his agreement.

The Baron snapped his fingers and one of the guards waved to the far valley slope. Goss, Coral, Tolat and Suth all stood in alarm. Rillish and Kyle remained seated with Karien'el. A small party started down the far valley side. A file of figures escorted by a few others. It did not have the look of an ambush.

'What is it, Sergeant?' Rillish called.

Goss answered, 'Looks like prisoners, Fist.'

'Yes, Fist,' said the Baron. And he stood, grunting and rubbing his legs. He invited Rillish and Kyle to the front of the tent. 'Please accept these officers of the Overlord as a gesture of our goodwill,' and he smiled once more.

In that bared-tooth savage grin Suth read the message: . . . *that you will kill each other off and save us the trouble.*

Rillish offered a slight bow. 'Our thanks, Baron. Until we meet again, then.'

The grin broadened. 'Yes. Until then.'

* * *

Corlo lay against the cold dank wall of his pen, legs drawn up to his chest, arms wrapped tight, not caring whether he lived or died. He'd done his shameful job – done what the Stormguard wanted of him – and now he lay cast aside, apparently forgotten. It was probable that the only reason he lived and was not chained along some frontier of the Stormwall was his prudent captors' awareness that he may be needed again.

Gods, not again. Surely not. His lie would see Bars through this season. Of that he was sure. After that . . . all that was too far away to care any more. He had betrayed too egregiously. The lie burned too virulently in his chest. *Yet surely some of them must still survive! Somewhere!*

Now he lay jammed in with the worst of the Stormguard's cullings. Dumped among those imprisoned within what was itself one immense prison. The murderers, the incurably rebellious, and the just plain mad. He was dying of starvation. Food came on plates shoved through a narrow slit. The strongest fell upon it and wolfed it down, leaving none for the rest. And since Corlo chose not to rouse himself he went without. Such was life without rules beyond individual gratification.

He set his head back. A cold breeze chilled him here below the single narrow chute that opened to the outside. No one spoke to him. Not only was he a foreigner; all here knew a hopeless case when they saw one. He had now what Hagen had identified as 'the look of a jumper'. It was too late now. Even if he wanted to he hadn't the strength to fight for his share. He would fade away. He rubbed at the metal torc round his neck alloyed with magic-deadening otataral. Too late. He'd planned to have Hagen wrench it from him when the time was right. So much for his grand plan for escape.

It was just too awful. All this effort to remain alive to help Bars – only to deceive him beyond all excuse. It was too much.

How many days had passed? He knew not. The glow from the deep chute that allowed light here far within the bowels of the Stormwall came and went. The engorged heartbeat of waves pounded ceaselessly through the stones.

Farewell, Halfpeck. I wish you better luck. May you see your way out. We made a good show of it. Almost made it, too. Crossed half the damned world only to fall short of Quon Tali, into the hands of these provincial, blinkered, ignorant religious fanatics.

Damn them to Hood's deepest vault.

Some time later Corlo was roused by yells and blows in the cell. Guards had entered and were swinging truncheons right and left as they worked their way through the prisoners. They appeared to be searching for someone.

Oh, damn, no. Not again. No. Never. I'll not . . .

Hands took hold of him, lifted him.

No! Damn you! I'd rather die!

He tried to fight but he was too weak. The effort blackened his vision and he knew nothing more.

He awoke lying on a pallet of straw. He no longer shuddered uncontrollably; warmth flowed over him from an iron brazier in the middle of what was a long hall where wounded lay on either side of the narrow walk between. *Some sort of infirmary overflow. Gods, no. They couldn't need him again so soon, could they?* His heart clenched. *Could there be trouble with Bars?*

Someone sat next to his pallet. He smelled hot stew that sent his stomach churning.

'Eat,' the someone said.

'Go away.'

The person leaned closer, said, lower, 'You must eat, Corlo.'

Corlo turned his head and there sat Jemain, First Mate on board their ship, the *Ardent*, before the Marese sank it off the coast of Fist. 'Queen's mysteries, Jemain! What are you doing here?'

The skinny fellow shrugged, grinning. 'I'm a trustee. Been keeping track of you. When I heard you were here I pulled a few favours.'

'But they wanted to keep us separate . . .'

The man lost his grin. 'Well, they seem to have forgotten who came with who. They have bigger worries, hey?' He stirred the stew, offered a spoonful to Corlo, who ate it. 'Anyway . . . I came because I have news. I met someone. A woman . . .'

'Good for you.'

'A sense of humour. A good sign. You're recovering. No, this one fought like a demon on the wall and when I mentioned the name Bars she reacted like she knew him.'

Corlo's stomach coiled, tensing. He tried to sit up. *Hood no! Not someone else!* 'Who!'

'Do you know the name Shell?'

Corlo stared. *Surely not Shellarr? How could they have captured her? Unless . . .* 'Was she blonde?'

'Yes.'

'Attractive?'

The man almost blushed. 'Yes.'

'A mage?'

Jemain frowned. He stirred the stew, offered some more to Corlo, who ate absently. 'She wore no neck torc . . .'

Corlo sat back. 'The woman I know as Shell is a mage. She would've had a neck torc.'

'Unless she's hidden it from the Chosen.'

Suddenly tired, Corlo shut his eyes. 'You say she fought well?'

'Well enough to catch the attention of the Stormguard,' Jemain said bitterly.

Shell was Avowed. Mage or not, that alone would place her among the most formidable here on the wall . . . 'Who was with her? Do you know?'

'She came with others. A few. I could dig around.'

Corlo nodded, eyes shut. 'Yes. Find out who she came with. Names. Descriptions.' Struck by a new thought, he opened his eyes. 'Who else are you in contact with? Who do you know of?' The man was quiet for a time; Corlo glanced over. Gaze lowered, he was stirring the stew. 'Do you know who's left, Jemain?'

Gathering himself, the man nodded. 'Yes, Corlo. I know.'

'Good. Who?'

The man pressed the wooden bowl into Corlo's hands. 'More of that later. That is enough for now. I have to go ask around, yes?'

Corlo grasped the man's wrist as tightly as he could; which was hardly tight at all. 'Who!'

Jemain pressed him back. 'Don't worry yourself, Corlo. Rest. That is enough for now. I'll have more information in time.'

'You're coming back?'

'Yes. Once I find out more.' He stood. 'This woman, Shell. She might be Avowed?'

'Possibly.'

'Good. I'll ask around. Good to see you.'

'And you.'

Jemain squeezed his shoulder then moved off. Corlo lay back, stared at the stone ceiling. *Halfpeck, then. Maybe Meek, Dropper, Joden and Peel. The old Blade. Surely them. Surely of everyone they would have survived. And this woman, Avowed? Probably not. Why would they infiltrate the Stormwall? Bars was convinced that under Skinner the Guard had turned from its old mission. Were they here to finish him off? But why come at all? Surely Bars is contained where he is. Yet he remains among the Avowed; he'll always be a threat to them.*

Very well . . . He found the spoon and stuck it into his mouth to suck on it. He'd have to see. And if there were Avowed of the Guard here, then in a way he hadn't really lied, had he?

* * *

The drain of requisitions for supplies, stores and men led Hiam to the length of Stormwall administered out of Ice Tower, north of Kor. It lay to the east beyond a tall headland and this Hiam climbed alone, cloak tight about him, spear held at an easy angle. Reaching the crest of the pass he was surprised to be challenged by sentries out beyond the obscuring snowfall.

'Halt! Who is there!'

Irritated, Hiam called back: 'By what authority do you challenge a Stormguard on the wall itself?'

'Advance!'

The sentries were not Chosen Stormguard themselves, a fact that eased Hiam's mind, for that would have been an egregious waste. The men were in fact two Theftian recruits carrying shields and swords. 'You are?' one demanded.

'The Lord Protector come to see Master Stimins.'

The two gaped at him, then each other. They sheathed their swords. 'Our apologies. We are just here to warn people off. There are repairs ahead – dangerous footing.'

Hiam cocked a brow. 'Really.'

'Yes, ah, sir. Master Stimins requests that no one continue on.'

'And do you think this prohibition includes me?'

The two shared another glance. 'Hard to say,' one murmured, scratching his neck.

The other shrugged. 'We got our orders.'

Fighting a smile, Hiam studied the butt end of his spear as he tapped the ice rime glittering on the stones of the walk. 'Orders . . . That I can understand. What to do then? It is a thorny question.'

The two shared frowns. One stamped his feet. The other held his hands over a brazier on an iron stand next to their post. They seemed to be hoping he would just go away.

'Perhaps,' Hiam suggested, 'one of you might escort me . . . onward?'

One shot a glance to the other. 'Dunno. Maybe.'

'I'll let Master Stimins know you were most vigilant.'

The two relaxed, letting out pluming breaths the wind snatched away. 'Well . . . okay,' one allowed. 'I'll take you. Gnorl, you stay on guard.' He invited Hiam onward. 'This way.'

Hiam followed, a rueful smile hidden behind the narrow slit of his helm. He didn't bother pointing out that he'd run up and down the wall since childhood.

Cresting the tall headland they descended to the low beach overlooked by the Ice Tower and its curtain wall. As they drew closer Hiam caught glimpses of that arc of curtain wall through the intervening gusting snowfall and he halted as if frozen himself.

Lady deliver us!

A great waterfall of blue-green ice enveloped lengths of it. The ice coursed over and down the rear of the wall, frozen in the act of falling. Figures worked like dark struggling ants upon the ice, hammering and chiselling, while others stood guard, facing the smashing waves.

What has happened here? Has it collapsed? 'Take me to Master Stimins,' he snarled to the guard and started down, slipping and staggering upon the slick rock steps. He found the Master Engineer directing repairs from the base of Ice Tower. He came upon the man suddenly, the blowing snow parting. Over the driving wind and the shuddering impact of the waves the engineer was yelling directions to a handful of workers. Hiam presumed these to be his crew chiefs. Upon seeing Hiam the men straightened, saluting, and Stimins' back flinched, becoming rigid. 'Dismissed,' he told the men, who bowed to Hiam and disappeared off into the driving snow.

'When were you going to tell me?' Hiam demanded.

Stimins slowly turned. 'You have the entire wall to manage, young Hiam. I hoped to spare you this worry.'

Hiam grunted, accepting that, though he was outraged. 'Well, I'm here now. What are you doing about this?'

The old man gestured up the length of the walk to where equipment, rope, and blocks of stone lay jumbled and veined in ice. 'I'm raising the wall.'

'*Raising it?* During attacks of the Riders?' Hiam was astounded – yet what else were they to do? He scanned the sea: the waves churned wind-chopped, but no burgeoning surge drove up the inlet, not today. Not now. Hiam could sense an assault to the hour just by the pitch of the wind. 'How goes it?'

Stimins shook his nearly bald head. 'Work is too slow. We're losing too many men. The Riders smell blood. We need more guards.'

Yet all the Chosen were assigned – and each was vital to his position. The truth was, they had no men to spare. Due south of here, though, lay the city of Kor itself. The Riders could not be allowed to breast this section. A new question occurred to Hiam. 'If there was no collapse, no break. Why here? Why now?'

The old man looked away, his mouth wrinkled tight. He examined his gnarled twisted hands, which were wrapped in rags. 'I'd hoped to spare you, Hiam. It is not welcome news . . . the truth is, the wall has not lowered . . . the sea has risen.'

Hiam stared. Rising? All along the wall? No wonder the butcher's bill had climbed so – he'd thought it their thinning numbers. But no. It was worse. For who can fight the sea? Yet . . . was that not what their ancestors had done for generations? How dare they do any less? *Lady – why do you test us so? Is our devotion lacking? Is this a punishment?*

He gripped his spear until his hands numbed. *Very well, Blessed Lady . . . you shall witness. Our piety, our fervour, shall humble all who witness it!*

'What of the west, the Wind Tower and the weakness there?'

Stimins nodded. 'I believe that also follows from the rising sea. All the flaws are emerging now under this increased pressure.'

Hiam snorted. *You have the truth of that, Master Engineer. Flaws in more than just the wall. And those flaws must be hammered away else the Lady will allow us to fall.* 'Very good, Stimins. You'll have whatever you need.'

'More guards for the work gangs?'

Hiam thought of the latest communiqués from loyal sources in Rool. Troops massing in Lallit for transport. All good signs. Yet reports also of the invader fleet in Banith. The Betrayer's forces meaning to invade there? Ridiculous, with Rool to pacify. They would need it as a foothold. The Betrayer would not abandon it. The fleet was merely over-wintering in calmer waters. They meant to repair and refit.

He just had to hold on until that Roolian manpower arrived.

Again, Hiam's instincts spoke to him. They may not have the numbers, but they had their champion, revitalized of late. And other skilled prisoners – even mercenaries. He would bring them all here; pour everything they had into this breach.

They would hold. They had to. They would be given no choice.

* * *

The Army of Reform crawled northward at a cripple's pace that did nothing for Ivanr's mood. Ahead of their outriders villages burned all across the landscape. Each cast a black plume of smoke that mixed and swelled, announcing open warfare between Imperial loyalists and Reform sympathizers. The smoke struck Ivanr as a fitting banner heralding their approach. Their numbers swelled further as sympathizers joined the army proper, or contributed to the swollen informal army of followers and refugees dragging along behind. All told he estimated their numbers at nearing fifty thousand. A huge force – in numbers. Largest yet of all the peasant uprisings and heretical messianic movements that he knew of from the past. Yet by his estimate less than a third could really be counted on to stand unflinching and fight.

He walked close to its centre now, completely disengaged from the day-to-day logistics and organization of command. So it was he could only watch while the army's unofficial sappers and engineers demolished many of the wooden buildings they passed. They piled the beams and lumber on to wagons for transport. Seeing this, he came to the dispiriting conclusion that Martal was preparing for a siege of Ring. The woman's lumbering carriages also rumbled here and there amid the disorganized crowds like siege-towers on the move. Seeing them heaving along reminded him of their commander's opaque claim that they'd brought their own fortress with them. Were they intended as a sort of mobile archers' platform? She must know she couldn't count on employing the same tactics as before. The Imperials would be ready for them this time.

A light drizzle fell, cold and discomforting. Its chill reminded him that much farther north the Korelri faced down the Stormriders in the name of their own defence – even as he and this army of heretics and polytheists sought to usurp the Lady's worship. Who was right? Was either of them? Again he wished Beneth were here, though he had never thought to discuss such matters with him while the man lived. What then was to be his role, if not teacher, prophet or inspiration? The question still tormented him and further blackened his mood.

A man waited to make his way through the layers of guards now surrounding him. Tall and sickly-thin: the old pilgrim. Ivanr nodded to allow him through. He approached, bowing, and paced Ivanr.

'You have news?' Ivanr asked.

The man's drawn face was grim. 'Yes.' The rain had plastered his dirty grey hair over his uneven skull.

'Troubling news?'

'Yes.'

Ivanr motioned to the overcast sky. 'Not a day for bad news.'

'No day would be good for this news.'

Does this fellow delight in being the bearer of bad news? 'All right. What is it?'

The man took a fortifying breath. 'We have word from reliable sources that the Priestess still lives.'

Ivanr stared at the man. 'Generous gods! This is *bad* news?'

'She is with the Imperial Army. They are bringing her with them.'

Ivanr rubbed the cold rain from his face as they continued to walk along. They were bringing her south – *to them*? 'And you are worried . . .'

'What they intend, yes. I believe they mean to make a spectacle of her death.'

Yes. That would make sense. A gruesome lesson in the uselessness of rebellion. Yet do they really believe that would terrify these people? It would only infuriate them. Strengthen their resolve, not weaken it. In fact, it may provoke a bloodbath. Could that be their real intent? To goad these peasants into a precipitous attack? I will have to warn Martal.

'Thank you . . . What is your name, anyway?'

A humourless tightening of the thin bloodless lips. 'Orman.'

'You served in Beneth's organization?'

'Yes, in addition to my preaching.'

Ivanr eyed him sidelong. 'When we spoke before . . . were you acting for Beneth?'

He shook his head, completely untroubled. 'Then, I spoke for the Priestess.'

'Well, I'm not one to meddle among Beneth's choices. So, what now?'

For a time Orman walked along in silence, hands behind his back, head cocked. 'With your permission I will travel ahead to Ring city. Early on we made an effort to seed the city with followers. Now we're pretty much locked teeth and throat in an unofficial battle for control of it.'

'How goes it?'

A clenched, pained look crossed the fleshless face. 'Poorly. These Imperials have finally caught on. They've sealed the roads north.

Forced refugees back into the city. They're not giving up any more ground.'

'I see. So . . . what is your prediction?'

He tilted his head. 'This time I believe the fate of the city will be decided by the battle. Whoever wins that will win the city – and half the country. Impartially speaking, the Imperials really should not meet us upon the field. They ought to garrison Ring, deny it to us, and watch our movement dissolve away goalless and unfocused . . .' He sighed, lifting his bony shoulders. 'But that they will not do. The way these uprisings have been dealt with in the past will dictate how the Imperials will handle this one now.'

He offered what might have been intended as a smile of encouragement, but which struck Ivanr as a death's-head leer. 'So you see, Ivanr. You may take their determination to meet us in the field as a potential disaster – I see it as already a half-victory.' With that the man bowed, and took his leave.

Ivanr wasn't certain what to make of all that. Either the man was an extraordinarily talented political agent, or he was a religious fanatic blind to everything but success. While he agreed that this lot did not have the discipline to last any protracted siege, the Imperial heavy cavalry playing to their strengths of warfare in the field did not particularly strike him as a mistake on their part. But he didn't serve on the intelligence side of strategy. Tactics was his strength.

The call came back through the ranks for an end to the day's march. The soldier in Ivanr was horrified: it was nowhere near dusk! At this rate it would take them another week to reach Ring. He dabbed his wet sleeve to his face. Such was the price of holding together a voluntary civilian army.

And as always, the Imperials watched and waited. He peered around, searching the rolling hillsides surrounding the loose, ranging force. There, on the distant flank, riders shadowing them. One of Hegil's few remaining cavalry? No way to tell from this distance. Probably not. He wondered why they weren't constantly harassing them, gnawing at their numbers. Perhaps the Imperials considered it beneath their dignity.

Perhaps they did not wish to discourage the rag-tag army from advancing to its destruction. A damned miserable conclusion to come to. He blew on his hands and wished he hadn't thought of it.

*

A constellation of camp fires lit the night to the east. Here, in a wooded depression, a single hearth of embered logs glowed a sullen orange. A man sat cross-legged before it, hunched, studying small objects pulled from a bag. Each piece elicited further exclamations of disbelief and outrage until the man scooped up the casting of pieces and thrust them home once again.

The crackle of brush snapped his attention round. 'Who is that?'

'It's Totsin,' snarled the newcomer, cursing and pushing at the dense bracken.

The man relaxed. 'Surprised to see you here. Don't you know it's dangerous to disturb a talent at work?'

Totsin straightened his shirt and pushed back his thin hair. 'Is that what you're doing? I'm looking for Sister Gosh. She's here, isn't she?'

The man shook the bag, squinted suspiciously at it. 'Yeah. She's here,' he said absently.

Totsin watched for a time, stroking his uneven beard. 'So, Brother Jool . . . what *are* you doing?'

Jool shook the bag next to his ear once again. A clacking sounded from it. 'The tiles are talking nonsense.'

Totsin's hand clenched in his beard. He took a quavering breath. 'Oh? I've always thought them unreliable, you know.'

Not answering, Jool smoothed the dirt before him then reached into the bag. He drew a tile, examined it in the faint light, grunted, and set it down.

'What is it?' Totsin asked in a whisper.

'Hearth, or Flame, inverted. Failure? Betrayal? A very troubling start.'

Next came another tile, this one of a very black wood. Jool snorted his disgust. 'Again. Always early. A strong portent – but of what?'

'What is that one?'

'The Dark Hoarder, inverted. Death? Betrayal ending in death? Or life, the opposite of cessation? How am I to read it?'

Totsin said nothing.

Another tile, this one of crude fired clay. 'Earth. Very unusual coming up this early. Could also mean the past returned, or consequences. It is aligned with the ancient earth goddess. Some name it the Dolmen.'

He reached in again and this time hissed at the gleaming white tile in his hand. 'Riders next. Prominent. Are these two associated now somehow? What are the relationships here: hearth betrayed, death betrayed, earth or past, and Stormriders? What am I to make of it?' Jool reached in again. 'One last choice.'

This dark wood tile he held up, squinting at it. 'Demesne of Night. Hold of Darkness. Related, how? A puzzle indeed.'

Totsin cleared his throat. 'I have a tile for you, Jool. I came by it recently.'

Jool did not look up; he was frowning at the spread of tiles before him. 'Oh? A new one?'

'Yes. Here it is.'

Distracted, Jool glanced up. Totsin tossed the small rectangle of wood; Jool caught it. 'What is . . . Gods all around! Totsin! You fool!' The man sprang to his feet, tried to throw the tile away but it would not leave his hand. He stared at it, horrified. 'We *never* – the Witch! *Her!* What have you—'

Then, a long hiss of comprehension, his shoulders falling. 'I see now. Hearth, home, betrayed: a traitor within the family. Death – mine. Dolmen – the past, your reasons. Night – now, this night.'

The hand holding the tile withered before their eyes, desiccating to a dead skeletal limb sheathed in skin cured to leather. 'The Riders, though,' Jool continued, wondering. 'What have they . . . wait! Four! Four fates foretold! Two greater and two lesser.' The man's face paled to an ashen pallor, sinking and withering. 'Fool you remain, Totsin. You slew me too early. What I foresee I now withhold – to your despair . . .' A last breath escaped dried lips and Jool collapsed, bones clattering, to fall in a heap of parchment-like flesh.

Totsin regarded the corpse. Bravado? Empty threat? What was he to make of that last message? Pondering it, he used a stick to push the tiles back into their leather pouch then cinched it tight. Nothing, he decided. It meant nothing. Too vague and unreliable, this technique . . . he'd never trusted it. A method for lesser talents only. He kicked dirt over the smouldering embers.

Only two left now. The two most dangerous.

* * *

After departing the Ancy valley, word came to the Moranth column that Borun and Ussü were to travel ahead by mount as they had been summoned by the Overlord. They took messenger mounts and used the system of changing-posts to transfer to fresh horses as they travelled west. Though a Moranth, and unused to riding, Borun endured the endless pounding with his typical stoicism. Ussü, however, hadn't ridden so hard in over two decades. The travel was a torture to him. His inner thighs were scraped raw; his back and neck ached as if struck all over by batons; and despite the constant agony he nearly fell off his mount as towards dawn he drifted into a fog of exhaustion.

At the next changing-post he lay down and threatened Borun with death should he disturb him. Prudently, the Moranth commander did not answer and withdrew. Ussü slept immediately, and seemingly just as immediately a knock came on the door. 'What is it?' he croaked.

'I have given you four hours,' Borun answered.

Ussü let his head fall back. *Damn.* 'Very well. I am coming.' Levering himself up he set his feet on the ground and straightened, groaning. *Gods, and Lady, I am too old for this. This trip alone will be the death of me.* He opened the door, leaned against the jamb. Borun grunted, seeing him.

'Food and fresh mounts await.'

Ussü shook his head. 'I cannot. You go ahead.'

'That is not the arrangement. We travel together. Now come.'

Ussü raised a palsied, liver-spotted hand. 'No. I haven't the strength. It's been too long.'

The featureless matt-black helm regarded him in silence, then Borun gathered the food into panniers which he threw over a shoulder. 'You are a mage – do whatever it is you do.' And he left the post's main room.

Ussü stared after him. *Damn if the man wasn't right.* He regarded the hand, drew on his Warren. Blue flame flickered to life around the flesh. *Anneal me*, he commanded. *Flames shall nourish.* Instantly the bone-weariness sloughed from him like slag in a furnace. He straightened, shocked and, frankly, rather terrified. Whence comes this power? There was nothing of the Lady in it; rather, she seemed to have stood aside and allowed it. Grudgingly, he accepted it.

My thanks, Blessed Lady.

At the changing-post beside the main crossroads for the road to Paliss, word came that they were to make for Lallit. Ussü took the orders from Borun's hands. 'Lallit? On the coast? Whatever for?'

'It does not say. But it is authentic. The seals and codes are correct.'

Ussü threw it back at the messenger in frustration. He needed to speak to Yeull! Why this detour to the coast? It was insufferable – and yet more riding! 'That's another four days!'

'Approximately. And we must go. There is no questioning this.'
'Still no word from Ancy?' Ussü asked the messenger.
'No, sir. You are ahead of the news.'
Borun dismissed the messenger. 'We'll take the Paliss road for a time then strike west.' He headed for the corral.
Ussü watched the man's armoured back. Here I am complaining and this man has yet to hear any word on his command. Surely they must be a good two or three days ahead of any Malazan advance – even if they broke through immediately. Still, he would do well to dwell less on his own troubles and think of those of others for a change.
Resigning himself to the shift in destination, he went to join Borun.

Three days' riding, plus the better part of three nights', brought Ussü and Borun near Lallit on the coast of an arm of Sender's Sea which many named the Pirate's Sea. These last few days they'd come across signs of the passage of many men and wagons and carts of equipment. It looked as if an army had been brought to the coast. All this further troubled Ussü. Could Yeull actually be here and not at Paliss? If so, what of the capital? Whatever was he planning? The Malazans were advancing; the reorganized Roolian Army ought to be massing and heading east to confront them.
Turning a last hillside in the long sloping descent to the coast brought the iron-blue expanse of the sea into view and the modest town of Lallit as well. Ships choked its narrow harbour and an encamped army surrounded the town. It looked like the assemblage of an invasion force. For an instant Ussü wondered whether they were looking at another Malazan force just landed on their west coast. But the dark brown of Rool flew everywhere, reassuring him. He and Borun exchanged a wordless look and continued on.
Sentries met them, and an escort was assembled to guide them to the Overlord. All the rest of the Sixth appeared to have been brought together from all frontiers. Elite native Roolian and Skolati forces fleshed out the numbers. Their escort brought them to the wharf and the gangway of a large man-of-war bearing Roolian pennants, plus the personal pennant of the Overlord, the old standard of the Sixth.
Here on the coast snow fell, driven inland by strong south-westerlies off the Ocean of Storms. The air was noticeably colder – the damp, Ussü told himself, nothing more. The Overlord's personal guard waved them up the gangway. Within the dim sweltering main

cabin they found the Overlord awaiting them. They drew off their thick travelling cloaks and Ussü knelt to offer obeisance to the shadowy figure behind the great desk piled with sheets of vellum, scrolls, and battered ledgers.

'Overlord. You ordered us to report.'

'And here you are,' the figure grumbled. 'Feed the fire. You've brought the frigid air with you.'

A guard set more wood on the iron brazier even though sweat now beaded Ussü's brow and steam rose from their travelling cloaks.

'You ordered our withdrawal . . .' Borun said, his voice sounding more hoarse than usual.

The figure leaned forward, arms on the desk. His vision adjusting, Ussü saw that Yeull sat wrapped in his usual layers. His black hair gleamed wet with sweat and his face held a pale fevered look. 'Is that an accusation?' he demanded.

'It is a question.'

The man grunted, sinking back into his tall-backed chair. 'You may have stalled the Betrayer a week or more but he would have crossed eventually. If not there, then elsewhere. Or divided his forces in multiple crossings. Yes?'

Borun grated, 'Possibly . . .'

The Overlord sneered. 'It would have happened. The Betrayer is determined to win through to the coast. He must. It is his strategy. His throw for all or nothing.'

'The coast?' Ussü asked.

Yeull's hot gaze shifted to him. 'You did not stop for news during your ride here, did you? Else you would have heard. Tell me, this second invasion force arrived in more than four hundred ships. What do you think happened to those once the Betrayer landed?'

Ussü shrugged. 'I imagine that in due course the Marese sank them. As before.'

Yeull seemed to growl his disgust. 'Hot tea!' he barked aside to a guard, and the man set about pouring a dark brew. 'No, my too-trusting adviser. In due course the Marese acknowledged defeat and sued for peace!' Yeull slammed a fist to the table, scattering vellum sheets. 'So much for them.' He pulled at the layered jackets and padded quilted jerkins he wore draped about his shoulders. 'And now we are flanked.'

Flanked? Ah, the coast! Gods forfend! They are here?

'You are abandoning Rool,' Borun judged, far ahead of Ussü in matters of strategy.

The Overlord nodded. 'Yes.'

Ussü was completely confused. Abandon Rool? To go where? *Why won't he stand and fight?* 'You too are capitulating?' he blurted and instantly regretted it.

The Overlord was quiet. Sweat gleamed like a sheath on his face. His gaze was like a heated lance stabbing at Ussü's brow. After a time he drew a shuddering breath, gulped down his steaming tea. 'We travel to the real battle, my ignorant adviser.'

A grating snarl sounded from Borun's helm. 'They strike at Korel!'

Ussü felt as if he would fall faint. The exhaustion, the heat, these revelations. It was all too much. He wiped a hand across his slick brow. 'That would be insane. The entire island would rise against him.' He searched the dim room for an empty chair or a stool.

'Your faith is a lesson to us all,' the Overlord commented from the gloom. 'That must be why she favours you so much.'

But Ussü was not listening. His breath would not come. It was too close, too constraining. He felt as if the ship were suddenly in a storm. Armoured hands gripped him and sat him down on a ledge. A hand forced his head down to his knees. 'Breathe,' Borun ordered.

The blackness swallowing Ussü's vision abated. He panted while his heart slowed its constricted panic. Borun was speaking: 'You are too quick to abandon Rool. Let me march south. We may yet stop him.'

'True,' the Overlord granted, sounding surprisingly tolerant of such questioning. 'We may. But I have opted to substitute the possibility of victory now for assured success in the summer.'

'Oh? How so?'

Ussü looked up, blinking. A guard offered him a glass of tea, which he took with gratitude. It was a herbal infusion he recognized, very resuscitating.

'The Korelri are desperate for manpower. We have struck an agreement to provide it. Further, we will stand with them to repel any Malazan attempt to break them. After this, come spring when the Stormriders have retreated and the Korelri stand idle . . . well, just imagine what we could accomplish returning to Rool accompanied by the iron might of the grateful Korelri.'

Ussü stared, amazed. Would this work? The Korelri had never before interfered in any of the old internecine warfare and feuds; so long as they received their tribute, they were content. Yet if Greymane struck at their island in an attempt to break their power, and the

Roolians stood with them . . . an alliance! The advantages would be incalculable.

'And my command?' Borun rumbled.

Silent, Yeull regarded the Black commander for some time, his eyes slit almost shut. Ussü sensed a dislike bordering on disgust in that gaze – could this be jealousy? 'They will be last. Ships will be sent back. You may stay to await them.'

Borun bowed.

'And you, my High Mage . . .'

Ussü straightened, bowing. 'Yes, Overlord.'

'You will accompany me. Have you ever seen the Stormwall?'

'Ah, no, my lord.'

'It is a wonder of the world. And quite a sight. Especially this time of year.'

Ussü suddenly no longer felt so unbearably hot. He pulled the sweat-soaked clothes away from his chest. 'So you say, m'lord. So you say.'

CHAPTER X

> There resides just outside Thol a famous anchoress who lives sealed within her prison home, her only communication with the outside world a narrow slit through which food may be passed. Pilgrims from all over the isles visit this sacred woman, who has forsworn the profane world for her contemplation of the sacred. You may sit next to the bricked door with its narrow window and partake of her wisdom earned through five decades of self-imposed exile from the world. Locked within her tiny cell, nothing is beyond the reach of her judgement.
>
> *Holies of the Subcontinent*
> The Abbey, Paliss

ENTERING BANITH, GREYMANE ESTABLISHED HIS HEADQUARTERS in the warehouse the Moranth Blue occupied. Devaleth was pleased to see that when the High Fist and Admiral Swirl met, they shared a long clasp. Admiral Nok, she'd heard, was not present as the man had famously sworn a vow never to set foot on land again. The two immediately sat down to discuss tactics. Orders went out to the Fists, Rillish and Khemet Shul, who were in the field overseeing the disposition of the troops.

While she was pleased by the High Fist's cheer, what he intended was now absolutely clear to her and the immensity, the audaciousness of it left her reeling.

Kyle noticed, and invited her aside. 'You are unwell?'

Her voice was shaky as she answered, very low, 'Do you have any idea what this man is actually going to go through with?'

'A landing on Korel, yes.'

She stared at him, shocked that he could say that so casually. 'It is clear you are all from elsewhere. What—' She stopped herself, searching for the right words. 'What does he intend regarding . . . regarding the Stormwall?'

The young man did not look sure himself. He felt his way through it as he spoke: 'I believe he intends to break the power of the Korelri here in this subcontinent. That he sees that as the only way he can truly win here.' He was nodding as he finished. 'And I agree,' he added half to himself. 'As to the Stormwall . . . The Malazans may have to step into the Korelris' place for a time.'

Devaleth twisted her hands across her stomach where they clenched, knuckles white. 'If you do that you will be trapped there for ever.' And she walked away, gaze lowered.

Fist Rillish entered, and saluted. 'You requested my presence, High Fist?'

Greymane leaned back against his table, which was cluttered with ledgers and curled orders. He pushed back his long iron-grey hair, and for a time eyed the man from under his heavy brows, his blue eyes stormy. 'Yes. Fist. We are disembarking for Korel with all speed. You know that. However, the worst option is that we may be repulsed. In which case we will need a secure port to return to. Banith, here in Rool, will be that port. Therefore, we cannot entirely abandon Rool.'

Devaleth's stomach clenched in dread. *Oh, no, Greymane – do not do this to him . . .*

The Untan nobleman paled, swaying. 'High Fist,' he whispered, his voice cracking, 'I beg you. Do not separate me from the Fourth.'

'I will leave four thousand troops with you.'

'Captain Betteries, or Captain Perin, surely . . .'

'A captain cannot be the effective administrative head of a country, Fist. You know that.'

'Greymane,' Kyle murmured, 'perhaps—'

'You're staying too.'

Kyle flinched upright. '*What!*' He stared in disbelief. 'You will need me for the landing!'

Greymane met his gaze: he seemed to be trying to tell the lad something. 'With you here, Kyle, I'm confident at least Rool will remain in Malazan hands.'

'With your permission . . .' Fist Rillish grated, turning abruptly and leaving. Kyle glared his confusion but Greymane looked away, lowering his head, mouth clenched. Muttering a curse under his breath, Kyle stormed out to find the Fist. Bowing, Devaleth followed.

She found them down on the wharf. The Fist was staring out over the harbour where the Blue vessels were readying to disembark. Already troops were heading out on launches for the larger men-of-war anchored in the bay. Kyle was standing nearby, also deep in thought. A chilling wind off the bay clawed at all of them and clouds roiled overhead, coasting inland.

'You must be very angry with me,' the Fist said, casting Kyle a quick glance.

'Angry? With you?'

The man shrugged, still staring out over the bay. 'If it weren't for me you'd be accompanying him, yes?'

'I think he is right in keeping you here,' Devaleth said. 'If only he'd done it differently . . .'

A strained smile from Rillish: 'Diplomacy is not Stonewielder's strength.'

'We need to be with him. The landing will be butchery.'

'No,' Devaleth snapped, fierce. 'It could easily go so badly – you will be needed here.'

The Fist took a deep breath of the icy sea air then turned to face them. His face was pale, the lines at the mouth savage. His greying hair blew about, neglected and unkempt. 'The High Fist has made his choice. We cannot but obey. Even with Yeull fled to Korel with the majority of the Sixth there still remain the Roolian militia, straggling units, renegade companies, and this self-appointed "Baron" to deal with. We will more than have our hands full.'

'That is not reason enough to leave us behind,' Kyle ground out.

'You are not considering another reason,' Devaleth said, her gaze arched. 'I believe the man has just saved both your lives.'

Kyle and Rillish shared a rueful glance, then she saw in their faces the realization: as High Mage, she would be accompanying Greymane.

*

Suth charged up the stairs of the inn the 4th Company had occupied when it entered Banith, threw open the door to his squad's room and began pulling his equipment together. Pyke lay on one pallet while Wess lay on another, apparently asleep.

'Get a move on,' he told them, quickly packing his roll. 'They're lining up to board.'

Pyke watched, an arm under his head, a mocking smile at his lips. He raised a bottle and took a sip. 'Haven't you heard?'

'Heard what?'

'We ain't goin'.'

Suth looked up from his packing. 'What?'

'We're stayin'.' Pyke held the bottle on his stomach. 'Garrisoning Banith here. Sweet berth, if you ask me. We'll be pulling in protection dues in no time. Maybe there'll be some girls who need extra protection, if you know what I mean.' He winked.

Suth gripped his sword, newly sharpened and wrapped in its belt. *He goes to find a grinder and now this happens?* He threw it down. 'You're full of shit, Pyke.'

For once the man wasn't nettled. He grinned, sipping his wine. 'Go ask fat-arse Goss. He's downstairs.'

Suth waved him a gesture and stormed down the stairs. He found the sergeant, and most of the squad, at a table towards the rear. 'What's this?' he demanded, standing over them.

Goss sank back in his seat, a tall stoneware stein before him. 'It's true,' he growled, sounding defeated. Yana nodded, head in her hands, elbows on the table.

'Imparala Ar take them! That is so full of shit!'

Someone cuffed Suth from behind, a trooper he recognized from the 10th. 'Good luck with these old ladies here in Banith – watch out for their canes!' The next table over burst out laughing.

Suth waved him off with a sick laugh of his own. Len kicked out a chair. Suth threw himself down. 'Who else?'

'The 11th, the 6th, a few others,' Len answered.

'The 20th?'

Len shook his head. 'They're going.'

'Sure – they get to go!' Yana snarled.

'It'll be damned ugly,' Goss warned, taking a deep drink. Len frowned down at the table. Keri looked pained, either for herself or for those going, Suth wasn't sure.

Lard just sighed. 'An' we're gonna miss it. I was so lookin' forward to it.'

Suth eyed the big man. He really couldn't say he was looking forward to it; he no longer needed to clash swords to see who was stronger or faster. The reason he wanted to go was to be there for everyone else – they'd all be needed for this ugly set-to. 'I can't fucking believe it.'

Goss was nodding. 'Welcome to the army.'

*

From the windows of his office Bakune watched the occupying Malazan Army march through the streets of Banith. *So they march in and they march out; Malazans go and Malazans come. Our old overlords had been Malazan yet somehow these feel different. But then I wasn't there when the Sixth first marched in. I imagine this is what they must have looked like then too: disciplined, hardened, the veterans of invasions on five continents. But after a few decades of occupation, now look at them . . .*

He turned away to his desk. Paperwork cluttered it. Demands from the religious hierarchy that Banith pay for repairs to the Cloister and Hospice. His denial of said demand: the church can pay for it. Though, given their disarray, there was no way of telling when that would occur. Demands from citizens for recompense regarding billeting and the occupation of rooms. Lost income, damages. Bakune could only shake his head. Didn't they understand that these were their *conquerors*? They could do as they pleased. So far no one had been killed on either side: *that* was the important fact.

And his request for an audience with this new High Fist – though he was far from relishing meeting the greatest fiend of the age. The Betrayer, Stonewielder, Greymane himself! Who would have thought it? A figure out of the old tales mothers used to scare their children.

Now here to scare them in truth.

So far, to his relief, his request had gone unanswered. He'd dealt with only minor officers to date, captains and lieutenants. Brusque and rigid all, but reassuringly professional in their demeanour. It was all cautiously encouraging – but then, no doubt the Sixth had also been similarly professional. In the beginning.

And Ipshank? Where was he? Gone to ground? He missed the man's counsel, especially now. Damn the man for disappearing when needed most.

A knock at his door. 'Enter.'

Captain Hyuke of the City Watch entered, and slumped down into a chair. He brushed thoughtfully at his fat moustache. Bakune regarded him. 'Well?'

'They're leavin' all right. Shippin' out for Korel. Chasin' after the Overlord. Gonna have it out with him. It's outta our hands now . . .' He shrugged.

As it ever was. 'And so?'

He continued grooming the long moustache. 'They'll leave some kinda small contingent behind, course . . .'

Bakune glared impatiently. 'Yes?'

The man lifted his shoulders in a regretful hunch. 'Well, there'll be trouble. People will start gettin' ideas. There'll be ambushes, killin'. Then there'll be retribution, arrests, executions. Things'll escalate. It'll be ugly.'

Bakune pressed his fingertips to his temples. *Damn all the gods! An insurrection. That was the last problem he needed right now. Just when things were settling down.* He regarded his Watch captain. 'You'll just have to keep that from happening then, won't you?'

The man scratched his scalp, examined his blackened fingertips. 'Well, that'll put your name and mine at the top of their list, won't it?'

Bakune blinked. *Am I not already condemned as a collaborator? Have there not already been attempts on my life? Hasn't someone already tried to break into my house?* 'That would seem unavoidable. Unless you wish to quit? Or are you suggesting there exists an alternative?'

The man seemed to squirm in embarrassment. He coughed into his fist. 'Well, there is this Roolian general up in the hills . . . he already controls most of the south. Mosta the militia 'n' insurgents 'n' such swear loyalty to him. He's offered to quash all that violence. Keep a lid on things . . .'

Bakune sat back, his gaze narrowing. He did not like the direction this was headed. 'And?' he mouthed, already knowing the answer.

Again, an almost apologetic shrug from Hyuke. 'All you have to do is look the other way while he's recruiting and resupplying 'n' such, that's all.'

Bakune felt his gaze harden into an icy glare. *Play both sides. How distasteful. Was he to betray his vows to uphold the laws of the land? Yet whose laws? The laws of an occupying foreign military elite? What loyalty could they demand from him? Or reasonably expect, for that matter?*

He cleared his throat. 'And what guarantees can this *general* possibly offer that he will not launch any operations here in Banith? The Malazans are here, after all. I'll not have this city become a war zone!'

Hyuke nodded, pained. 'Oh, that won't happen. He gives you his sworn word. He's busy consolidating right now anyway. Bringing order to more provinces.'

'Eliminating his rivals, you mean.'

An embarrassed shrug.

'And does this Roolian general have a name, then?'

'Ah, well, that's his guarantee, you see . . .'
Bakune sighed, impatient. 'Yes?'
'The general's name is Karien'el.'

* * *

Lord Protector Hiam met Overlord Yeull in a pavilion raised to the east of Elri. Wall Marshal Quint accompanied him, as did his aide, Shool. The encampment of the landed Roolian troops sprawled like an instant city down the shore to the very strand. Ships lay anchored off shore. Reports from the regular Korelri guard had made it clear that far more than the agreed-upon ten thousand had disembarked. Arriving, Hiam saw this to be true. It occurred to him that any other ruler would view such a landing as an invasion. But no other ruler had standing behind him the Stormwall and the absolute truth of his indispensability.

Guards opened the heavy cloth flaps and Hiam ducked beneath them. Within, a wall of heat struck him like a fist closing on his chest. Overlord Yeull sat next to a great glowing heap of embers resting on a wide iron bowl. Next to him stood a tall slim man, grey-bearded, in pale creamy robes sashed at the waist. The Overlord stood, straightened a thick fur hide slung over his shoulders, and bowed.

Hiam answered the bow. 'Welcome, Overlord, to Korel.'

'Lord Protector. You are most gracious to allow us to land.'

Quint and Shool entered and Hiam introduced them. Overlord Yeull gestured to the man beside him. 'Ussü, my chief adviser.'

'I must say,' Hiam began, 'I was most surprised to hear that you would be accompanying your troops.'

Yeull sat, held his hands over the embers. The man acted as if he were chilled to the bone despite the crushing heat within the tent, his layers of clothes, his fur cloak, and the sweat dripping from his sallow brow. He nodded his assent to the point. 'I will not prevaricate, Lord Protector. I am here because the Betrayer, Stonewielder, is coming here.'

Hiam glanced at Quint, who could not keep the scorn from his expression. 'Really, Overlord? I rather thought you'd come here because the Betrayer had defeated you and you had nowhere else to go.'

The man leapt from his chair, blood darkening his face. 'How *dare* you! Here you are, hard pressed, with barely the numbers necessary to defend the wall, and I come offering aid – *and this is how you repay me!*'

The adviser, Ussü, eased the Overlord back into his seat. He raised his hands to speak. 'Please. Lords. Let us not quarrel. It seems to me that like any agreement both parties have something to gain and something to give. We pledge ten thousand in support of the wall – our half of a pact of mutual defence. Surely our presence is a welcome boon, yes?'

Hiam inclined his head in acquiescence. 'Well spoken, sir. You are welcome, Overlord. For so long as you contribute to the defence of the Stormwall, you may remain as guests in our lands.'

'And should there be Malazan landings here in Korel we will defend the shores,' said Yeull. 'Surely, in such an event, you too would fly to the defence of your lands.'

'Certainly,' Hiam responded. *No matter how unlikely.*

Ussü bowed. 'Very good. Then we are in accord. Our thanks, Lord Protector.'

Overlord Yeull inclined his head a fraction. 'Agreed.'

'Agreed,' supplied Hiam. 'And now, my apologies, but duties on the wall demand my presence. I really must return.'

'I understand,' said Yeull, thinly. 'Another time, Lord Protector.'

Hiam bowed. 'Another time.'

Outside the tent, the adviser, Ussü, joined their party as they walked back to their mounts: three of the few horses the Stormguard kept for extremely vital messages. Hiam nodded to him. 'Adviser Ussü, how may we help you?'

The man walked with hands clasped at his back, head bowed. 'Lord Protector, a small request.'

'Yes?'

'Word has reached me of your current champion of the wall . . .'

'Yes?'

'That he speaks Malazan, that is, Quon Talian, yet is not of the Sixth Army . . .'

'Yes. That is so.' They reached their horses. Roolian troops steadied them while they struggled to mount.

'I wonder if I may have permission to see him? To speak to him?'

Tightening his reins, Hiam shrugged. 'I do not see why not. If you wish. Shool, arrange it, won't you?'

'Certainly,' Shool answered as he fought to get his foot into the stirrup.

Ussü helped the aide steady his foot then bowed as they cantered off. *Poor riders, these Korelri. I wonder how much support we can count on when Stonewielder arrives. Very little, no doubt. I do not see this man pulling troops from the wall. And this champion. Malazan, yet not Malazan. Bars. An unusual name. Could he be* the *Bars? Avowed of the Crimson Guard? Practically unkillable, these Avowed. Imagine what I could accomplish with one of them . . .*

Ussü returned to the command tent. He found Yeull bent over the brazier.

'Lady deliver me,' the Overlord groaned. 'This cold is killing me.'

'M'lord, when can we expect Borun and the Moranth? Soon, I should hope. Greymane may be here any day.'

Yeull sank back into his chair. 'What's that? The Moranth? Ussü – no ships have been sent. Nor will they ever be sent.'

Ussü felt as if he'd been slapped. He stared, open-mouthed. So shocked was he that he almost took the man by his collar and shook him. '*What?* I do not see—'

Yeull roused himself, furious once more. 'See? See? You do not see? *Who* are the Malazan allies in this, Ussü? Did you not *see* those reports?'

'Yes. The Moranth, but—'

'Yes! The Moranth. Exactly! They cannot be trusted. They are foreign. You cannot trust these foreigners.'

We are foreigners, you fool! The man had just thrown away their greatest advantage! How was he to salvage this? How could he salvage it? Lady – give him strength! Ussü forced himself to move to a table where tea brewed. He took his time preparing a glass. Eventually, he cleared his throat. 'He will land here, south of Kor?'

'Yes. Of that I am certain.'

'How so, may I ask?'

The man's voice took on a cunning, almost insinuating whisper. 'The Lady guides me in these things, Ussü. Now go and prepare. We will meet them on the shore and they will drown in the waves.'

Ussü knew not to dispute that tone. He bowed. 'Very good, m'lord.'

*

As they rode north, Hiam gestured Quint up beside him. The Wall Marshal awkwardly urged his mount into a faster canter. 'So what do you think?' Hiam asked. 'And none of your usual smooth talk.'

Quint spat, hands in a death's grip on the reins. 'A lot *more* than ten thousand arrived, Hiam,' he pointed out.

The Lord Protector laughed. 'Is that the closest to an apology I'll get out of you?'

The man winced, his facial scars twitching. 'They came all right,' he admitted. 'But *he* came with them.'

Hiam shook his head. Poor Quint – the man apologizes then takes it away with his next breath. 'Yes, he came. And his men will buy us the time we need till the end of the season. Then, come spring and summer, we will help reinstall him. He will only be on his throne because of us. And our price will be high. Very high. We will keep him there for ten thousand men a year . . . for the next ten years.'

Quint's brows rose as he considered this immense number. He nodded his approval. *It seemed Hiam would have this ruler squirming beneath the butt of his spear. As it should be. Every ruler from Stygg to Jourilan ought to consider themselves so indebted to us. It was only right.*

'Sir,' Shool said, speaking up, 'what of this claim that the Betrayer, Stonewielder, is coming to attack us? His fleet is in Banith.'

Hiam just shook his head. 'Too much to hope for, I should think. Let him cripple his forces in some disastrous attempt at a landing. Then let the broken remnants limp back to Rool. It will be all that much easier to sweep them away come the spring.'

'But, Stonewielder . . .'

Hiam glanced back. *Ah, those rumours. Damn the apocalyptic leanings of these mystics of the Lady. I, too, felt their fascination once. There had been much alarm and uncertainty then . . . and I yielded to Cullel, allowing him to go. How I regret that now! It was . . . shameful.* He cleared his throat. 'He is only one man, Shool. One man cannot undo the wall.'

'Then we just have to last the season,' Quint growled.

Young Shool was quite shocked by this blunt admission. Hiam clenched his teeth – Quint never watched his tongue and he wished he would. This time, however, he could not bring himself to dismiss the grim forecast. *Yes, Quint. We just have to last.*

* * *

The Army of Reform finally reached the muddy snow-wreathed fields on the outskirts of the walled city of Ring. It gathered up its long trailing tail of camp followers, wagons, and petty merchants, into its own informal crowded township. The circumstances reminded Ivanr forcibly of Blight. Except that Ring city was some hundred times the size of Blight and they dared not enter it for fear of drowning in its sea of citizenry. In any case, smoke plumed over its red and black tiled rooftops and towers as Reformist factions battled Loyalists for control of precincts. One tall bell tower and chapel of the Lady burned even as Ivanr watched from the hillside overlooking the walls.

Inland, to the north, just on this side of the Lesser White River, lay the encampment of the Jourilan Imperial Army. Or rather, a tent city of thousands including the Emperor's eldest son, rumoured to have been blessed by the Lady herself. He would lead the charge of the Jourilan aristocracy, which would sweep these rag-tag upstart peasants from the field – or so he no doubt imagined. And Ivanr could not help but half agree. This time he imagined they could not count on rain or some other miracle to deliver them, though it was overcast and cold, damned cold. The depths of the Stormrider-induced winter that tormented this region so.

He ducked back into his tent. Martal was overseeing the disposition of the troops. He knew she would forbid it, but he intended to be there in the front line. It would hearten these citizen-soldiers to see him there. So far it looked as if the foreign woman was proceeding as before, arranging pike formations backed by archers. Ivanr pulled his robes tighter about himself and paced his tent, unable to eat. The Imperials had seen this trick already and he'd spotted their response: their own archers and infantry milled in huge numbers in that encampment.

They would answer volley for volley. And who would win? Time, it seemed to him, was not on *their* side. And somewhere within that sprawling tent city was the Priestess herself. The Imperials threatened to execute her tomorrow, at dawn. What would be the army's response? They had already lost Beneth. He would have to be there in the front lines to sense their mood, to respond, and, perhaps . . . to intervene.

A sigh from behind made him spin, shortsword appearing from his robes. Sister Gosh sat cross-legged on a carpet. She arched a brow at the pointed weapon, and Ivanr sheathed it beneath his robes. The old witch looked exhausted. Her thick layered skirts and shawls were dirtier than ever and she was haggard, her hair a rat's nest of matted dirty knots.

'Where have you been?' he growled, though he was relieved to see her.

'Hiding.'

'What? Hiding? Why?'

The old woman pulled a silver flask from within her shawls, took a quick sip and sighed her pleasure. 'Because I'm being hunted, that's why.'

'Who?'

'Don't know. Some betrayer, I'm sure. There's almost none of us left. If anyone other than I approaches you, don't trust them, yes?'

'If you say so.'

She relaxed, letting out a long breath, and eased her shoulders. 'Good, good.'

'What's going on?'

The woman's gaze took on a measuring cast as she seemed to examine him. 'The end of everything, Ivanr.'

'What? The end of the world?'

She grimaced her disgust. 'No, no! Just change. The end of one order and the possible beginning of another. Though some do choose to see that as the end of everything, yes. In three days it will come. All I can see is that you must remember your vow, Ivanr. That is all that comes to me. Remember that.'

'Well, if you say so. I will try.'

'Very good.' A spasm took the woman and she grimaced, forcing down the pain. 'I'm sorry that I cannot be of more help, but I will be fighting my own battle – you can be sure of that.'

'I understand. Will I not . . . see you?'

Grunting, the woman tried to rise. Ivanr leapt to help her up. 'Thank you. Who is to say? Perhaps we will see each other again. I do not know. But I don't think so.' She crossed to the tent front.

'What of the battle?'

Sister Gosh paused at the flap. 'Trust Martal, Ivanr. Trust her. Yes?' She arched a brow again.

He inclined his head in assent, smiling. 'If you say so.'

She did not appear convinced by his contriteness, but accepted the gesture all the same. 'Fare well, Ivanr. May all the gods guide you.'

'Fare well.'

After she left, he sat for some time, reflecting. Yes, trust Martal. Trust this foreign Malazan. That was the question, wasn't it?

Through the night he was woken by the noise of construction, of mattocks banging and heavy weights falling. But no alarms sounded and he eased back into sleep – it seemed Martal was constructing her siege weapons. Rather too early, he thought.

In the morning he broke his fast with hot tea and bread. When he pushed open the tent flap he was looking at a blizzard of swirling snow, and beyond that the walls of a fortress. He stared, turned a full circle. Encompassing the entire Army of Reform camp rose plank-and-beam walls extending between the tall carriages that now reared like towers in castle battlements.

By all the gods above and below! A fortress! The damned woman has built a fortress!

He walked through the camp, trying not to gape. How did she *do* it? Reaching the nearest wall he noticed that the inner sides, backs and fronts of the carriages had been disassembled. They now stood as open-backed, two-floored archers' platforms. Their bottom floors were almost entirely taken up by vicious-looking ballistae that appeared able to shoot multiple bolts in a fan-shaped pattern. The woman *was* ready for her own siege. Nodding to the troops nearby, he climbed a ladder to a narrow catwalk that ran behind the wall. Turning left and right, he peered all along the curve of the fortress.

Amazing – but really, she didn't mean to yield the field to the Imperials, did she? They'd just stand back and starve them out. The soldiers gathered at the wall did not appear pleased by their accomplishment; they were almost all staring silently out over the fields and Ivanr turned. There, halfway between the armies, stood a pyre of heaped wood.

The Imperials had also been busy last night.

While Ivanr watched, a detachment of some fifty horsemen slowly approached from the Imperial side. With them came a cart pulled by an ox and in the cart a slim figure in rags. Behind, the heavy cavalry were already in line, mounted and armed, pennants limp. *Bearing witness*. More and more men and women of the Army of Reform gathered now on the walls. He saw Martal in her black armour gazing from a nearby carriage.

Gods. What will happen? Will they rush out in a maddened fury? Isn't that what these Imperials want? Disorder, blind rage?

Yet he sensed no rage around him. Only a quiet watchfulness; a collective breath held.

The detachment gathered to one side of the pyre. The woman – the Priestess, Ivanr could only assume from this distance – was dragged out. A priest of the Lady read charges, all in silence through the blowing snow. A tall figure in banded armour that glittered as if chased in gold led the detachment – the Emperor's eldest son, Ranur the Third? He sat slumped forward, helm under an arm, apparently bored.

The woman was pulled up the tall heap and tied to a pole. Brands were thrust into the piled bracken, but due to the snow and sleet the pyre was reluctant to start. The Imperial soldiers tried to coax the fire to life, but it only smouldered. The woman stood straight throughout it all, unmoving, not even attempting to speak. Often, Ivanr knew, such victims had their tongues cut out prior to their execution.

The crowds of the Army of Reform massed on the walls and carriages and had to be pushed back as the plank-and-pillar construction could not support such a weight. The soldiers were sullen, but cooperative. The anger was now palpable to Ivanr – a simmering dark rage born of offence at the indignity being played out before them.

The gold-armoured figure dismounted, waving and giving orders. The woman was dragged from the smoking pyre and forced down to her knees. The man drew his sword. First, he pointed the blade in their direction in a gesture that needed no words, then he raised it over his head in both hands and brought it down in a clean sweeping cut. The Priestess's head fell away and the troopers released her body, letting it slump into the mud and melting snow.

The wall Ivanr stood upon seemed to shake as hundreds flinched as one with that stroke.

Through the blustering snow the Imperials unlimbered a pike, set the head upon it, and left it standing on the field. They then mounted up and rode off, the ox cart bringing up the rear.

So ended the Priestess who brought the message of tolerance and worship of all deities to the subcontinent. What legends would arise, he wondered, from this day? That the fire refused to harm her holy flesh? That she went bravely to her end, scorning her tormentors? That the very sky wept to see it? For his part, Ivanr saw a sad and tragic end to a young life. A corpse in the mud and a head on a pike. He saw waste and a useless unnecessary gesture that solved nothing. Why did she comply? What lesson was there here for anyone?

Horns blaring within the compound brought Ivanr out of his reflections. *The call for forming up? What was Martal thinking?* He went to track her down. Pushing his way through the milling infantry, he came to the side of her big black stallion, took hold of her stirrup. 'What are you *doing*?'

She peered down at him, steadied her mount. 'What I must, Ivanr. And I'm sorry . . . she meant something to you, I know that.'

'You build walls then you charge out on to the field? You're doing what they want!'

'Let's hope they think so.' She kneed her mount forward.

Yet perhaps you are, Martal. He climbed the nearest wall offering a view over the western fields. Crowds pushed a number of carriages aside and like an unruly mob the horde of pike-wielding infantry was disgorged from the fortress. They washed down the gentle slope, pikes upright, a rustling forest on the move. From the distant Imperial encampment horns answered the challenge. The heavy cavalry cantered forward.

Form up, damn you! What are you waiting for? More horns sounded, an urgent clarion call. The armoured mounts picked up their pace. Seven distinct waves sorted themselves out among the hundreds of cavalry. For now the lances remained upright, couched at hips – he knew they would not be lowered until the last possible moment.

Panic appeared to grip the pike men and women. They milled in a shapeless mass, flinching back towards the fortress walls. *Form up! Have you forgotten everything?* Then a final brilliant blast upon the Imperial horns and the pace surged into a charge. Lances edged forward at an angle. Ivanr felt the reverberation of tons of flesh and iron pounding the ground.

The infantry flinched back in a near-retreat to the walls, only to hold fast at the last possible moment, presenting a layered serried fence of iron blades. And in their midst Martal, mounted, bellowing orders.

Ivanr clenched the wood in a spasm as the iron wave of armoured men and horse came on, charging into the wall of set pikes. The crash sent rippling shockwaves through the massed infantry. Wood shattered, horses screamed, wounded coursers tumbled through two, three ranks. The charge penetrated much farther than any Ivanr had yet witnessed. Men and women scrambled over the fallen cavalrymen and pulled down those caught in the press, knives thrusting through gaps and visors.

Yet Ivanr watched with dread as behind, down the slope, the second wave now surged forward to charge, lances descending. Martal was waving, sending orders. Horns sounded the re-form. The mass of infantry retreated yet again to set their lines just behind the carnage of the first wave. Ivanr watched in amazement as the second came on regardless, unflinching, as if their own impetus would carry them through the mass of flesh and out the other side. Many leapt the fallen horses and men; some failed, clipping the corpses or wounded to tumble through the lines like thrown boulders. And into these gaps further cavalry pressed, lances shattered, drawing swords.

The impact penetrated even through to the wall, causing it to shudder as horseflesh and impetus struck unyielding iron. A new horn sounded among the Reform ranks: withdrawal.

Withdraw! Why even sortie in the first place? For this? Martal! What were you thinking?

And the third wave came thundering on. Pikes steady, the Reform infantry withdrew step by step, rear ranks filing back into the fortress. And beyond, far across the field, the Imperial archers were left far behind. *They'd outstripped their support! Was this—* A noise as of a forest of wood bending brought Ivanr's attention around.

The enclosed ground within the fortress was one solid mass of archers. Bows raised almost vertical, they strained, arrows nocked.

The third wave of cavalry smashed into the triple-layered wall of razor iron. The impact drove through to shock the wall as infantry hammered back into it. A nearby carriage rocked as Imperial cavalry pressed upon it. A barked order brought the archers on the wall rearing up, firing at will. No need for great range now, he saw: all that was required was a quick rate of fire. Secondary banging and clattering shook the carriage and he peered down to see the shutters swinging open. With a shuddering recoil the ballistae let loose, clearing the field before it in a blast of four-foot iron bolts.

Behind him a great thrumming shook the air and a sleet-like hissing rose overhead. The archers on the walls and carriages loosed as well and Ivanr flinched, ducking. The salvo came sheeting down for the most part just beyond the wall of pikes, though some did strike their own. The fusillade raked the field, leaving carnage behind. Complete slaughter. Horses fell kicking, crippled. Men tumbled, tufted like targets. The ground itself was stubbled like a field after harvest. The following cavalry waves heaved to right and left, sloughing aside, curving back upon themselves. A further salvo chased them off. The chevrons turned, coursing in a broad circle, unwilling to close.

The remaining pike infantry slowly withdrew by brigade, all in order, and the carriages were pushed back into place.

Ivanr looked out upon the field. Already snow drifted wind-tossed over bodies. Wounded called. Parties slipped out through narrow doors to retrieve Reform wounded, at the same time finishing off any Imperials. The Imperial cavalry cantered back to their encampment, pennants flying and plumes still high. He went to find Martal.

Aides surrounded her: she sat on a field stool while a bonecutter removed her armour. Blood splashed her left side. Her cuirass lay beside her and her mail-and-leather hauberk underpadding came off over her head revealing a deep gash high under her left arm. Whatever Ivanr might have wanted to say he set aside. When she saw him, a weary smile came to her glistening sweat-sheathed face. 'Not how you would have done it, eh, Ivanr?' she said while the bonecutter wrapped her torso.

'No,' he allowed. 'But maybe that's how it had to be done.'

'Not going easy on me, are you?' She winced as the cutter had her raised up.

'She has to rest,' the man said to Ivanr, who nodded. Two aides helped her walk off.

Drawing Ivanr aside, the grey-haired medic asked, 'Was that her?'

'Who?'

'This morning. Was that the Priestess?'

Ivanr paused, thinking. *How to answer that? Gods, what an awful choice to have to make!* Finally, he nodded. 'Yes. I think it was.'

'But nothing happened,' the man said as he wiped the blood from his hands.

'I'm sorry?'

'When she died – nothing happened.'

Ivanr took a deep breath. 'No. Nothing. She was just a woman who carried a message. And that message hasn't died, has it?'

The old man nodded, taking his meaning. 'Perhaps that is part of her message.'

'I believe so.'

He bent closer, lowered his voice. 'And this morning . . .' He inclined his head to the fields beyond. 'What is your estimation?'

Once more Ivanr considered his answer. Personally, he thought it a draw but he knew he mustn't say that. He said, loudly, so that all could overhear, 'Every day they haven't broken us is a victory for us.'

The old man's answer was a knowing smile. He wrapped his bloody knives in a length of stained leather. 'Now you're talking like a leader.'

He was left thinking about that. Depending upon how badly Martal was wounded the lead may indeed fall to him. His vow said nothing against giving orders. It was long past the time he ought to talk to Captain Carr regarding what further surprises Martal might have set aside.

*

If Prince Ranur the Third was in charge of the assembled Jourilan Imperial forces, he gave them no time to recover from the blunting of their first cavalry charges. Ivanr failed to track down Captain Carr before alarm horns blared from the walls of the fortress. The splendidly armoured counts and barons of the lands were driving their massed crossbowmen and archers out on to the field. Ivanr recognized the coats of Dourkan mercenaries and Jasstonese free companies among the ranks of the local peasants and burghers.

Normally, a cavalry sortie would scatter such forces, but the Army of Reform's cavalry, so greatly outnumbered for so long, had been reduced to almost nothing. Its commander, Hegil Lesour 'an 'al, now fought on foot in charge of a brigade. Before the heaving lines of the Imperial archers could be cajoled into range for a volley on the fort, horns blazed again, summoning the Reform pike units to debouch. Ivanr ran to a wall to watch as carriages were pushed aside and the infantry jogged out. A forest of the tall pikes rustled and clattered, held upright. More horns called and broad lines formed then advanced upon the Imperial skirmishing crossbow and archer forces.

Ivanr thought this lunacy. The skirmishers could dance round the pike formations; were these Martal's orders? And who was in charge? Martal's wound was too severe, surely. These pike men and women were exposed to counter-charges from the cavalry. It was worse than foolish to sortie. *Yet she could not relinquish the field to these archers, could she? They would ring the fort and grind us down.*

Sure enough: movement among the flags and pennants of the Imperial cavalry. They would answer this challenge. Far across the field, ranks of the heavy cavalry assembled before tents and wagons of spectators. Spectators! They'd brought courtiers from Jour. Perhaps members of the Imperial family as well. Gods. So sure were they of crushing these insolent peasants.

And before today Ivanr would have half agreed with such an estimation. But the dawn execution of the Priestess before the eyes of all these men and women who had set everything aside, risked everything they knew in their life, to answer her call, seemed to have changed that. He sensed in them a grim, annealed resolve that perhaps had been within them all along, which before today he had failed to notice – or, he could admit, had discounted.

Yet on the field the harassing crossbow mercenaries and archers had brought the pike units into disarray. Seeing their chance, the Imperial cavalry sounded a call and the distant reverberation of hooves reached Ivanr once more.

Form up! Ivanr urged from the wall; he cut his palms, so tightly did he clench the timbers. But the mercenaries and undisciplined Imperial archers – perhaps completely oblivious of the threat now plunging down upon them from behind – stubbornly kept the units engaged.

Horns blared and the knot of mounted guards and messengers of command parted, revealing the black-armoured figure beneath the Reform pennant. Martal! What was she doing? This would kill her! She was not gesturing: she seemed to have a death's grip on the pommel of her saddle. Upon the field the pike units milled, hafts clattering. Out of this malformed ungainly mass ranks formed as if by magic and once again the layered serried points faced the cavalry. Ivanr raised a fist, recognizing movements he and they had worked upon for months, now perfected out upon the field.

Only now did the milling archers and hired crossbow mercenaries recognize their peril. They were caught between the two forces. The Imperials did not hesitate; further horns sounded, announcing an increase in pace, and lances angled down. The hired skirmishers panicked, scattering, and the coursers charged through. Pennants and flag heraldry went down beneath churning hooves. Entire units disappeared, ground into the muddied field like chaff.

The charge shuddered home on to the layered pikes and the reverberations of the impact rippled through the entire massed square. He wondered at the training and discipline necessary to force a horse to impale itself on sharpened iron and an impenetrable crowd of massed humans. First and second ranks disappeared beneath tumbling horseflesh, the armoured riders caught amid stirrups and strapping, crushed and broken. Helms and other unidentifiable pieces of armour flew overhead. Yet the square held, solid and unmovable. The trailing courses of cavalry swung off, circling to assemble for another charge.

Away from the centre, however, things were not going as well. The archers and Jasstonese mercenaries who had withdrawn to the extreme left now punished the pike brigade of that flank. Men and women fell, helpless beneath the withering volleys.

A second wave came charging down upon the centre. A call Ivanr didn't recognize sounded from the Reform signallers and nothing immediately seemed to come of it. Then, just before the heavy cavalry struck, movement rustled amid the main square and men and women shifted aside, clearing three channels – effectively breaking into four smaller units. An extraordinarily dangerous move completed just as it should be, at the moment of impact. Many of the coursers struck home, smashing pike hafts and driving through into the ranks, but most of the horses curved aside despite the raking and thrusting of knee and spur, preferring these opened corridors.

The ranks then closed in upon the cavalry from either side. Heavy armour might prevent impalement but the impact unseated many riders. Mounts went down, snapping hafts thrust into flanks and necks. It was a slaughter as all those countless pikeheads of sharpened iron closed together like jaws upon the enemy.

Even as the second charge was obliterated the left flank collapsed. That brigade broke to run pell-mell to the rear, effectively abandoning the field. Horns sounded as Martal, or Carr, or some other commander, ordered the centre to shift to the left. The hired Dourkan archers and Jasstonese crossbow companies jogged forward into the gap, sending up harassing fire, but seeing another disciplined square marching down upon them – one fresh from mangling their heavily armoured superiors – they melted away.

No third massing of Jourilan aristocracy appeared. Either they had had enough for the day, or, as Ivanr suspected, so supremely assured of their victory were they that all those barons or dukes interested in taking the field this first day had already done so. Others would have their day tomorrow.

And Ivanr wondered how the Army of Reform could possibly survive another day like this. Martal's command group now turned to ride back to the fortress. He noted how closely two of her guard flanked her, covering her and simultaneously guiding her mount as she rode stiff and unmoving within her armour. He left the wall to be at her tent when she returned.

The men and women of the camp acted as if they had won a crushing victory. They cheered him, calling out, 'Deliverer.' The title surprised and irritated him, for behind it he sensed the cynical guiding hand of Martal. Two female pike infantry, dirtied and sweaty from the field, knelt in his way asking for blessing. The act embarrassed him excruciatingly, but he did not show it. Instead he raised them up and said loudly enough for all around to hear: 'Your bravery is our blessing.'

The tears that started from their eyes burned him for the betrayer and impostor he felt and he moved on quickly, clearing his throat and wiping his own eyes. *Damn them for tormenting me! Don't they see I'm not what they think? That they are casting upon me the weight of their own hopes? Their own dreams? No one should be asked to carry such a burden. It's impossible!*

He found a circle of guards turning everyone away from Martal's tent. They'd lifted her from her horse and now she lay within. The same bonecutter was removing her armour once more and cursing her and her aides as he did so. The woman's face was white with agony and blood loss, wet with sweat – or perhaps shock. She was barely conscious, her eyes staring sightlessly upwards.

The clenched, pale lips parted. 'Carr has command,' she hissed through clamped teeth.

'You still command,' Ivanr said. 'You will always command.'

'Ivanr . . .' she said, peering around, straining.

He knelt at her side. 'Yes?'

'I must be seen tomorrow! I must . . . no matter what!' Ivanr looked to the bonecutter, who shook his head. 'Do you understand?'

'Yes, Martal,' he answered, simply to quiet her. 'I understand.'

She eased back, letting go a taut breath. 'Tell him I tried. I tried my best. I would so like to have seen him again.'

'Who?'

'My old commander. Tell him that, won't you?'

Ivanr could not answer. *Her old commander! The Malazan . . . Greymane!* 'Yes,' he managed, clearing his throat, hardly able to speak.

'That's enough,' the bonecutter said. 'Everyone out.'

Straightening outside the tent, it took all the strength Ivanr possessed to fix upon his face an expression of resolve, even one of firm optimism. He entered the gathered crowd, which parted before him. He squeezed shoulders, set hands on bowed heads, and answered their questions and worries: yes, she was wounded but she was recovering. She would lead them tomorrow. Never fear. Tomorrow they would finish the Imperials. The Black Queen would see them through again.

Yet he hardly heard his words or saw their faces. Instead Martal's parting words haunted him. *Her old commander . . . Greymane. The*

Betrayer . . . Stonewielder. Tell him she had tried . . . Tried what? I thought she'd been fighting for us! Yet what if all this time she'd been serving his command? And he was now back! But no – that was too incredible, too far-fetched. More likely she saw herself as remaining loyal to his . . . what? His . . . intent. Perhaps that was it. She'd been honouring his intent. And that – according to the Lady's priesthood – nothing less than the annihilation of their faith itself.

But Beneth chose her! He chose her. *A neat dovetailing of purpose? Nothing more? Perhaps so.*

Still, he was shaken.

That night sleep would not come. He lay restless until, giving up and rising, he threw a long loose jerkin over his shirt and trousers and went to a gap in his tent flap to stare out at the night. Overcast, as usual, the winter clouds scudding so low as to be almost within reach, yet stubbornly yielding none of their snow. Occasionally stars winked through openings only to disappear. Torches of pickets upon the walls flickered orange and red. The smell of an army in the field wafted over him: wet leather, unwashed bodies, the stink of privies too close for comfort.

'She's dead,' a man's voice whispered behind him.

He started, tensing. The fellow was an old man in dirty torn shirt, vest and dark trousers, bearded, with wild grey-shot hair. His eyes seemed to glow in the gloom of the tent. 'Dead?' Ivanr asked, his throat dry, even though he knew.

The man gestured him back in with a crook of a finger. 'First Beneth, now Martal. Leaving . . . you.'

Ivanr considered rolling backwards, a feint to the right . . .

Deep crimson flame alighted on the man's hand and he bared yellowed teeth in a knowing smile. Ivanr let the flap close. 'You are a mage. The Lady doesn't usually permit such things . . .'

'Special dispensation for those who cleave to the path of the righteous.'

'Which would be . . . ?'

The smile twisted into a sneer. 'Save your sophistry for the sheep outside.' He gestured and a vice clamped itself round Ivanr's body. Invisible bonds tightened like rope in a crushing agony. He could not breathe, could not shout. His vision darkened.

Then relief as the bonds dissipated, seeming to shred. Ivanr drew a shuddering breath. Blinking, he saw the mage frowning, uncertain.

'There is some sort of passive protection upon you,' he muttered. 'How . . .' His eyes widened and he glanced about in sudden alarm. 'No . . .'

The tent flap was thrust aside and an old woman entered – if anything she appeared even older than Sister Gosh. She was lean and wiry, dark as aged leather, her wiry hair up in a tight bun. The man bowed, his tongue wetting his lips. 'Sister Esa.'

The old woman, Sister Esa apparently, was pulling the gloves from her hands. 'I was hoping you would come, Totsin.'

Totsin edged around the tent as if searching for a way out. 'Now . . . Sister Esa . . . let's not jump to conclusions.'

The old woman's gloves came off, revealing hands twisted like claws, long nails broken and thick like talons and black with dirt. She gave a strange gurgling hiss and her lips drew back over teeth now black as well, and needle sharp. Ivanr flinched away, horrified. *Soletaken?* She launched herself upon Totsin.

The two wrestled in silence, the woman straining to set her claws or teeth into the man, he holding her wrists, head twisting aside. They fought, gasping and panting. The woman's hands and teeth edged ever closer to the man's flesh until she shuddered suddenly, her back arching in anguish. She fell to the floor, spasms twisting her limbs. The old man straightened his clothes and spat upon her.

'The Lady is with me, Esa. And now she has you . . .'

Ivanr leapt to his pallet and spun, his shortsword in hand, to slash Totsin. Incredibly, the man flicked his head aside, the blade merely gashing across his face. He clamped a hand to his head. Blood welled between the fingers. Ivanr closed, but searing pain bit into one ankle and he fell: the old woman had him.

'I leave you to the Lady,' Totsin gasped, rage and agony in his voice. He disappeared in a moil of greyness that enveloped him then vanished, leaving Ivanr alone with Sister Esa. He almost called for help, but caught himself – *gods, if this got out it would terrify everyone!*

The hand clenched, its talons cutting into his flesh and grating the bone. The head rose, eyes rolled back all white. The hair on Ivanr's neck stirred as a voice gurgled from the throat: 'Embrace me, Ivanr, and I will forgive you . . .'

'I'm sorry,' he said, and brought the blade down through the neck.

Some time later steps in the tent roused him and he leapt up, shortsword readied. It was Sister Gosh, pipe in mouth, staring down at the wrapped corpse of Sister Esa. A sudden fury took him that only now did she appear. 'Where were you?' he demanded. 'Together you might've taken him!'

She shook her head. 'I told her not to step in. We can't fight the Lady.'

Ivanr fell back on to his pallet, exhausted. 'Well, he got away.'

She let out a lungful of smoke. 'I think we'll meet yet.'

'And then what?'

She drew hard on the pipe and its embers blazed. She peered at him from deep within the crow's feet wrinkles at her eyes. 'Then we'll see.'

Ivanr grunted at the predictable, maddening opaqueness. He hung his arms over his knees. 'So . . . is she really gone?'

'Yes.'

'Did he . . .'

'No. The wound.'

He grunted again, accepting that. In other lands, he knew, such wounds could be treated by healers with access to Warrens. But here, the Lady denied all. That alone was more than enough reason for her destruction. How many needless deaths all these ages . . . ? 'Well,' he said, gazing at the dirt floor, 'I don't know if *we'll* last tomorrow.'

'Keep them fighting, Ivanr. You're here to do more than defeat these Imperials. More eyes than you know of are on this confrontation. The walls of Ring city are within sight. You have to show that these nobles can be stood up to. That there's a chance.'

'What are you talking about?'

'We'll see. Tomorrow.'

He gestured to the decapitated corpse. 'And her?'

'Have some men you trust take her off and bury her. Now, before dawn.'

He nodded. 'And you?'

Sister Gosh had crossed to the flap. 'I don't know. I'll do what I can. Before, I said we may not meet again. Now I'm even more sure of that. Good luck to you.'

'And to you.'

She ducked from the tent. Ivanr lay down again to try to steal some rest before dawn.

* * *

After Shell and her partner, Tollen, the Malazan Sixth Army veteran, had stood short stints at various posts along the wall, two Korelri Chosen came for them. They were in holding cells, separated. The Stormguard didn't seem to know what to do with Shell, being female, and so they emptied out a pen for her private use. Personally, she thought it was more for their sensibilities than hers. She could squat to relieve herself just as easily anywhere – it was they who seemed all shirty about it.

The two were fettered again and led off along one of the maze of corridors that ran like a rat's nest within the Stormwall. It was a long walk, much farther than any previous one, and took up more than the day. Deep into the evening they were tugged up stairs to exit a minor tower – the kind that only bore numbers – in this case, Tower Fourteen. From here they walked into the punishing frigid wind and sleeting snow. They'd been given tattered old cloaks, and Shell retied the rags she had wrapped over her sandalled feet and up over her legs, her head and neck, and finally her hands as well.

The wall climbed before them, high above the shore below, more of a connecting corridor than a working part of the Stormwall. At the crest of the pass it fell steeply in lethal sets of stone stairs to a section that looked to span a narrow inlet. Snow flurried in Shell's face as she hunched, scrabbling with her numb fingers for holds and grips to help herself down. Tollen descended facing the stairs, almost flat on all fours. Waves pounded below, reverberating like thunder. *Riders drove those waves.* She recognized the pitch of their force, their enmity.

The descent levelled to a smoother grade. Shell now made out a wide marshalling walkway more ice-choked than any she'd seen so far. It even seemed broached in courses of frozen rivers of ice. Stone blocks cluttered the walk, as did canted broken tripods. Ropes lay unusable beneath layers of ice. They passed a work gang where labourers hammered at a block to free it from its sheath of ice. One armed guard, a hired mercenary judging from his heavy armour, stood watch.

The two Korelri escorted them to a tower so layered in blue-tinted ice running in flows down its sides that it appeared as if the water had been poured. A single narrow doorway gave access to inner chambers where braziers burned, giving light and heat to close, damp rooms. Workers squatted, eating; bedrolls over straw crowded the wet stone floors. Down a narrow circular staircase they came to cells, more holding pens. Their fetters were struck and Shell was pushed into one, Tollen another.

Shell sat on the straw-littered raised stone slab she supposed was the bed and leaned back against the wall, only to flinch away – the stones were glacial and glittered with ice. Across the narrow corridor the opposite cell was occupied by a squat fellow in ring armour over leathers, rags at his feet and hands, his hair unkempt and growing a beard, leaning back asleep. He was much the worse for wear, but Shell would recognize Blues anywhere.

She whistled a call and one eye cracked open; he sat up, staring. Shell signed: *A Malazan soldier with me. Any news?*

Lazar is here. Fingers?

Don't know. I met someone who knows Bars.

Who?

Shell spelt: *Jemain.*

Blues shrugged. *Don't know him.*

Said he'd get back to me.

A second shrug. *We'll see.*

Shell said aloud: 'How is it here?'

'Damned desperate. Too many Riders, not enough guards.'

'Losing people?'

'Losing workers.'

'What're they doing here?' she asked.

'This is Ice Tower,' a new voice answered: Tollen. 'Always rough here. Looks like the waves are really cresting now.'

'Get some rest, damn you!' someone barked. 'You'll need it.'

Shell lay back, hugged herself. Whoever that was, he was right. Best think of what was to come. Don't let yourself get caught unprepared. And that accent . . . another damned Malazan?

Come the dawn, the nightshift of guards came trooping down the stairs exhausted, soaked through and shivering. A new shift was pulled together; neither Shell nor Blues was selected. 'How long you been here?' she asked.

'Only a few days.'

'How many of us prisoners are there here?'

Blues cocked his head, signed: *Thinking of breaking out?*

Can't stay for ever.

'Don't know,' Blues answered aloud. 'I'm beginning to wonder whether we should interfere . . .'

Shell stared at the man. A shiver took her; *good gods, that Blues should be uneasy about this . . .*

She jumped as a guard appeared to unlock her cell. He motioned her out.

'Good luck,' Blues called. 'Guard yourself.'

She gave him a nod. Sword out, the man forced her ahead up the circular staircase. At the top four regular guards covered her with cocked crossbows. Weapons cluttered the far wall. 'Take your pick,' one invited her, grinning. She eyed the spears and two-handed swords, but decided on a more conservative approach and selected sword and shield.

The guard motioned her to the door. 'Let's go.'

The door led to the corridor that exited the tower. Outside, the guard pointed to the right and they crossed the walkway, hunched, heads turned away from the punishing, cutting wind. They came to a work crew struggling with a tripod and block and tackle. The guard motioned Shell to the outer ice-entombed machicolations here. He hammered at the ice to expose an iron ring and shackled her to it. Waves pounded, soaking them with spray that shocked her though she'd felt its teeth before. Another defender squatted off to the right. He appeared to be an old man, wearing nothing but rags, his long hair and beard grey-shot and matted. Who was this fossil?

'Hey, grandfather,' she called, cupping her hands at her mouth. 'What are you doing here?'

The haggard head barely edged over to glance. She caught a glimpse of a gaunt, skeletal face as it turned away. The sight of that seeming death mask made her shudder.

A great bell-like resonance sounded then from the waters of the inlet. *That was new. Some sort of extra effort here? Maybe they think this is their chance.* She strained to penetrate the blowing snow. Far out, the surface of the waters seemed to bulge, swelling. *That's a lot of water – and it's headed for a very narrow gap!* Shell braced herself. Behind, the workers scrambled for cover. A block the size of a cart hung suspended from the tackle. *Raising the wall from the rear, working towards the front.*

Glancing back Shell caught the old fellow staring at her. He quickly glanced away. The tall bulge rolled inexorably down upon them. Like a tidal bore. Only generated by the Riders. Shell edged forward as far as she dared, peered over and down. They looked to have only some three fathoms of freeboard here. That surge could overtop them! Feeling a rising panic she glanced about, but no one appeared unduly alarmed. *Queen preserve her! This was what they fought here!*

The old man straightened, his arms loose at his sides. He appeared completely unarmed.

Shell edged back: the ice-webbed surge was almost upon them. She reached behind with one foot, sought a knob or irregularity to brace, found one.

The surge struck the wall; or rather, it began rising up the side of the wall. Shell's footing rocked backwards beneath her as if fluid itself. The water came on and on, swelling with Shell's own dread until it washed up over the top and swept her feet out from under her. Frigid glacial waters flowed over her. The shock almost took the life from her, but she straightened, braced against the flow, gasping in air, throwing her head back, to face a Stormrider standing atop the wall. The entity, wearing armour like shells sewn into a coat, thrust at her. She took the blow on her shield, swung a clumsy counter that the rider sidestepped. It circled, attempting to force her to put her back to the inlet. She dodged to forestall that. She shield-bashed but lacked the raw power to drive the Rider back. It slashed at a leg and she dodged back. It glanced behind her but she refused to look. Then it simply sank down into the receding waters to wash away in the flow. Shell was left standing, panting, her flesh in an agony of cold. She risked a quick glance behind: the tripod and block were gone, swept clean off the wall.

A loud high-pitched report, as of iron tearing, sounded from her right and she looked over: the old guy's post was empty. *Where—*

Hands took her throat from behind, lifted her from her feet.

'I knew I recognized you!' someone snarled. 'Skinner sent you, didn't he?'

With a despairing, almost bizarre feeling that this wasn't really happening, Shell recognized the voice. '*Bars!*' she gasped.

'No torc, I see,' he hissed. 'Going to wait for a wave then take me down while I'm busy, yes? Then off to your Warren. Looks like you missed your chance. Now . . . *where is he?*'

'No – you don't—'

Bars' frigid hands, like two wedges of ice, throttled her. 'Raise your Warren and I'll tear your head off. Now . . . where is he!'

'Who?' she managed, stealing a breath.

'Quit stalling! Skinner! Damn his betraying soul!'

Deceiving gods! Oponn, you have outdone yourself! Skinner! He was renegade now. His attempt to usurp K'azz failed and he was forced out – disavowed. And Bars thinks he's sent me! Shell drew upon all the strength those of the Avowed possess and yanked Bars' own hands a fraction apart while her legs kicked uselessly. 'Blues is with me!' she gasped before those iron fingers cinched like vices to cut off her breath utterly. Stars flashed in her vision and a roaring drowned out all sounds.

She came to lying in frigid water. A Korelri Chosen held a spear levelled at Bars while a regular guard helped her up. 'What is this?' the Korelri demanded.

'An old grudge,' Shell croaked, rubbing her neck.

'You are both finished then?'

Shell nodded. Bars crossed his arms. *Blues*, he signed, insistent. She nodded again.

'Your shift is done,' the Korelri told Bars, motioning him off. 'You . . . you stay as yet.'

Shell continued massaging her neck. Frankly, she *would* rather face the Riders.

They left her alone, staring out over the slate-grey waves whipped into white caps. After a time it occurred to her that the Stormrider had seemed more interested in damaging the wall itself than in killing anyone.

* * *

Suth sat on Banith's wharf, leaning forward on piled equipment, chin in his arms, watching the battered fleet of Blue dromonds and Quon men-of-war lumbering out of the bay. 'All the in-bred gods! I can't damned believe it.'

'Wish them luck,' Len said, saluting.

Lying back, eyes closed, Wess saluted the sky. Lard grumbled, 'Lucky bastards.'

Keri blew out a breath. 'Someone has to stay behind . . .'

'Hood take this Fist,' Pyke said. ''Cause a him we're missing all the action.'

Yana gave the man a look of contempt. 'You're glad we're staying, so stop your mouth.'

Pyke straightened. 'I'll stop your—'

'Store it!' Goss cut in.

'I need a drink,' Yana said, pushing herself up. 'Let's go.'

Suth stood and adjusted his cloak against the cutting wind. 'Aye. Let's go.'

'Your sweetie's still here,' Keri told Suth.

'Who?'

'That Barghast gal.' She made a fake grab for Suth's crotch. 'I hear once they get hold they don't let go.'

Suth flinched away. 'We ain't doin' nothing.'

Lard got a dreamy look on his wide face. 'Too bad. That sounds pretty damn good.'

They walked the near empty streets, heading back to their inn. Snow blew across the cobbles. They passed the occasional burned or boarded-up pillaged building, remnants from the riots and panic of the landings.

Yana flinched abruptly, hissing, a hand going to her side where a crossbow bolt had suddenly sprouted. Goss, Suth and Lard rushed the abandoned building opposite. Lard kicked down the boards covering the broken door. Suth charged the stairs, Goss following. Noise brought him to a rear room where a window gaped open. He leaned out: someone had let himself down, jumping, and now ran up a back alley. A slim gangly figure. A kid. A Queen-damned young kid. Goss arrived, a crossbow in hand: Malazan made. Suth shook his head in disbelief. 'Did you see him?' he asked.

'Yeah, I saw him. A kid.'

Suth blew out a breath. This was gonna be ugly. What could they do? They couldn't let it go unanswered. Everyone and their grandmother would be taking potshots at them. They had to respond. No choice. They went back down to see Yana.

Wess had his shield unslung and was covering her while Keri treated the wound. 'We have to get back to the inn. Lay her down,' she said. Goss nodded.

'Who was it?' Pyke demanded. 'Did you get him?'

'Just a kid,' said Suth. 'He got away.'

'A kid?' Pyke said, offended. 'So? Why'd you let him go?'

'I did not—'

Goss pulled Suth away. 'Shut that mouth of yours,' he warned Pyke. 'Lard, carry Yana. Let's go.'

Inside, they checked their rooms, laid Yana down and summoned a bonecutter. Goss placed Wess and Lard on guard then sat with Suth, Keri and Len. 'Started already,' he told Len, who nodded.

'What?' Suth asked.

'Insurgency. Attacks, killings, fire-bombings an' such. A vicious mess. Might get orders to pull back into the garrison.'

Len took a deep pull from his stein of beer. 'I hate occupations. Bad blood all around. Hate. Suspicion. We'll be prisoners in our own garrison.'

Goss just hunched, depressed. 'Reminds me of damned Seven Cities.'

*

Captain Betteries and Captain Perin joined Fist Rillish for dinner that evening in the commander's rooms in the old Malazan Sixth Army garrison. The stone fort was crowded, holding two thousand men and women when normally it would hold less than half that. The rest of the Malazan expeditionary forces were encamped inland, in the hills around Banith. Captain Betteries was a red-haired Falaran native, while Captain Perin hailed from north Genabackis, his skin almost as dark as a Dal Honese, but his face much wider and more brutal in features than the more refined lineaments of the Dal Hon. They had just finished a first course of soup when a steward opened the door to allow Captain Peles to enter. All three officers stood. Captain Peles waved for them to sit.

'Welcome,' Rillish said, inviting her to a seat.

Peles sat, as did they. Rillish wondered to see her now without her helm and thick mail coat. Her long silver hair was unbraided to fall loose; she wore a long-sleeved jacket over a pale shirt. And while most would not consider her battle-flattened nose and scarred cheeks beautiful in the narrow, stereotypical image of some floaty, cultured, urban lady, Rillish thought her extraordinarily attractive, even desirable. He discovered her answering his stare.

'Yes, Fist?'

He swallowed, looking away to pick up his wine glass. 'How are the security arrangements?' Captain Peles had been appointed chief of his guard.

'This garrison is a death trap. There's no well. The storerooms are too small. The arsenal is as empty as a merchant's generosity.'

'I agree,' Captain Betteries added.

'What would you suggest?' Rillish asked Peles.

'I suggest we withdraw to outside the town. Build our own fortress.'

'That would cut down on the nuisance sniping,' Captain Perin commented.

'What's the report?' Rillish asked.

'Two troopers wounded in separate incidents. Plus the usual vandalism, theft and physical assaults.'

The main course arrived. The news had blunted Rillish's appetite. *So soon. Occupations breed mutual disgust, harden divisions, and brutalize all parties.* Should they withdraw from town? Perhaps they should. Yet even if they went now, of their own choosing, it would look as if they'd been chased out. And so they were already effectively trapped. 'You have taken all the usual steps?' he asked Captain Betteries.

The man nodded, a little worse for drink. 'Arrested the local leaders. This acting Lord Mayor, who's also the local magistrate, apparently. A few others.'

'But I understand Admiral Nok had some sort of agreement with the man.'

'Better to have him where we can keep an eye on him.'

'Where is the Adjunct, may I ask?' Captain Perin enquired.

'With the troops outside the town.'

'And you, sir, Fist. I understand you have been here before?'

Rillish's jaws tightened. 'Yes, Captain. It was my second posting.'

Captain Perin seemed unaware of Captain Betteries' not-so-subtle glare for silence. 'Here, in Rool?' he asked.

'Yes,' Rillish answered, a touch tartly.

'Then . . .' The captain tailed off as he appreciated the dangerous waters he was entering. 'Ah . . . interesting.' He addressed his dinner. After a time his gaze turned to Peles, where it rested while they ate. 'You are of Elingarth?' he asked finally.

The broad-boned woman almost blushed. 'Around there,' she muttered into her plate.

'I am surprised. It is rare for one of the military orders to strike out on his or her own.'

'There are those of us who are selected to travel, to learn other ways, other philosophies.'

'A sound strategy,' Captain Betteries said.

Captain Perin was nodding as well. 'Yes. You could bring back information, useful knowledge. But you may also bring back dangerous ideas. The contamination of foreign beliefs . . .'

Peles cut up her fish. 'We do not follow the philosophy of purity versus pollution. That is a false choice, a false dichotomy. The truth is, nothing is "pure". Everything is the product of something else.

To name something "pure" is to pretend it has no history, nothing before it, which is obviously false.'

Rillish stared. That had been the longest speech he'd heard from the woman, who now blushed at the silent attention she was receiving from the three men.

'Well argued,' Captain Betteries said, and he took another drink.

Later that night Rillish sat in his offices reviewing quartermaster reports. After sorting through the entire pile of paperwork he came to an envelope addressed to him and sealed with wax. An aide's note said that it had been left by the front gate. He broke the seal and opened the thick folded paper, careful not to touch the inner slip – he knew of some who had been poisoned in this manner.

He read the short message once. Its contents obviously confused him as he frowned, puzzled. Then he read it again. The third time he snatched it up and stood, swearing and cursing. He summoned his aides.

*

The building was unprepossessing. It had the look of long abandonment, of having been looted then occupied by squatters for some time. It was deep into the night when Rillish arrived. He came alone, wrapped in a dark cloak. The name in the note was enough to assure him of the message's validity and of his safety. He waited in the main room among the rubbish and filth until a light grew above and a man came down the stairs, lamp in hand. The man was squat and muscular and bald. Seeing him, Rillish stared, amazed.

'All the gods above and below . . . Ipshank. You still live. I couldn't believe it.'

The priest appeared uncomfortable. 'Rillish Jal Keth. I don't believe we actually met.'

'No. But I heard much of you. You saw Greymane, then? You must have.'

'We met.' The man waved the lamp. 'Right here. Secretly.'

'Secretly? There's no reason for secrecy. All that was a long time ago.'

Ipshank set the lamp on a low table. He rubbed a hand over his bald pate. 'There are those who still remember. You. Myself . . . others. And the enemy remains.'

Rillish shook his head. 'It's over. Finished. You should have gone with him. How could you not have, knowing what he faces?'

There was a long measured acknowledgement from the man as he crossed his arms and hung his head. In the dim light the faded boar tattoos gave his face a death-like cast. 'That was what he said. That I should come with him. But I couldn't. My work is here. *Our* work is here.'

Rillish found himself a touch frightened of the man. 'What do you mean, ours?'

'I mean that Greymane – Stonewielder – goes to face his enemy while we must confront ours here. If we do not, then there can be no victory for us.'

'This is what you told Greymane?'

'Yes.'

'And he agreed?'

'Yes. He agreed by leaving you here.'

The sudden urge to flee gripped Rillish. He paced instead, his heart hammering. 'You *asked* that I be left behind?'

'Yes.'

'Why? Why me?'

The man sat on a low stool – perhaps only to set Rillish at ease. 'I'm sorry, Fist. I wish I could say that it was because of some innate quality you possess. That you were born to fulfil this role. That there was a prophecy foretelling you would be the one. Or that your father's father was one of the ousted rightful kings of Rool – one of a series of them, actually. Or some such nonsense.' He leaned forward on his crossed knees. 'But no. I'm sorry, there's nothing special about you. There you are. It's disappointing, I know, but that's how it is for everyone.' His wide, thick-lipped mouth drew down. 'And that just makes it all the harder, doesn't it? Not being special. Not having that funny mark or that omen at your birth. Just an ordinary person asked to step up to do the extraordinary.'

Rillish had been pacing the empty room, kicking at the litter. 'If this is your way of persuading me to help I can well understand your reputation as a difficult fellow. Just what is it you are asking?'

The man pressed his hands together as if praying. He set them to his lips. 'To help slay the metaphorical dragon, Fist.'

Rillish gaped. *All the gods, no. That was impossible. Yet this man obviously thought there was a chance. And he and Greymane were in agreement – or so he claimed. What evidence has he shown? None. Yet, Ipshank . . . he was one of those who remained loyal through to the bloody end.* He stopped pacing. 'I'll listen. That's all I can promise right now.'

Ipshank opened his hands wide and bowed his head. 'Good

enough. That will do for a start.' He stood, took the lamp to the gaping doorway and shone it out. 'First, there are some papers here I'd like you to go through.'

Shambling steps approached and two men entered, burdened by the large heavy chest they carried between them. Rillish thought one, a big fellow sporting a ridiculous long moustache, very familiar. An officer of the City Watch? They set the chest down. Ipshank invited Rillish to the low table and stool. He sat and the men opened the chest to hand over the first packet of an intimidating collection.

He read slowly, rather reluctantly. Then, with each document, he sat forward further, scanned each with greater intensity. He read through the entire night.

Come the dawn the guards were gone, and Ipshank sat leaning up against a wall, apparently asleep. Rillish sat back, pinched his gritty eyes and blinked repeatedly. *Gods, he was thirsty. A lifetime's work and dedication here. An amazing story to be pieced together.*

He eyed Ipshank. 'Should we let the man out?'

The priest shook his bullet head from side to side. 'No. He's already damned as a collaborator. If you release him you'll only confirm those suspicions and he'll be killed, or completely discredited. Every day he stays in the gaol is another day of rehabilitation for him.'

'Rehabilitation? I don't want to create a local leader here.'

One eye cracked open. 'Just who do you *want* as one?'

Rillish grunted, conceding the point. He stretched, yawning. 'So. What was it you wanted me to see? The Cloister and Hospice have been destroyed. Burned to the ground.' He eyed the priest anew. 'You didn't . . .'

Again, the head shake. 'No. Local adherents to the Lady. They wanted to incite hatred against you Malazans, so they torched it. Where else would the blame fall?' The man set his thick arms over his knees. 'No. Mainly, I wanted you to see evidence. Proof. Mixed in there are a series of interviews with minor workers for the Hospice: grounds keepers, cleaners and such. In those interviews are reports of a chest, a kind of box, brought out of the Cloister and loaded on to a wagon about a month ago.'

'Around the time of the landings.'

'Yes. I believe I know what was on that wagon, and where it went.'

'Yes?'

The priest took out a skin of water, tossed it to Rillish. 'Let me tell you a story, Fist. An old story whose particulars I have spent most of my life tracking down. Legends of this region tell of the three most precious relics of the Lady – the Holy Trilogy. Three sacred icons housed in chests. One, according to tradition, was lost in the great sinkhole, the Ring, far back during the attacks of the Stormriders. The greatest, as most know, was reportedly used to bless and sanctify the foundations of the wall itself. After which it was hidden away by the Korelri Stormguard. Most consider it to be housed in the great tower on Remnant Isle, the Sky Tower, guarded by hundreds of Stormguard. And they would be right.

'The third was the most difficult. After eliminating countless holy shrines, sacred cairns, monasteries and temples, I narrowed down its location to here, the great Cloister of Banith. It has since been moved – and I know where.'

'Paliss?' Rillish said, rousing himself from the hypnotic tale. He took a drink of the warm water.

'No. The caves of the mountain ascetics at Thol on the shores of Fist Sea.'

'Thol? That's more than ten days' journey by horse. You can't be asking me to pack up the army and march across the country to besiege Thol.'

The man shook his head, unperturbed by how outrageous Rillish made the request sound. 'No. This is for a small party only. And we must be there within the next few days, or so I believe.'

'Impossible. You know that. Only a mage travelling through Warren could manage that.'

'Or a shaman. And there's one here, nearby. A descendant of the native peoples of this region, tribes that can trace their roots to the ancient Imass themselves. The Lady scorns them, views their practices as beneath her. But all this time they have maintained their ancient ways, employed their Warren – a version of Tellann, I believe – quietly, without notice. Him we have to convince to help us.'

Rillish stared, amazed. *Gods, the man's actually thought all this through. Outrageous.* 'And,' he began, his mouth dry, 'what would you require of me?'

'Select a small party. Some twenty or so. And be ready for me.'

Rillish slowly shook his head in denial. An expression almost of horror clenched his face. 'Ipshank. Greymane *ordered* me to remain here. I cannot abandon my command. If I go I would be . . .' He could not finish the thought. 'Hood forgive me. I cannot betray his trust *again*.'

The priest displayed no sympathy. 'You have to. You have no choice.'

* * *

The Liosan were, if anything, rigidly formal and strict observers of manners and rules. Tight-arses, Jheval called them. Good to their word, they'd allowed the three of them the freedom of the camp. Kiska wanted to get away, of course, but not without her equipment. And so far their tiny guide had yet to show itself; that was either very reassuring, or very worrying. The huge lumbering ravens, however, were quite insolent in showing themselves, depositing great white smears as indelible signs of their presence.

After two days, or what large hourglasses housed in a main mess tent artificially dictated to be two days, they were invited to dine with the army's commander, Jayashul. They were escorted to her private quarters, and she met her at the hangings that separated off the rooms. A Liosan man waited within, sour-faced, his expression openly hostile. Jayashul invited Kiska to sit, then Warran, then Jheval. The Liosan male, introduced as Brother Jorrude, sat last.

Dinner came in numerous small courses of soup, bread and vegetables, none of which struck Kiska as particularly tasty or well prepared. *Bland, serious and practical. Like these people themselves.* She longed to escape this encampment and return to her mission. The only amusement of the night came from the faces Jheval made when tasting the food.

An after dinner tea was served, a watery green infusion utterly without flavour, and Jayashul announced: 'We are now prepared to mount an assault upon the Devourer.'

Kiska thrust aside her tea, spilling it. 'An assault? Shouldn't we determine just . . . what it is, first?'

Jayashul was undeterred. 'We know it is a powerful magus, or what some would name an Ascendant. No doubt quite mad. Perhaps brought on by exposure to your otataral dust, or some form of mental attack or breakdown. Merely visiting Chaos can induce such a reaction – it is not uncommon.' She turned to Warran. 'What say you, priest of Shadow?'

The priest had been very eager for dinner, and now he sat looking quite defeated by what had appeared on his plate. Kiska imagined he'd been expecting fish. 'It would be best, would it not, to examine this anomaly more closely first to determine all its particulars, before striking?'

Jayashul shook her head rather condescendingly. 'My dear priest . . . if one of our white hounds were to launch itself upon you with an intent to consume you utterly, would you take the time to enquire as to his pedigree or antecedents? No, you would strike! Defend yourself!'

Warran offered a thin smile. 'The hound would find in me a rather insubstantial meal.'

Jayashul thought nothing of the comment but Kiska shot the little man a sharp look. *Insubstantial?* Was the fellow playing games? Mocking this Liosan Ascendant. Perhaps mocking everyone, the entire situation?

A guard brushed aside the cloth hanging, and Jayashul looked up. 'He is here?' The guard nodded. 'Good.' She stood and everyone followed suit. 'The one we have been waiting for has arrived.' A man entered. He wore his long pale hair loose, and layered green robes. 'My brother. L'oric.'

The man's gaze swept them all. Then, as he was about to bow to Jayashul, he straightened, stunned surprise almost comical on his face, and his eyes returned to Jheval. 'Blood of my father . . .' he breathed. 'Leoman?'

Jheval's mouth twisted his chagrin and embarrassment. He bowed ironically. 'L'oric. As soon as I saw these Liosan I was afraid you would show up.'

'Show up?' L'oric echoed, disbelief in his voice. 'Leoman, your arrogance remains undiluted, I see.'

Leoman? The name was familiar to Kiska but she couldn't quite place it. L'oric turned his attention to her. Brother to Jayashul, but at first Kiska saw almost no similarity. His face was thin, but there was a certain haughtiness in its expression in which she saw the relationship. *This man should speak of arrogance! It marches emblazoned across his face completely unbeknownst to him.*

'Malazan, I see,' he mused. 'Claw, no doubt. Come to spy.' He turned to Warran. 'And a priest of that Shadow usurper. He is worried about the integrity of his stolen Realm, yes?'

Warran arched a brow. 'Stolen? The house was empty, unclaimed.'

L'oric's mouth pursed with distaste. 'The problem, I should think, is that by far *too* many claim that house.'

Warran's gaze narrowed in the first betrayal of annoyance Kiska had yet seen from him.

L'oric now bowed to his sister. 'Jayashul.' He indicated Jheval. 'What reason has this man given for coming here?'

'They say they came to investigate the Anomaly, the Devourer.'

L'oric's gaze was openly sceptical as he studied them in turn. Kiska felt as if she'd been mentally frisked for stolen goods. 'For what reason, I wonder,' he mused. 'All three must be arrested.'

'I have extended the status of guest to them.'

'Then you did so too quickly – you should have waited for me.'

It was now Jayashul's turn to reveal annoyance. Jheval laughed. 'Still the diplomat, I see, L'oric.'

The man frowned, completely unable to penetrate Jheval's taunt. 'This one, at least, must be chained. If only for our safety.'

Kiska couldn't contain herself any longer. It was stunning how these two could stand here speaking of them in the third person. 'We have done nothing!'

L'oric regarded her, bemused. 'How strange to hear a Malazan defending Leoman of the Flails.'

Leoman of the Flails! Kiska gaped at Jheval. The man at least had the scruples to appear ashamed.

'I am sorry, Kiska,' he said.

'Ah!' L'oric snorted, as if vindicated. 'He lied to you. Typical.'

'I believe we've established that,' Warran commented, arching a brow.

Leoman of the Flails. Follower of Sha'ik, and the last commander of the Seven Cities insurrection. The man who lured the Malazan Seventh Army to its greatest tragedy in the city of Y'Ghatan, where a firestorm consumed thousands. Possibly the greatest living threat to the Empire.

And a man she would have brought to Tayschrenn! Whom the Queen of Dreams pressed upon her! Could he have deceived her*? Surely not. But then . . . gods turn away! What was she to do?*

Kiska sat heavily, gazing at nothing.

'Perhaps,' Warran suggested, 'you might settle this on your own.'

L'oric gave a curt nod. 'Yes.' He snapped his fingers and a guard edged aside the cloth hanging. 'Take these three back to their quarters and put them under close watch.'

The guard's gaze flicked to Jayashul. Though obviously irked by her brother's infringement on her prerogative as commander, she gestured her agreement.

Kiska remained sitting until hands urged her up and guided her back to her tent.

She sat on her pallet, staring at the blank cloth walls long into the night. *Leoman. Had he planned assassination? The Queen of Dreams could not have been fooled. Did she then . . . approve?*

Her gaze fell to her hands. *Impotent. Deluded. Abetting!*

The hands clenched into white fists.

No. Never. I will kill him.

She stood, threw off her loose cloak and travelling jacket. She re-wound her sash wider and tighter, pulled on her gloves. Only now did she notice the noise without the tent. Many men and women moving about. She glanced out of a gap in the cloth opening: the Liosan were readying for their assault. *Utter insanity! What can an army do against a Void?*

She saw a detachment of five Liosan marching towards her tent, led by the man from the dinner, Brother Jorrude. *Damn! They might be . . .*

She pulled on her cloak, wrapped it around her and sat on the pallet, hands tucked within the folds.

A sharp knock on the tent's front pole. 'Yes?' she called.

'We must enter. Dress yourself.'

'What is it?'

'I will give you one more moment.'

'Enter, then. If you must.'

The flap was pulled aside and three Liosan stepped in, Brother Jorrude and two female soldiers. They peered about the empty interior of her tent.

'What is it?'

Brother Jorrude ignored her.

'Courtesy—'

'Courtesy?' the man cut in. 'You Malazans are not deserving of courtesy. I find your manners . . . offensive.'

Kiska smiled. 'Came away poorly from a previous meeting, did you?'

The man glared, gestured the others out, then followed.

Kiska gave them a moment then peered out of the gap in the cloth. They appeared to be gone. She bent to examine the cot. Two legs came off, giving her short batons as weapons. These she tucked into her sash at the rear. She went to the flap, tucked her fingers round the edge and waited for the alley in front to clear.

'There's too many for that,' a voice said at her back and she nearly jumped from the tent. It was Warran; the man was standing directly behind her.

'Don't *do* that!' she hissed.

'It looks as if we've all decided it's time to go.'

She eyed him, not liking that. 'What do you mean?'

'Jheval – that is, Leoman – has escaped.'

'I *knew* it! That was why they came here!' She regarded him anew. 'And you as well, it would seem.'

A modest shrug. 'I come and go as I please. These Tiste Liosan truly do not understand Shadow. To them it is merely some sort of bastard hybrid. A crippled, or inferior, Liosan. But it is not that at all. It is its own Realm. Separate and equally legitimate.'

In that speech she heard something new in the priest: pride, yes, but the touchy insecure pride of the outsider, or newcomer, to a very old and long-running game. 'Will you help me get away?'

The priest's answering grin was unnervingly sly. 'Of course.'

* * *

Pyke choked on his beer when Lard and Wess thumped down at his table. He finished drinking from the heavy tankard and wiped his mouth. 'What do you two want?'

'We're waitin' for Suth.'

Pyke snorted. 'Then I'm goin'.' He moved to rise but Lard grabbed his forearm. 'What's this shit?'

Suth entered, peered round, then sat at the table. He nodded to Wess, who yanked something from Pyke's waist – his money pouch. Wess upended it over the table. Silver and copper coins tumbled over the uneven planks and on to the floor. Pyke writhed to escape Lard's grip. 'You guys crazy? That's mine!'

Suth shook his head. 'I wasted my entire day following you, Pyke, from one shop to the next. Guess what I saw?'

Pyke wrenched his arm free and rubbed it, sneering. 'What's the matter with you guys? It's the routine. Why should we miss out?'

'We get paid,' Lard said.

A laugh from Pyke. 'When was the last time you saw any Malazan coin?'

'Coin or not,' Lard ground out. 'I signed on to fight, not steal.'

'Well then, you're just a stupid fucker, ain't you?'

Lard surged forward but Suth pulled him back, saying, 'You're digging a grave with that mouth of yours, Pyke. Consider this the warning it is. No more giving us a bad name, or we'll put you in the infirmary.'

Pyke bared his teeth in a derisive smirk. 'You can try.'

Suth sat back, disbelieving. *All the gods of the lands. How dense can a man be?* 'All right. Outside.'

Wess inched his head aside, his eyes to Suth's rear. Suth turned to see Goss approaching. The sergeant rested a heavy hand on Lard's and Pyke's shoulders, giving them all an evil smile. 'Good to see everyone together like one big happy family. Now kit up. We're on.'

The squad assembled in front of the inn. All were present, including, of all people, Faro. Yana only was absent as she was still recovering from her crossbow bolt wound. Suth had been named acting corporal. Len and Keri showed up last, jogging from the direction of the garrison. They cradled fat shoulder bags at their sides. Something in Suth shivered upon spotting those bags: whatever this was, it was gonna be ugly.

They marched east. Before they left the last outskirts of Banith, the 6th joined them led by Sergeant Twofoot. Suth couldn't miss the giant shambling Fish, the squad's muscle. The man held out a hand to Wess, who pressed a pouch into it. The two tucked rolls of leaves into their mouths. *Peas in a damned pod.*

Beyond the outskirts they passed tilled market gardens, leafless orchards and harvested fields of stubble and snow. They passed through Malazan checkpoints, were saluted onward. A mounted messenger joined up with them and led the way to a copse of trees north off the road. Here they were ordered to form up.

People advanced from the gloom of the woods. Suth recognized the Adjunct Kyle, Fist Rillish, and the mail-coated woman from the bridge battle, Captain Peles. With them was some squat meaty fellow who had the look of a wrestler, and an old man in ragged shirt and trousers, barefoot. One of the local tribesmen. The Fist stepped forward, studied their ranks.

'Troopers of the 6th and 17th. You have been selected for a special mission. We will be making a dash to a Roolian stronghold, a series of caves in the mountains. There, our objective is to acquire or destroy a small box or chest. If any of you should locate this object – *do not touch it!* It could be deadly. Call for the saboteurs.

'Now, you may be wondering how we could be making a dash to the mountains . . . well, you are Malazan troops. How many here have travelled by Warren?'

Suth looked round, curious, while a few hands went up – less than a quarter of the company. Goss' hand was up, as was Twofoot's, also most of the saboteurs'. Faro's hand wasn't up, which didn't surprise Suth; the man would hardly volunteer any information. Peering about, Suth was startled to see that someone new had joined their ranks at the rear: a giant. The fellow was nearly half as tall again as the average height. He was also by far the broadest across, as well. Suth stared, then remembered he was in ranks, and returned his eyes forward.

Fist Rillish was nodding. 'Very good. Those who have travelled before help the others, if necessary. Now, our guide for the quick journey will be this man.' The Fist indicated the elderly local. 'Gheven is his name. You will follow his orders explicitly. While we are in Warren, you will do as he says without hesitation or question. Is this clear?'

'Aye, sir!' came the bellowed response from all throats.

The Fist nodded again. 'Very good. Now, I requested you because I know you've been in the fire before. You can handle yourselves. Follow orders, be responsive and quick, and we'll be back before your lovers can miss you. That is all. Sergeants.'

Goss and Twofoot stepped forward. 'Squads! Form up double column!'

The 17th lined up next to the 6th, while the Adjunct and the Fist led with their party. Then they merely set off through the woods. The night was partially overcast. Occasionally, a crescent moon dropped silver beams across the tree trunks. It was chill, but not uncomfortable. 'Who's the big guy?' Suth asked Goss as they marched.

A shrug. 'Came with the priest. Strange feller. Don't see what help he'll be.'

'Priest?'

Goss gave him an amused look. He pointed to his face. 'Priest of Fener.'

Suth hid his annoyance: too damned dark to see, wasn't it?

'Where're we—'

Goss had raised a hand for silence. Crossbows were readied all up and down the two columns. The lines became ragged as some hesitated, anticipating a halt. But the order came back to keep moving. None should stop unless directly ordered to do so.

They marched, scanning the woods to either side, crossbows at shoulders. Suth caught a glimpse of some huge beast moving through a glade – of a set of gigantic antlers upraised, almost occluding a surprisingly fat and large moon. That none fired a bolt spoke of the strict adherence to the wait-for-go orders.

Suth stared back at that moon. He could've sworn it had been a sliver crescent last time he'd seen it. He was so absorbed he stumbled over Goss' heels and the man righted him. 'Ignore everything,' he told him. 'Unless it bites you.'

Suth nodded, chastened.

Things got very strange after that. The forest became extraordinarily wild and dense. Everyone released the tension on their crossbows and swung them on to their backs. Swords came out to hack a route. A mist rose, obscuring everything but the tall thick trunks and the vines surrounding them. Those vines occasionally snagged ankles and wrists but quick work from everyone hacked them away; Suth couldn't tell whether that catching was accidental or deliberate. Soon the mist was swept away by a lashing heated wind that halted them with its fury. Branches slashed them. Suth held a forearm across his eyes, head down. After the wind had passed smoke boiled over them, chokingly thick. It slowly dispersed as they felt their way onward. Ahead, the forest was a blackened wasteland of standing shattered trunks. Beyond that rose a wall of ridges and cliffs, bare and black, billowing plumes of smoke, flame-lashed and glowing, obscuring half the night sky.

*

Rillish steadied Gheven whenever he faltered, which was becoming ever more frequent. He wondered, not academically, what would happen if they were still in this strange Warren when the man died. Would they be lost for ever? It was selfish of him to think of it, but it was a worry. He studied the man's lined, sweaty face and received a nod of reassurance.

'She's anxious,' the old man explained, his breath coming hard. 'I sense it. There are things happening all across these lands. Control is slipping away. Now is our best chance.'

'And how are you?'

Gheven answered with a tired smile. 'I will manage. I have been hiding and watching long enough.'

Rillish answered the smile with one of his own then looked back to study the company. They were climbing the rocky slope of the crescent of mountains, the Trembling range, that contained the inland body of water known as Fist Sea. Somewhere ahead waited the cave complex of Thol. Below, the coming dawn revealed that at some time the forest had returned; the thunderstorm plume streaming from behind the peaks above was gone as well. A morning mist obscured the greenery of the forest, while the usual thick cloud cover now obscured the sky, seeming to pile up against the shoulders of the Trembling range.

The line of troops snaked below, the men and women dodging from cover to cover. Coming abreast of him, the priest Ipshank shot him a glance and Rillish directed his gaze to the elder. 'Can't you help him?' he murmured, keeping his voice low.

The priest shook his head. 'No. She'd sense me immediately. He's having a hard enough time obscuring the Adjunct's and my presence.'

'Are we . . . out?'

'Yes. Some time ago.'

Rillish nodded, relieved. 'As soon as there's cover I'll order a rest. Everyone's tired. We'll have one shift to try to get some sleep.' He waved for the sergeants. Now, his nagging suspicion returned that he'd not brought enough troopers. But Gheven had been adamant: he could manage no more.

So be it. They would have to succeed with what they had. The Adjunct, Kyle, had been insistent that he come. He had Captain Peles, who was extraordinary in a fight, Ipshank and Manask who were both legends, and two squads of Malazan heavy infantry. What more could any commander wish? It would have to do. After all, what could possibly be awaiting them here, in the middle of nowhere?

* * *

This time it was no Korelri Stormguard who came for Corlo; it was a regular Theftian guardsman. It would seem that now, at the very height of the season, the Korelri were too hard-pressed, too thin on the ground, to spare a Chosen for such a menial task. For his part Corlo took renewed comfort from this. The chances for their escape were looking better and better.

The guard manacled his hands behind his back then urged him on with the point of his spear. Jemain had not returned, but the wall was long, and gathering intelligence a chancy business. Corlo trusted the Genabackan could find him again should he need to. What worried him was the possible cause for his summoning. *Was Bars despairing again? Already? It rarely struck during mid-season. Was he just sick of it all? A reasonable reaction, actually. Just a little longer, Bars. I have news!*

He was urged east in a long walk. One of the longest ever. He'd never been this far towards the eastern end of the wall. It was mostly higher ground here, but for one notorious low-lying section. Ice Tower. His anxiety clawed ever higher in his throat as they headed onward for another day's march. He was startled at one point to pass a column of soldiers coming the opposite way: a detachment of fifty in Roolian brown. True soldiers, not frightened indebted citizens, or sullen criminals. Men well accoutred in ringed and studded armour, iron helmets, swords and shields. Had these Korelri struck some sort of deal with the Roolians? Looked like it.

The Theftian guard urged him onward down a treacherous icy descent to the curve of the Ice Tower curtain wall. Here he found chaos. Work crews struggled with stone blocks. Streams of ice coursed over the wall and down its rear where it disappeared into the driving snow. Guards waved them on as they might at a fire or some other catastrophe in any city. In the slashing frigid spume from the crashing waves, the guard hurried his pace. They both ended the journey running for cover into an ice-sheathed tower guarded by a single Korelri, his blue cloak trimmed in icicles, hoarfrost its own silver inlay on his Stormguard's full helm. Corlo stomped his feet and rubbed his hands in the guardroom, and wondered that perhaps such a sight was what lay behind the silver chasing on all the Chosen's armour: an imitation, or reminder, of the true inlay their sworn duty freely provided.

Within, a Korelri Stormguard motioned to the Theftian. 'Is this the one?'

The guard nodded, shivering too violently to speak.

The Chosen regarded Corlo from behind the narrow vision slit of his helm. 'Your friend has lost sight of his purpose again.'

Corlo felt his shoulders tightening. 'There is nothing new I can say to him.'

A gauntleted hand smashed across Corlo's face, sending him to the floor. He lay stunned. *These Stormguard were never subtle, and the time for subtlety has long passed!*

'Wrong answer. Convince him to fight or you both die. Am I clear?'

Corlo lay rubbing his jaw. 'Yes, sir. Very clear.'

'Good.' He picked up his spear. 'This way.'

The Korelri led him down narrow circular stairs past levels of holding pens, guardrooms, and crude dormitories no more than halls scattered with straw in which men lay dozing or sat passing the time, talking and playing dice. Down towards the bottom of these levels they entered a slim hall faced by cells. The Korelri stopped at one and peered in the tiny window. He turned to Corlo. 'Talk to your friend now. Convince him, or you'll stand the wall together.' He unlatched the door and pushed Corlo in.

Bars sat hunched against the far wall, elbows on knees, head hanging. He was filthy. His skin was blackened, cracked and scabbed from exposure, his greying hair long and matted. Corlo slid down the wall near the door. What to say? What could he possibly find to say? All he had left were lies.

The head rose and Bars gave him a wink. He stared, speechless. *What was this?* His commander stepped to the door, listened, then grunted. He pulled Corlo to his feet.

'I have news,' the big man said.

'As have I,' Corlo stuttered, still surprised.

'Avowed are here. Shell and Blues. They say K'azz has returned, driven Skinner from the Guard.'

Corlo studied his commander, his pleasure at seeing the man revived and animated fading. *Gods, no. Jemain mentioned the* possibility *of Avowed . . . but has all this finally proved too much for the man? Has he gone mad?*

Bars pulled away. 'Don't give me that look. It's real. I've met them. We just need to locate the survivors of the crew then we're out of here.'

* * *

Borun spent his days in the tower of the Sea Gate in Lallit, gazing out at the iron-grey waters of Sender's Sea. The Moranth sub-commanders knew not to disturb him as every day that passed without news worsened his mood until any question, no matter how tentatively set, received nothing more than an icy mute stare.

Two more days passed without the arrival of the promised ships. Then, Sub-commander Stoven, a companion of the commander from their youth, was selected to approach and ask what to do next. The woman knelt on one knee behind Borun, head bowed. 'Commander. You have guided us faultlessly all these years. None question your choices. We ask . . . what are your orders?'

The commander turned. His arms were crossed. A great breath expanded his chest and his head moved from side to side, vertebrae cracking audibly. A long low breath escaped him. 'Rise, Stoven. You are right to ask. I have been . . . negligent. It would seem that for reasons we have yet to ascertain, we are on our own. Very well.

Round up all craftsmen, impress labourers. Begin construction of a defensive wall round the city. We may be here for some time.'

Stoven bowed. 'Commander.' Straightening, she peered out to sea. Her surprise was quite obvious despite her obscuring visor. 'Commander – look.'

Borun turned. A vessel was entering the small bay. That alone was not worthy of note: what was unusual was that it was a Moranth Blue message cutter. As it neared Borun made out flagging raised on its yards requesting truce and parley. He set his gauntleted hands on the weapon belts crossed around his waist. 'Well, Stoven. Let us go and see what our good cousins have to say.'

CHAPTER XI

When you do not recognize the wrongs of the past, the future takes its revenge.

Author forgotten

THE NEXT MORNING BROUGHT FRESH JOURILAN NOBLES. THEY looked eager to show up their brethren from yesterday with a murderous charge that would finally sweep these heretical rabble from the field. Ivanr, exhausted and aching from the struggles of the night, wondered if perhaps their confidence was not misguided.

He watched from the wall. By now he'd realized that his place was not in the ranks. Too many looked to him for reassurance and a kind of guidance that, for the life of him, he felt he could not offer. Yet look they did, and so he must be here, though he felt a fraud and feared that somehow he would fail and betray them all.

Again, the impressed Imperial infantry and hired mercenary companies were left to find their own way. Whoever was in command over there seemed to have no idea what to do with them, though he or she seemed to understand by now that they were somehow necessary. The noble cavalry ignored these foot soldiers and had already demonstrated that they were even ready to run them down should they find them in their way.

The Reform pike rankers marched out once more to meet the challenge. Ivanr knew they would be better off remaining behind the raised walls of this instant fortress – no matter how frail its timbers may be – but failing to emerge would be tantamount to surrender. *They* were the ones who had to prove themselves.

He scanned the ranks, searching for some sign of a commander.

Carr's banner was there along with the brigade colours. But what of Martal? What were they going to do? Everyone must be looking for her. So far, the official story was that she was too wounded to ride – he wondered how long that would last.

As it was, the marshalled nobles gave no one the chance to speculate. Almost immediately the front ranks urged their mounts forward. The pike formations took up long rectangles less than twenty deep, covering a broad sweep of field quite close to the fortress walls. He wondered if Carr was the one behind this new strategy. The heavy cavalry came on steadily; the Imperial infantry milled lost to the rear, apparently far less keen for action.

This morning he sensed a lack of confidence and crispness in the pike manoeuvres. Martal's absence was being felt. The oncoming cavalry seemed to sense this as well: the call for charge sounded and their pace picked up. Horns answered within the Reform brigades and movement began among the pike ranks, but it was confused and slow. Ivanr stared, sickened with the prescience that the manoeuvre, an effort to open another cleared corridor, would not be completed in time. This worst nightmare was realized as the cavalry charge descended too quickly for all ranks to face uniformly, all pikeheads to present parallel, and every member brace.

An eruption of flesh and iron as heaving tons of muscle ploughed all the way through to the rear to burst outward, pikes glancing aside, men and women trampled. The wedge of noblemen, emboldened, even galloped onward to the fortress walls. They swung alongside, hacking at the planking. One horse reared, kicking, and that bowed a section. Ivanr clutched a log as the wall shuddered where he stood. Archers loosed point-blank from the walks and carriage-platforms.

These heavy cavalry seemed to have come prepared for this eventuality as they drew ropes that ended in nooses and small grapnel hooks. These they threw over the wall. The defenders hacked at the ropes but the nobles spurred their mounts and that section bowed outward, wavering. A tearing and sickening snapping of wood announced its fall. The archers jumped, tumbling. A great roaring cheer went up from the Imperial camp.

Yet an answering roar swelled among the Reform army and Ivanr peered around for its source: there, at a carriage-platform, in her black armour, Martal directing the defence. But not Martal. Someone in her armour. The chant arose: *The Black Queen! The Black Queen!* She was sending orders to her signallers and the horns sounded.

The cavalry turned to find themselves surrounded. The call went up to close and the razor pikeheads and billhooks advanced from all around. The noblemen spurred their mounts to escape but they had no room to gather momentum. They could only hack at the pikeheads as they thrust at them. In moments they were slaughtered to a man.

Across the field another cavalry mass was hastily forming up. The Imperials had seen success and now it appeared they intended to finish things. Every remaining horse and rider looked to be being pressed into this deciding charge. A great dark mass of men and horses started on its way towards them. The very timbers under Ivanr's hands shivered as the ground shook.

Even though he knew the woman in Martal's armour to be just some female officer, Ivanr could not help but glance to that dark figure where she gave orders on the carriage-platform next to the gap; like everyone constantly checking, making sure of their charm, their talisman against defeat. *She'd been right – she* had *to be seen. She had to be here.*

This final total charge bore down upon them in a dark tide, spreading out to cover the entire battlefield centre. The thick rectangles of pike wielders hunched, braced, pikes static, holding the equidistance between sharpened points that had been drilled into them day after day, month after month.

Loose pieces of iron rattled and the timbers thrummed with the advance. Archers upon the walls and within, filling the interior of the camp, aimed skyward, arrows nocked. All eyes went to Martal, arm poised, waiting. The arm cut down. A great hiss momentarily drowned out the thunder of the horses' hooves. The salvo arched overhead, denser and darker than the constant cloud cover, to descend, cutting a swath through the centre and rear ranks of the cavalry. But the front ranks were spared and these charged onward, lances levelling.

The front chevron ploughed into the thick rectangle of men and women. Ivanr witnessed the front two or three, in places up to four, ranks disappear beneath the iron and bone and relentless momentum, but the formation absorbed all that terrifying punishment and held. A second wave now hit home but with less energy as all the carnage and litter of fallen horses and defenders impeded them. Countless horses went down, tripping and stumbling upon the gore.

A cheer went up from the Reform camp but it was short-lived as bow-fire now raked everyone: the hired crossbow and archer companies had advanced to support the charge. This time the cavalry did not wheel away to re-form; they remained, dropping lances and spears to unsheathe swords. A melee broke out and Ivanr had to stop himself from jumping the wall to join in. This could not be allowed. The pike men and women were at too much of a disadvantage. Many wore no armour at all.

But a new element had entered the field. Some sort of horde of irregular infantry armed haphazardly with spears and billhooks and scythes and lengths of wood had taken the left flank and were advancing across the centre. They mobbed the cavalry as they went. Ivanr had taken up a shield and he raised it now overhead to stand as tall as possible – the city! Damned civilians had taken to the field in the thousands! While he watched, this undisciplined mass took the cavalry from the rear to exact a bloody and thorough revenge. Men and women, young and old, pulled nobles in banded armour from their mounts to jab daggers through joints and visors. The merciless bloodthirst reminded Ivanr of the village he'd passed through and he had to look away. Around him the Army of Reform cheered its unlooked-for allies. Even those nobles who surrendered, throwing down their weapons – and probably expecting to be held for ransom – found themselves dragged off their mounts and torn to pieces. By this time the mob was turning its attention to the distant Imperial encampment and panic stirred among those bright pennants and gaily decorated tents.

He descended the wall to join the camp followers and Reform archers pouring out on to the field. His remaining guards followed him. He shook countless hands, squeezed countless shoulders, and lost all tentativeness in blessing all those who asked. The black armoured figure of Martal had remained upon the wall but when Ivanr looked back she was gone. What would the story be, he wondered. Succumbed to her wounds this night? A sudden turn for the worse?

In the carnage of the field he found no prisoners. He knelt to a wounded girl, a pike wielder, one of many in the brigades; it had been his experience that what women may lack in raw brute strength they more than made up in spirit, bravery and dedication to the unit. Her leg had been shattered at the thigh, trampled by a horse. She was white with shock and blood loss. All he could do was hold her muddied hand while the life drained out of her. He brushed the wet hair from her face. 'We won,' he told her. 'You won. It's over. Finished.' Through the numbing fog of shock she smiled dreamily, nodding. She mouthed something and he knelt, straining to hear.

'*Kill them all . . .*'

He flinched away, and looking up he saw a familiar figure. It was the old pilgrim, Orman, leaning upon his crooked staff. Now, however, a crowd of civilians surrounded him and he was quite obviously in charge. Orman bowed to him. 'Greetings, Deliverer.'

'You appear to be the deliverer this day.'

A modest bow of his balding, sweaty pate. 'Ring city is ours. Your example turned the tide.'

'I see.' Now he understood Sister Gosh's words. This day the struggle had been to win something much more important than a mere battle. The confidence of a people? When does the movement become the institution? The rebel, the ruler? When comes that tipping point? It seemed it could happen without one even noticing. The cynical twist on Ivanr's lips fell away and he lowered his voice. 'About Martal . . .'

Orman nodded. 'I know. I've been in contact all this time. It is up to you now, Ivanr. You carry our banner.'

'No.' He glanced down: the girl was dead. Gently, he lowered her head then stood. But the old man would not be put off. His gaze had hardened, unnerving him.

'Yes. You have no choice now.'

'You won't like it.'

The old man bowed. 'It is not for me to judge. You are the Deliverer.'

'Then stop the killing. There's been more than enough of that.'

Orman bowed again. 'I will give the order. But there are risks. The people want revenge. There are enthusiasts who call for the cleansing of all followers of the Lady—'

'No. None of that!'

The old man's tongue emerged to wet his lips. He adjusted his grip on the staff, uneasy. 'I will do my best to enforce your wishes, Deliverer.'

'Do so.' Ivanr dismissed him and went to visit Martal's tent. What was going on there? Had that final rumour been unleashed already? Surrounded now by thousands of cheering jubilant veterans of the Army of Reform, he suddenly felt completely, and terribly, alone.

* * *

The much diminished fleet of Moranth Blue dromonds and mixed Falaran and Talian men-of-war made good time westward across the Fall Strait and up the Narrows, or Crack Strait. Strong constant winds off the Ocean of Storms allowed them to make the journey in two days and two nights. Poring over the antique maps of the region, Nok and Swirl argued for a landing further west, towards Elri, but Greymane was adamant: the landing had to be south of Kor, hard up against the Barrier Mountains. The Admirals finally appealed to Devaleth, but she could not help them. 'I really do not know this shore,' she had to admit. 'Though I have heard it is rugged.'

Nok pushed himself from the low table of his stateroom. 'There you have it. Unsuitable for a landing, I'm sure.'

'Especially one that may be contested,' Swirl added.

But Greymane would not budge. 'It must be here. We are coming up on it. The landing must go ahead.' He looked to the last member of Command present: Fist Khemet Shul. 'Strike inland, take control of the highlands. Use them as your base. Retreat to Katakan, if necessary.'

The squat man nodded. The lamplight reflected gold from his bald blunt head. 'I understand.'

Devaleth looked from face to face: the two reluctant Admirals, the flat uninflected Fist, and the growling, coiled High Fist. She wanted to scream: *How can you do this?* But she knew she'd be dismissed out of hand. Best to swallow her dread, follow along, and do the most she could to ameliorate the certain disaster to come.

'That is all, then,' Greymane said, crossing his arms. 'A dawn assault.'

Fist Shul saluted. 'Sir.' Bowing, he left to see to his preparations.

Devaleth bowed as well. 'I'll try to get some rest, then.'

The three wished her a good sleep. When she pulled the door to the stateroom closed, Admiral Nok was making tea.

Outside, Devaleth leaned on a gunwale railing. It was after midnight, and they were passing the last of the Barrier range rising north of them into the night like a distant set of ragged teeth. The sea was calm though the winds were high. And those winds chilled her, coming directly off the Ocean of Storms and bearing a hint of the Riders themselves.

As tentatively as possible she opened up to passively reach for her Ruse Warren. The response almost overwhelmed her. Raw churning power taut with anticipation. *Something is coming. Ruse senses it, or carries it like the gravid swelling of power before its release. What is it? Our destruction? Whatever it might be it is immense; there is power here for the taking – more than I'd ever dare to take, or even suspected flowed there for the taking.*

Drawing back, what frightened her the most was the dread that before tomorrow was over, she may be driven to reach for it.

The day dawned with the fleet approaching the coast on a wide front. From the side of Admiral Nok's flagship, the *Star of Unta*, it looked to Devaleth as if these Malazans and Moranth had used up all their tricks and stratagems getting by the Skolati and the Mare forces, and now all they were left with was a plain straightforward assault.

They'd entered the lee of the Barrier range and many vessels had had to break out the sweeps to continue shoreward. It was clear that the rocky coast was too rough for the ships to anchor anywhere close and so crews readied launches. Ashore, bonfires burned and Devaleth could make out timber barriers and massed troops. The Roolians. Obviously Yeull also understood that this length of shore was the crucial landing place.

The vessels nosed as close to the shore as possible. Smaller cutters and sloops swept in closer, carrying as many troops as could be jammed on board. But while the water was still too deep for the men and women to jump off sheeting bow-fire met them, arcing up from massed archers. Devaleth's stomach clenched seeing the troops delay while launches and all manner of rowboats were readied. They were sitting targets!

The coast was so rocky and dangerous here, only the smallest boats dared approach, so only the barest handful of troopers could land at any one time. Parties slogged ashore in fives and tens through the waist-deep water, and, while Devaleth watched, overwhelming numbers jumped up from behind fallen logs and rocks to charge. She saw entire boatloads of infantry cut down one at a time before escaping the wash of the waves.

This is a catastrophe! And the Korelri haven't even yet lent their weight to the battle.

Then, just as Devaleth could not imagine things unfolding any more disastrously, batteries of mangonels, catapults and onagers opened up from the shore. A barrage of projectiles came streaming up from the hidden weapons. Devaleth jumped, flinching at the sight of the fusillade. She watched frozen in a sort of suspended fascination as the stones descended, roaring, amid the anchored fleet. Most struck only water, sending up massive jets of spray. But a few found targets and punched down through decking and hull. *This is insane! Where was Greymane? The fool! Yeull was waiting for them!*

But yet again she'd forgotten about the Moranth. The engines that had cast so much death and destruction among the Mare fleet now responded. The colour of the dawn changed to an orange-red as a great sheet of flaming projectiles arced up from the Blue vessels. She watched just as fascinated as this barrage passed over the immediate shore to land a good hundred paces back from the lip of the sand cliffs masking the coast.

A firestorm blossomed, roiling in fat billowing flames and black smoke. It spread in great arcs of incendiaries that reached like claws, secondary bursts scattering the inferno even farther. The blast reached Devaleth like a distant rockslide or titanic waterfall. She was shaken from the spell of that eruption by soldiers jostling her: the *Star of Unta* was unloading its some four hundred infantry on to launches and jolly boats.

Smoke now veiled the shore. Wave after wave of infantry from the Fourth and Eighth Armies heaved themselves over the sides of the boats to wade into the killing zone where the surf broke amid rocks and pockets of gravel strand. She could not quite tell if any foothold had yet been gained. The bodies that had not sunk now washed about, crowding the surf like driftwood.

Punching through the smoke came a continued barrage from the defending engines, only now aimed higher, to fall short among the crowded boats and knots of men. Great jets burst skyward with each impact, throwing troopers like rags. Some few struck boats, exploding them in a great eruption of wood splinters and disintegrated bodies.

A hand grasped Devaleth's upper arm and she jumped, gasping. It was Greymane.

'I was calling you,' he said.

She swallowed, her heart pounding. 'I'm – I'm sorry. I'm so . . . Is this as bad as it looks?'

The big man grimaced his understanding. 'It's ugly – there's no way round it. Attacking a hostile shore? You can only push and keep pushing. It's up to the troops now – they mustn't flinch.' He looked to shore, his pale eyes the colour of the sky. 'But I have every confidence in them.' His gaze returned to her. 'Now I have a request of you, High Mage.'

'Me?'

'A journey through your Warren. I'm needed elsewhere.'

'What?' She gestured to the shore. 'But what of this? You're needed here!'

He shook his head. 'No. It's no longer up to me here. I can only watch. Nok and Shul have their orders and they will see things through. I must go – believe me.'

'But the Lady . . .'

His lips crooked up in a smile. 'We're on water, mage.'

She sighed as she acknowledged defeat. 'Very well. Where?'

'West. I will let you know. In fact, you may sense it yourself.'

'All right. West. If you must.' She took hold of his forearm. 'Gods – it's been ages since I've done this.' She reached out to Ruse . . . and stepped through.

She found herself on a flooded plain, standing in shin-deep water. The sky was clear, deep blue. Greymane was with her in his heavy armour of banded iron, helmet pushed high on his head. He hooked his gauntleted hands at his belt. 'Where are we?'

'I don't know.' She turned full circle: flat desolation in all directions. The water was fetid, heavy with silt and muck. The stink, gorge-rising.

'Which way?' Greymane asked, wincing at the smell.

'This way.' She headed off, slogging through the flood. Her sodden robes dragged as she pushed through the water.

They came to a long low hill, like a moraine, and there washed up against its side lay a great line of pale things like a high-water mark. At first she thought them stranded sea-life, seals or porpoises, but as they drew closer the awful truth of them clawed at her and she bent over, heaving up her stomach. Greymane steadied her.

'God of the Sea preserve us,' she managed, spitting and gasping. 'What has happened here?'

'It's me,' Greymane ground out, his voice thick with suppressed emotion. 'A warning, or a lesson, from Mael.'

'*A lesson?*' She studied him anew. 'What is this? *What is going on here?*'

The man tried to speak, looked away, blinking back tears, then tried again. 'I'm going to do something, Devaleth. Something I've been running from for decades. Something that terrifies me.'

She backed away, splashing through the shallow polluted waters. '*No!*' A dizzying suspicion clenched her chest – she could not breathe. '*Stonewielder! No! Do not do this thing!*'

'It must be done. I've always known that. I . . . I couldn't summon the nerve, the *determination*, before. But now I see there's no choice.'

She pointed to the swollen rotting corpses, men, women, children, heaved up like wreckage. 'And what is this? You would do *this*!'

He bowed his head then raised it to look to the sky, blinking. 'I was handed two ghastly choices decades ago, Devaleth. Mass murder on the one hand – and an unending atrocity of blood and death on the other. Which would you choose?'

'I would find a third course!'

'I tried. Believe me, I tried.' He gestured off into the distance. 'But it hasn't stopped, has it?' He added, more softly, 'And do you really think it will?'

She had to shake her head. 'No. It won't. But . . . the price . . .'

'It's the only way to end it. Everyone is in too deep. A price *must* be paid.'

Devaleth hugged herself as if to keep the pain swelling in her chest contained. 'I . . . I understand. For us the time for easy options is long past. And now our delay has brought us to this.'

'Yes.'

She bowed her head. *Gods – you are all a merciless lot, aren't you? But then, how can you be any better than your worshippers?* She started off again. 'This way. I feel it. It's unmistakable.'

She found the locus: a great current coursing through the flood where the water fairly vibrated with power. Here she brought them out of the Warren to appear in the shallows of a long wide beach that led up to a wooded shore.

Greymane turned to her. 'My thanks. You didn't have to . . .'

She waved that aside. 'I understand. It's time we made the hard choices. And I understand now why you pushed everyone away. Your friend Kyle. Us. All of us.'

He winced at that. 'Speak to him for me, won't you? I . . . I couldn't tell him.'

'Yes.'

'And give my apologies to Rillish. He proved himself. He deserved better.'

'I will.'

'Good. My thanks.' He started up the beach, turned back. 'Tomorrow. You'll have till tomorrow. Get everyone into the hills – and see Nok through this. It's up to you.'

'Yes. I'd say good luck, but I can't bring myself to. I'm sorry.'

The High Fist nodded. 'Goodbye. Good luck to you.' And he bowed his head in a kind of salute.

Devaleth watched till he disappeared into the forest of this unremarkable length of coast. *A forest soon to be swept utterly away should the man succeed – which isn't guaranteed, either.*

She summoned Ruse and returned to the Warren.

Her return journey was uneventful. The shallow wash remained, either the remnant of a flood, or a flood from an earth tremor, or some such thing. She could not tell. She avoided the moraine but bumped up against waterlogged corpses sunk in the water. Though their flesh was disintegrating in a cloud around their bones, these bodies appeared unusual: very gracile, the bones curved oddly, the skull narrow, limbs elongated. Very pale, of course, as the bleaching of the water accomplishes that. But still, very pale indeed.

Unnerved, she hurried on. When her sense of the Warren told her she'd found the place of her entrance she reached out once more to step through.

And she entered a maelstrom of noise and smoke and screaming. Malazan dead carpeted the tidal interzone of algae-skirted rocks and pools. Troopers hunched for cover among those rocks. Arrows and crossbow bolts whipped past her and she quickly raised a shield from Ruse to deflect them. Launches and jolly boats choked the shore, abandoned or half sunk.

What was going on? Why were they still here?

Furious, she slogged over to the nearest crowd of soldiers. 'What are you doing!' she demanded.

The troopers gaped at her. One, a sergeant by his armband, offered a hasty salute. 'Beggin' yer pardon, High Mage, ma'am. It's them shoreward cliffs. Their archers beat back every charge.'

She studied the cliffs: some three fathoms of loamy soil, no handholds, no gaps. 'Very well. Looks like you can use some help.'

The sergeant nudged the troopers near him. 'Yes, ma'am. An even exchange, every time.'

'Prepare yourselves . . .'

Ruse called to her. It practically sang. Yes, yes, she answered. *So be it.* She extended her arms to reach out over as wide a front as possible. *Come. Rush through. Rise.* She tugged the waters behind her, urging them into a swelling, a great roll or front that came surging upward. She sensed the enormous Blue dromonds and men-of-war anchored behind in the bay as tiny toys bouncing far above her consciousness. And she pushed.

Yells of alarm rang out around her but she did not turn.

An immensity now leaning forward behind her, rising inexorably. The weight was impossible, but she allowed it to flow through her, onward, promising release just ahead. A wave took her from behind, climbed her body and kept mounting ever higher. She sensed the launches and jolly boats surging overhead, men and women momentarily suspended, counter-balanced in their weight, kicked forward.

The surge struck the cliff like a tidal bore and was pushed upward, bulging, rising. It washed over the lip, taking with it everyone along this stretch of the landing, to burst outward in a great release of pressure, washing onwards, diminishing.

The surge sank around her, leaving her sodden, exhausted, and she slouched on to a rock. Water rushed round her knees, charging back to the sea, dragging the loamy soil with it, and peering up she saw the cliff eroded into draws that ran now like small waterfalls. A huge launch, some two fathoms in length itself, tottered on the lip of the cliff before sliding backwards, empty.

Troopers of the Fourth and Eighth splashed in from either side, charging, cheering, urging one another on. The charge thickened into a constant stream of soldiers as the entire landing converged on this gap to claw themselves up the slope. When next she raised her head for a look, a guard of troopers had her covered in a barrier of overlapping shields. She rubbed at a sticky wetness over her mouth and her hand came away clotted in blood. Nosebleed – of course.

Some time later the self-appointed honour-guard straightened, saluting, and, after bowing to her, jogged off. Devaleth turned to see the Blue Admiral, Swirl. The Moranth draped a blanket over her shoulders.

'High Mage,' he began, wonder in his voice, 'I am amazed. Had I known – we would have merely stood aside to let you clear the way.'

She shook her head. 'That wasn't me. I just tapped something abiding within Ruse. Something so immense the mere possibility of it allowed this.'

The Blue Admiral tilted his helm. 'I confess I do not understand. Does this bear on the High Fist's last orders?'

'What were they?'

'Fist Shul is to strike inland, take high ground. The fleet is to withdraw from the coast.'

She jumped up, tottering, clutching the blanket. 'Yes! That is it. We must withdraw to the centre of the Narrows. Shul will take the troops. He, all of us, we have until tomorrow.'

The Admiral bowed. 'We will complete the unloading as soon as possible, then. Will you not return to the flagship?'

She nodded her relief. *Gods, yes. I can feel her pushing against me. Raging. Full of hate and poison. Best to get away as soon as possible.*

She took a step and would have collapsed but for the Admiral's catching at her arm. Dizzy, she thanked him. He waved guards to him, ordered them to return her to the flagship. Despite her distaste for displaying weakness, she allowed them to walk her to the nearest boat.

*

'What do you mean he isn't here?' Overlord Yeull stared at Ussü as if he were somehow responsible. 'This is his landing! His moment! Why wouldn't he be here?' The man's gaze darted about the tent, feverish, wild. 'Where is he? He must be found!' The eyes, white all round, found Ussü. 'You! Find him! I command you! Find him and destroy him!'

Ussü drew breath to disagree but one look at the man hunched over the brazier, blankets and a fur cloak draped over his shoulders, hands practically sizzling over the embers, convinced him not to argue. He bowed. 'I am your servant.'

The man glanced to him as if startled by his presence. 'What? Yes! Go!' He waved Ussü out.

Outside the darkened command tent, Ussü adjusted his robes and considered the Overlord's degenerating condition. *He always was unreliable – now, who knows what whim might take him? Things did not look promising.*

Still, they were here in Korelri. Should these Malazans even gain a foothold, like a shallow wave they would break against the wall. He crossed to his tent, ducked within. His Roolian soldier attendants were still wiping up the blood from his earlier efforts. One was casting sawdust on the bare ground. The corpse had been wrapped and carried off. How the Lady mocked him for clinging to such crutches. Still, he remained reluctant to throw himself entirely into her hands.

'Another prisoner, magus?' an attendant asked.

'No. That is all for now.' No need to scry anew. Greymane was not here, that much was certain. Still, where was the man? It troubled him also that he could not find him. What was he up to? If he had sufficient power at his disposal he could locate the fellow – but not power pulled from the Lady, not yet. He wasn't that desperate yet. But perhaps from another source . . .

'I have need of a horse,' he told an attendant. 'Have we any?'

'We brought a few across, sir. For messages.'

'Very good. Prepare one.'

The man bowed and left. Ussü began packing a set of panniers. Should the Malazans gain a foothold then it would be an infantry battle, hedge-jumping and door-to-door skirmishing. Not his campaign. It seemed the Overlord had given him his mission, and thinking on it, he did believe it important. This man, Greymane, Stonewielder, must be planning something, and he, Ussü, the Lady's erstwhile High Mage, was the only one with the slightest chance of locating him.

Outside, the horse was brought up and he mounted. Wishing the men good luck, he urged his mount inland. He was a good few leagues off, climbing the gentle rolling hillside, when something tugged at him from the Strait. *Something's gathering.* He reined in and turned. Shading his eyes, he could just make out the distant Blue and Talian men-of-war anchored in the bay. *What were they up to?* Then he felt it: the puissance literally pushed him backwards. *Ye gods, what was this? Ruse, awakening? Had an Ascendant taken to the field?*

A great wave bulged in the bay, heaving shoreward. *That renegade Mare mage!* Sweeping the shore clear! Where came she by such might? Too much. Far too much for him to contest. That was one battle he had to concede. She could have the shore – but this was her one and only throw. He still had many more. He sawed the reins around and made inland as fast as he could urge the horse.

* * *

Warran took Kiska through Shadow – just how he did it she wasn't sure. He simply invited her to walk to the darkened rear of the tent and she found herself stepping on much farther than its dimensions. The gloom then brightened to the familiar haziness of the Chaos region and she turned to him. 'Where are we?'

'Within the boundary threshold of the Whorl itself.' The short fellow clasped his hands at his front. 'Myself, I have no wish to go any farther.'

'But it was dark . . .'

'To those looking from the outside, yes. It would appear that those within create their own local conditions.'

Kiska peered around, dubious. 'I don't think I understand . . .'

The old priest cocked his head. 'Some say every consciousness is like a seed. Perhaps that is true. I know of small pocket realms that act in this manner. Perhaps we create our own – for a time. Now I understand why the Liosan would come in such numbers. Their local conditions would be that much stronger, and more enduring.'

'Enduring?'

Warran gave a serious nod. 'You don't really think you can forestall the eroding effects for ever, do you? Eventually you will be consumed.' He raised a finger to his lips. 'Or perhaps you will drift in nothingness dreaming for ever . . . Hmm. An interesting problem . . .'

Kiska stared at the ragged fellow. 'That's supposed to reassure me?'

Warran blinked. 'Does it? It certainly wouldn't reassure me.'

Exasperated, she raised her arms to turn full circle. 'Well, which direction should I go?'

'I really do not think it matters. Here, all directions lead to the centre.'

'All directions lead – that doesn't make any sense!'

The priest pursed his lips, head cocked. 'You could say it has its own kind of logic . . . you just have to learn to think a different way.'

'You sound as if you've done this before.'

The greying tangled brows rose in surprise. 'Time is wasting. You'd better start searching.' He raised a finger. 'Oh! I took the liberty . . .' He reached into his dirty torn robes and pulled out Kiska's staff.

Mute with wonder, she accepted it, then stared from it to him: it was taller than he. 'How . . .'

He waved goodbye, started off. Over his shoulder he called, 'Take care. Remember the logic!' He'd taken only a few steps when he disappeared.

Kiska stared, squinting. Was that the border of her own personal space? The thought unnerved her utterly. She squeezed the staff in her hands, feeling emboldened by its familiarity, and started off in the opposite direction from the one in which the priest had gone.

She had no sense of time passing, of course. It might have been a moment, or a day, but eventually the sky darkened, seeming to close in until she jogged beneath a night sky blazing with stars that showed no constellation she knew. The ground to either side fell away in steep slopes down to an equally dark abyss, leaving a narrow walk, and here someone was waiting for her.

It was Jheval-Leoman, arms crossed, an almost embarrassed look on his wind-tanned face. Kiska noted he once more wore his morningstars on his belt – that damned priest! She lowered her staff. 'Keep your distance.'

He held up his opened hands. 'Kiska. I have no vendetta. Believe me. My only motive is to get you damned Malazans off my back.'

She motioned him to walk ahead of her. 'So you say. But I can't trust that, can I?'

He let out a long breath, his arms slowly falling. 'No. I suppose not.' He walked ahead of her. 'I've been thinking about what you told me of this manifestation, and I'm worried. You said Tayschrenn didn't create this—'

'Agayla would not deceive me! I trust her completely!'

He turned, walking backwards. 'Kiska. She did not object to me . . .'

She stopped. Objections crowded her throat but none could escape. Agayla was deceived? Hardly. She didn't know? The Queen of Dreams, ignorant? Even less likely. And yet . . . how could she accept this criminal? Nothing less than a mass murderer?

A dark shape caught her eye ahead. A figure, prone, wearing dark torn robes. *Tayschrenn!* She dashed ahead.

'*Kiska!* Wait!'

She dropped to her knees next to the figure, an old man on his back, thin, with long grey hair. 'Tayschrenn!' She touched a shoulder. 'It's me . . .'

The figure stirred, turning over. A hand grasped her wrist. Kiska stared, stunned. For it was not Tayschrenn. The man stood, his grip on her wrist inhumanly strong. He was sun-darkened, with a great hooked nose and black glittering eyes. 'And you are?' he grated in accented Talian.

Kiska could not speak, couldn't think. *Impossible. All this . . . impossible . . .*

The avid eyes slid aside, narrowing. 'And who is this?'

Kiska followed his gaze to Leoman, kneeling, bowed.

'Arise,' the man growled.

Leoman straightened, inclined his head in obeisance. 'Greetings, Yathengar. Faladan, priest of Ehrlitan. The Seven bless us.'

The man, Yathengar, pushed Kiska away. He took an uncertain step, his gaze furrowed. 'Leoman? In truth? Leoman – Champion of Sha'ik?' He clasped Leoman's shoulders and laughed. 'The Seven Gods are not so easily swept aside, yes? How they must have schemed to bring us together! We shall return, you and I. All Seven Cities will rise aflamed! You shall be my general. We will destroy them.'

Leoman bowed again. 'I am yours to command.'

To one side a brightening disturbed the uniformity of this island, or eye of calm, at the centre of the Whorl. Yathengar peered aside, frowning. 'What is this?'

Leoman shot Kiska a warning glance. 'Tiste Liosan, m'lord. This place touches upon their Realm and they are here to destroy it.'

'Fools to challenge me here. I will sweep them aside like chaff.'

Leoman had backed away a step. 'No doubt, m'lord.'

Kiska eyed him – what was the bastard up to? Has he deceived everyone? Every friend or loyalty he has ever established, he has betrayed. And now he would whip this madman upon the Liosan? Was there no limit to his debasement? Was it all nothing more than gleeful nihilism?

Leoman looked up, directing her gaze to the sky. Unwilling to cooperate, she reluctantly glanced up anyway. And she saw it. A tiny bat-like dot flapping overhead.

Her gaze snapped back to him, her heart lurching. The man took another careful step away from Yathengar. She followed suit.

'Watch, Leoman,' the priest commanded. 'See how I have grown in might here.'

Leoman bowed again. 'Yes, m'lord.'

Kiska cast quick furtive glances to their little guide. It descended to the rear, behind them, where the ground fell away to the dark abyss that seemed to surround them. It disappeared, arcing down into the gulf, and Kiska's gaze rose to Leoman, appalled.

He nodded, his gaze steady, insistent.

And she, hardly able to breathe, terrified, nodded back.

Leoman kicked her staff over the edge. Yathengar turned. 'What?'

Kiska leapt into the black emptiness. A surprised roar burst behind her. Then, a bellow of pure outrage: '*Leoman!*'

It seemed Leoman could not help but remain true to his character.

* * *

Bakune imagined himself the most coddled prisoner in the history of Banith's Carceral Quarters. Guards smuggled food and wine to him; guards' wives whispered news from the countryside through the grate of his door. Even the commander of the quarters, Ibarth, a man who once openly scorned his judgements from the bench, appeared at his door to express his horror at the Malazans' treatment of him.

'Imagine,' the man had huffed, 'after all your efforts to be civil. These Malazans are barbarians!' He assured Bakune that he'd have him out in an instant if it was up to him – but that the Malazans had his hands tied.

Bakune gave his understanding and the man fairly fainted his relief; he wiped his flushed sweating face and bowed his gratitude. News came only later via a guard's wife that the Roolian resistance had named Bakune a patriot of the freedom struggle – a title he personally could not make any sense of.

The next night he was startled awake by a rattling at his door. A guard holding a lantern gently swung it open to wink and touch the side of his nose in a sort of comical pantomime. Bakune stared sleepily at the man. Whatever was he up to?

Another fellow slipped inside, wrapped in a cloak, hood up, a heavyset great lump of a fellow who sat on the end of his pallet. The guard set the lantern on a hook and backed away.

Bakune eyed the figure. 'And who are you?'

The man threw back his hood. 'Really, Assessor. Don't you recognize old friends?'

It was Karien'el, just as fat, nose just as swollen, if a touch more tanned. Bakune jumped up. 'Whatever are you doing here? You're a wanted man!'

'I was here in town so I thought I'd break you out.'

That silenced Bakune for a moment. He flexed his arm, massaging it and wincing. 'Here? In town? Why? I told Hyuke there was to be no trouble here.'

Chuckling, Karien'el raised his hands. 'Granted. The Malazans can have this pimple.' He pointed to Bakune. 'It's you I want.'

'Me?'

Karien'el chuckled again, shaking his head. 'From anyone else I would take that as false modesty – but not you. I know *you*. That's why I want you, I need an administrator. One I can trust.'

'An administrator? What for?'

Karien'el lost his grin. 'Gods you're dense, man! For the bloody kingdom, that's what!'

Bakune sat heavily. 'There are others much more qualified . . .'

Karien made a farting noise. 'Lady forgive you, but you're taking all this fairness too damned far. Why them? Why not *you*? No, at this point it's all about relationships. I *know* you. For example, I know you won't waste both our time by scheming against me. Or trying to undermine my power to further your own.' The man raised his eyes to the ceiling, sighing. 'You have no idea what a relief that would be.'

Bakune couldn't quite believe what he was hearing. 'But the Malazans . . .'

'Neither the new Malazans nor the old Malazans have the men to hold the kingdom. And they both know it. It's ours for the meantime – and we're already fighting over it. Oh, they can try to retake it. But until then someone has to enforce order.'

Bakune looked him up and down. 'And that would be *you*?'

If the man was offended he didn't show it. 'Or the next lucky bastard in line.' Leaning over, he tapped a knuckle on the door.

Four armoured soldiers crowded the hall. Karien'el nodded to them and stood, letting out a long tired breath. 'Welcome to the struggle, Chancellor, and Lord High Assessor of Rool.'

The guards bowed. One gestured up the hall. 'This way, if you please, m'lord.'

Outside, it was a dark overcast night. Snow lay gathered against walls, melting, the streets glistening with water. He was hurried into a covered carriage. Two of the guards sat with him. Karien'el excused himself, saying he still had other business. Bakune did not like the sound of that, but he could hardly show such ingratitude now after the man had broken him out of prison.

As they rattled through the streets he peered out at lit windows. The town appeared just as it had, if a touch quieter, if not anxious. The garrison, he noted, sat completely black without sentries or watchfires. 'The garrison is dark,' he said to a guard.

'They moved out. They're building a fort outside the town.'

'Ah. And us? Where are we headed?'

'To Paliss, m'lord.'

Paliss? The capital? He sat back astounded. Karien'el controlled the capital? All the gods sustain him! He'd imagined a tent camp near some front, not the High Court itself! And without any interference from Karien'el, as well. Just as Karien'el said he knew him, so too did he know Karien'el. Just as he had no interest in ruling, so did Karien'el have no interest in the law itself.

But he mustn't get ahead of himself. He found a horse blanket under the seat and pulled it over his legs. He flexed his hand – still a touch numb. Karien'el would have to win out, after all. And if he did . . . *then* he would have his chance to put his stamp on the laws of the land.

And he most certainly intended to.

* * *

For some reason the city of Ring made Ivanr uneasy. He preferred to stay out in the field, occupying his tent in Martal's fortress, with a view of the city walls. He and the wrapped bodies of Martal and the Priestess. Many flocked to him now, begging for his blessing, hounding him. Inside the city it would be ten times worse.

He was the inheritor of a polytheistic movement nurtured and prepared by Beneth, inflamed by the Priestess, directed by Martal, and now in control of over half of Jourilan – and it terrified him. He had no idea what to do, or how to proceed. What next? March on the capital, Jour? Already Orman was harassing him with intelligence from the Dourkan border: news of Imperial loyalists negotiating for an alliance against the Reformist movement. He was no politician! Orman could handle that; he seemed to relish it.

He rested a hand on the cloth-wrapped body of the Priestess, the head and body reverently brought together, packed in salt, and lovingly bound. *Such a small frame to have brought about such enormous change! Yet, as the churgeon said, nothing happened. Why did you allow it? Did you see, in the end, that nothing short of your complete sacrifice to the cause could assure their complete devotion as well?*

'Deliverer!' a young girl's voice called from without. Ivanr stirred from what was perhaps the closest he'd come to prayer in many years. Gods! Not another one!

He tossed aside the flap to see a young girl lying prone, hands out before her. 'Stand up!' he grated, much more ferociously than he meant. She stood, quivering her fear. 'It's all right. Don't be afraid. Worship as you wish. There are no proscriptions now. The paths to the Divine are infinite.'

She nodded, gulping. 'Yes, Deliverer. My father sent me. He is too old to come. He believes in your message of forgiveness.' The girl visibly gathered her nerve to plunge on: 'My lord, with the death of the Black Queen there is such anger among the troops. They thirst for revenge . . . M'lord, in the city they are rounding people up. People accused of worshipping the Lady. They are killing them all.'

'*What!*'

The girl flinched, falling prone once more. 'No! Not you!' He glanced about the tent, found his staff. 'Show me.'

The streets were utterly deserted but for roving bands of Reformist troops, drunk, breaking into shops, looting. Along the narrow streets of two-storey shops and houses many gaped empty, ransacked from the rioting. Looted broken furniture and private belongings littered the street along with the burned remains of bonfires and street barricades.

After a few blocks, the girl leading, it became easy to find the source of the trouble as the echoing roar of shouting and cheering reached him. They came on to a market square. A great crowd of Reform troops mixed with Ring citizens, obvious victors in the bloody street-to-street civil clashes, choked the square. Some had even climbed broken statues and fountains for a better view, and everyone was peering across the way to where an informal archery range had been set up. Reform archers fired down the narrow cleared alleys between the crowds to targets of crossed lumber on which men and women hung limp, studded with arrows. A great cheer greeted every volley.

Enraged, Ivanr bulled his way forward. He slammed men and women aside and stepped out to where tables supported bows and quivers of arrows. Archers gaped at him, astonished, and most lowered their bows. All save one, a youth who deliberately ignored him to take his time firing one last shot into a woman hanging by her arms. The shot went true, though the woman's body didn't flinch, supporting as it did an entire forest of arrows.

Two quick strides brought Ivanr to the fellow and he slapped the bow from his hands. 'How dare you, you evil bastard!' he raged. The archer whipped round and he found himself staring straight into the scarred young face of the boy he'd rescued.

For Ivanr everything stopped.

The noise from the crowd faded to nothing. Even his vision darkened at its edges. He staggered backwards, his heart lurching as if impaled. *Gods forgive me! No!* The boy's face was different now – a kind of habitual cruelty twisted it. The youth snatched up his bow and defiantly nocked another arrow. *No! Please . . .* Ivanr started forward, reaching out for him. *Please don't do this – I'm sorry. I didn't mean . . .*

The youth spun about and fired point-blank into Ivanr's chest.

The answering roar of the crowd dazzled him. He stood confused. Hordes crowded in upon him. Hundreds of hands snatched the youth, tearing his clothes, his hair. The boy seemed to disintegrate before his eyes. All he could think of was that there was something he meant to do; he just couldn't quite remember what it was. Someone was talking to him – the man's mouth was moving but Ivanr couldn't make out his words among all the roaring noise. He peered down at the palm's breadth of shaft and fletching protruding from his chest. *Something had to be done about this!*

He asked the man if he could help him, or thought he did, but he couldn't hear his own voice. Hands guided him to a room, sat him on a straw pallet. Breathing was hard now – the arrow had taken a lung. But he was of Toblakai stock, and hardy. He stayed conscious, even when an army bonecutter leaned him forward to snip the shaft at his back, then, looking to him for permission, yanked the arrow out from his front. Ivanr convulsed in a great spewing mouthful of blood. The bonecutter bound his torso in muslin. Eventually Orman appeared, accompanied by Hegil.

'I'm so sorry,' Orman told him, actual tears in his eyes.

'They're saying it was an assassin sent by the Lady,' Hegil said.

Ivanr shook his head. 'Stop them,' he said, his voice papery dry.

'Stop?' Hegil asked. 'Stop what?'

'The killing. No more.'

The two shared glances. 'Yes,' Orman told him. 'Yes, Ivanr. Do not worry. Ease your mind.'

Bowing, they left. He heard speaking outside but couldn't quite make out the words. He was alone, straining to draw breath. Orman may have given his word to stop the killing but outside, on the streets, if anything the noise was swelling. Ivanr feared the attack on him had shattered all restraint. He tried to stand, but tensing his chest stole his breath completely and he almost blacked out.

The door opened and a young woman crept in like a mouse. A mouse dragging a huge stick with it. She looked up to see him staring at her and choked off a yell. It was the girl who had summoned him into the city. 'They are saying you are dead!'

Ivanr, who had been pressing a hand to his chest, let it fall. 'Who is saying?'

'Everyone! On the streets. They are emptying entire quarters.

Dragging families on to the streets. There is no sense to it. It's just bloodletting, nothing more than bloodlust.'

He gestured for his staff. 'Give me that!'

Together with the support of the staff and the girl, he managed to stand. 'My shirt – there.'

She dressed him and, one hand on her shoulder, the staff in the other, he limped outside. Guards turned, amazed. Two were his sworn bodyguards. These two looked at him, stricken with remorse.

Ivanr surveyed the gathered soldiers. 'Attend me,' he commanded simply, and they fell to their knees.

As he limped along within his circle of guards, Ivanr clenched back his pain and asked, breathless, 'Where should I go – the centre of things?'

'The Cathedral of Our Lady. Loyalists are fleeing there. The garrison of Stormguard on the Ring have come ashore. None dare attack them.'

Stormguard? Yes, dragging old men and women into the street is one thing, taking on the most ferocious warriors of the region is quite another.

A broad open plaza surrounded the cathedral. They found it a churning sea of citizenry and Reform soldiers. Ivanr's guard cordon pushed its way towards the wide front stairs. Ivanr heard chants to burn the entire structure to the ground. The tall oaken doors gaped open, guarded by four Stormguard. Even as Ivanr approached, Ring citizens, including entire families, darted up the stairs under a hail of rocks and rotten food to run inside. Within, he glimpsed a solid mass of pale terrified faces staring out.

Silence spread like ripples through the crowd around his passage. People pointed, shouting their surprise, even reverence. Ivanr raised his arms, staff in one hand, even though the gesture sent slashes of agony through his chest. He motioned for his guards to part and he climbed the trash-littered stairs alone.

'Citizens of Jourilan! Hear me! The time for killing has passed. There will be no more blood spilled!'

A momentary lull in the crowd's noise followed that, only to be filled by fresh screams. Those nearby pointed behind him. Ivanr turned to see a Stormguard descending the wide stairs, his thick blue cloak wrapped around him, spear held up straight. Ivanr's guard charged forward but he waved them back.

'You lead this rabble?' the Korelri called, his voice lazy with self-assurance.

‘They seem to think so,’ he answered, fighting down the pain, dizzy with it.

‘Well.’ The man stamped the butt of his spear down on a stair, regarded him through the vision slit of his rounded full helm. ‘We within remain true in our faith. We are not afraid to die.’

Ivanr was afraid that if he coughed he’d collapse, but he cradled his chest, said, ‘But you *are* afraid of something.’

The Korelri waved a hand. ‘We fear nothing.’

‘You are terrified of change. So scared you’d rather die than face it.’

The man took a step back. His eyes widened within the helm, then he waved again. ‘Faugh! Play your games of rhetoric and argument elsewhere, apostate. We here are pledged to the Lady – flesh and blood – we merely wait for her to collect us.’

Flesh and blood. Ivanr stared. *Gods! Could this be . . . deliberate? How many crowded within? Perhaps a thousand souls? Such an enormous blood sacrifice! All in the name of the Lady! No! I mustn’t allow this.*

The Korelri had turned his back on the crowds, deliberately and mockingly, and stalked back to the doors. Ivanr scanned the mass where brands now flamed as bonfires burned in the square. Wood and trash arced through air to strike the cathedral walls.

‘Come and die!’ the Stormguard bellowed from the doors.

Ivanr raised his arms wide, staff in hand. ‘No! I forbid it! The way of the Lady is to worship death. I ask you to worship life!’

Many heeded his call, but too many out of reach of his voice continued throwing tinder and shattered furniture. *It would only take one spark to light a conflagration!* Ivanr’s heart spasmed. He could not breathe; his vision darkened.

He gathered all his remaining strength and clasped the staff in both hands before him, bellowing, ‘*No! The time for vengeance and vendetta has passed! No more retribution! I forbid it!*’ And he slammed the staff down on the stone stairway.

The crowd hushed at the echo of that great crack of wood against stone. All was quiet for one brief instant. Then Ivanr collapsed.

It may have been his delirious dimming consciousness, but as he lay sprawled it seemed that a roaring overbore all noise. The earth moved beneath him. It heaved, rocking, accompanied by a great landside rumbling. Shrill panicked shrieks penetrated even his fading hearing. Hands lifted him up. He blacked out, seeming to float in their tender grip.

* * *

It was an ants' nest of tunnels and caves that seemed to go on for ever – always deeper into the bowels of the mountains that bordered the inland lake, Fist Sea. They went side by side, the Adjunct and Rillish leading. The local Drenn elder, Gheven, who had brought them through Warren, walked in the middle of the column. All they had met so far were emaciated ascetics who gaped at them, or priests of the Lady who, unarmed, launched themselves upon them, gibbering and clawing with their naked hands. All these Rillish ordered bound and left behind.

His arm aching, Suth slung his shield on his back. He couldn't tell if they were making any headway at all. Every cave and length of low-ceilinged tunnel looked like every other. It was dim, dusty, and so confined that many of them couldn't straighten. His leg was almost numb. *This was ridiculous; there was nothing here.* Pyke was grumbling that very thing to Lard. Yet ahead, the bullet head of the bald priest, Ipshank, ran with sweat and his brow was deeply furrowed. Maybe there was something . . . but where was it?

Discipline held, however; the complaints were few, and sotto voce. Goss and Twofoot saw to that. They came to one length of tunnel boasting several cut openings. The column stopped – some obstruction ahead. 'What's the hold-up?' Pyke snarled, hunched. 'These guys don't know anything!'

'Stop it up,' Lard growled, 'or I'll do it for you.'

'You and who—' Pyke was beginning when an armoured figure stepped out of the nearby opening and thrust a spear completely through Lard, the point bursting from his back. Blood splashed all over Pyke. '*Hood's balls!*' Pyke howled, falling backwards.

All up and down the line men in dark armour stepped out of openings to thrust into the column. Suth fumbled, trying to swing his shield forward. The enemy wore cuirasses and full helms enamelled a deep blue, with silver inlay.

'Korelri Stormguard!' Gheven yelled, amazed.

Suth abandoned the shield and parried for his life. The wide-bladed razor spear-tips thrust expertly; he couldn't get past them to engage the wielders. Troopers fell up and down the line, run through like pigs.

'*Clear the deck!*' a woman yelled. Squeaky.

Suth threw himself flat, pulling Gheven with him.

The eruption – in this narrow confine – blasted away his hearing and his breath. He lay stunned in a darkness of swirling dust while earth fell on him. *Had the ceiling collapsed?* He was blinded and choking on the dirt. Terror threatened to strangle him. Then hands yanked him up. He fought at first but the hands weren't at his throat so he clambered to his feet, staggering and running into things and people he could not see in the gloom. Roaring filled his hearing; he could just make out a trooper ahead and set a hand on the man's shoulder. Someone clasped his belt from behind. In this manner, as a troop of blind men and women, they felt their way through a tunnel, seeking clean air.

They collapsed into a cave, coughing and gasping. Two troopers guarded the entrance, shields at the ready. He peered round, wiping at his eyes. He saw Squeaky, Pyke, Faro, the elder Gheven, a few of Twofoot's troop, and the giant Manask, who was on his knees, the broken haft of a spear sticking from his wide stomach. He was struggling to wrench it free.

Suth went to Squeaky. 'What happened?'

'A partial collapse. We're cut off.'

'*Shit!* Now what?'

'Let's get outta here!' Pyke yelled. 'Those are Korelri!'

'Shut the Hood up!'

Manask yanked the spear from his layered armour. He raised it up high. 'I will lead us through this maze!'

'You can find your way through?' Suth asked him.

The man looked offended. 'With my refined senses? Of course!'

Suth grunted his agreement then went to the 6th's troopers. The clash of fighting from some other tunnel reached them and everyone stilled. Panicked yelling, then a muffled explosion shook everyone again. Dust and dirt sifted down from the rough uneven ceiling. *Going to bring this entire complex down on them!* He nodded to the three troopers, recognizing Fish. 'Suth,' he said.

'Corbin,' said the short stocky one.

'Lane,' said the other, his arm slashed and dripping blood.

'Looks like we're cut off,' Suth explained.

'Happens to me every night,' Fish said morosely.

'What's the plan?' Corbin asked.

'The big guy, Manask, says he'll lead us out.'

'Sounds like a plan,' Lane said.

Suth nodded to this tacit acceptance of his offer. 'I want the saboteur, Squeaky, in the middle in case things get hot. I'll back up Manask. You, Fish, back me up.'

'I can't even *stand* up in this friggin' mouse house,' Fish grumbled.

'Lane, take the rear with Pyke.'

'Oh sure!' Pyke yelled. 'Rear! Who put you in charge?'

'Put a rag in it,' Squeaky snarled.

Suth went to the Drenn elder. 'You walk with Squeaky here.'

But the elder's dark eyes narrowed to slits. 'No. I am sorry, soldier. But the Korelri are *here*. This changes everything. I will go for help.'

Suth studied him, uncertain. 'You mean your Warren? Here?'

The elder wiped the grime and sweat from his face, gave an apologetic shrug. 'Well . . . we can hardly pretend to be hiding now, can we?'

'True. Who – where will you go?'

The old man looked pained. 'I can only think of one place . . . but I am sorry, I cannot make any promises.'

'I understand. May the gods speed you.'

Pyke pushed his way to them. 'He can take us all with him! We can escape!'

Suth restrained himself from striking the man. 'We stay with the mission.'

'I don't like that Warren anyway,' Fish said to Lane. 'Looked dangerous.'

Lane nodded his profound agreement.

Pyke peered round at them. 'What's the matter with you all? We're gonna get killed! You're all crazy – I could do better on my own!'

'Do your job or I'll kill you myself,' Suth said, matter-of-fact.

Pyke straightened, slowly nodding. 'Fine. Okay. We're fucked anyway.' And he threw up his hands.

Suth turned to Faro, raised his chin. 'You're being real quiet.'

The little man raised and lowered his shoulders. 'Just pretend I'm not here,' he said, and gave his sharp-toothed smile.

That is bloody easier said than done. He looked to Gheven. 'What do you need?'

The man peered round the rough cave, carved from the broken sedimentary rock. 'This will do. I can go from here.'

The troopers backed away to give him room. He crossed to the rear of the cave and pressed his hands to the rock. He bowed his head in concentration, and stepped into the wall, disappearing.

Suth turned to Manask. 'Looks like you're up.'

The giant fellow threw everyone a huge grin. 'Do not fear! I will winkle out the secrets of this maze in no time! Come!' He lumbered in an ungainly duck-walk out into the tunnel. Suth followed, shield and longsword ready.

It was slow going. Manask's great bulk completely blocked Suth's forward vision. At every cave opening the man paused to poke in the broken haft of his spear and wave it around. Then he waved an arm. Finally, he hopped forward with a shout: 'Ah-ha!'

The third time he did this he reeled backwards accompanied by the thumping of heavy objects striking something. The giant staggered on to Suth. Two spears stood out from his thick armour like proud quills. 'You see!' Manask puffed, winded, 'one merely has to disarm them!'

Suth squeezed past and into the chamber. The Korelri Stormguard had already swung shields round and were prepared. Suth engaged one, Fish another. Suth fought extremely carefully: he probed the man's defences, kept him busy. Openings came but he recognized them as traps meant to draw him out. Facing the Stormguard he quickly understood everyone's dread – the man was fully the finest swordsman he'd ever faced: fearless, aggressive, and quick, a full-time professional fighter. But the Malazan infantry were trained for crowded shield and sword work. It was their lifeblood. These Korelri appeared to fight as individuals. Suth thought he and his squadmates might have the advantage in these circumstances.

A spear thrust over Suth's shoulder. The Korelri blocked, but the point continued on, passing through his shield to impale him in the chest and push him back to the wall, where he hung from the haft like an insect. 'Two can play with pointed sticks!' Manask exulted, and he brushed his hands together.

Alone, facing outrageous odds, the second Stormguard gave no hint of asking for quarter. He backed against a dirt wall, shield ready. 'Drop your weapons!' Suth ordered. The full helm merely slid side to side. Eyes hot for battle glared out of the narrow vision slit.

Damned fanatic. They didn't have time for this. He, Fish, Corbin and Pyke spread out in an arc before the man. *Useless! To prove what?* Suth tightened his grip on his longsword, steadied his breathing.

The Stormguard looked past them all, gaping. 'No!'

A crossbow fired just behind Suth made him flinch. The bolt took the Stormguard in the throat and the man slid down the wall, gagging. Suth turned to see Faro calmly tuck the slim weapon back under his cloak.

'Let's get going, shall we?' Faro said, raising his brows.

Suth nodded, swallowing. *Ye gods! Forget this man is with them? Not damned likely.*

Manask led them onward, but their pace did not increase. Distant yells, the clash of fighting, and, occasionally, a report of munitions would reach them. They came upon scenes of battle: fallen Stormguard and dead troopers; caves blasted by munitions; tunnels partially collapsed. Suth was shaken to find Len dead, run through by a spear. *Len? You too? Somehow I'd imagined it couldn't happen to you. I'm so sorry. You were a good friend. Looks like maybe Pyke's finally got things right.*

Squeaky knelt over the body for some time while everyone kept a nervous watch. Her final act was to close his eyes – the man's shoulder bags had already been scavenged.

Soon after that the earth shook, sending them all to the beaten earth floor huddled for cover. Dirt came tumbling down in a wash of dust that blinded and choked. After the shaking passed Suth gingerly eased himself up, wiping his face and coughing. When they had all straightened, beating at their cloaks and clearing their throats, they glared at Squeaky. She glared back, raising her hands.

'Hey! Don't look at me. There's no way we brought *that* many munitions.'

They continued through the half-collapsed tunnels. Suth couldn't tell if they were making any headway, but he didn't challenge Manask as he didn't think he'd do any better choosing left from right, or which carved chamber to enter. It was a senseless jumbled warren of tunnels to him. Eventually, it seemed they'd been walking, hunched, on the adrenalin knife-edge of fear for far too long, and he called a halt. They chose the best defensible cave they could find, set a watch, and lay down to try to get some rest.

Suth stood his watch with Lane, then had his turn to lie down. Though he was exhausted beyond care, sleep would not come. He couldn't shake Pyke's words. *How many left now? What of Goss, Wess and Keri? Still alive? These Stormguard are butchering us! This obviously isn't what Rillish and that priest had in mind.* It seemed to him that he'd just closed his eyes when a bellow wrenched him awake. A sword slammed into the dirt where he'd just been lying. A Stormguard stood over him, pulling back the blade for another thrust, and Suth swept a leg, bringing him down. He leapt upon the man, found a gauche scabbard at his side, drew the weapon offhanded, and thrust it home up into an armpit. The Stormguard shuddered, but threw him off and leapt to his feet. He and Suth faced off, crouched, circling. A shape fell upon the Stormguard, Faro leaping, two long daggers flashing, and they collapsed in a tangle. Suth cast a frenzied glare around the darkened cave. Jammed shoulder to shoulder, troopers grappled with Korelri. A Stormguard duelling Lane retreated towards Suth so he stabbed him low in the back then drew his own blade. He saw Fish go down, dragging a Korelri with him. Manask was holding the corpse of one in front of himself, using it as a shield with which to bash another back until Corbin took the Stormguard from the side.

In that instant of fevered rush it was over – though to Suth it seemed to have happened in a half-lit sort of slow-motion. Dust drifted now in the dead air and he stood still, panting. He, Manask, Faro and Corbin alone stood. Of the Korelri attackers who had seemed everywhere, Suth counted a mere five. *Five! Gods below! Still, they were lucky to be alive at all.*

Peering around, he saw Squeaky slouched up against a wall. She'd been gut-stabbed. He knelt at her side; she lived still, but had lost a lot of blood. Her breaths came shallow and quick, like a child's. 'He took it,' she told him.

'Quiet.'

'No. *He* took it. That prick, Pyke.'

'What?' He straightened, cast a quick glance around the cave: no Pyke, alive or dead. 'Where is he?'

'Who?' Faro asked.

'Pyke, the bastard. Who was he on watch with?'

'Was with me,' Fish said from the floor, breathing through clenched teeth.

Suth knelt next to Corbin, who was staunching the wound in the man's side. 'What happened?'

The man gave a weak shrug. 'He took one side. I took th' other. Later, I looked over an' he was gone. Run off. Them Korelri charged in.'

Suth sat back stunned. *Deserted! Takes the munitions and runs off. Leaves them unguarded.* A blinding white fury made him dizzy. *Why didn't I kill him? All those chances. And now this!* He went to his bedroll: he'd been sleeping in his hauberk and now he pulled on the rest of his gear.

'What's the plan?' Corbin asked.

'I'm gonna find and kill the fucker.'

Corbin spat aside, nodding. 'Sounds like a plan.'

'Not the mission,' Faro warned from where he squatted cleaning his knives.

'To Hood with the mission! This is personal!'

The scout – *Hood take it, a Claw* – stood. He brushed dust from a sleeve. 'Can't let it get personal. Doesn't do. I can't go that way.'

'Fine. Manask?'

The giant picked up a spear. 'He can't have gotten far.'

'Corbin?'

The trooper squeezed Fish's shoulder. 'Let me kit up.'

'Good.' He went to Squeaky. 'Take it easy now. We'll be back. Just . . .' The woman was staring, head sunk. Suth brushed a hand down her eyes to close them. He stood. 'Let's go.'

In the hall, Suth nodded farewell to Faro, who answered the nod – very slightly – then padded off silently to disappear into the gloom. Suth watched him go, thinking that of all of them, that bastard would win through.

There wasn't much of a spoor to follow. It was night-dark. Corbin carried their lamp. The Korelri had tramped all through the tunnel, but Suth walked ahead to do the tracking – somehow he'd lost faith in the giant's skills. It seemed to him they'd been doing nothing more than wandering randomly yesterday. Some tunnels bore a distinct slope and he calculated that Pyke would follow the slope downward, hoping to reach a way out. So it was they retraced some of their way, keeping to the tunnels, always downward.

Distantly, the reports of renewed fighting reached them as reverberations and muted roaring echoed down the tunnels and they would freeze, listening. But it was very far off now. Ahead, down a side tunnel, a bright golden glow spilled out of an opening. Suth edged up to take a quick look. He recoiled immediately. What he'd glimpsed inside made his shoulders slump.

'Come!' a voice called, inviting. 'You are looking for someone, yes?'

Suth leaned his head back against the curved tunnel wall, took a fortifying breath, and stepped in. Corbin and Manask followed. It was the largest of the chambers they'd yet seen. Some sort of rough temple complete with pillars of living stone. Candles and lamps lit the room. Across its centre, in two rows, waited ten Korelri Stormguard. The one at centre front was holding Pyke by the scruff of his neck.

'This is yours perhaps?'

'He's not one of ours any more,' Suth ground out.

'Oh? Then you would not mind if I did this?' The man raised a knife to Pyke's throat. Pyke struggled furiously, but he was gagged and bound.

Suth frowned a negative. 'Go ahead. Save us the trouble.'

The Stormguard nodded. 'Yes. I do not blame you. Do you know that when we caught him he offered to sell you out?'

Suth studied the wriggling fellow. So much for your stupid lone wolf chances, fool. Didn't come to much, did they? Peering beyond, though, Suth glimpsed the clean white light of day shining in from a side opening. *Damn! Pyke did come across an exit, but the Korelri had it covered. Haven't missed one trick yet, these bastards.*

Manask, Suth noted, was edging back to the opening. *Good idea.* 'Do as you like,' he told the Korelri.

The man dragged the curved blade across Pyke's throat, bringing forth a great gush of blood that splashed down his front into the dirt before him. His legs spasmed and the Korelri let him fall like a slaughtered animal carcass.

'Run, my friends,' Manask told them, and Suth and Corbin darted from the chamber, the giant following. Suth's last sight was the Korelri waving forward his fellows.

They ran pell-mell through the dim tunnels. Suth's poor vision caused him to run headlong into some corners. Picking himself up, he saw that Manask was far behind – the giant could hardly run squatting down as he must.

Bloody Hood! He waved Corbin back, pointed to a narrow cave opening, the cell of an ascetic. 'Have to do.' They waited for the giant then backed in. Manask's great bulk utterly choked the portal.

Suth could not help but laugh, staring as he was at the man's gigantic padded backside. 'Manask, this must be your worst nightmare!'

'Gentlemen,' he rumbled, 'I shall be the obstruction which cannot be dislodged!'

'I'm all choked up,' Corbin said, laughing.

But Suth lost his smile when he heard the big man grunting and his thick layered armour wrenched from impacts. *Brithan Troop take it! There was nothing they could do but wait for the man to die then be hacked to pieces!*

'Manask! Back in!'

'No, my friends,' he gasped, struggling. 'It would appear that I am truly stuck!'

If not back, then forward! Suth gestured to the man's broad padded back. In the near-absolute gloom Corbin's gleaming sweaty face showed understanding. The two pressed themselves against the tiny chamber's far end. 'One, two—'

An eruption punched the air from his chest and something enormous fell upon him, pinning him to the ground. *Cave-in! Buried alive!* Dust swirled, blinding him and filling his lungs. Groaning sounded from someone else trapped with him – Corbin perhaps.

The dust slowly thinned, and, blinking, Suth saw that the considerable bulk of Manask was lying on him. He struggled to move his arms to edge himself free. Then someone else was there, a skinny form, coughing in the dust as she heaved on the huge fellow. With her help Suth eventually managed to slide free and he stood, brushing dust from himself. The woman was Keri, her bag of munitions across her chest. 'What are you guys *doing*?' she demanded, glaring at him as if he'd been off on a drunken binge.

'Sightseeing,' Suth growled. He peered down at Manask: the man's unique armour was ruined, shredded, revealing an unnaturally skinny chest. He knelt to press a hand to the throat – alive, at least. Just stunned. And Corbin? He pulled him out by a leg, slapped his face. The man came to, coughing and hacking. Suth helped him up.

'What do we do with him?' Corbin asked.

'Leave him,' Keri said. 'No one's around. C'mon. The Korelri are regrouping.' She waved them into the tunnel. 'Come on!'

Suth reluctantly agreed. He picked up a spear, secured his shield on his back, and cuffed Corbin's shoulder. They followed Keri up the tunnel.

* * *

Corlo lay on the straw-covered ledge that was his bed in his cell deep within Ice Tower. The bars facing the walk rattled as someone set down a wooden platter – dinner.

'Corlo,' that someone whispered.

He cracked open an eye: it was Jemain. He sprang to the bars. 'What are you doing here?' He peered up and down the empty hall. 'When did you get here?'

But the skinny Genabackan did not look pleased to see him. He gave a sad shrug. 'Word is out on Ice Tower. No one wants to come here. Then I got a message, and they were happy to get a volunteer. How are you?'

'I'm fine! What about you – what word? Who have you found?'

The man positively winced: he looked unhealthy. The cold had scoured a ruddy rash of chapped skin and cracked bleeding scars. Glancing up the walk, he took hold of the bars with both hands. 'Corlo . . . when I saw you in the infirmary you looked so bad . . . I thought you knew, then.'

Something urged Corlo to back away, to shut the man up. A clawing fear choked his throat. 'What are you saying?' he managed.

'Then, when I found out you didn't know . . . well, I'm sorry. I couldn't bring myself to tell you.'

'Tell me what? Tell me, damn you! Out with it!'

Jemain backed away, as if frightened. He held his hands to his chest, hugging himself. 'I'm sorry, Corlo. But . . . there's only us. Us two. We are the only ones left.'

'No! You're lying! There are others. There must be! I saw Halfpeck!'

Jemain was nodding. 'Yes, he lasted for a time. But he too died on the wall.'

He too? All the gods damn these Stormguard! Damn them! Then what he'd promised Bars struck him and he almost fainted. *Queen forgive him, he'd told Bars there were others!*

'I'm sorry,' Jemain said. 'I couldn't bring myself to tell you.'

Corlo fell to his knees. He clasped the bars as if they were the only things keeping him alive. Then he laughed. *Gods, have your laugh! Justice is served, Corlo. How does it taste? It tastes . . . just. Yes. It tastes just.* He raised his head to regard Jemain, who was watching him with tears on his cheeks. 'Thank you, Jemain. For telling me. It seems we have come to the end of our lies. We can go no further with them.'

'You will see Bars?'

'Yes. He's on the wall now. I'll see him later.'

'What . . .' The man wet his lips. 'What will you tell him?'

'The truth. What he deserved long ago. The truth.'

'And then . . . ?'

Corlo shrugged, unknowing. 'Then we'll leave the wall.' *One way, or another.*

'How will he take it?'

Very poorly, I expect. 'Never mind, Jemain. Stay out of his way until I can speak to him, yes?'

The man nodded, rather relieved.

'Good. And thank you. It's good to finally know . . . anyway.'

'I'm very sorry.'

Corlo urged him on. 'Yes, I know. Better go.'

A wave goodbye and the man backed down the hall of cells. Corlo watched him go then rested his forehead against the frigid bars.

'I say you don't tell him,' said someone from across the hall.

Corlo started up, a blistering curse on his lips, but something in the bearded, ragged-haired head at the grate opposite stopped him. And the man spoke Talian. 'You're Malazan?'

'Yeah. Tollen's the name. Listen, there's some four or five Avowed here in this tower. Enough to take this entire section of wall. And I want to get my fellow veterans out. We need your boy Bars. So don't say a damned thing.'

Four other Avowed? So Bars had it right! Shell hadn't come alone. Corlo was quiet for a time, coming to terms with this proof. Then he snorted. 'He deserves the truth anyway. And I don't take directions from some bastard Malazan.'

'I'm trying to save your damn-fool life, Guardsman!'

Corlo pushed himself from the door. *Save a life! That's just what I told myself every time I spoke to Bars. I was trying to save his life. Well, lying is no way to do that. Better to be thought a betrayer, a traitor, than that.*

*

Atop Ice Tower, a Korelri Stormguard arrived and bowed to Section Marshal Learthol, who was in conversation with Wall Marshal Quint. 'The captive has been delivered.'

Learthol accepted the message. Quint gave curt wave. 'Good. Let's hope we can squeeze the last of the season out of this champion.'

Another Chosen stepped forward from the shadows of the chamber and the Korelri guard stiffened, bowing again. 'Lord Protector.'

Lord Protector Hiam acknowledged the bow. He addressed Learthol: 'I understand there are others here just as promising . . .'

'Yes. A surprising number of skilled prisoners of late. We must keep a close eye upon them.'

The Lord Protector studied the oil flame of the communication device of this uppermost chamber. 'Yes, Section Marshal. And we must take care to watch this flame. If calamity strikes we will have to summon aid quickly.'

'Yes, my lord. I must say, we are honoured by your presence.'

The Lord Protector waved such sentiments aside. 'Where else would I be, Learthol? You'll have more support soon. These Roolians will fill the inconsequential gaps. Easing the load for us. Soon you will have the numbers you should have had all along.'

'My thanks. But we would have held regardless.'

'Of course.' The Lord Protector stared into the flame for a time, then gazed at Learthol as if not seeing him. 'That will be all. Thank you.'

Bowing, the guard and the Section Marshal exited, pulling the door shut behind them.

In the relative quiet the howling wind returned to punish the shutters, which were seized in ice on all four sides. Quint's scarred face twisted as he studied the Lord Protector. 'You have news?'

A slow assent from Hiam. 'Yes. This *overlord* and his Roolian troops have been pushed back from the coast. The Malazans have struck inland towards the Barrier range.'

Quint slammed the butt of his spear to the flagging. 'They would take Kor!'

Hiam pressed a hand to one iced shutter. 'Perhaps . . .'

'Perhaps? What else could they intend?'

'They might . . .' Hiam wrenched open the westward-facing shutters. Cutting winds whipped through the chamber, snapping their cloaks and clearing a table of clutter and pages of vellum. The oil flame of the communication beacon was snuffed. Hiam stared down the ice-encrusted wall, where beneath fat hanging clouds and driving snow raging waves were breaking almost even with the wall's outermost crenellations. *All is grey – iron-grey, both sea and stone.* 'They might make a strike for the wall,' he admitted.

Quint slammed shut the leaf. 'Good! We will crush them!'

Hiam gave the ghost of a smile. 'Of course, Quint.'

'Yes!' The Wall Marshal relit the fat wick of the oversized lamp. 'Perhaps the Lady has drawn them here to destroy them.' He studied his commander through narrowed eyes. 'Had you not thought of that, Hiam?'

The Lord Protector was startled. *No, indeed. I had not considered that . . . Lady forgive me! My faith is shallower than I suspected. I must pray long tonight.* He answered Quint's steady gaze. *Living Spear of the wall. You know no doubt, Quint. The Spear does not reflect – it strikes!*

Rubbing his brow, Hiam acknowledged, 'No, Quint I hadn't thought of that. My thanks for reminding me that the ways of the Lady are beyond our knowing.' He squeezed the older man's shoulder. 'With you as our pillar, we shall not fail.' And he passed by to descend the narrow circular staircase, leaving Quint alone in the light of the guttering flame.

That evening Hiam was taking a hot dinner of stew with Section Commander Learthol. There came a knock at the door and a Korelri Chosen bowed. 'Lord Protector, the adviser to the Overlord has arrived. Shall I admit him?'

Hiam sipped his tea. 'Yes. Have him brought up.'

The man bowed. 'Lord Protector.'

'I have heard stories of this one,' Learthol said, after the Chosen had left. 'They say the Lady permits him the practice of his witchery.'

Hiam nodded. 'Yes. There is precedent in history.'

Learthol stroked his long chin. 'True. There are stories of a pair of travelling sorcerers. She did not destroy them.'

Hiam waved a hand. 'I understand they were merely passing through. They were of no consequence.'

A knock came at the door and Hiam called, 'Enter.'

The guard showed the man in, then, at a sign from Hiam, departed. The man, Ussü, bowed. His robes were travel-stained and wet with rain and snow. His long grey hair was plastered to his skull and he was shivering. Rising, Hiam gestured to a chair. 'Please sit. You are just arrived? What word from the Overlord?'

Sitting, the old man extended his hands out to the small stove in the middle of the chamber. 'Thank you for receiving me, Lord Protector.'

'Not at all.'

'No doubt you have heard the news from the south.'

'Yes. These Malazans have gained a foothold.' The man winced, whether at the bluntness of his phrasing or the use of the word *Malazans*, Hiam wasn't sure.

'Yes, Lord Protector. They have struck inland for the foothills and the Barrier range.'

'And the Overlord?'

'Is marshalling his troops in order to pursue, I understand.'

Hiam offered the man some tea. 'Excellent. If they dare to move north we will have them caught between us, yes?' *And should they dare approach? What could we possibly spare to meet them? Blood and iron, of course. As we deliver to all who would defy the Lady.*

Ussü accepted the small cup. 'Yes, Lord Protector.'

'And the Overlord sent you to reassure us, perhaps?'

'In truth, Lord Protector, I am come on another errand. I wish to question your champion. If I may.'

Hiam grunted a laugh. 'Your timing is impeccable, Adviser. You can have him. Just this afternoon he lost his mind. Went berserk. Tried to murder his cellmate – a companion of many years. Madness is a terrible thing. It can drive us to betray everyone around us. Sometimes for the most insignificant, or imagined, slights. Who is to know the reasons behind the breaking of a mind?' And he shrugged.

'That is a shame, m'lord. I'm sorry you lost so able a fighter. Still, he may be of use to me.'

Hiam scooped up more of his stew. 'What is it you require?'

The Roolian – Malazan, Hiam corrected himself, and a damned mage – blew out his breath. 'Oh, a private chamber, shackles, strong aides to help me. And chains, sir. Your strongest chains you use for hauling stone blocks.'

Hiam was rather taken aback by these requests. Still, these he could manage. *And, who knows? Perhaps something will come of it.* He nodded. 'Very well. I believe we can pull something together.' He turned to Section Marshal Learthol. 'Would you see to it?'

Learthol dabbed his mouth, stood. 'This way, Adviser, if you please.'

Standing, Ussü straightened his heavy sodden robes and bowed to Hiam. 'My thanks, Lord Protector.'

Hiam watched the man go, Learthol bowing as he closed the door, and he wondered: had he just made an error? Still, the Lady permitted the man his infringements – she should be the final arbiter, not he.

*

Ussü worked on his preparations long into the night before, exhausted, falling asleep at the work desk of the chambers provided. The next morning he awoke to hands and feet numb with cold, and frost thick in the corners of the stone chamber. The wind battered the one shuttered window. A servant arrived with an iron brazier stoked with charcoal and a modest meal of bread, goat's cheese and cold tea.

Two Theftian labourers arrived later, with orders to serve him. These he set to work fitting iron pins into joints in the walls, and securing lengths of chain. When all was in readiness, he briefed the two with detailed instructions as to how to proceed, then left to request the Champion be moved to his chamber. He decided not to be in sight until the man was secured: there remained the slight possibility that he might recognize him as a Malazan and become suspicious.

From down the hall he watched while the man was marched, manacled and under guard, up to the room. On first setting eyes on the fellow he was aghast: this emaciated, haggard, tattered wretch was the Champion? Still, anyone else carrying such half-healed wounds, frostbite, and exposure damage would surely be dead. That he was apparently able to ignore all these mutilations spoke well for the coming experiment. He waited to give time for the man to be securely chained, then entered.

The subject was laid out on a thick oaken table at the centre of the chamber, gagged. His legs were together and straight, wrapped in chain lengths secured to pins in either wall. His arms were together as well, stretched up over his head and extending down towards the floor, wrapped in chains, and secured to a pin sunk in the flagging. Ussü leaned over the grimed, stinking fellow to peer into his eyes.

Nothing. No apparent awareness. Merely a dull stare straight up at the ceiling. Catatonic? Just as well. All the easier for his purposes. Yet . . . lack of a will to live would *not* do . . . He began cutting the rags from the man's chest.

'You do not know me,' he told him, 'but I believe I know you.'

Tearing away the rags, he went to a table where his instruments had been laid out. 'I must admit that when I heard that the Korelri Champion was a Malazan who denied being a Malazan . . . and named Bars, well, I became intrigued.' He glanced back, and there, around the fellow's eyes – a slight tightening? 'I, as you can tell, am Malazan. Sixth Army, to be exact. Cadre mage Ussü at your service.' Knife in hand, he bowed.

He pressed a hand to the arc of the man's naked ribs, testing, prodding. 'You, on the other hand, are Bars, Iron Bars, Avowed of the Crimson Guard.'

Ussü stepped back, reconsidering. Perhaps the stomach cavity? Less risk of harming a lung, but still, such bleeding. It drains the life force. The man's eyes flicked sidelong to catch sight of him; the jaws shifted as if nearly summoned to speech.

'Yes. Imagine how much the Empire would pay for a living Avowed to study. Quite a lot, no doubt.' The man's astounding chest capacity decided things for Ussü. More room than had ever been offered before. It would be the front. He waved to his aides to take hold of legs and arms, then leaned over the man. 'But that is not why we are here. They say the Avowed cannot be killed.' He held the keen obsidian-bladed scalpel up before the man's eyes. 'This is what we are here to test.'

The chains crashed and rang, almost singing with strain as the subject convulsed.

Ussü flinched back, a hand on the man's side as one might calm a spooked horse. But the bindings held – so far. He rolled his sleeves up. He traced the line of the cut between ribs, nodded to his aides, and slit the flesh down through the muscle.

Gagged, the subject howled incoherencies, writhing and twisting. Ussü went to his instruments and selected his largest, most sturdy rib-spacer. He returned to the subject. 'I'm told,' he said conversationally, 'that this is a worse agony than even trained torturers can inflict.' He pushed the sharpened, toothed edges into the cut then struck it home with a heave of his bodyweight. Foam blew out around the edges of the gag and the eyes burned a blazing white-hot fury. *Good! Rage will stoke the will to live.*

Ussü began turning the spacing screws. 'Not that I am implying any sort of parallel between myself and some brute torturer. For the analogy breaks down here, you see? The torturer requires something from his victim and is attempting to draw it from him – or her. Yet I require nothing from you.'

Which is a half-lie. I require that you live. 'I, however, am motivated purely by curiosity and the pursuit of knowledge.' Ussü paused in the turning. *Does that not then make both torturers and I knowledge-seekers?* He cocked his head, considering. *The knowledge I seek is not held by anyone else . . . that is a fundamental distinction.* Nodding, he continued widening the gap between the ribs.

Something shook him then – not the subject, and not the waves slamming with mind-numbing regularity against the tons of stone beneath, but something new – an earth tremor. Ice outside the walls crackled as the entire structure rolled slightly, as if an immense giant had laid a gentle hand against the tower. The aides shared terrified glances. Ussü merely attempted to measure the extent of the displacement. *Interesting . . . such tremors are common on Fist, but I understand rather rare events here in the Korel Isles.*

The movements subsided with a diminishing of the landslide roaring accompanying it. Ussü returned his attention to the subject, dismissing the event. He'd entered high on the torso as he'd decided to come in above and between the lungs. The subject had stopped writhing, as even the slightest motion now induced waves of intense agony – or so he intuited. The gap large enough, he wiped his hand on the side of his robes, then, keeping it flat, like a knife-edge, worked it down into the blood-filled cavity.

The subject convulsed as if axe-struck, bellowing fury and anguish in a storm of mouthings and roaring. Ussü rode out the convulsion, hand up to his second knuckle in the man's chest. After the waves of twitching passed, Ussü carefully began edging aside organs and pushing down through films of tissue to reach the heart, cradled as it was in its protective pocket of fat and muscle.

Incredibly, the subject was still conscious. Just half an arm's length away the eyes blazed at him like promises of Hood's own vengeance. Ussü pulled his gaze away: he'd brushed the heart. It was time to summon his Warren. He reached out, mentally, opening himself to the wash of energies, and was seized by a torrent that nearly threw him off the body. *Gods! What lay behind such might? There was something here – some mystery beyond this Crimson Guard. They'd touched something. Something dormant, or hidden, with this vow of theirs.*

No matter. There lay future researches. For now, the task at hand. Ha! At hand! In hand, perhaps. Where was Greymane – the Betrayer – Stonewielder?

He reached out, seeking him. The extraordinary might available to him drove Ussü's consciousness far to the west, and there he found his man. An aura shone about him like a sky-gouging pillar, and the grey stone blade he carried in his hands streamed a molten puissance Ussü's Warren interpreted as a blinding sun-flare. The earth rolled about the man as if it were a cloth, shaken, and the merest echo of that release cast Ussü away from the body like a blow. He struck the stone wall and slid down, stunned.

His aides shook him awake. Coming to, he flailed, groggy. Then he stood, worked to catch his breath. He grasped one's shirt. 'The Lord Protector! Where is he! I must speak to him!'

The aides, Theftian labourers, merely gazed at one another, baffled. Snarling, Ussü thrust them aside to stagger for the stairs. 'Stay here! Watch him!'

*

Hiam was with Master Engineer Stimins discussing the potential damage from the tremor when the Overlord's adviser, Ussü, burst in among them. Blood stained his robes, hands and arms, as if he'd been groping his way through a slaughterhouse. Two nearby Chosen drew blades on him. Hiam took one look at the man's stricken gaze and waved the guards aside.

'Lady forefend, man, what is it? What's happened?'

'Who named him Stonewielder?' the Malazan demanded, almost frenzied.

Hiam felt his jaws clenching. 'We do not discuss that,' he ground out.

'Who! Dammit, I *must* know.'

Master Engineer Stimins caught Hiam's gaze, cocked a brow. Hiam gave him curt assent. 'There are locals on these islands. Indigenous tribals who survive here and there, such as in the Screaming range. They first named him Stonewielder. There are long-standing predictions of the wall's destruction. As old as the wall itself. They claimed he fit them. The stone's revenge against the wall – that sort of nonsense.'

The Malazan mage had been nodding his agreement, as if in confirmation. 'Yes. You here in Korel dismiss the Warrens – but they are real. One is named D'riss. The Warren of the Earth. The very ground beneath our feet. This . . . weapon . . . many claimed Greymane carries. Just now I found him, and *it*. It channels D'riss directly, Lord Protector. The might of the earth. And it has just been unsheathed against the wall. I felt it. Far to the west the Stormwall is being shaken to its roots. You felt the tremor, didn't you? There is worse to come at any moment.'

Hiam met Stimins' gaze. *Poor man. Driven mad by the Lady. Yet . . . the old predictions. The land throwing off the wall, and the old Lord Protector Ruel's vision: the wall collapsing in a great shuddering of the earth, the Riders pouring through to cover the land . . .*

'Calm yourself, Adviser—' he began.

'Calm myself?' the man fairly choked. 'The end is coming. I go to prepare for it. I suggest you do as well.' And he lurched away.

The Chosen guards looked to Hiam for orders to pursue him, but he shook his head.

'I don't like this mention of the west,' Stimins breathed, his voice low. 'I'd have preferred it if he'd claimed it was here – overtopping. But not out there, to the west. Not an undermining . . . Send a message,' he suggested. 'Status report.'

Hiam gave a thoughtful nod. 'Yes. There's been a tremor, after all.' His nod gathered conviction. 'Yes. I'll be up top. See to the repairs.'

Stimins snorted. 'Wouldn't be anywhere else, would I?'

CHAPTER XII

We cannot learn without pain.

Wisdom of the Ancients
Kreshen Reel, compiler

THE FIRST SIGN STALL HAD OF TROUBLE WAS MEMBERS OF THE WORK gang standing up from their hammering to stare southwards. Stall pushed himself from the rock he'd been leaning against and, taking up his spear, drew his cloak tighter about himself. Evessa straightened as well, sent him a questioning look. He motioned to the rock field far below, where a lone figure climbed the rugged slope that sprawled down from the rear of the Stormwall. Taking up her spear, Evessa waved to Stall and the two took their time picking their way down to the man.

Closer, Stall saw him to be a bull of a fellow, apparently unarmed, full helm under an arm. Against the cold he wore a plain cloak and thick robes in layers over his armour. He and Evessa spread out to stand ahead of the fellow, to either side.

Stall planted his spear, called, 'Who are you? Name yourself!'

The man did not answer immediately. He peered up past them to the slope where the rear of this section of the curved curtain wall soared like a fortress. The gang peered down from among the rocks where they worked on the buttressing ordered by Master Engineer Stimins.

The stranger nodded to himself, took a deep breath, and drew on his helm. 'I suggest you go now,' he told them in accented Korelri.

Stall lowered his spear. 'You'll have to come with us for questioning . . .'

Kneeling, the man pressed a gauntleted hand to the bare stony ground. Stall and Evessa shared a look – was the fellow touched? Stall began: 'Don't give us any . . .'

The ground shook. Rocks clattered, falling. Grating and roaring, the larger boulders shifted. Evessa cried out and had to jump when the huge rocks she stood upon ground together. The reverberation fanned out around them into the distance, from where the echoes of scraping and shifting returned ever more faintly. The workers cried out, scattering, clambering among the rocks.

Stall returned his attention to the stranger to see that he now carried a sword: a great two-handed length of dull grey. The man's eyes glared a bright pale blue from the darkness of his helm. 'Go now!' he commanded. 'Warn everyone to flee!'

Stall looked to Evessa, cocked a brow. The Jourilan woman inclined her head; Stall nodded. The two backed away. The man was clearing stones from the ground before him. Stall and Evessa picked up their pace, waving away the remaining workers watching them, uncertain.

'Run, you damned fools!' Stall yelled.

*

So which would it be? Greymane wondered while he stood waiting to give everyone time to put more room between he and they. The greatest mass-murderer of the region? Or a semi-mythical deliverer?

Both, I imagine. It could not be avoided. Many would die. And rightly or wrongly he would be blamed. Yet was he not just one link in an unbroken chain of causality stretching back who knew how far? Albeit the final one.

Devaleth's argument returned to haunt him – not that he didn't know the same doubts: what guarantee did he have that the Riders would not overrun all the lands? Objectively, that much water didn't exist in the world. Subjectively, every observation, action, and account supported his conclusion.

They would strike for the Lady.

Just as he should have when he had his chance. Regrets choked him now. He hoped Kyle would not be too angry with him – he'd had to keep everyone at arm's length. The fool probably would have tried to follow him!

And were the troops free of the coast? Certainly they should be by now – especially with Devaleth forewarned. And she should reach Banith as well, through Ruse. Yet what of every other coastal settlement of the region? Were they not all threatened? Yes, many would die. But at least after that it would be over. It would not go on eternally, year after year, as it had for centuries.

Or so he told himself.

Enough! Enough self-flagellation. It was too late then; it is even later now. What he should have done long ago awaited him still. Time to act.

A short thrust first, I think. To warn everyone what is to come.

He knelt, raised the stone sword, point down. *Burn, accept this offering and answer. Bless my intent. Right this ancient wrong. Heal this wound upon the world.*

He slammed the blade down into the earth.

At first nothing happened. The blade slid easily through the exposed stone. A kind of silence grew around him. Then came a vibration, the ground uneasy, shuddering. Up the slope boulders slid, subsiding. Rocks tumbled to either side. Far above, where the wall met the overcast sky with its embrasures, lift-houses, and quarters, clouds of birds erupted from their perches to take flight in dark swaths. Enormous hanging accumulations of ice, some longer than a man, snapped away, plunging down the rear to smash to the rocks below. Tiny figures raced madly back and forth.

Run while you can. Greymane yanked the blade free. Setting his left foot back firmly, he raised the sword straight up overhead to its fullest extension. Tensing his body, he snapped the blade down as if to gouge a slice from the earth. The rough stone blade struck the granite in an eruption of force that shuddered straight up to his grip. A crack split the rounded worn bedrock, shooting off ahead to disappear beneath the jumbled scree slope. Kneeling, he kept his death's grip on the length of carved stone. Water appeared from among the jumbled rocks. It shot down over his knees in a frigid sheen.

Oh shit. I'm under *the wall.*

Well, he chided himself, you didn't really think you'd survive this, did you?

A bell-like booming resounded from the towering wall. Two lift-houses built up over the rear fell away in a litter of fractured stone to tumble like doll's houses down the curved face and explode in shards of wood and stone at the base. Cut blocks of the curtain wall, each perhaps as large as a man, shifted, dirt and moss cascading down. Water shot from the lowest in a jetting spray, darkening the rocks of the slope.

Greymane yanked the blade free. *Enough? Well, best make sure of it.*

He raised the sword again. *One more. Then run like a madman.*

This time he swept the blade down as if he were sinking it into water. The naked time-gnawed bedrock parted in a gap that took even his grip. The very ground around him seemed to sink then flex upwards like a struck drum. Boulders the size of houses heaved aside to crash and tumble like catapult stones. A grinding screech as of a death-shriek sounded from the distance where the rearing curtain wall wavered as if struck by a giant's battering ram. Then it bulged outward at its base, stones shifting, and water burst forth in a gushing, heaving rush.

Time to go. Greymane yanked but his hands, sunk in past his wrists, would not give.

He yanked again, pushing off with his legs, but his hands and wrists were caught in the exposed granite bedrock.

He snapped a gaze to the flood rushing down the retaining field. Far along the curve of the curtain wall a watchtower, some five storeys tall, toppled achingly slowly, looking like a child's toy so far in the distance. The top courses of the curtain, undermined, now gave way in a series of puzzle-pieces. They tumbled, an avalanche of gargantuan stones, into the exposed gap beneath. He had a momentary glimpse of the Stormwall's interior architecture as the fallen walls revealed its outer casework of dressed stone blocks on either side of a driven fill of rubble.

The wall was breached entirely now, through to the bay beyond.

Greymane yanked again, frantic, but his limbs would not budge. He stared down at his hands, trapped in the raw living stone, and only then did the beautiful poetry of it dawn upon him and he threw back his head to laugh aloud. *Oh ye gods, you have outdone yourselves! Laugh at the fool mortal, for only now do I see it. Stonewielder indeed! Yes. You scheming bastards and bitches!*

'Damn you all to Hood's deepest pits!'

The foaming flood struck him. His feet were swept from under him; he was trapped under the raging flow. Branches and other driven trash smashed into him and he could hold his breath no longer. The air burst from his searing lungs in a froth of bubbles.

He never drew another.

As his consciousness faded he thought he felt hands grasp him there beneath the surface. He did not know if it was his delirious fancy or not, or what it might mean, for all went to dark then and he allowed himself release without regret, without anger, without expectation of anything.

*

The waters of the Ocean of Storms, risen far above ancient levels, tide-swollen, driven by the sorceries of the Stormriders, poured through the gap in a burgeoning flood. The course gouged its way south, always seeking low ground. Entire swaths of forest were swept aside as the flash flood raced downhill, gathering ever greater momentum as it went. Farmhouses, fields, roads, stone walls, all disappeared as this sudden new river scoured a widening channel down to the bedrock of the island.

A chance subtle rise in the landscape spared the fortress city of Storm. Its citizens had just picked themselves up from a rare earth tremor. Many had walked out into the streets to peer at the new cracks in the cobbled roads and arcing-down walls. They heard the distant roar and went to the walls to watch astonished as to the east a new channel thundered past as a true waterfall. And, for a time, the city was entirely cut off from the rest of Korel. These citizens later swore to catching glimpses amid the flow of brilliant sapphire flashes and gliding ominous dark shapes.

Racing far more swiftly than the fastest charger, the churning waters crashed through the last forested reach of land to pour over, then entirely grind away, the shore beaches and sand cliffs down into Crooked Strait. Here the waters melded into the narrow strait, ever rising, forming from shore to shore a great swelling hump of water coursing to the east and to the west. The wavefront climbed higher than the topgallant of the tallest vessel. Entire fishing hamlets disappeared without a ripple beneath this heaving peak more than five fathoms deep. It raced faster than any ship or messenger. It overtook fleeing vessels, submerged low-lying forested islands. Left behind in its passing lay an entirely new coastline, resculpted and washed clean.

*

Deep in thought, Hiam climbed the narrow circular stairs of Ice Tower. Chosen hurried up and down, pausing to salute, which he answered absently. *This tremor; could it really be as bad as the Malazan seems to think? Every mage who practises his or her witchery eventually goes mad – that is the most obvious explanation.* Everyone, he imagined, must be thinking of those mystical prophecies: the earth cracking open to swallow the wall. But this was no supernatural event; it was just an earth tremor, common enough in many regions of the world.

Unprecedented events were unfolding, yes, but that was no reason for panic.

Reaching the communication chamber he adjusted the flame to burn its highest then bashed open the west shutters. The frigid wind sliced into the chamber again but this time it did not snuff the flame. He lowered the metal sleeve, dug up a scoopful of the flaring dust and tossed it on to the flame. The dust burst into a hissing white glare that made him flinch away, covering his face. Hunched, head turned away, he worked the sleeve up and down, signalling the tower on top of the western pass.

Wind Tower: report.

Wind Tower was the westernmost of the main fortresses.

He waited. The request had to travel the entire length of the wall then back again. The answer came much more swiftly than he had anticipated; it seemed this tremor had put everyone on edge.

Wind Tower not responding.

That was the Tower of Ruel's Tears, its eastern neighbour.

Tossing more dust on to the flame, Hiam signed: *Status?*

After a time the answer came: *Ruel's Tears not responding.*

That was the Great Tower north of Elri, their main fortress on the Stormwall.

Disbelieving, Hiam threw more dust on to the flame, signed: *Status! Status!*

A long silence during which the wind moaned and gusted, seeming to mock him. Then, mystifyingly, from the neighbouring tower, the Tower of Stars: *Pray!*

Hiam threw himself to the western window, stared through the eternal blowing snow to the high pass where the glow of the guard tower shone like a beacon in the overcast gloom. While he watched, it was snuffed into darkness, and something billowed around it: something like a blizzard cascading down the pass along the wall, driving for this last reach of the wall and Ice Tower. Hiam clenched the window: *Lady, what was this? A true catastrophe such as struck ages ago? Was this truly the end? Lady, what have we done that you should turn your face from us so?*

Lady, forgive us . . .

The avalanche struck like a wall of white. Hiam was thrown to the floor, which bucked and hammered him. Enormous crackling fractured his hearing and he understood that the gargantuan shelves of blue-black ice that sheathed the tower were breaking off its sides. Further blows rocked and shuddered the tower as these shards, the size of wagons, came thundering down to slam bursting on to the top of the wall.

The quake passed quickly, the last of the shudders reverberating off into the distance like a passing storm, or rockfall. Unwilling to believe it was actually over, Hiam gingerly picked himself from the floor. He went to the window and peered out, half expecting a vista of ruination, but what he saw filled him with admiration and awe.

We still stand! The wall is intact!

Magnificent ancestors, you have not striven in vain! Lady, we have taken the worst and endured! Is this your message? If so, I am ashamed. How pathetic my faith.

Certainly, the damage was horrific. The worst of his imaginings . . . but nothing like a fracture or failure. Outer machicolations had fallen away; rear buildings had collapsed, coursework along the upper reaches appeared misaligned; cracks worked down the wall of the tower. But this was all merely cosmetic: the basic structural curve of the curtain wall appeared sound. Beyond that curve, however, the waters of the bay appeared unusually disturbed: great counter-waves slammed back and forth, and froth and spume jetted straight up in a clash of forces far out in the bay.

I'll need to inspect the damage. He ran for the stairs, but before he got two full turns down he found the way jammed by fallen rubble. He stared at the barrier, almost uncomprehending. *No! Not now! Not when I'm needed most!* He threw himself at the great stone blocks, heaving, pulling.

Lady, no! Please! I beg you to forgive me!

*

Deep under Ice Tower in the holding cells Shell stood pressed up hard against a glacial wall. That first tremor had terrified her. Here she was far below a stone tower on an ancient crumbling wall perched above a cliff over a sea! And now, though she dared not raise her Warren, she could feel it twitching, pulling at her. Something was happening. Something shattering.

A contingent came filing down from standing the wall. Shell saw Blues among them. The man had a hand to his forehead, wincing. A regular guardsman urged him on with a poke of his sword. Seemingly without effort Blues yanked the blade from the man's hand then clouted him on the side of his head and he fell senseless. The file of prisoners shuffled to a halt, completely uncertain what to do. Blues leaned against a wall, blinking and shaking his shaggy head.

'You sense it?' Shell called.

'Sense it!' the man groaned. 'Gods! My head's gonna explode. I've not felt this since Genabackis when we faced the Warlord . . . In fact, I would've sworn it was impossible . . .'

'What?'

The man stared about, suddenly panicked. 'Everyone, take cover! Get into doorways!

'What is it?'

'Quiet! Listen!' The man backed into a cell doorway, gripped the edges.

Shell tried to still her breathing. She felt her Warren crackling with energy at her fingertips – *just as during the worst magery engagements! Enormous power has been unleashed!*

Then she heard it: a rumbling seeming to arise from beneath her feet. The wall struck her, slamming her across the cell into the sleeping ledge. Stone shrieked, grinding and hammering. Dust and dirt rained down, choking her breath and blinding her while the floor bashed her. *She was going to die crushed like a beetle!*

Eventually, though it seemed to last an eternity, the rumbling and up-and-down shaking passed away. Ominous groanings, creakings, and the cries of wounded filled the silence. The door to her cell burst into the chamber, iron bars rattling.

'Shell!' Hands pulled her up: it was Blues, the side of his head a dust-coated smear of blood. 'Are you all right?'

She brushed at the pulverized rock dusting her clothes. 'Yes . . . yes! I think so. Who else is here? Lazar?'

'He's up top last I saw. What about Bars? Corlo?'

'They took him up the tower. Corlo . . . I can't say.'

Blues helped her out. 'Let's see who's here.'

Together they dug out all who could stand. They found a good many Malazan veterans, including Tollen. But no sign of Jemain or Corlo. For Bars' sake she hoped they hadn't been buried under tons of stone.

The Malazans formed into a party, headed by Tollen. They scavenged all the weapons they could find. 'We're heading up!' Tollen called to Shell.

'We should all go together,' Blues said.

Tollen spat. 'This tower won't stand for ever. Gotta go.'

'Good luck,' Shell called.

Tollen raised a hand in what might be taken as an abbreviated version of the Guard salute, then nodded his party up the stairs.

'One quick peep is all it would take to make sure no one's left,' she told Blues.

He frowned a negative. 'Too early for that yet. No lower levels?'

'Yes, but no prisoners down there.'

'The infirmary then – where's that?'

She nodded, suddenly certain. 'Yes! The infirmary! Jemain is sure to be there.'

'All right.' Blues searched around and came up with two sticks, each about the length of his forearm. With these he headed up the stairs. Shell followed, unarmed as yet.

Fighting soon sounded from above. They passed three floors to find the way blocked by the Malazans. Tollen pushed his way down to them, spat again. 'Blasted Stormguard's blocking the way.'

'Overbear them,' Blues said. 'What's the matter with you marines?'

Tollen snorted, then drawled, 'There's just the one.'

'One?' Blues pushed past the bear of a fellow. 'Let me through.'

Tollen offered Shell a wink. 'This I gotta see. The Lady's Grace is on this one . . . He won't go down.'

'The *Lady's Grace*? What's that?'

Tollen eyed her sidelong. 'You'll see.'

Shell followed. She had to walk over four dead Malazans, each bearing ferocious impalement wounds. They'd reached the main guardroom that allowed access to the surface. A lone Korelri Stormguard blocked the way amid the rubble, spear held upright at rest position, arms wrapped under his cloak. It was an older man, his short hair pepper-grey, his face savagely scarred. But what was most strange was the faint blue aura that played like a flame about the man and his spear. *Energies raised over him – and so strong as to be visible even without her Warren.*

'Form up to stand the wall, prisoner,' he told Blues.

'Shit!' Tollen murmured behind her. 'Now I know him. Wall Marshal Quint. The one Chosen we didn't want to meet.'

Blues advanced into the room. He held his two sticks straight down, angled slightly outwards from his body. 'Let us pass and we'll make no trouble.'

Quint's scarred face twisted in an almost otherworldly contempt. 'Pass? You can pass all right. You're needed to stand the wall. The Riders are stirring. Now's your chance to serve the Lady.'

Indeed, the waves were hammering the wall, but even Shell, new as she was to the place, could hear the difference: the arrhythmia of their pounding, and the relative weakness. It was as if they were drawing off – but it was far too early for that.

'We decline the honour of dying for your Lady,' Blues said.

The man levelled the spear. 'Why? You're going to die anyway.' And he thrust. Blues blocked the spear with his crossed sticks and lashed out, kicking the man back. He grunted, recovering instantly, to drive Blues back with a series of short thrusts. Shell was startled: Blues was their mercenary company's weapon-master; no one could stand before him. Certainly, there were those who could outlast him or overbear him, such as Bars or Lazar, or Skinner, for that matter, but in technique and ability with any weapon the man was peerless among them.

They duelled in this manner for a time, neither able to penetrate the other's guard. Shell watched, her amazement growing moment by moment. Who were these Stormguard? Obviously, she saw now, their reputation was not overblown.

Snarling his disgust, the Chosen, Quint, stepped back to point his spear. 'You've talent, I'll grant you that. A shame you refuse to put it to the proper use. But now we're done. Let's see how you like a touch of the Lady's Wrath.'

The aura that played about the man intensified at his hands, flaring to a brilliant glow. Shell had no time to call out a warning before it shot like a lance from the spearhead to strike Blues full in the chest. He staggered back, the aura dancing about him, sizzling. He smacked backwards into a wall with a sickening crunch that brought down another rain of dust from the roof, but he did not fall.

Quint gazed at him, utterly astonished. 'How is this? You live?'

Blues wiped blood from his cheek and mouth and shook himself like a dog. 'I felt something like that before, Wall Marshal. On another continent, and from another supposed *god*. I seem to have built up a tolerance.'

Quint struck a ready stance. 'Then we'll just have to settle this the old-fashioned way.'

Blues sighed, shook his head. 'No. I don't have time for this.' He raised his arms and Shell saw his D'riss Warren come to him, the Warren of Earth and Stone. He thrust his arms out, sending an answering blast of power that struck the Wall Marshal and knocked him flying backwards to crash through the heavy panelled door and tumble out on to the cluttered, ice-strewn wall.

Tollen let go a low whistle that Shell seconded: *yes, it's easy to forget that the man is also one of the Guard's strongest mages.* She stepped through the wreckage to Blues' side. 'Decided to test the waters, did you?'

Blues gave an embarrassed shrug. 'I guess the Lady's too busy to care so much right now.'

The Malazans and other prisoners pressed forward. 'Let's go,' Tollen called.

Outside, enormous shards of shattered ice choked the walk. Gouges had been taken out of the sides and entire buildings were gone – having slid off the rear, or collapsed. A great crack ran down the side of the tower, the dressed stone blocks shattered. A howling wind rampaged through the debris, driving pulverized ice into Shell's face. As they stood peering for a way through the carnage, a figure straightened amid the shattered wreckage, throwing off slivers of broken ice: Wall Marshal Quint.

'Won't this guy stay down?' Blues grumbled.

'Now you know how it feels,' Tollen complained.

Blues caught Shell's eye. 'Let's see if he can swim . . .' He was gesturing to raise his Warren anew when a blast of power erupted between him and Shell, tossing them both aside. Shell had a momentary glimpse of the waters foaming and lashing next to the wall before slamming down with a bone-snapping impact against stone.

*

When Ussü returned to his chambers he found the door open, his two aides fled. *Very well. Good help and all that* . . . The Crimson Guard Avowed, Bars, lay as before. Ussü tested the pins and lengths of chain, giving each a yank. Strong still.

The real blast was on its way. Where to sit it out? The chamber boasted a sturdy desk built of thick timbers. *Beneath this? Too undignified.* He went to the doorway, blocked the door open, pressed himself up against one jamb. Have to do.

He heard it just before it struck. How appropriate, he judged, that it should come rumbling like the avalanche and landslide that it was. Then a jolt threw him from the doorway and he tumbled about the hall like a doll kicked by the floor. Bone-juddering fractures announced the calving of huge shards from the tower's sheath of ice. A crack shot through the roof, beams exploding. Pulverized rock showered down upon him.

As the shaking stilled, he stirred, groaning, shook dust from his hair. He staggered like a drunk to his room through the fallen rubble of the hall. Within, he found an icy wind cutting about the chamber; the falling ice had torn the shutters from the window. His subject lay stretched over the thick table as before, arms and legs pinioned. Ussü pressed his ear to the man's naked chest, ignored the ugly gaping wound oozing blood.

A steady beat! As strong as before. It was as if nothing had happened! Thank you, my Lady. With such seemingly inexhaustible strength to draw upon – imagine what I can accomplish!

He brushed the dust and litter from the man. Pulled the larger stones and fallen grit from the wound. Would the Riders bother to strike here? Somehow he didn't think so. They had their breach elsewhere. No, it would be the Malazans. This was their chance to finish things. Shattering a section of the wall was one thing – stone and wood can be repaired. Truly crushing the Korelri would be another.

It was hard to think with such enormous forces pressing upon him. The gathering might felt like a mountain suspended above his head. A vast displacement was bearing down through the Narrows. And he, even from this far, felt it like a giant's boot crushing him.

And what of the Overlord? He raised his Warren and cast his vision south. What he saw made him lurch, almost sickened. *No! You fool! The man had his army marshalled still within sight of the coast! Why wasn't he in the highlands? Had he no idea – but no, of course not. Gods! I must warn him!*

Ussü threw himself upon Bars. He savagely pushed his hand into the wound, parting the glutinous scab of blood and fluids to quest down amid the organs. His fingers slid down around a lung and through the tears in the fat and muscle fibre surrounding the beating heart. Pressing his head down close to the subject's chest he closed his eyes and reached out to take the additional energy needed for a sending. Grasping this, he projected his consciousness southward.

He found Yeull wrapped in layers of blankets and furs, standing outside watching his tent burning to the ground. Chaos surrounded him, soldiers running about. 'Overlord!' he called, peremptorily, to be heard above the riot. The man's eyes flicked about, searching. His mouth drew down, frowning even more.

'What witchery is this?' he murmured, his gaze slitted.

Yeull, he knew, was seeing the faint and wavering image of himself, Ussü, outlined by his aura energies. 'I have news! A warning!'

'A warning?' The Overlord spread his arms. 'Rather late it would seem.'

'No! Worse – why are you still here? Why have you not struck inland?'

Yeull's gaze became creamy with a kind of satisfied cunning and his mouth crooked up in a half-smile. 'Best to give the Korelri a good scare, yes? They'll appreciate us all the more once we've rescued them from these invaders . . .'

Ussü could not contain himself any longer. All he had endured from the man came rushing up, choking him like swallowed vomit. '*You loathsome cretin!* Because of your childish scheming—'

'Hey? What's that? Has the Lady driven you insane, man?'

'Just listen to me and flee! Run! Order everyone to high ground! Abandon everything!'

Yeull scowled his confusion. 'What's that? Run? Whatever for?'

'A huge wave! A flood—' Ussü broke off as outside Ice Tower, just beneath his feet, another mage suddenly announced his presence by raising his Warren. 'Just order everyone to run for high land! You are warned!' And he broke away from Yeull as the man opened his mouth to ask for more explanation, or to object.

Drawing upon his and the Lady's power and the life energy of his subject, Ussü quested passively down through the tower to find the mage. *A practitioner of D'riss – and strong. Very well. I will have to strike hard, make sure of it immediately.* He began drawing and coiling power, gathering it into one stored blast to unleash in a single gesture. When the potentiality was almost bursting beyond his control, he projected it down the tower and released it.

The blast shook him high in his chamber. The entire tower groaned and shifted. More dust rained down, and somewhere a beam shattered in an answering explosion.

*

Fingers decided he'd had enough of life without access to a Warren. These damned Stormguard had snapped the otataral wrist-torc on him and since then life had been nothing but one long indignity. They forced him out into the frigid cold to chase those damned Riders off the wall – nearly getting him run through! And all the while he was as sick as a dog and would like to die – if he could!

Then someone unleashes Burn's own fury against the Stormwall and wearing this torc all he can do is watch while the tremor strikes, bringing down the tower around him. He'd be dead, he knew, if it weren't for the Vow. Apparently the otataral does nothing to impede its effectiveness. He's crawled over broken stones, up rubble-choked stairs, dragged himself over flattened burst bodies, and now he's lying outside on the wall, smeared in crap, somewhere along this blasted wall, gods know where, stranded! Two broken legs and no way to bloody heal himself.

Panting, almost delirious with pain, he raised his head to study the belt-knife he'd taken from one of the corpses. *Only thing for it* . . . He pressed his right hand, palm up, to the frozen stone flagging and set the edge of the knife to the wrist. *Goodbye hand! So much for rope climbing.*

'You really ought to be dead,' someone rumbled over him.

Fingers peered up, blinking, close to passing out. '*What?*' Whoever this was, he was a giant of a fellow, occluding almost all the sky.

'You are a mage, yes?'

Swallowing, Fingers managed a faint 'Yes.' Then he cried out a yell, his vision blackening, as the big man yanked on his right hand.

'You want this off, yes?'

Fingers could only hiss, '*Yes.*'

'Very well. All others are dead, as far as I can see. Only we two survive here. I am leaving. But before I go, remember, I, Hagen of the Toblakai, rescued you.'

Fingers nodded. *Yes, certainly, Hagen, yes. Whoever.*

The giant twisted the torc and Fingers yelled again as the fellow nearly broke his wrist. Then it was free and Fingers felt his Warren blossom open to him once more. He sighed, almost ecstatic, and felt like hugging the great shaggy ape. But the fellow, Hagen, had merely pushed off, running for the rear of the wall. Fingers stared uncomprehending as the giant increased his pace, faster and faster, until one huge bounding leap took him up and over the rear of the wall to disappear.

He gazed for a time at the blank section of stone where the giant had jumped and thought, *Was that really a Toblakai?*

Then, blinking and shaking his head as if to awaken from a trance, he set about healing his legs so that he could at least stand – not that he had any feel at all for the tricky Denul Warren.

*

On the cluttered stone floor of the infirmary, amid the toppled beds, fallen instruments and shards of stone, Corlo lay staring up at a titanic wooden beam fully a foot wide and a foot thick, yet split right through and hanging directly overhead.

Someone was next to him, talking, but he ignored the man. *Fall*, he urged. *Fall, you bastard! Cut me in half!*

The fellow was saying something about a saw and cutting – Corlo just wished he'd go away.

Why by all the gods above and below am I still alive? What have I done that was so terrible to deserve such punishment? Why have I been singled out like this? Aren't you done with me? What more could you possibly squeeze from me?

Something bit at his leg and he peered down. The man – Jemain! – was cutting off his leg at the knee. *Jemain is cutting my leg off!*

Corlo lunged for his neck. He hooked his fingers around Jemain's throat but the fellow easily pushed him down – *he was so weak! Why was he so weak?* One arm pressing on Corlo's chest, Jemain returned to sawing at the knee.

When the iron teeth slid under his kneecap Corlo passed out.

*

Shell awoke lying on her side. Her right arm was numb and it was an agony to breathe any deeper than the shallowest of gasps. *Ribs broken.* Only the instantaneous raising of Blues' Warren had saved her life in that attack. As it was, she hadn't fared so well. From where she lay she could see Lazar, close to the shattered crenellations, engaged in a duel with two Stormguard, both of whom carried the flaming aura of what they called the Lady's Grace.

Possession would be her word for it.

On the far side of the wall, the escaped prisoners, Malazans mostly, fought Korelri holding the stairs, Wall Marshal Quint among them.

But at the centre of the marshalling walk Blues was taking terrible punishment from this new mage who had suddenly announced himself. *A mage? She thought these Korelri had no mages. And of terrifying power, too!*

The driving energies were pushing Blues back towards the crumbling forward edge of the wall. Beyond, the seas raged, frothing and tumbled – the tremor must have struck there as well, underwater. As for the Riders, they appeared too preoccupied to take advantage of the chaos here. Waves still struck, however, still overtopping in washes of bitingly chill waters with every other strike.

Around Blues all the ice sizzled and melted in the wash of energies unleashed by this mage. Steadily Blues was being pushed to the lip of the wall. Obviously, this Korelri meant to drive him over the edge.

Gods! And she could not help! Just tensing her chest sent lances of agony through her and she winced, screwing shut her eyes, tears freezing on her cheeks.

Then a hand on her chest and relief – blessed easing. She sucked a shuddering breath deep into her lungs and opened her eyes to see Fingers kneeling next to her. He grinned his encouragement. 'Looks like Blues has finally dug up a real threat.'

Drawing one more wonderful breath, Shell gave him a nod and together they threw all they could muster against the mage.

*

More of these enemy mages! Ussü was surprised, but with the resources now at his command he was more than ready for them. The wellspring of power that sustained this Avowed seemed limitless; while the Lady's blessing, though thinning, continued. Along that flow of energies he sensed an awareness, the Lady herself perhaps, distracted, flailing, directing one quick vicious command his way: *Slay them all!*

Most certainly, Mistress. Ussü bore down, hammering this D'riss mage – why wouldn't the man fall? He seemed impossibly resilient to the might he was pouring down upon him. *Die, damn you! How could you possibly still live? Who is this prisoner? Another Malazan cadre mage?*

The body beneath him convulsed then, almost shaking him loose. Ussü snapped open his eyes to see just a hand's breadth away this subject, the Avowed, aware and glaring, burning rage into him. Ussü stared back at the man. 'You're conscious?' he breathed in wonder.

The gagged mouth drew up in a ghastly smile. The muscles of the arms and chest tensed – even around Ussü's wrist they tensed, and the man strained on the chains binding him. His face flushed, veins starting out and writhing. Ussü could not believe what he was witnessing. What did the man think he could . . . Then it occurred to him: the earthquake! Gods, no! He snapped a glance to the floor. The stone blocks were now uneven, jostled. The iron pin positively vibrated, quivering, grinding.

Oh no. Gods, no. Please do not play with me so. He clenched his hand, raising another thrashing convulsion from the man. 'I have your heart! Stop! Or I will crush it!'

The ghastly, almost insane smile remained fixed at the gagged mouth.

No! Stop! You don't—

The pin rang as it snapped free. The arms flattened Ussü to the man's chest.

Yet Ussü kept his grip, staving off the combined attacks of all three mages. The chains fell away with a clash. The Avowed pulled down the gag. 'Now I have *you*,' he grated.

Ussü twisted his fist: the organ laboured, squeezed in his hand. The man's eyes glazed in agony, fluttering, his arms weakening. 'Who will die first, I wonder?' he asked.

Bars shook the chains off his arms. He snapped a hand to Ussü's throat. 'You're forgetting,' he panted, hoarse with the unimaginable torture he'd endured. 'I can't die.'

'*Yes you can.*' And Ussü clenched with all his might, meaning to pulp the shuddering ball of muscle in his fist. But Bars' hand clenched as well, crushing Ussü's throat, cutting off his breath, the life force from his lungs. As Ussü's life slipped away from him he suddenly saw far into the wellspring of the inexhaustible might sustaining this Avowed and he understood its source. He gazed at the man's flushed twisted face, not a hand's breadth from his own, appalled by the magnitude of the discovery. He opened his mouth, meaning to tell him: *Do you have any idea—*

Bars squeezed until his clenched fingers cramped, shook the body one last time to make sure of it, then relaxed his grip on the corpse. With his other hand he gently, oh so damned gently, grasped hold of the wrist where it entered his chest, and slowly, as tenderly as possible, pulled.

The anguish returned – torture beyond anything he'd ever experienced before. White blinding fire blossomed again in his mind. All his death-wishes were as nothing compared to his desire to be free of this agony. Anything! Death would be as the most soothing balm. Infinitely preferable.

The hand came free with a sickening sucking noise. Revolted, Bars threw the body aside only to wince, gasping and cradling his chest. He stayed like that for some time: sitting up, curled around his wound, arms wrapped round his chest. The slightest move was an ordeal beyond any consideration.

After a time someone was at the door. Bars cracked one eye for a look. It was Blues. The man entered gingerly, as quietly as he could, stepping over litter. Bars raised a finger to forestall him. 'Don't fucking touch me.'

Blues eyed the fallen mage, nodded solemnly. Bars pointed to his chained legs. Blues waved and the chain fell away. Gritting his teeth, Bars eased one leg down to the floor, then the other. Blues closed to help but Bars waved him away. 'Let's get out of this Hood-damned hole.'

Blues stood aside of the door. 'Damn right.'

They were on the stairs, Blues ahead, casting quick worried glances back to Bars, when someone called from a blocked room: 'Hello! Is that someone? Hello?'

Bars straightened up from cradling his chest, his eyes huge. 'Jemain? Is that you?'

'Yes. Bars?'

Bars gestured to the blocked doorway. Blues motioned and stones began grating aside. Jemain's anxious face appeared in a gap. 'Bars! Corlo's here – he's hurt.'

*

On the wall, Fingers tried to raise Shell, who, grimacing and hissing, pulled her hands free: 'Wait! Listen!'

'What?'

'Grab hold of something, now!'

Fingers faced the bay, grunted, 'Aw shit . . .'

A wave smashed into the battered crenellations, overtopped easily and kept coming at them. It pushed loose blocks aside then struck them, submerging Shell. She held on, straining not to be washed off the wall and cast over the rear to shatter on the rocks below. Through the slurry of deathly cold water she saw the shimmering armour of a Stormrider standing before her.

She threw her head back, gasping in air, panting, her limbs shivering almost uncontrollably. The entity peered down, regarding her. Its sword remained sheathed at its side, no lance in evidence. Its helm shifted as it looked about. Then it raised an arm, the scaled armour flashing iridescent, seeming to salute her, and backed away.

Fingers appeared at her side, supported her. Together they watched while the entity reached the outer shattered crenellations and stepped back to fall away.

'What was that all about?' Fingers asked, stuttering.

'I think they're done here.'

'So're we,' Fingers growled. 'C'mon.'

Down one way they saw the Stormguard righting themselves where they blocked the one access leading off the wall. Of the

Malazans Shell saw no sign. Fingers motioned the other way; there Lazar fought splashing through the thinning waters, duelling two Stormguard both still glowing with the aura of the Lady. She and Fingers raised their Warrens.

Their combined strike smashed the two Chosen from the wall, casting them tumbling out into the white-capped waves, where they disappeared. Holding her numb side, Shell joined Lazar to peer down over the broken lip of the wall to the waters foaming below. 'Thanks, you two,' Lazar said, breathing heavily. 'Those boys just wouldn't go down.'

'Neither would you,' Fingers remarked, as he came limping up behind.

Lazar drew off his full helm and steam plumed in the frigid air from the sweat soaking his hair and running down his face. He drew in great breaths, blowing and gasping; then, peering out over the inlet, he froze. '*Damn Hood . . .*'

Shell looked over and her flesh prickled with true terror. A wave was approaching up the narrow bay – a wave unlike any she'd seen before. More a mountain of water, webbed in slush and topped in white spume, already looming far taller than the wall itself.

'Oponn's throw,' Fingers breathed.

Lazar punched Shell's arm, making her wince. 'Let's go!'

They met Blues and Bars at the tower entrance. Jemain was following behind, carrying an unconscious Corlo, one of whose legs now ended at a wrapped stump. 'We have to go,' Fingers told Blues. 'Now.'

'What about the Malazans?' Shell asked. She looked to where four Korelri Stormguard remained, Quint included, holding the stairs. Only a few fallen Malazan bodies were visible.

'They ran for the high pass,' Blues said.

'Good luck to them,' Fingers added.

Shell warned: 'Blues – take us.' Quint had motioned to his brother Stormguard and they were approaching.

'All right, all right!' Blues answered. 'We're gone. Stand close.'

*

Quint rounded the side of the tower to find the wall . . . empty. The foreigners had fled; they'd used their alien Warren witchery to escape. Movement out over the inlet caught his eye and he stared. At first he couldn't believe what he was seeing – the scale was all wrong. No wave could possibly be that tall, that immense. A small voice whispered in the back of his mind: *It is the prophesied end of the Stormwall come upon them after all. First the earth shakes then the waters come to reclaim the land – was that not the ancient warning of the end of the world?*

Quint looked to his spear, its gouged and battered blade, the Lady's Grace thinning, so faint, then to this titanic approaching crag of water greater than any he had seen in over fifty years, rearing now over him taller than six fathoms.

Damn you . . .

He raised the spear, shaking it in the searing extremity of his rage.

Damn everyone! Damn everything! Damn—

The mountain of water slammed into the wall to tumble, undercut, overflowing like a waterfall, washing, scouring, unstoppable. When it thinned, draining to both sides from the course of the wall, the stone core remained, uneven, punished, gouged of everything, empty of all movement.

On into the evening a fresh layer of snow began to fall over all: the grey undisturbed waters of the inlet, and the bare stones of the wall where no footfalls marred it. Through the night it froze into a fresh clean layer of frost and ice.

*

All through the fighting below Hiam knelt, praying. He prayed for forgiveness. For penance. And for guidance. He ignored the cries, the blasts and the upheaval. Hands clasped, eyes screwed shut, entreating, begging. *Lady! Please answer! How have we displeased you? Where have we transgressed? Please! In the name of our devotion. Will you not grace me with your guidance?*

At one point something enormous ploughed into the tower in an avalanche roar that seemed the end of the world. The impact drove Hiam against a wall and left the tower tilted, threatening to fall at any moment, but he did not turn from his single-minded observance. Surely his zeal would be rewarded now, at this moment of testing.

After a time he knew not how long – nor did he care – an answer came. The Lady's voice whispered as if into his ear: *You failed me, Lord Protector!*

He bowed to the floor, abject in his piety. 'My Lady! How? How did we fail? What was our transgression? Let us make amends.'

Amends? You failed! They are upon me! You let them through! You swore to protect me!

'M'Lady, our holy concord remains between us. We will protect the lands as we swore—'

The lands? The lands? You protect me! Me! And you have failed even at that simple task, you wretched fool.

Hiam sat up, puzzled. 'We swore to protect all the lands – under your blessing and guidance, of course.'

The lands? You fool! Your blood protected me from my old enemies! And now they are coming!

'Our blood protected . . . you?'

Yes! Fool! Blood sacrifice forestalls them. But now they are through! What is left to me? Who will— Wait! I sense them close. The ancient enemy. They have followed me even unto here. How will I hide? You! Why did you not die for me? Do so – now!

And the Lady's presence snapped away, leaving Hiam reeling. His mind couldn't catch at anything. His hands went to his neck. All this time . . . then all this time . . . No. It was too terrible to contemplate. Too horrific. A monstrous crime.

He rose from the floor, backed to a wall as if retreating from an invisible enemy. It was a lie. A deception. Somehow. But no. That had been the Lady. He knew her presence.

He had finally come to the true foundation of his faith and he wished he'd never done so.

His scorched thoughts turned to all the brethren who had preceded him – good men and women all. So many. Down through the ages. His heart went out to them in an ache of love that could not be borne. Countless! All trusting to the truth of their cause . . . Yes, trusting and . . . used.

He crossed to a gaping window, stared out at the snow-flecked night without seeing it. He knew what to do. What was one more death? He would die – but not for her.

No. Most certainly not for her.

Hiam climbed up on to the windowsill and threw himself from the tower, to tumble down into the heaving white-capped waters below.

* * *

Dockworkers among the maze of waterfront wharves serving the Korelri capital of Elri were still discussing the morning's tremor – how the tall pilings wavered like ships' masts! – when, before their eyes, the tide suddenly withdrew to an extent unheard of in any account. Fish lay jumping and gasping in the tidal muck abandoned by the waters. The rotted stumps of ancient docks reared like ragged teeth far out into the mudflats of the bay. Citizens still dazed from the shaking gathered on the waterfront to watch this eerie phenomenon.

A strange greenish cast grew in the sky to the west. A sound like a distant windstorm gathered. People stopped talking to listen and watch, hushed. Something was approaching up the bay – a wide green banner or wall hurrying in upon them like a landslide. The noise climbed to a raging whistling rush of wind that snapped cloaks and banners away. Citizens now screamed, pointing, or turned to run, or merely stared entranced as the wall swelled into an over-topping comber now breaking some seven fathoms high. It crashed through the shoreline without slowing or faltering and rushed on inland, taking villages, roads and fields on its way to slam smashing through the south-facing fortifications of Elri, demolishing those walls, toppling stone guard towers, gouging a three-block swath through jammed houses and shops.

As the water slowly withdrew it left behind a stirred, glutinous mass of brick, mud, shattered timbers and building stone. It sucked everything loose with it down the slope and back out into the bay, never to be seen again. And it left behind an empty shoreline of mud a full rod beyond its original contours.

*

Far within the channel maze of the saltwater marsh east of Elri, Orzu pulled his pipe from his mouth to sniff the air and eye the strange colour of the sky to the west. He leapt to his feet, threw the pipe aside and set his hands to his mouth, bellowing: 'Everyone aboard! Now! Quick-like!' The Sea-Folk stared, frozen where they squatted at cook fires or sat tying reeds. 'Now!' Orzu ordered. 'Abandon it all! Cut the ropes!'

Cradling her child to her chest, Ena clambered on board. 'What is it, Da?'

'The Sea's Vengeance, lass. Now tie yourself down.' Aside, to another boat, he roared, 'Throw all that timber overboard, Laza! Lighten the load.'

Ena wrapped one arm in a rope, tried to peer over the great fields of wind-lashed reeds bobbing taller than any man. A storm was hurrying in upon them. It cast a light over everything like none she'd ever seen before. It was as if the entire world was underwater.

Something was coming. She could hear it; a growling, rising in intensity. 'Is it another shudder of the great earth goddess?' she called.

'The old sea god's been awakened. And he's angry.' Orzu gestured urgently. 'Mother! Drop that baggage and jump in now!'

The boat lurched. Ena peered over the side: the waters had risen. She glanced back west in time to see some dark wall advancing like night, consuming the leagues of waving grasses.

'Here it comes!' Orzu bellowed.

The vessel slammed sideways, twisting like a thrown top. Ena banged her head against the side, struggled to shield the babe pressed to her breast. When she next looked up they were charging north, water-borne, bobbing amid a storm of wreckage: uprooted trees, the roofs of huts, driftwood logs, all in a churning mulch of detritus mixed with a flux of mud. She watched a cousin's boat become wedged between the boles of two enormous logs and crushed to shards. Her family members jumped to the roof of a hut spinning nearby.

The wave carried them over the sand cliffs bordering the marshlands and on inland, ever slowing, diminishing, thinning. Until finally, in its last ebbing gasp, it lifted them up to lie canted on the slope of a hillside far from the sight of the coast. She sat watching in wordless amazement as the waters swept back as if sucked, leaving behind in their wake a trail of ugly churned mud, soil, and stranded oddities such as the wall of a reed hut, or their boat itself: a curious ornament for a farmer's field.

Orzu thumped down next to her and gave her head a look. 'Are you all right then, child?'

'Yes.'

'And the babe?'

'Yes.'

'And you, mother!' he yelled.

'Fine, no thanks to you!' she grumbled.

'Do you think our friends had something to do with this?' Ena asked, still rather dazed.

Orzu slapped the boat's side. 'Well . . . that I don't know. But now I guess I'll have to do what I've been threatening to do all this time.'

'Which is?' She wasn't certain which of his threats he might be referring to.

'Take up farming.'

Ena snorted. That might last a day.

'Let's round everyone up then,' he said, patting all his pockets in search of his pipe.

*

The reassembled armies of Rool waited while its commanders, led by their Overlord himself, debated strategy. The camp had been cleaned up from the fires and panic of the series of tremors. Thankfully, while there had been some property damage, and some horses had been lost as they ran terrified, there had been little loss of life.

In a new tent, huddled next to a brazier, though he somehow felt warm enough for the first time in a decade, the Overlord Yeull was of the opinion that these invader Malazans, elements of the Fourth and Eighth Armies, must have fared much more poorly in the rough highlands, where landslides and rockfalls were so common.

A knot of army officers stood together, rather nervously eyeing the Overlord where he sat slumped, his face set in its habitual glower.

'Do they mean to come upon Kor from the mountains?' a young captain wondered aloud.

Yeull snorted. 'They're fools. They don't know the country. The Barrier range is a maze of defiles and razorback ridges. They'll starve.'

The officers, none of whom had ever set foot in Korel, nodded sagely.

A messenger entered, bowed next to the Overlord to whisper, his voice low. The Overlord frowned even more. 'What?'

The messenger gestured outside. Scowling, Yeull pushed himself erect, straightened his thick bear cloak – though he was tempted to throw off the suffocating thing – and headed for the entrance. 'Let's have a look.'

The officers followed. Outside, Yeull shaded his eyes to gaze to the south-west where the coast curved in a bay that gave way to a headland. The tide appeared to have withdrawn significantly when it should be in. Mudflats lay exposed in an ugly brown and grey swath. Yeull ground his teeth. *More Ruse trickery from that traitor bitch? What could she have in mind?*

Ussü's warning came to him but he pushed it aside. The man had reached the end of his usefulness. The Lady appeared to have finally dragged him into senility. In any case, they were safe here so far from the shore – he'd made sure of that. Nothing to . . . He squinted out past the bay, where the strait appeared to be experiencing unusually rough conditions. Something was coming into the bay. A tall bulge of water like a tidal bore, but fast, faster than any wave he'd ever heard of.

Amazed shouts sounded around him; soldiers pointing.

That was a *lot* of water and the bay was very shallow. Yeull's gaze traced the long gentle rise up from the shore cliffs to their camp.

Lady, no . . . It could not be possible. No. I refuse to believe it.

The great rolling bulge was not only impossibly tall, it was also impossibly broad: it stretched all the way across the bay, perhaps even across the strait itself.

It numbed his imagination just to try to conceive of that volume of water, and that amount of destructive potential bearing down upon him.

The damned end of the world, just like these crazy Korelri were always going on about.

The wave did not strike the shore so much as absorb it, continuing on without any hesitation. Soldiers now broke to run in open panic.

Yeull stood his ground. Officers called begging for instructions but he ignored them. *No. Impossible. It will not happen.*

The churning front of mud, silt, sand, tumbling shore wreckage, even suspended hulks from the shore assault, all crashing and spinning, now came flying up the grade towards them. Its blasting roar was as of an avalanche. Yeull's shoulders sagged. *Gods damn you, Greymane. This is you, isn't it? This is why these Chosen hated you so. These Korelri fanatics finally met someone as crazy as them. Don't you know your name will go down as the greatest villain this region has ever known? Malazans won't be able to enter this region for generations – you've lost all these lands for ever . . .*

Inexorable, blasting two stone farmhouses to rubble and splinters as it came, the wavefront ploughed into the camp. It swept over tents, collected supplies, masses of men. Yeull's last sight was of a maw of crashing tree trunks headed right for him.

*

On board the Malazan flagship, the *Star of Unta*, Devaleth had waited through the night and the dawn of the next day. At her urging the combined Malazan and Blue fleet had withdrawn to the centre of Crack Strait. Here they'd waited while, as far as she could tell, nothing happened. To their credit, neither Nok nor the Blue Admiral Swirl approached to pester her with questions or demands for explanations. They had accorded her the title High Mage, and seemed also willing to grant her due credibility as well.

All that changed in the early morning when a rumbling as of a thunderstorm rolled over the massed fleet. Devaleth looked to the west. *That was a much greater report than she'd been expecting. To have reached them this far, so loudly . . .*

Then far off, through the Warren of Ruse, she felt the sea lurch. Sea-Father forgive them! It was like the undersea tremors they taught about at the Ruse Academy. Immense volumes of water displaced, creating . . . She backed away from the side of the vessel. Nok stood nearby, concern on his craggy narrow face.

'What is it, High Mage?' he asked.

She found her voice, pulled her hand from her neck. 'A wave, Admiral. Much larger than I had anticipated. A great flood. We must run before it. Order the fleet to spread out, head east – now. I will do all I can smooth our passage.'

Nok bowed, went to give the orders. After he went Devaleth gripped the side to stop her weakened legs from giving way. *Smooth our passage! Laugh, great Sea-Father! May as well try to hold back an earth tremor with one's bare hands. Everyone must be warned of this.*

*

Captain Fullen, temporarily in command of the garrison at Banith, had a heart-stopping moment shaving when an apparition flickered into existence in his tent. He almost cut himself fatally when he jerked, surprised, as a hollow distorted voice spoke: 'Commander . . .'

He spun, pressing a cloth to his cheek, to see a shimmering image of the Mare mage, the new High Mage. 'A great wave is approaching,' the woman continued. 'You may have until noon. You must take steps to evacuate Banith immediately. Take all steps necessary. Admiral Nok orders this.'

The image wavered then disappeared. Fullen stared where it had appeared, wiped the blood and soap from his face. *Togg deliver him . . . just like the old tales of how things used to get done in the Empire. And he'd thought he'd never see the like!*

He ran from the tent, bellowing orders as he went.

A similar apparition appeared in many coastal cities, Balik and Molz in Katakan, Danig and Filk in Theft.

In Stygg, deep within the pleasure palace of Ebon, its ruler gaped at the image, heard its warning, then quickly acted upon its appearance: he gathered together all the twenty self-styled sorcerers, warlocks and witches he paid to protect him from such things and had them executed immediately.

Only in Mare, at Black city and Rivdo, were the warnings given any credence, though they originated from a damned traitor.

*

Devaleth also attempted to reach to the west, to Dour and Wolt in Dourkan, but the shattering disruptions she met in Ruse threw her back and she could not reach.

After sending what few warnings she could, she sat to gather her strength. She reached out to Ruse, extending her summons as far as she ever had – the burgeoning puissance nearing from the west called to her but she kept away, knowing it would consume her in an instant. Instead, she decided upon an old water-witch's trick from her youth: sea-soothing. Like oil upon water, the localized rounding off of rough water. It was simple, easy to sustain, and this would free her to concentrate upon drawing from the yammering waterfall of power coursing through Ruse – potency that would flick her to ashes in a moment's slip of concentration.

Horrified cries rose but she did not crack open her eyes. Ropes suddenly drew tight about her, binding her to a cabin wall, but she was far gone from her flesh – she rode the shockwave itself as it coursed through Ruse. Above a swelling roar Nok's voice sounded, ordering more sail. Devaleth worked to gather a pool of calm: a smooth surface like a slick of oil that would ride above the churning froth bearing down upon them. Accomplishing this, she worked now on spreading it to protect as much of the fleet as she could reach.

The roar intensified beyond bearing; nothing could penetrate its ear-shattering continual thunderclap. The *Star of Unta* suddenly lurched forward, picking up speed like a child's toy. It struck an impossible forward attitude. A rope's explosive snap penetrated the roar; boards groaned. Equipment tumbled down the deck, rolling and crashing for the bow. The ropes constraining Develath held her back. Someone screamed, falling forward, rolling along the decking. She fought at the limits of her strength – not to maintain the workings of the Warren, but to hold back the immense forces striving to break through her grip like an enraged bear striking at the thinnest of cloth. If even the smallest fraction of it should squeeze through it would annihilate her and the vessel together.

The *Star of Unta* now rode a waterfall slope, its angle pitched almost straight down. *The crest! We were upon the crest!* Devaleth bore down with all her might to maintain the mental contours of the sea-soothing charm. How grateful she was for its simplicity, its time-honed elegance. *And we in Mare sneer at these water-witches! They know what works, and do not mess with it!*

With another ominous chorus of groanings the vessel heaved itself flatter, falling at the stern. A mast-top snapped, falling with a deck-shuddering crash. Devaleth maintained her concentration, moving now with the wavefront, easing the passage of every vessel she could reach.

Someone was kneeling with her and a wet cloth was pressed to her brow. The coolness and the gentleness of the gesture revived her immensely. She dared slit open one eye: it was the old Admiral, Nok.

'How did you know that would help?' she ground through her clenched teeth.

'A mage named Tattersail told me – long ago.'

She grunted – of course. This man has seen them all.

'Well done, High Mage,' he said. 'I believe we are through the worst. And that was the worst I've ever seen. The end of the world.'

'No. Not the end of the world, Admiral. The end of *their* world.'

Nodding, he squeezed her shoulder and rose; instinctively, he understood that he'd distracted her enough, and withdrew.

Once the titanic wavefront had swept on far enough – far outstripping the lumbering progress of the vessels – she relaxed. She tried to rise but fell back, tied down. Utterly exhausted, she cleared her throat to croak, 'Would someone get these ropes off me!'

Sailors untied her and then the Blue Admiral, Swirl, gently attempted to raise her up but she could not move. Her vision suddenly swirled pink and all sounds disappeared. Agonizing pain seized her joints. *No! The depth-sickness! It had her! In the panic she'd neglected her protections!*

Yells of alarm rose around her as she suddenly, explosively, vomited up great gouts of bile and water.

* * *

Ivanr had returned to his weeding. It was heavy work; he'd been away for some time. It was demanding and he was out of shape. *How it hurt his chest to bend down!*

Someone was following him but he ignored her.

'Ivanr,' she called. 'Your work is not yet done.'

Don't I know it – just look at the mess of this garden!

'Your garden lies elsewhere . . .'

He turned on the annoying voice to find himself staring down at the small slim form of the Priestess. *You are dead.*

'And you will be as well if you keep retreating from your duty.'

Duty? Have I not done enough?

'No. A life's time would not be enough. The fight is unending.'

I know. He gestured around. *You see?*

'Exactly. You are needed. Think of it as . . . stewardship.'

Someone else can manage that. He bent to his weeding, wincing, and holding his chest.

'No. It has fallen to you – not because you are somehow special or singled out by fate. It is just that your turn has come. As it came to me.'

He straightened, studied his muddy hands. *That I can understand, I suppose. None of this stupid special chosen nonsense.*

'Yes. It is your turn – as it is everyone's at some time. The test is in our response.'

He slowly nodded, looked up at the sky. *Yes. The test is how you answer. Yes.* He rubbed his hands together. *I suppose so . . .*

'Ivanr?' another voice called, this one an old woman. 'Ivanr?'

He blinked his eyes, opened them to the hides of his tent outside the city, on his bed. It was day. The old mage, Sister Gosh, was leaning over him, the long dirty curls of her hair hanging down.

'Ivanr?'

'Yes?'

She sagged her relief. 'Thank the foreign gods. You're alive.'

'I thought you said we wouldn't meet again . . .'

She waved her hands. 'Never mind about that. I was wrong. Now listen, order Ring city evacuated. You must! It is vital! You will save countless lives. Now do it!'

'Order the city evacuated?'

'Yes. A great flood is approaching. Call it the Lady's Wrath, whatever. Just order it!'

He frowned. 'I can't say *that* . . .'

'Just do it!' she yelled.

He blinked, surprised, and she was gone. Guards flew into the tent, glared about. Then, seeing him awake, they fell to their knees.

He cleared his throat, croaked hoarsely: 'Evacuate the city.'

The guards glanced to one another. 'Deliverer . . . ?'

'Evacuate the city!' He squeezed his chest. 'It . . . it is doomed. Empty it now.'

Eyes widening in superstitious fear and awe, the guards backed away. Then they bowed reverently. 'Yes, Deliverer!' And fled.

Ivanr eased himself back down into his bed. He massaged his chest. Gods, how giving orders hurt!

*

Sister Gosh straightened from where she'd taken cover from the gusting frigid wind next to cyclopean stones that anchored an immense length of chain, the links of which were as thick as her thigh. The huge chain extended out across a wide gap of water between the tips of two cliffs, the ends of a ridge of rock that encircled a deep well that was supposedly bottomless. The Ring. Metal mesh netting hung from the chain – a barrier to anything larger than a fish.

She studied the rusted gnawed metal of the chain, pulled a silver flask from her shawls, up-ended it in a series of gulping swallows then shook it, found it empty, and shrugging threw it away. She set both hands upon the final link and bent her head down to it, concentrating. Smoke wafted from the iron and a red glow blossomed beneath her hands.

'It's just you and I now, Sister Gosh,' someone said from behind her.

Sighing, she turned to see Brother Totsin, the wind tossing his peppery hair and the tatters of his frayed vest, shirt and trousers. 'Thought you'd show up.'

'The Lady is with me, Gosh. I suggest you join as well.'

Sister Gosh sighed again. 'The Lady is *using* you, fool. And in any case, she's finished.'

'Not if you fail here.'

'I won't.'

Totsin frowned, disappointed, as if he were dealing with a recalcitrant child. 'You cannot win. The Lady has granted me full access to her powers.'

'Meaning she owns you.'

His greying goatee writhed as he scowled his irritation. 'Be the stubborn fool then. I never liked you.'

'I'm relieved to hear that.'

He launched himself upon her. Their arms met in an eruption of power that shook the stones beneath their feet. Rocks tumbled down some ten fathoms to the blue-black waters of the Hole below. The gargantuan chain rattled and clacked to vibrate in a frothing line across the gap. The flesh of Sister Gosh's hands wrinkled and cracked as if desiccated. She snarled, bearing down further, her face darkening in effort. A satisfied smile crept up behind Totsin's goatee.

Like an explosion a crack shot through the chiselled stone beside them anchoring the chain. Snarling, Totsin twisted to heave Sister Gosh out over the Hole. Black tendrils like ribbons snapped out around him, yanking him backwards, and the two released their mutual grip with a great thunderclap of energy.

A new figure now stood upon the narrow stone perch, tall, emaciated, dressed all in black, his black hair a wild mass. 'I have come back!' he announced.

Edging round to face both, Totsin nodded to the newcomer: 'Carfin. I am surprised to see you again.'

'The truth at last, Totsin. The truth at last.'

A rumbling swelled in the distance as of a thunderstorm, though only high clouds obscured the sky. Sister Gosh and Carfin shared alarmed glances.

Totsin laughed. 'Too late!'

'Not yet,' Sister Gosh snarled, and she threw everything she had at him.

The blast of energies surprised Totsin, throwing him back a step. Carfin levelled his Warren as well. The coursing power revealed far more potency than even Sister Gosh suspected of him – it seemed his sojourn within his Warren had granted him much greater confidence in his abilities. Totsin flailed beneath the cataract streams coursing upon him then, grimacing, leaned forward, edging in upon them. Carfin gestured again and a cowl of black snapped over the man's face. His hands leapt to the hood, grasping, tearing it into shreds. Sister Gosh yelled as she drew up a great coil of might that she snapped out upon Totsin. He flinched back, crying aloud, and stumbled off the lip. Sister Gosh kept her punishment centred upon him all the way down, and, though she could not be sure, she believed he struck the water far below.

'Thank you,' she gasped to Carfin.

'It was nothing.'

She turned to the anchor stone and the chain. 'Quickly now.'

Each pressed hands to the final link, stressing, heating, searching for weaknesses. The water, she noted, now ran far higher on the chain than it had before. Thunder rising in pitch announced the approach of something enormous emerging from Bleeder's Cut.

'What was it like?' she asked while they worked.

'What was what like?'

'Your Warren. Darkness. Rashan.'

'I don't know,' Carfin answered, straight-faced. 'It was dark.'

The metal glowed yellow now beneath Sister Gosh's hands. Drips of molten metal ran down the sides. 'You mean like that slimy cave you live in?'

Carfin clapped his hands and the metal of the link suddenly darkened to black beneath a coating of frost. It burst in an explosion of metal shards, Sister Gosh yanking her hands away. Screeching, grinding, the immense length of iron dragged itself down the lip of the cliff to flick from sight. Away across the gap water foamed and settled over its length as it sank.

'It is not a cave,' Carfin told Gosh. 'It is a subterranean domicile.'

The ridge of solid rock they stood upon shook then, rolling and heaving. A titanic bulge of water came coursing over the bay created where Bleeder's Cut met Flow Strait. The wave, more a wall of water, flowed over the Hole and with it went swift glimmering flashes of mother-of-pearl and brilliant sapphire.

Sister Gosh and Carfin sat on the lip of the stone. These flashes of light sank within the nearly black waters of the Hole. They seemed to descend for a long time. Then eruptions frothed the surface, greenish light flashing, coruscating from the depths. Over the Hole the surface bulged alarmingly, as from the pressures of an immense explosion. Then they hissed, steaming and frothing anew. Fog obscured the pit of the Ring, hanging in thick scarves.

The afternoon faded towards evening. Sister Gosh watched the undersides of the clouds painted in deep mauve and pink. More shapes came flashing through the waters to descend into the Hole. Shc fancied she saw the shells of their armour opalescent in emerald and gold. Reinforcements?

Whatever was down there was a long time in dying. Eruptions blistered the surface anew. Lights flickered like undersea flames. It seemed a full-blown war somewhere far beyond the ken of humankind.

Slowly, by degrees, the ferocity of the struggle in the depths appeared to wane. Evening darkened into twilight. Carfin amused himself making shapes of darkness dance upon the stones. Seeing this, Sister Gosh growled far down in her throat. The shapes bowed to her, then diffused into nothingness. Carfin sighed and shifted his skinny haunches. 'Now what?'

'Now everyone and their dog will be a hedge-wizard or seasoother.'

Carfin wrinkled his nose. 'Gods. It'll be awful.' He rose, dusted off his trousers. 'I'll stay in my cave – that is, my domicile.'

'Good riddance.'

'And to you.' He stepped into darkness and disappeared.

Now that's just plain showing off.

Below, swift shapes passed beneath the soles of her mud-covered, tattered shoes, coursing out into the bay. Far fewer than had entered, that was for sure. So it was over, here at least. What of elsewhere? Did the Riders fare as well against their other targets? Who knew? She was dog-tired. So tired she wondered whether there was a boat somewhere on this damned island.

* * *

Suth and Corbin followed Keri through the tunnels. They stayed close as the woman showed an alarming willingness to throw her Moranth munitions wherever she wished, and at the least hint of danger.

Almost hugging her back, Suth asked, 'Did the old man send you to help us?'

She sent him an irritated glare over her shoulder. 'What old man?'

'Never mind. So, they sent you to find us? All alone?'

She stopped in the dimness of a tunnel, turned on him, an explosive shrapnel munition called a sharper in one fist. 'Listen, Dal Hon. Alone is better, right? That way I can throw these without having to worry about your sorry arses, right?'

Suth raised his hands in surrender. 'Yes, okay! Whatever you say.'

'Damned straight.'

Corbin raised the lamp. 'What's the hold-up?'

'Numbnuts here,' Keri muttered. Corbin and Suth shared commiserating looks. 'This way,' Keri ordered, and headed off.

Suth expected Stormguard to jump out from every corner. He was shaken by their ruthless competence. They were ferocious opponents. Of their separated party only he and Corbin remained on their feet. Both squads had been ravaged, and Suth frankly doubted any of them would live to see the light of day again.

Keri led them through sections of half-collapsed tunnels, the scenes of confrontations where the dead lay where they fell, Stormguard and Malazan alike. Suth recognized the body of Sergeant Twofoot, nearly hacked to pieces. A faint yellowish glow ahead signalled a light source and Keri halted. She made a tapping noise, some sort of signal. It was answered differently but apparently correctly for she straightened, waving them on.

They entered a guarded chamber holding all that was left of the team: Fist Rillish, bearing many cuts, the Adjunct Kyle, Captain Peles, her armour gashed and helm dented, the squat priest, Sergeant Goss, Wess, and a few of Twofoot's squad.

Goss squeezed Suth's shoulder. 'The others?'

'Too wounded.' The priest, Ipshank, straightened from where he'd been sitting. 'Manask . . .'

'He was wounded, unconscious last we saw.'

Fist Rillish came forward. 'And the elder, Gheven?'

'He left by Warren to get help.'

Ipshank grunted at that. 'Good. But we can't count on it. We must press forward.'

Fist Rillish turned on the man. 'Why? Tell me that. We are outnumbered. I see no reason to lose anyone more.'

Ipshank nodded his understanding. 'Yet we must.'

'Why?'

The priest looked to Kyle who watched, arms crossed, the grip and pommel of the sword at his side glowing in the dim light. 'Because I believe Greymane is going to use his sword, Adjunct. And when he does we must be ready to finish what he has begun – else it will all be for nothing.'

Perhaps unconsciously, the young Adjunct's fist went to his own sword to close there, tight. He shook his head, in a kind of rueful self-mockery as if at some joke known only to him, and on him. 'I understand, Ipshank. I will go on. No one need accompany me.'

'I will, of course,' Ipshank answered.

'And I,' the Fist added.

'And I,' said Captain Peles.

'We're all goin',' Goss rumbled, and signed *Move out*.

They advanced unopposed through sections of the tunnels. The Adjunct and the Fist led, followed by Captain Peles and the priest, then the regular troopers including Suth, Corbin and Wess. Sergeant Goss brought up the rear. Suth wondered at the lack of opposition but he overheard the Fist opining that they'd withdrawn to guard their target. Ipshank now guided them, choosing corners and which chambers to pass by or enter.

Eventually they reached a widening in the excavation that ended at solid stone. Tall double doors reared in the naked cliff bearing the sigil of the Lady, the white starburst. After glancing about, wary of ambush, the Adjunct approached, tried the doors, found them closed and secured. He drew his blade. In the dimness it glowed like pure sunlight. Two-handed, he struck directly down into the middle where the doors met, and hacked through in a ringing of metal. He kicked a leaf and it swung heavily open, crashing against stone. They crowded forward.

It was a temple to the Lady. A long columned hall gave way to a wider chamber. Daylight streamed in from high up through portals cut into the rock. Awaiting them were gathered some twenty Stormguard. Behind them two priests flanked the tiny figure of a young girl who held before her a chest of dark wood glowing with silver tracery.

'Retreat, heretics,' one of the bearded priests called, 'or be destroyed by the holy wrath of the Lady.'

They spread out, the Adjunct and Fist Rillish taking the centre of the line. The Adjunct edged forward. He did not bother answering. One priest stamped his staff against the polished stone flagging and the Korelri spread out, drawing blades. A faint blue-green flame, an auora all too familiar to Suth, arose around the two priests. They touched their staffs to the Stormguard before them and the flames spread from man to man down the lines.

On Suth's right the priest Ipshank growled, 'Shit.' He shouted: 'They'll ignore wounds now!'

Suth knew this from prior experience. The priests howled some sort of invocation to the Lady and levelled their staffs. The flames leapt across the chamber to strike the Adjunct and Ipshank, who flinched, stepping back, grunting their pain and raising arms to protect their faces, but neither fell back.

The Korelri charged.

Suth fought with sword and shield. The Stormguard attacked first with spears.

Keri raised a sharper but the Fist yelled at her to stop. Cursing, she swung the bag to her rear and drew two long-knives. The Adjunct leapt forward, swinging. His blade struck a Stormguard but was deflected away in a shower of sparks and crackling energy.

'Who protects you?' a priest yelled at the Adjunct.

Ipshank grasped a spear thrust at him and held on though his hands smoked. The stink of burning flesh wafted over Suth. The troopers from Twofoot's squad fell. Keri stepped into the gap, parrying. Suth was almost taken by a thrust as he peered over, terrified for her. A spearhead grazed her face, then another took her in the thigh and she fell. Goss hacked two of the Stormguard but they would not fall, and, momentarily surprised, the sergeant was thrust through the stomach. Wess and Corbin held the gap but were close to being overborne. Then a huge figure came bounding into the room to join them: Manask, his armour hanging from him in shreds. He'd somewhere found a great halberd, which he swung, beheading a Stormguard. The headless body tottered and fell.

The Stormguard facing Ipshank freed his spear and thrust the priest in the side. The man fell to his knees. Fist Rillish stepped into the gap and the arcing blue-green flames shifted to envelop him. He screamed, smoking, and fell writhing in agony. Captain Peles let out a howl and hacked about her in a blind raging fury.

Then the earth moved. It kicked everyone from their feet, bucking and heaving. A great shriek of pained rock tore through the chamber. Rubble fell over them. A stone struck Suth, felling him. Dust and pulverized stone filled the chamber, swirling through broad beams of daylight. Then the reverberations and tremors eased into stillness and all was silent but for settling rock and the distant crash of surf.

The last tumbling stones clattered into the distance and Suth came to. He shook the dust from his face and helmet. The lancing pain in his shoulder was nothing compared to the crushing weight of the block of stone trapping his sandalled foot. Pushing with both hands, he managed to yank it free of the slim gap that stopped the great block from utterly flattening it. Around him, through the swirling dust, men and women groaned, rousing themselves. Daylight streamed through the dust and Suth blinked, trying to make sense of what he saw.

It seemed that the massive tremor had caused a landslide, or fault, and the far wall of the chamber had been shorn away with a portion of the rock it was cut from. Wind gusted through the chamber, lashing the dust away, and Suth had a bird's view of the broad Fist Sea and its curved mountainous borders. Standing on this new cliff edge was one remaining priest, blood glistening through his torn robes down one side, one hand tight upon the girl, who still gripped the chest to herself, her eyes huge. Four remaining Stormguard stood before them, swords out.

Advancing upon them came Kyle, helmet gone, his black hair a tangled mess of dust and wet blood. Suth found his sword among the broken rock and pushed himself erect to follow. Also staggering up from the rubble came Fist Rillish and Captain Peles.

Before Kyle could engage a waiting Stormguard, the priest gestured and a lance of the green-blue fire shot out to strike him in the chest. He reeled backwards, grunting his pain, but he did not fall.

'Who protects you?' the priest bellowed again, enraged, foam at his mouth. 'It is of the earth! I sense it! Who dares!'

Kyle's arms fell as he stared, shocked. 'The earth . . . ?' he echoed, wonder in his voice.

At that moment the Stormguard charged. Suth met one in a desperate delaying strategy, giving way, yielding, hoping beyond hope that one of his companions would finish their own opponent and come to aid him. Beside him, Fist Rillish fought with his two swords, exhausted, parrying only, hardly able to raise the tips of those slim weapons. Captain Peles fought doggedly, the only one of them to have retained a shield, which she hunched behind, refusing to give ground.

Kyle, recovering, hacked down the Stormguard and advanced upon the priest. Seeing death coming to him the priest howled his fury and thrust both hands out in a blast that threw up a cloud of dust, blinding everyone and bringing down further rocks, shaking the uncertain perch of the very cave. Suth, blinking, wiped an arm across his eyes, coughing. The Stormguard lashed out with a cut, judging his distance expertly from that mere cough, slicing Suth across his chest. The Korelri raised his sword for the killing stroke but lurched aside instead, falling. It was the priest, Ipshank. The man gripped the Stormguard's helmed head between his broad wrestler's hands and twisted, snapping sideways. The crunch of cartilage and vertebrae cracking made Suth flinch. He helped Ipshank to his feet.

Behind the Stormguard, the lashing wind tore the dust away to reveal the Adjunct down and the priest of the Lady exulting, laughing, the child yet at his side, frozen in horror, frozen in terror. That triumphant smile fell away, however, as a new figure bounded in from the side, rolling, closing with the priest – Faro. Before the priest could even react the Claw stitched him with countless knife-thrusts. Gaping his disbelief the man stared, unmoving, until Faro kicked him over the edge. Then the Claw turned to look down at the girl and raised his gleaming wet blades.

'No!' Fist Rillish yelled, charging past the Stormguard. The Korelri slashed his back as he passed. The Fist yanked the girl from Faro's side.

Suth engaged the Stormguard, Ipshank limping just behind. 'Do not touch the chest!' the priest yelled.

Shrugging, Faro lazily advanced on the Stormguard Suth faced and the Korelri turned to keep the two of them before him. All this time Captain Peles exchanged ringing blows with the only other Korelri standing. They seemed to have made a pact to see who could outlast the other.

Shifting, panting, his foot numb and almost useless, Suth tried to bring the Stormguard's back to Faro. Ipshank yelled then, next to him, 'Rillish!'

Suth snapped a quick glance to the cliff edge. The Fist, his hands on the shoulders of the girl before him, was slowly leaning as if drunk. His eyes rolled up white and he tottered backwards, his hands slipping from the girl's shoulders. He disappeared over the edge.

'*No!*' Peles howled and she smashed the Korelri facing her in a blurred storm of blows, literally crushing him to the ground before charging to the edge. Ipshank ran as well.

'Yield,' Suth gasped breathlessly to the last standing Stormguard.

The Chosen snorted from within his helm. 'Don't be a fool.'

'You're the fool,' Suth answered, and nodded to Faro.

The Korelri snapped a quick glance to Faro, and as he did so the Claw flicked a hand. The Chosen flinched, his arms jumping like a puppet's, then he sank to his knees and fell on his side. The handle of a throwing blade protruded from the narrow vision slit of his helm.

Suth limped for the cliff edge. Here he found Captain Peles, her helm thrown aside, white hair a matted sweaty mess, panting, gulping in great breaths. Out over the yawning gulf, straight-armed, she held the child by her shirt. The chest lay to one side.

'Don't do it,' Ipshank was saying in a low calm voice. 'Don't give in to it. Don't. You'll never forgive yourself.'

Tears ran down the woman's grimed, sweaty face. Her lips were pulled back from her teeth in a savage frozen snarl.

No one dared move. Far below the waves pounded, white-capped, insistent. Rocks tumbled and clattered down the freshly exposed cliff.

'Don't yield to it,' Ipshank said, not begging nor commanding, simply matter-of-fact.

The woman drew three great shuddering breaths, seemed on the verge of weeping, then threw the child to Ipshank and stalked away, her hands over her face.

The priest held the girl to him. 'Get everyone up,' he told Suth.

A dash of water from a goatskin woke Kyle, who groaned, stirring. Whatever was supposed to have been protecting him appeared to have insulated him from the blast, as his only wound was the gash that split his scalp. Manask had escaped death yet again by virtue of his extraordinary armour, which even in its shredded state had protected him from an immense knife-edged stone that pinned him down. Suth and Kyle levered the stone aside and pulled him up. Pulverized rock rained from the fellow like flour. Goss they woke, then Kyle set to binding his wound. Wess they found buried under great blocks but alive. Corbin lay aside, motionless, covered in rock dust. Suth found Keri unconscious from loss of blood. He went to work binding up her leg.

Faro merely cleaned his blades. Captain Peles sat aside, head sunk in her hands. Ipshank called from the cliff edge where he sat, the girl in his arms, asleep or unconscious. 'Look at the sea . . .'

Finished with Keri's wound, Suth came to the edge. Some disturbance ran like a line across the surface of the inland body of water for as far as he could see. And it was approaching the base of their cliffs with unnatural speed.

'Manask,' Ipshank called. He gestured to the chest with a foot. 'I want this as far out to sea as possible . . . but don't touch it!'

Manask bounced his fingertips together as if deep in thought. 'You know . . . we could get a fortune—'

'*Manask!*'

He raised his hands in surrender. 'Just a thought!'

Ipshank pointed. 'The sea.'

'Yes, yes. If we must. Simplicity itself!' the giant answered – though far less a giant now as he was missing his great thick mane of hair, revealing his bald head. And he had lost or kicked aside his tall boots. His layered armour hung from him in loose, torn folds.

The big man selected one of the Korelri spears. He pushed the butt end through a grip of the chest then carefully extended it behind him, sideways. Everyone moved aside.

With a savage flick he snapped the spear forward like a kind of throwing stick, flinging the chest far out from the cliff. Suth followed its fall. So small was the chest, and so great the distances involved, he could not see it striking the surface.

Almost immediately, however, a froth arose among the waves. A glow flashed, bluish and lancing, slashing, as if striking out. Bright shapes coursed among the waves, closing from all sides. Within that patch the water foamed as if boiling.

Kyle stepped up to the edge next to Ipshank and stood watchful, hands at his belt. The squat man eyed the youth, his gaze concerned. 'We don't know for certain . . .' he began, but the plainsman shook his head and turned away. As he went Suth saw him wipe at his face.

Manask elbowed Ipshank. 'All finished with this nonsense now? A lifetime's quest fulfilled, yes?'

'Let's hope so,' the priest ground out.

From the rear of the cavern, behind them all, Captain Peles yelled out: 'Attend!'

Suth turned on his wounded foot, wincing. There, filing in, came Black Moranth one after the other, until some twenty faced them. Suth would have groaned aloud if he wasn't so appalled. Captain Peles faced them, sword readied. Kyle joined her, and Wess staggered over to them.

'I could use my preternatural skills to sneak away – but I will stand by your side,' Manask told Ipshank.

'What a comfort.'

Suth glanced around for Faro, to discover that the Claw obviously did not share the giant's sense of comradeship. He drew his sword to limp up to Wess' side.

Then an old man slipped out from among the ranks of the Moranth: the Drenn elder, Gheven. 'I'm sorry we are so late – we were held up by collapsed tunnels.'

Suth stared at the man, uncomprehending. 'You . . . brought the Moranth? To help?'

One of the Blacks bowed. 'I am Commander Borun. We have contracted with our cousins the Blue to lend you aid. I apologize for our tardiness.'

Kyle lowered his blade. 'You are with the Blues?'

'Yes. Our obligations to the Overlord ended . . . dissatisfactorily.'

Suth could not think of anything to say; he exchanged an uncertain look with Wess, who appeared hardly able to stand on his feet, a gash down his entire side running with blood that soaked his leg.

'See to the wounded,' the commander told his troops, and they fanned out over the cavern.

Suth brought Gheven to Ipshank.

The old man peered out over the cliff, where lights flashed like an undersea eruption beneath the waters of the Fist Sea. 'I dared not hope,' he breathed.

'Let's hope they were successful elsewhere as well.'

'I fear not,' the old man said, his voice low.

Kneeling at the unconscious girl's side, Ipshank stiffened. 'What do you mean?'

'I mean I still sense her. She has not been utterly destroyed.'

'Where?'

'The Tower, I think. If I should guess.'

Ipshank grunted his agreement. 'Hundreds of Korelri guard that place. Too many.' Rising, he rubbed a hand over his shaven pate. 'I can't ask any more of anyone here.'

Gheven was quick to nod. 'Yes. I understand. We can only hope.'

'Yes.' Ipshank raised the girl in his arms, grimacing against his wounds. 'Let's get out of here.' He called across the chamber: 'We should go, Adjunct. Collect the others.'

Kyle signalled his assent to the Moranth commander Borun, who then passed on the Malazan hand-sign *move out* to his troops.

Suth watched while the Moranth assembled a stretcher from Korelri spears and a cloak and laid Keri on it. Two picked up Corbin. Another raised Goss; Manask waved aside numerous offers of help. They filed out, following Gheven. Suth noticed that Kyle stood peering out over the cliff for some time in a long lonely vigil, and that he was the last to leave.

* * *

Shell stepped out of Blues' D'riss Warren on to a muddy flattened wasteland of sluggish channels and humped, scoured-clean sand bars. She peered about mutely, as did the rest of the Crimson Guard.

'Is this the right spot?' she asked Blues, who'd been the first to emerge.

The man was looking around, still dumbfounded. 'This is it. I don't understand – wait! The wave. There must have been a huge wave here as well. The marsh has been swept over.'

In the distance a weak tendril of white smoke climbed into the twilight sky. They slogged their way to it. Lazar carried Corlo. Jemain helped Bars stumble along, his chest now bound. Fingers followed, coughing, leaning from side to side to press alternating nostrils closed and blow.

They found a dreary camp amid the wet sands, consisting of Orzu and a few of his numerous sons. The old man, pipe in mouth, rose to greet them. 'I knew you would come,' he said with a smile, holding out his arms.

Blues clapped the man's back, then held him at arm's length, frowning. 'The girl . . .'

'Ena,' Shell said.

'Ach! She is fine. It is too cold out here for her and the babe.'

'Baby?' Shell echoed.

The old man grinned with his stained rotten teeth. 'Aye, a babe. Shell, she is named. Good name for the Sea-Folk, yes?'

Shell nodded, rather dazed.

'You still have boats?' Blues asked.

The man waggled his head. 'Well . . . a few.'

Blues waved the matter aside. 'Don't worry. We don't require one any more. We'll make our own way. We just stopped to let you know . . .' His voice tailed off as Fingers, aside, suddenly turned away and raised a hand for silence.

Shell looked over as well: *something* . . .

Blues peered south also, his gaze slitting.

'What is it?' Orzu asked, pulling his pipe from his mouth.

Shell sensed them now: *Crimson Guard, but not. The Disavowed. Those who followed Skinner in his throw to take over the Guard, exiled by K'azz.* Her gaze went to Bars. *And* he *is come as well.*

Hugging himself, Bars slowly straightened. Awareness came to his eyes. 'He's here. *The bastard's here!*'

Orzu now clamped his lips shut, his gaze moving between them, calculating.

'What's south of here?' Blues asked, his voice taut.

Orzu shrugged, bewildered. 'Why, there's nothing. Nothing at all. Just Remnant Isle. But no one's there.'

'Nothing? On the island?'

Orzu pursed his lips. 'Well . . . there is the—' He stopped himself.

Blues turned to eye the man directly. 'Talk, old man.'

Orzu studied his pipe, turning it in his hands. 'Trust me, outlanders. You don't want to go there.'

Bars took a step towards Orzu but Blues raised a hand, halting him. 'We need to know. Tell us.'

Orzu's sons had risen as well and hands had gone to belt-knives and staves. The old man waved them down. 'A tower, foreigner. The Stormguard's sanctuary, hidden far back from the wall. But you cannot go there. Too many of them.'

'I'm going,' Bars ground out, his voice rasping.

'No you're not,' Blues said.

The man gulped an objection, his eyes widening, shocked. '*What?*'

Blues raised a hand. 'I'm sorry – you're in no shape.'

Lazar gently set Corlo down next to the fire. 'We'll need everyone,' he said.

'Blues,' Shell breathed, 'you and I and Fingers are under no constraints now.'

The short Napan leaned his head back, looking skyward. Shell held out a hand: a few fat raindrops struck from the darkening clouds. Blues threw down the sticks at his belt, gestured to the Sea-Folk youths. 'Give me those knives.'

The two looked at Orzu, who waved for them to do so. They handed over the thick curved blades. Blues hefted them, testing their weight and balance, then shoved them into his belt. Jemain handed Bars a sword he'd scavenged in Ice Tower. 'Lazar and Bars and I will stand together.' Blues looked to Shell. 'You and Fingers will switch in and out of Warren, covering us. I'll take us through.'

Bars turned to Jemain, who'd crossed to Corlo. 'If I don't come back . . . well, you and Corlo will make it back from here.'

Jemain nodded. 'Yes. And . . . thank you, Captain.'

Bars swallowed, looking away.

Shell caught the old man's eye. 'Say goodbye to Ena and the babe.'

Orzu forced something like an encouraging smile, bowed. 'Fare you well.'

'Closer,' Blues ordered.

They came out on a bare rocky shore that looked to have recently been washed over by a very high tide or large wave: fresh torn seaweed lay draped atop boulders and the dark water-staining rose all the way up to the base of a wide plain tower that sat atop the very centre of this small isle.

Shell immediately raised her Warren, that of Serc, the Warren of Air and Storm, and flickered in and out, covering Blues and Bars and

Lazar as they carefully climbed the slope. She knew that elsewhere, hidden, Fingers was doing the same.

She saw the scene in two differing frames. In one, the three men climbed the unremarkable barrier of rough uneven boulders, while in another the telltale marring and scars lingered of enormous energies expended and horrendous damage given and taken. Bodies lay among the rocks – slain Stormriders that she stepped right over. Their armour appeared to be a mixture of their sorcerous scaled ice over mundane materials such as shell, cold-forged copper, and exotic hides. They were fair, with pale hair. The characteristic features she saw among the corpses reminded her of the Tiste Andii.

The three reached the top and here Blues called to her. She stepped out of her Warren right next to him. He gestured ahead. Dead Korelri Stormguard were piled before the single, now blasted open, doorway to the tower. 'Anyone?' he asked, raising his chin to the tower.

She studied it from her Warren. 'No. None remain alive within.'

Fingers appeared, gestured, *Sighted*.

They closed on the tower wall, slid along around it. There, down the slope at an open sorcerous gateway into a roiling greyish Warren – Chaos? – the Disavowed. She recognized the Dal Hon mage Mara with her piled curled mane of hair, and Shijel, who favoured two swords and always fancied himself a match for Blues. More ducked through the gate, disappearing even as she watched.

But last, in his long coat-like glittering black armour, Skinner, holding a chest bound all in silver fittings.

Bars charged out from cover, bounding in great running leaps from boulder to boulder down the slope like some sort of hunting cat. '*Skinnerrrrrr!*' he roared as he went.

'Bars!' Blues yelled, then, 'Shit!' And ran out after him. They all followed, clambering pell-mell down the rugged bare rocks.

Skinner's helmed head snapped round, then leaned back as the man laughed. 'Bars! Is that you? You look like Hood's own shit!'

Mara and Shijel paused, but Skinner motioned them in and they disappeared. He edged one step backwards, right to the lip of the flickering portal, while Bars closed. The helm cocked as the man judged his timing. 'Lost them all, did you, Bars?' he called. 'Always were murder on your people . . .' and, laughing, he stepped back, disappearing just as Bars came crashing down on the spot.

The gateway snapped away with a rush of air. Bars lay writhing at the water's edge, snarling, striking the stones. They joined him there, weapons bared, Shell's heart hammering. *Skinner!* From her Warren the man's aura had appeared even stronger than the last time. As for the chest . . . the quickest snatched glimpse of the astounding potency carried within still left glowing afterimages in her vision.

'What damned Warren was *that*?' Bars snarled from where he lay.

'The Crippled God's,' Shell said. 'Skinner's thrown in with him. The Dragons Deck readers claim that the Fallen God has made him King of his new house, the House of Chains.'

Bars pushed himself up, hugging his chest, anguish twisting his face. 'He's his errand boy too.'

'What's with the chest?' Lazar asked.

'A fragment of the entity charading as the Lady,' said Shell.

'A fragment?' Blues repeated, alarmed. 'As in the other name for the Crippled God . . . the Shattered God?'

Fingers sat heavily on a boulder. '*Shit!*'

Shell stared across the dark waters of the small crater lake surrounding this isle, to the near-black cloud cover obscuring the night sky, without seeing any of it. *All that strength collected by the Crippled God. Added to him! What have they allowed here? What further catastrophes may very well be laid at their feet?* She shook her head in mute denial.

Lazar cleared his throat. 'We should go.'

Blues blinked, shaking off his thoughts. 'Yeah. We'll go get Corlo and Jemain.'

'K'azz must be told of this,' Shell said.

But Bars waved a negative. 'Not our fight. We just want Skinner.'

'K'azz will decide,' Blues said, finishing the matter, and he waved everyone to him.

Moments later the isle was empty but for the hundreds of corpses, silent but for the ragged surf surging over the rocks. Then kites and crows assembled wheeling overhead, gathering from all around, while an army of white crabs came scrabbling and feeling their way up among the rocks.

EPILOGUE

SUTH LAY IN HIS HAMMOCK AND LUXURIATED IN THREE CONsecutive days of relative inactivity – other than repairing his gear, and the usual make-work of cleaning the vessel. He was on board the *Velenth*, a Roolian merchantman commandeered for transport. The reassembled Malazan expeditionary force was returning to Quon Tali, and Command had yet to get round to formally reassigning him, Goss, Keri and Wess. He lay, an arm over his eyes, and tried to sleep while the great mass of vessels slowly made its way back through Black Water Strait.

He'd almost succeeded when Sergeant Goss' voice rumbled: 'Your presence is requested up top,' and the man yanked his leg.

Suth fumbled to regard his sergeant: the man was up again now that the few healers they had could access their Warrens. 'What? Not more damned scrubbing, *please.*'

But the sergeant looked more serious that he had in days. 'The High Mage is here. She has some questions for you.'

Suth stilled, knowing the instinctive nervousness every trooper feels when the high and mighty take an interest. 'What about?'

'Can't say.'

'Did she question you?'

'Yes.'

'And?'

The man gave a negative shake of the head. 'Don't think I'm stupid enough to dick with a High Mage's inquiry. Now let's go.'

Suth pulled on his boots and, hunched over in the cramped quarters, made his way through the maze of hammocks to the companionway. Up top it was still cold, but the air did not have the ruthless bite it used to. It was the wind that made one shiver. The massed cloud cover was still thick, but breaks were appearing, widening the farther south they went. Goss walked Suth to where the High Mage waited next to the ship's side. With her was the unmistakable figure of the tall and broad Captain Peles, unarmoured in her long padded aketon and leather trousers.

The two were in plain view as all the troopers crammed on to the undersized vessel kept a respectful distance, as did all the sailors passing to and fro in their running of the ship. Suth was quite tense; everyone was full of the High Mage's accomplishments: single-handedly breaking the shore defences during the landing, saving the fleet from the titanic sea-wave. It seemed the Empire had finally once more found a mage worthy of the title.

Suth saluted them both. 'High Mage. Captain.'

'At ease,' the High Mage said. She invited him to stand with her next to the side of the vessel and turned to face outwards, looking over the water. 'Only private place on any crowded ship,' she said with a wink.

'Yes, ma'am.'

'Now, firstly, be assured this is no official inquiry . . . no effort is being made to assign blame or censure. Is that clear?'

Somehow that failed to reassure him. 'Yes, ma'am.'

'I merely want a clearer picture of the events at Thol. That is understandable, yes?'

'Yes, ma'am.'

The woman let out a long exasperated breath. She pushed the unkempt mousy curls of her greying hair from her face. 'Relax, marine. That's an order.'

'Yes, ma'am.'

A hard one-eyed glare from her. 'Now, I've questioned your squad-mate, Keri – she's recovering quite well, by the way . . .'

'Glad to hear that, ma'am.'

'And to your best recollection did no one touch this chest after the young child dropped it?'

'No one, ma'am. Ipshank was most insistent.'

'Not even Manask when he threw it into the inland sea?'

'No, ma'am. He used a spear.'

'I see. And you are sure you saw it fall into the sea?'

'Yes, ma'am. Quite sure. I saw it thrown and fly out and then the sea foamed like boiling soup. Why, do you sense her?'

The High Mage chose not to take offence at the question. She shook her head. 'No. It's just Manask . . . the man's notorious . . .'

'Ipshank was watching.'

She turned to put her back to the side, nodding. 'Yes, well, thank the gods for that. He seems to be the only one who can exert any control over the man . . . And finally, Kyle, the Adjunct. Did you overhear anything from him before he went his own way?'

Suth thought back to the confusion and upheaval of their arrival back in that flood-panicked town. He and Wess rejoined the garrison – he never saw the Adjunct again. But before they went their separate ways he did overhear him and Ipshank talking. 'I believe he said something about heading back home.'

'I see. Thank you, trooper. Now, you accompanied Fist Rillish on a number of missions, did you not?'

'Yes, ma'am.'

'Well, before you go, and I have told this to Captain Peles here already . . . But I was the last to see Greymane, and I just want you to know that he spoke well of the Fist before he went. Since you served under him I wanted you to know that.'

'Thank you, High Mage.'

'That is all.'

Suth saluted and rejoined Goss.

The rest of the afternoon was spent reordering stores. All that time the High Mage and Captain Peles had the side of the vessel to themselves. They were there long into the evening as well.

Down in the hold, while Wess slept as usual, Goss and Suth watched the crowd gathered around a square of wood inscribed with a circle where cockroaches, released from a bowl in the centre, raced for the edges. The crowd of troopers let go huge roars with every race but they spent most of their time attempting to snatch up the escapees.

Uncrossing his arms, Goss winced and loosened his shoulders. 'It'll be a sergeancy for you, certain.'

'I don't particularly want it.'

Goss let go an irritated snort. 'Haven't you learned anything yet, man? The army doesn't care what you think. What you think doesn't matter. You'll take what they give you even if it's a dead dog and you'll say yes, sir, thank you, sir!'

Suth couldn't help a rueful smile crooking up his lips as he said, 'Yes, sir, thank you, sir.'

Goss grunted his approval. 'There you go. Now you're learning.'

* * *

The freak wave that rolled over the docks of Ring city had smashed boats in their moorings, demolished the wharves, and driven on to wash through the sea-front blocks. The worst of the damage was the countless souls it then washed out to sea as it retreated taking everything with it. Yet only a few days later the first boat dared approach Ring again. They found the great sea-chain fallen and submerged. Carefully, they oared their small fishing vessel onward, over the broad Hole itself, the first to do so since anyone cared to keep records.

Here the water was so clear, so calm, it was as if they floated hundreds of feet above nothing. Ernen, who owned the boat, squinted at the surrounding rock walls. 'Where's their keep, their quarters?' he asked of the three dock-front youths who'd agreed to accompany him. 'See anything?'

'No.'

It had been old Ernen's idea. 'Them Stormguard were gone, weren't they?' he'd argued. 'Probably run to Korel. So they must've left gear behind, yes? All that silver inlay. All them fine swords and armour an' such. A rich haul just waiting for the first one to dare . . .'

And so they snuck out at night, made their way across and entered. Now he waved them to one side, pointing into the gloom. The youths peered at one another, terrified in the dim glow of their covered lantern.

One fumbled at his oar then let out a horrific scream, flinching from the side and making everyone jump. 'Riders!'

'Quiet!' Ernen ordered, sitting still, listening. They all sat motionless as well, straining to hear. But only the murmur of the waves returned, echoing and hollow. Ernen cuffed the lad. 'Ain't no Riders here!'

'Something's down there,' the lad whispered, hoarse.

Huffing, Ernen extended his neck to peer over. He stared, squinting, then his eyes widened and he let go an oath, making a sign of blessing. The lads joined him.

Below, unknowably far down in the black depths of the Hole, a figure glimmered. The unnatural clarity of the water allowed extraordinary detail. An armoured giant of a fellow in a full helm and holding, point-downward on his breast, a great grey blade.

Ernen knew him to lie impossibly far below, but it was as if he could just reach down and touch him.

'Who, what, is it?' one of the lads breathed.

'A guardian,' another said. 'Must be a guardian ready should the Lady return!'

'It's just a body . . .' Ernen began, but the youths ignored him, all talking excitedly about what a great warrior he must be, and so the old man waved the subject off and grabbed the oars.

'Where are you going?' one asked.

'For the cliff. They must have a dock somewheres . . .'

The lads were horrified. 'You can't do that! You'll disturb him!'

Ernen stared. 'What? Disturb who?'

'The Guardian!'

'It's a body! Sunk to the bottom of the Hole!'

The lads yanked the oars from his hands. 'We're not disturbing him. No one should come here at all.'

Ernen looked to the night sky. 'Oh, for the love of all the damned foreign gods . . .'

'Don't be disrespectful,' one of them warned, rather sniffily.

Ernen muttered something and sat back against the pointed bow, crossed his arms. Damned pious idiots! A month ago they would've turned him in for cussing the Lady, now they're all against her. He shook his head. Damned youth – so certain of everything. Walk everyone off a cliff, they would!

* * *

At his bench on the High Court of the Newly Sovereign Kingdom of Rool, High Assessor Bakune listened to the advocate for the defence detailing the intricacies of the twisted bloodline governing the competing family claims to the Earlship of Homdo Province. He blinked his eyes to force them open wider, set his chin in his hands. He glanced out of a window where spring's thinning cloud cover allowed a glimpse of clear blue sky.

He sighed.

Roolian troops of the Baron, now General, Karien'el caught up with the ex-Lord Mayor of Banith near the frontier of Mare. Along the side of the east trader road they found his great carriage abandoned, empty. Not much further down the mud track, in a gloomy inn, they found the man himself, hunched by the fire, his fine fur cloak grimed and torn of its silver chains of office.

The sergeant of the detail dragged over a chair, reversed it, and joined the man at his table. The ex-Lord Mayor didn't even glance up from studying the flames in the cobble and mortar hearth.

The sergeant cleared his throat. 'So . . . where is it all?'

Rousing himself, the man rubbed the stubble on his drawn cheeks, blinked his bloodshot eyes, and lifted the tankard before him, only to frown and peer down into it. 'Innkeeper!' he called. 'Another!'

The sergeant yanked the tankard from his hand and slammed it down on to the table. 'Where is it?'

Ex-Lord Mayer Estiel Gorlings blinked at the sergeant. 'Where's what?'

'The entire contents of the Banith treasury, y'damned traitor!'

The man's lower lip began to tremble. Tears started from his eyes. He wiped his face with a fisted knot of cloth. 'It's gone,' he wailed. '*Gone!*'

The sergeant made a face. 'Pull yourself together, man. What d'you mean, gone? You can't have spent it already – have you?'

'No!' Estiel leaned forward, lowering his voice. 'It was stolen. I was robbed!'

'Robbed?'

'Yes! He jumped out upon us in the forest—'

'*He?* One man? You, with all your guards?'

'Yes!'

The sergeant crossed his arms, eyed the man as if disappointed. 'You'll have to do better than that.'

The one-time Lord Mayor reached out a hand, beseeching. 'Truly! He overcame the guards, picked up the chest and walked off into the woods . . .' His voice dwindled away into an awed silence as if even now he could not believe what he had seen.

The sergeant snorted his scorn. 'No one man could overcome all your guards then walk off into the wilds with one of those huge chests – they're made of iron!'

'I'm telling you he did!' Furious, Estiel attempted to push himself up, only to slump back into the chair, on the verge of weeping. 'The guards took what was left and deserted me – the ungrateful bastards! Now here I am. Stranded. Penniless.'

'Stranded no longer.' The sergeant waved his men forward. Two grasped the thick furred shoulders of the cloak and heaved the man up. 'We'll find out where you buried all that coin. Don't fool yourself.'

As the man was dragged off he raged at the sergeant. 'No! I'm telling you! He stole the chest. *He's* the thief! Not me! And he was a giant of a fellow. A giant!'

* * *

In the midst of a grassed slope beneath the gleaming snow-topped Iceback range, Ivanr stopped walking. Idly rubbing his chest, he turned to the mule train of followers tagging along behind – the last clinging remnants he could not shake off. They attended the two wagons of their blessed martyrs: the Priestess and Black Queen. 'Here,' he told the girl close behind.

'Here?' she repeated, uncertain, peering around. 'But there's nothing here!'

'We'll raise a modest building . . . a monastery, I guess, is what it'll have to be.'

'You would live here, so far from the capital? Please return with us, Deliverer. You must rule.'

Ivanr growled something deep in his throat. *Weren't they through with this?* 'No. Everyone should know their limitations. I'm no ruler. I'm just . . . a gardener.'

'We will build the mightiest monastery in the world! Eclipsing even Banith!'

Ivanr waved his hands. 'No! No . . . just a small building. With a garden.'

'And training grounds for weapon practice,' and she raised the staff she still carried.

Ivanr felt his shoulders falling but he fought against it and smiled his encouragement. 'Well, think of it more as a kind of meditation . . .'

* * *

Kiska awoke lying on a sand beach. She blinked, staring up at an empty night sky. Completely empty. Not overcast nor occluded by clouds, but clear and open yet pitch dark. A night sky utterly devoid of stars.

Strange. Was she in Kurald Galain, the Warren of Elder Night?

She sat up. Her staff lay nearby in the sand. And what strange sand . . . it too was black, yet as fine as any sand she'd felt. She stood. A surf broke gently against the charcoal shore. Kiska stared amazed: a sea of white light. Liquid brilliance shimmering and lapping, no different from any other sea. It extended out to a strange horizon that seemed to go on to a dizzying extent.

I've gone insane.

To one side a headland of rock extended out into the sea of light. Thankfully, it held a green-grey hue in contrast to the stark black and white all around. A figure was approaching from that headland, arms out, smiling beneath his moustache: Leoman.

She set her hands on her hips. 'Where in Hood's Realm are we?'

He gave a maddeningly unconcerned shrug. 'Not there, I assure you.'

'Then *where*?'

He raised his arms, turning full circle. 'Welcome to what I call . . . the Shores of Creation.'

Something told her that the man might be right. 'And what are we going to do here? How do we get out?'

Leoman raised a finger. 'Ah! I was going to ask a fellow . . . but I'm having a hard time getting his attention.' He gestured up high into the sky.

Kiska stared, squinting. 'Who?' Then movement – something enormous ponderously shifting above. A giant. And not some Toblakai or Thelomen. A titanic being the size of a mountain straddling the shore. Kiska knew that if she were next to his foot she wouldn't even be able to see over his toe. And he, or it, was doing something: moving or carrying a huge boulder the size of a fortress . . .

Kiska found herself sitting once more on the sands.

Leoman was sitting next to her. He nodded. 'Yes. I did that too.'

She sank her head into her hands. *Gods! She was lost! Utterly lost! Her quest to save Tayschrenn a failure! Hadn't the Queen of Dreams foreseen this? Why did she send her? She was . . . gods . . . she was castaway!*

To her horror she felt tears burning up within her eyes and she swiped at them, furious. Beside her Leoman sighed with pleasure and lay back. He folded his arms behind his head.

She glared at him, snapping, 'What are you so pleased about?'

He took a deep calming breath. 'Kiska, I've made a lot of enemies over the course of my life . . .'

'I'm sure of *that*,' she muttered.

'. . . and I feared I'd never be free of them all. Yet,' and he gestured around, 'here I am! Finally able to sleep utterly at ease. Completely free of fear! What a blessing!' And he closed his eyes.

Kiska stared, unbelieving. Now she knew it was worse. It wasn't that she was castaway. It was that she wasn't *alone*. She was with *him*. This useless, lazy, unmotivated lump.

She pushed herself up. 'Well *I'm* not content to do nothing here. *I'm* going to find a way out.'

He made a noncommittal noise, his eyes closed.

Kiska stalked off. *Useless shit! Why should she have to do all the work?*

Behind her, lying on the sand, a smile crept up Leoman's lips.

* * *

The Shadow priest, Warran, stood alone on a modest slope watching the Liosan army, battered but victorious, come staggering back to their camp. He saw their leader, the ferocious Tiste Liosan woman, another daughter of the Ascendant Osserc, come limping back, supporting her brother L'oric, his nose, mouth and shirt-front dark with blood.

There. Well. That's one thing settled, at least!

He held his hand out and a short walking stick appeared. He leaned upon it. His expression was one of satisfied contemplation.

'Aren't you done here yet?' someone asked next to him.

He looked to the empty sky, then glanced to one side. It was a slim man in a loose dark shirt and trousers, with a rope draped round his neck which he held in both hands. 'It just so happens that yes, I am.'

'Thank the Ancients – you've wasted enough attention here.'

'The creeping loss of Emurlahn is not to be ignored.' He raised a finger. 'No one steals from me. Not even a fish.'

The other furrowed his thin brows, opened his mouth to make a comment, reconsidered. 'Well, this was never a threat.'

'You are too sure of yourself.'

'My confidence has gotten us where we are.'

'As has my wariness and paranoia!'

Each glared at the other until Warran's slit gaze slid aside and he murmured, 'At least I think so . . .'

The other began fading away. 'We're too busy for this . . .'

Warran let out a tired breath, began thinning into transparency as if wafting away into shreds of shadow. 'But I was enjoying the unravelling of the Whorl, the desolate landscape, the useless flailing of the Liosan . . .'

In moments both were gone.

* * *

Kyle sat on piled cargo amidships of his contracted Katakan trader. The Isle of East Watch passed as a dark jagged hump to the south. The sun warmed him; a welcome relief from the months of bitter, unnaturally intense winter. Shading his gaze, he looked back to Kevil Horn, the southern tip of Fist.

If he ever returned it would be too soon. He was sick of all these lands and their useless, internecine warfare. Waste, that's what it was . . . all a sad waste. He'd return home – if he could find it. He wasn't exactly sure where it lay. East of Genabackis, he believed. It had been years now and what did he have to show for all his trouble? A weapon that brought him more attention that he wanted, new scars, and painful memories.

Maybe he'd look up his old friends from the Guard: Stalker and his cousins, Badlands and Coots. See what they were up to. Anything but remain here, in these lands.

They'd taken his friend. Sleep well, Greymane! You were right not to tell me, or to bring me along. I'd have stayed with you . . . but then, I can think of worse deaths than falling at the side of a friend. Something, it seems to me, these Korelri understand.

He reached to his neck to pull out a frayed leather strap and a small amber stone that he rubbed between thumb and forefinger. The words of that last Fistian priest returned to him: *Who protects you? It is of the earth!*

Could it be true? Another old fallen friend still with him? The amber stone had come from Ereko, a giant like these Toblakai and Tarthinoe – in fact he'd claimed to be of the race that was their ancestors. And he'd claimed the very earth as his mother. Perhaps he was with him in more than memory . . .

He released the stone to gently feel at his ravaged scalp. He had no way of knowing, but he would like to think so. In any case he was free of them all now: free of these Korelri, the Guard, and especially he was free of these damned Malazans. He'd go home where there were only the plains, the animals, and the hunt. It would be good to return to that honest, uncomplicated life.

He'd had a bellyful of war and death and great powers grinding people underfoot as they groped for advantage – it sickened him. He had nothing but contempt for it and he felt almost weightless now that he was out of their clutches.

Yes, he'd look up his friends, Stalker and his cousins. They'd come from the lands north of his birth plains. A land of mountains and forests. A land the elders of his clan named . . . *Assail.*

* * *

The crew of a fishing boat daring the rich waters south of Malaz Island was astonished when something heavy yanked on one man's line. A crewman at the side swore he saw something bright flash beneath the boat, but when nothing more occurred they turned to the line. They were fearful, yet it was no longer the season of the Stormriders and so they warily pulled, to see a man's body entwined in the gut. They heaved him into the boat and were even more astonished when he suddenly took a great shuddering breath and clutched at them.

'Take me to Unta,' he gasped.

Talia was sweeping the courtyard of the litter from the spring windstorms. Little Halgin pelted back and forth across the court defeating hordes with his stick sword under the careful eyes of their nanny. Talia was worried; they were expecting a number of foals and she wondered if they had room. And the harvest from last year – not what they'd hoped for. It would be a challenge to make do. She continued sweeping for a time, considering options: selling a few of the horses perhaps, though that was something she would never have imagined less than a year ago.

There were a lot of things I wouldn't have imagined less than a year ago.

Then the silence struck her. She looked up. Little Halgin was standing still, peering down the road where some old man was coming, limping carefully along with the help of a tall walking stick.

Inside, the twins started crying, screeching for their feed.

But she stared as well, watching. Something. There was something familiar in the shoulders, the head . . .

Halgin threw aside his stick to run up the road. Talia took one step to follow but stopped. Halgin was yelling something – a word she couldn't hear for the roaring in her ears. Then the nanny was there holding her up and the twins were crying. Talia straightened, forced herself to steady her breathing. She urged the nanny inside to calm the twins.

Down the road the man had thrown aside his stick and Halgin had jumped up into his arms and he carried him now, walking more strongly. Talia almost tried to rearrange her hair but wiped instead at her face. Then he was there before her and she thought she would burst. *Oh gods . . . my prayers. You answered my prayers!*

'Look, Mama,' Halgin said, grinning happily.

She nodded seriously. 'Yes, Halgin. I see.' She cupped his face – *so lined and thin! Gods, you have tormented him. His beard so much greyer!* She clasped his hands in hers. 'Rillish Jal Keth. You are home.'

'Yes, Talia,' he said, his voice thick with emotion. 'I'm finally home.'

GLOSSARY

Adjunct: in the Malazan Imperial hierarchy, an officer selected to stand in for, and represent, any High Fist or sufficiently ranked commander

Agayla: a witch of Malaz Isle

Ascendant: a title ascribed to any sufficiently powerful individual. It can only be given, never claimed

The Chosen: another name for the Stormguard, used mostly within the Korel region

The Crimson Guard: a mercenary company that has famously sworn a vow of eternal opposition against the Malazan Empire.

The Fallen One: another name for the entity variously known as the Shattered God and the Crippled God

Fist: another name for the island east of the Korel archipelago. Also sometimes applied to the entire region.

Imperial Fist: Malazan Imperial title denoting a commander, military or administrative.

Jayashul: 'She who Brings the Dawn'. Daughter of the Ascendant Osserc

Janzerian Cuirass: a type of branded armour.

L'oric: a mage, and son of the Ascendant Osserc

Our Lady the Blessed Saviour: a goddess worshipped in Korel and regions as its one and only true defender and care-giver. Also known as Our Lady, or the Lady

The Priestess / Sorrow: a Letherii convert to the cult of Dessembrae

The Star of Unta: Admiral Nok's flagship

The Stormguard: a religious military order worshipping the goddess known as Our Lady the Blessed Saviour, and dedicated to the defence of Korel and all lands of its subcontinent

The Stormriders: a sea-borne race apparently hostile to terrestrial life, currently contained within a body of water known variously as the Ocean of Storms, or Storm Strait. Also known as Riders

The Stormwall: a discontinuous series of battlements raised along the Korel north coast to defend against the sea-borne Stormriders determined to sweep across the land

Tiste Liosan: 'The Children of Light', people of the Warren of Light, a realm known to some as Kurald Liosan, or Kurald Thryllan

The Queen of Dreams: an Ascendant, also known as the Enchantress

ABOUT THE AUTHOR

Ian Cameron Esslemont was born in 1962 in Winnipeg, Canada. He has a degree in Creative Writing, studied and worked as an archaeologist, travelled extensively in South East Asia, and lived in Thailand and Japan for several years. He now lives in Fairbanks, Alaska, with his wife and children and is currently working on his PhD in English Literature. His previous novels, *Night of Knives* and *Return of the Crimson Guard*, are also set in the fantasy world he co-created with his great friend Steven Erikson.

To find out more about the world of Malaz, visit www.malazanempire.com